THE ART
OF WAR

THE ART OF WAR

A NOVEL

STEPHEN COONTS

St. Martin's Press ≋ New York

THE ART OF WAR. Copyright © 2016 by Stephen Coonts. All rights reserved. Printed in the United States of America. For information, address St. Martin's Press, 175 Fifth Avenue, New York, N.Y. 10010.

www.stmartins.com

Library of Congress Cataloging-in-Publication Data

Names: Coonts, Stephen, 1946– author.
Title: The art of war : a novel / Stephen Coonts.
Description: First edition. | New York : St. Martin's Press, 2016.
Identifiers: LCCN 2015038676 | ISBN 9781250041999 (hardback) |
    ISBN 9781466839205 (e-book)
Subjects: | BISAC: FICTION / Espionage. | GSAFD: Spy stories. | Suspense fiction.
Classification: LCC PS3553.O5796 A88 2016 | DDC 813/.54—dc23
LC record available at http://lccn.loc.gov/2015038676

Our books may be purchased in bulk for promotional, educational, or business use. Please contact your local bookseller or the Macmillan Corporate and Premium Sales Department at (800) 221-7945, extension 5442, or by e-mail at MacmillanSpecial Markets@macmillan.com.

First Edition: February 2016

10   9   8   7   6   5   4   3   2   1

To Gilbert F. Pascal and Jerry A. Graham

Warfare is the greatest affair of state, the basis of life and death, the way to survival or extinction.

—Sun Tzu

THE ART OF WAR

PROLOGUE

SEPTEMBER, SOUTH CHINA SEA

The waist catapults fired, one after another, and two F/A-18C Hornets launched into the clear early afternoon sky. They came together in a loose formation as they climbed and were soon checking in with an E-2 that had launched on the previous cycle. Its call sign was Moon Glow.

The leader of the two-ship section was Lieutenant Jerry "Cracker" Graham. His wingman was Lieutenant (junior grade) Dyson Wade, a quiet youngster with a diffident, respectful manner, so his squadron mates called him "Mad Dog."

"War Ace Three Oh Seven, Moon Glow. The situation is fluid. The Chinese destroyer is apparently trying to swamp Filipino fishing boats around the shoal, and a Philippine patrol boat is at least an hour away."

"Roger," Cracker Graham said, and eyed his computer. The distance to Scarborough Shoal was 138 nautical miles. He led Mad Dog up to twenty thousand feet and pulled the power back almost to idle and let the nose drift down a few degrees. *Got to save some fuel somewhere,* he thought, and wiggled in his seat to get comfortable.

As the air intelligence officer had stressed at the brief, conflict around Scarborough Shoal, a coral atoll about 120 nautical miles west of Luzon, was centered on fish.

Filipino demand for fish was estimated to be a bit over three million tons a year. China was expected to produce sixty millions tons of fish this year and import another four million tons to feed its people. "All in all, nearly a half billion people reside within a hundred miles of the South China Sea," the briefer had said this morning before they launched, "and of necessity, fish is their main source of protein. Unfortunately fish are a finite resource, and the South China Sea is already severely overfished."

Geologists suspected there might be oil under the floor of the South China Sea. That possibility had stimulated China into building a runway on an artificial island they constructed on Fiery Reef in the Spratly Islands, the ownership of which was claimed by China, Taiwan, Vietnam and the Philippines. At 9,500-feet long, the runway would constitute an immovable aircraft carrier in the middle of a disputed ocean. The Chinese already had an airfield in the Paracel Islands, about 150 miles southeast of Hainan Island, and now they wanted one in the Spratlys.

Be that as it may, the United States was trying to keep peace in the region between its allies and the ever-hungry Chinese dragon. So Cracker and Mad Dog were flying down to Scarborough Shoal to take pictures with handheld digital cameras of any ships or boats they found there. The photos would, of course, be passed on up the chain of command to be given to the diplomats, who would try to keep hungry people from shooting at their ancient enemies and upsetting the apple cart of world trade.

On the flight schedule, the mission was called "surface surveillance." Due to budget constraints in today's peacetime navy, this crumb was all that was available. Cracker didn't complain. This flight was a good excuse to get off the ship for an hour and a half in a hot jet fighter and log another catapult shot and arrested landing. Zip through a blue sky towing Mad Dog around. Another great navy day. Ho hum.

He picked up the Chinese destroyer, if that was what it was, on his radar scope, a mere blip, at sixty miles as he descended, power back, letting gravity do some of the work. He saw it at forty miles, a speck far away on the glistening ocean.

He glanced left. His wingman was about a hundred feet below him, several hundred feet aft, about five hundred feet away in a loose cruise formation. "How you doing over there, Mad Dog?"

"Terrific."

"Contain your excitement, you animal."

"Contain, aye."

As he closed, Graham could see that the destroyer was trailing a broad wake. A bow wave showed white. Now it was turning toward a small ship, the mother ship, surrounded by what looked like open boats.

Cracker put his fighter into a left circle around the ship at three thousand feet. Mad Dog was high and out to right, probably at five thousand feet. Cracker engaged the autopilot and fiddled with the camera that rode on a strap around his neck. Got it on, pointed it, focused and pressed the shutter. Held it down. It would snap several photos a second.

As he watched through the viewfinder, he saw the destroyer swamp one of the fishing boats with its spreading bow wave and turn a smidgen toward the larger mother ship, which seemed to be trailing a net. It was, perhaps, doing four knots. The destroyer didn't slacken speed. It headed straight for the mother ship, doing at least thirty knots.

The angle was changing as Graham circled, but with a nudge or two of the stick, he brought the plane around enough so that he could keep the viewfinder on the destroyer and its intended victim. The destroyer closed the distance at a charge. Then, at the very last second, it swerved and sideswiped the mother ship. The destroyer heeled from the impact; the mother ship ground down the side and came to a stop in the destroyer's wake.

"I'm going down for some close-ups, Dog. Stay high."

"Roger."

With the camera in his left hand, Cracker Graham punched off the autopilot and pointed the nose down. He went by the swamped open boat at 250 knots, saw men in the water as he held the shutter down and the camera pointed, then soared over the mother ship at a few hundred feet. Her side was damaged and she was listing, dead in the water.

The collisions were deliberate, Graham knew, and the sight of men in the water, perhaps drowning, infuriated him. From Oklahoma, by way of Texas, Graham well knew the story of the poor fishermen. They had lost their boat, their livelihoods, and perhaps their lives, all on the altar of great-power politics.

He made one low orbit, made sure he had photos of the sinking boat, men in the water and damaged mother ship, then added power and nudged his Hornet into a climb. The destroyer was already a couple of miles away, streaming a broad wake.

Graham abandoned the camera and turned hard out to the west. Added full power on both engines. Kept the nose up and turned south. He accelerated away, climbing. "You got me in sight, Dog?"

"Roger. I'm at your seven o'clock, five grand."

Graham leveled at ten thousand feet, accelerating. Then he dipped the left wing in a wide, sweeping turn and headed back for the destroyer, maneuvering to place himself astern of it, and lowered his nose. As he dived he plugged in both burners, pushed the throttles all the way forward.

He descended toward the surface of the sea, checked his radar altimeter, kept diving and accelerating. The electronic countermeasures gear picked up a fire control radar aimed at him and gave him an audible warning as he slipped through Mach 1 and kept accelerating. He was carrying two drop tanks, which would limit his maximum speed. Still, he was delighted to see Mach 1.3 on the meter as the radar altimeter deedled, signaling he had gone below two hundred feet. He was out of the dive, almost level now, the destroyer rushing toward him. That was an optical illusion, of course; it was he who was hurling toward the Chinese warship at well over the speed of sound. He pointed his nose ever so slightly to the right of the warship and let the Hornet descend to just below the masthead.

The captain of the Chinese destroyer, on the wing of the bridge, got a glimpse of the fighter behind the ship and turned his head to look. He heard nothing. The Hornet was well ahead of the roar of its engines, which were in full afterburner.

The captain focused on the oncoming fighter. The thought occurred to him that the plane was going to hit the ship—then it shot past, level with him, thirty feet from his head. At a little over a thousand knots, it passed him in less than an eyeblink. The concussion of the trailing sonic boom hit him like a fist, breaking both his eardrums and rupturing blood vessels in his nose and eyes. The pain was intense. He fell to the deck of the bridge, blood pouring from his nose. He didn't hear the glass on the bridge windows shattering or see the bridge team clapping hands to their ears . . . too late. Had the captain been able to look, he would have seen the fighter's nose rise to forty degrees above the horizon, and with both burners secured, soar up into the clear blue sky.

Cracker Graham got on his radio. "Moon Glow, War Ace Three Oh Seven. I need Texaco ASAP." Texaco was a tanker. Graham had used a prodigious quantity of fuel with his afterburner antics.

Meanwhile Mad Dog had spotted another ship only six or so miles away, dead in the water. Curious, he cut his throttles and made a slow pass by the ship at five hundred feet with his camera clicking. Then he climbed away, chasing his leader.

. . .

Back aboard the carrier, both pilots turned in their cameras so the photos could be downloaded. In the debrief to the air wing intelligence officer, Graham mentioned that he made a low pass by the destroyer and told how the destroyer had locked him up with a missile guidance radar. He didn't tell the debriefer just how low he had gone.

The pictures of the damaged Filipino ship, sinking boat and men in the water made an immediate splash. Op-immediate messages shot back and forth between the battle group commander and Washington. The following day the Pentagon released three of these photos to the press; they were on the evening news two hours later. Another international incident.

Mad Dog's photos were classified and not released. Photo interpretation experts concluded the stationary ship he had photographed was a Chinese seismic survey ship.

As the days turned into weeks, the oil and gas exploration ship was photographed repeatedly by carrier aircraft and several P-8A Poseidon patrol aircraft operating from a base in the Philippines as it went about its business in the South China Sea near Scarborough Shoal.

CHAPTER ONE

Attack where they are unprepared. Go forth where they will not expect it.

—Sun Tzu

The yacht had once belonged to a sultan's son—his name was still on the registration papers—but now it belonged to the Chinese navy. The sultan's son didn't know that, of course. He thought he had sold it to a shady German who was going to flip it to a Russian mafioso. The name of the yacht was *Ocean Holiday.*

It was a nice yacht, over 150 feet long, with tanks for enough diesel fuel to cruise halfway around the world. Sleek, clean and white, it was equipped with two bikini babes, a South African captain and British first mate, a Chinese crew and a Russian couple in their late sixties who slept in the owner's stateroom.

This miserable March night in Baltimore harbor, the captain anchored the yacht in the lee of a tramp freighter waiting for space at the pier to off-load a cargo of containers full of shirts made in China. The wind was blowing the rain almost sideways, and visibility was down to less than a mile.

Conditions are ideal, Lieutenant Commander Zhang Ping thought. He was the yacht's steward and real captain. The Chinese crew was composed of picked men, divers and frogmen. Their skills in the kitchen and dining room weren't so hot, but no one had come down with food poisoning on the voyage, and none of the non-Chinese, all of whom were being well paid for their parts in this little drama, had complained. Not that the non-Chinese aboard the yacht knew the mission—they didn't. They had been chosen because they needed money and had flexible scruples. Especially the captain, who was a fugitive wanted on a child molestation charge in Greece . . . under another name, of course.

Ocean Holiday had cleared customs and immigration earlier in the afternoon. Ship's papers and passports for everyone aboard had been inspected and entered into the laptop computers the Americans carried. Agents from the American Department of Homeland Security had also come aboard and inspected the yacht from stem to stern. They had even used Geiger counters to check for radiation. Finding nothing amiss, they had nodded at the customs officer in charge and left on a launch.

The wind was gusting, even in the lee of the freighter, so the captain had anchors lowered forward and aft to hold the yacht steady.

She was riding with only running lights and a small light on the bridge at midnight, apparently buttoned up.

Belowdecks, the Chinese were busy. They used a cutting torch to open up an empty fuel tank in the lowest part of the ship, amidships. That done, they placed the panel they had cut out to one side and entered with flashlights. A wealth of gear was hidden inside this secret compartment: scuba tanks and wet suits, diving gear, tools and an underwater sled.

Several inches of water stood in this compartment, water that had apparently leaked around the seal that encircled a hydraulically actuated door in the bottom of the ship. When it was opened, water would enter the compartment and fill it to just below the hole cut in the bulkhead.

Before the door was opened, all the gear in the empty tank had to be offloaded into the passageway. Everything. Then the gear had to be tested. Four men donned wet suits, and the others helped to ensure all the gear was operational and ready. The scuba tanks were filled with compressed air, regulators tested, tools arranged on deck, then loaded into knapsacks, weight belts weighed one more time. The battery in the underwater sled was carefully tested. Finally the engine was started and quickly shut down. It needed water to cool and lubricate it, so a short test was all that could be done.

Zhang Ping supervised everything, checked everything. Although he was the senior diver aboard, he wasn't going on this swim. The men who were he knew and trusted because he had trained them.

At last, at four in the morning, satisfied that everything was ready, Zhang ordered the door to the sea opened. The hydraulic mechanism opened it a crack, and water flooded in. When the compartment was as full as it was going to get, the door was opened completely.

Satisfied, Zhang opened a waterproof box lying in the passageway and extracted an automatic pistol. He picked up a loaded magazine, pushed it home and chambered a round. With the safety engaged, he inserted the pistol in his right rear pocket.

Zhang climbed ladders back to the bridge. The South African was alone there. "All quiet," he reported.

Zhang checked the bridge inclinometer. As expected, the yacht now had a two-degree list to starboard. The naval officer swept the harbor with binoculars. Lights glowed in the fog, but nothing was moving. He walked to the unsheltered wing of the bridge and inspected the freighter lying nearby. She was also dark, with only running lights showing. No people anywhere on her topside passageways. Her containers lay stacked like children's blocks on her deck.

Zhang lit a cigarette and smoked it in silence. He was keyed up and used iron self-control to ensure it didn't show.

He could hear the faint rumble of distant jet engines, no doubt from airliners coming and going from the Baltimore-Washington airport. They were invisible above this fog. Now and then the distant wail of a siren. Police, perhaps. Waves lapping at the side of the yacht. Wind sighing against the half-open bridge door, which swung back and forth as the ship moved and the wind played with it. He checked the radio on the overhead of the bridge. It was tuned to the harbor control frequency, and the volume was on. It had been busy during the afternoon and evening, but now in the moments before dawn it was silent.

The green line in the radar scope in the mount in the center of the bridge swept round and round, hypnotically. The outline of the shore was fixed upon the scope, as if it were engraved there. All the blips in the harbor were stationary. No, there was one moving . . . He watched it. A small blip—a boat. The boat moved parallel to the shore and headed west, toward the inner harbor, until the blip was blocked by the bulk of the freighter alongside.

Zhang was on his fourth cigarette when the fog began to gray from the coming dawn. The South African was asleep in the captain's chair.

The dawn came slowly. Fortunately the fog began to lift, so more daylight reached the surface of the harbor. Then, finally, two cigarettes later, the sun rose into the remaining fog.

The radio was squawking and the captain was on his feet, calling the kitchen for coffee. Zhang took a last look at the radar picture, scanned the harbor and the nearby freighter one more time with binoculars, then went below.

The four men wearing scuba gear were standing in the passageway outside the fake fuel tank. They had on masks and flippers and were ready.

"Use the lights as little as possible," Zhang said. "Go."

They slithered into the water inside the tank, turned on the sled and dropped it through the door in the hull into the water. Then the last two submerged.

The waiting had been hard. They would have to use lights to work under the freighter's hull, and at night the lights might have been noticed. With day here, there was little chance.

Zhang looked at his watch. Two hours, he hoped. If there were difficulties, perhaps three. They had to open the container that had been welded against the freighter's hull well below the waterline, remove the bomb, reseal the container and bring the bomb here, to this yacht.

There was no way they could get the weapon into the yacht. It was heavy—almost seven hundred pounds—and bulky, and there wasn't sufficient room. They would suspend the weapon under the yacht with cables that attached to underwater hooks. Then they would load the sled, close the hull door, pump out the water and get under way.

The underwater container had been attached to the freighter, which regularly made round trips between Shanghai and Baltimore, in a Chinese shipyard, and the bomb inserted. The container could ride along as part of the hull without the knowledge of any of the crew, who might talk, and hopefully would remain undetected by port authorities anywhere the ship called. Of course, the bomb could be triggered in any port, but this operation required deniability. The freighter would be long gone when the bomb detonated, months later, and would never have entered Hampton Roads. The yacht would take the weapon from the freighter and deliver it.

The Chinese had thought about putting the bomb aboard the yacht in China, but concluded that if for any reason the yacht were searched and the bomb and Chinese scuba divers were found, Chinese culpability would be undeniable. So the freighter brought the bomb to America, and it would be aboard the yacht for the absolute minimum time.

While he was waiting, Zhang Ping went to the kitchen and got a bowl of rice with pieces of fish in it, some chopsticks and a glass of hot tea. He ate there in the kitchen, drank the tea and poured himself another. When it was gone thirty minutes had passed. He climbed the ladders to the bridge.

The South African, Vanderhosen, was nervous. He was walking the bridge, listening to the radio traffic, glancing now and then at the freighter.

"If we are caught here, we will spend a long time in prison," he said.

Zhang didn't think that comment worth a reply. Vanderhosen thought the Chinese were drug smugglers, an ancient, honorable, profitable profession, although criminal. If he had known about the warhead, he would have been petrified.

Zhang paid little attention to the man, who didn't have long to live. Vanderhosen, the first mate, the Russian couple and the two Ukrainian whores who decorated the upper decks in Mediterranean ports would be shot and buried at sea as soon as they were out of American waters. Then the Chinese crew would merely be delivering a yacht to a Greek buyer, with papers to prove it.

Vanderhosen wasn't frightened—he wouldn't have slept in the captain's chair if he felt the cold fingers of mortal terror—just tense, now that the sun was up. He knew the sled was out.

"It goes well," Zhang said, to mollify the man.

"Umph."

"A few more hours . . ."

Zhang saw the harbor patrol boat first. It was heading this way. The radio squawked to life. They were calling the yacht.

Vanderhosen stepped to the mike and acknowledged.

"You need to move your vessel to its assigned anchorage. You can't stay there on the edge of the channel."

"We have had a problem in the engine room," Vanderhosen replied matter-of-factly. "It will take several hours to set right."

"Do you need assistance?"

"No. Our engineer is working on it."

The patrol boat swept on past. "Keep us advised. Move to your anchorage as soon as possible."

"Wilco, mate."

Vanderhosen hung the microphone in its bracket, then translated the English for Zhang, who was was watching the patrol boat motor away.

When Zhang turned to face him, Vanderhosen said, "This is a nice little operation you've got here, mate. Maybe I could get some sort of permanent job with you people."

"Perhaps," Zhang said. He grinned. The South African liked to see smiles and relaxed when he did.

Zhang glanced again at his watch. The divers had been gone an hour.

"Have the girls come up on deck and exercise," he told the captain. "Tell them to wear tights." Vanderhosen picked up the ship's phone and dialed their stateroom.

That should mollify the harbor patrol, Zhang thought. To maintain discipline, he had forbidden the women's company to the crew. Vanderhosen and the first mate, however, had been making nocturnal visits to their compartment. He thought Zhang didn't know about it.

The Chinese naval officer permitted himself a tight, private smile, and lit another cigarette.

The fog cleared away, but the rain continued to drizzle. The half-open bridge door swung back and forth, back and forth, as the wind, now a gentle breeze, swept the bridge of cigarette smoke.

The first mate replaced the captain on the bridge. His name was Lawrence. He had obviously been drinking heavily and was nursing a hangover. And he was nervous. He eyed Zhang, the water and the freighter.

Lawrence had been involved with a Chinese gang in Hong Kong smuggling opium when the authorities caught on to his activities. He still thought he was involved with drug smuggling, but this time in an operation controlled by a high official in the Chinese government. After all, corruption was ubiquitous in the Orient, and he was promised a large sum of money, some of which had already been paid, so why not? He still had his mate's ticket, so he looked good to port authorities the world over.

The harbor was busy now, with boats coming and going, an occasional ship moving into or out of the pier area, cranes off-loading containers, the radio squawking at odd intervals, police boats patrolling. On the freighter the crew was moving about occasionally. A wisp of smoke came from her stacks.

That freighter could be called to move at any time. That was the rub. Commander Zhang stood and watched everything, ignoring Lawrence, and waited. He was good at waiting. The captain and mate thought the man had no nerves. He did, but he had learned many years ago to keep his emotions tightly controlled. His one outlet was cigarettes.

Out on the wing of the bridge he could see the women exercising on the fantail. They were wearing Lycra that showed off their legs and butts, and tight sweaters. They would have been cold if they hadn't been working out. Zhang smoked his weed to the filter, flipped it into the harbor, and when back inside lit another. Lawrence was trying to drink coffee. His hands shook so badly that he slopped some onto the deck.

The second hour came and went. The minute hand on Zhang's watch crawled so slowly he had to force himself not to look at it. However, every now and then his gaze did sweep across the ship's clock on the bulkhead.

Two hours should have been enough. The divers must be having a problem.

There was no way to communicate with them, so he had to hope that they could solve it. If they couldn't, they would be back for more air in their tanks and he would get a report then. How much air did they have? At a shallow depth, but working hard?

Here came the harbor boat. A man stood on the fantail with a loud-hailer.

"We have a problem in the engine room," Zhang told Lawrence. "Another hour, at least, then we'll move the yacht."

The boat came right alongside and slowed to a stop with a burst of reverse thrust on the engines. It wallowed there as its wake rebounded off the hull of the yacht. Every man aboard, all four, were watching the women. Finally one of them called to Lawrence on the bridge wing. "*Ocean Holiday,* you must move to your assigned anchorage. This yacht cannot remain in the channel."

"We are working on the engine," Lawrence replied.

"Do you need a shipfitter? Or a tug?"

"In an hour we will know. Can you give us one more hour?"

"One more." The harbor boat began to move, the wake boiled, and it accelerated away. The man with the loud-hailer saluted the women.

Lawrence translated for Zhang, then stood on the bridge wing a moment, looking at the water, his hands braced on the rail. The water was dark and dirty and undoubtedly cold. After a moment he pushed himself away from the rail with an effort and came back inside the bridge.

A crewman came up the ladder to the bridge and reported to Zhang in Chinese. "It's under the yacht. The divers are getting new tanks, then will attach it to the hooks."

"The condition of the package?"

"It appears to be in perfect shape, sir."

Zhang merely nodded.

The crewman left.

It. A nuclear warhead. Transported to America in a waterproof container below the waterline of the freighter. Ten megatons.

"I want to get off this yacht," Lawrence said loudly in Chinese as Zhang puffed contentedly. Unnaturally loud. He had made his decision and had decided to announce it.

Zhang eyed the man. "That wasn't our agreement."

"I've gotten you here. I've been paid enough for that, and I am not going to the police. I just don't want to go back to China."

"I may need you again. This vessel must have two licensed officers."

"Now listen," the mate said, wiping a bit of drool off his chin. "I am in this as deeply as you are, and I don't want to go to prison. You can put me ashore when you start down the bay and we'll just forget—"

That was as far as he got. Zhang took one step toward him, leaped and kicked. His right foot caught Lawrence under the chin and the mate's head snapped backward. His body went with the kick. It skidded on the deck and lay absolutely still, the head at an unnatural angle. Zhang stepped closer for a look. The man's neck was obviously broken, his eyes frozen.

Zhang left him there. The second hand on the bulkhead clock went around and around. Zhang smoked another cigarette.

Twenty minutes after Lawrence died the crewman was back. He glanced at Lawrence's body, then saluted Zhang. "It's secure under the vessel. The divers and sled are aboard, the door to the sea is closed, and we are pumping the compartment."

"Very well. Send two men up here to get Lawrence's body. He fell down a ladder and broke his neck. Put him in his bunk and lock the stateroom door."

"Aye aye, sir."

"Get those women on deck below. Make preparations to get under way. We will back down on the stern anchor, raise it, hose it off and stow it, then move forward and pick up the bow anchor. You know the drill. When you have Lawrence tucked away, wake the captain and send him to the bridge."

"Aye aye, sir."

After the sailor had left, a wave of relief swept over Zhang. Ignoring the body on the deck, he seated himself in the captain's chair.

They were halfway there. Halfway. Now to plant the bomb.

He reached for the book of charts they had used to navigate up Chesapeake Bay to Baltimore and flipped through it. He quickly found the one he wanted.

Norfolk, Virginia. The biggest naval base on the planet.

Zhang lit another cigarette and studied the chart, as he had dozens of times in the past month. There were, of course, no marks on the paper. Still, he knew every depth, every distance. His finger traced a course.

There. Right there! That was where he and his men would plant the bomb.

Seven days later *Ocean Holiday* passed the Cape Henry light on its way out of Chesapeake Bay and entered the Atlantic. Lieutenant Commander Zhang steered a course to the southeast. A few degrees north of the equator, three hundred miles from the mouth of the Amazon River, on a dark night with no surface traffic on the radar, Zhang rendezvoused with a Chinese nuclear-powered, Shang-class attack submarine. Swells were moderate.

Both the yacht and sub could be seen by satellites, of course—even through the light cloud layer, by infared sensors—but the chance of a satellite being overhead at just this moment was small, since the crew knew the orbits and schedules of most of them. The night and clouds shielded the vessels from anyone peering through an airliner's window, which was the best that could be achieved.

Captain Vanderhosen, the Ukrainian prostitutes and the Russian couple were dead by then and, like Lawrence, consigned to the sea in weighted sacks that Zhang had brought on this voyage for just this purpose. Demolition charges were set as near the keel of the yacht as possible and put on a timer, and every hatch on the vessel was latched open. The life rings around the top decks were removed. Four of the Chinese rode the ship's boat over to the sub. One man brought it back for another load of people. Zhang Ping went with the final boatload of crewmen.

He was standing on the sub's small bridge when the demolition charges detonated and the yacht began settling. He stood watching for the four minutes it took for the yacht to slip beneath the waves on its journey to the sea floor eighteen hundred feet below.

When the mast went under and there was nothing on the dark water to be seen by searchlight except a few pieces of flotsam and a spreading slick of diesel fuel that would soon be dissipated by swells, Zhang went below. Sailors from the sub chopped holes in the bottom of the ship's boat and the flotation tanks that were built in under the seats. Then they cast it adrift and watched as it too settled into the sea.

Sixty-five minutes after the sub surfaced, it submerged.

CHAPTER TWO

Whoever rules the waves rules the world.
                                    —Alfred Thayer Mahan

Six miles away and two hundred feet below the surface of the ocean, the officers and sonar technicians of USS *Utah* listened to the dead-in-the water surfaced Chinese submarine and the gurgling noise of the sinking yacht. They knew exactly what made the noises. And they wondered what was going on.

Utah had picked up the Type 093 Shang-class sub as it exited the Chinese sub base at Sanya, Hainan, four weeks ago, and listened to her submerge. The American sub had fallen in trail about six miles behind her quarry and had no trouble maintaining that position. The Chinese sub was quiet, but that was a relative term. At 110 decibels, she was much noisier than *Utah,* which was a Virginia-class attack boat with all the latest technology. *Utah* was so quiet she resembled a black hole in the ocean and was undetectable by Chinese sonar beyond the range of a mile at this speed. She never once got that close.

The American skipper was named Roscoe Hanna, and he was an old hand at following Russian and Chinese boomers, as well as conventionally powered Chinese Kilo- and Whiskey-class boats. This was the first time since he'd assumed command of *Utah* that he'd had the luck to latch on to a nuclear-powered boat. The Chinese diesel-electric subs were noisy on the surface and easy to follow because they couldn't go very deep and they had to surface, usually at night, to recharge their batteries. The difficulty level rose geometrically, however, when two or more of them operated together. Chinese nukes, on the other hand, spent more time in port than they did at sea, probably because their reactors were unreliable and the boats needed copious maintenance.

"What's the name of this boat?" someone asked. Research in the ship's computers couldn't come up with a name, merely a hull number in the class.

"It's a Chinese military secret," the chief of the boat decided.

"The *Great Leap Down,*" the XO quipped, so that is what she became to the American crew sneaking along behind her.

Hanna and his officers had been ecstatic four weeks ago in the South China Sea when they realized they had a nuke on the hook. Then the ecstasy faded and mystification set in. The Chinese sub didn't stooge around the South China Sea or the Gulf of Tonkin, or head for the Taiwan or Luzon Strait. She submerged, worked up to eighteen knots and headed south.

Occasionally, at odd times, the Chinese captain would slow down and make ninety-degree turns to ensure no submarine was behind him, its noise masked by his propeller, and he would maintain that slow speed for a while to listen, "clearing his baffles." While he did that, *Utah,* in trail, also listened. The Americans wanted to ensure that their boat wasn't being trailed in turn by a Chinese or Russian sub. No, except for the Chinese attack sub and *Utah,* the depths were empty.

After a half hour or so, the Chinese sub resumed cruising speed. A half hour to listen, then go. The routine must have been on the Plan of the Day. On a similarly predictable schedule, the *Great Leap* routinely slowly rose from the depths and descended again, no doubt checking the temperature and salinity of the water at various levels, and once poking up her comm antenna for a moment, probably just to receive message traffic from home.

Captain Hanna and his officers remained alert. Russian subs occasionally used a maneuver known as a "Crazy Ivan" to try to detect trailing U.S. submarines. The Russian sub would make a 270-degree turn and come back up its own wake, trying to force any trailing sub to maneuver quickly to avoid a collision, which would make noise and alert the Russians to the trailing boat.

Yet the Chinese maneuvered only to clear their baffles. The *Great Leap Down* held course to the south. Rounding the swell of Vietnam, the course became a bit more westward.

The noise the Chinese boat made appeared as squiggles, or spikes, on computer presentations. The sonarmen designated the unique noise source with a symbol, then recorded and archived it. A movement of the noise source left or right meant the contact was turning; up or down, ascending or descending; getting quieter or noisier, slowing or speeding up. Following it required care and concentration, made easier by the fact that every maneuver the Chinese sub made changed the frequency of the sound. Taking on or discharging water to change her buoyancy, speeding up or slowing the prop, moving the rudder—all of that was displayed instantly on the sonar computer screens in *Utah*'s control room.

"My guess is she's headed for the Strait of Malacca," the navigator said to Captain Hanna, who was standing beside him studying the chart.

"Into the Indian Ocean?"

"Well, maybe."

Hanna seemed to recall that at least once before a Chinese boomer or attack boat had passed through the Strait of Malacca into the Indian Ocean. Normally they stayed in the western Pacific to intimidate their neighbors and strengthen Chinese demands for complete control of the China Sea. Yet this one was on a mission, going somewhere. As the navigator had predicted, it went past Singapore and northwest right through the strait between the Malay Peninsula and the island of Sumatra.

"Maybe she's going to India to show off Chinese technology," the captain mused.

Yet out of the strait, the *Great Leap Down* turned southwest, around the northern tip of Sumatra and through the Great Channel between Sumatra and the Nicobar Islands, into the Indian Ocean. Then it set a course for the Cape of Good Hope. *Utah* followed right along.

"This is one for the books," the XO said one evening at the wardroom table. "Maybe she's going to the States. The captain and his crew might be defecting, like *Red October*. Maybe she'll surface outside the Narrows and nuke into New York harbor."

"France, I think," the chief engineer opined. "Maybe they are going to France for a refit or upgrade. Visit the Riviera, ogle the women, perhaps buy a French sonar."

"Why not a pool?" suggested the navigator. "Everyone picks a place and we each put in a twenty, then whoever gets the closest to this guy's final destination wins the pot."

The officers liked that idea and mulled their choices for a day. The destination was defined as the farthest point from Hainan Island that the Chinese sub reached before it retraced its course. "I'll take a circumnavigation," the junior officer aboard said the following evening when he dropped his twenty on the table. "I think we're following a Chinese Magellan."

"You're entitled to your opinion twenty bucks' worth."

With the pool set, the off-duty officers went back to the wardroom Acey-Deucy tournament.

Captain Hanna began fretting the fact he was completely out of communication with SUBPAC. *Utah* could not transmit messages when submerged. It could, however, receive very low frequency radio signals, which literally came through the saltwater. When summoned, he would have to report. He decided to let his superiors know what he was doing without waiting for a summons. He prepared a long report, told SUBPAC where he was, what he was following, the condition of his boat, and his intentions. He had it encrypted and ready for a covert burst transmission, then slowed and let the Chinese sub extend the range. Poking up his stealthy comm mast would create only a little noise, but better to be safe than sorry. When the distance was about fifteen nautical miles, he rose to periscope depth, sent off his message and picked up incoming traffic, then quickly went deeper and accelerated.

The *Great Leap Down* was ahead of him, somewhere, yet she was, he hoped, still on course two-five-zero. He didn't want to close on her too quickly, so he set a speed just two knots above the boat he was shadowing. Getting back into sonar range took two tense hours. Finally his quarry reappeared as squiggles on a computer screen. The computer recognized the signature; the assigned symbol appeared. Got her again!

And so it went, day after day, averaging about 330 nautical miles every twenty-four hours. Around the Cape of Good Hope and northward into the Atlantic. Occasionally they heard commercial vessels passing on various headings, and now and then storms roiled the ocean, putting more sound into the water from the surface. The ocean was not quiet. It was a continuous concert of biological sound: shrimp, fish, porpoises, whale calls and farts. Amidst all this there was the steady sound of the Chinese sub boring along, slowing, listening, turning, speeding up, rising or descending.

"Man, I feel like we're following Captain Nemo in *Nautilus,*" the chief of the boat remarked one boring day, a comment that drew laughter.

The fact that the *Great Leap* rarely raised her comm antenna and never her periscope left Hanna with something to think about. A secret mission?

Despite the mystery, Hanna was enjoying himself immensely. He had been in subs his entire career, working for the opportunity to command his own. Now that he had that command, he was savoring every single day of it, for it would be all over too quickly. He visited every space in the boat every day, inspected, asked questions, praised, cajoled, encouraged, looked every one of his officers and sailors straight in the eyes. With the tight spaces, submarines were intimate places. There was no place to escape even if you wanted to. Roscoe Hanna loved the whole experience.

Finally, one day off the Amazon, the *Great Leap* slowed to three knots and began a giant square-search pattern. The slow speed allowed her sonars to listen with maximum efficiency. *Utah* kept well away from her.

On the surface, ships came and went occasionally. Single and double-screw freighters and tankers.

On the night of the third day at this low speed, the *Great Leap* turned into the center of the search pattern. A double-screw small vessel was approaching from the northwest. The *Utah* sonarman on duty recorded her sound signature and assigned her a symbol.

The *Great Leap* came up to periscope depth. She remained there for twenty minutes, then began blowing her tanks. The sound was unmistakable. Captain Hanna had the sound put on the control room loudspeaker, so everyone could hear it. There was no danger the Chinese boat would hear the noise that was now radiating from *Utah* since she was making so much herself.

The small vessel rendezvoused, then killed her engines. The buzz of a small outboard engine came from that location. After a while sounds of small explosions, then the sinking sounds.

Utah heard the prop of the *Great Leap* begin to turn and her ballast tanks flooding. A mile away from the sinking site, at a depth of two hundred feet, she turned to a heading of south and began accelerating.

A day later it seemed likely she was heading back for the Cape of Good Hope, to round Africa and reenter the Indian Ocean.

While the officers squabbled over the money in the destination pool—the junior officer was holding out for a right turn around Cape Horn and a transit of the Pacific, a circumnavigation—Captain Hanna composed a report to SUBPAC, with a copy to SUBLANT since he was now in SUBLANT's ocean. The next day, after the *Great Leap* had slowed and cleared her baffles, then accelerated away, he rose to periscope depth and sent the encrypted report, recorded the messages waiting for him on the satellite, then set off again to follow the Shang-class attack boat . . . as it turned out, all the way around the Cape of Good Hope, across the Indian Ocean, through the Strait of Malacca and northward to Hainan.

In the wardroom of the *Utah* a victor was named in the Acey-Deucy tournament, the *Great Leap* destination pool was awarded to the lucky winner, who had given the matter some thought and picked the Azores as his entry because it was close to Europe and a lot of other places, and another Acey-Deucy tournament was begun.

Utah's report of the Atlantic rendezvous and the subsequent sinking of the small surface vessel raised eyebrows at submarine headquarters in the Pentagon and in the Office of Naval Intelligence. This secret rendezvous was obviously for a purpose, but what was it? The National Reconnaissance Office was tasked to find satellite imagery that might be of help. When ONI finally received the sound signature of the rendezvousing yacht, the computer records from the acoustic arrays lying on the ocean beds and harbor entrances of the American East Coast were studied carefully. A candidate emerged. *Ocean Holiday*. She had cleared Norfolk in late March bound for Barbados. She never arrived there. Routine inquiries of port authorities around the Atlantic basin were negative. Cuba and Venezuela didn't bother to answer the telex messages. Still, even if *Ocean Holiday* had visited those countries, she had left them and rendezvoused with the Shang-class Chinese attack boat just south of the equator, in midocean. And sank there.

A covert operation? Was a Chinese spy taken aboard secretly in the United States? Presumably her Chinese crewmen and South African captain, the two Ukrainian women, the old Russian couple and anyone else aboard had transferred to the submarine and had been taken back to China.

Why? No one knew.

The information was shared with the CIA. Perhaps it would eventually become part of a larger picture.

There the matter rested. The Americans had done all they could, so for them, now, the matter became another unexplained happening in a world full of them.

As it happened, a Chinese mole in the National Reconnaissance Office noted the request for data searches of satellite images for *Ocean Holiday*. He had no idea why the request was made, nor was it unusual. It was simply one of many. He included it in his weekly report to his handler, who serviced him through a drop in a Chinese restaurant in Bethesda, Maryland, whose owner had no idea his premises were being used to pass messages back and forth to spies. It was used simply because the handler, supposedly a Chinese American, liked the food and the restaurant was a plausible place for him to visit regularly.

CHAPTER **THREE**

Politics is the womb in which war develops.
　　　　　　　　　　　　　　　　—Carl von Clausewitz

In late July the report from the spy in the American National Reconnaissance Office landed on the desk of Admiral Wu the senior officer in the People's Liberation Army Navy, or PLAN. In China, the navy was not a separate armed service but, like the air force and rocket forces, merely a branch of the army, though with its own officers, ratings and uniforms.

The report was quite simple: The Americans had searched their satellite archives for images of *Ocean Holiday*. Without more, the report raised a host of questions, none of which could be answered, including the most important one: Why?

Admiral Wu well knew the mission of *Ocean Holiday,* knew of the voyage of Hull 2 of the Type 093 class to a secret rendezvous, knew of the return of Lieutenant Commander Zhang and his crew to China, knew of his report of the successful completion of his mission.

The one conclusion that could be reached was that the Americans knew something. Something had made them suspicious. What?

Certainly not the fact that *Ocean Holiday* never arrived in Barbados. Or anywhere else, for that matter. Without a worried ship owner or insurance company or anxious relatives complaining and asking questions, a search of satellite imagery was unusual, to say the least.

Or was there an inquiring relative of the ship's captain, the mate, the Ukrainian women or the Russian couple? He sent for Lieutenant Commander Zhang, who had approved and vetted those people; the commander of the submarine forces, Rear Admiral Sua; and the skipper of Hull 2, Type 093 class, Captain Zeng.

Three days later the three officers stood in his office. He bade them be seated and passed around the intelligence report. And he asked, "What made the Americans order a search of satellite records of this ship? Why did they do this?"

When no one had an answer, or even a guess, Admiral Wu questioned Zhang closely. He had, he said, chosen the captain, mate and passengers partly because they had no family ties. It was possible they had lied to him, but unlikely, he thought.

Wu led Zhang though the mission, which was documented in his report, day by day after the yacht reached American waters. The question-and-answer session took an hour. Zhang was frank with the admiral—all had gone as planned. There wasn't a single incident he could point to that would arouse the slightest suspicions.

Seemingly satisfied, Wu began on Captain Zeng. "Were any ships or submarines in the rendezvous area?"

"No, sir."

"Were you intercepted and trailed by an American submarine?"

"No, sir."

Wu raised his eyebrows. "You mean, not to your knowledge."

"No, sir," Zeng said stoutly. "I took every precaution. My boat was not followed. We never came up to periscope depth and used the scope or the radio during the entire voyage, which was made submerged except for the rendezvous at the prearranged place and time. Our sonar functioned as it should. We had our best sonarmen in the submarine force on board for the voyage. No, sir. We were not followed."

"Rear Admiral Sua, have any of your boats ever been followed while at sea?"

"The conventional diesel-electric boats have, sir. But none of our nuclear-powered boats have, to the best of my knowledge." Wisely, the sub admiral used the caveat. He continued, "We even surfaced a boat in the middle of an American carrier task force conducting flight operations, to their consternation. The incident was reported worldwide. The Americans were completely surprised, shocked and embarrassed by our capabilities. They lost much face."

The question-and-answer session went on for another twenty minutes, then the officers were sent to an outer office. Admiral Wu wanted some time alone to mull his choices.

He got out of his chair, went to a window and lit a cigarette.

That Sua had mentioned the Americans losing face was interesting. Sua couldn't prove a negative, of course, but the fact that the Americans were grossly embarrassed had impressed him, convinced him that what he wanted to believe was indeed true. Never would he have willingly suffered such a humiliation. So he offered it as proof, which, of course, it was not.

Wu well knew the ingrained inability of Orientals to admit mistakes or embarrass their superiors, to lose face. Some of them would defer to erroneous decisions made by their superiors even if it cost them their lives. This cultural attitude was so ingrained that huge mistakes in the Chinese military acquisition process cost untold billions of yuan and long delays. Wu had fought this cultural foible his entire career, trying to get ships, submarines, missiles, aircraft and, finally, China's sole aircraft carrier designed, built and operational. At times he thought the shipyards, engineers and naval officers would rather build it wrong and pretend it worked than admit a mistake.

Zeng's and Sua's careers were in submarines. Nuke subs were the future. If they were already vulnerable to American submarines . . . well, in a shooting war they wouldn't last long.

Zhang—he had been entrusted with a great mission. Would he admit a mistake or an unforeseen glitch? Probably not.

Ultimately, Admiral Wu decided, how the Americans got interested in *Ocean Holiday* didn't matter. Today. What mattered was whether they knew her mission.

The Beijing politicians wanted the fish in the Yellow, East and South China Seas, and the Gulf of Tonkin and, someday, the Philippine Sea. The latest surveys suggested that huge oil and natural gas deposits could be there. Using stolen American technology, the locked-up petroleum could perhaps be captured in huge, economical quantities. In the years ahead an assured source of petroleum at a reasonable cost would be vital to fuel China's growing industries. Imports cost great wads of foreign currency and were subject to the vagaries of Middle Eastern politics, which in turn were driven by religious feuds and racial dreams. China's politicians also wanted to take over Taiwan, a goal that was popular with the Chinese masses. The politicians used the media to stoke the fire, to feed Chinese nationalism and justify military expenditures; and indeed, they would get Taiwan sooner or later. But first, the Yellow and China Seas. To intimidate the other nations around this basin, Korea, Japan, the Philippines and Vietnam, China needed a navy that looked impressive.

Not a navy that could win World War III, but a navy that could cow the neighbors. And the United States, whose navy ruled this ocean.

As Wu analyzed the problem, it really didn't matter if U.S. submarines had a technological edge on Chinese submarines. What mattered was that Chinese ships and submarines were better than those of any of China's neighbors who might be inclined to fight for their rights. The Americans—well, they had sold their souls for cheap Chinese goods for Walmart. American corporations were investing billions in China. The Americans would not go to war over Vietnam's or the Philippines' rights in the China Sea. Probably. The trick was to raise that probability to a certainty, and the way to do that was to weaken the United States Navy, to do it in such a way that it could never be proven who was responsible. Japan made that mistake when they attacked Pearl Harbor in 1941; the Americans knew precisely who was responsible and vowed revenge, which they took in full measure.

The admiral finished his cigarette and lit another. He stood at the window with unseeing eyes, thinking back.

"You have the floor, Admiral," the Paramount Leader had said. The Central Military Commission met behind locked doors in an underground conference room deep inside the August 1st Building in Beijing. The Paramount Leader was also chairman of the CMC, general secretary of the Communist Party of China and president of the People's Republic of China. He was a technocrat, one of the new generation, ten years younger than the admiral, and a politician to the core. A champion of the military, he gave them the money they needed to build weapons for the twenty-first century. Consequently the military were among the chairman's most ardent supporters. But support was a two-way street: The military needed the party, and the party needed the military to enforce its will upon the people. Neither could exist without the other.

Admiral Wu recalled that he had pushed his chair back and stood. Every eye in the room was on him. He had made a bold proposal ten days before. That day was the time for decision. Yes or no.

The admiral was the senior officer in the People's Liberation Army Navy. He knew that the Central Military Commission had already met and discussed this matter. That this item was on today's agenda meant they hadn't yet said no.

"Comrades, we have before us a historic opportunity, one presented to us by the vagaries of American budget politics and the excellence of our cyberespionage program. There are risks, which I will discuss, and yet great rewards if this thing can actually be accomplished.

"As you know, the United States heavily influences events and politics in the western Pacific and the countries around its rim, including China. Especially China. America cannot be ignored or disregarded because of the power and might of the United States Navy. That navy keeps the puppets on their throne on Taiwan. That navy prevents China from claiming the oil it needs from the seabeds of the China Sea. Lower-cost domestic oil would stimulate our economy, slow the drain of foreign exchange. Our future rests on our economy. We must control the China Sea. The American navy lowers our influence with all our neighbors, except, of course, the one we wish we did not have, the People's Republic of Korea."

Admiral Wu's small audience of seven men—four politicians and three other uniformed officers, the senior officers of the military—chuckled, which relaxed the admiral, who was at heart a gambler. He was willing to bet China's future on this one weird chance that fate had sent their way. He had to convince them.

"Comrades, it will take two generations for the Chinese navy to match the United States Navy ship for ship, plane for plane. It matters not how powerful our army, how mighty our air force. Upon the sea and under it, the United States Navy rules. We have been given an opportunity to change the odds. To level the playing field for at least twenty years."

The admiral pushed a button, and a photo appeared on the screen at the end of the table. In it were five aircraft carriers, nestled to piers. Beyond them were a variety of other ships, including assault helicopter carriers, destroyers and frigates. At the bottom right of the photo in English were the words "U.S. Navy photo."

"Two years ago," the admiral said, "the American navy brought all five of their Atlantic Fleet carriers into their biggest East Coast base, Norfolk, Virginia, at one time. One, *Enterprise,* was there to be decommissioned, and one was there to began its refueling cycle." Everyone at the table knew these ships were nuclear powered. "The other three were ordered into port by the administration, which was in a budget squabble with Congress."

The admiral paused. "Someday the Americans might do it again, and if they do, it will give us another opportunity, a once-in-a-lifetime chance to halve the United States Navy's striking force, and incidentally, stop construction on future carriers for years to come."

He pushed another button, and on the screen appeared a map of the Norfolk, Virginia, naval base. The carriers were nestled against the piers, which stuck out into the wide mouth of the Elizabeth River. They were labeled with names. Farther south, the piers were filled with other ships, ten destroyers, a helicopter assault ship, several supply ships . . . every pier was filled.

Wu zoomed into the map to show the ships. The map had been generated by the naval technical staff, with overhead shots grafted onto the map. Wu knew these weren't the exact ships that had been in Norfolk last December, but he didn't share that with the other people in the room. Finally, he zoomed out so the audience could see the naval base against the peninsula, the navy yard to the south, up the Elizabeth River, and the Oceana naval air station twenty or so miles away, quite prominent with its crossed runways. The civilian Norfolk airport was there, too, equally prominent, only ten miles or so from the carrier piers.

The admiral pointed out the amphibious base at Little Creek, and the minesweepers and other small combatants based along the northern shore of the peninsula. Then he moved the center of the map north, across Hampton Roads, and stopped it on the dry docks and shipyard of the Newport News Shipbuilding Company. Carefully labeled in Chinese characters were the hulls of three aircraft carriers under construction there, in various stages of completion.

Smoking today and recalling that event, Admiral Wu remembered the expressions on the faces of his audience as they looked at the naval power on display in the graphic.

Then he said, "Comrades, they are indeed going to do it again. In late December of this year the five current American aircraft carriers assigned to the Atlantic Fleet will once again all be in port, along with most of their escorts. Five carrier battle groups. The opportunity will be historic, and it may never come again."

The Paramount Leader lit a cigarette. He puffed it a couple of times, then said, "Comrades, I think I speak for everyone." He placed the cigarette in the ashtray in front of him and forgot about it. "We do not want war with the United States. Such a war would be fought here, not there, and could only end badly. Such a war would be unthinkable. Trade would be disrupted, the economy pitched into depression, and even if we avoided military defeat, revolution would follow." Here it was again, the Communist bugaboo. If they lost control of the people, the party and everyone in it were doomed.

Indeed, in this era of intertwined national economies, a complete breach in national relationships seemed impossible. Strategic thinkers had pondered these matters at great length. The world was a far different place than it was in 1941.

Admiral Wu had his arguments ready. The real problem, he thought, was the worldview of the Chinese leadership. Beijing was the center of their universe; the world outside of China was primordial ooze, populated by savage barbarians. Yet he wasn't going to say that. What he said was, "The Americans do not want war either. They are soft, decadent, fat and fond of worldly goods, many of which are made in China. And they have problems around the world. The Middle East, North Korea, Africa, South America, horrible drug problems in their cities, an unarmed invasion of Mexicans . . . War with China is the last thing the Americans want. A complete break in relations would hurt them as badly as it would hurt us. We must arrange a situation that cuts the American fleet down to size—cuts it in half—yet gives us and them plausible deniability. They won't like it, but all their alternatives are worse."

"Can it really be done?" the Paramount Leader asked. The chairman was a career party man, shrewd, unscrupulous, fashionably corrupt and extremely ambitious. To stay on top of the heap he had to keep the party's members convinced he was going in the right direction. Wu tried to read his mood. Was he dubious, or did he like the proposal and want reassurance from Wu to swing the opinions of the other men in attendance?

Wu went with his gut. "Yes, comrade, I believe it can," he said positively. He well knew he was betting everything he had, his career, his position, his future, perhaps his life. Yet he believed he was right. Gambling was a way of life for many Chinese, Admiral Wu among them. When you have a good hand, you have to bet it. Shove everything you have onto the table.

"That is what the Japanese thought when they sailed for Pearl Harbor in 1941," the chairman shot back. "Gut the American fleet and all would be well. A short, fast war. A fait accompli. The Americans would soon plead for peace on terms favorable to Japan. So they thought. It didn't work out that way."

"The Japanese made a surprise attack as they declared war," Admiral Wu shot back. "We shall not declare war. The Americans may *suspect* we are responsible, they may even privately *know,* but the public will assume an American nuclear weapon exploded aboard a warship. We will be surprised and shocked and offer sincere condolences. Americans don't trust their government, which has lied to them repeatedly. The decision makers will weigh the possible consequences of any response on the scale that measures human souls. Those decision makers will bow to public opinion and elect to follow the easy path."

Wu paused, then added, "*We* shall reap the harvest."

He pushed another button on the projector, and a second map appeared, overlaid over the first. On this one was a red spot under the second carrier pier.

It was at the center of a circle. The circle was large, encompassing the entire naval base, the runways, most of the city of Norfolk, much of Virginia Beach and, across Hampton Roads, the Newport News Shipbuilding Company.

The men around the table looked at one another. "A chance of a lifetime," one muttered, and his listeners nodded.

"Tell us of your preparations, and how it can be done," the Paramount Leader said.

That was then.

Today the plan was well along. If the enemy didn't get wind of it.

Wu stubbed out his weed and walked back to his desk.

He thought about what the Americans knew, thought about bureaucracies, about the friction and jealousy and incompetence that infected them all, including the Chinese ones. Could the American intelligence apparatus, even if given a peek, understand its significance? Would they devote the time, energy and money necessary to derive more of the picture? Would they understand it even if they did? Or would the tidbits they knew merely become more noise in a noisy universe?

Wu thought he knew the answer. But just in case, he would be ready. Enormous stakes required heroic efforts. He would leave nothing undone. Nothing!

Choy Lee lived in an apartment house on the seaward side of Willoughby Spit, a long arm of sand that stretched like a finger from the north side of the main-land that contained Norfolk out into the James-Chesapeake waterway. A crooked finger, because it was pointed northwest. The interstate highway ran along it and at the end, old Fort Wool, disappeared into the tunnel that led under Hampton Roads to Hampton and Newport News, on the northern side of the James River estuary.

At one time the north shore of Willoughby Spit was lined by huge, ram-shackle wooden boardinghouses standing shoulder to shoulder. They were gone now, demolished to make room for apartment and condo complexes. It was progress, maybe.

From his small balcony that faced Hampton Roads, Choy Lee could watch U.S. Navy ships coming into and going out of the Norfolk naval com-plex. Going in, the ships had to go around Willoughby Spit, over the tunnel, then turn ninety degrees to the south and go up the Elizabeth River to the Norfolk naval station, or, farther up, the Norfolk naval shipyard at Portsmouth.

Going out, they rounded the spit and headed east for the exit from Chesapeake Bay into the Atlantic.

On blustery or rainy days Choy Lee would often drive out to the public parking area on the end of the spit, adjacent to the tunnel entrance, and fish. He was an avid fisherman and caught more than most of his fellow anglers did. Choy Lee also had a boat, an aluminum runabout with an outboard engine that he pulled around on a trailer behind his SUV. On good, calm days he often motored out into Hampton Roads or down the Elizabeth River adjacent to the naval piers, there to fish and drink beer all day. It was a pleasant life.

As it happened, Choy Lee was also an enthusiastic amateur photographer. He used a Sony Cyber-shot, very reasonably priced, with a nice zoom capability. He shot pictures of fish that he caught, sunsets, sunrises, storms over the water, rainbows, other fishing boats . . . and occasionally a passing warship. The backgrounds of the photos often contained ships sitting at piers. He sent a lot of these photos to his sister as attachments to long, chatty e-mails and posted some of the more innocuous ones on Facebook.

Unfortunately, Choy Lee didn't have a sister. The person in San Francisco who received the e-mails encrypted them and forwarded them on to an address in Beijing. The system avoided routine NSA scrutiny because the unencrypted e-mail was to an American address, not a foreign one. His bland Facebook posts went all over the world. The encrypted e-mails were merely drops in the raging river of data that flowed through the Chinese cyber-espionage system.

A friendly fellow, Choy had a girlfriend, Sally Chan, whose father ran a Chinese restaurant that Choy liked to visit. They went to movies together, or to dinner at other modest restaurants in the Norfolk/Virginia Beach area, and occasionally Choy took Sally out in his boat to fish. She didn't like to touch the live bait or fish, when he caught one, but she laughed like an American and was pleasant and breezy.

Her presence made Choy feel happy. Life was good. Choy wondered how long it would last. Did he really want to go back to China? He thought about it occasionally, and somehow found himself thinking about life with Sally, in America.

In early August another Chinese American joined Choy, or so his cover story ran. The man was really Lieutenant Commander Zhang Ping of the PLAN. Five months had passed since Zhang had planted the nuclear weapon in Norfolk. The two seemed like old friends, or new friends in a strange land. Zhang found an apartment he rented by the month in a building near Choy's. The two were soon fishing together and running the boat down the Elizabeth

River. Zhang took many photos of Choy with Choy's camera, shots that were e-mailed on to Choy's apparent sister. Some of them, but certainly not a majority of them, had as the background the carrier piers of the Norfolk Navy Yard, usually empty. In late June a carrier came in, then another. Huge ships: Zhang had never seen anything like them. Although some tankers exceeded the carriers in gross tonnage, those ships rode low in the water.

The carriers, with their huge flight decks and sides rising sixty feet above the waterline, were visually stunning. Their islands, which rose another seventy or eighty feet above the flight deck, topped by a collage of antennae, appeared small from any distance, like a lonely house surrounded by endless rice paddies. The deck of one of the carriers was full of airplanes parked cheek to jowl. The tails of the planes stuck over the sides of the flight deck.

Zhang Ping was impressed by the sight. He knew, of course, the mission of these ships: power projection. They controlled the surface of the ocean within a thousand miles of wherever they happened to be and projected power onto the land. Their planes could hit targets anywhere within a thousand miles of saltwater, which was a great huge chunk of the earth's surface. America had ten of these ships, all nuclear powered, all at sea about half the time, in all the major oceans of the earth. Three more were currently under construction right across the James River at the Newport News Shipbuilding Company, which was, incidentally, the only shipyard in the world capable of constructing these monster warships.

Zhang thought it delightful, relaxing, to boat up and down the Elizabeth River or along the Chesapeake coastline, or to sit on the end of Willoughby Spit on summer evenings drinking beer and looking at a carrier or two berthed at the navy base while watching and listening to helicopters buzzing about and tactical jets roaring into or out of the base's airfield, Chambers Field.

Zhang Ping and Choy Lee tended their hooks, kept fresh bait on, watched their bobbers and listened to the jets and choppers. Life that summer was very pleasant, for them both, but Choy was worried. He knew nothing of the bomb, of course. He suspected he had been ordered to nursemaid Zhang because his English skills were nearly nonexistent. Certainly Choy's control wouldn't order him home suddenly and leave Zhang stranded in a country where he didn't speak the language. Yet why was Zhang here? The question gnawed at him.

Of course he told Sally that Zhang was here, a cousin, he said, from the mainland. Here on a tourist visa.

In September the days began to cool. More fronts moved through, morning fog became more frequent, and often the days became windy. On windy days the Elizabeth River and James Estuary became too choppy for Choy's boat. In October frontal systems with low clouds, copious rain and high winds moved through the area, followed by balmy, beautiful days with lots of sunshine.

Ships came and went. A carrier battle group came in, stayed a week, then went back out.

Zhang Ping became more withdrawn. He was smoking more now, watching the naval base for an hour or so morning and night. He watched the tugs, other harbor craft, fuel barges, became familiar with the rhythm of activities in the naval base, looked for anything out of the ordinary. And didn't see it.

There was nothing to do but wait. Still, with every passing day the waiting became more difficult.

Choy Lee picked up on Zhang's mood. He ascribed it to the fact that Zhang was alone in a strange land and could only speak to Choy, and other people with Choy's help. Cultural shock, Choy thought.

CHAPTER FOUR

The object of war is not to die for your country, but to make the other bastard die for his.

—George S. Patton

CIA Director Mario Tomazic liked to spend his free weekends at a cottage on the eastern shore of Chesapeake Bay, on a waterfront lot beside the wide mouth of a river estuary. He didn't have many free weekends; he was lucky to get one or two a month, but when he could arrange to get away this was where he came. He found fishing relaxing, and with his little runabout he could motor out and fish and drink beer and sit in the sun and look at the sky and clouds and recharge his batteries for the week ahead. He needed those weekends. Badly. They were especially sweet when his daughter and her kids came; he got a chance to play grandfather and teach the kids how to fish.

On the downside, there was the Friday afternoon traffic eastbound across the Bay Bridge, and Sunday evening it was a very slow go westbound. The Bay Bridge funnel was just something he had to live with, one of those things you can't do anything about.

If he hadn't bought this place years ago for a very modest sum when he was a colonel, he wouldn't buy it now. It was too difficult to get to on those rare free weekends and would be too expensive. His wife had loved the cottage by the water. Loved to birdwatch and do her watercolors, many of which decorated his office at Langley and his condo in town. She had died of cancer some years back. Still, he saw her presence everywhere at the cottage on the shore, the little house with a lawn that ran down to the water's edge and a small pier where water lapped nervously.

Tomazic was a retired army four-star, a "terrorism" expert according to the press, and that so-called credential and his record in Iraq had gotten him nominated for the CIA job by the president. He hadn't wanted the job, but when the powers that be wanted him for something important that needed to be done, he didn't have it in him to refuse. The military does that to you. Regardless of your personal desires, when the boss gives you a task you say "Yes, sir" and do it to the very best of your ability. That attitude becomes ingrained.

He was up at dawn this October Saturday morning. His daughter and the kids were still asleep, and would be for several hours. He'd had had a nice visit with them last night when they arrived, and now they were sleeping late. Tomazic couldn't have slept past 5 A.M. if his life depended upon it. Hadn't done so in forty years.

He drank a cup of coffee and watched the dawn peep through high clouds. A little wind, but not much. He ate a protein bar for breakfast, got his fishing rod and tackle box, then slipped out of the house and pulled the door shut behind him. Walked across the lawn the seventy-five feet to the pier.

God, it was a beautiful morning!

His boat was a sixteen-foot aluminum thing with a tiny outboard motor, one he wouldn't use this morning. He would just row out into the river a bit and drift down to where it emptied into the bay. That lightly churning water was a good place to find hungry fish.

Mario Tomazic checked the boat out, saw that it had ridden well since he put it in the water and got it ready to go yesterday evening. He loosened up the lines, put his gear on the dock where he could reach it and started to step aboard.

He never made it. The boat shot sideways away from the dock about a foot, to the limits of the ropes holding it. Something grabbed an ankle and he was pulled into the water between the boat and the pier. Tomazic whacked his head on the side of the boat as he fell in.

Woozy, shocked and confused, he found himself being dragged under the water by two strong hands.

Tomazic immediately began struggling. The hands shifted. One was on an arm and the other was on his back, pushing him down. Tomazic twisted, saw a faceplate in the murky water. A scuba diver! His free fist shot out and hit the plate, shattering it.

The hands were ruthless. They spun him and pushed him face-first deeper into the water, almost to the muddy bottom.

He couldn't breathe! Couldn't get a grip—couldn't get free. He struggled with all the strength of a drowning man, which he was, as the panic and terror swept through him . . . to no avail.

It was all over in less than half a minute. Involuntarily Mario Tomazic tried to breathe, which filled his lungs with water.

When he stopped struggling, the diver held him under another minute, just to make sure, then released the body. He checked his wrist compass, then swam away underwater.

It was four in the afternoon when Jake Grafton joined the deputy director of the CIA, Harley Merritt, two very senior FBI agents, and the chief of the county police on Tomazic's pier. The driveway was jammed with police and FBI cars, plus a mobile crime lab in a panel truck.

Tomazic's body was long gone.

"It looks as if he was trying to get into the boat and slipped," the senior FBI agent said. "Whacked his head on the gunnel there—you can see the blood—and then drowned right between the boat and the pier."

"A freak accident," the county mountie said hopefully.

Jake Grafton stood surveying the estuary, the other piers along the shores with their boats, and the houses he could see between the trees. Not even a trace of traffic noise. Some people stood in their yards across the placid brown river looking at the commotion over here. Still, this was a calm, peaceful place this Saturday afternoon. Where death had just visited.

"We've interviewed people in all the houses on both sides of this waterway," one of the FBI men said. "No one saw anything. Had to have happened early, like a little after dawn. The director was obviously going fishing. His pole and tackle box are still here on the pier."

"Any other boats anchored around here this morning?" Jake asked, still scanning the shorelines.

"Some out in the bay, but they left early. Long before we got here."

"An accident," the police chief said, almost like a prayer. He was about seventy pounds overweight and cinched his gunbelt tightly under his gut. The marvel was that the gunbelt stayed in place.

"I want to be damn sure," Harley Merritt said. "I want any satellite imagery of this place we can find for study. And I want a lockdown on all these houses on both sides of the river until we can interview everyone in each and every house—everyone. The police can help with that. Then I want complete bios done on each and every one of these people. Anyone who has left the area is to be tracked down and interviewed. I want to know who all these people are, why they are here, the whole enchilada. And FBI—"

"We know how to do an investigation, Mr. Merritt." The FBI senior man was a bit testy.

"I know you do. But this is a national security investigation, not a bank robbery. I want you to seal off this area right here and send down divers. I want them to sift the mud. I want anything and everything there is to be had around here."

"Jesus Christ!" the police chief said. "I know this guy was a big spook dude, but . . . Hell, people drown somewhere on the edge of this bay nearly every weekend, some weekends two or three of them. Get tight as ticks and—"

"And I want to keep this out of the press until Monday," Merritt said. "We'll make an announcement then."

"You gotta be shittin' me!" the local cop said disgustedly. "The ambulance crew has already put the guy's name on the air. It's out there, man."

Merritt seemed to take that with good grace. He did glance at Grafton, who was deadpan.

"Thanks, Chief, for all your help. We'll need more of it the next few days."

"If the county has to pay overtime, we'll send you a bill."

Even as the chief spoke, a helicopter came in from the west and began slowly orbiting the area where they stood. It had a television station's call letters on the side of it, and a big human eye.

The junior FBI man put his hand above the police chief's right elbow and escorted him away.

"What have I forgotten, Jake?" Harley Merritt asked. He was a former college basketball player, about six feet five inches tall, and had hands like dinner plates. He had thought he wanted to be a lawyer, but the agency had recruited him because of his language skills. His management skills and bureaucratic smarts had taken him up the ladder.

"Who found him?" Jake asked.

"His daughter. About nine this morning. She was still in her robe. Saw the boat was still there, came down to the pier and saw his fishing gear, then saw the body floating."

"Tough."

Merritt sighed. "The FBI took her and the kids home. They sealed the house and are searching it now."

He turned to the FBI special agent and spoke with a hint of apology in his voice. "I know you and your agency know how to investigate. I'm merely asking you to pull out all the stops. Do everything you can think of. I know you can't prove a negative, but if there is anything . . . anything at all that doesn't look right, that even hints that the director might have been assassinated, call me. Day or night." He passed him a card. "My private cell is on there."

"We should have preliminary results from the autopsy by Monday."

"Call me, and have a courier deliver a hard copy to me at Langley."

"Yes, sir."

Harley Merritt stuck out his hand and the FBI agent shook it. Jake did likewise. Then the two CIA officers strolled away, up the lawn, passing a team of people carrying lights and scuba gear.

"If it wasn't an accident," Merritt mused, "and of course it probably was, then it was an inside or an outside job. What foreign power stands to gain something by Tomazic's demise?"

"Damn if I know." Jake Grafton was a retired two-star admiral, the current head of Middle Eastern ops for the agency. He was a lean six feet, with a nose a bit too large for his face, a square jaw and gray eyes. His thinning, graying hair was combed straight back. No one had ever called him handsome. Still, he had a presence. His wife thought it was a mix of competence and self-confidence. Whatever, he radiated a calm demeanor that seemingly couldn't be shaken. That Harley Merritt had called and asked Grafton to come to meet him and the FBI here was testimony to the professional regard Merritt held for him, and Jake knew that.

"I want you to go back to the office," Merritt told Grafton, "and get all the security codes to Tomazic's office, desk, files and computer. The computer will have to be examined by the IT guys. You dig into the rest of it."

Jake knew what Merritt wanted. If Tomazic had been murdered by someone in the CIA, Merritt wanted a trail. A trace. A sniff. Something.

"He was only with the Company about eighteen months," Jake said.

"I know that. But maybe someone got scared. Frightened people do really stupid things."

"Anything else?"

"Monday we'll do a full-blown staff review of everything on our plate. I'll alert the other department heads and the staff. Have them come in tomorrow and get after it."

"If someone inside the Company murdered him, then everyone is suspect," Grafton pointed out. "Did you check where I was at dawn this morning?"

Harley Merritt gave him his frozen stare. "We have to trust people, even in this business. Especially in this business. I trust two, you and me. If it turns out that you're bent and I'm still above ground, I'll kill you."

A trace of a smile played on Jake Grafton's features. "I'll keep that in mind," he said.

In front of the dead man's house, Harley Merritt got into a bulletproof executive sedan, one trailed by a car containing a driver and two armed guards. Jake Grafton watched the two vehicles thread their way around all the police and FBI vehicles and turn left on the street.

Mario Tomazic normally rode around Washington in a guarded limo, too. But not on his getaway weekends. On those precious escapes he left the guards in Washington and drove his old pickup to the Eastern Shore. And there it sat, right in front of the garage door, getting a preliminary look from two FBI agents. A tow truck was backing down the driveway to hook it up. In Washington the pickup would get the full treatment and give up any secrets it had. If it had any.

Jake walked across the grass toward his own car, a five-year-old Honda. When he got the call from Merritt this morning, he had been at his weekend house in Rehoboth Beach. He pulled out his cell phone and called his wife.

"It's already on the news, Jake," Callie Grafton said when he told her the director was dead. "I was watching the story on TV. How very sad."

"Yeah. Going fishing, then drowning right there by the pier."

"So when will you get back to the beach?"

"Monday night, maybe. I'm going back to Washington. Gotta go to the office."

"I have a class on Tuesday I have to be back for." Callie was a linguist. This semester she was teaching a few classes of Chinese at Georgetown University, just to keep her hand in.

"Monday night. I'll come get you then. We'll eat dinner on the way back to Washington."

Traffic on the Bay Bridge wasn't bad Saturday afternoon. Most people were still trying to get out of the Washington metro area, not return to it.

As he drove, Jake Grafton thought about the vicissitudes of life. His career had given him an intimate acquaintance with violent death. He had seen a lot of it, combat, operational accidents, murders . . .

Was Mario Tomazic murdered? He didn't have an opinion because he had no facts to base one on. The general was a good man. His family and colleagues were going to miss him. That's more than many of us get.

.   .   .

That evening at CIA headquarters in Langley, Virginia, Jake Grafton turned over the director's PC and laptop to the IT department, along with the registered access codes. Maybe they could get something out of those two devices; Jake certainly couldn't, and he wasn't going to waste time trying.

When he was again alone in the director's office he opened the desk and filing cabinets. All were locked, of course, but he had the codes. The desk contained mostly office supplies: some pencils, paper clips, a stapler and a half-dozen pens with the general's favorite color of ink: green. Some pocket change. A laundry receipt. A staple puller. And a pocketknife, a two-blade Schrade, old but sharp, made in the USA. That was the crop.

On the desk were pictures of the general's deceased wife and his grown children with their families. Jake took the photos out of the frames, made sure there was nothing else there, no notes or telephone numbers or access codes, then put the frames and photos back together.

He tackled the file cabinets last. Got them open and started on the left-hand cabinet, reading every file, from the left side of the top drawer to the right. The files were all in red folders marked prominently TOP SECRET. Was there any other kind? When he finished with the top drawer, he moved down. At three in the morning he'd had all he could stand, so he crashed on the couch in his office. He got back to it about noon on Sunday, after he ate a sandwich at the cafeteria.

The files contained mostly political summaries. Problems in Egypt, South America, Venezuela, Cuba, Russia, Iran, Iraq, Afghanistan, Syria . . . the list went on and on. Europe was there, summaries and guesses and analysts' notes. Current CIA operational files and notes were not in the director's drawers. Conference notes and synopses of meetings with other federal agencies were. Tomazic had half a drawer devoted to the agency's contacts with the Department of Homeland Security and another half drawer full of National Security Agency proposals, meeting minutes, notes and so on. Jake Grafton signed his name on the access sheet of every file he opened.

Jake was still reading files and Tomazic's green-ink notes when the sun came up Monday morning. Harley Merritt came in at seven. Rumor had it he owned a couple of late-1960s muscle cars that he liked to work on in his garage and take to weekend car shows, where you'd sit around in a parking lot in front of your car on a folding chair and visit with fellow car nuts. Merritt was married, of course, for the second time, as Jake recalled, and had the two kids by his first marriage in college somewhere. His family was something Harley Merritt rarely talked about. With him, it was usually all business.

"Well?" Merritt said. He was a no-holds-barred bureaucrat brawler. There was no forgive-and-forget in Harley Merritt. If you went against him, you had better know your ground. Jake had gone head to head with Harley twice and won; the third time he had lost. Still, apparently, the deputy director respected him.

Jake sighed and stretched. "If there is something nefarious here, I haven't found it." They discussed some of the agency's most sensitive operations, those that seemed most likely to cause a foreign response if uncovered. Three of these covert operations Jake knew nothing about until Merritt briefed him; he didn't have a need to know. Now he did. He supposed.

"The FBI says they should have that autopsy report later today," Merritt said, tossing it off as if he had other things on his mind. "They're still working on the crime scene and neighbor interviews. We'll also get satellite imagery, what there is of it, later today."

"Won't be much," Jake muttered.

They both knew that all they would see would be images from satellites sweeping over in low earth orbit, on their way to photograph something interesting. Or perhaps some imagery from a geosynchronous satellite that would be nearly useless due to the distance and the fact the satellite wasn't really focused on the area of interest.

They spent another thirty minutes discussing ongoing operations; then Merritt shot a glance at his watch and charged off.

Jake Grafton locked the director's desk and cabinets and office, then walked the corridors to his own office. His executive assistant, Robin, handed him a cup of coffee. She was a nice lady with a head of huge hair. The coffee was hot, black and delicious. He told Robin about his visit to Tomazic's weekend retreat on Saturday afternoon, and the bare facts as he knew them about Tomazic's death, then went into his office and lay down on the couch for a nap. He was asleep in less than a minute.

The ringing phone woke him up at 11 A.M. He got off the couch and answered it. Robin. "Sal Molina to see you."

"Send him in."

Jake was putting on his shoes when Molina came in and closed the door. A Hispanic lawyer in his fifties, Molina carried an ample spare tire and wore comfortable clothes. He didn't have to dress up for cameras since he was strictly a behind-the-scenes operator at the White House. No one knew what his exact duties were, including, probably, Molina. He had been with the president ever since the big dog got into politics.

Molina dropped onto the couch beside an unshaven Grafton and watched him tie his shoes. "Bad weekend, huh?" he said.

Grafton grunted.

"Too bad about Tomazic. Hell of a guy."

"Yeah."

"So where are we?"

"Damned if I know. The FBI is investigating . . . we're looking at stuff. I spent the weekend in Tomazic's filing cabinets in his office. Seen about three-quarters of it. A lot of it's new to me. Need to know, and all that."

"Want some coffee?"

"Sure."

Jake opened the door and asked Robin for two cups, black.

He sat down behind his desk and yawned.

Molina dropped the bomb. "The president has decided to appoint you interim director."

Slightly stunned, Jake stared. "Merritt's the deputy director. He can handle it."

"He's career CIA. Congress and the public are in a sweat over NSA snooping. He's signed off on a lot of those decisions."

"You said interim. Merritt can handle the job until the new director gets Senate confirmation. Find a squeaky-clean retired four-star admiral or general, or a washed-up senator that the voters can't stand anymore, and appoint him, or her, to the job on a permanent basis."

"Oh, we're going to do that. But until then, the boss wants you."

"What does Reinicke say about this?" Paul Reinicke ruled his own fiefdom, the Office of the Director of National Intelligence. With his staff, he was supposed to coordinate and evaluate the intelligence product of all of the United States' intelligence agencies, sixteen in total, including the CIA, the NSA, the FBI, the U.S. Army, Navy, Marine, Air Force and Coast Guard intelligence arms, and the stuff put out by a variety of other agencies, including the Department of Homeland Security, Treasury, State, and some others. The office was created by Congress in 2004 in response to the September 2001 terrorist attacks. Tomazic had thought the new layer of bureaucracy was a typical political response: Appear to be doing something, even if it is only a reorganization.

"No one asked Reinicke," Molina replied.

"Terrific," Grafton muttered.

Robin knocked. Jake shouted, and she brought in two cups of coffee and scooted back out, pulling the door shut behind her.

Jake sipped at his cup.

"Don't you want to know why the president wants you?" Molina asked.

Jake waved it away. "I've listened to you blow smoke before."

"It's because you're old Mr. Smooth."

"Right."

"You have a lot of friends on the Hill."

"And a lot of enemies," Jake shot back. "In the administration, too, as a matter of fact. Like Jurgen Schulz." Schulz was the national security adviser. "Why don't you name him interim director?"

"He'd be out of his depth, and you know it. And he can't stand Reinicke."

"For once, he and I agree on something," Jake said.

Sal Molina sighed and slurped.

"I don't want the job."

"You're refusing a request from the president of the United States?" Molina said that as if Jake were Jonah refusing a commission from God.

"Yep."

"How about saluting and saying 'Yes, sir'? You military types are all supposed to do that."

"Bullshit," Jake Grafton said.

The telephone rang again. Robin said it was Merritt. Jake took the call.

"The preliminary autopsy results are in. Tomazic drowned, all right, but he has some bruises on his left wrist and back. Plus the gash on his head where he probably hit the boat. Funny thing is, the 'lividities' occurred just seconds before death. Just enough time for some local capillaries to pop, then his heart stopped."

"What do they make of that?"

"Well . . . it's suggestive, they say. Suggestive of what they didn't say. But the interesting thing is that divers found a piece of plastic under the boat. Clear plastic. They say it might have come from a scuba diver's mask faceplate. Got to do some research on that to be sure, though."

"How long was that piece of plastic in the water?"

"No guesses yet, but not long. No algae on it."

Jake sat digesting the information. Finally he said, "Thank you, Harley."

"I'll get back to you."

Jake cradled the instrument and sat staring at the wall. After a bit he let his gaze wander.

Sal Molina sipped on his coffee, now getting cold, and watched the man behind the desk. The skin on Grafton's face showed the marks of too much sun through the years. Then there were those gray eyes. Everyone meeting Jake Grafton for the first time noticed the eyes. If he was angry, those eyes were cold as a North Atlantic breaker.

Grafton had been a navy attack pilot in his youth. He had absorbed the lessons well. For years he was the Pentagon's go-to guy when crises erupted here and there.

Grafton was correct about one thing: National Security Adviser Jurgen Schulz had argued vociferously this morning against giving Grafton a jot more power. "He's a loose cannon," Schulz said, "who can't be trusted. One of these days one of his little plots is going to blow up in his face, and this administration is going to be the party that gets badly burned."

The secretary of Homeland Security thought someone with more political savvy should be installed immediately as interim director, then senior leaders of the president's party in Congress should be sounded out about possible permanent replacements.

The president heard them all out, thanked everyone and shooed them off. When they were alone, he asked Molina what he thought.

"Grafton," the president's man said. "I'd pick him for my team for anything from softball to hand grenades to nuclear war. That said, frankly, sometimes Grafton gives me the willies. He plays his cards close to his vest, doesn't keep his superiors informed, and he's perfectly willing to ignore all the rules. Yet he always gets results. Not the results we thought we wanted, but usually the best possible outcome."

The president mulled it while he twirled a pencil in his fingers. He instinctively distrusted the intelligence bureaucracy. And the military bureaucracy. Too damned many secrets and hidden agendas. On the other hand, Grafton got things done, he hadn't stepped on any politicians' toes lately, and this appointment was only an interim, "acting" deal, until the president could get a loyal man appointed and confirmed.

"Okay," the elected one said. "Grafton it is. Go tell him." The president made a dozen or two decisions a day, and he wasn't going to waste more time on this one.

"Sometimes I get the feeling with Jake Grafton that I'm up on the back of an infuriated tiger," Molina told the big boss, "and I'm about to fall off."

"As long as he's our tiger."

"He's America's tiger, not ours. You can bet your tiny little political soul that no one owns him. Appointing him acting director won't get you any points with him. With some of those people in Congress, maybe."

"What the hell could happen in three or four months?" the big banana asked rhetorically. "He'll do until we get someone else. Go tell him."

That was this morning. Molina was jerked back to the here and now when Grafton cleared his throat. He had the president's man skewered with his gaze.

"I'll take the job," he said.

"What made you change your mind?"

"Mario Tomazic was probably murdered."

Molina rubbed his eyes. *Oooh man! Here we go again.* "Okay," he said.

"You go tell Merritt that the president wants me. Better make it good. He knows this agency inside and out, and I am going to need him just as much as Tomazic did."

"Sure."

Jake stood and walked Molina to the door. "I should be thanking you, I suppose, but I won't. I will tell you this. If Tomazic was murdered, we'll get the people that did it. You can bet your bottom dollar on that."

"Umm."

"Better tell the president that before he signs the interim appointment letter. If I'm in, I'm all in."

"Jake, this administration can't afford another intelligence scandal."

"I understand. But I didn't kill Tomazic. If someone did, it's a problem that will have to be faced . . . regardless of where the trail leads or who over at the White House doesn't want to hear about it. You can tell Reinicke and Schulz I said that."

Molina took a last good look at those cold gray eyes, grunted, then left.

Jake Grafton went out to the coffeepot and poured himself another cup.

On Willoughby Spit, Zhang Ping and Choy Lee watched a thunderstorm roll out in the estuary. Dark, malevolent, flashing lightning and vomiting an opaque cloud of rain, it was impressive.

Zhang wondered what would happen if a bolt of lightning struck near the warhead, but after a few seconds' thought he stopped thinking about it. If the warhead exploded, he and everyone within fifteen miles would be instantly, totally dead. He wouldn't even feel the transition from this life to the next. Actually, that would probably be a pretty good death. No debilitating old age, no loss of dignity, no shameful last-second thoughts. Click. And he would be gone to the next adventure, if there was one, which he doubted. But he would be beyond earthly concerns. That was an absolute fact.

Zhang and Choy had just loaded the boat onto its trailer after a reconnaissance down the river to look over the naval piers and generally snoop around. Everything normal. Absolutely normal.

Now they were in the SUV watching the storm.

"Want to go get a beer?" Choy Lee asked.

"Why not?"

Choy started the engine and pulled the transmission lever into drive.

That evening he took Sally to a movie, a soapy love story. Sally snuggled up against him in her theater seat and held his hand. Just like the American girls up and down the rows near them.

She *was* an American, of course, third generation. She spoke not a word of Chinese and merely giggled when he spouted some occasionally. Unlike Chinese girls, she didn't cover her mouth with her hand when she smiled or giggled. She showed off perfect white teeth that her father had paid a whopping orthodontist bill to provide. Choy thought she was very charming. And her hand was warm and firm, supple, sensuous.

He felt very, very good. Maybe he should marry this woman. Maybe he should ask her. But there was Zhang. If it weren't for him, Choy could just cease his activities for his controller, get a job, probably move, and Chinese intelligence would be out of his life and a part of his past. They would never find him among three hundred million Americans.

He would need a job, of course, because without the controller the money would stop. But jobs were plentiful in America if you were willing to work hard and had a little bit of intelligence.

Choy Lee thought about all this and held Sally's hand and let the sensations of life and love warm him gently.

CHAPTER FIVE

If men make war in slavish obedience to rules, they will fail.
—Ulysses S. Grant

Coffee cup in hand, Jake Grafton walked down the hall to the director's office. After a short word with an executive assistant in the outer office, he punched in the code on the door and went in, closing it behind him. Today rain was hammering against the double-pane security glass of the office window and wind was shaking the branches of the nearby trees, which Grafton could have seen if he had looked, but he didn't.

Acting director!

He didn't know where to start. Soon, perhaps tomorrow, he would have to talk to the department heads, see where the agency's budget was and how the draft budget for next year was coming together, review all the big irons in the fire . . . and he was going to have to find someone to run Middle Eastern ops. There was no way he could do the director's job and that one, too.

The CIA was a huge, global operation. Not that the agency's staff was the sole outfit in the government charged with gathering foreign intelligence, because they weren't. Still, this agency was supposed to collect, analyze and pass on the intelligence it collected to the director of national intelligence, Reinicke, who was supposed to pass it on to senior decision makers in the White House, and in military and civilian agencies and departments.

Well, he decided, the more he knew about what was going on in the world, the sooner he could get on top of this job. He set his coffee cup on the desk, opened the director's file cabinets and started in where he had left off.

An hour into the mess, he found a Top Secret memo, or report, generated by the Pentagon's IT staff. If had been forwarded to Tomazic by the chairman of the Joint Chiefs. Copious amounts of Tomazic's green ink were all over the margins and footers.

The Chinese had hacked into the Pentagon's computers. The signature of Chinese computers was unmistakable in the telltale mouse droppings. U.S. Navy operational schedules were compromised. Apparently all of them. Nuclear submarine schedules and missions, aircraft carrier task groups, port calls, manpower problems, projects, budgets . . . It looked as if they had seen everything except technical data and ship plans. No, wait. Maybe they had cracked into those files, too.

When he finished the printed report, he started on Tomazic's handwritten notes. "Chinese espionage a huge problem. Their new stealth fighter an obvious clone of the F-35. Must get a handle on this. Our encrypted communications are obviously compromised—if the Chinese know what the messages might say, then they are easier to crack. How do we keep them out of this closet? Can we keep them out?"

He stared at the memo. After scanning it quickly, he reread it slowly, carefully, ensuring he got every word and nuance.

"Or should we simply let them look?" Tomazic had written in the right-hand margin.

Grafton took out his pen and wrote in blue ink, his favorite, "Can we get into Chinese navy's computers?"

The phone buzzed. "Mr. Merritt, sir." Robin must be overcaffeinated, he thought, calling him sir. The last time she got on a sir kick she wanted a promotion and pay raise.

Jake opened the door. "Come in, Harley."

"I just had a long talk with Sal Molina," he said. "Congratulations."

"I didn't ask for this job," Grafton muttered as he sat down on the couch, "permanently or on an interim basis."

"I didn't either," Merritt said blandly.

"The job was offered, so I took it. If it had been offered to you, you would have taken it, too."

"Yes, I would have."

"Harley, I need your help. If Tomazic was murdered, we have a serious can of worms buried somewhere. We're going to have to turn over every rock to find it. If there are physical clues that the killer left, the FBI will find and follow them. They will look into Tomazic's private affairs, family life, military career, old enemies, all of that. We must start on our end, a motive due to his job as director of this agency. I want you to head up that staff review you ordered this morning. We have got to rule out people inside the Company, if we can, and try to decide if anything the Company has going could have stimulated a foreign government to kill him. Someone wanted Mario Tomazic dead for a reason. Let's see if we can find it."

"We may find a half-dozen reasons."

"Or none," Grafton said wearily. "Tomazic wasn't the CIA; he was one man. You can't kill a bureaucracy, no matter how hard you try."

"We don't know that he was murdered," Merritt objected reasonably. "Assassinated. We may be snipe hunting."

"Assume it's murder until I tell you it wasn't."

Merritt thought about that, then nodded once. "Okay."

Grafton eyed the man, sizing up his body language. Yeah, Merritt was disappointed, but he was a professional.

"I didn't want this job," Jake said, "but I've got it. Let's talk about how we can get me up to speed."

He had a short interview with both of Tomazic's executive assistants, telling them he had been told the president was going to appoint him interim director and he wanted them on the job tomorrow morning at eight o'clock. Then Jake Grafton left. He went to the parking lot, got in his Accord and motored off for the beach to pick up Callie. The gate guard gave him his usual friendly wave. Fortunately he was on the front end of rush hour so got around the Beltway and over the Bay Bridge without much trouble.

As he drove he thought about Callie, his wife, about how she would take the interim appointment thing. They were married after the Vietnam War, while he was a young attack pilot. She had loyally supported his naval career, done all the things officers' wives were supposed to do, while she continued to work as a teacher of languages at the college level. Hell, she knew seven or eight, last he heard. On the other hand, lately she had been dropping not-so-subtle hints about retirement. He spent too many hours at Langley. With his navy retirement pay as a two-star, bumped up some due to more federal service, they didn't need any more money to live comfortably. They were already socking away a large chunk of his salary now.

Retirement. He had done a couple of years of that before going to the CIA. Flew all over the country in his Cessna 170B. Still had it, but hadn't flown it in six months. No time.

What was he doing at Langley that someone else couldn't do? Couldn't do as well or better? Didn't he and Callie deserve a few years of retirement while they were still hale and hearty? After this interim thing. Then, he thought. Then. Get the plane out. Go on some cruises. See some of Europe. Maybe Israel. Spend some time with daughter, Amy, and the grandkid.

Jake Grafton promised that to himself.

He arrived in Rehoboth Beach on the Atlantic about seven o'clock Monday evening. Callie was packed and ready. After a kiss, he hit the bathroom, showered, shaved and changed clothes. He felt better. At least the director's office had a shower, and he vowed to use it. He topped off his suitcase, loaded their bags into the car, locked up the house, and off they went the other way, back toward Washington.

"It was on the evening news Saturday night that Mario Tomazic is dead," Callie said. "Big write-up on Tomazic in the newspaper this morning. I kept a copy of the *Post* in case you didn't see it."

"We couldn't sit on it," Jake explained. "The local sheriff was there, plus the county coroner. There was a news chopper overhead before I could get out of there."

"Drowned!" Callie exclaimed. "With his daughter and grandchildren asleep in the house. How horrible!"

"Yep."

Jake concentrated on driving.

"Was it an accident?" Callie asked suspiciously. She could read him like a book.

"Maybe. Maybe not . . ." He decided to be honest. "Probably not."

"Who in the world?"

"Damn if I know."

"So is Merritt going to run the agency until a new director is confirmed?"

"No. I am."

"*You?* For Christ's sake, Jake! *You?*"

"Yep. President's choice, according to Sal Molina. I didn't want the job— don't want the job—but thought it over and said yes."

"Oh, my God!" his wife moaned. "There went our holiday season!"

"You getting hungry? I thought we could stop somewhere ahead and get a hamburger."

"Amy is coming in two weeks, bringing the grandbaby," Callie said bitterly. "And you'll be locked in at the office. Damn it!"

"No, I won't. You'll see."

"Why can't you just retire, for God's sake?"

"Tomazic was probably murdered, Callie."

"Maybe, you said."

"It's just an interim appointment. I'll be acting director. Get to use the director's parking place for a couple months, shower in his office, deal with the Beltway trolls for a while, make lots and lots of new best friends, then that will be that."

His wife sat watching the countryside go by. Jake had been lukewarm to the idea of retirement in the past, told her he'd think it over. Now this!

The silence was broken several minutes later when Jake asked, "You want a hamburger or Subway for dinner?"

"Whatever."

Callie Grafton was peeved, but as she sat watching the road unwind before them she tried to put it all into perspective. She had known Jake Grafton was a warrior when she married him, way back when, and he had proved it many times since. Mario Tomazic was not Jake's personal friend, but he was a brother officer, and Jake stood by his fellow warriors. It was in his DNA. Tomazic's fight was his fight. She bought it when she married Jake and she bought it now. She sighed inwardly. She was ready to ditch it all and do the grandparent thing, let life slow down, hang out with other retirees. Jake obviously wasn't. And perhaps he never would be. He could smell a fight from a mile away, and he found the prospect irresistible. That was who he was.

She had never liked the president, had voted for the other man, but thank God the stupid SOB had the sense to appoint Jake as interim director. He couldn't have found a better man if he had scoured the earth for candidates. No doubt Sal Molina had something to do with it: Callie had heard Jake mention his name several times. Molina was the president's right-hand man, his brain trust, if any of those idiots in the White House had any brains. Many pundits assured their readers daily that they didn't.

"I love you, Jake," she said.

He glanced at her, flashed that grin that had always warmed her and said, "I love you, too, Callie."

The Graftons got subs and soft drinks at a gas station/convenience store, and when they were rolling along munching and slurping, Callie asked, "Didn't Tomazic have some bodyguards? Where were they?"

"He always gave them the weekend off. Didn't want them underfoot when he went to the Eastern Shore."

"So will you get bodyguards?"

Jake glanced at Callie. That had slipped his mind. "Well, I guess so. When the interim appointment gets announced."

"Twenty-four/seven, or are you going to do the free-weekend thing like General Tomazic?"

Jake put the rest of his sandwich back in the bag. He thought about bodyguards as he drove along.

Callie wouldn't let it lie. "If someone somewhere wanted the director of the CIA off the board, you may be next."

Jake pulled over to the side of the road and removed his cell phone from his pocket. He scrolled through his contacts, picked one and touched the screen.

A two-week vacation was a rare treat for me. My name is Tommy Carmellini. Forty-eight weeks a year I am a wage slave for the CIA as a tech-support guy, which means I install and monitor listening devices, break into computers, bug embassies, that kind of thing. However . . . every now and then I get dragooned by Jake Grafton, head of Middle Eastern ops, for special assignments. I had just returned to the States from one of those in Egypt a couple of weeks ago and managed to finagle a vacation.

An old college buddy and I had used the last eight days to free-climb some cliffs in Yosemite. It had been a few years since I had that kind of a workout. I was sore as heck the first few days. Feeling fit and studly now. Mom's bathroom scale said I had dropped seven pounds. My trousers were loose, and I was using a new belt notch.

It had been a delightful interlude . . . until I got a good gander at her new boyfriend, Cuthbert Gordon. He was in his early seventies, short and not carrying any extra weight, with a huge white handlebar mustache and a tan that looked as if it came from a bottle. And he was a talker.

I could hear a cell phone ringing. In the kitchen. I felt my pockets. Maybe I had left it there.

Gordon was prattling on. ". . . retired from the university on Long Island and decided to try California. Teaching a couple of courses on investing at the community college here just to keep my hand in. A mutual friend introduced me to your mom. Wonderful lady. We're thinking about an Australian vacation next month. It's spring down there. I've been to Australia and New Zealand about a dozen times through the years and love it. Skin diving, the beaches, sightseeing . . . I think it's perfect for your mother. I'll pick up the tab, of course, and—"

"Tommy," Mom called from the kitchen, "it's for you." I kinda thought it would be, since it was my phone. "Some man named Jake."

Uh-oh. A call from Jake Grafton out of the blue was not good news. Hadn't been yet, and doubtlessly never would be.

"Excuse me," I said to Mr. Wonderful. I put my glass of merlot on the stand beside the chair and went into the kitchen.

Mom held her hand over the telephone mouthpiece and whispered, for the eighth or tenth time, "Isn't he terrific?" She was smiling brightly.

I didn't have a high opinion of Mom's taste in men. This one was even smarmier than the last one I met, three or four years ago. That one had been married five times and had all his chest hair waxed out every week or two . . . but I digress.

I relieved her of the phone.

"You're calling about my promotion, right?"

"Hey, Tommy." Yep, it was Jake Grafton. "Have you been following the news?"

"No. It's called a vacation. Has war been declared?"

"That's next week. How about coming back ASAP? I need you."

I gave it a second to let him know I was unhappy, as if he cared, then said, "I'll get a flight tomorrow."

We said good-bye, and I hung up the phone. "My boss," I told Mom. "I'm going to have to go back to Washington tomorrow."

"Did you get a promotion?"

"No such luck." Mom was also kinda slow on the uptake.

"I'm sorry, Tommy. I thought Bertie and I could take you into San Francisco for an evening." Bertie, no less. Ye gods!

"Next time, maybe."

When she broke the news to the boyfriend, he asked me, "Who do you work for, anyway?"

"It's a government job," I said evasively. I tried to remember what lie I had told Mom. Did I say I worked for the GSA or FHA? Or was it Freddie Mac?

"Tommy is in housing," she told Mr. Wonderful with a proud smile. "Mortgages and all that."

"Mortgages, eh?" he said. "I made a lot of money in mortgages—back before the crash, of course." And away he went, regaling us with his adventures in secured debt instruments as we sliced up our dead animal and vegetables.

After dinner, while Mom made coffee, I flipped through her stack of old newspapers. Found that the agency director, General Mario Tomazic, had drowned this past weekend. More riots in Egypt, the revolution in Syria was heating up again, North Korea was making more threats, another city had filed for bankruptcy . . . looked as if life on this old planet was perking perilously along as I climbed cliffs. A call from Jake Grafton—could this be about Tomazic? Hell, drowned is drowned. Wasn't a thing I could do for the guy, whom I had met only once, except wish him a happy hereafter.

Obviously something was up, but I wasn't really curious. Sort of bummed about not getting to do some more climbing. On the other hand, one evening with Mr. Wonderful was quite enough.

"Would you like some dessert, Tommy? I fixed your favorite, blueberry pie. Bertie likes it, too."

"Sure, Mom."

Afterward I helped her clean up. Slipped a knife and fork that Mr. Wonderful had used into the side pocket of my sport coat when Mom wasn't looking.

"That was a short call from that Jake," she remarked.

"Yeah. He always acts like Ma Bell is personally charging him for every word." I let it drop.

Curious phrase, "I need you."

The last time Grafton thought that only I could properly handle a chore, I spent a couple of months camping in the African outback. I said a silent prayer. No more camping, please! And I damned well didn't want to go back to Egypt. Or Iran. Or Iraq. Or . . .

Maybe Grafton just wanted me to bug someone's embassy. As soon as possible, as if there were any other time schedule in the spook business. Knowing what the other guys were actually saying to each other, their real negotiating strategy, their real assessment of the international situation, was the gold standard of intelligence. I kinda hoped that was all there was to it, but doubted it. I knew Jake Grafton too well.

On the way upstairs after coffee and blueberry pie, I swiped a manila envelope from Mom's tiny office and carefully deposited the filched knife and fork in it, taking care not to smear any fingerprints on the handles. I wondered if Cuthbert Gordon also waxed off his chest hair.

In Mom's guest room I used my cell phone to make an airline reservation to get myself, complete with body hair, back to Washington, Sin City USA. Washington wasn't hell, but you could see the smoke from there. And smell it. The good news was that when politicians died, they didn't have far to go.

After I broke the connection I looked at that cell phone with distaste. I may be the only person in America under seventy who loathes the damn things. I left it in my stuff here at Mom's when I went climbing, but now I was back tethered to the thing. Aaugh!

CHAPTER SIX

All warfare is based on deception. . . . Attack him where he is
unprepared, appear where you are not expected.

—Sun Tzu

Accidental deaths are difficult to arrange. That is why murderers and hired
assassins usually kill their victims the tried-and-true traditional ways,
with gun, knife, bomb, garrote, poison or blunt instrument. Amateurs rarely
use accidents because they miss out on the satisfaction that comes from using violence on an enemy. Professional assassins don't have enemies; they have
targets. So when an assassin has time to set it up and wants to keep police guess-
ing for a while, accidental death is the logical choice.

Fish was a professional. Had been since he got out of reform school at the
age of eighteen and an up-and-coming mobster paid him to whack his boss.
Fish did the job cleanly and fatally, leaving the police with no clues. The mobster was appropriately grateful and began steering business his way. Five
years later, Fish was paid to whack his benefactor, and did so. He had no sense
of loyalty, none of the so-called higher emotions. He was a sociopath without
a shred of conscience. Smart, too. He read up on police methods, knew most
of the latest scientific discoveries used in forensics and was a methodical crafts-
man. He also enjoyed his work in the same way a fine mechanic enjoys repairing a well-made machine. He knew how to do it and he did it well. That
was enough.

His nickname, Fish, came to him early in life. His childhood acquaintances
labeled him a "cold fish," later shortened to Fish. He didn't care one way or
another.

Tonight he sat in a stolen car in the parking lot of a large apartment complex near the Potomac in Georgetown. He was waiting. Had been since six that evening. Now, at twelve minutes after ten, his target arrived in a limo followed by a car containing two guards. The target got out of the car, muttered something to the driver, flapped a hand at the guards in the trailing car and went inside the building.

The limo and guard car soon disappeared into traffic.

From where Fish was sitting, he could see the windows of the target's apartment on the eighth floor. Sure enough, six minutes after the target entered the building, the lights in the apartment came on. Fish rolled down the window of the Lexus, chosen because it would blend in perfectly with the other cars parked nearby, and lit a cigarette. He smoked it down and crushed it out and put the butt in his pocket. Time passed. After an hour, he lit another.

He was patient. He watched other cars arrive and people enter the building. He paid attention to the sights and noises from the street. Listened with the window down and occasionally smoked a Marlboro.

At two minutes before midnight, the lights in the target's apartment went out. Or almost out. There was a suggestion of a light in one window, perhaps a night-light or an adjustable light that functioned as one.

Thirty minutes, precisely, after the lights went out, Fish reached behind him and took a small box from the backseat. He opened it on his lap. Two remote controllers were there. He selected one that he had previously labeled, turned it on, waited for a green "ready" light, and when he got it moved the control lever forward, then full aft. He looked again at his watch, turned off the power and put the first controller away.

He had allowed ten minutes in planning for the next stage, so he lit another cigarette and sat smoking it as he watched the windows of the target's apartment, checked traffic and the rare pedestrians, watched two more cars arrive and their drivers and one passenger go inside the building, and he listened. Listened to the night. Listened to life happening up and down the length and breadth of the great city.

When the ten minutes had passed, Fish opened the case and removed the second controller. He turned it on and waited for the green light that indicated it was ready to use. Meanwhile he started the engine of his car.

The green light came on. Fish aimed the controller at the window and moved the joystick full aft, then full forward.

Five seconds later he saw the glow in the apartment window, which quickly grew brighter. Then the apartment exploded. The windows blew out in a gout of fire.

Fish put the controller back in its box, closed the box and laid it on the seat behind him. He snicked the gearshift lever into drive and fed gas. Thirty seconds later he was rolling eastward, paralleling the Potomac, toward the center of town. Two minutes passed before he heard the first siren. He lit another cigarette.

The newspapers carried the story on the front page. Navy Rear Admiral (ret.) Jake Grafton had been appointed by the president as the new acting director of the CIA. I bought copies of three of the papers before boarding my plane in San Francisco and read the stories as the big bird winged its way eastward toward Sodom on the Potomac. According to the White House propaganda minister, the president needed several months to find a suitable candidate to be permanent director, nominate him or her and let the Senate do its advise-and-consent role.

Staring out the window as we flew over the Rockies and out over the Great Plains, I wondered what in the world Jake Grafton needed me for. He certainly wasn't going to give me a big promotion and a department to run. Maybe he wanted me to bug the Oval Office. Or maybe not. With Jake Grafton, predictions were worthless.

I'd worked with him enough the last few years to know how his mind worked, which might best be described as unconventionally. He didn't go from A to B to C and thereby arrive at D. He went straight from A to D. He was usually sitting on D while I was trying to figure out where B was. So Grafton was now acting director while I remained a grunt in the spook wars.

My old 1964 Mercedes 280SL coupe was right where I'd left it in the long-term parking lot at Dulles Airport. I threw my bag in, stuck the key in the ignition as I said a little prayer for the battery, then gave the key a twist. The starter ground a while before combustion began. I pumped the accelerator. After a pleasant roar, the old gal settled into a rocking idle with clattering valves. One of these days I am going to be forced to choose between trading cars and becoming a long-distance hiker.

It was nearly six in the evening, but I figured with his new elevation and all, Grafton would still be at the office. I confess, I was kinda curious about the sudden summons from an all-too-rare vacation. I tooled over to Langley, showed my pass to the gate guard and was admitted to the grounds.

I knew where in the complex the director's office was, of course, although I had never before had occasion to visit the inner sanctum. The secretary in the outer office looked at my building pass and matched the photo to my dishonest phiz. I tried to look handsome. She had a nice jawline and good eyes, which I happen to like in women. Her long blond hair was tied up in a ponytail. Her legs were under the desk, so I couldn't tell about them. Everything in sight looked great, though. She was at least a Goddess Third Class. Perhaps even a Goddess Second Class. Goddesses of any rank are rare, in my experience, especially in government service. The plaque on her desk said her name was Jennifer Suslowski.

"Do you have an appointment?"

"Unfortunately—"

"Admiral Grafton is in conference right now. Perhaps—"

"I have just returned from Moscow with Putin's evil plan for world domination. Send him a note that I'm around and I'll go get a sandwich. See you again in a half hour or so."

In the cafeteria I got a turkey sandwich and a cup of lukewarm coffee. While I ate, I eyed up some of the egghead chicks and the seminary crowd, who were huddled over their tables and talking about anything but shop. The guys at the next table were discussing the football fortunes of the Redskins, who were trying desperately again this year to rise above mediocrity. At the table on my other side they were talking about the demise of the late director— was his death accident or murder?

Murder? The word jolted me.

A television mounted high in one corner of the room was airing a news channel. Finally I began paying attention. There had been a fire in an apartment building in Georgetown in the wee hours this morning. At least seven people died, including Director of National Intelligence Paul Reinicke, a retired air force four-star general. Police suspected a gas line leak, they said.

The White House press secretary had some wonderful things to say about Reinicke, whom I had never met. By reputation, which was merely Company shop talk, he was a paper-shuffling boob who demanded that intelligence analyses be edited to conform to his view of the world, which, amazingly enough, mirrored the worldview of the White House and National Security Council staff. "He'll be greatly missed," the press secretary said. Nothing was known yet about the other victims. Three people were hospitalized in critical condition with burns.

The director of the CIA, now the DNI. Being a big weenie in Washington was getting unhealthy.

A half hour later I was back looking at the director's secretary, the goddess without a wedding ring. She glanced at me as I seated myself in one of the three empty chairs, and kept on with whatever she was doing on the computer. After a minute her phone buzzed. She answered it and talked in a low whisper. When she hung up, she said to me, "You may go in now."

I went. Gave her a smile in passing, a deposit for the future. She didn't smile back.

Grafton was pounding the keys of his computer when I entered the director's office and closed the door. He didn't look up, just said, "Hey, Tommy. Grab a chair."

The director had pretty good digs. A wall-to-wall carpet, of course. A flag on a pole behind the desk, oil paintings on two walls, drapes for the windows, three padded chairs and a couch, motion detectors mounted high in the corners, infrared sensors. There were three doors, the one I had entered and two others, both closed.

When Grafton quit typing and swiveled toward me, I said, "Congrats. Maybe. Can I have your old office?"

"This job is temporary."

"I read that in the papers, but who believes any of that stuff?"

He passed over the secretary's note. It was a printed form. The block labeled TO SEE YOU was checked. There was a handwritten note: "Mr. Carmellini with Russian plan for world domination. Will return at 7:50."

I passed it back. "Is she demented?"

"Quite the contrary."

"I'll work on her in my spare time. If I have any."

"You won't. I want you to put surveillance cameras in my condo building and the garage where I park my car. Rig it up so Callie can look at it on her home computer."

"Okay. I can requisition the stuff I need. I'll need a signature on the form."

"I can do that. I want it done as soon as possible. Callie is worried."

"It'll take me a couple of days if I do it by myself. If I can get some help, just a few hours."

"Okay."

"You going to want the system monitored by anyone besides your wife?"

"I was thinking of your friend Willie the Wire. And you and me."

"Why not a tech-support dude?"

"The less talk around here, the better. And for what it is worth, Callie likes Willie."

"She and I may be his only fans on this little round rock. I'll see if I can get this chore done in the morning."

"Fine. Then I have another little chore for you. Paul Reinicke, the DNI, and six other people were killed in an apparent gas explosion in his apartment building last night. Three badly burned, two less so. The explosion took out Reinicke's apartment, the apartment above him and the two on either side. The fire department managed to save the building, but it was touch and go."

"I saw a bit about it on the television in the cafeteria."

"I want you to work with our FBI liaison officer. Mario Tomazic drowned, Reinicke blown up . . . It begins to smell to high heaven."

"Can't the liaison guy handle it?"

"It's a she. And yes, she's an FBI agent on temporary assignment to us and very competent. I want you right there beside her."

I didn't like anything about this. I didn't know anything about law enforcement except how not to get caught. Hanging with cops wasn't on my bucket list. "Why does she need help?" I asked.

"I don't know that she does. You're there as my eyes and ears."

"Why me?"

"Because I'm giving you an order. I have transferred you to my staff."

"Oh, wow. I'm floating upward through the goo toward the top. Is there a promotion or pay raise involved?"

"Ah, no."

"You're the boss," I replied.

"Don't you forget it." That was the Jake Grafton I knew. The old attack pilot. Retired admiral. Warrior extraordinaire. A real softie.

I noodled it a bit. "How did this ace FBI female get to be the CIA's liaison person?"

"Her name is Zoe Kerry. She was in a couple of shootouts. Killed some people. We had an opening and the FBI wanted to give her some easier duty for a while so she could get her head on straight, so they sent her to us."

I was less than thrilled. "Zoe Kerry. By any chance is she related to Unbelievably Small?"

"I don't know. Ask her."

"How come I don't get some easy duty occasionally?"

"You have my phone number. Day or night."

"Just what am I supposed to be looking for?"

"If I knew that, I wouldn't need you on this, Tommy. Use your head. Now I've got work to do. Beat it."

"Aye aye, sir." I stood, saluted and stalked out. Damn him anyway.

The secretary was still at her desk.

"You'll be delighted to hear," I said softly, leaning forward as if I were sharing a secret, "he was *very* impressed with my work obtaining Russia's diabolical plan."

"I am so happy for you." She didn't smile.

"And now I'm off to more fabulous adventures. I need the office number of the liaison people, please." I flashed her a winning smile so that she would know I was a trustworthy son of the Red, White and Blue.

Jennifer consulted her Tippy-Top Secret list and gave me the info.

I decided today wasn't the day to try to get better acquainted with Jennifer. There was always tomorrow, I hoped. I thanked her, blessed her with another gracious smile and made tracks.

Zoe Kerry, the FBI's former ace shooter and now CIA liaison to that fearsome federal agency, wasn't in her cubicle at the Liaison Office, which handled agency relations with Congress and other federal agencies. I knew the head guy, Charlie Wilson, and chinned with him for a minute. He knew, he said, that the director's office was sending me down here temporarily.

Wilson was a tennis nut, ten or so years older than me, who always looked harassed. Dealing with the people on Capitol Hill takes a certain talent, and he had it. Still, he looked as if he had ulcers. I got comfortable in one of his two guest chairs. "I need a favor," I said.

"Like what?"

I fished Mom's envelope from my coat pocket and dropped it on his desk. "That's a knife and fork with fingerprints. Some mine. I need to know who else's prints are on there." The only way he could get them, of course, was to have the FBI lift the prints, classify them and run them through their database.

"Got a file number?"

"Nope."

"For Christ's sake, Tommy. You gotta have a file number. You know that."

I leaned forward a little and whispered, "It's a secret."

"If this is some broad you're trying to make, forget it."

"I don't need fingerprints for that. Can't you make up a file number?"

"Oh, hell."

"I'd really appreciate the favor, Charlie."

"If it's anybody but Joe Six-Pack, you are going to have some explaining to do."

"Thanks." I got out of my chair, shook hands, said I'd see him tomorrow, then headed for the barn.

I picked up milk and eggs at a convenience store and bought a sub on the way home, home being an apartment in the Virginia suburbs. I had moved there from my place in Maryland to get a slightly better commute, lower taxes and an easier drive to and from Dulles Airport. Given my travels hither and yon, I didn't own a pet, not even a goldfish, so the dump was always lonely. Especially after ten delightful days in glorious California.

The super had my mail, which consisted of a few bills and lots of junk flyers. I found a college football game on television and left it on for the noise. Sipped a beer, ate the sub, put my underwear and dirty shirts in the washing machine, settled in on the couch to finish the beer . . . and woke up in the wee hours. Ah, the glamorous, exciting life of an intelligence professional.

FBI Director James Maxwell ate dinner with a group of friends every Tuesday night at the National Press Club in Washington, where he was a member. He treasured the social interlude and rarely missed a Tuesday evening dinner unless work obligations prevented it. He tried to ensure they didn't.

None of his five friends, all male, were in law enforcement. They consisted of a banker, a scientist at the Naval Ordnance Lab, a newspaperman, a novelist who used to be a college professor, and a retired investor. They had been fraternity chums in college and had kept up their friendship through the years, kept it up by working at it. The ironclad rule at the dinner table was no shop talk. Sports, politics, international affairs, movies, food, cigars and families were the usual topics of conversation. None of his friends mentioned the recent demise of the CIA director and national security adviser because they knew the FBI was investigating, and Maxwell certainly wouldn't. He left all that at the office. He wouldn't talk about ongoing investigations to anyone outside the FBI or the Justice Department, not even his wife.

One of the attractions of the National Press Club was the people you ran into there. Of course there were the media types, newspaper editors, reporters and columnists, television personalities and talk show hosts, lobbyists for every industry and cause under the sun, and the occasional senator or congressman or big-business mogul. These were the people who made Washington the center of the universe. The movers and shakers. A word here, a handshake there, a smile, and James Maxwell felt like one of them. He liked that feeling. There were times when he needed it.

So this evening he finished his dinner and had one more drink with his friends—he wouldn't be driving—and wished them good-bye. He paused to chat with a senator for a minute or two.

Fish drove up in a garbage truck behind the press club, where the three big Dumpsters were located, and was gratified to see the limo was still parked over against the side of the concrete wall, out of the way. It had been there the last three Tuesday evenings when he checked. And this Dumpster area had no security cameras aimed at it. He had checked that, too.

He stopped the big garbage truck in the street and, using his mirrors, backed it in toward the nearest Dumpster. This truck was equipped with a power lift that picked up the Dumpster and emptied it into the bed of the truck. The truck beeped as he backed it up. Almost to the Dumpster, but not quite. A light rain was falling, and he had the windshield wipers going. Little wind.

He put the transmission in neutral, set the parking brake and climbed down from the cab. Walked around to the driver's side of the limo. There was about three feet of clearance between the car and the concrete retaining wall. The driver of the limo was sitting in it, wearing earphones. An iPod, it looked like.

The driver saw him coming and ran down the window. Fish put his hand in his right coat pocket.

"Hey," the driver said.

Then Fish shot him. Didn't take the pistol out of his pocket. Fired right through the coat. The bullet slammed the driver sideways. Fish removed the revolver from his pocket, checked that the hammer wasn't jammed with a piece of cloth, then looked at the driver. He had taken a round in the neck. Fish leaned in and shot him in the head. Then he put the revolver back in his pocket.

Fish walked around the front of the limo and climbed back into the cab of the garbage truck, which was idling nicely. As he surveyed the street—it was nearly eleven o'clock, and no pedestrians were around—he picked up the 12-gauge pump shotgun on the seat beside him and checked it. Safety off. He pointed it at the driver's door, so when he opened the door and started to climb out the weapon would be pointed in the right direction, ready to fire. He had used a hacksaw to cut the barrel down to twelve inches, so the front bead sight was gone. No matter. At this range, he would merely point and shoot.

He waited. Listened to the idling diesel engine.

He had waylaid the driver of the garbage truck an hour ago. Killed him as he climbed out of the truck. The driver was now in the bed with the garbage.

Ten minutes passed. Fifteen. Twenty. About twenty-three minutes after he shot the limo driver, Fish glanced at his watch. He wasn't nervous, was in no hurry. He was ready, had a good plan, and it would work. He knew it would. He kept his eyes on the truck's right rearview mirror. In it he could see the back door of the club that led out onto the loading platform.

Two minutes or so later he saw three men come out that door. That was right. Maxwell and two bodyguards. They crossed the loading platform and went down the stairs behind the truck and a green garbage Dumpster.

Fish opened the driver's door and stepped out, with the shotgun pointing.

Then they were there, coming from behind the Dumpster, heading for the limo. He had the shotgun up.

The first shot was for the lead man. The man in the middle, Maxwell, soaked up the second round of #4 buckshot, and the third man got the third round. All body shots.

Fish worked the slide again, catching the third spent shell in his hand, then closing the action. He picked up the two spent shells at his feet, then walked over to the men lying on the concrete. They were bleeding profusely from torso wounds. Fish was taking no chances. He fed two more shells from his left coat pocket into the magazine of the shotgun and shot Maxwell in the head, blowing it apart. Pumping the gun, he shot each of the others in the head. Picked up the spent shells.

He went back to the truck, opened the door, tossed the shotgun into the passenger seat and climbed aboard. Brake off, transmission in gear, he pulled out onto the street and drove away.

The next morning I coffeed, ate two boiled eggs and called my lock-shop partner, Willie Varner, also known as Willie the Wire. "How's everything?" I asked.

"You just out of jail, or was it the hospital?" Willie was habitually surly, and more so in the mornings. I had lived with that for years, ever since we went into business together.

"Hey, I've been out of town."

"This shop is a business, Tommy, and as a co-owner, you should check on it more often."

"I'm in business with a black Bill Gates. I trust you, dude."

"The women come in to see the Great Carmellini. And I need you to sign job bids."

"And I need some help today," I told him. "I'll be there around ten o'clock. We'll close the shop and open it tomorrow."

"Any money in this?"

"Contract wages. By the hour."

"Well, a little extra pocket money would be helpful," Willie admitted.

"Have any bids ready to sign. I'll see you at ten or thereabouts." I rang off.

Willie Varner was about twenty years older than me, and probably the best lock picker alive. He had taught me a lot. He gained his skill picking hotel locks and carrying out the guests' luggage, unfortunately without their permission. The second time he got out of prison for those activities, he decided to go straight. That's when he and I went into the lock-shop business together. Despite his abrasive, sour personality, he was my best friend and he could keep his mouth firmly shut. I trusted him, for one very good reason: He knew if he crossed me no one would ever find his body.

Zoe Kerry was a hard-body of medium height, with short dark hair and short fingernails without color. She had a nice jawline and a pleasant face without laugh lines. I tried to decide if she was a runner or tennis player or just an exercise nut.

"Name's Tommy Carmellini," I said. "Grafton sicced me on you. I'm supposed to follow you around."

She eyed me without enthusiasm. "He sent me a memo."

"Great."

"Why did he send you?"

"He didn't say." I shrugged.

She thought I was lying, which was ridiculous. She also thought I was a boob, and maybe that was the best way to play it.

"I don't think he likes me," I said earnestly. "But they have to give me something to do while I'm waiting for my court date. Grafton said you were FBI on assignment."

"Admiral Grafton."

"Yeah, that Grafton. He said you shot a couple of folks and came to us to unlax and rewind." I smiled.

"Umph."

"So what's on your agenda today?"

"The agenda is finding out where the FBI was on Paul Reinicke's and Mario Tomazic's accidents, and now James Maxwell, the FBI director."

I goggled at her.

"Maxwell, two bodyguards and his limo driver were assassinated last night. Haven't you heard?"

"No." I don't normally listen to the news or read the paper in the morning, as both of them have detrimental effects on my digestive system. But I didn't share that personal info with her.

She gave me the bare-bones particulars. She was slightly distracted.

"Did you know any of the three of them?"

"One of the bodyguards."

"I'm sorry," I said, and meant it.

"He was . . ." She left it there.

"Unfortunately I cannot accompany you today," I said apologetically, "as I have another errand. Tomorrow, perhaps."

"I'll try to stifle myself until then."

"Of course."

It was about ten thirty when I showed up at the lock shop with all the goodies stowed in the car. Willie and I transferred them to the shop van, which already had all the tools we would need arranged in belts and bins inside. We were a one-stop lock shop, modern as hell and really up to date. Willie was already in his lock-shop coverall, so I stepped inside and pulled one on over my trousers and shirt.

As I dressed, Willie said, "So, spy, who we gonna bug?"

"Jake Grafton."

He stared at me. He had obviously been reading the papers, too, and knew that Grafton was the new acting director. "You're shittin' me, right?"

"Nope. At his request. Actually, I think, at his wife's request."

Willie mulled it. He still had all his hair, now flecked with gray. If you could have gotten a suit and tie on him, you might have labeled him distinguished. He did indeed own such an outfit. He bought it to be buried in. I saw him wear it just once, a few years back.

When we were rolling along toward the Grafton pad in Roslyn, he said, "Man, they're poppin' these big government dudes one after another. I saw on the morning TV that the director of the FBI, Maxwell, got shot to death last night. Behind the National Press Club. You hear about that?"

"Yes."

"Shotgun. Him and two bodyguards. His driver was whacked as he sat in the limo. Four FBI dudes, deader than hell."

"This morning?"

"Well, near midnight, I heard on the TV. They're still lookin' for the shooter. A fuckin' hit. Four FBI dudes, just like that."

I didn't say anything.

Willie motored on anyway. "Third big government honcho this week, the TV babe said. Tomazic, Reinicke, now Maxwell, the FBI head weenie. Room at the top, that's what they're making. Room at the top so all the people in the chain can move up one notch. Like a cakewalk. 'Ever'body take one step forward.' I kinda figure it's raghead terrorists or some frustrated paper-pusher who never got the promotion he figured he'd earned."

"You think?"

"Kinda looks like that. But maybe it's someone gettin' even. Maybe he'll get the warden at that federal pen in Williamsburg, South Carolina, next. That cocksucker gave me a really hard time. Told me I was too sassy. He didn't like no sass, y'know, and him bein' the warden and all, he don't have to take much. None, actually. He ran that damn prison like he was Adolf Hitler's bastard kid on a mission for God."

I didn't care much for Willie's prison reminiscences, but it was no use trying to change the subject once he got into one of his moods. I drove and thought about the job. And about killers with shotguns. In Roslyn we pulled around the Graftons' condo building into the service area and locked up the van. I sent Willie on a reconnaissance to see who, if anyone, might be watching the building while I went up to the admiral's condo and knocked on the door. Callie Grafton opened it.

"Hi, Tommy," she said. "Come on in." I entered, and she closed the door behind me.

Mrs. Grafton is my idea of the perfect lady. She still had her figure and erect carriage, she was attractive, and she was pleasant with everyone she met. She had brains. In her sixties, she was the kind of woman that some men my age wish they had had for a mom. I sure did. Mine was a ditz.

Anyhow, she had been married to Jake Grafton since they were in their twenties. What she saw in him I'll never know. Oh, he was polite enough and smiled occasionally, but he had my vote for the toughest man alive on this side of the Atlantic. He was also smart, determined, fearless and, when necessary, absolutely ruthless. Maybe his wife had found a warm and fuzzy spot in him somewhere, but I had never seen it. If he had such a place, I thought, it was probably microscopic.

Mrs. Grafton had the television on. I paused to watch for a minute or two. The DC police had found an abandoned garbage truck that had apparently been the Maxwell killer's getaway vehicle six blocks from the National Press Club. The driver of the truck was dead on top of the garbage in back. Already someone had come forward who had seen the garbage truck parked behind the press club.

Mrs. Grafton watched with me. "What's going on, Tommy?"

"I don't know, Mrs. Grafton. But the admiral asked me to wire this place up. Do you have a Wi-Fi system in the condo?"

"Oh, yes. Do you want to see it?"

"Please."

It was under the television.

I walked through the condo, looked things over, then came back to her. "I brought Willie Varner with me. You know him?"

"We met in Paris. He's a nice man." I had never before heard Willie called nice, but I kept a straight face.

"He and I own a lock shop in Maryland. Willie's a little rough around the edges, but he's good people. He's downstairs now. What we would like to do is put some surveillance cameras in your place here, everywhere except the bathrooms and master bedroom. The cameras have their own batteries, which will run them for a couple of weeks before they will need to be replaced. We'll also put some cameras in the hallway and down in the lobby, in the other building entrances and a few outside. All of them will send their signals to your Wi-Fi system, which will put the feed onto the Internet so we can monitor it from different locations. Is that okay with you?"

She wasn't thrilled. "I suppose this is necessary."

"We'll also install a battery backup to your Wi-Fi system, so if the juice goes out in the building, it will still work. We'll put a broadcast terminal with a battery backup on the roof to boost your system."

She took a deep breath and said, "If you think this is necessary."

And that was precisely the reaction I expected from Mrs. Jake Grafton. The thought crossed my mind that in her own way, she was as tough as he was. Likes attract, not opposites.

"I think this is the most reliable system we can install quickly," I said. "It can be defeated, but only by someone who knows it is here and how it works. It won't deny access, but it will give anyone monitoring it warning."

"Okay," she said.

"We'll get to work outside first, and do the interior last. Be a couple of hours before we get back to you."

"I'll have some lunch ready whenever you are."

We left it there. I closed the door behind me and took the elevator down to find Willie.

The cameras we installed were digital, of course, and very small. They looked like smoke detectors. The satellite transmitter on the roof took about an hour to wire up, backup battery and all, and another hour to tie in to a CIA satellite com channel. As I worked I tried to picture the mind-set of the killer who gunned down the FBI director and two bodyguards.

Whoever he was, he was no amateur. No disaffected office worker. He was cool and deadly. Maxwell may or may not have been armed, but the bodyguards were. Undoubtedly he didn't give them time to draw their weapons. Just boom, boom, boom.

Mrs. Grafton did indeed have ham and cheese sandwiches, chips and coffee waiting when we got back inside. With a trapped audience, Willie was in seventh heaven. Talking with his mouth full, he delivered himself of opinions about national politics, the Redskins, the Nationals, women, taxes, the mayor, potholes and *Downton Abbey*. I was amazed at the comments about the PBS TV show. I didn't know he watched. You learn something new about the human condition every day.

After lunch, while Willie installed the cameras in the condo, I loaded a program on Mrs. Grafton's iPad and her iPhone, did mine, too, and checked that the cameras were working as they were supposed to. "I'll also load this onto the admiral's iPad and phone and any computers he wants to monitor this stuff at work. I'll check on the system occasionally, and so will Willie. We'll have this stuff up and working by tomorrow morning."

She thanked us and offered us some cookies. Willie took two handfuls, and we said good-bye.

On the way back to Maryland I said to Willie the Wire, "I didn't know you watched period British shows."

"You need to get some culture, Carmellini. Without culture you're one-dimensional. I noticed that in you. Women do, too. It's holdin' you back, man, professional life and love life." He started munching another cookie.

"I wondered what the anchor was," I replied.

"Culture, dude."

"I'll get a quart next time I'm in Walmart."

Willie changed the subject. "You know that killer dude who did Maxwell may be makin' the rounds. Those surveillance cameras we put in today won't stop buckshot."

"No," I agreed, "they won't."

CHAPTER SEVEN

Whenever peace—conceived as the avoidance of war—has
been the primary objective . . . the international system has been
at the mercy of its most ruthless member.

—Henry Kissinger

The next day I popped into the director's suite and met the four secretaries
and two executive assistants. The secretaries were women in their fifties
who had worked their way up the food chain to the head honcho's office. I assumed there were pay raises involved. They were nice ladies, and way too old
for me. The executive assistants, however, were a different matter. At least the
female one was. She looked to be in her late twenties. Her name was Anastasia Roberts. She was black, shapely and brilliant. I liked the way her agency
ID dangled between her breasts, which were just the right size and shape. She
was tall, with the top of her head coming up to my chin. I didn't see a wedding ring.

The guy, Max Hurley, was also on the right side of thirty, about five foot
eight and whippet thin, with cordlike muscles. He had a head of hair that stood
straight out and scraggly facial hair that he didn't shave but once a week, if
that. I figured him for a long-distance runner. He wasn't wearing a wedding
ring either, but these days, many married people didn't.

I had heard about the EAs, and now I was meeting them. These folks were
geniuses the Company recruited from Ivy League colleges and elsewhere in
government. They were going to be superstars in a few years, so they started
in the director's office to learn the ropes fast and went on from there. Folks
not quite as intellectually gifted called them geeks, and I suppose they were.

Anastasia Roberts gave me a hard look, shook the offered hand and said, "I've heard of you."

"I won the Company camping award last year."

"That must have been it," she said coolly.

Hurley chimed in. "Admiral Grafton said you are going to be working with us," he said, scrutinizing me.

"He told me that, too."

"Welcome aboard."

I assumed that was nautical humor. I smiled to show I was just one of the guys. "So how long have you been with the Company?"

"Eight months," Roberts said.

"A year," Hurley replied.

"Where did you work before you came here?" I asked, aiming at both of them.

Hurley answered first. "This is the first job I have ever had. The Company recruited me as I was finishing my doctorate."

"Dr. Hurley. Cool." I glanced at Roberts.

"I was over at the White House," she said. "I'd had enough and floated my résumé, and the Company hired me."

"And what did you do over there?"

"Political staffer. Memos and such."

"We have paper to push, too."

"And you?" she said.

"I've been here a while. Mainly tech support."

"I've heard that you worked with the admiral before."

"Occasionally." I changed the subject, to where they lived, how did they like DC and so on.

We were still chatting a few minutes later when Jennifer, the desk person, sent me in to see Grafton.

I installed a program on his computer, iPad and cell phone so he could see the video from the cameras we planted that afternoon in his condo. We sat and watched for a few minutes.

"Too bad about Maxwell," I said, trying to jostle him.

"Hmm," he murmured.

"Willie made an observation I thought cogent. He said these cameras won't stop buckshot."

Jake Grafton swiveled his gaze to me. "There's a killer out there," he admitted.

"He's pretty damned good at his business, too," I observed.

"What do you suggest?"

"Bodyguards around the clock. Don't cross the street without looking both ways."

"Go see Joe Waddell in Security. He'll have two armed men in a van a block or so from my building around the clock. Give them the address for the feed and the password."

"I'll stop in and see him before I go home tonight."

Grafton made a noise and turned back to the monitors. Callie was in the kitchen on the phone.

"I didn't think you wanted just everyone listening to you and Mrs. Grafton, so video is all you get."

He didn't say anything. Just flicked from camera to camera.

"Retirement might also be an option. Your wife doesn't want you dead."

"Stay with the FBI liaison officer tomorrow," he said. "Then brief me tomorrow evening."

"Aye aye, sir," I said, and immediately regretted it. I was already starting to sound like Hurley. I closed the door behind me.

When I got home about seven o'clock I got a dinner from the freezer—meatloaf, mashed potatoes, gravy and corn—took it out of the box and punched holes in the top with a fork, then stuck it in the microwave. As it nuked, I turned on my laptop and went to the Grafton feed. Watching the video, I thought about Tomazic, Reinicke and Maxwell. Accidents normally come one at a time, randomly, I've noticed. Three big intel dudes dead in a week were two too many. Maybe I was getting paranoid. I told myself that Grafton probably had it already figured out and just hadn't bothered to tell me about it. Or anyone else, I suspected. Damn him anyway.

I called Willie. "You been watching this Grafton feed?"

"Yeah. Writin' the times down. This hourly rate is goin' to work up to a nice chunk of change. Might even finance a trip to Vegas whenever Uncle Sugar shits me a check."

"You going to watch it this evening?"

"Hell no. I got a date. She's fixin' dinner. Gonna try to get laid."

"Good luck."

Finally the microwave beeped and stopped humming. I ate my gourmet repast on the countertop while the video from Grafton's condo and building played on my laptop. Washed the grub down with beer. Sooner or later, I told myself, I was going to have to get a life.

I had finished the frozen dinner and was working on my second beer when Callie answered the phone in the kitchen.

I wondered if Joe Waddell had those two guys in the van on station yet.

I got busy with my phone and set it up so that I could get the Grafton feed on it. Then I took a shower and changed into jeans and a sweatshirt. My pistol and shoulder holster were lying on the bed. The gun was an old Walther in .380 that I picked up cheap a few years back at a gun store. I looked at it with disgust. Compared to a 12-gauge shotgun, it was a peashooter. What I needed was full-body armor. I donned the holster and put the pistol in it.

Jake Grafton drove to Tysons Corner, then wound his way into a building complex. The seal of the Office of the Director of National Intelligence was on the guarded entrance. He showed his CIA building pass to the uniformed federal security officer on duty and was admitted to the parking lot.

This bureaucracy had been created after 9/11 because of political necessity. Prior to that, the director of the CIA had served as the national intelligence director. But the politicians had to do something after the 9/11 terrorist strikes, so a new agency was created—one that now had about 1,750 federal employees, another layer of bureaucracy to push the raw intel through before it got to the decision makers. Grafton thought it a wonder the U.S. government knew anything at all. But perhaps someone somewhere slept better knowing all these bureaucrats were on the job, except of course for weekends, vacations, federal holidays, sick days, snow days, office parties and all the rest of it.

He went into the building, showed his CIA pass again, walked through a metal detector and was escorted upstairs to the assistant director's office.

The assistant director was a serving navy vice admiral, three stars, named Arlen Curry. He rose from the desk flanked by flags when Jake entered. The escort left and shut the door behind him.

"Sorry about Reinicke," Jake said. "And Maxwell."

Curry, in uniform, motioned Jake to a chair and took one himself three feet away, situated at a ninety-degree angle. Curry crossed his legs.

"Who's going to be named acting DNI?" Jake asked.

"I don't know. No one at the White House has said squat to me."

"Yeah," Jake said. "You know that they named me acting director of my agency, so we'll be working together."

"The White House called me on that. Sal Molina. Congratulations. If you want them."

"I don't. What I want to know is why Mario Tomazic died."

"I don't think Tomazic drowned all by himself," Arlen Curry said, biting off his words. "I don't think the explosion that killed Reinicke was an accident. Maxwell and his bodyguards and limo driver certainly didn't commit suicide with number-four buckshot."

"Number fours, eh?"

Jake Grafton leaned forward and put his elbows on his knees.

"Want a drink?" Curry asked, and stood. "By God, I do."

"Sure. Whatever you have."

"What I have is bourbon. No ice." He pulled a bottle from his lower right desk drawer and produced two glasses, which looked reasonably clean. He poured a healthy shot in each and handed Jake one. Then Curry returned to the chair he had vacated. Both men sipped in silence.

Jake let it lie. They talked about the international situation, about the current ins and outs of the intel business, but Curry had nothing to say that Jake didn't already know. After a few more minutes, Grafton thanked Curry for his time and extended his hand.

Curry stared at the door after Grafton left. Then he looked at his watch and found he had a few minutes before the next meeting. He got busy with the stuff in the in-basket.

I found the surveillance van a block from Grafton's building in Roslyn, around the corner, parked in an alley. It had the name of a local plumber painted on both sides and was dirty and scruffy; still, the antennae on the roof gave it away. If I could find it, so could a bad actor bent on murder. That was something to think about. I drove slowly through the neighborhood, looking. A mom-and-pop pizza shop across the street, a coffee shop, a dry cleaner, a little sit-down Mexican restaurant . . . and a large, six-story parking garage. Beehives of condos rose in every direction. Down the hill a block or so was an entrance to the Metro. A nice urban neighborhood on a hill overlooking the Potomac, with a subway stop. If you wanted to live in close, yet not in the District, this Virginia neighborhood was about as good as it got.

Only a few minutes after nine. People were still on the street, which was lined with parked cars. Cars flowed past on a regular basis. The windows of the condos were all lit up. People were inside reading, watching television, socializing, relaxing after a day at the office. Last night when Maxwell walked out of the National Press Club, that street looked benign, too. But it wasn't. There was a killer on the loose. Or more than one. That fact gave this street a sinister tone tonight.

A car pulled out of a parking place at the curb, so I pulled in. Killed the headlights and engine and sat watching the screen of the cell phone. Mrs. Grafton had the boob tube on, but she was making something in the kitchen.

After a half hour sitting there contemplating the state of the universe and watching people on the sidewalk and in cars, I locked the car and walked across the street to the pizza joint for a beer.

When Jake Grafton was behind the wheel of his car he checked his watch. Ten after 10 P.M. He checked the list of contacts on his cell phone and called the chief of naval operations, Admiral Carter McKiernan. He called him on his private home number.

"Yes."

"Jake Grafton, Admiral. I'd like to stop around in about thirty minutes and see you."

"Can't it wait until tomorrow, Jake?"

"I'm up to my eyeballs, Admiral. I'd like it to be tonight, and off the record."

"I'm not in bed yet. Come on over. You know where I live?"

"Yes, sir."

"I'll tell the gate guards to admit you."

"About half an hour, sir."

"Right."

The CNO lived in a mansion on government property at the old Washington Naval Yard. At this time of night, traffic into the district from Silver Spring was light. McKiernan was a naval aviator and had actually been the air wing operations officer aboard *United States* when Jake was the air wing commander. He had been a lieutenant commander then, selected early for commander. *God,* Jake thought, *that was a long time ago.* McKiernan had been selected for nuclear power school, and had gone on the usual career path to executive officer of a carrier, commanding officer of a supply ship, then commanding officer of a carrier. From there he had been promoted to rear admiral and had worked his way up the ladder. He was bright, loved the navy and knew how to lead. Jake had followed his career from a distance and had been pleased with each and every promotion.

Grafton wondered if Cart McKiernan would be candid.

· · ·

I watched people on the sidewalks and in passing cars and trucks from the window of the pizza joint across the street from Grafton's condominium building in Roslyn. The place was well lit and cheerful and smelled of wonderful comfort food. One guy worked the counter and phone; through the pass-out window I could see two more making pizzas in the kitchen. There were three couples and one guy with two kids in there munching pie when I arrived, laughing and whispering and relaxing after a day at desks somewhere. Other people came in from time to time, replacing the folks leaving, or to get a take-out pizza they ordered by phone. That phone. It was at the far end of the counter and never stopped ringing. I made myself at home on a counter stool where I could watch the street.

I was sipping a beer when I saw the homeless man pushing a shopping cart full of junk come slowly up the sidewalk from the direction of the Metro stop. He turned into the alley between Grafton's condo hive and the one just down the hill. Going to mine the Dumpster behind the building, probably, or homestead a place to sleep.

I signaled for the bartender, who came over wiping his hands on a white towel. "How long would it take you to make me a pizza to go?"

"About twelve minutes or so."

"Do you have one already made up you could stick in a box?"

"What kind?"

"Whatever you have ready to go."

"I'll see." He was back a minute later. "Yeah, we got one we can warm up in about two minutes. Sausage, pepperoni and olives."

"Fine."

The derelict came out of the alley between the buildings, crossed in front of Grafton's building and went down the alley to the loading dock and Dumpster behind it.

I watched him on the video on my cell phone.

When the pizza came, I paid for it and the beer and left a tip. "Thanks," I said, and hit the door.

I crossed the street. My jacket was unzipped so I could get to the gun under my shoulder easily, if need be. I tried to whistle as I walked down the alley. My lips were too dry and I had to lick them. I got some noise out, but if there was a tune there I don't know what it was.

The derelict was half in and half out of the Dumpster. He was bent over the lid of it with his upper body inside and his feet out.

I waited until he straightened up and could see me.

"Hey, dude. Can you eat a pizza?"

He eyed me and the pizza box. "Yeah."

He climbed down. He had a couple of days' worth of stubble, and his clothes looked dirty enough. I looked at his hands and neck. Fairly clean. Through the years and various adventures, I have noticed that men who never bathe take on a rich, ripe odor, not too bad. That's after they quit stinking. I was downwind of the derelict, and I couldn't smell that odor. Nor was he stinking.

He was about five feet nine inches tall, and compact. He looked fit, not skinny and starving like an alcoholic or drug addict. He had even features and brown eyes, a tad too close together, wide cheekbones and a chin that should have been a trifle smaller if he was ever going to get a job posing for magazine ads or strutting in front of a television or movie camera. Maybe he didn't have those ambitions.

I glanced at his hands as I handed him the box containing the pizza, said, "Eat it in good health," and started to turn away.

"Was you gonna throw it away?"

"Yeah," I lied. "Got it for my kid, who just called and said he was staying at a friend's house tonight. Not a pizza person myself."

"Thanks," he said, and opened the box.

I turned my back and walked around the corner of the building and up the incline to the street.

Fish watched Carmellini until he disappeared around the building. He wiped his hands on his trousers and helped himself to a piece of pizza from the box. Still warm. As he munched he looked around at the building, the four cars parked in this area, the Dumpster. He stood thinking about the four FBI dudes last night.

Man, shooting them had been fun!

He shook his head at his own stupidity. *Shooting people is just a job,* he told himself. *You get to liking it too much and they're going to get you, sooner rather than later.*

He tore another bit off the pizza, popped it into his mouth and chewed, savoring the tomato-and-cheese taste as his eyes roamed across the rear of the building.

That guy . . . a good Samaritan, or a security guard?

Not that it mattered. *He'll never see me again,* Fish thought, and tore off another piece of pizza.

.   .   .

Cart McKiernan still had every hair he had been born with, Jake Grafton thought, although it was salt-and-pepper now, not jet black. His eyes still smiled when his lips did. Square jaw, good teeth—he looked like the admiral from Central Casting. "Send me an admiral for my movie." They would send McKiernan.

Tonight he was in sweats. He had a towel around his neck. "Was on the treadmill," he apologized as he led Jake into the kitchen. "Want a beer or drink or something?"

"Got a Diet Coke in the fridge?"

"Sure."

McKiernan filled a glass at the tap with water for himself and led his guest into the den. High ceilings, at least ten feet, Jake noticed. A packed bookshelf. Comfortable furniture. Naval paintings from the days of sail on the walls. Seeing Jake look at them, McKiernan explained. "They're on loan from the National Gallery."

"Nice."

"What's on your mind, Jake?"

"As you probably know, Admiral—"

"Cart. Always Cart to you."

"Yessir. Cart. The president appointed me acting director of the agency after Mario Tomazic drowned—"

"I read about it. Congratulations."

"I'm not sure congrats are in order. I feel like the guy getting strapped into the hot seat for the big jolt. In any event, I'm trying to get up to speed. Found a file in Tomazic's office that said the Chinese have hacked into the navy's database and are reading ship deployment schedules and the like."

"Yeah, I know about it."

"Can we talk here, in your den?"

"It's swept every week. They did it yesterday, as a matter of fact. I think we're okay."

"Without going into it too deeply, I can tell you NSA is also into their computers. The Fort Meade folks tell me they are sharing summaries with you and your intel staff. The reason I came tonight—I would like your private, confidential, not-for-publication assessment of Chinese naval intentions."

Cart McKiernan wiped his face again with the towel and took a healthy drink of water. "The picture isn't good, Jake. The Chinese are building massive amphibious capabilities and pumping up their naval assets. I think they're capable right now of winning a short naval war with Japan and Taiwan, and invading Taiwan. The staff thinks they also have designs on the southern Ryukyu and Senkaku Islands. That would give them the seabed between those islands and the mainland. Needless to say, geologists think the oil deposits there are probably as large as those in the Gulf of Mexico."

"What about the United States?"

"They have already stated publicly that their nuclear ballistic missile subs could strike American West Coast cities, killing up to twelve million Americans. Those are their figures."

"Jesus."

"I don't think he's going to help us with this," the admiral said drily. "What we have is the U.S. Navy. And that's about it."

Jake Grafton took a deep breath, then said, "It boils down to their assessment of what our reaction would be if they reacted to a 'provocation' by Japan or Taiwan. If they think we won't aid our allies, or can't aid our allies, we're screwed."

"The White House says we will stand by our allies," Cart McKiernan said flatly.

"Right."

"We have treaties."

"Treaties are only paper when the shooting starts." Jake Grafton worked on his Diet Coke. "How about the Middle East, Syria and Israel and Iran and all of that?" he asked.

McKiernan scratched his nose. "What can I say? American foreign policy has been a disaster. Militants killed the U.S. ambassador in Libya. Nothing happened. The president was going to bomb Syria, then he decided to leave it up to Congress. He made a deal with Iran, which didn't abide by their agreements. American credibility has gone into the ceramic convenience. Every holy warrior, tyrant and raghead wannabe has read the writing on the wall. America will do nothing. Yet when the shit really hits the fan and the public and Congress go berserk, the White House will call the United States Navy. Which has had its budget slashed and so forth."

Jake Grafton sat trying to digest it. Finally he said, "What's in your naval database that the Chinese might be interested in?"

The change of subject didn't cause McKiernan to miss a beat. "Submarine and carrier operations, for one," he said promptly. "When they stage one of their little propaganda productions in the Far East, you can bet they've read our ship schedule and know what we can do to respond and what we can't."

McKiernen made a gesture of frustration. "And if the Chinese are into our stuff, Russia probably is. Maybe al Qaeda. Iran. North Korea. God only knows. The only people who don't know our operational plans are our own people. We never tell our sailors anything, so they feel like they're being jerked around without reason."

"So you assume the navy's computer systems are all compromised."

"Yep. Everybody but Americans knows that all the Atlantic Fleet carrier task groups have been ordered to Norfolk on December twenty-second."

Grafton stared at the CNO. He certainly didn't know that.

"We did it before when the president and Congress got into a budget squabble," McKiernan continued. "The debt limit will have to be raised again by year's end."

"Doesn't anyone remember Pearl Harbor?"

Cart McKiernan leaned forward. "The United States Navy is following orders. The orders came straight from the White House."

Grafton's thoughts tumbled around. "Who at the White House?"

"Man, the National Command Authority. That's the president. I'm just a sailor. I take orders and I give orders. I suspect the president wants those five carriers in port over Christmas so he can argue that without a higher debt ceiling from Congress we can't afford to operate the navy, but no one on Pennsylvania Avenue has told me that. And, oracle that I am, I guarantee you they won't say it. Ever. Still, I suspect that's the reason they did it last time. And they won. Congress caved."

"Can't you finesse them?"

"How? If I don't obey orders, they'll fire me and get someone who will. You and I both know that."

"If anything happens to those five carriers, there will be rejoicing in Beijing."

"Tell me about it. And in Tehran and Damascus and Moscow and Benghazi and Pyongyang and a dozen other capitals around the globe."

"I know you're going to take every precaution."

McKiernan nodded. "Every precaution anyone in the navy can dream up. All of them. Helicopters overhead day and night. Two attack subs submerged in Hampton Roads and two just outside the entrance to the bay. SEALs in the water around the ships. Armed fighters aloft. Boats containing sailors armed with Browning fifties patrolling twenty-four/seven. That area will be a quarantine zone for boats and a prohibited area for airplanes. We'll shoot down any airplane that comes within ten miles of those ships. We did all that the last time, and nothing happened, knock on wood. Still, I'm going to sweat bullets until we get those task groups back to sea."

Jake slapped his thighs and stood. "Thanks, Cart, for the briefing. The agency will do everything we can to keep you informed."

"I know you will, Jake. I was going to call Mario, but after he drowned I figured you were probably up to your ass in alligators. You've saved me some sweat."

They said their good-byes, and Admiral Cart McKiernan escorted Jake to the front door and locked it behind him. Grafton looked at his watch. It was a half hour until midnight.

He got in his car and pointed it toward Roslyn.

I was sitting in my car when I saw Grafton's blue Honda Accord come up the street and turn into the parking garage. We didn't put cameras in the garage—I didn't even know if Grafton had an assigned parking space or just took whatever was available—but I planned to put Willie on it first thing in the morning. I had been eyeing that garage all evening. It was a perfect sniper's perch.

I sat there in the car holding my breath until Grafton came out of the garage and walked across the street to his building. He used a keypad on the front door, opened it and went in.

I followed his progress to the elevator and, when he reached his floor, down the empty hallway to his front door. He walked as if he were tired, I thought, but at nearly midnight, I would have been surprised if he weren't. He used the key and went in.

When the door to his pad was closed behind him, I started my car and headed home.

The next morning at seven I called Jake Grafton at home. I figured he was up and getting ready to go to Langley. He said he didn't have an assigned parking place in the garage. Nobody did. He was curt, no doubt from not enough sleep. Then I called Willie Varner. I figured it would take a day to install cameras and rig up a battery-operated Wi-Fi and booster transmitter on the roof. I went to Langley, got the stuff and took it over to Willie.

"Two days," Willie said, surveying the stuff.

"Get busy, dude."

"Go spy something, Carmellini."

Back at Langley, I headed for the Liaison Office. The Company liaises with everybody, Congress, every federal agency, police departments . . .

Zoe Kerry was waiting for me. "Where have you been?" she demanded.

"It's a secret. If I told you, I'd—"

"Let's go." She marched out of the office, and I trailed along behind her.

She had an agency sedan, a relatively new one that rode nice. I was thinking some more about trading cars when she asked, "Was that bullshit about waiting for a court date?"

"I'll prove my innocence. You'll see."

"Bullshit."

"It takes practice to be a good liar, so I work at it. I rarely tell the truth if a lie will serve."

"Gimme a break."

"That was the truth, by the way."

"Just keep your mouth shut today. Okay? Don't get in my way."

"I'll be a fly on the wall."

There was a conference about Mario Tomazic's death in the Hoover Building. Lots of conferences this day in that building, I supposed, since the FBI director, Maxwell, had just got spectacularly murdered. Yet if they were in a frenzy, it didn't show much. The special agent in charge of the Tomazic investigation, a woman named Betty Lehman, chaired our meeting. It consisted of reports about various lines of inquiry and a spirited back-and-forth about how many agents should be put on what.

When Lehman thought she had it all, she said, "People, so far you haven't given me any evidence that Tomazic's death was anything but an accident. There is a very real limit on how many assets, for how long, we can devote to this unless someone somewhere gets something that points to murder. Something. Anything."

From the Hoover Building we went over to look at what was left of Reinicke's apartment building. Kerry's phone rang repeatedly, and she did a lot of listening. We found a place to park, then walked four blocks to the building. It was a mess. Looked as if a bomb had gone off in one corner, seven or eight stories up. The entire exterior walls of two apartments were gone, along with windows and glass and all the furniture from the small balconies. The exterior was extensively fire-blackened. Lots of windows missing. Crews of men were nailing up plywood, probably to preserve the scene for investigators.

Kerry led me to an unmarked van parked near the building. Right beside it were two vans from the fire department. Police cars were scattered around, and we had to step over some flaked-out fire hoses. Debris all over the parking lot. Some of the cars still there had been damaged by falling objects.

Inside the van we met the FBI guy, who was seated across a small metal desk from a senior fire guy, who wore a uniform. Kerry and I had to stand. She introduced me to both men.

"What is the CIA doing here?" the FBI guy asked, looking at me. I had to break my promise to Kerry.

"Liaisoning," I said.

"That is what Ms. Kerry is doing. She'll tell you everything we want passed along."

"I can go outside, if you like, then pump her after we leave."

"Fucking spooks," he grumped. "Like we have secrets. Listen all you want."

So I stayed. I got his name so I could put him on my Christmas card list.

"Definitely a gas explosion," the fire official said. "What triggered it, we don't know. We hope to find out within a couple of days."

They yammered some more, talked about how the gas lines were routed, about the building's maintenance records, emergency repairs and so on. No one offered us coffee.

When Kerry's cell phone began ringing again, she glanced at the number and went outside to answer it. I followed her. I wandered away a bit so as not to be seen eavesdropping, but I listened hard. Stuff about the investigation into Tomazic's enemies. Apparently he had stepped on some toes on the way up in the army. I knew he also had a strained relationship with a son who had had serious drug problems in the past. Part of the conversation, I gathered, was a follow-up on the son's whereabouts and current drug usage. I kinda doubted that a doper could manage to drown someone without being seen by neighbors, but what the hey. The experts were looking under every pebble.

As we walked back toward the car, Kerry asked what I thought.

"If Tomazic was murdered," I said, "it was by a pro. No one saw anyone, there are no traces of anyone's presence, except that piece of plastic under the boat, and no weapon was used. It would have had to be a swimmer with scuba gear."

"Yes. And Reinicke?"

"Not enough information. Gas lines occasionally leak, and houses and apartments occasionally blow up when they do. Usually the occupants smell the stuff, though. Wonder why none of the survivors said they smelled gas?"

"Maybe some of the victims smelled it but didn't have time to get out."

"If this one was murder, too, the people doing it are very good. If they are the same ones."

"Lots of ifs," she said.

"If it was murder, the killer or killers are callous bastards. Seven dead, three badly burned."

She gave me a hard look. "Yes," she agreed.

We ate lunch at a McDonald's. She tried to pump me a little, and I didn't give her much. I told her how many years I had been with the agency, that I was from California originally and lived in an apartment house in Virginia.

I asked her a few questions, equally innocuous. She opened up a bit. She was from Ohio, went to Ohio State, had been in the FBI for ten years.

"So those shootings . . ."

"I don't want to talk about them."

"I understand."

Zoe worked on her salad a bit, then said, "Killing someone, even an asshole who is trying to kill you . . . It's like playing God."

I nodded sympathetically. Her delivery had changed, both the tone and the way she delivered her words. I finished my first Quarter Pounder, took a sip of coffee, then unwrapped the second burger while I eyed her. The muscles in the side of her neck were tighter. Her eyes were fixed on me, as if she were trying consciously not to lose eye contact.

"Post-traumatic stress, they said. I thought about quitting the agency, but they talked me into giving it a while. Took me off major crime investigations. Sent me over to your outfit. Said maybe time would help."

"Is it?"

"I don't know." Zoe Kerry thought about that for a while. "I don't know if I can face another dangerous situation. I just don't know."

That was the high point of the day. We stopped by the Hoover Building again, visited the lab and looked at the piece of diver's faceplate, if that was what it was, chatted up the scientists, then rode back to Langley.

As she parked the car I picked up her clutch purse, then handed it to her as she got out. She went somewhere, presumably to the Liaison Office, and I rode elevators and strolled corridors to the director's suite. Grafton had someone in there. They left after ten minutes, and Jennifer Suslowski admitted me to the stronghold.

"Thought I'd better report in person."

"Okay. What does the FBI think?"

"God only knows. But I had a little tête-à-tête with Zoe Kerry over lunch. She says she doesn't know if she can face another dangerous situation."

"Okay."

"She was lying. All the tells were there. It was fiction. PTS my ass. That broad could pull the trigger on anybody and wouldn't lose a minute's sleep over it."

Jake Grafton ran his hand through his hair.

"And she had a shooter in her purse. I picked it up. Makeup doesn't weigh that much."

"She's a sworn officer. They probably require her to be armed."

"Yeah. PTS. Light duty."

He picked up the phone and asked Jennifer to call the assistant director of the FBI, Harry Estep, whom Jake had worked with on several prior occasions.

While we were waiting, he said, "You got a gun at home?"

"Sure."

"Wear it."

The phone rang. Grafton got to it. "Sorry to hear about Maxwell, Harry . . . I know you're busy as hell . . . I'm sending a man over tomorrow morning, Tommy Carmellini. He will want to see one of your personnel files."

A pause.

"Zoe Kerry."

Another pause.

"I know all that. I want him to read her file. Everything. Supposedly she was in a couple of shootouts. Performance evals, psychologist's evals, all of it."

After another pause he said, "Thanks, Harry. See you at the White House tomorrow at ten. You're coming to that soiree, right?"

He listened a bit more, then said good-bye and hung up.

"Ask for Alice Berg in the director's office," Grafton told me. "We're violating the privacy laws and personnel policies. Don't take anything or copy anything. Just look."

"Yes, sir."

He picked up the phone. "Jennifer, send an e-mail to Alice Berg in the FBI director's office. Tell her Tommy Carmellini will be armed tomorrow when visiting, and at all other times when he enters the building."

There was a pause; then he cradled the instrument and looked at me.

"Thanks, Tommy."

"Don't mention it, boss."

He ran out of words right there and sat staring at a paperweight, an A-6 Intruder hold-back bolt. I got out of my chair and closed the door behind me.

I drove over to Roslyn to see how Willie was doing on the surveillance system in the parking garage. Almost done. We took a break for dinner at the pizza joint. I had my phone on the table and studied the feed from the Graftons' building while we waited for the pizza and sipped beer. "I watched it four hours today," Willie said. "About a hundred bucks' worth, before taxes."

When I had had enough I pocketed the phone. After we finished eating, Willie didn't reach for his check. I remarked on that.

"Hey, man," he said, deadpan, "you got a big expense account and a wallet full of fake credit cards. Stick it to Uncle Sam."

"Yeah."

"This is pretty good pizza."

"Health food."

"I had the all-meat for lunch. I paid for that."

I paid both our tabs, left him there and headed home.

CHAPTER EIGHT

Tragically, making war may be what humans do best.
—Ralph Peters

The place where they parked the van wasn't ideal. They were sitting beside a fence on a narrow lane of asphalt, in dry-land farm country fifteen miles north of Denver International Airport. Frank and Joe—not their real names—were assembling the drone in the back of the van. Cheech, a *nom de guerre* that he had chosen, was outside with the hood up, apparently tinkering. Chong—he picked his name too, after Cheech had his, so none of the men he worked with would know his real name—was the man in charge, and he sat in the passenger seat with a handheld aviation radio.

He glanced again at his watch. They had about an hour to wait, if he had all this timed correctly. Another passenger jet went overhead, about four thousand feet above them, heading for the airport. They came in more or less an endless stream, about two a minute.

He turned the frequency knob on the radio to 125.6, the Automatic Terminal Information Service, and adjusted the volume control. "Denver Airport Information Foxtrot. Temperature one-seven. Dewpoint, three. Check density altitude. Overcast at fifteen thousand, visibility seven miles. Wind two-two-zero at twelve, variable fifteen, gusts to twenty. Landing Runways One Seven Left, One Seven Right, One Six Left, and One Six Right. Altimeter two-niner-niner-eight . . ."

Chong switched the radio to 119.3, Denver Approach. "Denver Approach,

United Four Two Eight, at Anchor at flight level one-nine-zero with information Foxtrot." Anchor was a published GPS waypoint.

"United Four Two Eight, Ident."

There was a pause.

"United Four Two Eight, I have you in radar contact. Proceed Kippr"—another waypoint—"and cross at one-one-thousand. You are cleared for the approach ILS One Seven Right." ILS meant Instrument Landing System, a precision instrument approach, which was routinely used even in good weather.

Now came the read-back, which ensured the pilots of the approaching plane had heard and understood their instructions. "Four Two Eight, direct Kippr and cross at one-one-thousand. ILS One Seven Right."

Chong turned down the volume and glanced behind him. Frank and Joe had the drone assembled and were testing it in the back of the van.

The bird was an AeroVironment RQ-11 Raven, a hand-launched remote-control drone. This one had been extensively modified and weighed 5.2 pounds, a pound more than the Raven in military service. It carried the usual CCD color video camera and a small, specially constructed bomb. The bomb weighed fourteen ounces and its attaching hardware, detonator and receiver two more ounces.

The Raven had a pusher prop powered by an electric motor. Power for the motor, sensor and controls came from a lithium ion battery. This particular bird was the Digital Data Link version, one of the newer ones. AeroVironment had manufactured and sold to American and allied forces over twenty-four thousand of the things at last count. This Raven had been purchased from a Spanish army major in Barcelona who had no idea who the buyers were or what they intended to use it for. Nor did he care. He was paid ten thousand euros, enough to save his house from foreclosure, and that was enough for him. He reported the Raven and its control box destroyed in a storage shed fire that he set himself. There was no investigation.

Chong consulted the map of the Denver airport on his lap as Denver Approach instructed the next plane to fly the ILS approach to runway One Seven Right. DIA had four parallel runways, 16 Left and Right, and 17 Left and Right, so there was no way to pre-position the Raven until they knew which runway the target plane was assigned.

The Raven had its limitations. The airport approach corridor was four miles wide, and the drone flew slowly. Its cruising and climb speed was about thirty-five miles per hour, a bit faster in a dive. And it would have to climb five thousand feet here, up to ten thousand feet above sea level, where it would be fighting that wind from the southwest, which would probably be stronger at altitude. It might make thirty to thirty-five miles per hour in the climb, which would take a bit over six minutes from launch. Then it would have to be positioned southwest of the interception point so it could make its run-in in a descent, at max speed.

The timing had to be exquisite.

The color camera hung on gimbels under the nose of the craft. The gimbels on this one had been modified so that instead of looking down, the camera could look five degrees above level at max elevation. Still, to see the coming airplane and intercept it, the Raven would have to be higher than the plane. The video from the camera was displayed on a laptop computer, which was interfaced with the drone controller.

"We're ready," Frank said.

Chong looked at his watch. Watched the second hand sweep. Listened to the radio chatter, waiting . . .

"United Four Two Eight at Kippr at one-one-thousand inbound."

"Roger, Four Two Eight. Switch Tower on one-three-three-point-three."

Eight and a half minutes from the Anchor fix.

Chong lit a cigarette and stared at the road running away in front of the van. Uh-oh. Here came a pickup. He used binoculars. Farm vehicle. Driver, no passengers. Looked like one large round hay bale in the bed of the thing.

As the radio chattered on, he watched the truck approach. It didn't slacken speed, merely moved over a bit and went cruising by. Hispanic driver. No muffler.

Chong swung the binoculars. No one in sight in the fields to the left or right. There was a mobile home about a mile away to the left, but the yard was empty of people. Two vehicles there. They hadn't moved in the last hour. He checked the mirror on his door frame. Only the farm truck in sight, going away along the prairie road.

"Denver Approach, Air Force One at Anchor at Flight Level one-nine-zero with information Foxtrot."

"Roger Air Force One. Squawk Ident . . . Ident received. Radar Contact. Cross Kippr at one-one-thousand. You are cleared for the ILS Runway One Seven Right approach."

"This is it," Chong said to Frank and Joe. "One Seven Right. Launch it." He reset the timer on his watch and watched the second hand begin to sweep again.

Frank and Joe opened the cargo door and got out. Joe was handed the

Raven. Frank played a moment with the control box, which was about the size of a video game controller and was wired to an antenna that was stuck to the roof of the van with a suction cup. The genius of the Raven design was that all the microchips and processors that made the thing a stealth observation platform were housed in the controller, not the drone. The bird was too small for most radars to acquire and nearly silent. It was essentially undetectable at altitude when airborne, an invisible eye in the sky. Today the controller was augmented with a laptop, which was programmed with waypoints and a flight plan.

Joe took five steps away from the van, turned to face the wind. The prop on the Raven spun up. Joe waited until Frank yelled, "Ready," then he tossed the Raven into the wind. It climbed away quickly and was soon merely a tiny dot against the dirty gray sky. Then it was lost from sight.

The radio continued to chatter. "Frontier One Nine, hold at Anchor at Flight Level two-three-zero as published. Expected approach time four-nine after the hour."

"Is this that NOTAM closure?"

"Affirm. Advise when in holding . . ."

Apparently the FBI had gotten Grafton's memo; I had no trouble carrying my gun through security at the Hoover Building. In fact, after I showed my CIA ID, I was escorted around the metal detector and straight to a conference room on the fifth floor. My escort, a young man of about twenty-four or -five years of age, looked bored. He asked me no questions at all, merely sat and played with his iPhone until a plump woman in her fifties came in carrying several paper files.

She laid them on the desk in front of me.

"I kinda thought all this would be on a computer," I said.

"We're trying, but not yet."

"Okay."

She sat down across the table from me. With two sets of eyeballs on me, it was going to be difficult to filch anything, if I got the urge.

Well, Zoe Kerry hadn't been lying. Born in Columbus, Ohio, the daughter of a midlevel retail executive and his schoolteacher wife. Majored in accounting at Ohio State. Passed her CPA exam. Joined the FBI eleven months later. They did an extensive background investigation before ordering her to the FBI school at Quantico: It looked like the usual drivel. Her neighbors and high school teachers liked her. Her brother they liked not so much. He had gotten in trouble several times as a kid, didn't go to college, had a couple of DUIs. Was unemployed as of the date of the last interview. I wondered what he was doing now.

Her shooting scores at Quantico raised my eyebrows. They were excellent. So were her classroom grades. She sailed through the obstacle course and did well at the cross-country. Graduated in the top quarter of her class. Bully for her.

The second file held Kerry's record at the FBI, ten years' worth. Assignments. She did five years in New York, then four in San Francisco. Then back to DC. Evals, lie detector test results (they gave them annually now to everybody, apparently), even expense account claims and amounts allowed. Promotions . . . I settled in to read her performance evaluations as the gray-haired lady watched me like a hawk. The young stud was playing a computer game on his iPhone.

The shootouts were six months apart in San Fran. She had been assigned to the antiespionage task force there. There were references to file numbers. A fellow agent, male, was killed in the first one, and she dropped the villain, a suspected Chinese agent. In the second one, a civilian bystander was killed, and Kerry killed the gunman, also a suspected Chinese spy, a mole at Apple Computer. Given temp leave after each shooting, she was cleared to return to duty by the psychologist after the first shootout, but after the second she was sent to Washington for further evaluation. No mention of what that psychologist found or recommended. Presumably Zoe Kerry came to us from there.

I reached for a notepad in front of me and jotted down the file numbers of her shooting scrapes. Then I tore off the top sheet and passed the slip of paper to the watching hawk.

"I'd like to see these files, please."

"Are you done with those in front of you?"

"Yes, thank you."

She picked them up and left the room.

The game player yawned. I looked at my watch. I had been reading this stuff for an hour and a half. I wondered how long it would take for Zoe Kerry to read all the crap in my files at the CIA, which were, I assumed, digitized now.

Ten minutes passed. My escort was still on his iPhone. I reached for the notepad and tore off the top sheet. Wrote down Kerry's address and Social Security number and birthday on the bottom, below the place that held the impressions of the file numbers. Folded the sheet and put it in my pocket.

Another ten minutes passed. It was getting along toward eleven o'clock. The door opened and a Type A individual in a natty dark gray suit and power tie strode into the room. My escort snapped to attention.

He walked over to me and stuck his hand out. "Tommy Carmellini? I'm George Washington Lansdown, special agent in charge of records."

I rose to my feet. I was about three inches taller than Lansdown, and I saw a fleeting expression of irritation cross his features. He was accustomed to being the biggest stud in the room. We pumped hands. "Pleased to meet you."

"I'm afraid the files you asked to see are ongoing investigations," Lansdown stated, not a bit apologetic as he looked up into my shifty spook eyes. "Department regulations do not allow us to share those files with other agencies. Not only are they sensitive, they contain investigative notes that may or may not be true that could impact innocent individuals. And, of course, unauthorized disclosure might adversely impact successful prosecution of the guilty."

I refrained from commenting that I wasn't going to mention a word of anything in their hush-hush files except to my boss, the acting director, but refrained. A comment like that would merely bounce off Lansdown. Obviously, it was going to take more horsepower than I had to induce the FBI to share.

"Thank you for your cooperation, Mr. Lansdown. I'll pass your comment along to my boss, the acting director, Admiral Grafton."

Lansdown wasn't going to waste another minute on me. "Escort him out of the building," he said to my guard, then nodded once in my general direction and strode out.

I followed my handler like a good dog.

Chong found it impossible to stay in the van. He got out and looked in the side door at Frank and Joe huddled over the screen of the laptop studying the readouts. Chong looked at the picture on the video screen, a transmission from the color video camera in the Raven, held the radio close to his ear and waited. The drone was now level at ten thousand feet on the altimeter, flying upwind at a stately fifteen knots groundspeed.

Air Force One called Kippr and was told to transfer to the tower frequency.

Chong dialed it into the radio and was in time to hear the tower roger the call of the Air Force One pilot.

Chong told Joe, "He just crossed Kippr at two hundred ten knots. Kippr is five minutes from us. He'll be abeam us at nine thousand six hundred feet, ready to dirty up."

"Three more minutes, I think. Then I turn the bird to intercept."

They had practiced this interception a dozen times using a fighter plane that flew a similar track, at the same height and airspeed. The last four interceptions were good, but there were a lot of variables, not the least of which was wind, which would change the drone's velocity and require a heading correction of some magnitude.

They didn't have to fly the Raven into the big Boeing, merely get it within three hundred feet. Then its integrated controls would trigger the explosive charge the Raven carried, generating a large pulse of electromagnetic energy that should be enough to overcome the light shielding in the plane's computers and control system, burning them out. At that point the 747 would become uncontrollable. The electromagnetic pulse would fry iPhones, computers, pacemakers, the air data computer, the fly-by-wire, the engine controls, all of it. The plane would crash. Presumably all the crew and passengers would be killed. Including the president of the United States.

Chong used his binoculars to sweep the fields and roads. No one around. No traffic on the road since the farm truck went by. He pointed his binoculars to the north and searched the sky. The seconds ticked by.

"There it is," he told Frank.

"Turning to intercept."

Chong focused his binoculars on the oncoming plane. It should have its flaps out, be slowing to gear speed. He just couldn't tell from this angle, which was almost head-on, but looking up.

"Got him on the camera . . . Damn, we have a tailwind. Drone is making ninety over the ground."

"Don't lead him too much."

"Denver Tower, Air Force One with you, approaching Japex. We have the glideslope."

"You are cleared to land, Air Force One."

"The bird is going too fast. It's too high and won't come down."

"Try to detonate it right over him."

Frank was good, really good, but . . .

"Drop the gear," Chong whispered at the Air Force One pilot.

If the plane would slow, Frank could get the drone down.

"Shit, the wind changed. It's driving the Raven to the east. Too fast."

Chong glanced at the video presentation on the laptop. The drone had missed the big Boeing to the right. Frank was turning back toward it, steeply, and the camera picture blacked out. The turn was too steep.

Chong heard the Boeing and looked up. The president's plane was passing overhead.

"We missed it," Joe said, the disgust evident in his voice.

"Recover the drone and let's get the hell outta here."

"Sorry," Frank said.

"We'll try again when he takes off. He's only going to be here four hours."

I found Zoe Kerry in the CIA cafeteria eating a salad. I dropped into the seat beside her. I had two hot dogs with chili, mustard and onions on my plate. "Hey," I said.

"Where you been, Carmellini?"

"Doing serious hot important things."

"Shit."

"Yeah. This is the CIA, after all. How goes the investigation?"

"The piece of plastic they found under Tomazic's boat was from a diver's scuba mask faceplate. They even have the brand name."

"How long was it in the water?"

"Less than twenty-four hours."

"So it begins to look like murder?"

"Yes."

Boy, this would stir them up. In addition to the director of the FBI, the director of the CIA was also murdered. I could visualize the headline.

I ate my hot dogs. The chili they used in the cafeteria was actually pretty good. And real beef hot dogs. God only knows what part of the steer the meat came from, but parts is parts.

Kerry was still messing with her salad when I finished off the dogs and took a long, slow sip of coffee. Not as good as McDonald's, but acceptable. The upside to not being a gourmet is that you are easily pleased.

"How about friend Reinicke?"

"The fire investigators don't have much to go on. They are sure the epicenter of the explosion was in Reinicke's apartment. Natural gas. Hell of a fire. Not much left. Tomorrow, maybe, or the next day. If there is anything to find."

"You up for dinner tonight?"

"No."

"Is that no never, or no tonight?"

"Never is a long, long time. Let's just say, not tonight."

I gave her my most charming let's-get-laid-soon smile, picked up my tray and headed off for more serious hot important things. She actually gave me a small smile in return. It must be that old Carmellini charm that worked so well for dear old Dad, and Granddad . . . and Great-Granddad . . .

I got in to see Grafton about three that afternoon. He was on his computer. I waited, and when he finished he swiveled his chair to me. "Anything?"

I told him about the morning visit. About the special agent in charge of records, George Washington Lansdown. Tossed the piece of notepaper on his desk. He picked it up, held it under the light so he could see the faint indentations of the file numbers.

"Is this worth following up on?" he asked.

He wanted an opinion. So I gave him one. "They don't want to share it, so presumably it is interesting reading. Her computerized files that the dragon lady said didn't exist might be, too."

"Kerry lied about PTS."

"And she is sitting on Tomazic's murder, which may be coincidence or cause and effect. She says that piece of plastic in the water came from a scuba diver's faceplate. If there was a diver in the water when Tomazic drowned, it was murder."

"I heard about that." Grafton sighed and rubbed a hand over his hair, smoothing it down or scratching his dome. I don't think he even knew he did it when he was thinking.

"I'll see what I can do about this," he said, nodding at the notepaper. "Thanks, Tommy. Stick with her."

"Yes, sir."

After Carmellini closed the door behind him, Jake Grafton looked again at the file number indentations. He held the paper up to the light and jotted down the numbers on his own notepad. Then he picked up the phone and called the FBI assistant director, Harry Estep. After ten minutes and two executive assistants, he got through to the man himself.

"Harry, Jake Grafton. My man Carmellini came over there this morning and read Zoe Kerry's files. No problem there . . . Thanks. Anyway, he wanted to see the two files she got in shootouts over before she came here . . . Uh-huh . . . Case files."

"You know we can't show you those, Jake."

"Oh, bullshit, Harry. Like I'm gonna call a reporter. I've got this woman waltzing around Langley and I'm up to my ass in Chinese spies and she was involved in a couple of their messes. I'm curious."

"Sorry, Jake. Department of Justice regulations."

"I hate to put our professional relationship on that basis, Harry, but you're pushing me."

"I have my orders."

"Have a nice day," Jake Grafton said, and hung up.

Chinese espionage seemed to be cropping up with distressing regularity, he thought. A coincidence, or cause and effect? The CNO, Cart McKiernan, was worried about the Chinese, and Jake had the greatest respect for him. Just that morning at a department head meeting he had asked for a synopsis of everything the agency knew about Chinese cyber-espionage and naval force readiness. Once again, he was appalled at the reliance of the U.S. intelligence services, including this one, on satellite reconnaissance and electronic intelligence. Only spies on the ground could tell you what the other side was thinking, and unfortunately the United States had far too few of them. In part that was because the U.S. intelligence services had both traitors and moles, who had in the past betrayed human assets with fatal results.

But there was nothing to be gained by fretting over what America didn't have.

Grafton looked up a telephone number in his private address book and dialed it on his secure outside line. After the third ring, a female voice answered.

"Sarah Houston."

"Jake Grafton, Sarah. How're things?"

"You know, after I read in the papers that you were the new acting director at Langley, I wondered how long it would be before you called me."

Grafton smiled. Sarah couldn't see it on the phone, of course, so he let it show. Houston was at the National Security Agency, the intelligence service that used batteries of supercomputers to monitor electronic communications all over the planet. Some of their activities in the United States had been revealed to the press by Edward Snowden, another traitor, a revelation that had caused a political firestorm worldwide and crippled the service. Just how much, no one in the know was saying.

"I thought after Snowden you might be looking for a job," Grafton said.

"You never know," she replied coldly. "If they can me, I'm thinking of buying an RV with my severance money and becoming a gypsy."

"We could always use you over here."

"Wouldn't that be lovely?"

"The reason I called, I need some help."

"Well, duh. I didn't think you were calling to wish me Happy Birthday or Merry Christmas."

"Happy Birthday and Merry Christmas. Just in case. I need some help getting access to a couple of FBI files. They are being sticky, and I want a look. Probably nothing to it."

He paused to give her a chance to say something but got only silence.

Grafton continued, "They're case files. May I give you the numbers?"

"Damn, Admiral. You're going to get me sent right back to prison."

"Not unless you've lost your touch."

She said a word that was illegal to use on the telephone. Grafton had helped the U.S. attorneys prosecute her a few years ago. She pled guilty to thirty-seven felonies and went to prison. Then he had gotten her out, not paroled, but temporarily released, when he needed her hacking and data-mining expertise. She was still temporarily out, unofficially, but with a new name, a new life story, a new driver's license and a new Social Security number. Still, the prison sentence was always there, hanging over her neck like the sword of Damocles. Grafton knew she resented him for it. Owed him and resented him.

"You want the whole files or a synopsis or what?"

"Whatever you can get."

"Give me the numbers," she said flatly.

Grafton read them off. "Call me if and when," he said, and read off the number of the secure phone in his office.

"It'll be a day or two." Her lack of enthusiasm was palpable.

The admiral ignored it. "Fine," he said heartily and closed with "slave labor is so rewarding."

She hung up on him. Jake Grafton smiled again and cradled the instrument.

Chong had the handheld radio transceiver tuned to the Denver Ground Control frequency, 121.85. The wind was still out of the south, and the cloud deck had come down to ten thousand feet. He knew that because he had listened to the Automatic Terminal Information System. Denver was still landing and taking off planes to the south.

But the airport was silent just now, without a single airplane in the air. That was because the president's plane was about to depart, so all traffic into Denver was holding at various fixes all over Colorado. Planes waiting to take off were still at the gate. No doubt the passengers in the terminals were peeved beyond endurance, calling on their cell phones, worrying about connections and missed business meetings, and queued up at the restaurants, bars and restrooms. All to prevent a suicider from ramming the president's plane as it took off and climbed to altitude.

Air Force One had called for its clearance twenty minutes ago, probably while the president's motorcade was en route from the University of Colorado in Boulder, where the president had made a speech to his favorite fans, liberal college students who knew in their hearts he was on the side of history and the angels.

The van was slowly cruising a dirt farm road south of the airport, parallel to and a mile or so north of the east-west highway that ran by Front Range Airport, a general aviation airport, and out across the high plains through various hamlets on its way to Kansas.

Joe and Frank were in the back with the Raven, its battery fully charged, its little EMP bomb wired up with its detonator and ready to pop. The concussion would destroy the Raven, of course, and pieces of it would flutter down into the pastures, there to be found by investigators. The van would also be found, abandoned and burned to ensure there were no fingerprints and DNA samples to be obtained from it. Not that it mattered. The four men would be long out of the country by the time FBI and Secret Service investigators put it all together.

Good luck finding us, Chong thought. Not that the Americans wouldn't try. They would move heaven and earth to find the president's assassins. They would never give up, but the trail would lead them nowhere.

All the precautions had been taken. Every possible lead was a dead end. Months had been spent setting up this operation. He sat there holding the handheld, scanning the roads for security vehicles and thinking about loose mouths. The only possible way for the investigators to find them, Chong believed, was a wagging tongue, a tongue loosened by alcohol or the need to inflate an ego.

He didn't know the other men's real names, nor did they know his. They all had separate escape routes, passports that would not be questioned. The plan was as solid as very careful, well-financed professional criminals with adequate time to prepare could make it.

All four of them would be rich, of course. Rich and ready for a life of leisure, women, the good things in life. By God, Chong was ready. He assumed the others were, too.

The radio hissed, and then words came out. "Denver Ground, Air Force One ready to taxi." So the president was aboard, the plane was buttoned up and the engines were turning.

"Air Force One, taxi Runway One Seven Left. Route at your discretion." In other words, the airport was empty of taxiing airplanes, so the ground controllers didn't care which taxiways the pilot chose to get his plane to Runway One Seven Left. Other pilots listening on the frequency must be green with envy.

One Seven Left. The departure route would be behind the van.

Cheech turned the van around in the road, carefully so it wouldn't go into a ditch, and drove a half mile or so, until Chong told him to stop. They were on a tiny swell in the prairie, and he could see the entire runway with binoculars.

There it was! Taxiing.

He looked east along the highway, then stepped from the van and looked west. The road was empty in both directions. He swept the binoculars around the fields north and south. Some horses, a few cattle. Fences, plowed wheat fields . . . and little else.

"Let's get ready."

Cheech shut down the van and climbed out. Opened the hood.

Frank and Joe piled out. Got the Raven ready to fly.

Chong stood beside the van with his binoculars up. He watched Air Force One taxi toward the departure end of One Seven Left. No doubt the tower would clear the pilot for an immediate takeoff and he would roll as soon as he taxied onto the runway.

"Launch it," Chong said over his shoulder. As Joe threw the Raven into the air, he dialed the tower frequency into his radio, 133.3.

"Under control and climbing," Frank reported.

"Air Force One, Tower. You are cleared for takeoff at your convenience."

"Roger that. Cleared to go."

The big Boeing reached the end of the taxiway, turned broadside to Chong for just a moment and sat there. It was at least four miles away. Parked along the runway were several small security vehicles and a fire truck.

"A thousand feet and climbing," Frank said. "Tell me when to turn to intercept." He was climbing the Raven into the wind, southwest.

Now the president's plane began to move. Onto the runway. Slowly, probably so it wouldn't jostle anyone still standing and moving around. Chong doubted if the pilot was going to tell the president to sit, fasten his seat belt and turn off his iPhone.

"We got company coming," Cheech said from his station in front of the van. "From the west."

Shit!

Chong checked the oncoming vehicle. An airport security pickup with emergency lights on the roof. They were off just now.

Air Force One was rolling. Frank took a look over his shoulder.

"Turn it," Chong told him, then tossed the binoculars onto the seat.

Joe stepped behind the van, out of sight of the oncoming vehicle, now only a hundred yards away. The engines of the Boeing 747 were just barely audible.

The pickup slowed. It was going to stop. Chong reached into the passenger seat and put his hand on the pistol, a Beretta in 9 mm. Took the safety off.

As the pickup stopped, the jet lifted off. Still coming this way and climbing, although not too steeply. The sound was swelling.

Two guys got out of the truck and approached Cheech, who was busy under the hood with his back to them.

Cheech backed out and looked up at the plane, now almost overhead. The officers, walking toward him, did, too.

As it passed and the noise crested and began to dissipate, one of them shouted, "What are you doing out here?"

Cheech had already reached down behind the radiator and lifted the submachine gun off its restraining hooks. He turned, firing. One three-shot burst for each officer. Both went down as if they'd been sledgehammered.

As Cheech ran toward the security truck to check to see if there was anyone else, Frank shouted, "Five seconds."

They never heard the small EMP bomb go off. The jet continued on its course for several seconds, the engines at full power, then began a gentle turn to the right. The nose drifted down. The turn steepened and the nose dropped further. Then the giant plane, now about two miles away to the south, went into the ground at about twenty degrees nose-down and thirty degrees right-wing-down. It exploded on impact.

Chong shouted, "Let's get the fuck outta here," pulled the antenna from the roof and tossed it into the van.

With all four of them in the van, Cheech started it. On the off chance that the EMP burst would be close by, they had spent a week shielding the electrical system.

The van roared away in a cloud of dust, leaving the two security officers lying in the road. One managed to stagger to his feet. He had been wearing a bulletproof vest. He had several broken ribs and massive contusions, but he was alive and conscious. He staggered to the pickup, got the door open. Reached for the radio on the dash and keyed the mike.

Nothing. The radio was fried.

It didn't compute. He didn't understand. He tried it several times, then remembered the two-way radio on his belt. Got it out, ensured it was on, then tried to talk. It too was dead.

Only then did the conflagration of the burning airplane two miles south and the rising column of black smoke sink into his consciousness.

They didn't say anything on the ride into Denver. The enormity of the crime they had just committed seemed to crush the words from them. Two police cars with lights flashing and sirens howling roared past them going the other way. Then an ambulance. And another. And a fire truck.

Finally, as they were nearing the public parking garage downtown where they had left the cars, Chong said, "Everyone got their tickets and passports?"

All yeses.

They had selected this garage because it didn't have security surveillance cameras. Cheech went up to the sixth level. Their cars were where they had left them, and no one was around. Cheech wheeled the van into an empty stall.

He shut down the engine and reached for his seat belt release. Chong shot him an inch above the right ear, then turned and put a bullet into the heads of Frank and Joe, one at a time.

Bang, bang, bang, just like that.

He tossed the gun over the seat.

He got out, pulled out his bag that had held the binoculars and from it took a large plastic bottle of charcoal lighter fluid. He squirted some on Cheech and everything in the front seat. Closed the passenger door. Opened the van door and squirted Frank and Joe. Emptied the bottle on everything in sight, then tossed the bottle in.

Patted his pocket, felt his car keys and got out his cigarette lighter. Stepped back a few feet, lit a cigarette and tossed it into the van.

And waited. Nothing.

Just when he thought he was going to have to do it again, the entire interior of the van lit off with a whoof that nearly knocked him down.

Chong walked, not ran, to his parked car, unlocked it with the key and got in. Started it, pulled out of the parking place and drove down the slanting alley away from the van on fire, down level by level, drove toward the exit to the street and the rest of his life, which was stretching out before him like a sunlit, shining road.

CHAPTER NINE

History does not long entrust the care of freedom to the weak
or the timid.

—Dwight D. Eisenhower

The news of the crash of Air Force One brought the United States to a stand-still. And within minutes, the rest of the world. People who had lived through the assassination of JFK when they were young were flooded with memories and stunned into silence. First reports indicated the plane had gone in nose first, at a twenty-degree nose-down angle at least, and the resulting explosions and fire with a column of black smoke were soon on television, giving anyone watching little hope.

As it happened, I was in the office with Grafton's two new executive assistants, Max Hurley and Anastasia Roberts, going over the memos Grafton had scrawled in the margins of every report and intel summary. We saw them all, from confidential to Tippy-Top Secret intel. If ever someone wanted to know what was going on in the Company, all they would have to do was subvert one of the director's EAs. That thought had zipped through my noodle and was bouncing around in there when the receptionist ran in with the news, "Air Force One has crashed in Denver."

We locked stuff up as fast as we could and headed for the conference room, which had a television. It was already on. Two of the secretaries were standing there watching it. We joined them. Dead silence as we watched the column of rising black smoke go up into the blue sky and be twisted away by the breeze.

"They must all be dead," Anastasia murmured. "Including the president."

"Did you know anyone on that plane?" one of the secretaries asked, a plump woman who liked to bring homemade desserts to work.

"Probably many of them. They won't announce the names for hours, I suppose, until they get the relatives notified."

"Oh, how sad!"

I overheard that exchange but didn't turn to catch Roberts's reaction. I was concentrating on the announcer and the pictures, as no doubt hundreds of millions of people all over the world, in schools, offices, airports, homes, bars and brokerage firms were also. The video was hard to watch, live television pictures from helicopters and a news crew on the ground. The effect was mesmerizing and horrific. A picture of a smashed airliner always stirs a visceral reaction. Nowadays everybody flies in those things, sooner or later, so seeing one crumpled like tissue paper and on fire gets to your gut. The only good news was that for the people on the plane it was over quickly. The announcer didn't mention that bright spot, however.

The announcer must have been listening to his producer, however, because he said the nation's cellular telephone system was paralyzed as everyone, everywhere, tried to call their family and friends to alert them to the disaster.

The spell was broken fifteen minutes later when the first report, soon confirmed, came out that the president was not on the plane.

"Oh, thank God," three of the women said in unison.

He had stayed behind in Denver for a secret conference with senators and governors from his party to plot political strategy, the announcer said.

The nation and the world breathed a collective sigh of relief. At least the American head of state was still alive. Even though about 150 staffers, aides, Secret Service agents, communications specialists, and a few reporters were aboard and presumed dead.

In the room where I was, we all clapped. It wasn't that we were political friends of the prez, because I doubt if we all were, but he was the head of state, and it was a huge relief.

About that time I realized that Jake Grafton was standing against the back wall, watching the tube.

After a while the secretaries wandered off, back to their desks, but we three EAs stayed glued to the tube. The stock market was gyrating madly. When it closed at 4 P.M. Eastern Time, the Dow was down a couple of hundred points.

Two hours after the crash, the first accusation, by an airport security guard, that the plane had been brought down by a drone aired on a Fox News affiliate and was picked up by the network we were watching.

A burned-out van containing three bodies was found in a Denver parking garage and surrounded by FBI, local police, Secret Service and Homeland Security agents. Hundreds of uniformed and plainclothes officers converged on the crash scene, the roads around the airport and the burned-out van. Thousands of people were questioned, surveillance video was confiscated for review, roadblocks were set up, and several million people in Colorado were severely inconvenienced.

An obviously distraught president appeared on television. He was being briefed, he said. He was overwhelmed by the tragedy that had struck his official family, amazed that by a quirk of fate he wasn't on that plane and had no answer to the question of why the plane had taken off with the Air Force One call sign, which was supposed to be used by the executive Boeing 747 only when the president was aboard.

"I don't know," he said. "Apparently it just happened. We'll have to wait and see." He asked that all national flags at government and post office buildings nationwide be lowered to half mast. "The nation has lost a lot of really dedicated public servants. Their families have my sympathy."

After he said that, I realized Grafton was gone.

By six that evening I was the only person left in the conference room. The network anchors were speculating about causes. If there was a drone involved, it sounded like murder. A terror strike, or an assassination attempt? Or was it just an aircraft accident?

Zoe Kerry joined me, and together we watched the wrap-up. The fire in the wreckage was out and it was covered with foam.

That was when I remembered the surveillance system I had installed at Grafton's house. I found Grafton standing by the reception desk with Anastasia Roberts. She was telling him that she had been called by the White House and asked to inform several families that their loved ones were dead.

"Sure. Go do it," he said. "And give them our condolences."

"I may not make it in to work tomorrow."

"I understand."

Roberts strode out, and he turned to me. "Tommy, I can't get on the Internet to check the system at my house. Seems the satellite feed should be working, but apparently it isn't. Security had the van come over here to augment grounds security. I think Callie should be home from the university by now. Would you run by there and make sure everything is okay?"

"Sure. On my way."

I said good night to everyone who was still there, including Jennifer Suslowski, grabbed my jacket and headed for the stairs. Now I was worried. If I were a hit man, a disaster like this would have been the perfect time for a little improvised mayhem. With every possible witness, and my victims, glued to the tube, I would have a rare opportunity.

In the parking lot I tried my cell phone. Couldn't get a connection. Everyone in the world was calling someone. I tore out of the Langley lot and headed down the GW Parkway into Roslyn.

Thank God the Graftons lived close, not an hour and a half away out in the suburbs.

Fifteen minutes later I drove by their place, looked it over, then drove into the garage across the street and parked on the top deck. Lots of cars, but not another soul did I see on my way up. I walked down, looking for people on each level. One car drove in on the third deck, parked, and a guy in a suit got out. Fiftyish, a little overweight. His tie was loose, and he had obviously had a few on the way home. It was that kind of day.

I wondered if he knew anyone on that crashed plane. Heck, I wondered if I did. About the only White House denizen I knew was Sal Molina. I wondered if he . . .

I jaywalked across the street and headed for Grafton's building. Kept my eyes moving, looking for guys sitting in cars, people leaning out of the open garage . . .

Nothing. Paused in front and tried to get the surveillance video on my cell phone. It wouldn't log on to the network. Technology, ain't it great?

Went into Grafton's building, pushed the button on Grafton's mailbox. After a moment, "Hello."

"Mrs. Grafton, this is Tommy Carmellini. May I come up for a moment?"

"Sure, Tommy."

The door clicked; I entered the empty lobby and summoned the elevator. Up I went.

The door opened into an empty hallway. I walked down it to the Graftons' door and knocked.

Callie Grafton opened the door. Talk about a classy lady! Smart, erect, trim and still gorgeous—if and when I commit matrimony I want a lady like Callie Grafton!

"Hello, Tommy. Come in."

I did so. "Sorry to barge in on you like this, but the Internet is overwhelmed and we couldn't get the video from the cameras. I thought I'd drop by to check on you."

"You've heard the news about Air Force One, of course."

"Oh, yes. Terrible."

"Have you had any dinner?"

"Uh . . . no. Have you been here all afternoon?"

"No. I just got home about a half hour or so ago. I'm fixing a salad for dinner. Will you join me?"

"I'd be delighted if you'll give me a few minutes to look around."

"Of course. Whenever you are ready."

I checked the Wi-Fi under the television. Still working normally, as far as I could tell. Then I went out of the apartment and rode the elevator to the top floor, used the stairs to the roof. The door was locked. I used my little assortment of picks and got it within a minute.

Up on the roof I went over to the unit we had installed to send the Graftons' Wi-Fi feed to the satellite.

It was offline. I looked it over. The battery had been removed, and someone had used a blunt instrument on the thing. It was as dead as Benedict Arnold. The old battery wasn't there. Installing a new one, assuming I had one in my pocket, wouldn't make it work.

Someone had come up here while the Internet was off and fixed this thing good. That meant they had recognized the cameras on the outside of the building and in the hallways for what they were.

I reached under my sport coat and fingered my popgun while I looked around the roof. Whoever had done the dirty deed wasn't there now. I walked around the edge of the building's roof, looking. There didn't seem to be any access to the roof except through the door by which I had entered. The nearest other building was at least fifty feet away across a driveway and lawn borders. Fifty feet is a lot of space to cross.

Oh, man! I felt naked. I could be in a sniper's crosshairs right now. Right goddamn now!

I slid down behind an air vent and sat looking around, trying to think.

I wondered when the Company guys in the van left. Not that it mattered.

The fact that Reinicke had been killed when his apartment exploded crossed my criminal mind.

I couldn't stay here. I was up and running at full tilt in a heartbeat. Got to the door and shot through it. Went down the stairs and along to the elevator and took it down to Grafton's floor, the seventh.

Went down the hall and let myself in.

Went to the kitchen and found Callie. "Forget the salad. We need to leave now."

"Now?" She looked at me without understanding.

"Get your coat and purse and let's get out of here. Now."

Callie Grafton was quality. She was certainly Mrs. Jake Grafton! She didn't even stop to put the salad makings in the refrigerator. She merely walked to the closet by the front door, pulled out her coat and purse. I held the coat for her, and then we walked out. I made sure the door locked behind us.

We left the building and walked across the street to the pizza joint. I explained while we walked. "It looks as if someone visited the building while you were gone and the Internet and cell phone net were down. They're still down. The crash of Air Force One. Everyone and their brother and sister and spouse and girlfriend are trying to get on them. Whoever was in the building sabotaged the repeater I put on the roof and may have entered your condo."

We went inside and installed ourselves at the bar so I could see anyone crossing the street to the Graftons' building. "Let's wait here for the admiral," I said. The television on the wall was still covering the crash of Air Force One.

She took several deep breaths as I surveyed the crowd. About ten people, all drinking, watching the news on television.

I turned back to Callie. "No doubt I'm being paranoid, Mrs. Grafton, but the DNI, Reinicke, was killed when a gas leak in his apartment exploded. Someone may be trying to kill the admiral the same way. Probably not. But there is a chance. Say one in a hundred. Why risk it?"

"You really think—"

"I'm paranoid, sure. But the admiral sent me over here to check. And I've checked, and I think the thing to do is wait for him and you two spend the night somewhere else. Tomorrow, when things calm down, we'll have some experts go through your place."

The barman came down the counter. "A drink? A menu?"

Mrs. Grafton said, "I'll have a glass of chardonnay. And a salad with vinegar and oil. Tommy?"

"Bourbon. Neat. And a salad like the lady's."

We had had finished our salads and each had a couple of drinks when I saw Jake Grafton's old Honda pass by. I intercepted him on the street after he came out of the garage.

He came in, got a quick update from Callie and glanced at me with those gray eyes.

"Thanks, Tommy," he said.

Zhang Ping and Choy Lee watched the coverage of the crash of Air Force One on a television in Choy's apartment. He had a big flat-screen television made in China that he had bought at Walmart.

Zhang's English was improving—he listened very carefully and watched a lot of television—but he had a long way to go, so Choy translated whenever the announcer was saying something that he thought Zhang might like to know.

Outside the wind was howling down Chesapeake Bay. Forty knots, at least, Zhang thought. When he got home tonight he would open his window a crack and turn on the heater, so he could hear the wind sing and not get chilled.

Zhang liked his apartment, which was three times bigger than the flat in which his parents had raised him. It was the nicest place he had ever lived. If his mother were still alive, she would have been overjoyed to see it.

His kitchen, with its appliances and big refrigerator, was a constant source of delight. So was his bathroom, with the heater and white ceramic toilet that flushed and swept everything along to some mysterious fate, out of sight and mind. He knew the sewage didn't go into the bay—this was *America*! Not China, with its dozen hundred million poor people. That was the world Zhang had escaped when he joined the PLAN. And here he was, watching American television, listening to the wind howl outside, with his comfortable, pleasant apartment to return to in a few minutes.

Zhang wondered what the Americans were thinking about the assassination attempt. Were they angry, amused, frightened? They didn't like their president very much, Zhang believed. Only one in three people thought he was doing an adequate job. Apparently it was a sad case of voters' remorse. That thought led Zhang to muse about public opinion polls, which were a strange thing in his experience. No sane person would ask thousands of people in China what they thought about the government, then publish the results.

Finally Zhang bid Choy good-bye, and was soon outside, feeling the wind tear at him as he walked the quarter mile to his building. The wind whipped his hair and tugged at his clothing. It reminded him of nights at sea, when he was a cadet and, later, aboard his first ship.

Unfortunately those days were behind him now, and would probably never come again. Still, in the interim, he could enjoy the wind.

He opened his window an inch or two and let the singing night wind into his apartment.

Savor the days, he thought. *Savor being alive. The end will come too soon.*

With Choy's help, Zhang bought a pickup truck the next day. It was two years old and had no rust. Although he had a driver's license, this was the first vehicle he had ever owned. Well, he really didn't own this one, since it was purchased with Chinese government funds but he liked it anyway.

Choy made some telephone calls to get insurance for the truck, vanished into an office and came back with a sheet of fax paper. "We're good to go," he said.

Zhang drove it out of the sales lot with Choy in the right-hand seat.

"I only have an international driver's license," he told Choy. "Will that be a problem?"

"Not with your passport and tourist visa. And this insurance binder." He folded it up and put it in what he called a "glove compartment," a drawer with a door that hinged downward, below the dashboard on the passenger side.

As he drove along with a wary eye on traffic and the road signs that told him speed limits and others that had names of places and arrows, Zhang tried to stay in the proper lane for turns. One had to decide far in advance of a turn which lane was best and pick a hole in traffic to get into it. American drivers, he had noticed, were very touchy about someone cutting in front of them and quick to blow their horn and glare. Or raise a middle finger. Driving required concentration.

Finally he took Choy home and dropped him off, then went motoring by himself.

As he drove, Zhang thought about Choy. How far could he be trusted?

Of course Zhang knew about Choy's girlfriend. He had met her on several occasions when they went to the Chan restaurant, where she worked. She smiled a lot at Choy. And everyone else.

On a long-term assignment, naturally a man needed a woman occasionally. Paying for sex was dangerous since the police kept their eyes on prostitutes. A girlfriend was good cover for Choy.

But how much help could he expect from Choy before the man became suspicious? He was on a low-grade assignment and had never been trusted with tasks more onerous than taking photos and sending them to an Internet dead drop.

How loyal was Choy?

If Choy saw too much of Zhang's preparations, he could compromise the operation if he talked too freely or got arrested. On the other hand, without him Zhang would be on his own without a translator. It was a nice problem, and Zhang turned it over and over in his mind.

CHAPTER TEN

Fear is the beginning of wisdom.

—William T. Sherman

The Graftons spent the night in the spare bedroom of my apartment. I insisted. Yet I was kinda ashamed when Mrs. Grafton saw how messy the dump was and how little grub I had in the fridge. I was starting to mumble an apology when Mrs. Grafton said, "It looks better than that rat's nest Jake lived in on Whidbey Island when I married him. I stayed there for weeks and loved every minute of it."

Grafton used my landline telephone to call the office and talk to the security head, Joe Waddell.

"The president's plane going down triggered the security procedures," Grafton explained to Callie and me after he finished talking with Waddell. "Protect the most important stuff first."

We watched television until eleven o'clock, trying to wind down, and then the Graftons toddled off for bed. Thank heavens I had some clean sheets on the bed in the spare bedroom and clean towels in the bathroom.

When they were tucked in, I poured myself three fingers of bourbon. After one sip, I rooted in my dresser and pulled out my Kimber 1911 .45 automatic. I loaded the eight-round magazine and snapped it into the pistol. Chambered a round and lowered the hammer. I resolved to get a shoulder holster for it as soon as possible. The little Walther hadn't given me much comfort on Grafton's roof.

I grasped the loaded Kimber. This sleek contraction of machined steel and springs could kill eight men, or one man eight times. Loaded, it was heavy. Maybe three pounds. I was pleased again at how well the pistol fit my hand, which is larger than average. The cold steel and heft made me feel powerful, in control, which of course was the illusion of the gun. We are all tossed on the stormy seas of fate, at the mercy of men and forces beyond our power to comprehend, control or deflect. Sometimes we need an illusion. *You worthless tiny piece of flotsam on the tide of life, this gun gives you power.* Isn't that the way it goes? I caressed the Kimber and threw it on the bed.

I sipped on the whiskey while looking out the window. Thought about the guy or guys who entered Grafton's building in broad daylight, or at least early evening, and took out the satellite repeater on the roof. One guy, I suspected. Two would have been more noticeable. People might remember. Probably just one guy. Whoever he was, he was a cool customer. If it was the same guy who did Reinicke and Maxwell, he was also damned dangerous.

The homeless Dumpster diver that I had treated to a pizza came to mind. I could see his face, his trim physique, the sober, quick eyes . . . He could have been mining the Dumpster for pop cans to sell by the pound. Or looking for credit card and identity information he could sell to an Internet thief. Or he could have been casing the building, setting up a hit.

I sipped whiskey and thought about the possibilities. And wondered what Jake Grafton was thinking. He was a bunch of IQ points smarter than me, older and more experienced, and he understood the evil in men's hearts. Me, I'm just a thief. But Jake Grafton, he was a twenty-first-century prophet. And warrior.

I wondered if he was still awake, staring at the ceiling.

My Internet service came back on about midnight, and my cell phone beeped a few minutes later. My mom had tried five times to call me earlier that day. Some things never change. On reflection, I decided I was fortunate to have a mom who wanted to hear my voice. I figured she might be still awake in California, so I gave her a call. When we said good-bye, I finished the booze and fell into bed. I slept with the Kimber under my pillow.

The next morning I fed the Graftons a bachelor breakfast of hard-boiled eggs and Pop-Tarts. Callie looked at the Pop-Tarts as if she had never seen one before. She daintily ate half of one, probably just to be polite. She liked my coffee, though. The admiral put too much salt on his eggs, then poured on a lot of Cholula sauce, which in my opinion is Mexico's great gift to the world. With all that salt, I wondered about his blood pressure. He liked my coffee, too—Kroger's best.

I left when they did. At Langley I spent the morning with Zoe Kerry liaisoning with the FBI. They were down to a couple of agents working on the Reinicke explosion. The special agent in charge had the grumps. What could you say when most of your troops were jerked out from under you and sent packing willy-nilly off to Colorado? Nothing nice. That was what the team leader said. Grumpily.

Jake Grafton was summoned to the White House for a ten o'clock meeting. The conference room was packed, standing room only, but as interim director of the CIA, Jake got a seat at the table. Up the table were National Security Adviser Jurgen Schulz, the president's chief of staff, Al Grantham, Assistant ODNI Director Admiral Arlen Curry, Acting FBI Director Harry Estep, the head of NSA, and Sal Molina. Molina looked glum.

In front of everyone on the table was a list of the people who died yesterday aboard Air Force One. Jake glanced at the list. He flipped to the back page and found there were 132 names on it. Then he scanned the list for names he might recognize.

When the herd was more or less assembled, someone said, "The president of the United States," and everyone stood. The president walked in and took his customary seat at the center of the table on the side opposite Jake. He had obviously returned secretly to Washington last night. He looked tired.

"Please be seated," he muttered as he looked around at the familiar faces.

The president said a few laudatory words about the dead staffers, nothing memorable. Then he got down to it.

"It was just my sheer dumb luck that I wasn't on that plane. I wanted to meet with some people in Denver after the university event without the press getting wind of it, and that was why the plane used the Air Force One call sign when it departed.

"I talked to the head of the National Transportation Safety Board a few minutes ago, and his crash investigators don't yet have any indication why the plane crashed. Considering that the plane is a burned-out wreck, it may be weeks before the investigators get the technical end of it sorted out. And yet, the burned-out van that was found in that Denver parking garage had a piece of gear in it, damaged but recognizable, that the army says is a drone controller. I asked how a drone could crash a plane. They say if it had a small electromagnetic pulse weapon on it, an EMP warhead, that could knock out all the plane's electronics, including the flight control computers, if it detonated close enough with the plane in the air. Folks, if that box is indeed a drone controller, it looks like the people in that van tried to assassinate the president of the United States."

The president let that sink in for a moment before he resumed. "The FBI and Colorado law enforcement are investigating. There were several bodies in the van, badly burned, so it will take a while to identify them. As of this morning, no one knows how many people were in the van that are unaccounted for. We may have one or more murderers out running around. It stands to reason that if we do, they may be trying to get out of the country. I've asked Homeland to seal the borders as tightly as possible, but you know how that is. This murder event, terror event, attempted assassination, whatever, appears to have been carefully planned, and if so, an escape route was on the play card.

"Finding out the identity of the people who brought down that plane is now our number one security priority. Are they domestic or foreign? Is a foreign government involved? I want to know, the families of the victims want to know and the American people want to know. Your job is to help us find out.

"I'm now going to turn this meeting over to Jurgen, who will give your agencies and departments various assignments. Harry Estep at the FBI will be everyone's point of contact, and he will report three times a day to Jurgen, who will personally brief me three times a day."

The president surveyed the group, then stood. Everyone in the room scrambled to his or her feet and stayed there until he was out of the room.

The meeting went on for another hour. When it was over and everyone had their marching orders, Jake lingered to see if Sal Molina wanted to talk. Apparently he didn't. Molina and Al Grantham walked out together engaged in conversation.

Zoe Kerry and I were back in Langley about noon. Grafton had just returned and put me and Max Hurley to work drafting memos to the department heads, whom he wanted to see immediately. Hurley and I attended the meeting and sat in the back where we could take notes and run for files if required. Harley Merritt was there and sat beside Grafton.

The department heads were four men and three women. All of them looked like competent and capable civil servants, which I hoped they were. In the next few weeks I suspected I would find out, one way or another. In my sojurn at the Company I had already had run-ins with a couple of them. Still, I was big enough to let bygones be bygones.

Grafton summarized the White House meeting and said, "We have our marching orders. We are to conduct a nation-by-nation intelligence review to see if we can find any hint or trace of a covert operation to assassinate the president."

"What about the murder of Mario Tomazic?" Merritt asked bluntly.

"Have we found any hint of a possible foreign motive for wanting him dead?" Grafton asked.

"Not yet. But we have only gotten our feet wet so far."

"What if we assume the murder of Tomazic and the attempted assassination are linked? Will that help?"

It might, the assembled brains decided.

"In any event, let's get at it. The president said this morning that finding the identity of the culprits behind the downing of Air Force One is our number one national security priority. You will use as many of your people as you need to get this done, without letting our intelligence gathering go into the toilet in the interim. You'll have to use your best judgment. All vacations are canceled, effectively immediately. Call anyone on vacation and tell them to get back here. If you need to work people ten or twelve hours a day, that's fine with me. Saturdays and Sundays, too, if necessary. However, I'd like to ensure everyone gets at least one day a week off. If we don't do that, people will burn out."

There was more, and it took another half hour. Then Grafton ran the EAs out and huddled with each of the department heads for a half hour or so apiece going over what was happening in their shops.

Hurley and I got back to work. There were intel assessments to review, and Grafton's notes to turn into memos, plus all the usual paperwork that infects every federal bureaucracy. I learned that the EAs were supposed to attend to all this, prepare short memos for Grafton, write stuff for his signature, maintain his calendar, answer queries from other government agencies, all of it. Already I was missing Anastasia Roberts. Hurley and I had secretaries, so we put them to work.

By six that evening I was exhausted. We let most of the secretaries go home and kept drafting memos about every whisper on the planet for the boss to read. How he managed to wade through this stuff on a daily basis was a mystery to me.

Grafton kicked out the last department head about six thirty and asked for me. I went into his office with a pile for his in-basket and placed it where it belonged.

He got up, shook my hand, moved the chair around for me to sit in and called for coffee. When he was ensconced in his executive leather chair behind the desk and we both had hot steaming cups of java, he said, "The DC bomb squad went through my place this morning. There were three sticks of dynamite in my desk, a small homemade bomb. If I had opened the little drawer where I keep my pencils and pens, the dynamite would have exploded. Thank you, Tommy."

I didn't know what to say. Just thought about it. Finally I said, "That guy was a pretty cool dude, waltzing in and out, never knowing when the Internet might come back on."

"He's stopped fooling with accidents," Grafton mused. "Now it's just plain murder, like with Maxwell."

"Why? I don't understand why."

Grafton used the eraser on a pencil to scratch his head. "If we knew that, we'd know who."

I thought about it. "He won't come back if all he's after is a high-ranking official to pop. There are thousands of them. Well, hundreds, anyway. If he does come back, it's because someone wants you, specifically, dead."

Grafton just grunted. I didn't know if that was a grunt of agreement or "opinion noted and filed."

"Where are you sleeping tonight?"

"Amy's house in Laurel." Amy was the Graftons' daughter. "Callie went there this morning. But we gotta go home tomorrow night. All our stuff is there."

"I drafted a memo for your signature. It's in the in-basket."

He dug it out. As he read it, I thought it was a pretty good job for my first executive decision. The memo was to Joe Waddell in security, telling him that he was to provide two armed guards at Grafton's residence around the clock starting at eight o'clock tomorrow morning. They were to wear bulletproof vests, carry weapons and be visible. Every exit except the front door was to be sealed so it couldn't be opened from outside. Only residents of the building with proper ID were to be admitted. The guards were to carry handheld radios and report in every hour on the hour. Two men around the clock were also to be stationed in front and back of Harley Merritt's house in Bethesda.

Grafton reached for a pen. "You draft this?" he asked with eyebrows up.

"Yes, sir."

He signed it. "You got a future pushing paper," he said. He tossed it across the desk. "This morning at the White House it was pointed out that there aren't enough federal security officers to guard every public official in this town, even the agency and department heads. Not to mention the members of Congress, all five hundred and thirty-five of them, and the Supreme Court justices. Homeland recommended bringing in army troops, but the president said no. He's worried that it will look like the federal government has panicked."

"In light of the bomb in your condo, maybe it's time to panic," I said.

"I would bring in troops now, if it were my decision," Grafton said thoughtfully. "One more assassination of a high public official will certainly create real panic. Which is worse, another death or the appearance of overreacting?"

I was used to the way Grafton thought through problems. He was just thinking aloud, so his listeners could see where his thoughts were going. Sort of like shining a flashlight on the forest ahead, trying to see the trail hidden in the darkness.

"How about you riding over to Amy's place with me tonight," Grafton continued, "and picking me up in the morning? Starting tomorrow night, I would appreciate it if you would plan on sleeping at my place until things calm down."

I shrugged. "Sure. I can go home with you. Before we leave this evening, I want to stop by a gun store in Tysons Corner and buy a shoulder holster." That .380 automatic I was packing made me feel underdressed. I wanted the Kimber under my arm.

The phone rang. Harley Merritt was outside.

I left as Harley Merritt was coming in. I gave the receptionist, Jennifer Suslowski, the signed memo as I passed. She didn't smile. It was a tough day for everyone.

Harley Merritt had been on the telephone with various intelligence chiefs around the world—MI-6, the Mossad, plus the German and French intelligence agencies. "I asked them to review their intelligence and see if they had a glimmer about who might have tried to kill the president," he told his boss. "But you know how that is. Everything is a matter of degree. There must be at least a dozen tin-pot dictators and holy men and Taliban chiefs who would welcome the credit for offing the American Caesar."

"Maybe something will strike someone as worth mentioning," Grafton replied.

"That's a damn thin maybe."

"NSA?"

"They're tied up in knots. Gotta have a warrant to sample the river flowing out of their fire hoses. We'll have one by tomorrow, by God, but their hands are tied until then."

"So how are we coming on searching our own house?"

Nothing looked promising. They were still evaluating intelligence from various sources and ongoing covert operations two hours later when Tommy Carmellini returned.

On Willoughby Spit the wind had eased to perhaps twenty knots that evening, but the rain was steady. It had been too bad to take the boat out, so Zhang Ping and Choy Lee had contented themselves with a quick check of the carrier piers from the viewing area at the south end of the Hampton Roads tunnel, then had driven over to Newport News to see what they could of the shipyard and the three giant ships under construction there. As they ate lunch at a shipyard workers' diner, Choy Lee listened and Zhang concentrated upon his sandwich.

On the car headed back through the tunnel, Choy gave his impressions.

"All they talked about was the attempted assassination of the president. They don't like the president very much, they say, but he is the head of state, and an attempt to murder him is an attack upon the United States. The workers are unhappy and belligerent."

Zhang only grunted. He had no idea who was behind the assassination attempt. If his superiors in China, or the political leaders there, had arranged that covert operation, which had apparently almost succeeded, he assumed they were unhappy at their failure. Much loss of face. Privately he wondered if assassinating the American president six weeks before the big event was wise.

Oh well, it wasn't his decision. It was one of the cards life dealt. If the Americans increased the security around the base because of it, he would just have to deal with that.

Success for this mission was everything. Zhang Ping knew in his soul that the future of China depended upon it. Nothing—nothing—could be allowed to interfere with that. Admiral Wu had impressed that fact upon him.

He glanced at Choy Lee behind the wheel. Choy did not know why his surveillance of the naval base and the roadstead were important. Nor did Zhang intend to tell him. If they were arrested, the less Choy knew the better. Of course, if arrest appeared imminent and he had the opportunity, Zhang would kill Choy to ensure he never had a chance to tell what he did know or surmised. Choy Lee didn't know that either.

Zhang lit another cigarette and cracked his window to carry the smoke out.

After a few moments, he told Choy, "I need to buy a boat. One with a cabin that we can take out into the bay on days like this. With two outboard motors, I think."

Choy grinned. "I like to look at boats," he said. "I know some marinas where boats are for sale. Want to go look now?"

"Certainly."

CHAPTER ELEVEN

Enlightened rulers and sagacious generals who are able to get intelligent spies will invariably attain great achievements. This is the essence of the military, what the Three Armies rely on to move.

—Sun Tzu

In my opinion, a shotgun is the perfect home defense weapon. The ranges are short, you don't have to be much of a gun person or marksman, and any bad guy hit by a load of buckshot between ten and thirty feet away will be instantly dead or disabled. No one soaks up an ounce and quarter of lead, then proceeds to do you bodily harm.

I marched down to the CIA armory with Grafton's authorization in my hot little hand and soon was looking at a couple of Remington pumps, both well used, which was fine with me. One didn't have much finish left on the stock and had a couple of pitted places on the barrel and action where rust had done its thing. It was also pretty dinged up. The other was in a little better shape but didn't have much bluing left. I worked the action, checked the safeties, pulled the triggers and pronounced myself satisfied. The guys gave me four boxes of #4 buckshot—they came five to the box—and I walked out feeling like I was ready for World War III. The barrels were a little long, but I had plans to fix that.

After I delivered Grafton from his daughter's house to Langley the next day, I stopped by the lock shop that I owned with Willie Varner.

He wasn't happy to see me. "When the Internet came back on, Grafton's place was full of cops. What the hell was that all about?"

"While the Net was down someone planted a bomb in Grafton's desk."

"You're shittin' me!"

"Nope."

"Well, it's a damn good thing I didn't jump in the shop van and go motorin' right over to see what was what," Willie declared. "I might've met the murderous dude face-to-face."

"Yeah."

"Being a convicted felon and all, you know I can't legally own a shooter, Tommy. I might've been killed."

"Hey, you didn't go, and I knew about it, and I went."

"But . . . a bomb!"

"Stop sweating the program." In the workshop, I removed the shotguns from the gun cases that held them and put the first one in a vise. Willie watched. I used a hacksaw to cut off the barrel right in front on the forearm. Still had nineteen inches of barrel left, so I was legal. No more front sight, though, but at close range you don't aim one of these—you just point and pull the trigger and trust to Remington and whoever made the ammo to take care of the rest.

"What, pray tell, are these shotguns for?" Willie asked as I sawed away on the second one.

"Grafton and I are going to bunk over at his place for the foreseeable future."

"You idiot! You're hopin' that bomber dude comes back!"

"Yes," I admitted. I hadn't thought about it until Willie said it, but, yes, I would welcome a chance to perforate his hide.

"Assassins tryin' to kill the prez, mad bombers runnin' around loose, and now you're gunnin' up to play cowboy." Willie stalked out.

After I finished cutting off the second barrel, I dressed up the muzzles with a round file, oiled them lightly and worked the actions repeatedly. Loaded each one with five shells, then worked the actions and ejected them.

They would do.

Back at the office I got into the executive assistant gig big-time. I was impressed with the competence and brains of both Roberts and Hurley. They had only to glance at a document or memo and they instantly understood it, memorized it and were able to relate it to the big picture. I felt outclassed and way behind the curve. I quickly became convinced that executive assisting wasn't my thing. I muddled on, however, always the good soldier. I don't know if that is a vice or virtue. I thought that if and when I screwed up too many things, Grafton would find something else for me to do. Like steal something. That was my best skill set.

At night I went over to the Graftons'. The first night the admiral and I inspected his desk carefully. The thing was covered with black fingerprint powder, which was ridiculous. No self-respecting criminal these days left fingerprints.

"You know," I said to the admiral, "I may have seen the guy who did this." I told him about the Dumpster diver and the pizza. "Maybe I should go through mug books and see if I can spot him."

Jake Grafton was dismissive. "This man isn't a street hood, Tommy. He's a pro. There is little chance he has an American arrest record. It would be a waste of time."

Callie gave me the guest bedroom. She seemed to accept the situation as another adventure to be lived through. She paid close attention when I showed her how the shotgun worked, how the safety worked, how to pump the action. She did it a few times, pointed the thing and pulled the trigger.

"It's going to kick," her husband told her, "but you'll be so scared you won't notice. After the kick, work the action and shoot again. Keep shooting until there is nothing standing to shoot at or you run out of shells, whichever is first."

I loaded the gun and she took it to the bedroom.

I figured my car was the best place for mine. It was there now, already loaded.

So we settled into a routine. I ate better at the Graftons' than I did at home since Callie didn't do frozen meals. At the office I struggled on executive assisting. Roberts and Hurley did the bulk of the work and left me stuff that was simple and they thought I wouldn't mess up. They checked me afterward anyway. I found I spent a lot of time with Grafton's calendar. He could either see you at two o'clock or he couldn't. He was busy as sin. Department heads, meetings with the new acting director of the ODNI, big FBI bananas, foreigners, probably some foreign intelligence agency—he talked to them all or had meetings or ran over to their office in a bulletproof limo with two armed guards and a trailing car with two more shooters. He didn't tell me what he was getting out of all of this, of course, but the stuff we EAs drafted or filed or arranged let us see under the corners occasionally.

The news about the attempted presidential assassination dribbled out. Dental work proved that the dead men in the van were Russians. The bodies were too badly burned to obtain fingerprints or postmortem photos of faces or tattoos, if they had ever had any. Somehow the fact that the three dead men were Russians leaked to the press, which provoked a small international political crisis. The Russians took offense.

We soldiered on anyway.

Sometime that week Charlie Wilson, head of the Liaison Office, called me. I stopped by his office twenty minutes later. He was steamed and it showed. He waved a sheet of paper at me. "I got an FBI report on those fingerprints you gave me. They have their knickers in a real twist. Where did you get them?"

I decided that this time perhaps the truth was best. "From my mother's boyfriend. Smarmy bastard. I didn't think there was a word of truth in his head. What's the crisis? Who is he?"

Charlie took a deep breath and rubbed his face. Then he stared at me. "That straight?"

"I wouldn't lie to you."

"Carmellini, you started lying before you got out of diapers and have never stopped. If you told me this was November I'd check the calendar to make sure."

"Come on. Who is he?"

Wilson passed me the paper. There was even a mug shot photo, with a booking number. He must have been plastered when they snapped it. It was Cuthbert Gordon, all right. But that wasn't his real name. He was Alfred Bruno, a Cleveland mobster who ratted on his pals and was now in the witness protection program, with a new identity, a new past and a small pension. I was surprised, and it showed on my face, I guess.

"You really didn't know, did you?" Wilson said, slightly amazed.

"I didn't. That's why I brought the tableware in here. I wanted to know. I thought he might be some kind of creep who relieved single women of their savings. Mom is something of a ditz, but she doesn't deserve an asshole. Like this one." I looked again at Bruno's photo. True, the day of his arrest had not been one of his better days, but . . . Man, he looked ready for a coffin.

"Okay," Charlie Wilson said. "I'll buy that story until a better one surfaces. Let me give you the gospel. I just got off the phone an hour ago with some FBI weenie in witness protection. He was royally pissed. Said if we—that's this United States government agency—messed with one of Justice's star witness in some creepy spy caper and exposed him, heads would roll. If he got whacked, they would move heaven and earth to find who blew his cover and have the loose-mouthed bastard prosecuted. Have you got that?"

I nodded.

"How old is your mother?"

I told him.

Wilson calmed down two degrees. "She's an adult, presumably rational and presumably not a virgin since she claims you. This is her problem, Carmellini, not yours. If you make it your problem, the shit is going to hit the fan and you are going to get splattered. Have you got that?"

I nodded again.

"Don't ever ask me for another personal favor. Not one. Our relationship with the FBI is too important to throw a handful of sand into the gears for personal reasons."

"Uh, is there any way I can get Mom's knife and fork back? She inherited—"

"For the love of God! Give me that sheet of paper and get out of here."

I took one last glance at Alfred Bruno's sour, soused puss, handed the sheet back and disappeared. Poof.

The Wednesday before Thanksgiving Jake Grafton received a call from his NSA spy, Sarah Houston. "I'm calling from a pay phone, Admiral. I got the info you wanted on those two FBI files."

"Great. Shoot."

"The files are counterintelligence files. Zoe Kerry was on a team working them out of San Francisco. One of the two dead men was suspected of espionage. For the Chinese. Kerry said he tried to kill her, so she had to kill him in self-defense. The other man she shot, six weeks later, was a supposed onlooker who tried to intervene violently in the attempted arrest of a spy. Why he did that is anyone's guess. The alleged spy got away."

"Any follow-up by the FBI?"

"The usual routine suspension and investigation, which cleared her on both of the shootings for lack of evidence. There was no proof that they were anything but what she said they were."

"You read the files. What do you think?"

Silence. After a moment, Sarah Houston said, "No witnesses, no conflicting stories from fellow agents, none of the usual friction. Maybe it went down the way Kerry said, maybe it didn't."

"Chinese spies?"

"Yep."

"Thank you, Sarah. I'm going to request that your agency transfer you to the CIA. How do you feel about that?"

More silence. "Are you giving me a choice?"

"Nope. A heads-up. I need your skills over here."

"I'm not going to have to work with Carmellini again, am I?" Sarah and Tommy had been a number but had broken up a couple of years back, for the second or third time.

"I'll try to keep him busy somewhere else in the building."

"When?"

"Next week, if the paperwork sails on through."

"I'll be holding my breath." She hung up on him.

When he found out that the president was not aboard Air Force One when it crashed, Chong had a bad moment. The big money was for popping the big banana, not for whacking his staff and a few reporters.

Damn, they should have gotten him as he flew *into* Denver! He was on the plane *then*!

As he thought about it, Chong realized that the president missing the plane was just one of those illogical, unpredictable twists that life throws at people with appalling regularity. The real question was, would the client pay off anyway? After all, Chong and the guys had done the work and taken the risk. The job was to crash the plane, and they had accomplished that feat. It wasn't Chong's fault if Whosis huddled in a secret plotting session with his political allies and sent the plane on without him.

Chong thought about every aspect of the hit, looked at it from every angle, as he drove through the Rockies to Utah. He changed cars in the long-term parking lot at the Salt Lake City airport. He drove out of the lot in a Mazda he had parked there two weeks ago and spent the night in a ski resort in Alta, where he had a reservation. The season was just getting started, the desk clerk who checked him in explained. Some man-made snow, but it wasn't very good.

Chong smiled and said he would make out. He thought the authorities would be looking for a running man, so he didn't run.

He ate well, watched television news morning and evening and skied for a couple of hours each day. Real snow was falling, and fast. The skiing got better.

The fifth day, he hit the interstate heading north into Idaho, and from there drove for Seattle. Spent another night in a sixty-nine-dollar room in Walla Walla, Washington, and had another good meal, a New York strip, at a local steakhouse.

He was feeling pretty good about the getaway. He listened to radio news every hour on the hour as he drove. The authorities were keeping their cards close to their vest. The burned-out van was being examined by forensic experts, but the findings were not being released. The FBI had figured out that a drone equipped with some kind of EMP weapon was the most probable cause of the Air Force One crash. What other information they had, the authorities weren't saying. The attorney general, however, was promising that those behind the attack would be apprehended and brought to justice if it took the entire assets of the Justice Department to do it.

Between news broadcasts, Chong listened to syndicated talk shows, all of which had conservative hosts who lambasted the administration over domestic and foreign policy and hammered the president over his vacations at taxpayer expense. They also lamented the tragedy of the deaths of the people on the plane. Reporters had been busy. They had human interest vignettes on many of the victims. Each host seemed to have his own idea about who might be behind the attack, but they kept their speculations generalized, no doubt to skirt the libel laws. Chong did learn that two separate Islamic jihadist groups had claimed responsibility.

After three days on the road, Chong rolled into Seattle. It was raining lightly, as usual. After a comfortable night in a hotel, he drove to Sea-Tac Airport and parked in the long-term lot.

The car he had parked here he had purchased two months ago for cash from a guy who had an ad in the newspaper. It still had the old license plate on it. A green Chevy with fairly high miles, it was dirty as Chong walked up to it. Tires still good. He unlocked it, threw his small bag in the backseat and got in. He picked up the passenger-side mat and felt around.

Yes, the credential case was still there. He pulled it out, checked to ensure he wasn't being watched, then opened it. The passport and driver's license were there, along with a thousand dollars in cash. The passport and driver's license were real enough, but the name was not Chong's.

He put the case in his inside pocket and automatically took another look around.

Dum te dum. Chong inserted the key into the ignition and twisted it.

The bomb under the hood contained six sticks of dynamite, more than enough to blow the front end of the vehicle to smithereens and drive enough dashboard pieces and engine parts aft into Chong to kill him instantly. He never felt a thing as bits of flying windshield glass, plastic and metal flayed his face to the bone. The cars parked nearby were heavily damaged by the blast.

The fireball rose spectacularly as bits and pieces rained down on parked cars for a hundred yards in every direction.

Fish was two blocks away at a bar when he felt the concussion and saw the rising cloud, which spread into a glowing minimushroom in the wet gray sky. He looked at his watch and took another sip of beer.

The man beside him, who had supplied the dynamite and detonator and pointed out the green Chevy, said, "You are very good at what you do."

Fish glanced at him and sipped the last of his beer. "Our mutual friend said you would wire the money immediately. By the close of business today."

"The money will be there."

"It had better. I know where you live, and of course, so does our mutual friend." Fish scrutinized the man's face. Apparently satisfied, he rose from the table and walked out of the bar. He didn't look back.

The Chinese agent took a deep breath and exhaled slowly. He felt nervous around Fish. The man wasn't normal. Of course, any man who made his living killing people would, by definition, not be "normal." But great missions made it necessary to use many different kinds of people.

Fish would not betray him: He knew that. Nor would he betray Fish. He was what the American law would classify as a "co-conspirator" and would be equally as guilty as Fish. That fact was his protection from Fish, the reason the assassin didn't kill him after he collected his money.

Of course, Fish had no knowledge of why the man in the green Chevy had to die. The Chinese agent had been very careful not to even hint about the reason for the hit, nor did Fish ask. The reason, he suspected, was because Fish wasn't curious. The assassin just didn't care.

He reviewed the operation again. Chong's preparations had been carefully watched. The dynamite and detonator were stolen, so a chemical trace would reveal nothing. The capacitor and wires were equally untraceable. Fish had left no fingerprints. The explosion and resulting fire had taken care of any stray DNA Fish might have left in the car.

All in all, a clean hit. All the men who had brought down Air Force One were dead. The FBI would soon hit a wall that prevented them from going any further on their trail.

The man signaled the waiter for another glass of wine and through the window watched the smoke rising from Sea-Tac's long-term parking lot. Chong had been an assassin, too. Such men usually ended badly.

Perhaps when this was over, something could be done about Fish. As insurance.

CHAPTER TWELVE

If everyone is thinking alike, then somebody isn't thinking.
                                                        —George S. Patton

Thanksgiving was at the Graftons', with all the trimmings. Turkey and ham, stuffing and gravy and corn, with pumpkin pie with ice cream and Cool Whip for dessert. I ate until I thought I would pop. I visited with Grafton's daughter, Amy, and her husband, Peter, and cooed over the grandbaby. I drank a bit too much red wine, then retired to the guest room to watch some football. Fell asleep during the game.

Life does go on, even when you think the world has stopped spinning.

The next day, Friday, Grafton called me into his office and motioned me toward a chair.

He passed me three small brown envelopes. I opened one. It contained six X-rays of someone's mouth. "The forensic examiner got these," Grafton explained, "from the guys in the burned van. Dental experts say these teeth were worked on by Russian dentists."

"Far be it from me to dispute the experts. So where does that get us?"

"These may have been the drone operators who crashed Air Force One."

"May?"

"That is as good as we're going to get. Russians."

"So what do the Russian spooks say about all this?"

Grafton leaned back in his chair and propped a foot up on an open lower desk drawer. "The Russian embassy is promising complete, total cooperation.

Which means nothing. I suspect that in a week or two or three, they will send a note to State saying, 'Sorry about that. We can't identify them.'"

"Okay."

"In any event, I think a back-door approach might be worthwhile. Janos Ilin, the number two in the SVR, wants to meet me in Zurich. I can't go. I want you to meet with him, listen to what he has to say. We not only want to know who these people are or were, we want to know all about their associates and the men who controlled them." The SVR (Sluzhba Vneshney Rasvedki) was the Russian foreign intelligence service, the bureaucratic successor to the foreign intelligence arm of the Soviet-era KGB.

I didn't ask him how he learned that Ilin wanted to talk to him. I figured the less I knew about the machinations of the top level of the international intelligence business, the better. What I didn't know I couldn't tell, hint at or testify about. Ignorance may not be bliss, but they can't convict you for it.

I had met Ilin before. He was a tall, rangy Russian dude whose extreme competence erased whatever doubts you might have had about how good the SVR really was. I kinda suspected he was almost as smart, capable and ruthless as Jake Grafton, but without the admiral's scruples. Grafton and Ilin had crossed paths several times in the past. The problem was, for Ilin, that his bosses didn't know about many of his extracurricular activities. It went without saying that Grafton expected me to use every wit I had to ensure that Ilin's little secrets remained his little secrets. Knowing Grafton, he might say it anyway.

"When do I leave?"

"Tomorrow morning. Go see about airplane tickets and a hotel."

"Fake passport?"

"Yes."

"Where and when do I meet Ilin?"

"I'll tell you tomorrow."

Off I trotted to the ID office. The agency maintains thousands of fake identities for moments like this, with real credit cards, addresses, driver's licenses and the other paper bits that prove we are real people. All I needed was an identity that would withstand a quick check, not one I would have to live with. My new name was Harold W. Cass from Indianapolis, Indiana. The W. stood for Wallace. I hated the name Harold and decided if necessary I would be Wally to my new friends.

From there I went to the travel office. Zurich, Switzerland. Air reservations and hotel for Harold W. Cass. Maybe if I had to wait a few days for Ilin, I could ski down an Alp.

Fool that I was, I remember thinking, *At last! An easy job for a change. A nice hotel, a comfy bed, good food, toilet paper . . . aah. All with Uncle Sugar's dollars. God bless American taxpayers.*

Saturday morning when I dropped Grafton at Langley, I went over to my place and closed up the joint for a couple of weeks. I packed some winter clothes and debated about my ski boots, which I hadn't worn in years. Decided to rent some in Switzerland. Ditto skis.

When I got back to Langley, I went to the travel office, picked up my tickets and some expense account money, then zipped over to the director's office.

I had to wait to see Grafton. He was up to his eyeballs in it.

"Any message for Ilin?"

"I would take it as a personal favor if he could give us anything to help on the identity of the men who dropped Air Force One. Anything."

Grafton tugged at an earlobe. "You'll meet one of Ilin's private agents. I don't think she's SVR. I think she's a volunteer working solely for Ilin. As you know, he runs his own little intelligence network. I don't think the SVR knows about that. If they did, Ilin would be dead."

The hair on the back of my neck prickled as he talked and I felt a sudden flash of heat. "Her?" I managed. It came out a whisper.

"Yep. Her. Anna Modin."

That name didn't just ring a bell—it exploded in my head. A few years ago I had been desperately in love with Anna Modin. Then she disappeared. Several weeks later I received one postcard. Hadn't heard from her since. Obviously, Jake Grafton had. He knew where she was. Or the CIA did, which was the same thing since Grafton was now running it.

I sat thinking about things while Grafton busied himself with paper on his desk. Finally I blurted, "I don't want to do this."

He glanced up. "You know her and she trusts you. She was Ilin's choice as a go-between."

"Find someone else. I don't want to go."

He looked me squarely in the eyes. "I didn't ask you to go. I told you to."

I started to say something I would regret, and managed to choke it off before it hit the air.

"Make sure no one follows you or sees you meeting Modin or Ilin."

So this was secret agent shit. If it cost Anna her life, I was going to be partly responsible. I counted to ten. Then I counted ten more. Finally I nodded.

Grafton's face softened. "Tommy, this is the life Anna Modin has chosen.

She knows the risks as well as you do. Probably better. Keep your eyes and ears open and your brain working. I hope Ilin will tell us something that his government wouldn't share in the ordinary course of business. It's a possibility, anyway."

I nodded again.

"You will write nothing down, commit everything to memory and ask any questions you think apropos. Then come home."

"Where do I meet Anna?"

"I don't know. She works at a bank." He named it. "Devise an approach that ensures no one observes you meeting her. She will tell you how to meet Ilin or take you to him."

"Yes, sir."

"Any questions?"

"Nope."

"Get gone. I have work to do."

I closed the door behind me.

I parked my car in the lot and walked into the Dulles Airport terminal three hours before flight time. With the endless security lines at Dulles and the mobs of people, you must plan for the worst. After my morning interview with Grafton, it would have been a damned bitter pill to tell him I missed my flight because I wasn't a professional. Screw that. I was going to be on that plane if I had to ride in a wheel well.

I checked my luggage and got a boarding pass, then headed for the security line with my little carry-on. There was a bookstore on the way, so I glanced at my watch, saw I had a few minutes and decided to buy something to read on the plane. I didn't need to sit on that damn flying bus for eight hours thinking about Anna Modin.

I grabbed the latest Stephen Hunter paperback and a copy of the *Washington Examiner* and *The Washington Post,* both of which had big spreads about the progress of the investigation into the crash of Air Force One. I queued up behind a fat lady, waited while she paid for two handfuls of candy and chips with a debit card, then paid cash for my loot, waited for the clerk to bag it and headed for the door.

That's when a man walking by in the corridor caught my eye. It was *him*! The Dumpster diver! Sure as shooting. Amazing! Of all the millions of people in the Washington area . . . Well, people get in car wrecks every day; you just don't know when it will be your day.

He was pulling a little overnight bag, one like mine. Strolling along at a good pace at a ninety-degree angle going to my right. I could see his head moving back and forth, eyes scanning.

Decent dark slacks, leather shoes, a gray jacket. Wearing sunglasses indoors. No hat. I was only twenty feet behind him as he stepped on the escalator; I waited for someone to get on in front of me, then stepped on. Down we went to the luggage carousels.

He went over to number 18 and stood where he could watch the people gathering around. I stayed back, put a pillar between us, and tried to keep an eye on him by watching his reflection in the lost luggage window behind him. The thought occurred to me that guys who ride airplanes hither and yon don't often pay their bills by collecting tin cans from other people's trash and selling them by the pound.

My mind was racing. I would like to see what car he got into, get the license number. With that, assuming the car wasn't stolen, he was toast. The FBI could investigate him until they got sick of it. Of course, getting a squint at his ID would be even better. Assuming it wasn't fake.

I was weighing it, trying to decide what to do, when I risked a glance around the pole. He wasn't there!

I ran my eyes over the crowd. Found him, on the other side of the carousel. He had moved, and he was scanning the crowd. I took a step back . . . and he spotted me. Looked right at me. Our eyes met for just a second, but he recognized me. I saw it on his face.

He began moving. Heading for the tunnel that led to the pickup area. I abandoned my overnight bag, book and newspapers and went after him. Decided to take him down and look at his ID. It wasn't a conscious thought, but it was there. He was my meat.

He walked quickly, strode. Passed families and couples and singles pulling luggage. He was quick, so I broke into a trot. He disappeared down the tunnel.

I ran.

People kept getting in front of me. I dodged and juked like an NFL tailback. Hit one guy and went sprawling. Got up and charged on into the tunnel that went under the passenger drop-off area. Saw my guy limned against the light going out. I gave it all I had.

He was running along the sidewalk toward the taxi stand when I emerged. I charged toward him.

He stopped and grabbed a policeman. Pointed at me. I was running full tilt toward them and wasn't hard to spot.

The cop stepped in front of me and I took him out with a good stiff-arm and kept going. My guy was fifty feet in front of me and losing the race. I was going to get that son of a bitch. No way could he have a weapon after the unemployables of Homeland Security had searched and X-rayed him. I was six inches taller, thirty pounds heavier and a whole hell of a lot meaner than he was. I was going to put him in the hospital.

I slowly overhauled him on the sidewalk. Our audience was people in dashikis, Orthodox Jews, Muslims in head rags and Hindu women wearing spots, plus the drivers of the cars loading them and their stuff. I'll say this for the bastard—he could run. He was shoving people out of the way, which sort of cleared a path for me.

He veered into traffic and dodged a car that I went over by leaping on the hood. Then I had him. Tackled him. With him on his stomach, I gave him a kidney punch that would have felled an ox. The air went out of him and he went limp.

I was dragging him erect when the cops got me. There were four of them, and they had night-sticks and Mace. They grabbed arms and legs and put me on the ground. Four against one isn't fair. I think there were four, but there may have been a dozen. One of them popped me across the right kidney with that stick, and that about did it for me. I struggled to breathe as they slammed my face against the concrete.

They rolled me over, a cop on each limb. "Hold still, you bastard, or you're going straight to the hospital."

I stopped struggling and tried to talk. "I'm a CIA officer chasing a suspected bomber. Don't let him—"

One of them punched me in the stomach. Then they rolled me over and cuffed me while one of them helped himself to my wallet.

When they finally pulled me erect, the Dumpster diver wasn't in sight. That's when I remembered that I was Wally Cass from Indianapolis. They had a lockup in the basement of the terminal, and that's where they took me.

"You want to make a phone call, Cass, before we slam the door behind you and throw away the key?"

"Yeah."

I called the director's office. Needless to say, I got the receptionist, ol' tight-lips Jennifer. "This is Carmellini. Is Grafton there?"

"More Russian plans for world domination?"

"No, trifle. Let me talk to the boss."

"He's in a meeting."

"Tell him I got arrested at Dulles. I'll hold."

After a while I heard his voice. "Arrested?" he said.

I started to explain, and got about halfway through it when Grafton started to laugh. Actually it was a snicker. Or chuckle. He was snorting and trying to choke it off.

"I'm in the dungeon at Dulles, asshole," I roared. "Get someone over here to get me out." I slammed the phone down.

"Who was that you were talking to?" the cop watching me asked.

"The director of the CIA."

"Right." He raised an eyebrow. "We get guys like you ten times a week. You may be King Shit in Indianapolis, Cass, but you're just mouse shit here. Empty your pockets, turn them inside out and give me your belt and shoelaces."

As I did so, he added, "If you had a lick of sense, you'd have called a lawyer."

I settled into my own private cell. The place smelled of disinfectant and urine, the eau de jour of all the lockups I have ever been in. Willie Varner would toss his cookies after one good sniff. My back hurt like hell.

I'd been in there an hour when a grizzled sergeant with a scarred face came for me. "You really are a spook!" he said in amazement.

"Did the president call?"

"Your assistant director dropped by."

"May his tribe increase."

"You wouldn't have been arrested if you hadn't—"

"And you are really a bunch of damn fools. If you had bothered to ask why I was chasing someone, you might have made a significant arrest. As it is, he made a clean getaway. Congratulations. The next assassination in DC, I hope you bastards choke on it."

That certainly wasn't a nice thing to say. Maybe they didn't deserve it, but I was kinda pissed by then.

"The man running from me left a carry-on somewhere," I told the sergeant. "If you paragons of law enforcement get your act together, maybe you can find it. And my stuff. And maybe I can spot him on the videotape of people in the terminal."

Fish stood behind a car in the long-term parking lot, a huge affair of a hundred or so acres, packed with cars, and tried to catch his breath. The big man, some kind of athlete, running him down, and he didn't have a weapon. Just off the plane with no way to defend himself against a man six inches taller and thirty or forty pounds heavier who ran like a deer. He glanced back over his shoulder and saw that face—the square jaw, the look—and he knew ice-cold terror for the first time in his life. So he had run.

What to do now?

He had a car, parked somewhere in this flat monument to the air age, but they made videotapes of every license plate that went through the tollbooths. And he had driven his own car.

He tried to calm down and list his options. Time was pressing. Soon the man who chased him would get the police interested and they would start searching this lot. He had to be gone by then. Being gone meant wheels, since Dulles was twenty-five miles from downtown Washington.

He could steal a license plate and put it on his own car . . . but he didn't have a screwdriver. He could break into someone's car and steal that . . . but again, no screwdriver or pocketknife to strip the ignition wires. He could go catch a bus downtown . . . take a taxi . . . steal a police car . . .

A man walking toward him pulling a suitcase decided him. He let the man pass while he played with his cell phone, then, when he was twenty feet ahead, pocketed the cell phone and fell in behind him. A black guy, wearing a suit, maybe 160 or 170 pounds.

After walking another hundred yards and changing rows, the man pulled a set of keys from his pocket. Up ahead a car flashed its lights. Now it beeped. More lights flashing. The guy was playing with the fob as he walked. Some kind of midsized sedan.

Fish lengthened his stride. Came up behind the man silently and quickly as he reached his car. Grabbed the man and slammed his head against the sheet metal of the car, denting it. The man went down, dropping the keys. Fish picked them up, then opened the car door and looked inside.

Yes! The ticket to get out of the parking lot was over the visor.

He scanned around—no one watching.

Used a button on the key fob to open the trunk and lifted the man into it. Slammed the lid and looked around. No one staring or pointing or screaming.

He pushed the guy's suitcase onto the backseat, then got into the driver's seat and put on his seat belt. Inserted the key in the ignition. Started the car. Put it in reverse and carefully backed out of the parking space.

The car had been in the lot four days. Fish paid the lady with cash, then headed for Washington.

As he drove he thought about the man who had chased him. He recognized him—the guy who gave him a pizza when he was casing the Grafton building the day before the Internet crashed. That guy recognized him in the airport. Fish assumed the meeting had been by chance, a coincidence, one of those things.

He went over the situation again. The cops would scarf up his carry-on bag, with his fingerprints and enough DNA to trace his family tree. Maybe he could get some help to deal with that. The guy in the trunk could just stay there. He would abandon the car, wipe the steering wheel and door latch and trunk lid and walk away.

His real problem was the guy who chased him. True, he didn't see him plant the bomb in Grafton's apartment, but he put him there the day before. And he had chased him with mayhem on his mind. That guy . . . he was going to have to do something about that guy.

Fish sighed. His heart rate was back to normal. He kept his eyes on traffic and drove carefully. And thought about being scared. He had peeped into the pit and didn't like what he saw.

My flight to Switzerland left without me. When it pushed back, I was still in the airport cops' office looking at videotapes. And I found him. By six o'clock that evening, we had reviewed enough videotapes to determine that our John Doe had flown in on a flight from Seattle. The airline provided the passenger list, and we sat staring at it. Which one was he?

I tried to decide why our Dumpster diver didn't exit the secure area down the escalator to the baggage carousels, and concluded that he had probably missed the sign. I knew the Dulles terminal intimately since I was in and out of there at least six times a year, so that was a mistake I wouldn't make. These things happen to people unfamiliar with the terminal. Tourists from the provinces drop dead at Dulles every day when their bladders burst because they can't find a restroom.

Armed with his photo, the airport cops went to interview the airline personnel. One policeman sheepishly turned over the bag with my book and newspaper, and my carry-on, all of which were rescued by some family from Scranton on their way home from France. The Dumpster diver's carry-on wasn't found. Someone had probably helped himself. Or herself. Washington is that kind of town.

I called Jake Grafton on his cell. He listened until I ran down and said, "Schedule another flight. If they won't bump someone for tomorrow's, call me."

"Yes, sir."

"Nice try, Tommy."

"Thanks."

I went to the head to pee and didn't see blood. The cop who used a stick on my kidney would be disappointed. I had used my fist on the Dumpster man: I hoped he was pissing red.

The FBI was there taking custody of the tape with the face of our friendly suspected bomber on it when I left the terminal. I limped out to the long-term lot, rescued my Benz and went home to my closed-up apartment. Fixed myself a frozen dinner and a tall bourbon and thought about things. My back ached and my face was slightly swollen, bruised and abraded from intimate contact with a street. There was a ripped place in my shirt, which had a few spots of blood on it. My blood. My trousers and sport coat were ruined. I looked like a sailor after a Saturday night drunk.

About nine that night I called the airline and got myself on tomorrow's flight to Switzerland. There were several empty seats, the lady on the phone said. She had a nice voice.

"Are you on business or vacation?" she asked.

"Vacation," I lied.

"Have you ever been to Switzerland before?" she chirped.

"Yes." That was the truth. I tell it occasionally for variety.

"It's a gorgeous country—I'm sure you know that. You're going to have a wonderful vacation."

"I'm thinking of quitting my job and moving there," I said. "I know a thing or two about U.S. tax laws. Some bank might hire me as a consultant."

After we finished our tête-à-tête, I filled up a freezer bag with ice for my back and poured myself another drink. Found myself thinking about Anna Modin.

That evening Choy Lee and Zhang Ping ate at the Chans' Chinese restaurant. Choy ate there several times a week. The menu was in Chinese characters and English, which was a touch for the locals who were looking for something "authentic." The cuisine actually tasted similar to real Chinese fare, or close enough if you were Chinese and missing home badly. The owner, Sally's father, spoke a bit of Cantonese and stopped to talk to Choy and Zhang. The waiters were Americans, black and white, and didn't speak a word of the language. Choy chatted them up, drew out their stories and gave extravagant tips. That worried

Zhang, but Choy waved it away. "This is America," he said, and moved on to another subject.

Zhang regarded the restaurant people with open suspicion. Oh, he knew people had been bailing out of China for several centuries in search of a better life elsewhere, but for a patriot like Zhang, that fact, and those people, rankled. China was their heritage, who they were. And they had deserted.

It was just another little irritant about life in America. Not speaking the language, Zhang felt like a stranger all the time, and that disconcerted him. It also made him underestimate the acuity of the people he met, which was a grave mistake for a clandestine agent. He never gave it a thought.

All Zhang had to do was hold on, make sure the Americans didn't find the bomb, or if they did, start the countdown and run for it. This countdown— the experts assured him that he had twenty-four hours to leave the area after he initiated the detonation signal with a radio transmitter. Zhang didn't believe it. If he had been running the operation, the explosion would happen immediately after the capacitor charged, which took half a minute. Maybe it would, maybe it wouldn't.

If it didn't, keep on fighting. If it did . . . well, life had been a helluva trip.

When they were eating, Sally came from the kitchen and sat down beside Choy. Of course he introduced Zhang, his "cousin." Through Choy, Zhang gave his cover story in answer to friendly, innocent questions. There was no way out of it. She chatted some; then Choy said in English to Sally, "Could I pick you up tonight when you get off work?"

"Of course," she said. She bussed Choy on the cheek, and went back to the kitchen.

Zhang didn't know what had been said, but he had seen the glow on Sally's face. That was a woman in love.

When they finished dinner, Choy chatted up Sally's father, complimenting him extravagantly, and tipped the waiter, a skinny black man, the same way. Zhang climbed back into the SUV and told Choy to drop him at his building, which was fine with Choy, because he looked at his watch.

"What did you say to Miss Chan?"

"That I'd pick her up when she got off work."

Zhang nodded. That explained her look. She and Choy were going to be lovers tonight.

When Choy was out of sight, Zhang climbed into his pickup truck and drove to the overlook near the entrance to the tunnel that led under the estuary. It was dark by then, no stars or moon, with a good breeze down the bay.

There was a carrier in. Zhang used binoculars to study the lights of the carrier tied to the pier. She was a huge ship. Over a thousand feet long, ninety-five thousand tons displacement. She was lit up as if it were Chinese New Year.

He scanned the water that he could see. No boats moving. Nothing that was not the same as it always was. But there should be a harbor patrol boat. Zhang waited. Twenty minutes later it came down the Elizabeth River into view. Moving slowly with a spotlight playing about on the water.

Tomorrow, he would buy a laptop computer that he could use to download the triggering algorithm from the Internet. He would wait another week and buy a boat. He would need Choy's help with both purchases. If the man became suspicious, he would have to be terminated. To be on the safe side, he would also need to kill Sally Chan. Since they were lovers, Choy had perhaps told her things he shouldn't. If he disappeared, she might go to the authorities.

After he killed Choy, Zhang would be on his own. Zhang sat in the darkness with his binoculars watching the carrier and thinking about how he would accomplish his mission without Choy Lee.

CHAPTER THIRTEEN

Worry is the interest paid by those who borrow trouble.
—George Washington

Jake Grafton had been calling Schulz's office to report progress or the lack thereof in investigating the crash of Air Force One, as ordered. He never got through to the man and ended up talking to an EA. So after a day or so he just had one of his EAs call Schulz's EA. Sunday morning he was summoned to the White House for lunch with Jurgen Schulz and the other heads of intelligence and law enforcement agencies.

He was getting dressed to take Callie to church—she wanted to go a couple of times a month—so she sent him to the bedroom to change from the slacks and sport coat he ordinarily wore to work and had donned this morning.

"Your new gray suit," she said. "With a white shirt and your new purple tie."

"Hey, this is a working lunch," he protested.

"It's after church."

She had picked out the suit, which had been tailored to fit. He went and changed. After church the sedan with two bodyguards dropped Callie back at the condo and took Jake off to the White House.

He felt like the best-dressed man in the room when he greeted his colleagues and the secretary of Homeland Security, Lewis Warren. Sal Molina, wearing his usual sport coat from Sears, inspected Grafton's suit closely. "Wish I could afford a rig like that," he said.

"Eat your heart out." Jake plopped down beside Molina and started looking at the paper piled in front of him.

The menu was soup and salad. The soup was pretty good, tomato with peppers, so Grafton caged another bowl from Molina, who didn't want his. While he ate he looked the group over. All the usual suspects were there, Homeland Security, FBI, and a gaggle of staffers.

Plus Jurgen Schulz, of course. Schulz was a Harvard professor on sabbatical, loaning his brain and whatever it contained to the government to benefit his fellow Americans. Someday when the exigencies of politics pressed hard enough, presumably Schulz would go back to Harvard to teach a few classes a week to grad students and write a profitable big book about his adventures in Washington.

It was a working lunch, when meant they talked and ate at the same time. The big news came from the FBI man, Harry Estep, over the soup. A van had exploded in the Sea-Tac Airport long-term parking lot Saturday morning. One man dead. His teeth said he was a Russian. Some fingers were found with intact fingertips. More fingerprints came off his luggage, which was in the car. The prints had been sent to Interpol and Russian police authorities to see if someone could put a name, face and history to him.

"Who blew up the van?" someone who was not impressed asked.

"We don't know," Harry Estep said with his chin jutting a little. "We're investigating."

"What did they use?" the questioner persisted. It was a honcho from the NSA.

"Forensics says dynamite. American manufacture. Five or six sticks, at least."

"I think the *Post* this morning had a story on the van."

"I think so, too," Estep shot back.

The pieces of the drone recovered in the field near the remains of Air Force One proved it to be a military drone, a Raven. None had been reported stolen, so the army was conducting an inventory. That would take several more days. Meanwhile, of course, the trail of whoever stole it and the controller was growing colder. Still, Estep said, when they knew where the drone came from, the people who had access to them would be given intense scrutiny. Vehicles were being traced, and people remembered people, but without hard descriptions or driver's licenses with names, the going was slow. Denver-area motel and hotel records had been exhaustively checked, and possibilities were being eliminated one by one. The airport security guard who survived had been working with police artists to try to reconstruct the face of the man who shot him. Estep passed around the picture. It was so generic that it could have been anybody, Jake Grafton decided. About the only thing the witness was sure of was that the face he saw was clean-shaven and white. And the guy had a big gun.

This was all good solid police work, and in time a picture of what happened and a chronology might emerge. How much light it would shed on who and why remained to be seen.

Tommy Carmellini's adventure the previous evening at Dulles Airport was not mentioned by Harry Estep. Jake Grafton knew the FBI knew about it, so he didn't mention it either.

Vice Admiral Arlen Curry spoke for the intelligence community. NSA was mining telephone and Internet intercepts for clues. Another week would be needed, at least. Army and naval intelligence had no clues. Satellite surveillance had come up with a few photos of DIA at the time of the shootdown, but all they proved was that there was a van off the end of the duty runway that the president's plane had passed over.

Schulz broke in. "Admiral Grafton, what about foreign plots?"

"We have found no connection yet to any nation or group, sir. Or course, we are still reviewing information from our sources. Two al Qaeda clerics, one in Iraq and one in Pakistan, have claimed responsibility, but they lack credibility. Their claims made them popular in their mosques for a few days, though."

By the time they had finished their salads, the agenda of the meeting had been covered. Schulz kept them there for another twenty minutes firing questions. It was a waste of time, Grafton thought.

Schulz soldiered on. "People," he said, "the lack of progress in this investigation is totally unacceptable. Answers are out there buried under some rock or other. Your job is to turn over rocks and find those answers. Use some brains and common sense to figure out which rocks to look under. Keep me informed three times a day."

Then he got up from the table, and so did everyone else.

I have mixed emotions about Zurich. It's a modern European city, very civilized, with substantial buildings and views of the Alps and a gorgeous lake. They have nice hotels with running water, ceramic conveniences, plentiful toilet paper and decent restaurants. Every year when I filled out a Company dream sheet of foreign places where I would like to be stationed, Switzerland was always number two, right under Paris. I don't know why I bothered: I had never been sent anywhere I wanted to go, except Paris once, as an illegal.

If all there was to eternally neutral Switzerland was Swiss Army knives, expensive watches, ski towns and yodelers in the high meadows, no one would give the place much thought. But the Swiss long ago figured out how to profit from the troubles of others. They armor-plated banking secrecy, so Swiss banks were the place where Europe's Jews deposited their wealth in the face of the Nazi holocaust, drug cartels and terrorists transferred money to and fro, and people from all over the globe hid their wealth to escape the local taxmen or unhappy soon-to-be ex-spouses or ex-partners.

Someone once observed that the Swiss banking industry was a state-sanctioned criminal conspiracy. In any event, the Swiss bankers' passion for secrecy and flexible ethics had drawn the attention of most of the world's intelligence services for many years and would probably continue to do so.

In light of all that, I was reasonably certain that Anna Modin was Janos Ilin's spy in one of these Zurich strongholds. When I had known her several years back, she had just finished spying on a bank in Cairo that was used to finance Muslim terrorism. She convinced me she wasn't SVR but was a volunteer agent for Janos Ilin, whom she thought one of the few true Russian patriots. Be that as it may, Ilin himself was in the beating heart of the beast. Currently he was the number two dude at the SVR, and I had no doubt that if tobacco or cutthroat politics didn't kill him, one of these days he'd be the top dog.

I sat on a park bench in Zurich that early winter day watching the gray bank building where Anna Modin worked and thought about these things. And thought about Anna. Wondered how she thought about me. Did she miss me, regret that she walked away? I sure did. But like jilted lovers since the dawn of time who rejected suicide, I kept on living, and time scarred over the wound. Whole days went by, nights even, when I didn't think of her.

Snow started falling, pushed by a chilly breeze. I snuggled deeper into my midcalf-length coat and arranged the wool scarf around my neck. The coat and scarf were new, as were the hat and gloves. This exterior outfit was purchased this morning so I would blend into the Swiss professional crowd. I kept my eyes moving. If anyone was watching me, I wanted to know it. My urban anonymity seemed to be intact. Even the pigeons ignored me.

Maybe Anna's status as an unofficial spy was a distinction without a difference, considering the turmoil that has racked Russia repeatedly since Communism collapsed and the new ex-Communists swallowed capitalism whole. Spies are spies. I ought to know: I work for a spy agency. Believe me, in the spy business the right hand rarely knows what the left hand is doing. It's also kinda tough at times figuring out who the good guys are.

Me, I was lucky. I had faith in Jake Grafton, who was as close to an American warrior-saint as I was ever likely to meet. I think Anna felt the same way about Ilin. Maybe what Anna and I had in common was the need to believe in something. Or someone.

That thought made me slightly uncomfortable. Perhaps I should take religious vows and join a monastery, if I could find one that didn't do vows of chastity. Money I might possibly be able to live without, but not sex. Better yet, maybe I ought to be seeing a shrink on a regular basis. It might be informative to know what was actually happening inside my head, but I doubted if the shrink would tell me. They had their little secrets, just as I had mine. Not that I would ever tell them mine.

When the wage slaves began to dribble out of the money temple, I watched for Anna. Saw her, and my hard little heart gave an extra thump. I rose and followed.

Following someone through a city you don't know well is iffy at best. If they jump a bus or taxi, you gotta be quick, and even then, if you don't want your rabbit to burn you, it takes luck.

She queued up at a local bus stop, so I hoofed it back down the street and found a taxi. Got it, tried English on the driver, and he answered with a heavy German accent. The bus passed us, so I said, "Follow that bus."

He was dubious. I got out a wad of Swiss francs and waved them, so he pulled up behind it. I saw Anna get on.

Away we went, slowly, stopping here and there on the way to a suburb. People got off, people got on. Anna stayed on the bus, so we stayed behind it.

"You follow someone, yes?"

"Yeah. I'm a spy."

"Funny man."

"A bag of laughs."

"Why?"

"My wife is on the bus. I think she's meeting another man."

He nodded sagely. "Wives very . . ." After a bit he added, "How you say? Difficult?"

"Yeah."

I figured we had gone about three miles when Anna got off in an area of high-rise apartment buildings. I paid off the cabbie, gave him a nice tip and got out when she was a block ahead of me.

She never looked behind her. Either she didn't think anyone was following her or she didn't care. The entrance was a glass door with rows of names and buttons on the right side. There she was. Anna Modin, 6E. I was tempted to push the button, but stood there thinking about it. If she lived with someone, he or she might be there, and Grafton had been emphatic that no one was to see us together. At some point paranoia becomes a way of life if you are a spy. I suppose that's good life insurance, even if it doesn't do much for your personal or love life. On the other hand, hers was the only name on the flat.

It was a chance I refused to take. I wasn't going to be the one who blew her cover or put her life in jeopardy. I strolled away.

The next morning I was out front when Anna exited the building. I watched her walk to the bus stop. Even though I was about fifty yards away I had no doubt it was her. I knew her figure and walk. A knot of people gathered there, four from her building. Others exited and headed for cars, or stood on the sidewalk until people picked them up.

The bus came along, and Anna and her building mates climbed aboard.

I went to the entrance of Anna's building and waited. In a moment a woman came out. I caught the door and entered. Let the door close behind me.

There was no desk, so no receptionist or doorman. All self-service. Other people came down in the elevator.

I entered the stairwell and climbed up to the sixth floor, being careful to remember than in Europe, the first floor is the one above the main floor. Seated myself in the stairwell and waited. Thought about Anna. Tried to figure out how I felt about her. Gave up, finally, and felt sorry for both of us.

At ten o'clock I figured that anyone who lived with Anna was out if they were going out, so I went out onto the floor and found 6E.

Knocked. Loudly. No answer.

Got out my picks and went to work on the lock. It took about a minute for me to open it. No one came into the hallway while I was working. Nothing could be simpler. Actually, I felt like an idiot. I would have had the lock in twenty seconds if I hadn't been so clumsy. My mind wasn't on the job, which is a big no-no in this business. People who don't pay attention get arrested a lot or wake up dead.

I opened the door, completing the crime. I made sure it shut behind me. Once inside, I scanned the place, saw that I was in a small living room with a television, sound system and closet. I walked on, checking every room. One bedroom with a closet, a bathroom with a tub, a small kitchen with dining nook. That was it. From the evidence, only one person lived there.

I shed the coat and gloves and got busy searching. I was only interested in whatever she might have hidden that she didn't want found, so merely scanned the cupboards, small refrigerator and closets. Everything else I gave my full attention.

I know how to search a place, and I did it right. Putting everything back as it was made the job last longer, but I had all day. She had no photos of anyone, which I thought was kinda sad. Not a parent, child or man. No one. No letters from anyone. A few books were among her few personal possessions. A Bible in Russian and one in German. I carefully went through her clothes closet and dresser. Even went through the trash.

Two hours later I was convinced there was nothing hidden in the apartment. I scanned the fridge, decided that nothing there looked appetizing and settled on a package of freeze-dried soup in the cupboard. Just add water and bring to a boil, then serve.

There was a half-full bottle of Italian red wine with a cork stuck in it that I appropriated. I poured myself a full glass and sipped it while I waited for the soup to warm.

Wondered how Anna spent her evenings and weekends. I hadn't even seen a crossword puzzle or library book. She had some CDs to listen to, and maybe she watched television some.

After I had the soup, I sat in her most comfortable chair and worked on the wine. Felt as if I were invading her privacy, looking at a corner of an empty life that she wouldn't want me to see, if she had a choice. I felt sad. Wanted to leave, but didn't. I had a job to do, too.

Was I still in love with Anna? I thought not. Time doesn't just heal wounds; it kills passion.

When Sarah Houston showed up for her first day of work at the CIA, before she did the usual checking-in things, including forms and photos and fingerprints, she was escorted straight to Jake Grafton's office.

"Hey, Sarah. Sit down, please."

She looked around distractedly, taking in the wall-to-wall carpet, the flags, the paintings on the wall, then settled into a chair.

"Admiral," she said.

"Thanks for coming to work here. We really need your help."

"As if I had a choice."

She didn't, of course. Her real name was Zelda Hudson. She had once been involved in the theft of a nuclear-powered attack submarine. Grafton had laid hands on her, actually saved her from her co-conspirators, and she had been convicted of numerous felonies. Later, Grafton had sprung her from the clutches of the federal prison system with a presidential order and could get her sent back with a telephone call. None of that would appear in the agency's personnel records.

"After a bit," he said, "I'll have one of the EAs take you down to personnel for all the usual forms, photos, fingerprints and so forth. They'll give you an ID and access to some of our computer systems. We'll skip the polygraph exam. I would appreciate it if you stayed in character, from this moment on, as Sarah Houston, federal wage slave."

She grunted, which was about what Grafton expected. Houston was one heck of a hacker and data miner. If you wanted a computer genius of the first order of magnitude, you wanted Sarah Houston. If you wanted nice, you needed to keep on looking.

The admiral handed her the file that contained the memo on Chinese hacking of the U.S. Navy's operational schedules. He waited until she read it, including Mario Tomazic's handwritten margin comments.

"That is your first assignment," he said. "I want to know everything you can discover about what the Chinese have seen, what they know, what they don't know. Anything. Everything."

"You're going to give me access to the navy's computers?"

"Heck no. Hack your way in."

"What if I get caught?"

"Don't get caught."

"Okay."

"Then I want you to hack into the Chinese navy's computers. I want to read their stuff."

"The Chinese have an entire organization engaged in computer espionage and counterespionage," Sarah Houston objected. "Hundreds, perhaps thousands of people, thousands of *really smart* people. There's just one of me."

"Yeah, but you're the one I've got."

She stared into those cold gray eyes, which stared right back, unblinking, pinning her. Finally she lowered her eyes and said, "Terrific."

"As of today you are on my staff. We'll get you an office and all the rest of it, and you settle in and get after it. I would like a report as soon as you get your bearings."

She took a deep breath and nodded. Put the file back on the desk.

Grafton buzzed the receptionist. "Send Anastasia Roberts in, please."

He introduced the two women, told Roberts to take Houston to personnel. Then he stood and stuck his hand out at Houston. "Welcome aboard."

She took it, and her lips twisted as she tried to smile. "Thank you, Admiral."

Out in the hallway Roberts asked, "Is this the first time you've met Admiral Grafton?"

"No," Sarah Houston said without emotion. "We go back a ways."

"He's very nice to work for," Roberts opined.

Houston snorted silently. Anastasia Roberts obviously had never seen Jake Grafton in action. She didn't bother to reply.

Roberts dropped the subject, and started into the trivia of how one worked for an agency where everything everyone did was a deep secret. Apparently Roberts didn't know Houston had just come from the NSA, an equally mysterious bureaucracy, and Sarah didn't make an effort to enlighten her. Roberts had no need to know.

The sun had set and the twilight was about gone when I heard the key in the door. I was sitting in darkness in a chair with my back to a window.

The door swung open and Anna Modin stepped in. She closed the door, locked it, then turned around and saw me. In the dim light coming through the windows, she apparently couldn't recognize me.

She didn't panic. Didn't say a word. Merely reached for the wall switch and turned on the light.

"Hello, Anna."

She put a hand on the wall to steady herself. "Tommy?"

"Yep." I stood and stepped toward her.

"My God," she whispered, and wrapped her arms around me. Put her head on my shoulder.

I hugged her fiercely. That's when I knew: I still loved her.

We were sitting in the darkness of Anna's apartment, with only the lights from the street coming in, as we sipped the last of the red wine. Rain began streaking the window. There was so much to ask, and yet, no real place to start. We did long silences.

"How did you find me?" she finally asked.

"The CIA found you. Somehow. Jake Grafton sent me here with a message for you to pass to Ilin. Are you still in communication with him?"

"Yes," she said.

"I need to talk to him."

"He's not yet in Switzerland."

"When?"

"The day after tomorrow, I think."

I smiled.

"Oh, Tommy. I—" She stopped abruptly, rose from her chair and went to the bathroom. After a while she came back. In the subdued light it was hard to tell, but I thought she might have been crying.

She started back for the chair, but I reached for her and pulled her down to the couch beside me. Her presence was a tangible thing. I held her hand. It was warm and firm. And it clung tightly to mine.

After a while she said, "Are you hungry?"

"We can eat something here," I said. "Grafton didn't want us to be seen together."

She grimaced. "No. No! No! I refuse! We will go out. To a restaurant with light and music and laughter. We will eat a fine dinner and drink champagne. I am tired of wasting my life sitting in this . . ." She gestured. "This prison."

I wasn't going to argue. She rose from the couch, picked up her purse and said, "Come."

The rain had changed to snow when we exited her building. We walked the streets holding hands as the flakes came fast and thick. Her shoulder kept bumping into mine. She smiled. Her eyes were bright and glistening, and snowflakes melted on her eyelashes. She held my right hand for a while, then switched sides and held my left.

The restaurant was gay. Bright lights and a four-piece jazz band. We got a table in a corner away from the band where we could talk without shouting. I ordered a bottle of French champagne, and we sipped it, talking about little things. I let my eyes roam around occasionally, scrutinizing the patrons at the other tables. After a while we ordered.

Before our food came she went to the ladies'. Took her purse. While she was gone, I checked out the other patrons of the restaurant again. Looked over the waitstaff. Anna was known here, apparently a regular patron. If someone was keeping tabs on her, this was the place.

So I looked. Got out of sorts a little. In our line of work, it was impossible to ever take a day off. Caution became ingrained. And I was disobeying Grafton, which wasn't a thing to be taken lightly.

When she returned, as she walked between the tables she glanced around, taking people in, looking for familiar faces. It was a habit. Finally she sat and said, with her hand in front of her mouth, "I left a message in a drop."

"Okay."

"It may be more than a few days."

I shrugged. Grafton said to see Ilin, and I fully intended to obey that order. "If I don't get home before Christmas," I told her, "I'll send Grafton a postcard. 'Having a wonderful time. Glad you aren't here.'"

She laughed. I had always liked her laugh. "Maybe he'll fire you," she murmured.

"Then I won't ever have to go home."

We lingered over dinner, listened to jazz and sipped champagne and drank calvados afterward. I charged the meal to American taxpayers.

We walked back to her place through the snow, which was at least an inch deep. I glanced behind us occasionally for tails. We didn't have anyone following us on foot that I could see.

I said, "I have a hotel room. I don't want to compromise your cover."

She didn't say a word. Just gripped my hand tighter.

When I got her home she pulled me into her apartment and locked the door. She brushed the snow from my hair and eyebrows, ran her fingers along my cheeks. I helped her out of her coat and scarf. Her cheeks were warm and her eyes shining. Her lips were cool.

We began shedding clothes on the way to the bedroom.

She went to sleep in my arms. I held her, listening to her breathe, and thought about things. About Anna Modin and Tommy Carmellini and spies and nations and all kinds of stuff. I was thinking about the two of us when I drifted off.

On Willoughby Spit rain beat on the window and wind howled through the half-inch gap between the sill and the sash. Lieutenant Commander Zhang sat in a chair near the window in his room looking out into the darkness of Hampton Roads, watching the lights of a ship move slowly from left to right. She was apparently heading for the mouth of Chesapeake Bay and the open sea beyond. On this stormy night.

He knew that this curved arm of sand sticking out into the bay, Willoughby Spit, had been formed over the centuries, millennia probably, by the action of the surf and the wind. Grains of sand were moved and dropped, one by one.

Zhang pulled the blanket around his shoulders and opened his laptop. Automatically he checked the battery. Fully charged. He had downloaded the algorithm, and now he opened the program and looked at it. He would need a few pieces of computer hardware, which he had been told were available in any computer store. Now all he needed was a boat. One with a typical civilian radar.

He closed the laptop and automatically caressed it. He felt the chill of that early winter wind. The thought that this was probably his last winter occurred to him. Less than four weeks now. Twenty-seven or -eight days, then nothing.

Zhang didn't believe in an afterlife. No man knows anything from the time before his birth. We come from nothing and go back to the same state when life is over. Death is not a tragedy, not a disaster, but the natural order of things. After life, rest.

Unlike all these people in the Norfolk–Hampton Roads area, about a million and a half of them, Zhang was the only one who knew death was coming . . . twenty-seven or -eight days from now. Oh, we all know we are mortal, but even if we are fatally ill the death moment is unknown. The evil day is somewhere out there in the unpredictable, unknowable, amorphous future, someplace else, when we are older, when life is at low ebb, when our children's children are adults. Someday . . . when we are more ready.

He again felt the chill. Finally he turned out the light beside him and sat in the darkness listening to the rain's steady beat on the window glass . . . and the wind.

CHAPTER FOURTEEN

The art of war is simple enough. Find out where your enemy
is, get at him as soon as you can, and keep moving on.
                                        —Ulysses S. Grant

The next morning Jake was at work at seven thirty. As usual these days, FBI liaison Zoe Kerry was waiting in the reception area to give him his morning briefing on the investigations of the murders of Tomazic, Reinicke and Maxwell.

He waved her into the office and asked, as he took off his suit coat and put it on a hanger, "What has the FBI learned since yesterday that I don't know about?"

"Nothing, sir."

Grafton spun to face her. "Bullshit. Either the FBI is stonewalling you or they are incompetent. Which is it?"

"The priority is the attempted assassination of the president," Kerry shot back. She was still standing, looking at Grafton from halfway across the room. "We have only so many agents."

Grafton walked over to his desk and parked a cheek on the front of it. She found herself looking into those cold gray eyes as he examined her face. The scar on his temple, an old bullet wound, some said, was a reddish hue as he spoke. "The director of the FBI was murdered, gunned down on a street in the nation's capital, and the FBI isn't moving heaven and earth to find out who did it? I may be an old country boy, but I am not naïve enough to buy that crock of Pelosi. I want you to go to the Hoover Building this morning and tell your boss to tell Harry Estep that I want to be kept briefed on progress. You know as well as I do that the same people were probably also behind Tomazic's and Reinicke's deaths. Crack one and you've cracked all three. Tell Harry that I don't give a shit what he tells the press or the White House, but he'd better keep *me* informed. Got it?"

"Yessir." Her face was frozen.

"I hope so. I'm sure you'll have a complete brief for me tomorrow morning. If you don't, you and I will go to the Hoover Building and we'll see Harry Estep together."

"I understand."

"Get going."

She wheeled and left.

I read the latest from across the Atlantic in the *International New York Times,* which was thrown in front of my door at my hotel, as I ate breakfast in the hotel dining room. After reading the news and all the pieces of the op-ed page, pro and con, I sipped my coffee and gave silent thanks that I was here and not there.

Anna Modin was here, and that gave the day a glow I hadn't seen in a long time. Not since I first met her a few years ago. I sighed contentedly and poured another cup of joe from the thermos on the table. It was thick as Mississippi bottomland dirt and just as wet, but I had learned years ago that there wasn't a decent cup of coffee anywhere east of Boston. If you are going to be a traveling man, you gotta take your caffeine any way you can get it.

This contented sighing was largely due to the fact that I didn't expect Anna to hear from Janos Ilin for a while. I was taking Anna to a white-tablecloth, expense-account dinner every evening and staying late at her place. I refused to spend the night and be seen departing in the cold light of morning. As it was, I was disobeying Grafton and putting her at risk: No sense being a fool about it.

Underneath my bonhomie was the cold hard fact that this romantic interlude would come to an abrupt end in the near future. I had to go back to Washington. I wondered if I could talk Anna into quitting her job and coming along. Wondered if she loved me enough. Wondered if I was important enough to her. Wondered the same things lovers have been wondering since Adam and Eve were evicted from the garden.

Maybe this evening I would pop the question. Or tomorrow evening. Or the evening after that. I had asked her to marry me before, way back when, and been refused. Could I induce her to change her mind? Or had she already done so and was waiting for me to bring it up?

Maybe it was just a fantasy. Living together in the good ol' U.S. of A., home of baseball and the NFL. A little place in the suburbs with a flat-screen TV and cable and a barbecue out back. Because I was a tightwad, spent a lot of time overseas riding the expense account and drove a paid-for, worn-out old car stateside, I had some money saved up, enough for a decent down payment on a house. Plus a job, with a steady income. Private enterprises and corporations come and go, but nothing is steadier than working for Uncle Sugar.

So I was indulging in what-if reverie when I realized the man helping himself to the muesli on the breakfast bar was as tall and lean as Abe Lincoln. When he turned to pour a little milk into his bowl, I got his profile. Yep. It was Janos Ilin.

Damn! The bastard must have jumped the first jet from Moscow as soon as someone called him about the message from Anna.

I sipped on my java and glanced around the room to see who was with him. No one, apparently. He and I were the only guests in the dining room. Probably because it was a few minutes after ten and the honest guests of this fine establishment had gone off to tend to their business appointments or call on their Swiss bankers.

He sat down at a table against the wall, facing the dining room door, and went to work on his cereal. One of the waiters came from the kitchen with a pot of something hot. Water. Ilin looked through the tea bag selection and chose one. He had a copy of a paper, a local one to judge from the German-language headlines, and he got absorbed in that as the minutes ticked by. He never once looked my way, and I tried to ignore him. He talked to the waiter in German.

When he finished the tea and I had folded my *Times* and put it aside, Ilin rose and made his way down the corridor that led to the men's room. I waited three minutes, then followed him.

He was standing in the men's room facing the door. "Mr. Carmellini," he said when the door closed behind me.

"Mr. Ilin." He didn't offer to shake hands, so I didn't.

"We met once before, a few years ago. You were with Jake Grafton."

"I remember."

"How is he?"

"Acting director of the firm. Mean as ever."

Something like a trace of a smile crossed his face. "I have something for him. A map." He produced an envelope from a coat pocket and passed it to me.

I put it into the breast pocket of my sport coat. "Anything you want me to tell him about this?"

"It came from one of my agents in China. Waving it around in the wrong quarters could endanger his usefulness, not to mention his life."

"I'll mention his life anyway."

I removed the small brown envelopes that contained the dental X-rays from my pocket and handed them over. I explained what they were. "My boss would like to know who these men were and whom they worked for. The attempted assassination of the president has got the Americans hopping mad. Any help you can give will win you a lot of gratitude. My boss said he would take any help or information offered as a personal favor."

Ilin put the envelope in his jacket pocket. "I will give all the help I can," he said. "You will meet a certain man at the corner bar at the Willard Hotel in Washington at noon two weeks from today. You or Jake Grafton. No one else. He will join you and say, 'A mutual friend was talking about you the other day.' You will reply, 'Which friend? I have several.' If you cannot make the meet, or are followed, keep going back at noon on successive days."

"Okay."

He turned to the sink and began washing his hands.

I squared my shoulders and said, "I'm taking Anna back to the States with me."

"Oh!" He glanced at me. "Does she want to go?"

"If she wants to go."

He glanced at me with a look of amusement. "Are you asking permission?"

"No. I'm telling you." I turned and walked out.

Zoe Kerry had a report for Jake Grafton when he came to work the day after their confrontation. The three pages took twenty minutes for her to brief. Lots of minutia about all three murders, Maxwell's, Reinicke's, and Mario Tomazic's, and two pages of trivia about the shootdown of the presidential airplane.

Jake scanned the pages, asked a few questions and said, "There isn't one significant fact in this puree of trivia."

"We're working on it, sir. Early in an investigation, progress is often a matter of establishing negatives."

"You think?"

"Everyone in the agency wants these killers caught, and we're moving heaven and earth to make it happen."

Grafton sighed. "Every morning I want to see you in here with a report. Tell Harry Estep that I want to see evidence of a conspiracy. Any conspiracy. To commit any crime. From jaywalking to murder to stealing books from the Library of Congress. Anything. And I want any evidence any of your agents can find pointing to the identity of the killer of Mario Tomazic, the director of this agency."

"I don't think you are in our chain of command, sir."

Jake Grafton smiled. Perhaps. At least his teeth showed and his eyes turned cold. "I don't want to get into a pissing match with the FBI, and Harry Estep doesn't want to get in a pissing match with this agency. Discuss this conversation with him. I'm sure he will agree. I need to see evidence of a conspiracy, if there is one, so this agency can do the job for which it was created. And if the person or persons who killed Tomazic came from this agency, or from overseas, I need to know that so I can do my job. Wouldn't you agree?"

"Yes, sir."

"Tomorrow morning, Kerry."

She left, and Harley Merritt came in carrying his coffee cup and a file filled with things he wanted Grafton's opinion on. They got back to the serious business of global intelligence.

When Anna came home from work, I was sitting in the darkness waiting. "Oh, Tommy," she said, and dropped her coat and opened her arms. She gave me a great hug. Oh, man . . .

I already had a bottle of her favorite wine open and a glass poured. When she finally released me, I got her seated in her little living room and handed the wine to her.

"I saw Ilin today," I said.

"Oh," she said, surprise in her voice. "I had no message."

"He walked into my hotel dining room a few minutes after ten o'clock. We had a little conversation in the men's room."

"So you're going back to America?" she said. I tried to wring a clue from her voice and the way she said it, but couldn't.

"Soon," I said with nothing behind it. "I was thinking . . . Well, Anna, I was hoping you would come with me."

She stared. Completely forgot the wineglass in her hand and stared into my eyes. I stared right back.

"Will you?" I asked.

"Is this a marriage proposal?"

"I tried that once and it didn't work. I'm lowering the barrier. If I can get you over this little fence, get you to America, get you to see how great life would be with us together, then I'll try another proposal. See, I've thought this out."

She smiled at me. "I've been thinking, too," she said.

"If you have a Swiss passport you don't need a visa to get into the States. Do you have one?"

She nodded. Yes.

"Soooo . . ." I tried to contain myself. I reached for her hands. We were already knee to knee.

"Oh, Tommy. I—"

"Come on, kiddo. This is the best offer you're going to get today. Let's get on with life. Let's worry about Anna and Tommy. Nobody else."

She didn't say anything. The thought that perhaps I was pressing too hard occurred to me. "What have you been thinking?" I asked.

"That I was a fool not to say yes the first time you asked me."

That did it. She started laughing and crying at the same time and I started laughing and crying and we went on up into the stratosphere from there.

We managed to get on a plane to Washington, via London, the following morning. I used my Harold W. Cass credit card to buy both tickets. If the Company bean counters didn't like it, they could rat me out to Grafton and he could fire me.

Anna called her office from the airport and told them she was resigning. We checked our bags, went through security and walked the concourse holding hands. As we flew across Europe we talked about the future, not the past. I was pretty sure there wasn't much more of the CIA in mine. I was tired of going overseas for weeks, or months, often to places no sane person would even want to visit. Tired of pretending to be something and someone I'm not.

I had a law degree. Maybe I could go back to California and take the bar exam. What I knew for sure was that I didn't want to stay in the Washington, DC, area. I had been there for enough years to know I didn't like it. California! Yeah.

Changing planes in London, we had an hour to kill after we got to our gate. We walked into a bookstore/newsstand and I bought some newspapers. One of the stories at the bottom of the front page of *The Wall Street Journal* caught my eye. Homeland Security had been ordered by the White House to step up inspections on people leaving and entering the United States. Entering? The *Journal* predicted long lines for travelers. No kidding!

I stood there thinking about the envelope that Ilin had given me, which was in the breast pocket of my jacket. What if they found that? Confiscated it? Wanted an explanation? I was traveling as Harold W. Cass, Hoosier extraordinaire, with a fake passport issued by the U.S. State Department and a fake driver's license and AAA card, all issued by the documents section of the agency. What if customs got curious about the map? The computer should let my passport slide on through, but this map . . . I hadn't looked at it, but obviously Ilin had gone to a great deal of trouble getting it to me and thought it would mean something to Grafton if I could deliver it.

"Wait at the gate a moment," I told Anna, and went back along the concourse toward a Royal Mail storefront I had noticed walking up. It was about twice the size of a telephone booth. The gray-haired lady in uniform behind the counter had envelopes and stamps. I bought an envelope, stuck Ilin's envelope inside, and addressed it to Willie Varner at the lock shop. Bought enough stamps with my CIA credit card to get it all the way across the Atlantic, affixed them and dropped the envelope in the slot.

Feeling somewhat relieved, I strolled back to Anna, who was waiting at the gate. She smiled at me as I walked up and reached for my hand. A huge grin spread across my face. Life was looking up.

It was afternoon when we landed at Dulles Airport in the western suburbs of Washington. We got through immigration easily enough after the usual wait, me through the U.S. citizens line and Anna through the foreigners section, and found our baggage at the carousel.

The line to get through customs was severely backed up. From where I stood, I could see the inspectors pawing though luggage. Beyond the inspectors, against the wall, were armed Homeland Security officers in uniform, scanning the crowd. They didn't look bored. Which bothered me. The whole scene reminded me of my last trip through the Moscow airport. Guilty until proven innocent.

"Get in another line," I whispered to Anna. "If we get separated, meet me at Grafton's in Roslyn. You remember the address?"

She nodded. She was a professional. She had committed that address to memory years ago, when she was sent by Ilin to see Grafton. She glanced at me just once and went, no questions asked, pushing her cart with her suitcase and carry-on.

It took an hour for me to get to the head of the line. I surrendered my customs form, which said I had not bought anything abroad and had nothing to declare. Then I dumped my stuff on the conveyor belt and watched them x-ray both items.

The fun began when the stuff came out of the X-ray machine on the belt. An inspector there had my customs form in hand. He gestured at the bag and carry-on. "Open them up." He pointed to a nearby table. I carried the bags over and tossed them up.

After I opened them, I stood back when he gestured. He started through the stuff as if he suspected I was smuggling in a load of heroin or Cuban cigars. He emptied the clothes, felt the lining, wadded the clothes up and put them back in, then attacked the carry-on, which had the newspapers from London, a couple of books and my cell phone, which was off, a wall charger and my key ring. Plus a toothbrush and toothpaste.

When he had given all that stuff a very careful look, he gestured to a couple of the armed goons. "You need to go with these gentlemen. They will do a body search."

"Guess this is my lucky day," I said. "I hope they have warm hands."

"Don't get cute, buddy."

I thought that excellent advice. I was taken through a security door into a long puke-green corridor. The feds must buy puke-green paint in railroad tank cars. Lots of doors. They picked one halfway down on the left side and sent me in first. My bags were brought in, too. As two people searched the luggage again, meticulously, I was told to strip to the skin. Then I was given a body cavity search.

When the jerk finished and was taking off his rubber glove, I said, "I hope you enjoyed that."

"Keep talking, asshole, and we'll do it again."

There is a time and place for everything, I reflected, and this wasn't it. The guy tossed me a small towel to wrap around my waist; then I was led back into the corridor and into a room at the end that housed a major X-ray machine. I expected to meet Dr. Frankenstein, but I got an overweight guy wearing a white gown. He coached me through a complete body series. If I had had an implanted microchip or a diamond in my ear, they would have seen it. Ditto a condom of coke in my intestines.

"How do my lungs look?" I asked. "I had a chest X-ray scheduled. Maybe I can cancel it."

My technician ignored me.

Afterward, a heavyset guy with lots of tattoos took me back to the original cubicle, gestured to my pile of duds and told me to get dressed. When I was reunited with my luggage, I told the inked-up dude, "I assume you'll send the bill to Obamacare."

"Your tax dollars hard at work, Jack. Scram."

The whole ordeal took about an hour and a half. Anna was nowhere in sight when I emerged. I took the bus into the long-term parking lot. I sat there feeling pretty good about my decision to mail the map to Willie Varner as we rode the rows and people got on or off the bus.

My old Benz was right where I left it. The tires still had air. After I loaded my bags into the trunk, the door lock admitted me. I arranged myself behind the wheel and clicked the seat belt. Inserted the ignition key, said my usual prayer, and twisted the thing. Nothing. The engine didn't even make a noise.

I opened the door again. The dome light didn't come on.

Uh-oh! I got out, opened the hood and took a look. Yep. The battery was gone. Some asshole had stolen it. They hadn't taken off the terminal wires, but had cut them.

Welcome home, Tommy!

I was cussing when the realization hit me that I could have easily been dead. Instead of some lowlife stealing the battery, what if that Dumpster diver from Grafton's had put some dynamite under the hood? Was this a warning from the bomber?

I felt the icy fingers of the devil run up and down my back. And now I had Anna to worry about.

I took a taxi to Grafton's. On the way I played with my phone, got the video from the security cameras and saw Anna in the kitchen talking to Callie.

When the admiral got home at six o'clock, Anna, Callie and I were finishing off our second bottle of wine. He looked a little stunned when he saw Anna. Callie jumped right in. "Jake, Tommy and Anna are engaged."

She and Anna looked at each other and smiled, as if they knew something we males didn't.

Jake Grafton looked surprised. He gave me the once-over to see if I had lost it or suffered a severe head injury. After he decided I looked more or less normal, he made polite noises for a minute or two, "Congrats" and all that, then motioned for me to follow him into his office.

He closed the door behind me and demanded, "What the hell has gotten into you?"

"I'm going to commit matrimony. Hormones, probably. Anna and I got the urge at roughly the same time."

"What if she's a spy for the SVR?"

"If the FBI catches her doing nefarious stuff in the good ol' U.S. of A., they can prosecute her."

"I see. You know that you'll have to resign from the agency when the preacher signs the marriage license. Before the ink's dry. Why don't you two just shack up together?"

I tried to look horrified. "You mean, like, *live in sin?* The shock might kill dear ol' Mom. And I'd have to lie when I do the annual lie detector thing. You know how adverse I am to falsehoods."

Grafton threw up his hands. "Oh, hell. Okay, you win. The day before the wedding, you resign. Get married unemployed."

"Okeydokey."

He dropped into a chair. "Where's Ilin's stuff?"

"I mailed it to Willie Varner. An envelope that he said contained a map. The stuff you asked for he said would take a couple of weeks." I told him about the meet at the corner bar at the Willard.

"A map of what?"

"He didn't say, and I didn't open the envelope to peek. He said he got it from a guy in China. He said the guy had risked a lot and if anyone saw it his life might be in danger—all the usual crap. All of which meant hold it close. The thought struck me as I watched him that I was hearing precisely what he would have said if he were selling a map generated in a Moscow apartment to peddle to foreign spies for a thousand bucks a copy. I don't know what you paid for this piece of graphic art. Maybe there is a lost gold mine or buried pirate treasure under the X. I suspect there is a very slim chance you got a bargain, and a much larger chance you got screwed."

Jake Grafton watched my face as I spoke. When I ran out of words, he said, "Tell me what happened at the airport."

I sat down across from him and went through it as best I could.

He had questions. "Did you get the impression that they knew you weren't the guy on your passport?"

"Well, not really. But they were looking for something that they believed I had. I didn't think they were just randomly searching. They were hunting for something they *knew* was there."

He thought about that for a moment, then said, "Why did you decide in England to mail the thing?"

I shrugged. "An article in the paper . . . just a feeling I had. If they'd got their hands on it, as paranoid as they are, I'd be in a cell incommunicado until the very last terrorist goes to his reward in Paradise."

"That's the mystery." Jake Grafton regarded me as an unusual specimen. "Why did you decide to mail it and not carry it—carefully—upon your person?"

I shrugged as I thought about my answer. Finally I said, "Because I thought it was more likely to get here if it was delivered by the post office. Willie isn't on anybody's list of dangerous characters, so I sent it to him. Also, I knew his address."

Grafton sighed. Yeah, Willie was probably below the radar. If they were working off a list of the president's ten thousand worst enemies, Willie Varner, black ex-con, probably wasn't on it. "Let's talk about your car," he said. "Instead of stealing the battery, someone could have put a bomb under the car or under your hood."

"That thought occurred to me." I tried to keep my voice even.

Grafton grimaced. "The FBI says they can't find anything on that Dumpster guy you ran into at Dulles."

"I didn't think they would."

"Why not?" He regarded me with knitted brows.

"Just an itch between my shoulder blades. Something isn't right."

"A whole lot of things aren't right," Grafton said with feeling. "Welcome home!"

Mrs. Grafton insisted on fixing dinner. I sat and watched Anna's face as she chatted, ran her eyes over me, sipped a glass of chardonnay, gestured with her hands. I liked the way her eyes moved, the way she smiled, the way she tossed her head occasionally to get a stubborn strand of hair back from her eyes. I liked the sound of her voice, the accent, the way she chose words and made them sound. I wondered if I would ever get over the wonder of being with her.

Jake Grafton was apparently relaxed. He smiled and chatted and his eyes took in everything.

Of course it was Callie Grafton who got to the nub of it. She asked Anna, "You and Tommy—isn't this sudden?"

Anna looked at me and said, "I should have married him the first time he asked, several years ago, when I was here. Life gave us a . . . what do you say? . . . a do-over again?"

"A do-over."

"Yes. A chance to make another choice, a better choice." Her hand grasped mine. "He asked again, and this time I knew the right thing to say. The right thing for both of us."

Dinner was salad with chicken, with Callie's homemade dressing.

After dinner Grafton took me back to his office and gave me a pistol for my pocket. It was loaded. He put one in his pocket, too. "We'll talk more tomorrow. Let's go get the car and I'll drive you two over to your place."

"You still have guards in a van around the corner?"

"Oh, yes. I feel like a crime boss."

We got the car from the garage, after opening the hood and checking it out, and Grafton parked in front of his building in the loading zone. I went upstairs and hauled Anna's bags down, then went back for mine. We said good-bye to Callie, who kissed us both.

Traffic that evening was terrible. Everyone inside the Beltway was trying to get out. As we crept along in stop-and-go traffic, a fine mist of rain smeared the windshield. Grafton played with his wipers, and we chatted.

I have relived that drive in my memory a dozen times, and I can't recall what we talked about. Anna sat in the backseat behind Grafton, and I rode twisted around so I could see her. I remember her smile. She was so full of hope. Full of life.

Grafton dropped us under the awning of my building, so we were out of the misting drizzle as we unloaded the luggage. I got out my keys and opened the door to the building. Grafton wanted to help me carry the luggage, but I refused. Anna and I could pull it on the little wheels, and we had kept him long enough. I can't remember what I said. Thanked him, certainly. I remember him hugging Anna and shaking my hand and smiling broadly.

Then he held the door until we were through it. The elevator came as he drove away.

I remember thinking that if I had known I was bringing Anna home, I could have really cleaned up the apartment. Oh well.

I opened the door, let her precede me, then began dragging luggage in. The place smelled closed up. I had been gone a week. I went to the windows and opened them a few inches to admit some air.

I don't remember turning the lights on, but I must have. I think I gave her a tour of the place, both bedrooms, the kitchen, showed her the closets.

I asked her if she wanted something to drink. I have forgotten what she said. Maybe she wanted a glass of water.

Anyway, she was in the bedroom with her suitcase and I was in the kitchen when it happened. There was a huge concussion, like a car crash, and I remember being swept off my feet and flying through the air . . . I don't remember sound. No boom. None of that. Just the impact and flying through the air.

Then nothing.

When I woke up I was in this hospital bed, Admiral. How long have I been here?

A policeman came a while ago. I don't know when. Or maybe a fireman. Someone in uniform. He told me she died instantly. The bomb was apparently in the dresser. He said the blast was centered in that corner of the bedroom. He said a wall that was blown out whacked me in the kitchen.

So Anna's dead. And I can't remember much. How long have I been here? When are they going to let me out?

Do you know who did it?

Don't beat around the bush with me, Grafton. Tell it to me straight.

Who did it? Who put that bomb in my apartment?

Who murdered Anna?

CHAPTER FIFTEEN

If you know the enemy and know yourself, you need not fear the results of a hundred battles.

—Sun Tzu

When he came out of the hospital room, Jake Grafton found four men wearing casual clothes and light jackets standing in the hallway. They were covert operators from the agency: Travis Clay, Willis Coffey, Doc Gordon and Pablo Martinez. All had pistols in holsters hidden under their jackets.

"How is he?" Coffey asked.

"Has a concussion, some contusions, cuts and scrapes, a light burn and some memory loss. Doctor said nothing is broken or smashed. They want to observe him for a few days."

The four men nodded grimly. They all had worked with Carmellini on various occasions.

"So how about two of you on watch outside the door day and night. Twelve-hour shifts, staggered. No one but hospital personnel with the appropriate badges with photo ID goes through the door. If they take him out, one of you accompanies him and the other waits in the room. I told the doctor to arrange to have meals brought up to you from the cafeteria."

They nodded.

Jake took a paper from his pocket and handed each of them a sheet. It was a photo from a computer printer. "Study this photo and keep the paper in your pocket. It's from the video cameras at Dulles. Tommy recognized this guy there last week, chased him and had him in hand when the police interfered. The guy escaped. It's just possible this guy is the dude who tried to bomb my place and did bomb Tommy's. If it is him, he's a killer. I'd like him alive and able to talk, but don't take any chances. He's undoubtedly armed. If you have to shoot him, kill him."

They all nodded again.

"He's a little under six feet, Tommy said. White man, and fit."

"We have a name?"

"Not the one his mother gave him."

More nods.

"Call me anytime if you have any trouble. You have my cell number. If anything goes wrong. Anything."

"Yes, sir."

"You can visit him a little, one at a time, when the doctor says it's okay, but he needs rest."

"Yeah."

As Jake came out of the elevator in the lobby, he met Willie Varner coming in.

Varner recognized him.

"Let's chat," Jake said, and led him into the lobby and gestured to chairs. "How'd you learn about this?"

"Man, it was in the mornin' paper."

Grafton sighed.

"His girl really got it, huh?"

"Yes, she did."

"Same guy who tried to bomb you?"

"I don't know. Perhaps."

Willie ran his hand through his hair. "Damn," he said softly. "He called me from London. Said he was gonna get married." Willie sighed, remembering. "Never heard him so happy. And it all turned to shit."

Grafton described Tommy's physical condition. "He'll be out of here in a few days. No visitors."

"Man, the same asshole could walk in here and waste him."

"I have some men upstairs."

"Okay." Willie nodded his head and wiped his eyes. "Really tough shit for Tommy, man."

"He told me he mailed you an envelope from London. When it comes, call me. Don't open it. I'll send a man to get it."

"Okay. You know I'm still watchin' the video from your place from time to time. If anythin' happens, I can't call Tommy. Want me to call you?"

"Yes. If you can't get me, call nine-one-one."

"He really gonna be okay?"

"The doctor is hopeful. So am I."

Willie cussed a bit, then stood up, and they walked out of the hospital together.

When Grafton stuck out his hand in the parking lot to shake, Willie Varner seized it and gave it a pump. "You better find that bomber motherfucker soon," he advised. "If Tommy gets to him before you do, there won't be enough left of him to make a little dog's breakfast. Tommy's a good guy, and something like that wouldn't be good for his soul."

When he got back to Langley, Jake Grafton found Zoe Kerry waiting for him.

"Carmellini's place was blown up with a dynamite bomb. Four sticks, at least."

"What else?"

"The FBI is working it, Admiral. There's a security camera in the lobby, but it's on a twenty-four-hour loop. We took it and sent it to the lab, but . . ."

"What about that dude Tommy tackled at Dulles last week?"

"We're working that angle. Getting some resistance from Homeland. What their problem is I don't know."

"Tomazic?"

"No further information."

Grafton thanked her and sent her on her way. Then he had the receptionist call Sarah Houston. When she came into his office fifteen minutes later, he asked, "What have you got?"

"How is Tommy?"

She seated herself near the corner of Grafton's desk and put her file folders on her lap.

"Alive, with a concussion and cuts and bruises. A few days before they discharge him." Grafton eyed Tommy's former girlfriend. "No visitors, the doctor said."

Sarah nodded. "I didn't know he had a fiancée."

"They just decided to get married. He brought her back from Switzerland. He asked her to marry him once before, years ago, and she refused. She said yes this time. Came home with him and got blown up. Murdered. Sometimes life hands you a shit sandwich."

She didn't say anything to that, merely glanced at the files in her lap.

"What do you have?" Grafton asked, all business.

"The Chinese have indeed been into the navy's computer systems. I've got a report here. It will take a while to read." She passed it across.

"Anything jump out at you?" he asked as he glanced through it.

"I think the Russians have been in there, too. The systems are structurally weak."

"Terrific."

"They don't seem to have cracked the heavily encrypted stuff. Both powers have been into the low-grade stuff, such as ship schedules, port visits, that kind of thing."

"Okay."

"The thing I found a bit hard to understand—the navy has every carrier in the Atlantic Fleet scheduled into Norfolk over Christmas. They did the same thing two years ago during a budget battle with Congress."

"All of them?"

"Yep. All five of the battle groups. Some of the escorts will go to other ports on the East Coast, but the carriers will all go to Norfolk."

"Unbelievable," Grafton muttered. He didn't bother to tell Sarah he already knew of the navy's op plans for the carriers over the holidays.

"The navy has some light maintenance scheduled for the ships," she continued, "and they are apparently going to be generous with Christmas leave for the sailors. The ships will be there through New Year's, at least."

"Five carriers," Grafton mused, playing with a pencil while he scanned the report. "What else?"

"I'm recording phone calls on those numbers you gave me. You are treading on dangerous ground, Admiral."

"Anything interesting?"

"The White House staffers about lost it when the president's plane went down. That came as a huge shock to them."

"Did to me, too."

"They keep asking each other, 'What's happening?'"

Grafton used the eraser on his pencil to rub his head. After a moment he asked, "This guy Tommy tried to catch at the airport and you got the photo of, where is that?"

Sarah Houston said, "Homeland Security called the FBI off."

"Really?"

"Really. A couple of calls on that."

"Why?"

"I don't know."

Grafton collected his thoughts. "I think someone told Homeland Security that I sent Tommy to Switzerland. He was thoroughly searched at Dulles when he came back. He said he got the impression they were looking for something. That suggests the possibility of a leak in this agency."

She stared.

"I want you to get the cell phone numbers of all my staff and start recording their calls. And Zoe Kerry, the FBI liaison officer. If someone in this building is leaking classified information to other government agencies, I want to know about it as soon as possible."

"Why not just give that to the security people?"

"Because I don't trust them either," Jake said softly. His gray eyes pinned Sarah. "Someone murdered the previous director, Mario Tomazic, and as it stands, the motive could have come from within this building."

"I needn't remind you that evidence acquired through illegal means can't be used in court."

"You got that right. You don't need to remind me."

"Just saying." She stared back into those gray eyes, not the least intimidated.

"This isn't the Department of Justice, Sarah. It's the Central Intelligence Agency. We don't do prosecutions."

"Your responsibility."

"Absolutely. You are goddamned right." His voice rose. "The president appointed me, and I'm going to do my duty as I see it, come hell or high water. If the president or Congress or the FBI doesn't like it, they can do whatever they want with it. I didn't ask for this job, but I'm going to do my damnedest to do it to the best of my ability." His roar came down to merely loud. "If some son of a bitch is passing classified information to anyone not authorized to have it, I'll cut out the bastard's heart and eat it for breakfast. Got it?"

"Yes, sir."

His voice dropped to a conversational volume. "People are being murdered. Anna Modin was merely the latest. Tommy Carmellini was the one they wanted. Someone is doing this shit. There *must* be a reason. Give me a glimpse. A glimmer. Something there that shouldn't be. A word, a tone of voice, a hint. Anything."

Sarah had been fanged by Jake Grafton before, so this latest episode didn't raise her blood pressure. "Okay," she said evenly.

"I'll keep this report. You get these other people on the computer and record those phone calls. Listen to them. Anybody says anything suspicious, you bring it here as fast as humanly possible, or sooner. Got it?"

"I do have it, Admiral."

"Get cracking."

Sarah Houston left. Grafton stared at the door after she closed it.

Then he consulted his private telephone list and dialed a call. After he went through a switchboard and an executive assistant, he got the CNO, Admiral Cart McKiernan, on the line.

"Jake, how's everything?"

"Just fine, sir. I'm calling about those five Atlantic Fleet carriers that you have scheduled to be in Norfolk over the Christmas holidays."

"Okay."

"Who at the White House told you to schedule them that way?"

"Didn't even go through SECDEF's office. I got a call from some White House weenie. President's orders, he said."

"Which weenie?"

"Frank Harless. He's some sort of ass kisser or cigarette lighter or political guru over there. About a month ago."

"You sure it was him?"

"Yep. Told me if I didn't like it I could talk to Al Grantham."

"Did you?"

"Hell, yes. Told that son of a bitch that putting all those ships in one port was a really stupid idea. Asked him if he'd ever heard of Pearl Harbor."

"And . . ."

"And he told me that the order came from the president. I asked for it in writing."

"What did he say?"

"The subtle bastard asked if I wanted to retire early."

"Thanks, Cart."

"Yeah. You hear anything, anything at all, and I'll keep those ships at sea or dock them somewhere else. They didn't put it in writing. You know as well as I do that if anything goes wrong, they'll either flatly deny that they gave me an order or say that they merely suggested a course of action and expected me to use my best professional judgment. If *anything* goes wrong, it'll be the navy's fault. None of the mud or blood is going to stick to them. I've been there before and so have you. Fuck Grantham. And fuck the president. He can have a piece of my ass at the country club if he can catch my golf cart."

"Okay. Thanks."

"Any time, Jake. Don't be a stranger."

. . .

Lying in that hospital bed staring at the ceiling was the hardest thing I have ever done. The nurses and doctors came and went occasionally, took vital signs and said nice things. Every few hours one of the guys in the hall popped in, to stay only a few minutes. I had served with them all someplace and liked all four of them. They were guys like me, good on action and no great shakes with words. They tried to say comforting things, but nothing helped.

Anna was dead and I was just going to have to live with it. She didn't deserve to die that way, but what victim of insane, random violence does? With no evidence, I was sure that the Dumpster diver dude had fixed up the bomb in my dresser, the same way he had rigged up one to kill Jake Grafton.

If only I had been more careful. If only I had . . . checked the dresser myself? Then I'd be dead and Anna would still be alive.

The guilt ate at me. If-onlys are a poison that can kill you as dead as arsenic. They rob you of the will to live and destroy your ability to cope with life. At some point, all of us have to let go of what-might-have-been and go on down the road of life, wherever it might lead.

I wasn't ready yet. Anna's memory was still too vivid.

I wanted to get out of this damned bed as soon as possible and make some funeral arrangements. I was thinking about that when I realized that I didn't even know who her parents were, or where they were. Didn't know if they were even alive. If she had brothers or sisters. Maybe Grafton could get word to Janos Ilin somehow and he could see that they were told. They deserved to know. But he had probably already thought of that. Grafton was that kind of guy.

I also felt sorry for myself. That, and my guilt, made me feel like a real shit. If I got angry enough, maybe I'd pop an artery in my brain and stroke out. Dying right now or crippling myself wouldn't do. I had a score to settle with that bombing son of a bitch.

So I tried to calm down. The second morning I was conscious, I turned on the television. Problems overseas, problems here, the White House press secretary answering questions about the investigation into the Air Force One shootdown . . . I could feel my blood pressure rising, so I turned off the idiot tube.

Lay there in the bed thinking about Anna. And what might have been.

Oh God, why her?

When Willie Varner got the envelope from London in his mail and called Jake Grafton, the admiral climbed in his executive sedan with his bodyguards and went to get it himself.

"How's Tommy?" Willie asked.

"Doing okay, the doctors tell me. A couple more days. They think he can have short visits. If you want to go over to the hospital and visit for ten minutes or so, go ahead."

"By God, I will."

"They're going to have a psychologist visit him. You can expect that he's mired up to his eyeballs in post-traumatic stress. And guilt. Anna got it and he didn't."

"Yeah," Willie Varner said and nodded vigorously. "That's Tommy."

"That's everybody in his situation," Jake shot back. "We're all human."

"Most of us, anyway," Willie replied. "Not that bomber bastard. He's a fuckin' animal."

Riding back to Langley in the backseat of his executive sedan, Jake put on his reading glasses and opened the envelope. All that was in it was a folded map, which appeared to have been printed off a computer display. When he unfolded it, the sheet was about eighteen inches by eighteen. A map of the Norfolk, Virginia, area. At the center was Naval Base Norfolk. On the carrier pier was a dot. Surrounding the dot were concentric circles, five of them. Here and there were Chinese-language symbols.

Jake Grafton sat looking at the map. After a while he folded it back up and inserted it back in its envelope.

He thought about the possibilities. A: The map was real, put together in China. B: The map was fake, made by the Russians to slander the Chinese. C: The map was fake, drawn God knows where, and the number of people who might have made it was legion.

Assuming the map was made in China, what did it mean?

When he got back to Langley, Grafton had three Chinese-language experts come to his office. He duplicated the map, then had them translate the characters and mark them on his copy. The original went into an envelope that he stamped TOP SECRET.

He was studying the copy and its English translations when Harley Merritt came in for his daily appointment.

Jake handed the deputy director the map and said, "What do you think of this?"

Merritt pulled his glasses down from his forehead and began looking. After a while he said, "What is this and where did you get it?"

Jake told him.

"Holy shit," Merritt said.

"I want you to take the original"—Jake passed him the envelope stamped

TOP SECRET—"to the forensics lab. I want to know if this was made in China. Have them do an analysis of the paper and ink and the Chinese-language symbols. It looks like a computer print-off, but see what the wizards can learn. I want everything they can tell me. Everything. Then call the air force and navy and get some nuclear weapons experts over here. If that dot represents a nuclear explosion, I want them to estimate the explosive power of the weapon."

"Sure," Merritt said, fingering the envelope and duplicate.

"Keep the circle of people who know about this as small as possible."

Merritt nodded. Then he asked, "What are you going to do with this?"

"Nothing until the forensic and weapons experts have their say."

"Okay."

"Even if the map is a Chinese product, it can't tell us if this represents a contingency plan or an event that is going to happen."

"I understand."

"Our military makes war plans all the time. China's probably does, too."

They left it there.

"Our in-house investigation of reasons for Tomazic's murder is complete," Merritt told his boss. "Nothing. I am writing a report that I'll pass along when it is finalized, but there isn't anything worth mentioning in it."

Grafton nodded.

"If he was murdered, the motive isn't here at Langley," Merritt continued. "I'm convinced of that, and I put it in writing."

They moved on to other subjects. An hour after he arrived, Merritt left. Jake Grafton went back to studying the map. A retired navy attack pilot, Jake Grafton knew a lot about nuclear weapons. If this map represented the kill-and-damage zone of a nuclear explosion, the explosive power of the warhead would depend on whether it was detonated as an airburst or surface burst. An airburst could be delivered by a plane or an ICBM, or a missile fired by a submarine. Since the warhead detonated well above the target, it could be a smaller weapon.

A surface burst would need a more powerful warhead to do the same damage . . . and a surface burst would be more difficult to make happen. It would require a boat or ship or submarine to steam right up to the target, represented by the dot, and detonate the weapon. Unless the weapon was already there, planted on the bed of the harbor or inside something.

· · ·

Grafton put the duplicate in his desk and sent for his executive assistants. Regardless of everything else that was happening, he still had an intelligence agency to run. Anastasia Roberts and Max Hurley wanted to talk about Carmellini. "He's doing okay. The police bomb squad and the FBI are investigating. What they'll come up with may not help us find the bomber, or it might. We'll see. Tommy needs peace and quiet."

They nodded. Anastasia Roberts reported on her briefing to the White House that morning. Nothing on the possible Russian involvement in the assassination.

"Nothing from the Russian embassy?"

"No, sir."

They started in on the paperwork.

After they left an hour later, Grafton worked silently on the paperwork for a while, then went to the cafeteria for lunch.

He found Sarah Houston there and sat down beside her with his tray.

"How's Tommy?" she asked.

"Docs say he'll be back to normal soon."

"Good."

"Whatever normal is for Carmellini. I've known him for years and I haven't figured that out yet."

"Me either."

They chatted about the news for the rest of their lunch; then Jake asked Sarah to come up to his office.

When they were there and had the door closed, Jake asked about the telephone intercepts.

"Nothing to report," she said. "I would have called you if I heard anything."

"Good," he said. He opened his drawer, got out the map and handed it to her.

As she studied it he gave her his analysis. Then he said, "I know you're busy as hell, but I want you to search our database and the navy's to see if you can find anything suspicious about the Chinese navy."

"There is only one of me."

"Thank God for that."

"What am I looking for?"

Grafton considered. If he narrowed the search too much, something important or relevant might be missed. On the other hand, a report on the activities of the entire Chinese navy would be voluminous and possibly hide the hint he wanted. If there was anything there to be found.

"Let's just look in the Atlantic," he said. "North and South. Make it during the last year. Everything the Chinese navy has been doing in this hemisphere. There can't be that much."

"Okay."

"Thanks, Sarah."

Lieutenant Commander Zhang had never in his life seen anything like it. From where he stood looking over the piers of the marina, he could see at least a hundred boats, all for sale. Choy Lee was translating the jabber of the salesman, who sensed he had a sucker on the hook and was in a fine mood.

"Yes, sir," he said. "You folks surely came by at the right time. Lots of folks sell their boats in the fall because they don't want to pay the upkeep and storage and all through the winter. So I got lots of inventory and rock bottom prices. Got the lowest prices of anybody on the Chesapeake—that's why I sell the most boats. Ask anyone. They'll tell you if you really want to sell your boat, bring it here. And if you want to find a hell of a value in a boat, this is the place."

Zhang listened to all that in Chinese, eyed the man, then said to Choy, "Tell him I want a used boat with a cabin and small head, two engines, all the usual navigation gear. Plus an adequate aft platform to fish from and a built-in holding tank for our catch."

The salesman, a heavyset man with a crew cut and an enormous gut, with jowls to match, shook his head vigorously. "I got six or eight like that," he declared in an old-line Tidewater accent, which Choy appreciated but was way beyond Zhang's command of the language. "All good values. All good boats. Come on, I'll show them to you. Got the best one here in the showroom." He took them inside.

"Now you understand," the salesman said, "that a boat with two internal engines is going to be large and cost you a serious amount of change. This one only has one engine, but she's only two years old and is a sweetheart. Gonna make a great boat for somebody."

Zhang climbed up the ladder stand on the floor and went aboard. No doubt, it was a nice boat. He went below and looked at everything as Choy and the salesman chatted.

He was staring down through the open doors in the stern area at the single engine when Choy said, "This boat was repossessed by the bank when the owner couldn't make the payments. He'll sell it for fifty thousand dollars off the new price."

Zhang straightened up and said, "Let's see what else he has."

The fifth boat the salesman showed them was the one, in a slip on the third pier surrounded by boats that were too small or too big. Some of these boats were yachts, with prices over a million dollars. These Americans were amazing. What kind of person could afford such a . . . small ship?

This one was a twenty-eight-and-a-half-foot Boston Whaler with a small enclosed cabin and two large Mercury outboard engines of 225 horsepower each. Zhang eyed the Supermarine radar on top of the small bridge area.

"You probably know all about Boston Whalers," the salesman purred. "Unsinkable. You can cut 'em in half and both halves will float. Safest boat ever made, yes sirree."

"Will he guarantee that every system in the boat works?"

"Of course," the salesman replied after Choy put the question. "We'll take her out in the bay and make sure every single gizmo on this whole boat works like it did when it came from the factory four years ago. GPS, radar, depth finder, bathroom facilities, kitchen stove and refrigerator, both engines, the works. If something don't work, we'll fix it and you'll boat out of here like you were driving a new one. This is *our* business. All customers completely satisfied, yes sirree, that's our motto. No complaints. We make things right." He kept on with the sales patter, but Choy didn't bother to translate it, which Zhang thought just as well.

They left the marina, which was in an inlet on the south shore of the Chesapeake, heading north. Both engines purred like kittens. Zhang was at the helm. He looked left, to the west, but didn't see Willoughby Spit. It was too far west, hidden behind a head of land. He looked at the radar, ran the range out to maximum and saw the Chesapeake Bay Bridge to the Eastern Shore, ships, the shape of the shoreline. He brought the range in, played with the gain, brought it in to five miles, adjusted the gain again . . . It was a nice unit.

He ran the boat flat out on the step with the engines singing and a big wake pouring out behind, then at cruise speed, still on the step, maneuvering tightly. The boat responded like a racehorse. She heeled and ran and bucked the waves as the wind blew whitecaps on the bay and low clouds scudded overhead.

After an hour they turned back for the marina. Just a few miles out, the salesman leaned over the scope and pointed out the radar reflectors on pilings that marked the entrance to the inlet.

Zhang haggled and got the salesman to come down ten thousand dollars on the price. He had plenty of funds in his American bank account, but he didn't want the salesman bragging to his friends that a couple of Chinese fools paid the asking price, thereby calling unnecessary attention to Choy and himself.

Zhang played hard to sell. He had Choy demand another ten thousand off the price. When they didn't get it, they left. They came back an hour later, after lunch, and the salesman made free pier space part of the deal.

"You can keep her here at a berth through the winter, if you want, or let us haul her out and put her in storage for spring, whatever you wish. But you will have to have her out of here by May. We'll need our pier space for inventory."

Zhang agreed to all that and signed a paper that Choy Lee approved. Actually he signed a stack of papers, contracts, all printed in four copies. Then he wrote a check on his bank for the whole amount plus sales taxes.

When the salesman heard Zhang wanted to pay cash, before he had the documents prepared, his eyes widened. "Don't get many folks in here who don't wanta finance, 'less of course they're in the drug business. By chance, you guys ain't bringin' in shit, are ya?"

He laughed at his own wit, heartily, with his big gut pumping up and down. Choy Lee smiled thinly and didn't bother to translate for Zhang. *American humor is an acquired taste,* he thought.

CHAPTER SIXTEEN

Organized force alone enables the quiet and the weak to go about their business and to sleep securely in their beds, safe from the violent without and within.

—Alfred Thayer Mahan

Things were happening. In the next two days Grafton learned that the FBI had found the trail of the Air Force One shootdown team. Good solid police work had revealed their trail from the day they arrived in the United States until they died. Where they stayed, where they ate, telephone calls, even some fingerprints, none of which had yet been identified. The FBI was working with Interpol and police agencies worldwide, all of which seemed to be cooperating to the best of their ability.

Jake had his chauffer and bodyguards take him to the hospital to see Tommy Carmellini.

"How come I haven't heard from you?" Grafton asked me.

"My phone is dead. Or so the hospital staff said. It was in my pocket. Anyway, it's gone."

"I saw the doc. He wants to do another brain scan tomorrow."

"They already did one and said it was fine."

"They want to do another."

"Anybody got anything on the guy who blew us up?"

"No. We'll talk about it when you get back to the office."

"Where's my shoes and clothes?"

"Damn if I know. We can get you some clothes. The stuff in your place is a mess. The FBI salvaged what they could, a couple of your guns, a photo album, some of your CDs, a little bit of other stuff, but no clothes. Stuff was impregnated with chemicals and smoke. What are your sizes?"

He talked a little more, didn't say much. No sympathy. All matter-of-fact. Jake Grafton was no softie, not by a long shot. He looked like he had other things on his mind tonight. What they were he would never tell. He was also the most close-mouthed man you ever ran across. Kinda the opposite of Willie Varner, who was a Grade A gossip and told everything he knew, almost. Willie could keep a secret, if it was important. *If* he thought it important. But that was a big if.

When Grafton left I lay there in the bed thinking about Anna.

Finally, when the hospital had quieted down and the nurses had checked on me for the last time, I got to thinking about my car sitting in the long-term lot at Dulles Airport without a battery. If some scumbag had stolen the battery, that was one thing. But what if the bomber had stolen it, just to piss me off, giving me the finger, knowing that he had a dynamite bomb rigged in my apartment that was going to kill me dead in just a few hours?

The more I thought about that angle, the better I liked it. A pro would never have done that, but a killer who had a score to settle . . . well, he just might have.

It was something to think about.

When Jake got home Callie asked, "How is Tommy?"

"Depressed. He—" Grafton made a gesture. He couldn't think of anything else to add.

"When will they release him?"

"They were going to release him tomorrow, but I asked them to hold off a few days. They've taken his pants and shoes, so he can't jackrabbit unless he wants to do it in a hospital gown with no back."

"I understand."

"He wants to arrange for a funeral for Anna. I told him there's no hurry. The police scientists are still working with the remains. Nothing can be done until they release them."

She nodded. "Better take a shower and change clothes."

"What's for dinner?"

"Your favorite. Meatloaf, peas and corn."

"Thanks." He went to the bedroom to clean up.

. . .

It was a Tuesday morning when they told me I could go home that afternoon. I called Willie and asked him to come get me. Everything I owned was in the bombed apartment, and I didn't want to go sift through the rubble, if the cops would let me, which they probably wouldn't. I was going to have to do some serious shopping. Then the nurse came in and pulled out my IV and put a Band-Aid where it had been.

When Doc Gordon popped in I asked him to bring his pal. It was Willis Coffey.

"Hey guys. As soon as I get some duds I'm outta here. Grafton was supposed to send some over. Tomorrow at eight o'clock, I'd like to have all four of you guys come over to the lock shop." I gave them the address.

"What's the deal?" Willis asked.

"Tomorrow. Will you come?"

"Langley know you're being discharged?"

"Not from me."

"Well, we're supposed to be your guardian angels, so what the hell, we'll say we're still on duty."

"Gonna need Travis and Pablo, too. All four of you guys."

"Okay."

The nurse brought clothes that Grafton had sent over the day before. I got into them. Then I looked into a mirror. Still some half-healed cuts that were pretty scabby. The big one on the front of my head, up in my hair, still had stitches. The color of my bruises had mostly faded, and I was only a little sore. Good to go.

When Willie showed up, I rode out of the hospital in a wheelchair. The nurse was sweet, too. Willie brought the lock-shop van around, I thanked the nurse and climbed in, and we rolled.

"Where to?" Willie asked.

"Sears. Need some clothes."

"You got money?"

"Plastic. My wallet survived the adventure intact. Gonna use the Company credit cards."

"That's the spirit. Stick it to Uncle Sam. Ever'body else does."

After our shopping expedition and a gourmet repast at a Mickey D's, we went to the FBI headquarters downtown in the Hoover Building. It took me an hour, but I left with my guns and shoulder holster. A bag of ammo because the box split. The shoulder holster had two tears in the stretch material, but it was serviceable. I made a mental note to buy another holster when I had an opportunity.

I spent the night at Willie's place. He didn't have a spare bedroom, but he had a couch and a bottle of good whiskey. I checked the pistols, which seemed undamaged, and laid them aside. We drank, laughed, drank some more and finally cried. Then we collapsed.

I woke up in the morning on the floor with a hell of a headache. Willie had aspirin. I took three. Washed them down with coffee.

I got dressed in my new duds, put my Kimber 1911 in the shoulder holster and put it on. Put on a light jacket to cover it up and keep me warm.

When the guys showed up at the shop, I was ready to talk. The headache was almost gone.

"Here's the deal." I told them about my dead Benz stranded in the long-term lot at Dulles. "I need to go ransom the thing before the parking tab is more than the car is worth."

"I've seen your car, Tommy," Travis Clay said. "You may have already crossed the line."

"Yeah. Gotta install a battery and cables. But there are at least three possibilities. First, and most likely, some scumbag may have stolen my battery because he needed one and couldn't afford to buy it, and nothing may happen when I start diddling with the car. Second, the car could have a bomb in or under it set to pop when I open the car door or the hood, or try to start it. Finally, the killer may be sitting around watching, and even if there is no bomb, he may try to shoot me."

They discussed it. "Seems to me," Pablo said, "that a guy who needed a battery could have found one a little closer to home. Hell, Dulles is twenty-some miles from downtown, a dozen miles west of the Beltway."

Willie the Wire chimed in. "Kinda hard to figure a poor man goin' all the way to Dulles to score a battery and payin' a parking fee while he's doin' it."

After they had chewed the rag a while, Travis Clay said, "What do you want us to do?" No one suggested calling the bomb squad.

I grinned. These guys were all right.

"I don't want the son of a bitch dead. I want him alive to talk. If he's a little sore here and there and bleeding a little, that'll be okay."

They looked at each other and nodded.

"What are you gonna do with him afterwards? Or them, because there might be a couple of 'em."

"Nothing you want to know about. What you don't know, you can't testify to."

Everyone agreed with that assessment. America is full of low-information voters, who presumably are ignorant and happy.

Doc Gordon pointed out, "If there is any shooting out there, the cops and Homeland are going to be on us like fleas on a dog."

"That cuts both ways," I said. "That's why I kinda think we'll find a bomb in the car. However, this guy is nursing a serious grudge. There isn't a reason on the planet I'm a threat to anyone but him, and that's only because I saw him. My assessment is that there'll be a bomb, and he'll be close by to watch it go bang."

"Maybe," Willie said, and the others nodded

"It may be radio controlled," Travis pointed out. "He may blow it when he sees you, just for the kick. This guy strikes me as having that little piece of the devil in him. He makes his living killing people because he likes the work."

I got out a sheet of paper and a pencil and began drawing. "Let me make a diagram of the lot and let's figure out how we're going to snag this guy . . . if he's there."

The director's suite at Langley had a soundproof conference room beside the director's office. The room was really a well-disguised high-tech media center, complete with pop-up displays, projectors and screens. It could be accessed from the office or the reception area. It was equipped with the standard long table, a credenza and a small refrigerator filled with bottled water. All the screens and gizmos were hidden behind panels that could be moved with the push of a button. Jake used it when he had more people to talk to than his office could easily seat or when someone needed to make a presentation on the gadgets.

On the credenza he had a model of an A-6 Intruder that he had brought from his old office. He liked to glance at it from time to time because it reminded him of his youth, when his only problems were bombing assigned targets and staying alive. Somehow those concerns seemed easier, cleaner, than the challenges he wrestled with these days.

After his morning chat with Zoe Kerry, Harley Merritt came in with three scientists, who looked around as if they had never been in the head honcho's office. After the introductions, Jake asked. They hadn't.

He took his four visitors into the conference room, made sure the door to the reception area was locked and said, "Whatcha got?"

"The paper is Russian," Merritt said. "The map is apparently computer generated from an Internet database."

"Okay," Grafton said slowly, searching faces.

"The lettering appears to be standard computer stuff that the Chinese use."

"Bottom line?"

"Anyone with access to Russian paper who was savvy on Chinese computer tech could have made this thing."

Could be right out of Ilin's shop, Jake Grafton thought, although he didn't say it.

"If the dot represents the location where a detonation is expected," the weapons wizard said, "to get the kind of damage represented by the circles, we can estimate the potency of the explosion. If it's an airburst, at optimum altitude, which would be about nine thousand feet, something like two or three megatons would do it."

"Surface burst?"

"About ten megatons, more or less."

The experts launched into technical explanations, which Jake listened to carefully. The stakes were too high for guesses.

When they had all said everything they wanted to say, Jake had one last question for the weapons expert. "Assuming these circles accurately predict the damage a weapon would inflict, how many people will die in the Norfolk/Virginia Beach/Hampton Roads area?"

The expert, a young, prematurely bald Ph.D. who wore thick glasses and was already carrying a paunch, took time to consider. "The area is thinly populated, as metropolitan areas in the United States go. Very suburbanized. There is also a lot of water within those circles. This isn't New York or Boston.

"That said," he continued, "I would expect a million people to die instantly, and another million to die of their wounds or radiation poisoning within . . . say, six months. After that, maybe a hundred thousand will die of radiation poisoning within the next ten years. Finally the deaths will slow to a trickle. But people will suffer from radiation poisoning and die from complications until everyone, even present fetuses in vivo, who is within perhaps a hundred miles of the blast finally passes on eighty or ninety or a hundred years from now."

"A hundred miles."

"Yes."

"That takes in Richmond and a lot of the Delmarva Peninsula."

The expert nodded sadly.

. . .

After Merritt and the wizards departed, Jake Grafton sat staring at the wall, trying to get his mind around mass murder. In the navy he had been trained as a nuclear weapons delivery pilot. The indiscriminate horrors that nuclear weapons could and would inflict if used had had a profound effect on him then. Today, when he was forty years older, the effect was almost devastating. He sat immobile, trying to visualize the implications.

The danger, he knew, was that the problem would become so overwhelming that he would lose the ability to think about it rationally.

How did the Chinese think they were going to avoid war with the United States? Nuclear war? As horrific as an explosion in southeastern Virginia might be, nuclear weapons popping in densely populated Chinese metropolitan areas would slaughter people in the hundreds of millions.

He stared at the circles on the map on the table in front of him. Did they think America lacked the will or ability or guts to retaliate?

An attack on the United States. Any plan for that must have been approved at the very top.

If that was what this map represented. *Does it?*

What other explanation could there be?

The telephone on the desk buzzed. He picked it up. It was the receptionist. "Sarah Houston to see you, sir."

"My office. Send her in."

He extracted himself from the chair at the conference table, picked up the map and went into his office. Sarah was coming through the other door. He waved to the chair nearest the desk, and she seated herself.

"Hey," he said.

"I have a conversation that you should hear. I put it on your computer."

Jake didn't even sit. He bent, typed in some secret passwords, hit the ENTER button a couple of times, got to a screen he liked, then waved to his chair. Sarah switched sides of the desk and addressed the keyboard.

"You will have to turn up the volume on that thing," he said. "I usually leave it off."

Sarah played with the mouse and keyboard a moment; then came a sound of a phone ringing, then a male voice: "Yeah."

"Are you out of your mind?" A woman's voice, one that sounded familiar.

"Say what you want to say. I'm busy."

"Why did you put that bomb in Carmellini's place?"

"He saw me. And I owed him. What's it to you?"

"You know our deal. Only when I give you the target. Being unpredictable keeps you alive."

"You're getting your money's worth."

A click, then the humming of a dial tone.

Sarah hit a key. "Want to hear it again?" she asked.

"Whose phone?"

"Listen to the voice and tell me."

She played the conversation again.

"Zoe Kerry," Grafton said when the dial tone sounded.

"Yep. Her phone. She dialed a number that is a prepaid cell. No name."

Jake jerked a thumb, and Sarah vacated his chair. She walked around the desk, sat and crossed her legs. He collapsed into his and stared at the computer screen. As he watched, the screen saver began dimming the screen. After another minute, the screen went dark.

"Shit," he said.

"Do you want a recording of this, or the conversation put in writing?"

"A recording."

"I'll put it on a CD."

"Bring it to me personally. And we're not going to say anything about this to anyone. Especially Zoe Kerry."

She nodded her understanding.

"Anything else I need to know?"

"I'm working the phones, Admiral. Checking on the Chinese navy. When I get something, I'll make an appointment and come up."

He didn't look at her, just nodded.

Sarah got out of the office through the door ahead of the executive assistants, who were marching in with their piles of daily reports and memos and directives, all of which needed his attention.

After he had waded through it, a process that took an hour and a half, Grafton shoved the paper back at Roberts and Hurley and said, "I have a research job. Max, are you up for it?"

"Of course, sir."

"I want résumés of the careers of the top officers in the Chinese navy, say the ten most senior. I need it as soon as I can get it."

"Yes, sir."

"Hop to it," Jake said, and Anastasia and Max scampered out.

. . .

I'm certainly no bomb expert, and I never went to an EOD school. Somehow Grafton never sandwiched that one in. However, I'd watched the experts play with roadside bombs in Iraq and picked up a few things, so I probably knew a bit more about the subject than the proverbial man on the street, may he rest in peace.

Lying in the hospital I had thought about bombs, about fuses and batteries and how to trigger the capacitor to set the whole mess off with a big bang. It kept my mind off Anna Modin.

Driving out to Dulles late in the afternoon, I felt as if I were in some transition world, somewhere between reality and the world as I wished it to be. Anna was gone, to whatever comes next. I didn't even know if she believed in an afterlife. Somehow that never came up.

The only fact that I had hold of, that kept me going in a semi-straight line, was the fact she was murdered. Probably by the same bastard that had tried to kill Grafton. Who probably did kill the director of the CIA, the director of the NIA and the director of the FBI. Maybe he had something to do with trying to kill the president. I didn't know, but if I could just get my hands on the guy, I thought I could find out. If his heart didn't give out under interrogation.

Anyone can be made to talk, to tell everything he knows about any subject on earth, if enough pain is applied. Anyone: you, me, anyone, no matter how tough they are. Or almost anyone. There is a tiny number of people who can endure pain up unto their death and never talk. They are rare individuals. Still, the drawbacks to that technique of obtaining information are twofold. First, the sufferer is likely to tell you what he thinks you want to hear in order to end the pain, so you may be obtaining bullshit you think is gold. Secondly, applying the pain does things to a sane man that are impossible to explain or live with. The torturer becomes an animal.

I didn't think my conscience would be a big problem. All I had to do, I thought, was think of Anna and tightening the screw would not be difficult. That's what I told myself, anyway.

First, we had to catch the bastard.

Willie and I went shopping for a battery and the cables to replace the cut ones. We took the shop van. We also bought a mechanic's mirror, for looking under vehicles, plus a tiny camera on a flexible fiber-optic hose for looking into tight places.

At three that afternoon Travis Clay showed up at the lock shop with two tactical headsets they had borrowed from the Company. We tried them out. The other guys would have them, too. We would be on channel one. The other guys were already on their way to the airport. They would slip into the lot at intervals and do a look around, as surreptitiously as possible, then find parking places. We hoped there would be parking places. Although we were interested in an area of about fifteen acres in that hundred-acre lot, Dulles was a busy place and parking places were hard to come by. We would just have to do the best we could.

Everyone would be in place, surrounding the old red Benz, when Willie and I showed up at five o'clock to do our thing.

We chatted on the tac net on the way to the airport. Everyone in place. Not ideal positions, but at least they were arranged around the Benz. They had done some looking, but not much. If our rabbit saw them searching the lot, he would boogie. If he was there. We were hoping he was. I had my fingers crossed.

I had my Kimber in my shoulder holster. Willie wouldn't carry a gun even if he had one: He was a two-time loser, and being caught with a gun would have probably got him prosecuted as a habitual criminal, which would have meant a serious stretch in the pen, maybe life. He wouldn't have touched a shooter even if it had tits on it.

We put on coveralls with the name WILLIE'S LOCK SHOP emblazoned on the back. They looked as if they hadn't seen a laundry since last spring. Willie slid behind the wheel of the van, and I climbed into the passenger's seat.

On the way to the airport, Willie had second thoughts. "What if this guy has a bomb rigged up with radio control, Tommy? You thought about that? He see you near that car and push the button and drive off while you takin' the long slide to hell."

"I don't think that's likely," I explained. "He can't sit in that parking lot around the clock, and he hasn't the foggiest when I might show up. If I do."

"Man, 'less that fool's there, he put a bomb in your car to pop when the hood is lifted, it might blow up a couple of mechanics from Joe's Garage."

"You don't really think he gives a damn, do you?"

Willie shrugged. "Maybe not. But if there is a bomb in the car, he oughta be in the next state over. If he's got a lick of sense."

"Willie, if he had a lick of sense he wouldn't be assassinating people. This is a special kind of dude."

"Special," Willie agreed, his head bobbing.

"He likes killing people. Hold that thought."

"And us standin' round that ol' Benz beggin' him to do it to us. Talk about lackin' sense!"

Actually, I was kinda hoping this guy would take a shot at me. And miss, of course. Then the snake-eaters and I would have his homicidal ass to do with as we chose. As *I* chose. And I had plans.

Got to catch him first, though. Got to catch him.

We drove into the long-term parking lot, took a ticket and went creeping down the aisles. "Slow, man, slow," I said as I scanned every car in sight. "We're a couple of mechs looking for this dead car."

"In a lock-shop van!"

Well, it was the best we could do on short notice.

Fortunately, the area where the Benz was parked wasn't full. There were other cars creeping in, looking for parking places, and here and there people dragging suitcases on wheels and queuing up at the bus stops, waiting for a ride to the terminal, which was over a half mile away. Jets took off and landed, although the noise wasn't loud. Amazing how they had quieted those things the last few years. Now at the airport jet noise was just a background drone.

"There it is," I said, pointing. "Park right in front of it."

He did. I got out, went around back and opened the doors and took out the mirror. I didn't rubberneck. That was Willie's job. He stayed behind the wheel and was supposed to be looking right, left and ahead.

Of course, it was possible our bomber wasn't in the lot but was somewhere a good distance away, with a rifle. That seemed unlikely, although possible. Hell, anything was possible. The hairs on the back of my arms seemed to come to attention as I walked up to the Benz and looked 'er over. Looked in every window, walked all the way around the car, keeping moving.

I may be a stud, but I didn't have it in me to just stand there posing for a sniper. Then I slid the mirror, which was on a four-foot handle, under the car and began looking. It was an interesting device, with a twist-grip handle that allowed the operator to adjust the angle of the mirror. I did the driver's side first. Didn't see anything. Worked my way around. Looked up into the engine compartment, then under the passenger side, then under the trunk area. Didn't see a thing that wasn't supposed to be there.

After I had done the whole car, I put the mirror in the back of the van and took out the optical device on the flexible probe. It even had a little spotlight on it.

"You have the eyeballs going, right?" I said to Willie.

"No, fool. I'm takin' a nap."

I inserted the optical device under the bottom of the hood. Tried to get it over the top of the radiator for a look. I couldn't. The gap between the radiator and sheet metal was too small. After five minutes of trying, I gave up. There was nothing for it but to pop the hood and take a peek.

First I had to open the car. I had the keys in my pocket, but if there was a watcher, that wouldn't do. He hadn't used keys, and after all, this was a lockshop van. I got the tool we used to open cars after people locked their keys inside and slid it down between the driver's window and the outside sheet metal of the door.

Manipulated the flat tool a bit, and the lock popped.

I put it back in the van, like a careful workman, then opened the driver's door. Very slowly, alert for the slightest sign of resistance. There was none. I reached in, pulled the little handle to release the hood, then closed the door and went around front.

"There's a guy watchin' us," Willie said on the net. "Behind the van. He's out of his car, foolin' with a little suitcase and watching us."

"Got him." That was Doc Gordon.

I took the video probe over to the front of the Benz and reached inside to ease the hood off its latch. Then I planned to insert the probe for another look. I was trying hard to look nonchalant, just a workman doing his job.

"He's walkin' this way." Willie's voice in my ear. "He dumped the suitcase. Comin' quick."

That's when I looked. Yep, it was him. About a hundred feet away and striding along.

I dropped the tool and ran toward him. He was in the middle of the traffic lane. He stopped with his feet spread and raised a pistol he had been carrying down by his leg. I hadn't seen the pistol when I started toward him. It was too damn late to stop.

He took a two-handed grip, raised the weapon, which seemed to have a silencer on it.

I was going at him on a fast lope. I juked left, the pistol flashed and popped, and I faked right and went left again. Another shot, another miss.

Thinking about it later, I was amazed at how cool I had been as the assassin blazed away. Pulling my own shooter didn't even cross my mind. I wanted this son of a bitch alive. All I can tell you is that right then I guess I didn't give a good goddamn.

The fact that I was still running toward him must have made him lose the tactical picture. He never saw or heard the car coming up behind him. Doc Gordon's front grille caught the shooter in the ass and he went forward onto his face.

Doc slammed on the brakes and I sprinted up, kicked the pistol away. The guy was stunned. Spread-eagle on the pavement. I rolled him over. Yep. It was the Dumpster diver.

Doc was leaning out the car window.

"It's him, all right. Back up, then run over his elbow."

I stuck his right arm out and stood back. Doc leaned out the window and eased the car forward. The left front tire went right over the guy's elbow, crushing it. He screamed.

I dragged him out from under the car. Doc and Willie helped me put plastic ties on his wrists and ankles and gag him with a strip of duct tape.

Willie ran back to the van and backed it up. I told him when to stop. Doc and I picked up the guy and threw him in the back. Then we looked around. No one seemed to be watching. "We got him," I said on the net.

Doc retrieved the silenced pistol and the guy's suitcase and tossed them into the van. Then he closed the rear doors.

"All you guys get out of here," I said on the net. "See you tomorrow at the office."

Got mike clicks in reply.

"Go up to the Benz," I told Willie. He got behind the wheel and moved the van.

I took a last look around. Blood on the pavement. It would wash off when it rained again. Blood always washes off.

Willie climbed between the seats and took a look at our patient. "He's bleeding," he said to me.

"Put a tourniquet on that arm," I told him. "Use a plastic tie. Make it tight."

"So why did he come runnin'?"

"There's a bomb in the Benz and he thought I was going to find it."

Indeed, six minutes later I saw it with the optical tool. It was wedged near the firewall, with a trip wire taped to the front of the hood. With the hood almost down, there had been just enough room for him to work. Looked like five or six sticks of dynamite. Of course, if I had just lifted the hood all the way . . .

We would come back, disarm the bomb and install a new battery in the Benz later. We would also pick up the bomber dude's ride to see what we could learn from it.

I shoved the last of my gear in the van, climbed in and pointed at the distant exit from the lot. Willie put the van in motion.

The bomber was writhing in the back, moaning softly. He was hurting bad. I figured he was going to be hurting a lot worse pretty soon. I threw a blanket over him so the woman in the tollbooth wouldn't get a shock.

I put on my seat belt, sat back, took off the tactical headset and mike. Yawned. Snapped on the radio to drown the moans. Willie had it tuned to a DC rock station. The whanging of an electric guitar, insane drumming and incomprehensible lyrics matched my mood.

"Well, come on, Tommy. Gimme some cash for the parking lot tab."

I dug out my wallet.

Truth is, I felt pretty good. Better than I had all week.

Choy Lee was in love. He wanted to spend the rest of his life with Sally Chan. But he was a Chinese spy, monitoring American fleet movements, which seemed fairly innocuous in and of itself. He had told her months ago that he was an early retiree from Silicon Valley, which explained his income and his hobby, fishing. If he got married he could always keep up the deception, of course, until his control transferred him or ordered him home. Then he and Sally could drop off the edge of the planet into the beating heart of America.

However, the addition of Zhang Ping to his station worried him. He had reported every ship movement for months, without fail, and then came Zhang. Was he about to be ordered home? What if he proposed to Sally and she accepted? How would Zhang take it?

Now he and Zhang were spending every day in the new boat cruising around Hampton Roads, drift fishing, trolling or anchoring near one shore or the other and fishing. Fishing, fishing, fishing. Actually he fished and Zhang sat in the captain's chair in the little cabin and used binoculars, by the hour.

Today the temperature was in the mid-fifties and there was a twenty- to twenty-five-knot wind blowing under a high overcast that blotted out the sun. Zhang's laptop was in a stand near the helm, beside the radar scope and GPS. Earlier, when Zhang went to the head, Choy had examined it. A wire with a USB plug ran from the computer to a power outlet to keep it charged. There was another USB plug, too, and the wire for that ran into the console. Choy figured Zhang had wired it up one evening when he and Sally were in bed at a Virginia Beach motel. He wondered where it went. He didn't get to dig around to find out. When he heard the head flush he moved noiselessly back to his fishing rod and was reeling in to check his bait when Zhang came up the small ladder from the cabin.

As Zhang searched with binoculars, Choy thought about Sally. She was American to the core. Choy's occupation would horrify her. Her father's parents had fled China when the Communists were on the verge of victory and come to America. Her father had been born here and had served in the army during the Vietnam War. Her mother was a fifth-generation American from California. Both of them hated Communism and believed in the American dream with all their hearts. So did Sally. She had made that crystal clear on several occasions when some liberal commentator or politician on television spewed an elitist, anti-American viewpoint. "Crap," she called it, and changed the channel.

So what was he going to do? If he turned himself in to the FBI, perhaps he would eventually be released, and then he could marry Sally. She might forgive past sins, but she would never continue their relationship if she knew he was an agent of the Chinese military. Never. And he thought too much of her to try to keep his occupation a secret.

He felt a bite and set the hook. "Got one," he called to Zhang, who put down his binoculars and asked, "Should I move the boat?"

"I don't think so. It isn't that big."

After a ten-minute fight he brought the fish to the side of the boat. It was a rockfish, fifteen or sixteen pounds. He used a gaff and hauled it into the boat. Big, but no record. The biggest rockfish ever hauled out of this bay was over sixty pounds.

He turned, grinning like a fool at Zhang, who looked amused.

"How about that?" Choy Lee roared in English. Wait until Sally heard about this!

He put the fish in a cooler near the outboard motors that also contained ice, and sat down in the enclosed little bridge where Zhang was, out of the wind, to warm up and have a beer. Beer was one of the things he liked about fishing, even in December.

He would take the fish to Sally at the restaurant this evening. Maybe she and her father could cook it the Chinese way. He almost invited Zhang to come share it, then decided not to.

Zhang turned back to the radar scope. Two container ships were to the east, heading north for Baltimore. Another, a bulk carrier probably full of coal, was in sight coming down the bay, headed for the entrance to the Atlantic. Over by the mouth of the Elizabeth River a destroyer was coming out. When she was broadside to them heading east, Choy could just make out the number on the hull: 109. That would be DDG-109, USS *Jason Dunham*. He called out the name to Zhang, who merely nodded that he had heard. He was examining her now with binoculars.

Why was Zhang in America, here in Norfolk? His presence meant something, but what?

CHAPTER SEVENTEEN

War is hell.

                         —William T. Sherman

It was a few minutes after midnight when I called Jake Grafton. Checked on Willie's phone to see that he was home—looked like they were out or in bed, but I rang his house anyway. Woke him up.

He showed up at the lock shop at a quarter past one.

I was sitting in the front of the shop checking my notes when I saw Grafton park out front. I unlocked the door for him, then relocked it when he was inside.

"You got him, huh?" Grafton said.

"He's in back with Willie. Been jabbering his head off. I wrote it all down if you want to read it to save time." I told him about Travis, Doc, Willis and Pablo.

Grafton went through the door from the shop to the workroom. We had our bomber spread-eagle on the floor with a work light in his face. We had been manipulating his arm below the crushed elbow socket. The wound was swelled up to about the size of a grapefruit, and blood was leaking out. The pain, I imagine, was excruciating. The assassin stood it a while, then tried to answer questions to get us to stop. That worked for a bit, but when he wound down we would have to stimulate him some more.

Grafton took a long look at the guy. The odor of shit and piss didn't seem to bother him any. He kicked Fish's foot so he would open his eyes.

"What happened to his elbow?"

"Car ran over it. Doc Gordon hit him from behind. He was shooting at me. He must have figured that I would find the bomb in my Benz."

"How bad is the elbow?"

"Bones on both sides of the joint are crushed, I think. They'll probably have to amputate. See his fingers? No circulation. They're turning black."

"But he's still alive," Grafton said with a sigh. "That's good. I might think of a few more questions. Do you think he's been telling the truth?"

"He did some lying there for a while, but we got those kinks straightened out."

"These fingerprints on the last page?"

"His. He wasn't in any shape to sign his name, so we put ink on his fingers, left hand, and he signed with those."

Grafton gave me a look, then went over to the workbench, where we had Fish's stuff laid out. Looked at the pistol with the silencer, at the suitcase, which only held two bricks to give it heft, and at his cell phone and keys, which were on a ring. He picked up the phone, played with it a bit and pocketed it.

Then the admiral sat down in the only chair and rearranged the lamp over Fish so that he could read my notes. I turned up the volume of the shop radio so that Fish wouldn't be burdened by our conversation. "Tomazic, Reinicke and Maxwell. And Anna," Grafton muttered. "Put the bomb in my place . . ."

After a bit Grafton said, "So this is why you saw him at Dulles."

"He was coming back from Seattle. Did that job out there with a car bomb. He really gets off on car bombs."

Grafton read on. A couple of times he glanced at Fish, who was enjoying the respite from excruciating pain. No doubt his whole arm hurt like hell, but nothing like it did when I twisted his lower arm or stood on it or kicked it. Then he about jumped out of his skin. He screamed and screamed. Fortunately our little shop was in a strip mall and the tenants on both sides had gone home for the night. There was no upstairs. Willie checked the alley behind from time to time. Fish could scream his lungs out if he wished.

Actually I had to go easy on that arm. If I had really tugged and twisted, I think the lower arm would have separated from the upper arm; the socket looked that bad. Then it wouldn't have hurt anymore. Then I would have had to use a hammer on the left one and start all over. But I didn't have to do it. Fish got positively garrulous. He even volunteered things, which was hard to believe. Yet I saw it happen.

Grafton was studying the meat of the revelations. Who gave Fish his targets, whom he had seen in Seattle, where he got his dynamite and fuses, how much he was paid, numbers for contacts, where he lived, where he kept his money, where his weapons were, who he had killed since the day he got out of diapers until this evening, all of it.

"So this Chinese guy, who is Kerry's control, called him and sent him to Seattle?"

"So he says."

"His name?"

"He doesn't know it. The guy mentioned Kerry, called her a mutual friend."

Finally Grafton asked the stupidest question I'd heard in years. "Did you read him his Miranda rights?"

"Oh, sure," I said. "I carry a card in my wallet. Willie heard me."

"Good."

Grafton went back to my notes. Finally he folded up my sheets of paper and put them in his pocket.

"What do you want me to do with him?" I asked.

"Well . . ." Grafton considered. He didn't glance at Fish. "I'll make a call or two."

Jake Grafton went through the shop, made sure the outside door wouldn't lock behind him, went outside, got out his cell phone and called Harry Estep at home.

After eight rings, Estep answered the telephone.

"Jake Grafton, Harry. Sorry to wake you up."

Estep grunted.

"We've got a little problem that you can help us with. We've got the guy who killed James Maxwell. Among others. Our problem is what to do with him."

A long silence followed. Finally Estep said, "Jesus Christ. How'd you do that?"

"He planted a bomb in Tommy Carmellini's car at Dulles Airport. He was waiting around to see Tommy get blown up. Tommy and a few friends got him first."

"Has he talked?"

"I'm going to reserve that for the time being. He's in bad shape. A car crushed his elbow while they were trying to capture him. I'm afraid he needs to go to a hospital. I want you to send some people you trust to arrest him under a national security warrant and see that he is guarded around the clock, held incommunicado, available to no one."

"I hope you haven't fucked this up so we can't use his testimony in court."

"You know better than that, Harry. I doubt if he'll say a word without his lawyer by his side. Your guys can read him his Miranda rights and all that. Still, we're going to have to keep a serious lid on. If you like, I'll brief you tomorrow. As it is, he needs to go to a hospital."

"Who is it?"

"Goes by the name of Fish. His real name is Peter Vega. He's a professional assassin."

"Where is he?"

Jake gave him the address of Willie's Lock Shop.

"Vega, Vega. Is he Hispanic?"

Grafton sneered into the phone. "Damn if I know."

"Okay. Take him to Walter Reed. I'll get some people over there within an hour."

"Carmellini will run him over there." The irony of that remark was not lost on Grafton. "Come over to Langley about eight. I'll buy you breakfast."

"I know you're not telling me everything."

"Of course not. Eight o'clock. My office. See you there."

Jake hung up and went back into the lock shop.

Carmellini was sitting near Fish, not looking at him. The man was on the floor, moaning.

"Take him to Walter Reed," Grafton told me. "The FBI will have some people there to meet you. They'll arrest him and guard him around the clock. After the doctors get done with him, we'll jail him. Might need him later to tell his tale again. If he will. If he won't . . ." Grafton sighed. "He'll be a one-armed assassin, assuming that someday the country gets back to normal. And assuming someone hasn't permanently shut his mouth before that happy day arrives."

"Okay."

"Put a tourniquet on that arm. He's still bleeding. And tape his mouth shut. He talks to no one."

"Okay."

"So your Benz has a bomb in it?"

"Yes, sir."

"Call the bomb squad. You're no EOD specialist. See you in my office at ten." He glanced at his watch. "This morning. And don't forget you have an appointment at the Willard at noon."

"Yes, sir."

The admiral didn't look at Fish again. Said hello to Willie, who had been sitting on a stool watching and listening, then walked out.

When I came back from locking the front door, Willie was putting his jacket on. "Damn," he said. "That Grafton is somethin' else."

"Oh?"

"I was gettin' around to kinda feelin' sorry for this murderous son of a bitch after what you did to him, which God knows he had comin', but that Grafton . . . He ain't got a quarter ounce of sympathy in his whole body."

"Sympathy isn't one of his virtues," I agreed sourly. "And I'm running a little short of it myself these days. Let's get this asshole to a hospital before temptation gets the better of me. I'd sleep better nights if I killed him and dumped what's left in a sewer."

Admiral Cart McKiernan answered his phone after ten rings. He sounded sleepy, too.

"Couldn't you have called in the morning?" the CNO asked, after Jake told him he wanted to see him at eight.

"I need to see you in the morning, as soon as possible."

McKiernan sighed. "I have a Joint Chiefs meeting in the morning. Can this wait until lunch?"

"Yes, but I'd rather you come to Langley so I won't be seen around the E-ring. I'll buy your lunch."

"A free meal! How can I refuse? See you then."

Jake tapped on the glass that separated him from the driver's compartment. The driver opened the window. "Langley," Jake said.

Sitting in the chair behind the director's desk, Jake sighed. He now knew who had killed Mario Tomazic, Reinicke and Maxwell, planted the bombs in his condo and Carmellini's apartment, and gone to Seattle and killed one of the Russians who attempted to assassinate the president. Fish. Zoe Kerry had hired him for the DC hits. A Chinese man hired him for the Russian hit, a man Fish knew in Boston who was Kerry's control. Fish had dumped the bag, even giving Carmellini the name of his Boston contact and his telephone number, plus a description of the Chinese man who met him in Seattle.

All that was left was the why. Staring at the map of Norfolk on his desk, Jake thought he had a glimmer about the why.

Zoe Kerry. What did she know?

If arrested and interrogated, would she talk or clam up?

If she was removed from the board, would her controller sound the alarm . . . in Beijing or Moscow, to whoever paid for murder and mayhem? Who was the controller? Someone was providing the money. Kerry certainly couldn't be paying Fish for assassinations out of her own pocket.

He had told Tommy to take Fish to a hospital. He could be held there incommunicado and the word could be passed that he was not talking to anyone. Still, Zoe Kerry would eventually find out Fish was locked up. Criminals who commit serious crimes think they will never be caught; if they admitted the possibility, they wouldn't do the crime. What would Kerry do when she heard about Fish? Disappear?

He thought about it. With Harry Estep's help, she could be kept under twenty-four-hour discreet surveillance. Every phone call could be monitored. Except if she used a public telephone booth—that was the risk.

Kerry had had two shooting scrapes in cases involving Chinese intelligence operations in America. Had she tried to arrest spies or protect them? The Chinese had hacked into the navy's computer systems. Five carriers were going to be in Norfolk over the holidays, and presumably the Chinese knew that. He asked Ilin for backdoor cooperation, and Ilin produced a map of Norfolk that he said was Chinese, a map that could be construed as showing the blast effect of a nuclear weapon. A team of Russians tried to assassinate the president. A man controlled by a rogue FBI agent killed the director of national intelligence, the director of the CIA and the director of the FBI. The same man, perhaps, was paid by a Chinese agent to kill one of those Russians with a car bomb in a parking lot at Sea-Tac Airport, and did so.

Add it all up, and what do you have?

Jake wrote a note to the receptionist asking to be awakened when she arrived, put it on her desk, closed his office door and stretched out on his couch.

If the Chinese hacked into the navy's computer system, so could someone else. Like the Russians. Perhaps the North Koreans, but not likely. The Iranians had certainly been trying. Al Qaeda? The Venezuelans? What if . . .

If you are going to blow up half the American navy, why assassinate high-ranking intel officials? The director of the FBI? Why kill the president?

Who else was on Kerry's list? Well, heck, he was. He knew *that*. But why?

He was thinking about the map when he went to sleep.

. . .

In Norfolk, Choy Lee had dinner with Sally Chan in the Chans' restaurant. Sally's father cooked the rockfish, which he served on a bed of rice with some traditional Chinese vegetables. He and his wife joined Choy and Sally at the table. It was a convivial meal, full of good cheer, happy conversation and smiles. The conversation was all in English, American English.

Choy wondered what the senior Chans would say if they knew he was a Chinese agent. But mainly he wondered what Sally would say if he told her. Would she drop him like a hot potato and immediately call the FBI?

He considered the problem from every angle as he sipped traditional tea.

"You are so preoccupied tonight," Sally said. "What is on your mind?"

He shrugged. Now was not the time, nor was this the place.

"You need to get a real job," Sally said seriously, gazing into his eyes. "Fishing all day and loafing is not an honorable occupation for a man of your youth."

"I have earned my retirement," he said defensively.

"No doubt, but what are you accomplishing?"

"I catch good fish."

"Congratulations. Maybe you should become a commercial fisherman."

"You are serious, aren't you?"

"Indeed I am," she said, still watching his eyes.

"I'll think about it."

Sally Chan still had his eyes pinned. "I think you are in love with me, and I am in love with you. You haven't mentioned the L-word, but I think I know what is in your heart."

Choy Lee's blood pressure rose ten points.

He finished his tea and pushed the cup away. Like every other Chinese restaurant in America, this one gave out fortune cookies when the waitress brought the check. There was no check tonight, of course, but the waitress brought the cookies anyway. Choy smiled at her and examined the two on the small plate.

"Which one do you want?" he murmured to Sally.

"The one you don't pick."

He leaned forward, pretending to examine them, then seized the one nearest to him, broke it and extracted the small slip of paper. He unfolded it and read silently, "Important decisions await you."

He crumpled it in his fist. Popped a piece of the cookie in his mouth.

"What does it say?" Sally demanded.

"I don't know that I want to share. Open yours."

She did so, and read aloud, "Romance is in your future." She eyed him again. "Now yours."

Choy saw no way out. He passed it to her. She smoothed the paper and read it.

"Prophetic, I would say," she told him, and pocketed both of the small slips.

Choy Lee didn't smile. He sat staring at her.

CHAPTER **EIGHTEEN**

Invincibility lies in the defense; the possibility of victory in the attack.

—Sun Tzu

Lieutenant "Gnuly" Neumann and Lieutenant "Whitey" Sorenson were at the controls of a U.S. Navy P-8A Poseidon over the South China Sea on a routine surface surveillance mission. The Poseidon, the replacement for the navy's forty-year-old turboprop P-3 Orion patrol airplane, had a surface search radar in a pod on the belly, which had been lowered hydraulically so the radar's scan wouldn't be limited by the engine nacelles.

Two naval flight officers (NFOs) and three enlisted naval aircrewmen sat at the operators' stations along the port side of the aircraft behind the cockpit. Only the pilots had windows. Today they were busy tracking the ships and fishing boats in the South China Sea.

It was a dull mission. The plane and crew were based at the old naval air station runway at Subic Bay in the Philippines. The United States had turned over the base to the Philippine government in 1992 after the Philippine Senate demanded the U.S. military leave, but the rising aggressiveness of China had changed political reality in Manila. The Philippines decided they needed the United States as military allies. In 2012 the U.S. Navy was invited back to Subic Bay, the finest deep-water port in the western Pacific. Fortunately for the Americans, the saloons and whorehouses of Olongapo, the city beside the base, had welcomed the Americans back with open arms, as had all the Filipinos who once again had jobs at the base.

Gnuly was thinking about how the world had turned, again, when the senior NFO, Lieutenant (junior grade) Doug Shepherd, said on the intercom, "We have a high-speed bogey at three o'clock. Thirty miles and closing fast. On a course to intercept. It's above us and descending."

"How far are we from China?"

"One hundred and forty-five miles east of Hainan Island."

Oh hell, Gnuly thought, *here we go again.* The Chinese had already harassed U.S. patrol planes three times this year. Twelve or thirteen years ago, one hit a P-3. Killed the fucking Chinese bastard in the fighter—he went into the ocean—and the P-3 made an emergency landing in Hainan, where the Chinese held the crew for eleven days before releasing them. The pilot was now a commander; Gnuly had met him once. All these thoughts shot through his head in a second or two.

Gnuly left the plane on autopilot. A steady course might prevent some damn fool chink from inadvertently hitting him. Not that there was much he could do about a Chinese aircraft zooming around, with or without hostile intentions. The Poseidon had no antiaircraft weapons whatsoever. Nor was it aerobatic or supersonic. It was a military version of the Boeing 737-800, an airliner.

"Hell," Whitey said, and stared out his window, trying to catch a glimpse of the oncoming airplane.

Then he saw it, slightly above them, descending toward them. "Collision course," he said, his voice rising. "Right at us! Holy damn."

The airplane, a fighter, slashed right in front of them, missing by what seemed a few feet. The Poseidon jolted as it went through the fighter's wake. The fighter went out to the left in a climbing turn. Gnuly watched it. It was high, curving around to come in behind them.

"You guys in back get ready. This guy is gonna buzz us again."

"Or hit us," Whitey muttered. He concentrated on the instrument panel. If the autopilot kicked off, he wanted to be ready to hand-fly this beast.

The Chinese pilot came zooming in, seeming to aim his plane right at the cockpit. It looked like he was going to ram, yet at the very last second he dipped his wing and passed in front of them on knife-edge, a ninety-degree angle of bank, so close they could see his helmeted head in the cockpit. Extraordinarily close. Once again the Poseidon bucked as it crossed the fighter's wash.

"Jesus!" Whitey roared. "He damn near got us."

Gnuly took several seconds to get himself under control. He had thought they were going to die. "How close is the cavalry?" Gnuly asked Shep. He meant American fighters, of course.

"An hour away, at least," was the answer.

"Get on the horn. Get them coming this way. Have Mike tell base ops what is going on." Mike was the other NFO, Lieutenant Mike Fischer. "Give them our position. If we go down, at least they'll know where to look."

"Yep," Shep said, and changed radio channels.

"Got it," Mike echoed.

"There's another fighter a thousand feet above us, crossing our nose right to left," Whitey said. "Got him in sight."

"The wingman," Gnuly said.

"Yep."

"Gimme a camera, somebody. I want a photo if he comes by again."

The fighter did make another pass, but Gnuly was still trying to get the camera that had been passed to him turned on and focused when it came up the port side in afterburner and crossed right in front of them, seeming close enough to touch, its wingtip almost scraping the cockpit. Gnuly managed a photo as the fighter headed west, toward Hainan. It was at least two miles away when he clicked the shutter.

Then they were gone and the incident was over. Two fighters disappearing into the haze toward Hainan, the Poseidon still on autopilot, the crew wondering what it all meant. If anything.

It was an international incident, reported worldwide. Another Chinese-American incident. A Chinese spokesman said, "Continued surveillance by the United States threatens to undo previous diplomatic efforts."

Jake Grafton read the article in *The Washington Post*. So did Sally Chan, in Norfolk, in *The Virginian-Pilot*. Choy Lee read that article, too.

After two FBI agents showed up at the hospital, Willie Varner and I took the van back to the shop. We got into his car and headed back to his place, where I was bunking.

"I guess you don't need me watchin' that feed from Grafton's anymore."

"You're done."

"Maybe that Kerry bitch will kill someone else."

"I don't think so. Grafton will take care of her."

"Gonna be a nice little check, when I get it."

"Hold that thought."

Willie the Wire looked me over and shook his head. "This shit ain't good for your soul, Carmellini," he said. "Mine either."

"Meet you in hell," I muttered.

At his place he got out a bottle of bourbon, poured a glass neat, handed it to me, then went to bed.

I sipped bourbon and thought about the interrogation. I almost killed Fish when he told me about planting the bomb in my apartment. Of course, he had lots more to spill at that point, so I didn't. Just caused him more pain. Lots more. Killing him would have given me a lot of satisfaction, but it would have been an easy out for him. Toward the end, he was begging me to shoot him. That's when I was glad I hadn't finished him. Now I was wishing I had.

Ah me. Why is it we are supposed to be civilized, obey the rules of a civilized society, when the enemies of our society aren't civilized?

That was a conundrum I wasn't smart enough to solve.

Any way you looked at it, Anna Modin was dead. Gone. Gone forever, and I was left here to march on through this putrid morass of stupidity, self-interest and evil.

Was I feeling sorry for Anna or myself?

I finished off that glass of whiskey, drank one more, then stretched out on the couch. I was replaying Fish's screams in my memory when the alcohol put me to sleep.

Sal Molina arrived two minutes prior to Harry Estep. Jake Grafton handed him Tommy Carmellini's notes and a cup of coffee, and called for coffee for Harry when he got there. Both men read Carmellini's notes in silence. As they were reading, Robin knocked, then came in carrying two breakfasts on cafeteria trays. Jake nodded at her, and she gave one tray to each of the visitors. She looked a question at Jake, and he shook his head no. He would get something to eat later.

When Robin left, Estep angrily asked, "How'd Carmellini get this stuff outta this Fish guy? Vega."

"I didn't ask," Grafton shot back.

"Tortured him."

Jake Grafton shrugged. "I didn't ask because I don't want to know. There it is in black and white. Two days before, we intercepted Zoe Kerry talking to this guy on a cell phone."

"Intercepted?" Estep growled. "You got a warrant?"

"No."

"We can't use that in court."

"Want to listen?" He turned to his computer, and in less than a minute all three men heard her voice.

When the conversation was over, Estep said a cuss word.

"So what are you going to do about Zoe Kerry?" Grafton asked, eyeing the FBI man.

Estep lost it. "What the hell can I do? Fish, Vega, won't testify. This statement to Carmellini isn't admissible in court. That recording is worthless. The Justice Department won't prosecute. Kerry will just laugh at us."

"Well, you better think of something," Grafton said, staring at Harry. "You and I know those notes are the gospel. She sicced Fish on Mario Tomazic, James Maxwell, Paul Reinicke and me. He put a bomb in Carmellini's apartment and killed Carmellini's girl. He assassinated the last known man who brought down Air Force One, trying to kill the president. Fish says he did Carmellini on his own because he saw him, knew his face. You have several hundred agents investigating all these crimes, and Fish admits he did them. Now what the hell are you going to do?"

Harry Estep threw Carmellini's notes on Grafton's desk. They scattered all over. The admiral left them where they landed.

"Sal, you want to say anything?"

"Why?"

Jake Grafton took a sip of coffee, as if this were just another staff meeting. "Because he was paid."

"Who paid him?"

"Kerry."

"Who paid her?"

"I don't know. She does. Harry?"

Harry Estep was pale and sweating. His eyes bulged. He stared at Jake Grafton. "You . . ."

"Man, I just told you how it is. You're the interim director of the FBI. Until Sal's boss throws you under the bus. Now, Interim Director, what *are* you going to do?"

"Arrest her. There's nothing else I can do."

"I agree. She'll try to contact Fish sooner or later and smell a rat when she can't get him. Toss her in the can. But get busy investigating her. Not him. She's got a contact somewhere. Get a warrant to intercept her calls, search her computer. She's got a bank account somewhere that she uses to pay Fish, or she's got a mattress full of cash. That money is somewhere. Goddamm it, *find the money*! But don't get the idea you can let her walk around while you investigate.

If she realizes Fish is in custody and calls the money man or sends him an e-mail, he'll know the deception is over."

"So?"

"Damn it, don't you see? The murders were all a diversion to keep our eyes off the ball."

"What ball?"

"I'm not sure yet."

"All this on your say-so."

"I didn't set this up, you idiot. I'm just telling you about it."

"We'll decide what to do," Harry Estep snarled.

"Better get at it. She could be trying to call Fish even as we speak."

"Fuck you, Grafton."

"That remark won't help an iota."

"It makes me feel better. Got any whiskey in your desk?"

"No."

"Thanks for nothing," Harry Estep said, and rose from his chair.

"If you're going to arrest her, better get at it," Grafton said.

Estep was in a foul mood. "Unlike you, we have to get a warrant first." He strode to the door, opened it and slammed it shut behind him.

Molina rose from his chair.

"Not you," Grafton said sharply to the president's man. "Sit."

Molina didn't move.

"Harry has a full plate," Grafton said, "but you people at the White House have been living in la-la land and dancing between the raindrops. Now it's time to face the music. Sit down."

Molina sat.

"Whose bright idea was it to have the navy bring five aircraft carriers into Norfolk over the Christmas holidays?"

Molina stared. "Five carriers in Norfolk? This is the first I've heard about it."

"Unfortunately, the navy heard about it months ago. Maybe six months ago. Some White House weenie ordered the CNO to order all the Atlantic Fleet carriers to Norfolk for the holidays, and McKiernan obeyed. As it happens, government spending will hit the debt ceiling in early December, and Congress will probably be reluctant to raise it. Oracle that I am, I predict another round of posturing about the debt ceiling. Remember what happened the last time?"

Molina sat silent, looking at Grafton. The telephone buzzed.

Grafton answered it.

Robin. "Zoe Kerry is here to brief you."

"Tell her I'm busy. Tomorrow."

"Yes, sir." The receptionist hung up.

Grafton swiveled back to Molina. "Someone at the White House told Cart McKiernan to put those carriers in Norfolk over the holidays. The Chinese know about it; they've been hacking into the navy's computers. God knows what other nation knows our plans. The navy's computers are apparently easily hacked. They might as well make a public announcement. One nuclear explosion and half the fleet will be wiped out, a million lives lost." He pulled out the map Ilin had sent and handed it over.

Sal Molina stared at it.

"That's a Chinese product. A Russian spy got it, and a high official in the SVR passed it to me."

It took almost a minute for Molina to digest. "You're implying the Chinese government will destroy these ships."

"That's a distinct possibility."

"An attack on Norfolk?"

"It will probably be more subtle than the Japanese attack on Pearl Harbor."

"Subtle?" Molina was still trying to understand. "How?" he asked.

"The bomb may already be there."

Willie Varner and I were sitting in the long-term parking lot at Dulles at nine o'clock that morning in the lock-shop van watching airliners land and take off when the FBI's bomb squad showed up in an armored truck. One of the dudes got out of the passenger seat and came over to the van.

"Are you Carmellini?"

"Yep."

"Got ID?"

I showed the guy my CIA pass. He took a hard look, sighed and handed it back. I almost asked him for his ID, but thought better of it.

"That's the car." I pointed at my ride.

"A bomb in it, you think?"

"Yep. Under the hood. I have the keys if you want them."

He surveyed the cars, the sky, an airliner that serenaded us as it headed for Europe or Denver or wherever, and the people pulling luggage on wheels through the lot. He was a medium-sized wiry black guy with a buzz cut. He had a pinch of snuff in his lower lip. After a long look at my Benz, he spit on the pavement. "The office said I was to get the bomb out and let you have the car back."

"We already have the man who put it there, and he has confessed. There won't be fingerprints. Might be some DNA, but we don't need it."

"Wanna move this van? Back up a hundred feet and help keep people away."

"Okay."

"Gimme your keys." He looked at my Benz. "What year is that?"

"A '64."

"An antique. Kinda ratty. Aren't you about ready for a new ride?"

"I'm working up to it."

I backed the van up about a hundred feet and turned off the engine.

"See, ever'body thinks you oughta get a new car," Willie said.

"I just hope these guys don't blow up my car and themselves, so I'll have something to trade in."

"You the tightest dude I know," Willie grumped. "Kinda ashamed to be seen with you around that scruffy old thing."

"Let's get out and herd pedestrians."

Willie said a common cuss word, and we climbed out of the van. I kept my cuss words to myself; they didn't do me any good when I said them, so why bother?

The EOD specialists didn't blow themselves up. After they removed the bomb, six sticks of dynamite, from under the hood, the bomb squad guys drove away. Willie and I put a new battery in the Benz.

"Six sticks," Willie said. "Enough to spread you and this fuckin' clunker all over this parking lot. They'd have scraped you up with a spoon to get enough to bury."

"Yeah."

"Seriously, Tommy. You oughta think about gettin' into another line of work."

"I am, dude. I am."

"I've heard that song before outta you," he said disgustedly. "Three or four times. I'll believe it when I see it."

The Benz started on the first crank. After I gave him ten bucks for the toll-booth, Willie drove the van out of the lot, and I rolled out behind him. I was headed for a mall to buy some more new duds; then I had an appointment downtown.

Another line of work. No shit, Willie.

I was on the way to Washington on the limited-access road when it came over me, all of a sudden. I started sobbing and my eyes teared up.

I pulled over on the shoulder to let it pass. I couldn't stop sobbing.

About two minutes later a trooper pulled up behind me. He spent a moment in his car, probably calling in my license plate, then got out and walked up to the driver's side window. I ran the window down. I was a little better, but I must have been a sight. He took one look, sizing me up, and said, "Move your car when you can."

I nodded.

"A woman?"

I nodded again.

"Been there, buddy. You'll live through it." He turned and walked back to his cruiser and left.

Three minutes later I was my usual sour self, so I started the engine and got the Benz under way.

I stopped in the men's room on the way out of the mall and put on a set of my new threads. Underwear, socks, dry-clean trousers, leather shoes, a shirt with a collar that would take a tie when necessary, a sweater. Their off-the-rack sport coats fit me like I was wearing an empty feed bag with three holes in it. Plus a new belt. I was wearing new from the skin out.

On the way downtown, I called Doc Gordon, who was hanging around the Willard with a couple of other guys, looking for anyone who might be interested in little old me when I arrived. I circled the block a few times, keeping an eye on traffic. Reasonably certain I had no tail, I drove into the parking garage and wound my way to the top floor. Took the elevator down. No one paid the slightest attention to me. Doc was waiting when I came out of the elevator. He ignored me. Willis Coffey was seated in the lobby looking at a street map.

I ducked into the men's room and sat on the throne until five minutes of twelve, then walked out and went into the corner bar. Five people in there, four men and a woman.

On Friday evenings this bar was one of Washington's top meat markets for the professional and government crowd. If you looked the part and couldn't get picked up here, you were essentially without prospects. I took a seat at the bar, and the barman handed me a bar menu. "What'll it be?"

I considered. One drink at noon shouldn't put me over the edge, and God knew I needed it. I named a bourbon. "Neat," I said.

He nodded.

"Hell, make it a double."

"You got it."

I glanced around to see if I could spot my Russian spy. Nope.

Nothing on the bar menu screamed at me. I laid it down and looked out the window.

The bartender served my drink without comment. I sipped it and minutes passed. I watched reflections in the window. No one paid me any attention. The place gradually filled up. The patrons looked like lobbyists or political staffers, with a few lawyers sprinkled in for seasoning, the same crowd you see at noon in bars and eateries all over the downtown.

The whiskey tasted good. I thought about ordering another and decided against it. This afternoon I was going to have to tell Grafton I'd been stood up, and I should probably do it sober.

When the last of the brown liquid was behind my new belt buckle, the bartender asked, "Another?"

"No. One's enough."

"A mutual friend was talking about you the other day."

I did a double take. The bartender was a black guy, maybe fifty, with prematurely gray-tipped hair. Even features, no visible tattoos, maybe 150 pounds.

"Which friend? I have several."

"He just said he knew you, Carmellini. I'll bring your bill." In a moment he placed a little book containing the bill on the counter. I picked it up. It had the tab in there. I put my credit card, the government one, on top of the tab. The drink was going to be on Uncle Sugar.

When the book came back, I opened it and removed my plastic and a small brown envelope, pocketed them, then added a 20 percent tip to the credit card slip, signed it and launched off. Everyone ignored me.

Admiral Cart McKiernan came into Jake's office at the CIA headquarters at Langley at twenty minutes after twelve. Jake had two trays from the cafeteria sitting on the sideboard.

As they ate, Jake explained about Fish and handed the admiral Tommy's notes. After he read them carefully, McKiernan said, "So who hired this woman he took orders from?"

"I think it was the Chinese, but the evidence is thin. It's someone who invested a lot of money in the attempt to assassinate the president. And Fish doesn't come cheap."

"Why?"

"I think this whole mess is a diversion to tie up law enforcement and the intelligence apparatus. The real threat is elsewhere."

McKiernan abandoned his lunch half eaten. He pushed the tray back an inch. "Where?"

Jake passed over the map and explained how he got it, mentioning no names.

"Norfolk," the admiral whispered, staring at the map.

"The carriers and their escorts in port over the holidays. Maybe."

"How good is your maybe?"

"One chance in four. That's the best target around. But there are others. Washington, New York, San Diego . . . We could make a list."

"Well, this is easy. I'll send the ships somewhere else or keep them at sea."

"I don't think you should do that. At least not until the very last minute. There is an excellent possibility that *if* Norfolk is the target, the bomb is already there. Someone is watching it. If the watcher suspects that we know about the weapon, he might detonate it without waiting for ships. There are more than a million people in the Norfolk area, not to mention Newport News."

"But we don't know it's there," the admiral objected.

"We are going to have to find out. Search that harbor without anyone knowing we are doing it. And keep an eye peeled for the watcher, who may or may not have the ability to trigger the thing."

They worried the bone. "If the weapon isn't there, the attack must come from the air, from a plane or missile," Jake argued. "If it's a missile, we'll know who launched it. Ditto an airplane. That would start World War III with the Chinese. They can't want that. They want the ships off the board and the United States Navy's offensive power cut in half. That will force the United States out of the Yellow and China Seas, maybe out of the western Pacific. They'll blame the explosion on us. Say an American nuke detonated. Half the people in the United States, Japan and Europe will believe them; that's the political reality of our world today. You know that."

McKiernan made a face. "And of the half that believe it was the Chinese, half of those will want to do nothing, preferring to pretend it was an accident."

Jake said nothing.

The admiral mulled it. "If a bomb is there—and you have not an iota of proof that it is, other than a map that any kid with a computer could flange up—when was it planted?"

Jake picked up a classified file on his desk and passed it to McKiernan. "One of my staff dug this out last night." The file contained the report from USS *Utah* about shadowing a Chinese sub from Hainan to the South Atlantic. The sinking of the boat, the return of the sub to Hainan. In addition, there was the information on *Ocean Holiday.*

"It isn't much, I know," Grafton said. "But this is a real possibility. The people on the yacht planted the bomb, left U.S. waters bound for the West Indies, rendezvoused with the Chinese sub off the Amazon and scuttled the yacht."

McKiernan read every piece of paper in the file twice, then handed it back. "It fits," he acknowledged grudgingly. "Do the people at the White House know about this?"

"Molina has seen the map. Not this file."

McKiernan couldn't sit still. He walked around the office with unseeing eyes. "Another Pearl Harbor," he muttered. Finally he sat down again.

"Okay," he said. "Okay."

I drove the Benz back to Langley. Jennifer Suslowski, at the reception desk, waved me into Grafton's office. She even smiled at me. I was so stunned I forgot to smile back.

Grafton was in his reading glasses, sipping coffee and going over paperwork. He was always behind, I knew. Budgets, personnel, covert operations, intelligence summaries, reports . . . The paper flowed in faster than he could make it flow out. He had department heads, administrators and executive assistants, but still he was inundated. And like the captain of a ship, he was responsible for everything. Ask any congressman.

He glanced up at me and waved to a chair. "Get your car back?"

"Yes, sir. The FBI EOD guys got the bomb out without an explosion or a police riot in the parking lot and took it away."

"The Willard?"

I put the envelope on his desk. "It was the barman. He passed this to me."

Grafton nodded and fingered the envelope. He wasn't going to open it while I was sitting here.

He changed the subject. "I talked to Estep this morning. He's going to arrest Kerry, after he gets a warrant. That'll probably take all afternoon. Why don't you trot over to her apartment and take a casual look-see through her stuff before they get there? I've called personnel; they'll show you her file before you go. Leave her computer for the FBI. See if she's got a getaway bag packed and what's in it. Don't leave any prints."

I frowned, started to protest. I never leave prints. Jeez . . .

Protests would have been wasted. He was back reading, so I left.

I had other things on my mind when I went by Suslowski, so I don't know if she smiled at me or not. Probably not. She didn't waste more than one or two a day.

In personnel, the desk lady, a gray-haired woman with too many pounds and too many years for me, produced the file quick enough, but then wanted me to sign something. "The Privacy Act," she said by way of explanation.

I was a bit surprised. "Admiral Grafton called."

"We have our rules. You wouldn't want just anyone reading your file, would you?"

"Certainly not." Using my left hand and careful not to leave fingerprints on the access sheet, I scribbled something illegible. She was satisfied.

She stood and watched me flip through the file. I made notes . . . with my right hand. The desk lady commented. "I'm ambidextrous," I told her.

Kerry's DOB, address, telephone numbers . . . Langley CIA pass number, car window sticker, license plate and type. That was the same car she had ridden me around in. In two minutes I thought I had everything I needed.

The desk lady had her eye on me the whole time, making sure I didn't remove anything from the file. I made a mental note to tell Grafton that his sterling reputation cut no ice with the grunts. I thanked her and left.

I left Langley and drove over to Kerry's apartment house, which was in Tysons Corner, on the west side of the Beltway. Thick clouds above the buildings and trees. Gloomy, chilly day. Maybe it would snow. Or rain.

I found the building, right across the street from a McDonald's. Only one entrance. I had to wait for a garbage truck to exit. Then I drove in slowly and started looking for FBI vehicles. Up and down the rows I went. The lot was perhaps a third full, since it was only two in the afternoon. Their car was in the back row, backed in facing the front entrance. Two men, ties and sport coats.

I merely glanced at them and rolled on by. Her car wasn't here.

The lot had a driveway around the south end of the building that allowed you to go around behind it. I took it. A dozen cars back there, with room for maybe twenty more. Her car wasn't here either. Nor were there any FBI agents.

I parked at the far north corner of the lot and reached under the passenger's seat for my picks and latex gloves. Pulled on the gloves slowly, worked them up over my fingers and hands.

Checked my gun under my armpit. Not that I intended to shoot any FBI agents, but maybe I would get lucky with Zoe Kerry.

The back door had numbers and names in a list. Beside each name was a buzzer. Yep, 213, Kerry. I pushed the buzzer and waited. Jabbed it two or three more times and waited some more.

I started at the highest floor, which was four, and ran my finger down the buzzers, giving each one a blast. The little squawk box came to life. "Who is it?"

"Joe Wilson. I forgot my key."

The door beside me clicked. I pushed and was in. "Thanks," I told the squawk box.

I took the elevator. The door opened into an empty corridor. I looked at the sign on the wall. Apartment 213 was to the right, so I went that way. Rapped on her door, just in case. Silence.

It took me about thirty seconds to get the lock.

I went inside, closed the door and made sure it locked behind me.

The place looked as if Conrad Hilton had designed it fifty years ago. This was an old hotel, converted to apartments. I walked toward the sitting room, by the door of a bathroom and a closet on my left into the sitting room, or living room, which had a kitchen in one corner. There was a small refrigerator, a four-burner electric stove with an oven under it, a small microwave and a super-duper coffee machine that ground the beans and heated milk.

I needed to know what was here, yet I didn't have time for a leisurely search. On the plus side, I didn't need to make sure everything looked undisturbed. The FBI would tear this place apart this evening; they wouldn't know how she left it this morning.

The door that connected this room to what had once been another hotel room stood open. Big bed, a dresser, a nightstand, a desk with a printer on it, and a flat-screen television mounted on the wall. This room's hallway had been converted to a walk-in closet. The bathroom door had been altered so now it opened through the bedroom wall, not the hallway. I opened it. Beauty paraphernalia was scattered all over the counter and filled the drawers. I closed the drawers and moved on.

The problem was time. I had no idea how much I had. Five minutes, five hours? Or something in between.

She had a laptop computer in the living area, on the counter across from the kitchen. It was plugged in and charging. I passed it and looked out the window between the curtains, without touching them. I was looking at the parking lot in front of the building. Traffic went by on the street beyond. The FBI guys were still there, sitting in their car.

If she had a getaway bag, it had to be where she could get to it fast. In a place this small, she could get to anything fast.

I went into the bedroom closet and got busy searching.

Shoes, hats, dresses, slacks, boots.

I went back to the closet by the door to the apartment. It contained winter coats and boots and sweaters. I felt the pockets of the coats. There was something in one.

A derringer. Two-shot, .22 caliber. It was loaded. I felt in the pocket for extra cartridges. None. Tried the other pocket, which was also empty. Well, this was a hideout gun. If you needed more than two bullets, you needed a better gun.

I started to put it back where I had found it, then changed my mind. Pulled up my pants leg and stuffed it in my sock.

I got busy, trying not to be messy, but looking. Did the desk first. Checkbook, bank statements, receipts . . .

In addition to a couple of dirty glasses, the nightstand had two books on it. Library books. *The Aviator's Wife* by Melanie Benjamin and *Nancy* by Adrian Fort. Both books were three days overdue. There was also a magazine, *Cosmopolitan*: The cover proclaimed that the lead article was "Twenty-Four Moves That Will Drive Your Man Wild." I flipped through the books and magazine to see if she had carelessly left a note in Chinese in one. She hadn't.

I got down on my hands and knees and looked under the bed. A gym bag. I pulled it out, set it on the desk and opened it.

Jackpot. Right on top was a .38 caliber revolver with a two-inch barrel, loaded. Two speed-loaders containing cartridges were also in the bag. Two prepaid cell phones, and a little notebook with the first page full of phone numbers. There were letters by the numbers, a private code, no doubt. The next three pages had account numbers and passwords. Strings of numbers on the fifth page. The rest of the book was blank.

There was a U.S. passport. Kerry's photo, but the name was Janice Alice Johansson. And a Virginia driver's license with the same name.

At the bottom of the bag was money. Six bundles of currency, cash in bundles held with rubber bands, plus several credit cards. The name on them was Janice A. Johansson. The money was old bills, fifties and hundreds. I didn't count it.

I looked the printer over. Yep, it had copy function. I turned the thing on. While it was warming up, I peeked between the curtains at the parking lot. The FBI guys were still sitting in their car, windows rolled down, fighting crime.

I had been inside fifty-five minutes—way too long.

I copied the pages of the notebook that had writing, the ID pages and entry and exit pages of the passport that had stamps on them, the credit cards and driver's license. It took twenty sheets of paper. Another seven minutes gone. Turned off the printer and went back into the bedroom. Copied the phone numbers off of the cell phones onto the back of my paper stash, then put cell phones, notebook, passport and credit cards back in her bag and shoved it under the bed. After a last look around, I checked the FBI guys one more time, then went to the door. I glanced through the eyehole; the hallway, as much of it as I could see, was empty. I folded the paper lengthwise, then into a square and stuck the mess in my hip pocket. It was a wad.

I unlocked the door and stepped out. I pulled the door shut behind me and heard it latch. Just as I started for the elevator, another door opened. Apartment 209. A Chinese man came out. He couldn't know that I just came out of Kerry's flat.

He was about medium height, wearing a dark gray suit and maroon tie. Regular features, Asian eyes, balding. I nodded and kept on going. The elevator door was open. I stepped in, and got a glimpse of a reflection of the Chinese man in the marble trim on the wall. He was still standing outside his door. He had been watching my back. Obviously he didn't want to ride the elevator with me, so I punched the lobby button.

The lobby was empty. I headed for the back door. Went through it, stood under the overhang examining the parking lot. No people in or out of the cars. I went over to the Benz, unlocked it and got behind the wheel. Stripped off my gloves and shoved them and my pick pack under the passenger seat.

Looked at my watch. Thirteen after three. I drove out of the lot, around the building, past the FBI dudes and out onto the street, which was two lanes in each direction with a concrete median. I went down to the light, hooked a U-turn when the light turned green, and drove back to McDonald's. Parked facing the street.

The view across the street was pretty good. I could see the back of the FBI sedan and the front of the building. I fished a small set of 6x binoculars out from behind the driver's seat. Rolled down the windows so I could listen and treated myself to a piece of gum from a new pack. Sighed and tried to relax. I had a mild headache, and my muscles were sore. The December air coming in through the window was chilly, so I put on a jacket I had stuffed behind the seat. Drops of rain began to spatter on the windshield, and the breeze picked up. I rolled up the passenger window and left the one by my shoulder down.

The derringer was loaded with copper-clad solids. The serial number had been taken off with acid, which left a flat place. I put it back in my sock.

Damn Zoe Kerry!

I sat there savoring my memory of Fish's screams, and feeling the pain of what might have been.

At four thirty I needed a break. I rolled up the windows, locked the car and dashed into Mickey D's for a head call and a large cup of java.

I was back in less than ten minutes. Rain misting down. The FBI car was still sitting across the street. Those guys must have steel bladders or be pissing into their coffee cups.

Traffic was picking up. Cars began trickling into the apartment building lot across the street. People locked up their rides and went into the building. Lights in apartments began illuminating. The security lights on poles came on to fight the evening gloom. The rain stopped. Low clouds continued to churn overhead, and the breeze freshened again.

Cars drove into McDonald's. Some parked, some lined up for the drive-through. I tossed my empty cup behind my seat. After a bit, I turned on my ride and ran the heater for a while.

I glimpsed Kerry turn into the apartment lot at six fifty. At least, I thought it was her. There was a lot of traffic going up and down the street.

Watching through the binoculars, I got another fleeting look at her car rounding the building for the parking lot in back. I wondered if she had seen the agents in the car.

Zoe Kerry parked her car and sat for a second. She had indeed seen the dark government sedan and two heads dropping out of sight.

Worried, she went upstairs and used her key to open her door. She went straight to the window and, without touching the curtains or turning on a light, looked out at the brightly lit parking lot. She saw the agents, now upright, sitting in the two front seats of the sedan.

Taking her purse, she walked out of her room, leaving the door ajar, and knocked on the door of 209. The Chinese gentleman opened the door. The television was on.

Kerry walked in, watched the man close the door behind him. "Have you been watching the lot out front? There are two men in a car in the row closest to the street."

The man had venetian blinds on his window, now closed. He went to the window and looked. He turned back. "I haven't been looking."

"So you don't know how long they have been there?"

"No, but—"

"Did you see anyone you don't know on this floor today?"

"Yes. I was going down to check my mailbox, and I saw a man walking down the hall past my door. He got into the elevator."

Now she was really worried. "Did you get a good look at him?"

"Yes. A big man, about three inches over six feet. Wide shoulders, close-cropped brown hair, tanned face and neck. Clean-shaven, square jaw, dark sweater and dark trousers, leather shoes, no tie or hat. He was very fit, walked like an athlete. About thirty years of age, I would say."

Tommy Carmellini.

"Did he come out of my flat?"

"I don't know. When I saw him he was walking toward me. He passed and entered the elevator."

Kerry had always known this day might come, and she had made plans. It was time to go. "You haven't seen me today," she said. "I'll get in contact through the drop when I can."

She walked out, opened the door and strode to her apartment. Grabbed her getaway bag from under the bed and took a moment to glance again at the car out front. Still there. Watching and waiting for a warrant.

She pulled the door shut behind her and went out the rear entrance. Walked across the parking lot to an older Ford sedan that had been there for weeks. The FBI and CIA didn't know she owned this one. She got in, inserted the key. The engine started. The battery was only three weeks old.

She drove around the building and picked the lane that would take her to the sedan where the two men sat. Stopped in front of it and put the transmission in park, left the engine running. Got her purse, opened the door and walked to the driver's side. The window was down. She paused by the driver's mirror, where she could see them both. She knew the man behind the wheel, didn't recognize the other one. Neither was wearing his seat belt. Two empty coffee cups were in the cup holder, and a thermos between them.

"What are you doing here, Jay?" Zoe Kerry said, leaning down to look straight into his face.

"Aah . . ."

"Waiting for you," the other man said, reaching under his coat.

She already had her hand in her purse. She pulled her service pistol and shot them both, as fast as she could pull the trigger. She got the driver in the face, and a shower of blood and brains sprayed against the headrest. The man in the passenger seat had his pistol half out when her bullet hit him just below the chin. She steadied the gun, aimed and shot him again, in the head.

Then she turned and walked back to her car, putting her pistol back in her purse. She got behind the wheel and put on her seat belt. Zoe Kerry drove out of the lot, waited for a break in traffic, turned right and accelerated away.

I was watching Kerry's apartment, waiting for the lights to come on. When they didn't, I got worried. Now what? Were these federal cops still waiting for some judge to sign a warrant?

Seven minutes after I saw her car go around the building, I saw a car stop in front of the FBI car. I got the binoculars up. Kerry got out. Walked over to the car. Between the vehicles speeding by on the street, I saw her shoot into the car. Three little pops, almost inaudible over the traffic noise. A semi rumbled by. When next I saw the car, a faded blue, it was waiting at the entrance. Then she turned right and was gone, her taillights fading down the street.

There wasn't a chance in the world I could get out of McDonald's, run the Benz over the median and chase her. And no chance to turn right, go to the next corner, hook a U-turn and catch up with her in rush hour traffic.

What I did do was drop the binocs, turn on my headlights, drive out of Mickey D's, go down to the corner and U-turn to go back to the apartment building. Stopped in front of the parked sedan and walked over. One look was enough. No ambulance crew or doctor could help them now.

A woman came walking toward me. Middle-aged, wearing a coat, with a key fob in her hand. I got into my car, fished my phone from my pocket and dialed Jake Grafton's cell. Behind me a woman screamed. I glanced back. She was standing beside the government sedan looking in. As the phone rang, I put the Benz in gear and headed for the street.

I got back to CIA headquarters at a little after eight that evening. Grafton was in his office with Sarah Houston and Sal Molina. I had met Molina a time or two in the past and knew he was a heavy hitter at the White House, a dumpy fifty-something guy in rumpled slacks and a ratty sport coat. Sarah looked as gorgeous as ever; you would never know she had just put in a long day at the office.

Grafton didn't introduce me, merely asked, "What have you got, Tommy?"

I pulled the copy paper from my pocket and handed it to him, then sat down beside his desk facing Sarah and Molina. "These documents were in her getaway bag under her bed. New name, Janice Alice Johansson. Passport, driver's license, credit cards, a lot of cash, old fifties and hundreds—I didn't count it. Nice loaded snub-nose .38 Smith & Wesson, blued. Two speed-loaders ready to go. She had a notebook in there. I figured Sarah could do magic with all those phone numbers and account numbers."

"Tell them about the shooting," Grafton said.

I did so.

"After the shooting, you drove across the street and checked to see if either of the agents was still alive?"

"I did. They weren't. I left and called you."

"Why didn't you follow her?" Molina asked.

"It's a divided street with a raised concrete median. She turned right, I had to turn right. By the time I could get behind her, she was long gone. So I went over to see if I could do anything for the guys she shot. They were dead."

"You broke into her apartment?"

"Earlier that afternoon, before she got home."

"Why?" Molina asked.

"I told him to," Grafton said flatly. "He was obeying my orders."

Molina looked at his hands.

Jake held out the papers to me. "You and Sarah go copy this. Sarah, do your magic. Who the phone numbers belong to, what the other numbers are. Get a night's sleep and get on it first thing in the morning. Tommy, bring the papers back after you've copied them. I'll call the FBI with the passport and ID info."

Sarah and I trooped out, leaving Grafton facing Molina, who looked tired and angry. I don't know what he had to be pissed about. With the ID info we had, Kerry was going to get picked up sooner or later, and Molina wasn't in the car with the agents and consequently was still alive.

"So the men who shot down Air Force One were Russians?"

"Yes. Russian mafiosi. Four of them. Here are their names." Grafton held out a sheet of paper from the small envelope that had been passed to Carmellini at noon.

Molina glanced at the slip of paper, then handed it back. "Anything else?" he asked.

"They spent three or four months in China. Then their trail peters out. The FBI will tell you all about their activities in America."

"China," Molina muttered, and rubbed his chin. "How do you know this Russian of yours is telling the truth?"

"I don't know, Sal. Do I look like Diogenes?"

As the copy machine did its thing, Sarah said, "I'm sorry about Anna."

I grunted.

"Want to go get some dinner?" she asked.

"I'm not hungry." I eyed her. "I could use a drink, though. Or two."

After I returned Grafton's paper pile to him and Sarah locked hers up in a secure safe in her office, we left the building together. She drove her car, and I followed her. It was raining lightly again. Windy. A miserable damned night. The wipers merely smeared the windshield, and a trickle of water dripped from the roof seal above the rearview mirror.

Maybe I should have just sat in Kerry's apartment and waited for her. Cuffed her with her own cuffs and visited until the FBI got its paperwork blessed by a judge and came for her.

Ain't hindsight wonderful? I'm sure she could have answered many of my questions.

Of course, if I had stayed, I'd have probably killed her before the feds knocked on the door.

Now I kinda wished I had waited.

. . .

Sarah and I ended up at a chain bar/restaurant. Safely ensconced in a booth by a window, with a football highlights show on a television above the bar that I could glance at from time to time, we ordered. I decided I was a bit hungry and ordered some wings with my bourbon. Sarah ordered white wine and a salad.

After the waiter left, I told Sarah about the Asian gentleman who lived in apartment 209, right down the hall from dear ol' Zoe. "Great setup if he's her control," I mused aloud.

"The vast bulk of Chinese Americans are not spies," she said, "nor are all coincidences suspect, but it wouldn't hurt to check this guy out."

"You can do that?"

"It's what I do, Tommy," she said, slightly exasperated.

Rain smeared the window. Looked like it was setting in to rain all night.

"I'm sorry about Anna," Sarah said again.

I just nodded.

"I thought you were never going to get married."

"So did I," I said, a bit more forcefully than I intended. "I should have left Anna in Switzerland. She'd still be alive if I had."

Sarah frowned. "Don't start that what-if crap. Pretty soon you'll be wishing you had never been born. I know! I have a patent on what-if."

Sarah Houston had a good face. Actually, she was lovely, with big dark eyes that seemed to see everything. She had certainly made her share of mistakes though the years, enough mistakes for a dozen people, but she seemed to be trying to get on down the road. Maybe there was a lesson there for me. Sarah was no saint, and I wasn't either. Just two very mortal people.

Our drinks came. We didn't have much to say to each other. Superficial things about Jake Grafton and the agency and the state of the universe. I had finished my bourbon when my wings and her salad arrived, so I ordered another drink.

We finished eating and were watching the rain, each of us lost in our own thoughts, when she asked, "Where are you sleeping these days?"

I had been thinking about Zoe Kerry, wondering where she was tonight. Wondering if the FBI had alerted every badge-toter on the East Coast to watch for her. I abandoned Zoe and saw Sarah's reflection in the window. I turned my head to see her face clearly. Well, she wasn't drunk. Not with only one glass of wine in her. "At Willie Varner's," I said.

"Think he could spare you for an evening?"

"Is that an invitation?"

"Yes."

"Picking up men in bars is bad for your reputation."

She smiled. "I'll try not to make a habit of it."

"I accept."

I followed her home.

CHAPTER NINETEEN

War is not merely a political act, but a real political instrument, a continuation of political intercourse, a carrying out of the same by other means.

—Carl von Clausewitz

Finding the watcher or watchers at Naval Base Norfolk was an impossible task without bringing in hundreds of Homeland Security agents, FBI agents and police, and even that might not be enough. Or might cause the watcher to trigger the weapon, if he could. The best option, Jake Grafton thought, was finding the weapon or weapons that Grafton suspected were there without alerting the media or public. Or the watchers.

The navy brought in four SEAL teams. Each team was given a section of the anchorage to search, starting at the carrier piers and radiating outward. Their diving boats were navy dredges, which were used periodically to pull sediment from the bottom of the anchorage to keep it deep enough for the deep-draft carriers. Barges used to hold the dredged-up muck were rigged alongside with a sponson between the barge and dredge, leaving a gap that divers could use to enter and exit the water.

If the weapon was merely lying on the bottom, the dredges would of course pull it up eventually. Since the dredging went on year-around, presumably it wasn't there.

The SEAL officer in charge stood on the small bridge of the dredge and used binoculars to scan the pier. It had to be there, somewhere, he thought, in an area that the dredges wouldn't normally do. So he sent his men swimming in that direction after entering the water.

The SEAL commander, Captain Joe Child, and the commanding officer of the base, Captain Butler Spiers, had been personally briefed yesterday by the chief of naval operations, Admiral Cart McKiernan, in a guarded conference room in the base administration building. Sitting beside the admiral was a civilian; he wasn't introduced, yet Child recognized him from newspaper photographs. The man was Jake Grafton, retired rear admiral and interim director of the CIA. It was the most amazing briefing Joe Child had ever attended.

After he had explained the threat, McKiernan laid it on the line. "As you know, we already have plenty of security precautions in place, including airborne fighters, a restricted area over the base, continuous helicopter patrols. Still, in light of this threat, we are going to do more. We are starting those patrols tomorrow, a week early. All commands have been notified."

He paused to gather his thoughts. "We have a carrier at the pier now, *Harry Truman,* undergoing maintenance on her catapults and other gear, and she isn't scheduled to leave until mid-February. The *Ford* will be towed over from Norfolk tomorrow. The next carrier will be arriving three days from now, the eighteenth. Two more will arrive on the twentieth and the twenty-second of December. All will be here with their task forces, which means some amphibious assault ships and about eighteen destroyers. There isn't enough pier space for all their escorts, so they will make port up and down the East Coast.

"If we can't find a bomb—because it isn't there or we just can't find it—I am going to have all those ships except *Harry Truman* and *Ford* stay at sea. The drop-dead date for that decision is four days from now, December twenty-second."

"What if there are several weapons?" Captain Spiers asked.

"Even if we find one, we're going to keep looking," McKiernan replied.

"A nuclear weapon," Captain Spiers said. His face looked a little pasty. "Sir, we should be evacuating this base right now. Hell, we should be evacuating this whole area."

"That's been discussed. The decision has been made to tightly hold this secret. It is entirely possible that there are one or more watchers who will detonate the weapon if they realize we suspect it's here and we're looking for it. Trying to move a million and a half people a hundred miles from here can't be kept a secret. We'll just have to find the weapon."

Spiers licked his lips. "But if we don't?" he asked.

"Then we'll do what we can do, and hope for the best."

"Admiral, I have leave scheduled on the seventeenth," Spiers said. "My eldest daughter is due to deliver—"

"Cancel it. That's an order. Your duty is here."

"—our first grandchild," Spiers finished belligerently.

"I want an acknowledgment that I have just given you a direct order, Captain."

Spiers' Adam's apple bobbed up and down. Finally he said, "Aye aye, sir."

"Moving on, the SEAL teams will arrive tomorrow on transports. They have been told they are deploying to the Middle East. We'll need barracks for them, with no one else in them. The day after tomorrow, you will announce a security exercise, close the base and search it. Every square inch. Your people will not be told about nuclear weapons, but will be told to look for anything— and I mean *anything*—that isn't supposed to be there. All leave and liberty is canceled. No one, and I mean no one, goes on or off the base. The exercise will last until the twenty-second."

"We don't have berthing for all these people who can't go home," Spiers pointed out.

"Get cots and sleeping bags and porta-potties and berth your people in hangars. Set up chow lines. The ships' crews will be staying aboard their ships. Figure out the details and get at it, Spiers. Get enough food on the station to last two weeks, for your people and the crews of the ships in port."

"Yes, sir, but we don't have enough refrigeration—"

McKiernan's fist smashed on the table. "Then you'd better get a shitload of MREs anywhere you can find them," he roared. "Do I have to can you and find someone who can figure this out?"

"No, sir."

In the silence that followed that exchange, Captain Child pointed out, "Everyone these days has cell phones."

"The cell towers are going out of service even as we speak. We are sealing this base and searching every square inch of it. Understand?"

"Yes, sir."

"The story is the base is holding a security exercise. Get it in the newspapers and on television today. A routine security exercise. If there is a watcher, he or she will expect us to take extra precautions since we are going to have all these ships in port. We would be idiots if we didn't, and whoever planted this weapon knows that."

"Yes, sir."

Spiers had one last question. "How sure are we that there is indeed an armed nuclear weapon somewhere close?"

Jake Grafton spoke for the first time, his voice hard and flat. "Bet your ass it's here and you may not lose it."

"Who put it here?"

"You don't need to know that," Grafton said, staring Spiers straight in the eyes, almost as if he dared the captain to ask another question. Spiers lowered his gaze and rose from his chair.

Jake Grafton said, "Captain Child, one more word."

Spiers left, and Child sat down again.

"I want you to bring your EOD people in and have a long talk with them," Jake Grafton said. "As I analyze this problem, there are two ways this weapon, if it is here, can be triggered. First, it might be wired up to a clock mechanism and be merely ticking down to a certain date and time, perhaps Christmas Day. If so, it could be anywhere in the estuary or river or on the west side of the river in that Corps of Engineers storage depot. Wherever the thing is, it might have a triggering device that is waiting for a radio signal. This is the most likely prospect, I suspect, because it keeps all the bomber's options open until the last possible second, when the button is pushed triggering the thing. We can also assume that the triggering device is on or beside the weapon. Almost has to be to keep the wire runs short.

"Be that as it may, if the triggering mechanism is waiting for a radio signal, it won't be in ten or twenty or thirty feet of water. Or if it is, there will be a wire leading from it to some kind of metal structure that will act as an antenna and receive the transmission when sent and pass it on to the triggering device. If I were you, my first efforts would be to find an insulated wire attached to something metal. I'm no expert, but I suspect it could be darn near anything."

Captain Child nodded.

"That's it," Jake Grafton said. "Talk to the EOD guys and get their opinion. Most radio waves can't go through twenty or thirty feet of water. Perhaps the Chinese could use very low frequency waves that go through the water, but how will they know just when to trigger it, given that we can shut down the Internet or telephone networks at any time? I suspect it's more likely that there is someone close, and at precisely the right time to do maximum damage he or she will use a higher-frequency, short-range encrypted radio signal that will not penetrate water. That gives them maximum flexibility regardless of what we do to thwart them."

"The *Ford* is scheduled to be towed from Newport News to the carrier piers tomorrow," Child said. "She's been in dry dock for a year. The crew has been ashore. The media people want to film the arrival. Still, it's a good excuse for us to search the waters around the carrier piers and inspect the bottoms of every hull there."

The Chinese would know that, of course, Jake thought.

McKiernan didn't bat an eye. "Do it."

"Yes, sir," Captain Child said. He walked out and closed the door behind him.

The four-star admiral in command of the Fleet Forces Command, Sherman Fitch, was waiting when the CNO and Jake Grafton arrived at Base Ops to board the little executive jet to Washington. The CO of the base, Captain Spiers, was also there. McKiernan told him to dismiss the honor guard, which he did.

As Jake stood watching, Cart McKiernan took the man who owned the Atlantic Fleet aside for a private conversation on the ramp. It took ten minutes. Jake used the break to hit the head. When he got back, the admirals were shaking hands and saluting. Spiers saluted them both.

On the flight to Washington, McKiernan told Jake, "I told Sherm I wanted the orders drafted and ready for signature if and when I told him to send the ships elsewhere over the holidays. Didn't give him a reason, but demanded Top Secret security. Had to give him a heads-up. You can't turn a fleet on a dime. Without some prior planning, sending the ships elsewhere or keeping them at sea will be a fucked-up mess. Everyone will be talking, and it will be big news everywhere."

Jake Grafton said nothing. The decision was McKiernan's whenever he wished to make it.

The CNO changed subjects instantly. "Could the bomb be triggered from a satellite?" he asked.

"Not without an antenna, the experts tell me."

"An underwater acoustic receiver," the admiral mused, "waiting for a sound, like a sonar. Or a fish or depth finder."

"Perhaps," Jake agreed. "But those devices all have limited range and will require the triggerman to get relatively close, which would be difficult or impossible if we limit access to the anchorage, as you intend to do. Simple is usually better; less chance for a technical breakdown or unanticipated events blowing your preparations."

"That means a clock."

"Maybe. But let's let the SEALs search a while before we get esoteric."

"And how long will that be?"

"I don't know."

The CNO eyed Grafton. "Can you find the watcher?"

"We can try, Cart. That's all I can promise. It could be a civilian or sailor. The FBI and Homeland Security will give us some agents, a few dozen. The cover story is the security exercise at the base; our guys will do some discreet whispering about a terrorist threat. That's the best story because it allows us to question everyone about themselves and other people and look at ID. I've cleared it with Sal Molina. If the news breaks, the pundits and politicians will get their undies in a twist, and we'll just have to live with that. Still, don't get your hopes up. We'll need some breaks. And some luck."

"Why do I have this feeling our luck is running out?" Admiral McKiernan mused.

"Better have every ship in the fleet searched. If a bomb goes off in Norfolk, half the people on earth will think it was one of ours. We'd better make sure it isn't."

"The orders were issued yesterday."

Jake Grafton nodded and scratched his head. What if they didn't find the bomb in time, or the watcher got worried and triggered it? Or the Chinese somehow used a satellite to trigger it? It would be, he knew, the end of the America he had known and loved.

Or what if the news—or rumor—got out that the sailors searching ships and the SEALs searching harbors and buildings were looking for a bomb? Mass panic in southeastern Virginia. Packed roads, car wrecks, people driving like maniacs. Dozens would die. Moving some of the medically fragile might kill them. Those without transportation would shout that they were being abandoned to be cremated alive. Even if there was no bomb, the political repercussions of a panic disaster would make massive waves for years. That was Sal Molina's nightmare.

Jake glanced at the admiral. "What about that incident a few days ago in the South China Sea? The Poseidon that had a close encounter with Chinese fighters?"

"We can't back off," McKiernan explained. "Japan, the Philippines, South Korea and Vietnam can't go it alone."

"A carrier in the South China Sea to intercept the fighters?"

"We are going to escort patrolling Poseidons with air force fighters for a while. Truth is, we can't spare a carrier there right now. Our ships are committed to the hilt. We just don't have enough carriers if China presses harder."

And if five of America's carriers are wiped from the board, Jake thought, *America will face an impossible task of trying to juggle assets between the Middle East and western Pacific. There won't be enough anywhere.*

The FBI was on the Chinese guy in apartment 209 like stink on a skunk. They had a van parked in back of the place that could pick up any electronic emissions from the building, and two cars with two agents each in front and back. In addition, there was a car with two agents across the street at the Mc-Donald's and one a half block to the right of the apartment house at a gasoline station/convenience store.

I went to the van from the building on the next street, so anyone watching out the window wouldn't see me enter it. The sign on the side of it said it belonged to a plumbing firm, one with the slogan "We fix it up so it goes down."

Inside, I introduced myself and displayed my CIA card. They glanced at it and said, "They told us you might be by." Cooperation between federal agencies is a wonderful thing.

"Got something for you to look at," the guy introduced as Nate said, and passed me several photos. Sure enough, they had him. Taken from a surveillance camera that I doubted that he had seen, the blown-up photos were of an Asian man about fifty-five, with a distinguished haircut and even features, dressed well in a suit and tie, wearing a dark topcoat. No hat. "We got those this morning when he went out for a bagel and newspaper," Nate said.

"That's him," I said. "Who is he?"

"His car is registered to Jerry Chu. Wears Virginia plates. He transferred the registration from Massachusetts eighteen months ago. He used to work for Whitewater Encryption Systems. Born in California to Chinese immigrant parents, educated at Cal Poly. Whitewater was the fifth high-tech company he worked for. The personnel department there told the local police he resigned eighteen months ago. He left no forwarding address."

"Encryption systems," I mused.

"Yeah."

"This guy got a bank account?"

"At least one, at the Potomac Valley Bank."

"Safety deposit box?"

"No."

"Can I use my cell without screwing you up?"

"Go ahead."

I called Sarah Houston and kept it on a high professional plane. "Tommy. I have a question. Ever hear of Whitewater Encryption Systems?"

"Yes."

"Talk to me."

"They signed a contract a while back with Los Alamos National Laboratory to commercialize a new technology the wizards thought up. Supposedly it took the geniuses twenty years to develop. The tech harnesses the quantum properties of light to generate truly random numbers to encrypt data and messages. Not a prime number or square root of something. Quantum mechanics. Einstein would be impressed. In theory, using their technology, they can generate unbreakable crypto codes."

"How about in practical terms?"

"I don't know. I've never seen one."

"Why didn't NSA glom onto this and classify it?"

"Obviously they didn't want it. Perhaps because they didn't invent it. I don't know. You'd have to ask them, and of course, they won't answer."

"Thanks," I said, and started to hang up. *Very* professional.

"What do you want for dinner tonight?" she said.

That caught me a little off guard. I thought we had just had a one-night stand. But—

"Pizza?" I suggested.

"Ugh. Chinese."

"You got it."

I hung up. "Got any coffee?" I asked the tech team, who had pretended they weren't listening. Good guys. The coffee was from a thermos, and still warm. I drank it black.

I watched people come and go. Most went out the front of the building, of course, but the folks who came home late last night and couldn't find parking in front went out the back. Most of them seemed to be young professionals and were gone by nine in the morning. Then things really slowed down.

I was working a crossword puzzle in the *Post* at noon when Nate got a phone call. He listened a bit, then grunted and hung up. "He went out the front three minutes ago. Got in his car and drove away."

I got out my cell phone. "Give me your cell number." He did so, and I entered it. "Keep him out until I come out or call you."

"Sure."

I donned my jacket and put on my latex gloves. "The fire department has been briefed?"

"Of course."

I got out of the van, walked around the front of the vehicle and headed for the back entrance to the building. The day was not pleasant—a low overcast and a wet cold wind that was cutting on exposed flesh. I let myself in with a pass card the FBI had supplied and headed for the elevator. Was lifted all the way to the top floor. I didn't see anyone. So I took a smoke grenade out of my pocket, pulled the pin and tossed it down the corridor.

Then I took the elevator down to the second floor. There was a fire alarm mounted on the wall by the elevator. I broke the glass and pulled it. It went off with a noise loud enough to wake the almost dead.

I stood there a moment watching people trickling from the apartments. A couple of them got in the elevator, but it was disabled, so they used the stairs. I waited a few moments to ensure that everyone who was leaving was out, then went to work on the lock on 209. It only took two minutes; I knew what kind of lock it was and had the right picks. As I was working I heard the first fire siren.

I walked in, closed the door behind me and ensured it locked, and stood surveying the place, memorizing how the room looked, where everything was. It was automatic. The tough part was I didn't know what I was looking for. Something that tied Mr. Chu to espionage. What it might be I had no idea. And it might not be here, or I might not recognize it if I saw it. Sort of like hunting Easter eggs without knowing an egg from a rock. On the other hand, I had to make Chu believe no one had been in here. It was a nice problem. The good news was I had as much time as I needed. The fire department would keep everyone out of the building until I locked up and left.

I looked at the bedroom, the bathroom, the closets. This apartment was a mirror image of Zoe Kerry's. A desk in the bedroom with a laptop on it. A flat-screen television made in Korea. A wire for charging his cell phone on the nightstand beside the bed. No landline phone.

Remembering the recently departed Miss Kerry, the first thing I did was look under the bed. Chu didn't vacuum under there, apparently. I used a flashlight to examine the visible springs underneath and gave it a pass.

The way I figured it, if there was anything in this apartment to find, it would be something innocuous. The truth is, most spies don't keep anything, not a scrap of paper or a jar of invisible ink or a list of drops or code words . . . nothing that would indicate they are not who they say they are. Everything they need is in their heads. What I needed to establish was whether there was any physical thing here the FBI would like their experts to look at, and if so, what. If there was, they could get an arrest warrant and search warrant and remove Mr. Chu from the board. On the other hand, if he was indeed the control for a watcher in Norfolk, removing him from the board would take a serious gambler. Jake Grafton was that kind of guy, but I doubted if Harry Estep, the interim FBI director, was, and I suspected the folks at the White House didn't have that kind of guts. So I was sent to look. Everyone would be relieved if I found nothing. Including me. Especially me. Postpone the evil day.

I started looking. For something. Anything. I was careful, making sure that everything was put back as it was when I arrived. First I inspected the ceiling. It was plasterboard. The light fixtures would need attention. I examined the chairs to see if they had been used as stepladders. Apparently not. I looked at the bottoms. I decided to save the light fixtures for last, if I didn't find anything.

I went through the closet, looked in every pocket, took out the drawers inspected and repacked them, looked in the pillow cases, in the couch. Checked the cushions, unzipped the coverings, zipped them back up, examined the couch, lifted one end and looked at the bottom. Checked the pictures on the walls, which were prints of Chinese art.

Outside in the hallway I could hear the firemen as I worked. Dragging a hose, it sounded like, knocking on doors. Voices. They had been briefed not to bother with this apartment, and they didn't.

I did the bathroom. Looked in the water closet, felt around under the rim of the commode. Looked at everything. The only thing I didn't do was squeeze out his toothpaste. After a last look around to ensure I had left everything as it was, I moved on. The screws holding the faceplates onto the wall sockets had no marks on them.

In the bedroom I stood looking at Chu's laptop. The hard drive held the secrets, if there were any. But dare I steal it? I went through the desk. It was almost empty. A few pencils, a notepad . . . I held it up to the light at an angle and looked to see if anything had left an impression. Not that I could read Chinese characters. It was clean.

No books, no magazines. How in the heck did Chu spend his day? Watching Oprah?

The television sat on the dresser near the desk, arranged so he could watch it in bed. The back of the television looked benign. I examined the cable connection, saw that it came through a splitter; one wire went to the television, and one was trapped under the computer. So that was how he got on the Internet.

He was a tech guy, an expert in crypto, I assumed. I doubted if he was Whitewater's finance officer.

So did he have software on the computer? Doubtful. Only a fool would do that, and a fool he probably wasn't. He had spent years stealing high-tech secrets and passing them along to Chinese intelligence. That meant a thumb drive. Some people called it a jump drive. Some device that the computer's USB port would take.

Where the hell was it? Probably the same place as his cell phones—he supposedly had two—and that was in his pocket.

I went into the kitchen and stared at the boxes and cans of coffee. I glanced at my watch. I had been here for an hour and a half.

That was when I lost it. I dumped the ice tray from the freezer into the sink. Then the contents of the refrigerator and freezer into a garbage bag he had under the sink. I was getting frustrated. The place was too clean. It looked like a high-end hotel room, cleaned every day. Real people didn't live like this. I knew, *knew,* that this guy was dirty and *it* was here. Somewhere. *It.* I dumped contents of the boxes in the pantry in the middle of the kitchen floor. The coffee cans.

Nothing.

I got a chair and used a kitchen knife as a screwdriver on the light fixtures. They were empty. I left them dangling.

The kitchen had linoleum as a floor covering, and the rest of the place had wall-to-wall carpet. I moved furniture and got down on my hands and knees and inspected the edges, looked for holes. Saw none. Examined the faceplates on the electric outlets.

Finally I gave up. I stood looking. I had done it all. No cell phones and no thumb drive. I glanced at my watch. Two hours and forty minutes. I got out my phone and called Nate in the van.

"Carmellini. Chu out there?"

"Yeah. Watching the fire department. The smoke stopped rolling out about two hours ago, but they are still doing hoses and stuff."

"Grab Chu. I'm coming down."

"Arrest him, you mean?"

"Grab him. One man on each arm. Then get his keys and search his car."

I picked up his laptop and walked out. The door locked behind me. No one in the hallways.

They had Chu standing beside the van. He was surrounded by four agents. He saw me coming toward him carrying the computer. Our eyes locked as I walked up. This guy was probably Kerry's control, and he had helped kill Anna. I handed the computer to an agent, spun him around and made him lean against the side of the van with his hands on it. Spread his legs.

"Am I under arrest?" he said tightly.

I began feeling him all over. The agents had frisked him for weapons, but I wanted everything in his pockets. I turned them inside out. I laid everything on the ground. The phones and thumb drive had to be on him or in his car.

And by God they were on him! A thumb drive in his left coat pocket. Three cell phones. I jerked his belt off. Made Chu take off his shoes.

"Cuff him," I told the agents. As one of the agents bagged his personal possessions, I took the computer, thumb drive and phones into the van.

"You got something?" Nate asked.

"We'll soon see," I muttered. "Let me borrow your computer."

He pointed toward it. It was already on. I slipped the thumb drive into a USB port and clicked on the icon when it appeared.

A logo came up. Under the logo were the words **Whitewater Encryption Systems**. Under that was a prompt for a password, which of course I didn't have.

A sense of relief flooded over me. *Yes!*

I managed to smile at Nate. "He had it on him," I said.

When I called Jake Grafton to give him the news, he listened without a question. After I ran down he remarked, "The folks at the FBI and Justice aren't going to like that warrantless arrest."

"They aren't," I agreed.

"Why did you do it?"

"He was a neatnik. Nothing personal in the apartment. It felt like a hotel room, but with a little food and coffee. Whatever he had had to be on him."

"Well . . . let's hope what you found takes us somewhere. I'll call Harry Estep and kiss his ass, and you give Sarah that stuff as soon as you can get here. After she's mined it, she can pass it along to the FBI."

"That will add to their unhappiness."

"Everyone's unhappy," Grafton shot back. "All of us."

He hung up.

FBI Interim Director Harry Estep had already heard about the arrest when Grafton called him.

"That son of a bitch Carmellini was just supposed to search," Estep said bitterly.

"I know. He used his judgment and discretion, based on experience. We have Chu's laptop, a thumb drive with an encryption system on it and three cell phones. I'll let you know what we find, then send them over."

"Grafton, you bastard! Counterespionage is our goddamn turf. Not to mention the two agents that traitor Zoe Kerry shot dead. I agreed to let Carmellini search because I thought he knew the rules. I should have known better. You damned people don't play by the rules. I want that gear and I want it *right fucking now*."

"Get a warrant," Jake Grafton said, and dropped the phone onto the cradle.

CHAPTER TWENTY

For to win one hundred victories in one hundred battles is not the acme of skill. To subdue the enemy without fighting is the acme of skill.

—Sun Tzu

When Captain H. Butler Spiers, the commanding officer of Naval Base Norfolk, got home after McKiernan's brief he poured himself a glass of Jack Daniel's, added one ice cube and, still wearing his coat, went out onto the enclosed porch of his quarters. The temp was about fifty, and there was a breeze. The lights of the base made the overcast glow. He lit a cigar to go with the whiskey.

He knew what he was going to do, although he had refused to admit it to himself. When he had told Admiral McKiernan he wanted leave because his daughter was going to have a baby, he had been a wee bit less than honest. His daughter lived in an apartment complex just a few blocks from the community college where her husband was a history instructor. In Norfolk.

Spiers was never going to make admiral, and he knew it. Command of NB Norfolk was the final tour of a thirty-year career that had started in minesweepers. He then went to destroyers and after commanding one had been chief of staff for an admiral. After a tour as an instructor at the War College in Newport, he became CO of the base here, which was, by the way, a major command for an officer of his rank.

He and his wife, Katherine, Kat to her family and friends, had only one daughter, even though they had tried for more children. Her name was Ellen, or Ellie. She was something of a flake. She had never been a good student, yet, poorly informed or misinformed with only a few facts, she arrived at opinions about people, politics and morals that were unshakable, and always Liberal with a capital *L*. For Ellie, life was not complex but simple. And everyone who disagreed with her was wrong. She walked through life with a certainty and confidence that were awe-inspiring. The truth was, her father didn't like her.

Nor did he think much of her husband, Harold, another mediocre intellect who had managed a master's in history from some little college in Georgia that no one ever heard of and wormed his way into the substrata of academia, where he would undoubtedly spend the rest of his working days, happy as a termite. Harold and Ellie. A perfect match.

Kat was the one he cared about. She had doted on Ellie, everything for Ellie, and no doubt spoiled her. The news of Ellie's pregnancy had filled her with joy. She was going to be the world's best grandmother, just as she had been the world's best mom; it was her destiny, the yardstick by which Kat measured the value of her life.

She should have had three or four kids, Butler Spiers thought again tonight, as he had many times through the years. The real problem, Butler told himself, was that Kat hadn't really been cut out for life as a naval officer's wife. The constant transfers meant that she couldn't have a career. For a woman of her intelligence and education, that left her only one outlet, her daughter. Kat had concentrated too much love on one child, one of average intelligence, physical ability and attractiveness. The incandescent glow of her love had merely reinforced Ellie's inability to see the world from any vantage point other than the pedestal on which her mother had placed her.

Now the grandchild, a boy, was due in three weeks.

With a possible Chinese nuclear warhead ready to detonate at the naval base. Jesus Christ!

If it detonated, Kat and Ellie and Harold and the boy yet unborn would instantly perish. Kat didn't deserve that.

He had about finished the cigar when he heard her car in the driveway. He left the cigar in an ashtray and went inside. He had poured himself another drink when she came in, smiling.

She had spent a few hours with Ellie, talking about the baby to come. "They decided to name the boy Harold Butler," she told him, a grand announcement.

"At least they didn't decide to name him Herman," he said. Herman was his first name, and he hated it even more than Butler, which had been his mother's family name.

He took another sip of whiskey and led her out onto the porch. She hadn't taken her coat off, and he was still wearing his. He stubbed out the smoldering cigar and faced her.

"I want you to go back to Ellie's, get her and Harold and take them to your mother's place in Massachusetts. Ellie can have the baby there over the holidays."

She stared at him, trying to understand. "Harold won't be done with school until the end of the semester, five days from now. He can't leave."

"He can call in sick, and if that doesn't work, he can quit his job. He can get another job in New England. We'll help with the family finances until he does."

"Butler," she said, shaking her head, "I won't do it. And they won't go. Harold had a devil of a time finding this job. The baby shower is three days from now. Invitations have been sent. Two dozen women are coming, her friends and—"

"You must talk them into it."

"I can't. It's silly. I won't try."

He leaned forward and looked into her eyes. He didn't want to tell her classified information, but there was no other way. So he told it.

She had a few questions, then sat processing it.

"You can't tell them the reason," he said, even though in the back of his mind he knew she would have to, as he had. "If this gets out, there'll be mass panic. Everyone on the peninsula and over in Newport News will try to leave, and the roads are just too small. Worse, the watcher may hear of it and decide to detonate the weapon without waiting for the carriers. We don't know that he *is* waiting for the carriers, but it's almost a certainty. If the mission was simply to blow up the place, he could have already done it."

"Maybe the SEALs will find the bomb," Kat whispered.

"Perhaps," her husband admitted. "And maybe they won't. Do you want to save Ellie and Harold and the baby? Or not?"

"You'll still be here."

"I'm a naval officer. This is my duty post. I'm not leaving."

She went upstairs to pack.

Butler Spiers sat huddled inside his coat feeling very old. He had just betrayed classified information for personal reasons. If the powers that be ever learned of this, he was ruined professionally. He might even go to prison. If the bomb hadn't already killed him.

Yet he had to do it. He owed it to Kat. Owed it to her for the thirty years of her life that she had given him.

He finished his drink and went inside and poured another.

He almost wished the damn bomb would go off. For him, that would not be a tragedy.

The news about the routine security exercise at the Norfolk naval base made the Norfolk/Virginia Beach television stations' ten o'clock news. Choy Lee and Sally Chan watched some footage of ships and the base public relations officer's explanation on one of the channels as they lay in bed. They had eaten a nice dinner at a seafood place on Route 60, just west of the navy amphibious base at Little Creek. They ate and drank wine at a table by the window and watched the lights of ships come and go in the bay. Night had already fallen under an overcast sky. Afterward, they went to Sally's apartment and made love. Finally they turned on the news.

Zhang had never told Choy that the Americans were going to have five carriers in port over the holidays. Still, Choy was worried. Both he and Zhang were spies, reporting on ship movements, and the Americans were taking steps. Choy reflected that there were undoubtedly a lot of things Zhang knew that he hadn't told Choy.

Then there was Zhang's new Boston Whaler, with an iPad wired to the radar. At least, Choy thought it was wired to the radar. What it was for he had no idea, but it worried him. What would the Americans say if they found it? And they might. A Coast Guard boat could stop them at any time for an inspection. Safety or otherwise.

"What's wrong?" Sally Chan asked, snuggling against him.

The devil of it was that he was in love with Sally. At first this was supposed to just be companionship and sex, but somewhere along the way it had become more than that. Much more.

And Sally Chan was as American as apple pie and the Fourth of July. So were her parents. Oh, they were proud to be Chinese Americans, in the same way Italian Americans, Irish Americans and African Americans were proud of their heritage. But *this* was their country! What would Sally think if she knew he was an agent of the Chinese government? A spy? Reporting on U.S. Navy ship movements? Would she dump him? Call the FBI and report him?

Then there was Zhang. Somehow, lately, the mission had subtly changed. It was no longer photographing warships and reporting on their movements— Zhang was watching the carrier piers. The area around the carrier piers. Looking with binoculars at every harbor craft, watching for something. What? He never said, and Choy never asked. Somehow he knew that was the wrong thing to do.

Now a "routine security exercise." There hadn't been a security exercise at the base all summer and fall. Why now? Were the Americans looking for him and Zhang? Had the mission been compromised? Or was he just suffering the intelligence agent's normal professional paranoia?

"I love you," Sally whispered.

Choy had other things on his mind. He distractedly pecked her on the forehead.

When Jake Grafton got home that evening, Callie had beef brisket, salad, and cucumbers and onions marinated in vinegar waiting. They ate at the little round table just off the kitchen where they normally ate breakfast.

"When are you going to have Tommy take this security system out?" she asked. Jake had told her several days ago that the bomber had been arrested, although it hadn't been in the newspapers.

"Oh, I dunno," he said, frowning. "No one is monitoring it. Thinking about leaving it in place, just in case. You can never predict when—"

"I want it out," Callie said forcefully. "I am sick of looking at those little cameras or whatever they are and being constantly reminded that someone tried to murder us. That someone *did* murder Anna Modin. We've got to move on."

"Well . . ."

"If Tommy's too busy," she said, "I'll call Willie Varner and ask him to come do it. His lock shop is in the telephone book."

"Maybe you should call Willie," her husband said, surrendering gracefully. "Probably be quicker."

"So how was your day at the office?"

"Oh, you know, the usual. Got shouted at and shouted back. We progress, I think, but slowly."

Her voice sharpened just a bit. "Have the people at the White House said anything about nominating a permanent director?"

"No. I think their plate is as full as mine."

"Jake, you can't keep doing this CIA thing twelve to fifteen hours a day, seven days a week. There are other competent people."

"Right now we have a problem that soaks up my time," he explained. "It will be resolved in a few weeks, one way or another, and then I'll be a forty-hour-week dude or I'll resign."

She eyed him. "You're serious, I hope."

"I can't keep this pace up. You are absolutely right about that. I'll burn out and won't be any good to anyone. On the other hand, I owe it to the families of the people who got murdered to hang in there. People like Mario Tomazic's daughter . . . and Tommy Carmellini. I'm in their corner."

"Jake," she said, sliding her hand over his, "I understand, but I need more of your time. I am still very much in love with my husband. I don't want to see you just when you bring your dirty clothes home to exchange for clean ones. That wasn't why I married you."

He squeezed her hand and looked into her eyes. "A few more weeks, hon. Then it'll be over."

Or, he thought, *I'll be dead along with a few million other people and it won't matter.* Being Mr. Smooth, he kept that thought to himself.

Sarah Houston was still at work on the hard drive of Jerry Chu's laptop when I was ready to leave for the day. I had been watching over her shoulder. It was like watching someone translate Egyptian hieroglyphics; I didn't understand any of it.

"I'll be along after a while," she said. "Take my house key from my purse. It's there beside the desk."

Her lock was a Yale, and I could do them blindfolded, but I didn't brag. I took the key. On my way out the door she said, "I changed my mind about Chinese. I've had enough Chinese for one day."

"So have I," I said. On the way to her place I stopped at a supermarket and purchased a few items from the deli counter. Gourmet Tommy. Got a bottle of wine—twelve bucks—and some more coffee, since Sarah was almost out.

I was standing at the window thinking about Anna . . . and Fish and that bitch Kerry and good ol' Jerry Chu . . . when I heard Sarah rap on the door. I caught a glimpse of my face in the mirror as I went to open it, and paused a few seconds to rearrange it. Sarah didn't deserve me in a foul mood. Maybe she didn't deserve me at all. She could do a whale of a lot better.

I opened the door. She had a sack of stuff, too.

She gave me a kiss as she sailed by, headed for the kitchen.

Amazingly, I felt better. She could do that for me.

"What did you get out of that computer and thumb drive?" I asked as she put away groceries.

"It's going to take a couple more days. I doubt if I can ever crack the quantum code, but there may be a way to get messages before he encrypted them. That may be all that is possible."

"Um."

"Got all the numbers off the phones and sent the phones by courier to the FBI."

"They'll be pleased."

She eyed me. "Why do I have a feeling you shouldn't have grabbed that stuff?"

"It was an illegal arrest. No search warrant. No arrest warrant. Any half-decent lawyer can probably get the evidence suppressed, if there is any, and get Chu off . . . if he ever comes to trial. They have him on a national security hold right now, incommunicado."

"So why didn't you let the FBI get a warrant?"

"We don't have a week for them to dither. If a nuke goes off in Norfolk, the judge scrutinizing the affidavits and FBI agents standing in front of him will feel the floor shake and think there has been an earthquake. Poof, another million or two souls on their way up or down."

"So what did Grafton say about it?"

"Nothing to me. He might tomorrow, or he might not. With Grafton, you never know. You take a risk and everything turns out okay, he's happy. If I'd gotten Jerry Chu arrested on my say-so and nothing was found, not so happy."

"We still don't know if he's dirty."

"Oh, he is. I got a good look at his face." I yawned and stretched. "But if they want to fire me, I'm ready to go."

She opened the wine bottle, poured for the both of us and handed me a glass. After she had an experimental sip, she asked, "If they fire you, where would you go?"

"I don't know. Haven't thought much about it. Maybe trade the Benz in on a used motorcycle and just hit the road. There's a lot of America I haven't seen. There are days when I think I ought to be out there in the middle of it while it's still America."

She looked at me and I looked at her.

"When is Anna's funeral?"

"There won't be one. They released her remains and I had them cremated. She was in tiny little pieces." I had to swallow a couple of times. "I'm picking up the ashes tomorrow at ten and taking them to Hot Springs, Virginia. Gonna scatter them there. We had good times there, at the Homestead. I think she would have approved."

Sarah was watching me over the rim of her glass. After a bit she said, "The doctors amputated Fish's arm yesterday. Not enough circulation to his lower arm."

I didn't say anything. Just stood holding the wineglass, wishing I had killed the bastard.

"Tommy?"

"Your key is on the counter," I said, trying to keep my voice normal. "I'm not hungry. How about a rain check?"

I placed my glass of wine, still full, on the counter. Got my coat and let myself out.

Lieutenant Commander Zhang of the People's Liberation Army Navy also saw the television news feature about the "routine security exercise" at the Norfolk naval base, and although he didn't understand most of the English, the footage of a carrier coming into the carrier piers captured his attention. He resolved to buy a newspaper in the morning and have Choy Lee translate it for him. He was becoming more and more concerned about Choy's fixation upon Sally Chan, the daughter of the man who owned the restaurant, yet he still needed his translation skills. For a little while, anyway.

Zhang wondered what Choy had told Sally. Had he compromised the mission? Whispered secrets had a way of spreading quickly, like wildfire in dry grass.

He automatically fingered his cell phone, which was charging on his nightstand, and lit a cigarette. If Chinese agents in Washington or up and down the coast, or communications hackers in China, learned that the American navy had changed its plans and diverted carriers elsewhere, he would get an encrypted message on his iPad. Or a telephone call with a code word. Thinking about the contingencies, Zhang realized he must be ready to detonate the bomb with minimum warning. Better too early than too late. On the other hand, the richer the target, the greater the reward.

At heart Zhang was a gambler. Admiral Wu knew that, which was why he had chosen him for this mission. No panic, but a nice judgment about when to get as much as possible. That was what Wu and Zhang both wanted. That was what China needed if it was to become the major power in Asia.

He sat for a moment staring at the television with unseeing eyes, thinking of the Japanese navy's mistakes at Pearl Harbor on December 7, 1941. They had a great plan and they pulled it off magnificently, yet the ships they sank were battleships, obsolete weapons in the fledgling air age. The real prizes, the real strategic assets, were the U.S. Navy's three aircraft carriers. They were at sea when the blow fell on Pearl, so were untouched. Had the Japanese ignored the battleships and waited for the carriers, or lingered to hunt the carriers in the open sea . . . Well, undoubtedly the war in the Pacific would have gone a lot differently, and probably better, for Japan.

The Japanese also failed to damage or destroy the aboveground storage tanks at Pearl that contained the fuel oil the fleet burned. Had they done so, the Americans would have had to transport fuel from the American West Coast and would have had no place to store it, which would have severely limited the fleet's combat radius until new tanks could be constructed.

The Chinese plan was better than the Japanese. Today's American carriers were all nuclear powered, but the facilities to build, repair and refuel them were in Newport News; the explosion would put that shipyard out of action for years, if not for decades.

The Japanese overestimated America's readiness. Had they an inkling of the true state of affairs in Hawaii, they could safely have taken much greater risks and probably achieved greater, perhaps decisive, results.

Zhang didn't think he had made Japan's error. No, the danger here was erring the other way: underestimating the enemy's readiness. He had only one bomb, which would do catastrophic damage, and he had taken every precaution he could.

Zhang took a last long drag on his cigarette, stubbed out the butt and lit another. *Wait for the carriers,* he told himself. *But don't wait too long.*

CHAPTER TWENTY-ONE

If you're going through hell, keep going.
                                    —Winston Churchill

Kat Spiers managed to convince Harold and Ellie that they must leave. They refused to go, of course, as she had predicted, until she figuratively dropped the bomb: The Chinese were believed to have a nuclear warhead secreted at the naval base, and while the navy was looking, it might detonate at any time.

Being very human and mortal, Harold and Ellie agreed to leave. No one got any sleep that night, waiting, waiting . . . for the detonation. The next morning Harold called the college and pleaded a death in the family. He would return, he said, for the beginning of the next semester. Ellie e-mailed the women who were coming to the baby shower and said that, due to a death in Harold's family, it would have to be postponed. She would let them know.

Then they packed and got on the road about noon. Kat drove. Through the Hampton Roads Tunnel and up the interstate toward Richmond. They were so frightened they didn't relax until they were almost to Fredericksburg, when they decided to pull off and eat a late lunch at a Cracker Barrel restaurant.

The trio ate in silence, each absorbed with his or her own thoughts. Now that they were safe, relatively, the enormity of the disaster that might engulf every one of their friends weighed on them. Oh, Kat had stressed that they couldn't tell anyone, because the information was classified and might lead to panic. Mass panic. And if the media got it, it might even cause the trigger-man to detonate the weapon.

Heavy, Harold thought. *Very heavy.* Then he began thinking of his friends. He had a few he trusted, friends he knew who wouldn't tell anyone else, who would appreciate the opportunity to escape. If they knew. And what if he didn't tell them and the bomb went off? How would he live with that? *It is one thing,* he thought, *to take your wife and her unborn child to safety, but leaving your friends to die when it would be so easy to warn them?*

He made up his mind, and while he waited for his entrée to arrive at the table, he excused himself and went to the men's room. Sitting on a throne, he got out his cell phone and turned it on. He had six friends that he thought would do the same for him, if they knew. So he sent them an e-mail. The Chinese were believed to have a bomb at the Norfolk naval base. He had it on excellent authority that the navy was looking, but they might be too late. He advised his friends to leave the area. And, of course, not to tell any of *their* friends about this. No Facebook, no e-mails, no Twitter, no nothing. Just pack and go. Somewhere safe.

Then he pushed the SEND button and the little telephone sucked the e-mail into cyberspace.

He went back to the table and felt a little better. Yeah, he was taking his family to safety, but he had given his friends a warning. They had families, too. He attacked his hamburger.

Ellie played with her salad. Ate some of it and drank unsweetened ice tea. When she finished, she went to the restroom, taking her purse. She consulted her contact list. Thought about each one as she selected the name. The message ultimately had ten names, after she put over a dozen on and deleted a few after deliberation. She demanded that they tell no one else what she told them. She knew they wouldn't, because they were trustworthy and they would under-stand that the news could cause catastrophic damage if it got out. There were another twenty or so people on her list of contacts that Ellie wished she could tell, because they were so nice, but she knew she couldn't rely upon them to keep the secret, so she sent no warning. She told herself she was just being realistic and, being Ellie, dismissed the moral dilemma of warning some friends and not others without further thought.

When Ellie returned to the dining room, Kat excused herself. She too went to the ladies. She had two good friends from church, almost like sisters, who lived in the Virginia Beach suburbs. They weren't military, nor were their hus-bands. They had grown children and several grandkids. She told them the news she had gotten from her husband, not mentioning her source, and advised the strictest secrecy. Although she knew they would know her husband had told her—that was the power of the warning and the reason it would be believed—it wasn't fair to him to name him. She advised her two girlfriends to get out of the area as quickly as possible, taking their families with them. If nothing happened, well and good. If something did, at least they would be safe. And say *nothing* to anyone.

She sent the message and took a deep breath. Butler would be angry she sent it, but he would understand. It was he who had demanded she leave the area with her daughter and son-in-law. And the baby soon to be born. What a world this child would arrive in!

Feeling she had done her duty to her closest friends, both Christian ladies who had endured their share of adversity and then some, while not betraying her husband, Kat walked back to the table, left a cash tip, took the bill to the register, paid it with a credit card and accompanied Ellie and Harold to the parking lot and the waiting car.

Sitting behind the wheel with her seat belt on, she sent a text to Butler, who was probably in it up to his eyeballs. "In Fredericksburg," she typed. She put the phone in her purse, started the car and put it in gear. He never received the text. Kat didn't know it, but cell phone service to the Norfolk metropolitan area had been disabled on order of the military authorities. For the duration of the security exercise. However, the e-mails the trio had sent did go through, on landlines. The recipients would find them when they turned on their hardwired computers.

At one o'clock in the afternoon Captain Joe Child's SEALs finished searching the Craney Island Corps of Engineers Depot, across the broad mouth of the Elizabeth River from the carrier piers. They had been at it since dawn. Hundreds of acres of mountains of silt and mud dredged from the mouth of the Elizabeth River and the Hampton Roads estuary over the years made the task one of the labors of Hercules. To truly search that morose, stinking landscape would take a half-dozen bulldozers and a hundred man-years. All his forty men could do was walk over it with metal detectors and look for anything suspicious. That they had done.

Then they tackled the monstrous junkyard of old naval equipment. Bulldozers, vehicles of every kind and description, equipment that went on the highway or didn't, things taken off ships, stuff no one could name and stuff that was probably a worn-out one-off constructed for some project long forgotten—they looked, concluded that there was nothing there and gathered around their team leaders. Buses were waiting to take them to the next areas on the list. Child used a landline to call Admiral McKiernan, who had demanded to be kept personally informed.

McKiernan called Jake Grafton, who was at CIA headquarters in Langley. "They've done Craney Island," he said. "Results negative. The SEALs said it was like searching a hog pen for a diamond."

"It must be in the water, under a Carley float, on a tug or barge, somewhere in that yard."

"Or on a ship. Or it isn't there at all. I am beginning to like the idea it is on a boat that will come roaring in off the Chesapeake."

Jets were overhead, helicopters were buzzing around, the base was sealed due to the "routine security exercise," and Patriot missile batteries were standing by in case anyone penetrated the prohibited zone the FAA had established over the Hampton Roads area. The Coast Guard and navy patrol boats from the amphib base at Little Creek were patrolling around the clock.

"It's not on a boat," Jake said. "Too iffy. Too many things can go wrong. It's there now. It was there yesterday and it hasn't moved."

At two o'clock Sarah Houston came in with Jerry Chu's laptop, thumb drive and cell phones. "I've gotten everything I could and sent the rest to NSA. Maybe some of the mathematicians can make something of the crypto stuff, but it will take a long time." As Jake knew, NSA employed more Ph.D. mathematicians than any other company, university or government agency on the planet.

"Phones?"

"We have the numbers and are working them. Nothing for Zoe Kerry. But you knew there probably wouldn't be. If she calls him or he calls her, they will ditch the phone."

And ditto the watcher, Jake thought. If Jerry Chu had a number, it was in his head. And he'd never tell.

"Get a car and take that stuff over to the FBI. Sign a chain-of-custody form and get signatures when you turn it over. Then come back here. You and I need to talk about China."

"Yes, sir." She walked out with Tommy's trophies.

The autumn leaves were all gone, but the sun was out in the mountains of Virginia. I drove along with the top down and the heater going, taking my time. I thought about Anna for a while, then about our times together, all too brief, and then about nothing at all. I wondered where Zoe Kerry was. Not in the States, I decided. She was long gone. Not to China. I couldn't visualize her in China. She was a Europe kind of person. Germany or France, maybe Switzerland or Italy. Not the Balkans. Not Russia. Certainly not the Middle East or Egypt.

But somewhere.

Gradually she faded and there was only the road, the mountains covered with a forest of naked trees, waiting for snow. Waiting for winter. Under a clear blue sky with lots of sun.

When I die, I want to be buried on a day like this. A day sent from heaven.

The plastic urn with Anna's ashes was beside me, strapped into the passenger seat with the seat belt so it wouldn't come open in a crash. It was actually a small urn. They had cremated everything they could salvage, they said, but she was so close to the bomb . . .

The good news was that she hadn't felt a thing. Here one heartbeat and then gone forever. No transition. Just . . . gone.

Maybe Anna was lucky. I don't know. No old age, no debilitating illnesses, no nursing homes and endless painful medical procedures, no wishing her life had gone differently, no waiting for the inevitable end, no wondering when it would come . . . None of that. Boom. And she was gone.

But that bomb robbed her of a lot of good years. Robbed me of what might have been. Robbed us both of the happiness we so deeply anticipated. If life had worked out the way we wanted. So few things in life do. Work out the way you want, that is.

Another little tragedy. In a world full of them.

Aaugh! God damn it all to hell.

I drove through Hot Springs, by the Homestead, and took the two-lane highway south. Up the highway a ways I turned left on a side road, following the airport signs. Met no traffic. Wound all the way to the top of the mountain to the airport and parked next to the only vehicle in the lot beside the little fixed-base operator's terminal, a ten-year-old pickup. Went in and looked around.

"Can I help you?" the man at the counter asked. There were no airplanes on the ramp.

"Just looking."

I went back to the car, started down the hill. At the first overlook I pulled off. Unstrapped the urn, got out and stood looking over the mountains stretching away into the haze to the west. Looked at a hawk up high, circling. Tested the wind. It was from the southeast. No cars here, nor did I hear anyone pulling the grade.

I opened the urn and trickled the ashes out. The breeze caught them and whisked them away toward the valley below. Some of the bigger pieces reached the ground, pieces of bone maybe; the little stuff was lost on the wind. The rain and melting snow this winter would make the ashes part of the earth.

Good-bye, Anna.

When the urn was empty, I put the cap back on, got in the car and headed back down the mountain, back to Washington.

Zhang and Choy Lee spent the day aboard his Boston Whaler fishing offshore of old Fort Monroe in Hampton, across the roadstead from the mouth of the Elizabeth River. At least, Choy fished. Zhang sat at the helm with binoculars and watched the helicopters flying here and there over the base and the open water, the jets running high, navy harbor boats with a machine gun on the bow and two Coast Guard patrol craft. This activity was more than he had seen since he arrived in America, but Choy had translated the newspaper story about a "routine security exercise."

Zhang bought it. He knew the lengths his navy went to when their sole operational aircraft carrier, *Liaoning,* was in port, entering, exiting or under way. She was formerly a Soviet carrier, *Varyag,* bought from a Ukrainian shipyard 70 percent complete and towed on an epic voyage to the Dalian shipyard in China, where, after much study, her hull was completed and she was fitted with engines, radars, arresting gear and all the equipment necessary to turn the unfinished hull into a real warship, a carrier of armed warplanes that could project Chinese power for many hundreds of miles.

The Chinese also purchased three other retired carriers, hulks, incapable of operating aircraft, that they studied for years: the Australian carrier HMAS *Melbourne* and the former Soviet carriers *Minsk* and *Kiev.* Finally *Melbourne* was partially dismantled, and the two ex-Russian carriers were converted to resort/amusement parks to favorably impress the public with the future of their navy. For a reasonable amount, you and your wife, girlfriend or concubine could sleep, gamble and drink aboard a real warship. However, until these hulks were scrapped or converted, the PLAN had kept a watchful eye on them with harbor craft and helicopters. *Liaoning,* now operational and equipped with Shenyang J-5 fighters, was guarded day and night.

Unlike these complacent Americans, Zhang thought, the three Chinese fleet naval bases were closed to civilian maritime traffic. And spies.

Actually, the American navy's security operations were what he expected. Five aircraft carriers in port at one time, plus several helicopter assault carriers, was a juicy target. Better than Pearl Harbor in December of 1941. Much better. The Americans weren't such fools that they didn't know that. Yet the Chinese preparations were adequate. The attack would be a success.

He glanced at Choy Lee from time to time. Choy's usefulness was almost at an end. He thought Choy might suspect that, so he would have to be watched carefully. He seemed quite calm today. Had even caught a couple of fish, one big enough to keep.

Fortunately the day was fairly benign, with broken high clouds that the sun peeked through from time to time, not too much wind and only light chop. Six or seven miles visibility. Zhang lit another cigarette and went back to scanning with his binoculars and checking the radar presentation from time to time.

He was watching when he saw the blip of a large ship appear on the scope, trailed by two smaller ones, passing Point Comfort, heading into the bay. Using the binoculars, he saw a helicopter assault ship and two destroyers emerge from the haze, like ghost ships becoming real, on course westward, no doubt to moor at the carrier piers at the naval base. As she steamed along he watched her with his binoculars. She was a gorgeous gray ship, not as big as *Liaoning,* but impressive. Helicopters filled her flight deck.

He would, he decided, motor into the mouth of the Elizabeth River later this afternoon, at least an hour before darkness fell, for a look around. Then he would fill the tanks of the Whaler at the marina. Again. He filled them every evening, just in case.

Choy Lee would have been relieved if he had known Zhang thought him calm today. He had a big decision to make, and he was sorting his options. Since he hadn't decided what to do, he was here today, to give himself more time to think, and to watch Zhang and see if he could get a hint of Zhang's mission and plans. Choy sensed that Zhang's expectations were rising. He was more tense, never smiled, never made a joke. *He is waiting.* For what?

For the American carriers. Obviously. But why?

Zhang was watching the helicopter carrier now.

Should he tell Sally Chan of his suspicions? Would she go with him if he disappeared? Or would she demand he call the navy or FBI and tell them what he knew, and suspected? What would become of him if he did?

Bored, he took his cell phone from his pocket and turned it on. No service. Maybe he was too far from a tower.

But there should be cell service out here. There always had been.

He pocketed the phone. Thought about telling Zhang.

Something made him refrain. Zhang was using the binoculars again.

Oh God. What to do?

He went back to fishing.

The e-mails from Kat Spiers and her daughter, Ellie, and son-in-law, Harold, started a firestorm in cyberspace. By the time they were on the Washington, DC, Beltway, over ten thousand people in the Norfolk/Portsmouth/Virginia Beach area had seen some version of one or more of the e-mails and were forwarding them on to friends, acquaintances and co-workers. People from all walks of life received the news with varying degrees of belief and disbelief. Some thought the whole thing was a joke and said so. Others weren't so sure. Some people merely forwarded on the e-mail they received; others undertook to rewrite the message on other websites. The Chinese had a dozen bombs hidden on the naval base. Airplanes were going to drop bombs. Intercontinental ballistic missiles were going to wipe out the fleet. The missiles were already in the air. Or they were being prepared for launch. Some folks even added that the security exercise at the base was a war preparation.

A great many of the people who received these messages or read the Facebook posts didn't stop to ask themselves or anyone else if any of this might be true. They hustled the kids into the car when they got home from school—some went to schools to get their kids and told the school authorities why—threw in whatever duffel their car would hold, and headed for the roads out. Within an hour the roads were clogged. Traffic accidents began to slow the exodus.

The news reached the local television and radio stations at about the same time, which was lightning fast. Some producers just put the rumors on the air. Others called the public affairs office at the naval base to get their reaction. They were going to do a story about the rumors anyway, but would be delighted to give someone in uniform fifteen seconds to deny everything.

The public affairs officer, or PAO, at Naval Base Norfolk was Lieutenant Commander Heidi Fritzsche, and she was winding up the day's business when the first call came in. She listened, incredulous, and asked the television station dude to hold the line.

She rushed down the hallway to the CO's office and asked the civilian receptionist if Captain Spiers was still there. Informed he was, she rapped on his doorframe once, opened the door and rushed into his office.

"Captain, you aren't going to believe this, but WNOF just called. They say the news is all over the Internet that the Chinese are going to bomb the base. Their phones are ringing off the hooks. They want a comment from us."

Captain Spiers' face went dead white. He had to swallow twice to get enough composure to say, "If they are, they haven't told us about it."

"The Internet!" Heidi Fritzsche declared bitterly, and trotted back toward her office and the waiting telephone.

Butler Spiers buried his face in his hands.

Two minutes later, when he felt a bit more composed, he checked his Rolodex, picked up his telephone and called Washington.

Back in her office, Heidi Fritzsche's phones were ringing constantly. As quickly as her yeomen could field a call on one line, explain about the security exercise and hang up, the phone rang again. Heidi took a call from a man who said he was the manager of a large hotel—he named it—in Virginia Beach. "We're hosting a convention of Vietnam vets. They're lined up at the desk ten deep trying to check out. What the hell is going on out there at the base?"

"A routine security exercise."

"Not according to the Internet."

"We don't run the Internet. We're just trying to run our little corner of the navy." She hung up and fielded the next call, which was from the PAO at Naval Air Station Oceana.

"Heidi, the phones are ringing off the hook over here. Some of my staff have received e-mails saying that the naval base is preparing for a nuclear attack from the Chinese."

"For God's sake!"

"They say it's Pearl Harbor all over again."

Involuntarily Heidi looked out her window. Sunlight and shadow were marching across the lawn. The flag flapped vigorously on its pole. Beyond the roof of the next building, she could see superstructures and masts festooned with radars and antennae of ships at the carrier piers. A helicopter went by overhead. Cars and trucks on the streets.

"No one is bombing anything here," she shouted into the phone. "We're having a routine security exercise that's been planned for two months and announced to the public. Read your damn messages! And get a goddamn grip!" She slammed the phone down.

. . .

Anastasia Roberts broke the news to Jake Grafton. "We've received a call from the Pentagon. They're fielding inquiries from various networks and news-papers. It seems the Internet is full of messages saying that the Chinese are about to attack the Norfolk naval base. ICBMs are in the air, there are bombs hidden on the base, it's Pearl Harbor all over again. The stuff has gone viral on Facebook and Twitter and presumably every other Internet site on the planet."

Jake Grafton just stared at her. So she went on. "The public in the area around the base has panicked. Massive traffic jams of people trying to get the hell out. Cell phone towers are overloaded. People are driving the wrong way on the interstate lanes. Lots of accidents. Some of the hospitals and nursing homes are demanding help to evacuate their patients."

He made a face.

"The Pentagon has told everyone that the base is having a routine security exercise that's been planned for months. Maybe some people believe that, but a lot of people don't."

I wonder if the watcher will? he thought.

"And Sal Molina is on line one." Anastasia Roberts wheeled and left the office.

Jake picked up his phone and pushed the button for line one. "Yes, Sal."

"Have you heard the latest from Norfolk?"

"Yes."

"The president told the press officer to try to calm the media. He told me to call you and ask, 'What the fuck, over?'"

Anastasia stuck her head back through the door. She mouthed, "CNO on line two."

"I have another call, Sal. I'll get right back to you."

"Okay."

Cart McKiernan said, "Norfolk is in meltdown. The news got out, some-how. Maybe not—but rumors are flying thick and fast. They're on the Inter-net, and now television and radio. I'm going down there on a chopper from the Pentagon in about an hour. You want to go?"

"Yes. I'll bring Sal Molina."

So he called Molina back, cut him short and said, "Admiral McKiernan and I are going to Norfolk. You want to go?"

Molina didn't hesitate. "Yes."

"See you at the Pentagon helipad in an hour. Bring a toothbrush."

Jake called Harley Merritt and gave him a quick brief, told his secretary to alert his driver and security team, then went into his office bathroom and threw some things into his overnight bag. When he was in the limo on the way to the Pentagon, he called his wife and told her he wouldn't be home tonight.

"I've been watching television, Jake. Are you going to Norfolk?"

"Yes."

"Dear God Almighty," Callie said.

Although she was certainly no Internet junkie and didn't own a cell phone, Sally Chan heard about the panic in midafternoon from the television set above the bar in her father's restaurant. The place was unusually empty. She had the place settings on all the tables; her father was cooking in the kitchen; her mother was behind the bar inventorying the liquor, wine and beer. Mrs. Chan had turned on the television for the company.

Sally happened to glance at it, saw the news ribbon scrolling across the bottom and paused to read it. An afternoon soap opera was playing. "U.S. Navy spokesmen at Naval Base Norfolk and in the Pentagon have denied that the security exercise at the base is in any way related to the Internet rumor that a Chinese nuclear weapon is hidden on the naval base." There was more . . .

Within sixty seconds the network interrupted the program to air a live interview with the White House press secretary. Sally stepped behind the bar and turned up the volume. He was loose, smiling, as if all this were a big joke. "Debunking Internet rumors will be a new career for me—"

Sally changed channels, got a local station, which was airing footage shot from a helicopter of massive traffic jams on the interstates leading to the Chesapeake Bay Bridge-Tunnel and the tunnel under Hampton Roads. She and her mother stood mesmerized watching the camera pan from a height of perhaps five hundred feet.

Cars jammed the roadways as far as the camera could see. A breathless local announcer confirmed that people were fleeing the area as quickly as the roads allowed. Hospitals and nursing homes were demanding transport for patients. Now the camera depicted a demonstration that was almost a riot in front of Norfolk City Hall by a mixed-race crowd. One demonstrator, a fat woman, demanded the authorities transport people from the area who didn't own cars. "Get some buses," she shouted into the camera. "Get some city buses and get us out of here! Don't leave us to die like you did to the poor people during Katrina." Katrina was the last big hurricane to slam New Orleans.

There was more of the same on other channels.

Bedlam. Mass panic.

Sally turned off the audio of the idiot tube and poured two glasses of wine.

"What does it mean?" Mrs. Chan asked, fingering her glass.

"I don't know," Sally answered. She sat on a bar stool to drink hers.

"The Chinese again!" Mrs. Chan said with contempt. "Why do they always blame the Chinese? We are good Americans. We work hard and send our children to college and pay our taxes. We are good Americans, as good as anybody."

Sally wasn't listening. She was thinking about Choy Lee, supposedly retired from California high tech, yet he never talked about California or his life or work there. Perhaps there was a failed love affair, but why had he crossed the country to live here, and why did he do nothing? Except fish.

Then there was Zhang Ping, who spoke essentially no English. Why was he here? A pal from California, Choy said. Yet Zhang said little, even to Choy, except to occasionally ask him to pass along a compliment on the excellence of the family's food. He fished, too.

In the light of the almost unbelievable accusations about diabolical Chinese intentions at the naval base, all these little things became larger, more ominous. Who were Zhang and Choy?

If they weren't spies, why were they here?

But the whole thing is ridiculous, Sally Chan told herself. *A Chinese attack on the Norfolk naval base? That would start World War III. Wouldn't it?*

Torn by indecision, she watched the news. After a bit the local station stopped showing traffic jams and stories about panicked old people at nursing homes and poor people in the ghetto, and showed a photo of five carriers and two amphibious assault ships at the carrier piers during the Christmas holidays two years ago.

So how many carriers were going to be here this Christmas?

According to the television news person, someone had asked that question of the Pentagon, and had been rebuffed. "We never talk about future ship movements," a man in a blue uniform said on camera.

Sally Chan decided to call Choy Lee. She dialed his cell . . . and the call didn't go through. She tried again. Nothing. The fourth time his phone rang. After five rings the call rolled to his voice mail.

"Call me when you can," she said, trying to keep the panic out of her voice.

. . .

The superstory of the day hit the Chinese embassy in Washington like an incoming missile. No one there knew anything about the voyage of *Ocean Holiday* or the mission of Lieutenant Commander Zhang Ping, both of which were tightly held military secrets.

The staff put out a press release denying the rumors as vicious smears, and reported all this to Beijing in encrypted flash messages. Of course, the Chinese foreign ministry there had their own Internet sources, so they knew all about it.

The answer came back to the Chinese embassy in Washington thirty minutes after it was sent. The ambassador was to announce that he was going to Norfolk to tell everyone that China was being foully smeared by outrageous Internet lies, and to reassure the citizens there. And then he was to go. Immediately.

In the meantime, the embassy press officer was to point out to the American media that an outrageous slander like this one about the Americans would never be allowed on the Internet in China.

While all this was going on, Zhang Ping started his boat toward the mouth of the Elizabeth River. He had to use the channel over the Hampton Roads tunnel. The radar reflectors at each side of the channel showed nicely on his radar screen. As he closed the distance, Choy Lee pointed out the traffic backed up on the access road to the tunnel on Willoughby Spit. Zhang used his binoculars.

He could see that traffic was stopped. Trucks, cars, vans, everything. Flashing lights on police cars. A helicopter—no, two helicopters—hovering near the tunnel entrance.

He passed the binoculars to Choy, who focused, scanned the scene, then handed them back. "An accident in the tunnel," Choy explained. "This happens often. Last week the cars sat for an hour before a wrecker could get through from the other end to remove the cars."

Zhang recalled the incident. "Americans have too many cars," he said dismissively, and turned his binoculars to the amphibious assault ship and her escorting destroyers, which were ahead of him going through the channel over the tunnel. A harbor patrol craft was following the procession. Its machine gun was unmanned. Zhang wondered how long it would take for the crew of the patrol boat to go to action stations and man the weapon, if they were told to do so.

Choy Lee turned on his cell phone. It refused to log on to the cellular network. *Another day in America,* he thought.

CHAPTER **TWENTY-TWO**

A pessimist sees the difficulty in every opportunity; an optimist
sees the opportunity in every difficulty.
                                              —Winston Churchill

It was early in the morning in China when Admiral Wu was summoned to
the capital to meet with the Paramount Leader at a session of the Central
Military Commission. The staff was monitoring the media reaction in the
United States to the Internet rumors, of which they had translated quite a
sample.

The plan had not included a contingency for the Americans getting advance warning of the Chinese stealth attack on their ships, only two of which
were actually at the carrier piers.

Tomorrow, the eighteenth of December in America, the men gathered
around the table were told, the third one was scheduled to arrive. The final
two would arrive on the twentieth and twenty-second. All three were in
the Atlantic with their task forces bound for the entrance to the Chesapeake.

The choices were obvious: Abort the attack, detonate the bomb as soon as
possible, or await the carriers and detonate it then.

"Does the American navy know the weapon is there?" the Paramount
Leader asked the head of the intelligence service, who was in attendance.

"We have received no indication that they know, or even suspect. They are
checking the waters around the base, have tightened security, but we knew
they would do that. There is no indication they are doing anything that we

didn't think they would do. However, the local cell towers around Norfolk are out of service. A technical problem, the telephone companies said."

"Could these Internet rumors convince them that there is a weapon there?"

The intelligence chief didn't think much of that possibility. In his experience, the American military and political leaders used facts to make their decisions or what they thought were facts. Frightened people who knew nothing sending texts and e-mails and making Facebook and Twitter posts wouldn't sway them. "The Internet there is totally open," the spy chief explained. "People routinely use the Internet to accuse the political leaders of every crime known to man, everything up to and including treason, every hour of every day. The people in government ignore all that. The media ignore it. Their attitude is that if one ignores the Internet, it doesn't matter what is on it."

The Paramount Leader didn't share that viewpoint; nor did the other officials in the room. In China an open Internet could easily undermine support for the party, they thought. People who slandered the party in any forum were public enemies. Yet, he realized, this enormous gust of cyber-wind was happening in America, not here.

"Admiral Wu, your opinion."

"As long as the United States Navy doesn't believe a bomb is really there, the ships will come in to their berths at the carrier piers. If the admirals believe a bomb is there, the ships will be diverted elsewhere. We are monitoring their naval traffic and the internal naval traffic in the Pentagon. So far, we have seen nothing to that effect."

"So your recommendation is to wait."

"At least until the third carrier berths. Then we can reevaluate. But I say to you now, the repercussions of our attack will be vast. Our position must be that an American weapon accidentally exploded. The Americans never admit that nuclear weapons are aboard their ships, and everyone knows that they are. Their evasions will help destroy their credibility. The presence of our ambassador and his death will help sell the story of an accident. Nothing that has happened in America, or will happen, leads me to believe the current administration will ask Congress to declare war."

"No one declares war anymore," the Paramount Leader said unequivocally.

"War declared or undeclared would cause the current American administration to be thrown from office," Admiral Wu insisted. *"They know that. It will be the pole upon which all their thinking turns.* Two carriers are a small return for our effort and the risk. Three would be better. Five would make the gamble worthwhile. Let us not forget why this mission was authorized."

"What do your men in Norfolk say?" the Paramount Leader asked the admiral.

"We have heard nothing from them—there are two agents there—except routine Internet posts. The latest was yesterday. We cannot get through to them today since the cellular network around Norfolk is out of service. Temporarily. The telephone company says it is severely overloaded jammed with Internet traffic. So it has been temporarily shut down."

A chuckle went around the room.

The Paramount Leader didn't chuckle. "Could the Americans have captured the agents and be playing us?"

"To what end?" the intelligence chief asked. "That would be illogical. After all, if they have the men and the weapon, nothing will happen. Our attack will be a nonevent. We are sitting here wasting our time."

The chairman lit a cigarette and smoked it in silence. Everyone in the room sat silently, too.

A war with America would stop the Chinese economy dead in its tracks. Even an embargo of Chinese exports to America would be devastating. An embargo of all China's imports and exports would be something less than total war, but it would cause the nation to run out of oil and food. Yet there was small chance it would ever come to that. Even if the Americans *knew* the Chinese had pulled the trigger, they could plausibly deny that they knew. Could and probably would.

On the other hand, the Chinese people wanted China to be a major regional power. China needed the oil, natural gas and fish from adjacent seas. Its people demanded that other nations in the region respect them, their flag, their achievements and their ambitions. If *that* didn't happen, the rot would eventually set in and the future of the party would be in doubt. Lead or get run over.

When he stubbed out his cigarette, the Paramount Leader spoke conversationally to everyone in the room. "We will wait another day."

As the marine helicopter flew the 125 nautical miles south from the Pentagon helipad to Chambers Field at Naval Base Norfolk, Jake Grafton ignored the crew chatter on the intercom. He was thinking about the Chinese. If they planted a bomb in Norfolk and it did indeed explode, he thought they had seriously underestimated the reaction of the American people afterward.

The Japanese certainly did when they planned the surprise attack on Pearl Harbor, lo those seventy-some years ago. A large segment of the American population then was willing to exterminate the Japanese race from the planet. Admiral "Bull" Halsey caught the mood when he said, "Before we're through with them, the Japanese language will be spoken only in hell."

Total war. Absolute total war. At the least, the Communist Party would be finished in China, and chaos would once again cause the death of millions, tens of millions, hundreds of millions. In China.

That explosion would irrevocably transform America. Into what, Jake didn't know, but his head and heart told him the republic that had lasted since 1789 would probably not survive.

When the chopper settled on the tarmac, he roused himself from his meditations. Finally the engines died and the rotors stopped. He followed the admiral, his two aides, and Sal Molina down the little stairway to the concrete. One of the CNO's aides, a woman, was a rear admiral; the other was a captain.

Captain Butler Spiers and the admiral in charge of Fleet Forces Command, Sherman Fitch, were waiting to salute McKiernan. Inside the little Operations Building, Spiers led his visitors to a conference room, where one of the news networks was playing on a television.

Admiral Fitch grabbed the remote and killed the television audio. "The situation is totally out of control," he said. "Here and clear to Richmond. Everyone within a hundred miles is trying to get the hell out of here, including half our sailors. I have never in my life seen anything like it. Did you see the highways as you flew in? The interstates are giant parking lots, creep and go, for a hundred miles in every direction. Accidents everywhere. Riots in downtown Norfolk, Portsmouth, Suffolk and Newport News. Looting has started. The police can't control the mobs."

"None of that is our problem," McKiernan said. "Our problem is a bomb. Have you found it?" He addressed that question to them both.

"Every ship has been searched," Fitch said. "A quick going-over. Now they are emptying the storerooms and inspecting the bilges. Every ship in my command. Nothing that shouldn't be there except some marijuana and a couple of stills running on fruit juice."

"We're about halfway through searching the base," Spiers reported. "We've been through every building and are doing the manholes. The warehouses will take at least two more days to search with the people we have. SEALs are searching the piers and river and offshore, with no luck. We've even had a destroyer search with the new sonar. Nothing yet."

"Have you told your people what they're looking for?" Sal Molina asked the naval officers.

"We told them that a shape, a dummy weapon, had been hidden, and that was what we were looking for," Spiers said. "We're not looking for a lost diamond ring or somebody's poodle."

Fitch nodded. "I told the skippers what they were searching for."

"That's how the secret got out," McKiernan said heavily to Molina. To Spiers and Fitch he said, "You both made the right decision. In the age of the Internet, it was an impossible secret to keep."

"I suppose," Sal Molina said unhappily. He pulled his cell phone from his coat pocket, saw that he had no service and went out to find an empty room with a hardwired telephone so he could call the White House.

"The question is," Jake Grafton said, "what the Chinese reaction will be. They haven't detonated the bomb yet, but they may decide to do so in the next minute, hour, day or week."

"We've got to turn those ships around."

"We're screwed if we do," Jake said. "The instant the Chinese get wind of that, they may pop the thing. Why wait? You know as well as I do they're waiting for more ships."

"The *Lincoln* will be here tomorrow."

"I know, and they do, too."

"What remains to be done," McKiernan asked Spiers and Fitch, "to find this bomb? Or bombs? Are we looking at a day, a week, a month? How long?"

"We need to get the SEAL boss, Joe Child, in here."

"Call him."

Child was there in five minutes. He had been in Spiers' offices looking for him and been told he was in Base Ops at Chambers Field, so he had been on the way.

They were discussing what remained to be searched when Molina came back.

Another helicopter settled on the ramp outside the building. Jake heard it, glanced through the window and saw Harry Estep and National Security Adviser Jurgen Schulz walking quickly toward the Ops Building. Molina saw them, too.

They came into the conference room without fanfare and grabbed seats around the table.

"What the fuck is going on around here?" Schulz demanded.

"We're trying to figure that out," McKiernan answered coolly.

"All this crap about a Chinese bomb—what evidence is there that there *is* a Chinese bomb?" Harry Estep asked harshly. "Or a bomb, period?"

Several people started to talk at once, but Molina silenced them all without even raising his voice. "There isn't enough evidence to convince a jury of anything beyond a reasonable doubt," he said, "but this isn't a court of law. There is enough evidence to convince me—and the president—that the Chinese government *may* be plotting an attack on the United States. Or another country or group *may* be planning an attack that we will blame on the Chinese. I don't know if there is more than one chance in a thousand that there is a bomb. But I guarantee you, if one explodes, the aftermath will be absolutely catastrophic. Now let's cut the bullshit and figure out what the United States government is going to do to prevent an explosion. Admiral McKiernan?"

The CNO looked at Joe Child and Butler Spiers. "How long to complete the search?"

"To an absolute certainty, a month," Child said.

McKiernan made an angry gesture. "None of that! I want the bomb found by noon tomorrow." He looked at his watch. "You have nineteen hours. You two go get at it."

"Yes, sir," they said almost in unison, then rose and left the room.

When the door closed, Schulz said, "It doesn't really matter what you want. What about all these people on the base? What about the two million people in the metropolitan area?"

"I'm not God. I'm doing what I can do," McKiernan shot back.

"If our mad bombers are after the ships, why not get the ones that are here under way and stop any more from coming in?"

McKiernan introduced his senior aide. "This is Rear Admiral Suzanne Deighton. She is in charge of the navy's IT systems. Admiral?"

Deighton didn't hem and haw. "The Chinese have been reading our operational stuff for several years. Our latest analysis is that they may also be reading our encrypted message traffic."

"For the love of God!" Schulz roared. "And you have done nothing about it?"

McKiernan didn't turn a hair. He cast a cold eye on the national security adviser. "Don't play the innocent with me. Your staff has been told all about this problem. We do what we can with the money in our budget and the people we have or can hire. This isn't the time or place to cut up the corpse."

Molina said smoothly, "Admiral Grafton. Your opinion, please."

Jake Grafton's gaze circled the room. "If we tell our carrier battle groups to go somewhere else or remain at sea, the Chinese may learn of it and instruct the triggerman, or men, to blow the weapon. There will be no profit in waiting. On the other hand, if we bring all these ships in here and then they blow it, we have just screwed ourselves."

"That's the problem in a nutshell," Molina said softly. "Thank you, Jake."

The meeting broke up then. However, McKiernan, Grafton and Molina made no move to leave their chairs. The CNO signaled to Admiral Fitch to remain.

When everyone else had left, McKiernan said to Fitch, "I want you to put senior officers on two CODs"—carrier onboard delivery planes—"and have them fly out to the carriers that are due in on the twentieth and twenty-second. The admirals are to be told orally that they are to remain at sea until further orders. Nothing over the air, encrypted or otherwise. No crew Internet. No ship-to-ship voice. Absolute radio silence."

"Aye aye, sir. What about the *Lincoln,* which is coming in tomorrow?"

McKiernan and Jake Grafton exchanged glances. "Let her come," Jake said softly. "The Chinese expect her."

Cart McKiernan nodded. He was a gambler, too.

Zhang Ping used his binoculars when he was in the mouth of the Elizabeth River, only half a mile from the carrier piers. He ignored the two giant carriers berthed there, and the amphibious assault ship covered with helicopters, and studied the harbor craft. One seemed to be anchored. The Whaler was barely moving, to make it a more stable platform for viewing with binoculars. Still, the boat's motion made it difficult to discern details. He concentrated fiercely. As he watched, a man wearing a black wet suit and scuba gear came out of the water. People on deck helped him with his gear.

He knew what they were doing. Searching the water around the carrier piers, inspecting the bottoms of the ships, searching . . .

A harbor patrol craft came his way. Zhang put the binoculars in his lap. A man on a loud-hailer shouted something in English.

Choy Lee translated. "This area is closed. Turn around."

Zhang Ping wheeled the Whaler into a tight turn, pointed her north and added throttle. The twin 225-horsepower Mercury outboard engines began to sing. The Whaler came up on the plane.

Well, Zhang thought, *they are taking precautions. They are alert. Yet they are searching in the wrong place. By the time they get to the right place, it will be too late!*

Sally Chan was worried. Choy Lee hadn't returned her call, and when she tried to call him the cellular network was dead. The call wouldn't go through. There was no ring tone, nothing. High-tech junk.

The restaurant was empty. Her mother had gone home because there was nothing for her to do. The other waitress hadn't come in, and probably wouldn't. Perhaps she was in the traffic jam for one of the tunnels or highways out.

Sally was sitting at the bar nursing a glass of wine when the window in the dining area, next to the parking lot, exploded. Glass showered across a dozen tables.

As she went to look, she heard a revving engine and squealing tires. She found a brick under one of the tables. Only a few shards of glass remained in the window. The breeze came in the broken window.

Her father came from the kitchen to see what had happened. He too had been following the panic by checking the television occasionally. "We're Chinese," he said, unable to keep the disgust from his voice. "That's enough for some people."

"Stupid teenagers," Sally said.

She went for the broom and dustpan. The good news was that behind the restaurant in the area where the garbage cans were kept were six sheets of plywood under an overhang, for whenever a hurricane threatened. There hadn't been one in years, yet the plywood had been there since the last storm because eventually, someday, another storm would come. *That's life,* Sally thought. *A storm always comes sooner or later.* She began looking around for the hammer and nails.

She had finished nailing plywood over the broken window opening and was putting the hammer away when the telephone in the restaurant rang. She raced for it and grabbed the thing off its cradle.

"Hey, beautiful," he said breezily. "Just got into port. My cell phone isn't working."

"Where have you been?"

"Fishing. With Zhang. Why?"

"Have you talked to anyone, watched any television?"

"No."

"The Tidewater area is in meltdown. The roads are packed with people fleeing the area. The rumor on the television and Internet is that the Chinese have a bomb planted at the Norfolk naval base and are going to explode it. All hell has broken loose."

Silence. Then Choy's voice. "When we get the boat put away, I'll come over. You're going to stay at the restaurant, right?"

"Yes."

"See you in a while," he said distractedly, and broke the connection.

Sally stared at the phone for a moment, then put it in her pocket. That tone in his voice . . . that had been ominous.

Oh, she thought, *I am just being foolish. Choy Lee is a good man. He wouldn't be a part of mass murder! My God, a vicious rumor, and you are suspecting everyone. Sally, get a grip!*

She went back to the bar and made herself a gin and tonic with a slice of lime. Her father came in from the kitchen. "Go home," she told him. "Mom probably needs you with her."

"We're closed," he said. He kissed her and walked to the front door, turned the sign so it read CLOSED, and manipulated the lock so that it latched the door behind him.

Sally sipped her drink. After a bit, she turned off the television and sat in silence staring at the interior of the little business that had supported her family, and her, for over twenty years. This little piece of America.

The telephone call with Sally had given Choy Lee an epiphany. Suddenly the last six months of watching the fleet, Zhang and his boat—it all came into blindingly clear focus. A bomb! To destroy the United States Navy's ships! To destroy the heart of the American fleet!

He couldn't imagine how the news got out, nor did he care. It fit! He had no doubt whatsoever.

Zhang was still standing in the boat with the fuel-hose nozzle in his hand, filling the Whaler's tanks. Choy didn't wait to try out his poker face on Zhang. He walked across the parking lot, got into his SUV, started it and drove away.

If exploding a bomb at the naval base was indeed Zhang's mission—and Choy Lee believed it was to a certainty—then Zhang would kill him soon, if he didn't trigger the bomb. When he heard about the news stories, it would be one or the other, as soon as possible. And Choy didn't even have a gun.

He headed for the Chans' restaurant through almost empty streets. Everyone was trying to get out of town, Sally had said. Choy had never seen the streets so empty. He made good time, merely slowed at stop signs, and zipped along.

A *bomb*! That was *it*!

Yet, perhaps, when Zhang heard the news, he would merely trigger the bomb. Then Choy and Sally would be instantly dead. Along with a couple million other people.

For the first time in his life, Choy Lee felt on the edge of death. The eternal darkness was right there before him. And he hadn't even told Sally Chan he loved her.

The attendant at the marina did indeed try to tell Zhang Ping about the panic. Zhang didn't understand enough English to make sense of it. He merely smiled and looked around for Choy, who wasn't in sight. Perhaps he went to the restroom. The attendant looked at Zhang strangely, then shrugged and moved off down the pier.

Zhang maneuvered the boat into its slip. Double-checked that the master switch was off, unhooked the iPad, made sure the bumper pads were in place and the boat was properly tied in its berth, then put covers on everything.

Only when he was finished and walking to the parking lot with the iPad in his hand did he wonder what had happened to Choy. He turned on the iPad . . . and discovered he had no Internet service. He stood there, trying to make sense of it. The iPad got its Internet signal from cellular telephone towers. He wondered if the interruption in service was temporary, or if the authorities had turned them off. Perhaps it was just the iPad. He retrieved his cell phone from a trouser pocket and turned it on. No service.

In the parking lot he discovered that Choy's SUV was gone.

Zhang had a decision to make, and he made it quickly. He glanced about, looking at parked cars and pickup trucks and SUVs. No one in sight. A car was driving into the lot. The driver got out, then opened the rear door and picked up what looked like a brown paper bag full of beer or groceries. The guy was going out on a boat this evening.

Zhang came up behind him and, as he turned, grabbed his head and twisted viciously, breaking the man's neck. The bag fell and split, and six-packs of beer tumbled out. Zhang fished in the man's right-hand trouser pocket, found the car keys and shoved the body onto the backseat. The six-packs he picked up and tossed in.

A quick scan around to see if anyone had been watching. No one in sight.

Zhang got into the car, inserted the key into the ignition and drove away.

Chapter TWENTY-THREE

Everything in war is very simple. But the simplest thing is difficult.

—Carl von Clausewitz

I was sitting in Sarah Houston's office reading the news from Norfolk on my laptop while she manipulated her desktop computer, working on God knows what. The news was beyond bad; it was a major shitstorm. The story about a Chinese bomb had been twisted almost beyond recognition, but the kernel of truth was there. I confess, I wasn't surprised. A secret this big was too hot to hold; a leak was inevitable.

I wondered if Jake Grafton had leaked it. He was capable of it, certainly—he was a damned sneaky bastard—if he thought it would help us find the bomb before it popped, but I couldn't see how it would. I thought the opposite was probably true.

There was a little television on a table by the wall. I turned it on to one of the news channels. The politicians were running around with their hair on fire. Massive traffic jams on all the highways out of the Norfolk/Virginia Beach area. People were driving the wrong way on the highways, making cops dive for the ditches. Riots in Norfolk and Newport News. After three minutes, I strangled the beast. Blessed silence. Only the clicking of Sarah's computer keys. She could silence them, of course, but she hadn't. Maybe the noise helped her focus.

After a bit she stopped to make a note on a pad on her desk, tore off the top sheet and handed it to me. I looked at it. "Cuthbert Gordon, 7354 Vista Del

Mar." The city, state and zip code were on it. In case you have forgotten, ol' Bertie was my mom's new love interest.

"Thanks," I said, and tucked the note into my wallet, then put my wallet into my hip pocket, right next to my heart. Sarah got busy again on her keyboard.

I sat there relaxed, with one leg crossed, thinking about Anna Modin's ashes dribbling into the breeze.

My cell phone rang. It was in my shirt pocket. I pulled it out, didn't recognize the number, but answered it anyway. Maybe someone wanted my opinion on the exciting taste of McDonald's latest burger.

Grafton's voice. "Tommy, I want you to come to Norfolk. I need you."

"Take a while to drive down there, what with the traffic jams and all." I thought maybe a week would do it.

"A helicopter will pick you up at the Langley helo pad in half an hour. Be on it."

"Yes, sir."

After I had my cell phone back in my pocket, I checked the Kimber in my shoulder holster. Loaded and ready. Zoe Kerry's derringer was in my right sock, also loaded. Put my laptop in my office, make a pit stop on the way to the helicopter, and I would be ready to fly.

Sarah stopped tapping and swiveled toward me. "You going somewhere?"

"Grafton wants me in Norfolk. He's sending a chopper for me."

"That bomb might explode while you are there."

I shrugged.

She couldn't leave it there. "Don't you have anything to say?"

I didn't know what to say. We're all going to die. That's the way life works. The only issue of any interest is when. I kept my mouth shut.

"So aren't you scared? A little bit?"

"Should I be?"

"Tommy . . ."

Seeing the look on her face, I crossed to her, tilted her head up and kissed her on the lips as sweetly and gently as possible.

"See you in a few days, Sarah," I whispered.

Walking down the hallway, I felt like a shit. I just didn't have a good-bye scene in me. "Farewell, dear lady. Until we meet again, here or on the other side of the great divide." Fuck that.

Maybe the truth was I didn't give a good goddamn.

. . .

The panic in southwestern Virginia hit the White House like an earthquake. Sal Molina and Jurgen Schulz had helicoptered back from Norfolk. Molina thought he could feel the floor oscillating as people ran through the halls on errands that presumably would save civilization. He was summoned to the Situation Room, where the president was huddled with his national security team. Once there, Molina found that Schulz had panicked, too. He was in full cry when Sal walked in.

"It's that incompetent asshole Grafton, and that idiot admiral McKiernan. Those two fools think they can manage this mess! The hell of it is, there probably *is* a fuckin' bomb in the harbor, and those imbeciles sat there talking about finding it, a fuckin' needle in a fuckin' haystack. Goddamn chinks! I think we should get the Chinese ambassador in here and tell him that if a nuke goes off in Norfolk, we'll massively retaliate against China. We won't leave two bricks stuck together in that fuckin' commie paradise. We'll cremate every fuckin' chink between Vietnam and Mongolia. Every last one of the silly sons of bitches—men, women, children and comrades. *All of them!*"

When Schulz paused for air, Molina spoke directly to him. "Let me get this straight. You are advising escalating the crisis by threatening the Chinese with all-out nuclear holocaust. They have ICBMs with nuclear warheads, too. What if they decide there is no way off the cliff except to shoot first? Wipe out America and save as many of their people as possible?"

"They'll back down," Schulz insisted.

"What if they don't? Are we bluffing? Would you really do it?"

The silence that followed was broken when the president said, "Thank you, Jurgen, for that thoughtful advice. Any more thoughts, Sal?"

"Norfolk certainly is in meltdown. Somebody leaked the possibility of a bomb, sure as sin. That was inevitable, I suppose." Molina sighed. "If Grafton and McKiernan can find the thing before it blows, they will. If they can't, I don't think anything we do will matter much. A nuclear explosion in Norfolk, or anywhere else, will have profound, unknown consequences. If it happens . . . Well, I think we had better await the event and go on from there. Assuming that there is a United States left that we want to live in."

Jurgen Schulz started cussing again. Molina had never before heard a Harvard professor throw around so many of those fine old Anglo-Saxon words. Obviously Schulz was a connoisseur. Molina thought it a rare treat to hear those words delivered so passionately.

When Schulz ran down, the president said, "I don't know about you people, but I am going to have a nice quiet dinner, drink a couple glasses of wine and try to get some sleep. I suggest everyone here do the same."

"What about the congressmen and senators and the press?" his chief of staff asked. "They are besieging us."

The president eyed him. "And your point is . . . ?"

"We can't—"

"Oh yes we can." The president stood and walked out.

Sal Molina didn't linger. He went to his office, stirred though his telephone messages, then donned his coat and headed for home. He decided to buy a six-pack on the way, and a pizza. He used his cell phone to order the pizza, which the girl assured him would be ready when he arrived.

When he got to the Pearly Gate, St. Peter might ask, "So how did you spend your last night on earth?"

"Eating a Super Supreme Pizza and drinking three beers, sir. I couldn't think of anything else."

"Did you get the traditional crust?"

"Oh, you bet."

Zhang Ping was on his way to the Chans' restaurant when he passed a convenience store with a telephone kiosk mounted on the wall. America didn't have many of those anymore, not since the dawn of the cell phone age, so it was a rare opportunity. Zhang did a U-turn and went back to the convenience store, which was still open. Yet empty, with only the clerk behind the counter.

Zhang examined the phone mounted on the wall. The receiver was off the hook, dangling at the end of the line. Someone had pried open the coin box, ruining it. Zhang put the receiver on the hook, waited a few seconds, then put it to his ear. No dial tone.

Perhaps there was a telephone in the store.

He went into the store, walked to the cooler and selected a soft drink. Took it to the counter. Saw the phone on the ledge behind. The young male clerk was of mixed race, perhaps a quarter black, with tattoos on his arms and one running up his neck.

Zhang put the soft drink on the counter and reached for his wallet with his right hand.

The clerk picked up the bottle. That was when Zhang reached with his left hand, grabbed a handful of hair and slammed the man's face down onto the counter. With his right hand he delivered a karate chop to the neck. He heard the bones snap.

He pushed the clerk away, and the body fell behind the counter. Taking his time, Zhang Ping walked around the counter, picked up the telephone.

He dialed a number he had memorized six months ago. The call went through.

Ringing. Once, twice . . .

A male voice answered.

This was an unsecure line, yet Zhang threw caution to the wind. He had to know what was happening. The empty streets, the cell phones that didn't work, Choy's disappearance, the massive traffic jams on the exit roads . . .

In about a minute he had it all. The news was out. The rumor that there was a Chinese nuke hidden at the naval base had emptied the town. Mass panic. The authorities were searching.

"Do you have any instructions?" Zhang asked.

"No." That meant that the man had heard nothing from Beijing.

Zhang stood beside his vehicle in the empty parking lot listening to helicopters fly overhead, the low moan of jet engines . . . stood listening and thinking.

If Choy Lee hadn't betrayed him yet, he soon would. That was problem number one. Zhang decided to take care of it first.

He climbed back into his stolen ride, started the motor and headed for the Chans' restaurant.

The lights in the parking lot were still on. Choy's SUV was sitting in front, nose-in to the building., the only vehicle in the lot. Not another car sat in the parking lots of the other storefronts to his right and left. Sally's old Toyota must be parked behind the building. Zhang saw the plywood over the window and the CLOSED sign in the front door, which was undoubtedly locked.

If Choy had called the authorities, this lot would be full of police and government cars. It wasn't, so he hadn't. Perhaps there was still time.

When Choy Lee got to the restaurant, the door was locked. He pounded on it until Sally opened it.

Of all the things he had to say, the only thing he could think of was, "What happened to your window?"

"Someone threw a brick through it." She locked the door behind him and headed for the bar. He trailed along.

"Want a drink?" she asked.

"A beer."

When he had it, he sat down on a stool. Sally sat on another one at the end of the bar with her gin and tonic. The television was on. "Want to tell me about it?" she asked.

He stared at the video. And at the little ribbons with headlines running across the bottom.

"Talk or take your beer and get out," Sally said.

"I'm a spy," he managed.

"I thought you might be."

"Honest to God, I don't know a damned thing about any nuclear weapons. I don't even know if there is one. Or two or three or whatever. I've been watching the harbor, reporting on navy ship movements, since I got here. That's all I did."

"And Zhang?"

"I don't know about him. I thought he was a watcher, too."

"Maybe he's something else," she said, cool as a frosty morning.

"Maybe." He thought about it. His head began to bob up and down. "Yeah, he probably is. I ran out on him while he was tying up the boat this evening. He's making me nervous."

"Don't you think you should call the FBI?"

"Christ, Sally, let's you and me just get the hell outta here."

"How?" She gestured at the television, which was showing a sea of taillights on a highway somewhere.

He sipped at the beer. It was cold and delicious. Sally hadn't touched her drink since he sat down.

"You'd leave all these people here to get murdered by Zhang?"

"You don't know that he'd do that." He smacked the bar with a palm. "Damn, woman, we don't know anything, and if I make that call, you and I won't be able to get out of here, have a life of our own."

"Is that what you want?"

"Yes. I want to marry you. I'm in love with you, in case you haven't noticed." The look on her face softened.

"Lee," she said, "if there is only one chance in a thousand that there is a bomb hidden somewhere, we can't run. You have to call the FBI, and you have to tell them what you know. Help them find Zhang. Unless you do, there is no future for us."

"There won't be one if I do."

She didn't say anything to that.

"Why the hell do you think I haven't already called? I want a future for *us*."

"Do it now. There's the phone, right there on the podium by the door."

He turned to stare at it. He had seen Sally answer it a hundred times, taking reservations. He looked back at her. She was watching him.

"It still works," she said.

He walked over to it, picked up the receiver and got a dial tone. *Better call 911*, he thought. He dialed it. Got only a busy signal. He was going to have to call the FBI, see if anyone was in the office.

"Where's your phone book?" he asked.

She got it from under the bar and brought it over.

As Zhang approached the door to the restaurant, an old car with a bad muffler drove into the parking lot. The windows were down.

"It's another fuckin' chink," the driver said. White guy. Young.

Zhang heard the words but didn't understand them. He saw the shotgun barrel poking out of the rear window. He fell flat and rolled toward the front of his car as the shotgun boomed. The remaining window in the front of the restaurant dissolved into a cloud of glass fragments, most of which went into the place.

Choy Lee and Sally fell on the floor as glass fragments sprayed the room. Sally stayed down, but Choy risked a look through the front-door glass. He got a glimpse of Zhang, and the dark car rolling slowly. Then the shotgun settled on the front door. He ducked as it went off and the glass flew into the restaurant.

"It's Zhang," he told Sally, then grabbed her and ran for the back door.

Zhang Ping was shielded by his car and wouldn't have done anything if the old clunker hadn't stopped and the doors opened. Three guys put their feet out. Only one had a gun.

It was about ten feet to the guy getting out holding the shotgun, a kid with long sloppy hair. Zhang was on him before the boy could get the gun pointed. Jerked it from his hand and used the butt on his throat. The kid went down gurgling with a crushed larynx. He swung the gun onto the driver, another kid, and pulled the trigger. The driver's face instantly turned to a mass of blood as the shotgun boomed. This guy went over backward onto the asphalt.

The other young man who had climbed from the car ran. Zhang pumped the gun to chamber another shell, pointed it at the fleeing man, then lowered it.

He went over to the empty hole in the wall of the restaurant where the window had been and climbed through it.

The lights were still on. No one in sight. He glanced behind the bar, then ran into the kitchen. The rear door was standing open. He paused to pull the shotgun's slide back far enough to check that there was a shell in the chamber. He saw brass. He slammed the slide forward and charged out the door.

Sally's Toyota was in the alley. Now the motor howled, the tires squalled, and it shot forward. Zhang Ping aimed at the driver's window and fired. Not enough lead. He missed. Got the rear passenger window. He jacked the slide and tried again. The gun clicked. Empty.

He ran back through the restaurant with the shotgun in his hand, charged out the door and ran over to the body of the punk who had gotten out of the clunker with it. The kid wasn't dead. He was turning blue and twitching. Had pimples. Maybe eighteen or nineteen. Zhang patted him down, felt more shotgun shells in the kid's jeans. Helped himself. Got five of them, 12-gauge.

Then he jumped into the driver's seat of his stolen car. Took the time to shove three shells into the gun's magazine, racked the slide to chamber a round and put the thing on the passenger seat behind him. In seconds he had the engine running, checked that he would clear the clunker and backed up. Ran over one of the bodies. He felt the bump and ignored it.

Slammed the gearshift into drive and ran over the body again as he accelerated away down the street in the direction the Toyota had taken down the alley.

"So what do you think, Lee?" Sally demanded. "Is Zhang just a watcher? Is there a bomb?"

"Put on your seat belt," Choy shouted. He used his right hand to get his across his lap and latched, then turned right at the first street and stood on the accelerator. He was trying to figure out how to lose Zhang, who he knew to a certainty was coming after them. Choy didn't turn on his headlights; maybe that would help. No traffic on the streets—they raced from the glow of one streetlight to another, running stop signs and red traffic lights.

Sally brushed bits of safety glass from her hair. She had a few cuts on her face from the glass. Apparently none of the birdshot had entered the interior of the car, or if a few pellets had, they hadn't hit them.

"The police station," he roared at Sally over the howl of the motor. "Where is it?"

"I don't know," she replied.

He glanced in the rearview mirror and saw an SUV coming fast under the streetlights. No headlights either.

He took the next left as fast as he dared. The tires squalled.

The helicopter ride to the airport at Naval Base Norfolk took about an hour. From my window I could see interstates and highways due to the ribbon of headlights that filled them. Everyone was apparently going somewhere at five miles per hour. Or less. Whatever illusions I had about the power of the Internet these days, I lost on that ride.

The ramp was littered with parked helicopters. At least a dozen. Two civilian biz jets. Some military ones.

The sailor waiting when the chopper settled onto the ramp led me around all this aviation iron to the base operations building. We entered through the back door and climbed the steps to the main level, and got there just in time to watch through the front glass doors as a black limo pulled up and four men in civilian suits got out of it. A couple of high-ranking officers—they had a lot of gold braid on their sleeves—standing there shook hands and escorted them into the building. Chinese men. Probably the ambassador from the People's Republic, I figured, and some of his flunkies. I remembered learning sometime during the day that the ambassador was coming to prove that China had been maligned on the Internet by evil Americans.

They went along the hallway with the military brass and disappeared into an open door. The room was packed, I found out later, with every politician around, including the mayor of Norfolk and the governor of Virginia, plus assorted congressmen, senators, county officials, sheriffs, police chiefs and folks from the State Department. No wonder the ramp looked like a used-helicopter sales lot.

My sailor led me upstairs and along a hallway to a conference room, which was packed with people huddled around a big table covered with satellite photos, maps and drawings. Grafton was there, along with Admiral McKiernan, a captain or three, a couple of commanders, some warrant officers, people I took to be senior noncoms and a handful of civilians. There wasn't room for anyone else around the table. I stood against the wall and tried to make myself smaller.

I gathered they were figuring out what sectors of the base and harbor had been searched, and planning what to search next. One of the captains was marking up a map with a Magic Marker.

They left the room one by one, striding quickly. Finally there was just Grafton and me left. He motioned me over. Showed me the marked-up map. "What do you think?" he asked.

"Why did you use four colors on this thing?"

He explained the color code. Trust the military to use logic. This search was organized to the hilt.

"Beats the hell out of me," I said, and dropped into a chair.

Grafton fell into another, put his elbow on the table and rested his chin in his hand as he scrutinized the map.

"How come there are no colors out on Willoughby Spit?" I asked. "You going to search it?"

"We are using all our assets to search the base and harbor. Already searched Craney Island, that Corps of Engineers dump across the river. We don't have anything left to do beyond the base perimeter."

"Maybe the Chinese figured that would be the case."

"If it's in a house three miles from here," he mused, "the damage would still be the same."

"How'd they plant it, you think?"

"From a boat." He told me about the *Ocean Holiday*.

"How heavy is it?"

"Figure anything from seven hundred fifty pounds to maybe a thousand."

"So they didn't carry it through the streets to put it into someone's garage or basement."

"Unless they had a truck, probably not."

"Got to have equipment to handle something that heavy. And they didn't climb the seawall carrying the thing and trot across the runway and stuff it into a hangar or down a storm drain."

Grafton frowned and chewed his lower lip.

"I'd concentrate on the harbor bottom," I said, "all the stuff the navy uses to service ships, and the waterfront. As far as I could search."

"We've already done that in the harbor," Grafton said. He picked up the handheld radio from the desk and called several people, issued orders. "Instead of area A, take your people to Willoughby Spit. Start at the tunnel entrance and work east along the waterfront. Get your divers into the water off the beach."

He pulled some more people from another area and sent them south, up the Elizabeth River.

When he had done that, I asked, "How are they going to trigger this thing?"

"That's what the experts have been working on. If the trigger is underwater, it is extremely doubtful if it's a radio signal device. Only the very longest wavelengths will penetrate water."

"Maybe it's got a clock that's ticking," I suggested.

"That option deprives the bomber of any control. Most military minds don't work that way. The guys giving the orders want to be able to change the target, or in this case the timing, right up to the last possible moment. No plan survives contact with the enemy."

"So how *are* they going to do it?" I asked.

"Damned if I know," Jake Grafton admitted.

"I don't know anything about boats," I remarked.

"Neither do I," Grafton said. "Never owned one. Never even spent an afternoon on one. But I've heard guys talking. I was saving boats for my old age."

I couldn't resist. "Maybe it's time."

I don't think he heard me. He was scowling at the map, fingering the handheld radio.

After a bit Admiral McKiernan, another admiral, the CO of the base and Captain Joe Child, the SEAL team commander, came back in to consult the charts and talk to Grafton. More aides and department heads followed. Someone brought coffee. The room got so hot some junior man cranked the windows open.

Grafton and the brass discussed depth finders and fish finders, everyone put in his two cents, and then Grafton caught my eye and the two of us escaped.

The motor roared and the wind shrieked though the shot-up window as Choy Lee drove as fast as he dared through the boulevards and highways eastward toward Point Comfort and tried to think. Not a police car in sight. Zhang Ping had a shotgun. He was going to kill both Choy and Sally, so they couldn't tell the authorities what they knew.

Every few seconds Choy looked in his mirrors. He was still back there, a bit closer perhaps.

A fire station? No one there had weapons. A military base!

The amphibious base at Little Creek was ahead on the left. A mile or two more perhaps. He jerked his ride into a hard left turn, as fast as he dared. The tires squalled. Now right onto Route 60, a four-lane. Passed a couple of cars heading west. Pedal to the metal. The highway angled south and crossed a bridge over an inlet. There, the main gate! He slammed on the brakes to slow for the turn. No cars waiting to get in. The barrier was down. He ran through it, right by a sentry. Smashed the thing to splinters.

Kept going, accelerating, as he checked his mirror. The sentry came running from the booth—Choy hoped he had pushed the alarm—and stood in the road. He was still standing there when Zhang Ping swung his SUV into the lane and hit the man, sent him flying over the vehicle.

A traffic circle loomed ahead. Choy was going too fast. Brakes full on, he went around the thing with all four wheels sliding ... and he was heading back toward Zhang. He swerved the car left and sideswiped Zhang.

Glimpsed Zhang at the wheel at the instant of collision. Fighting the wheel, trying to go straight. But it was over in a flash, and Choy's steed was going off the road toward the right.

Jumped the curb, now going sideways into a tree. Smashed into it on the right side. The engine was still howling, but they were going nowhere. Choy flipped off the ignition as he roared at Sally, who was dazed from the impact, "Out, out, out!"

Both right doors were jammed, as was the driver's door. Sally's door was against the tree. Both rear windows were gone. Choy managed to get Sally out of her seat belt and climbed over the middle to the back. Then he grabbed her and pulled. "Wake up, goddammit, wake up and help or die!"

He risked a glance to his left.

That asshole Zhang was walking across the street with the shotgun in his hands.

Pulling with superhuman strength, Choy got Sally into the rear seat and shoved her headfirst through the right rear window opening. She was coming out of her daze and wriggling, trying to help, maybe.

Choy was pushing her legs through the opening when Zhang shot him in the back from a distance of eight feet.

Choy Lee collapsed.

He didn't hear the siren or see the navy pickup with flashing lights mounted on the cab screech to a halt in the street. The driver bailed out and used the truck-bed wall for a rest. Both arms on it, with pistol in hand.

"Drop the damn gun," the sailor shouted as he tried to align the pistol's sights.

He was aiming it when Zhang got off the first shot. The birdshot struck the sailor in the upper half of his face, putting out both eyes. The man fell backward to the pavement.

Zhang glanced again at Choy, who lay with his face against the right rear door of the Toyota. The shot charge had hit him between the shoulder blades.

Zhang walked, not ran, across the street to the stolen SUV. Reached in and grabbed the iPad.

The shotgun was in his right hand pointing as he approached the pickup, which was still running, with lights flashing and siren moaning. The wounded sailor writhed on the street with his hands on his face. Lots of blood. Near him lay his pistol. Zhang picked it up and stuffed it into his waistband.

Zhang Ping got behind the wheel of the navy truck, tossed the iPad on the passenger seat and put the vehicle in gear. In fifteen seconds he was out the gate and heading west on the empty highway. Only then did he fiddle with the switches on the dash and kill the siren and flashing lights.

It was two in the morning in Norfolk when the Paramount Leader and his lieutenants met with Admiral Wu and the other members of the Central Military Commission at the August 1st Building in Beijing. It was two in the afternoon there. Lots of military brass were also in attendance.

When Admiral Wu got a look at the faces, his misgivings grew exponentially. The Internet storm in America cast a serious cloud. Millions of American fingers were already being pointed at China. In the cold light of day the planned propaganda offensive that would cast the blame for a nuclear explosion at the Norfolk naval base on the American navy looked less and less likely to deflect the inevitable flood of outrage after the blast. "We are going to light a candle in a hurricane," the Paramount Leader remarked, which set the tone for the meeting.

Someone else remarked that the Internet poison from America was already seeping into China, despite the censors' best efforts. American outrage was one thing, but Chinese outrage threatened the party's control *here*. Control of the people of China was the one thing on this earth the people in this room could not afford to lose.

Admiral Wu argued that America would not, could not, go to war with China. Wu understood politics within the military and in Beijing, and he well knew he was betting his career right here, in this meeting. Yet, as he explained, this was China's best chance to change the balance of power in the western Pacific, tilt it in favor of China and her future. The American administration was arguing that the Internet rumors were just that, rumors without substance.

"If the American navy believed there was a threat, they would order their ships to go elsewhere, but they have not," he said. "Two carriers are there, and three carriers more are still planning on tying up in Norfolk, one in about ten hours, and two in a few days."

"But after the bomb explodes and the base and ships are destroyed, the American administration will face a tsunami of public opprobrium," one of the PLA's senior generals argued. "Caution and realpolitik considerations will be washed away in the demand to do *something*!"

"The Americans will not declare war," Admiral Wu stated flatly.

"They don't have to go that far," was the riposte. "An embargo of all imports from or exports to China will damage our economy severely. If the Americans can get Japan, Australia and the European Union to go along, several hundred million people will immediately be out of work. Can our economy withstand such a blow?"

"If we don't explode the weapon, they will eventually find it. That is inevitable."

"We can deny it is ours," someone shot back. "Since no damage was done, they can swallow the denial whole. And probably will."

The Paramount Leader made the decision. He didn't announce it; he merely looked at Admiral Wu and said, "Contact our agent and tell him not to explode the weapon. Tell him to leave the country as quickly as he can."

Blood drained from Wu's face. He said, "Sir, we have a problem. We have been trying to contact the agent for almost eighteen hours, and cannot. The cell phone network in the Norfolk/Virginia Beach area is off the air. Neither telephone calls nor e-mails can be delivered wirelessly. He called his contact via landline several hours ago, but the contact had no instructions for him. Unless and until he calls again, he is not under our control."

CHAPTER TWENTY-FOUR

When they get in trouble they send for the sons of bitches.
—Ernest J. King

Before he went to the marina, Zhang Ping stopped by his apartment and packed a backpack with food, water and a couple of packs of cigarettes. Then he turned off the lights for what he knew would probably be the last time and made sure the door was locked behind him.

Waiting for the carrier due to arrive later today would be about all the risk that could be justified, he thought, given that Sally Chan would probably tell everything she knew. He should have shot her, too. Another mistake. The carrier due on the twentieth, the day after tomorrow, and the one coming in on the twenty-second, two days later, were out of the question.

Yet, he mused, what did Sally Chan know? Whatever Choy told her, but what was that? Choy knew nothing of the bomb, nothing of the ships' schedules, nothing of the triggering device. True, he had seen the iPad hooked up to the boat's radar, but he hadn't said a word about it to Zhang. Could he have figured out what he was seeing?

Zhang didn't think so. The truth was, he didn't want to think so. This mission was going to cost him his life, and he wanted it to be worth his sacrifice. Three of those humongous aircraft carriers, ninety-five thousand tons each, their air wings, their escorts—*three complete battle groups* . . . That would be a *triumph* indeed! Not a victory on the magnitude of five battle groups, but he never expected to get all five. That was just a goal. Like every other goal, merely a target to aim at. It might be achievable in a perfect world, if the stars aligned and the enemy behaved just as he wished and nothing went wrong. However, perfection was rare in human affairs, Zhang knew; he had never expected to sail through without problems. Bagging three battle groups was a more realistic goal, one that would be a severe blow to America. He would be happy with that.

The navy corpsmen who took Sally Chan to the emergency room at the Little Creek dispensary tried to question her, but she had a concussion. The collision with the tree had bounced her head off the passenger's window.

As she lay in the hospital, her memories were jumbled. The brick through the window, Choy Lee, what he had said about Zhang, about watching navy ships, the shots, the chase, the crash . . . it was all jumbled up. She babbled to the nurses, the doctor and the lieutenant commander in charge of base security gathered around her bed.

In truth, even if she had been coherent, it wouldn't have mattered. The bodies lying in the parking lot at the Chans' restaurant had been discovered by people driving by, but landline calls to 911 went unanswered. Even if a dispatcher could have been reached, all the police on the Norfolk/Virginia Beach peninsula were out on the highways trying to salvage an impossible situation and save lives. Anarchy reigned. There had been at least five fatal accidents so far, another ten or twelve with injuries. Medevac helicopters were trying to get injured victims to hospitals in time to save their lives.

People were driving like maniacs: jumping medians, running along the berms and trying to cut back into line, going against traffic on divided highways, basically driving without a lick of sense. How many fender-benders there were no one knew. Blood was flowing. Casualties were trapped in wreckage.

There were no police available to investigate shootings in suburban mall parking lots, no one to put the pieces together, no one whatsoever to check out suspicious characters at local marinas.

Consequently Zhang Ping had no trouble getting the covers off the Boston Whaler, no trouble getting his backpack and iPad aboard, no trouble releasing the lines and getting the Mercury outboards rumbling. He advanced the throttles slowly and eased out of his slip, went down the channel between the slips at idle, then finally cruised slowly along the channel toward Chesapeake Bay without seeing another boat. The night was his.

And a fine night it was, with an overcast that made the moon gauzy. No wind. Temp in the low fifties.

By eleven thirty in the evening he was in the bay and shoved the throttles a bit forward. Well away from the marina, he put the boat on autopilot and hooked up the iPad.

The carrier due in later tomorrow was supposed to dock at one in the afternoon. That meant it would clear Cape Henry some time in midmorning, perhaps about nine or ten. It would be within the blast area by then. Any time after nine or ten.

The trigger had a timer on it. Zhang could set a delay on it by simply programming it into the iPad, up to twenty-four hours.

His fingers hovered over the iPad keyboard. He didn't know if the carrier was going to be on time. Nor did he know if the accompanying ships were going to enter with the carrier or be strung out for hours awaiting tugs to get them into their berths. Nor did he know if the trigger would accept a time delay or merely detonate when the capacitors were fully charged, which took about thirty seconds.

He set the delay for sixteen hours.

Zhang fingered the autopilot, turned it off and advanced the throttles. He examined the GPS display. He was two miles out into the bay.

With the radar going and the scope adjusted, he turned westward, toward the channel that led over the Hampton Roads tunnel. It was seven miles away.

He looked for the radar reflectors that marked either side of the channel. There they were, blossoming on the scope as dots of bright light when the sweeping radar signal illuminated them. They caught the radar beams, concentrated them and reflected them back.

Zhang took a deep breath, then pushed an icon on the screen of the iPad. That would encode the radar's signal being transmitted toward the reflectors. The one on the left, to the north of old Fort Wool, where the tunnel dived under Hampton Roads, that one had a wire leading to the bomb's trigger.

He waited for ten seconds or so, then saw the MESSAGE SENT icon.

Zhang looked at his watch—11:53 P.M. Unless he sent an immediate detonation message in the interim, the bomb would explode at 1553 this afternoon. The battle group should be at the pier or in the estuary by then.

Three battle groups.

A good haul.

Unless it exploded within the next few seconds.

Dying would be ridiculously simple. When it came, there wouldn't be time for a single sensation—not light, heat or concussion, sound, none of that—to register on his brain before he was vaporized and his molecules consumed in the atomic furnace. He would feel nothing. In fact, he would not even know it happened. Nor would any of the other people who were going to die with him in the heart of the detonation. All of them would simply cease to be. Those folks on the edge of the blast zone, however, were going to die hard. Zhang had never allowed himself to think about them.

Zhang Ping waited . . . and waited . . . and waited.

He turned his boat to the north and shoved the throttles forward to the stops. The boat came up on the plane.

Try to catch me now, he thought. *Too late! Too late for you.*

He was abeam the Grandview fishing pier in Hampton when he noticed the moon was gone. The overcast had thickened, and the temperature was dropping. Off Marsh Point, rain began smearing the windshield. He turned on the wipers.

The night was devoid of light. A few lights on boats and flashing lights from lighthouses were all that enlivened the gloom. The cockpit of the Whaler was illuminated dimly by eyebrow and instrument lights, and by the glow of the radar repeater and iPad screen. He adjusted the brightness of all of these.

Zhang steered into the mouth of the York River and started up it. When he had been assigned this mission by Admiral Wu, he and the admiral had discussed the fact that he would have to perish in the blast. After the weapon detonated, there he would be, a lone Chinese man without an escape plan in a country whose language he didn't speak or read. He would be captured quickly. And interrogated. The best that could happen was that he would spend the rest of his life in a cell. Now, with the trigger activated, the thought of running north up the bay as far as he could get in sixteen hours crossed his mind, but he dismissed the thought.

Lights along the banks of the river from houses. This was the town of Poquoson. He buttonhooked around the point and, using the radar, found a creek or inlet on the west side of Plum Tree Island National Wildlife Refuge.

After checking his depth finder to ensure he had enough water under the keel, he put the engines in idle and went forward, released the anchor. He backed down a bit, letting chain out, then killed the engine.

The rain increased. Held by the anchor chain, the boat rocked ever so gently, no doubt as artifacts of the swells that entered the bay from the ocean dissipated themselves in this placid backwater.

All the lights were gone now. Fog. He could feel it on his cheeks. The metal bits and plastic panels of the cockpit became wet to the touch.

He checked the pistol he had taken from the sailor at Little Creek. A Beretta M9. Nine millimeter. Fourteen rounds in the magazine and one in the chamber. He made sure the safety was on and stuck it behind his belt. The shotgun he laid across the empty passenger seat.

His cell phone had a nice charge on it. No service, of course. He plugged it in to charge anyway.

Zhang got a fresh pack of cigarettes from his backpack, opened it and lit one. Smoked it slowly, savoring the smoke.

Dawn was oozing into the fog when Zhang Ping settled down to drink a bottle of water, eat some boiled eggs and listen to the rain patter steadily on the little roof over the cockpit.

The thought that this was his last morning on earth never occurred to him. He felt fully alive, in control, his mission essentially completed. *Successfully.* A man can't ask for more than that from life.

He snuggled deeper into his jacket, sighed contentedly and lit another cigarette. The truth was, he was tired.

When he finished the cigarette, he flipped the butt into the water. He checked to ensure the anchor was holding. It was. He took the shotgun and went below, where he lay down on one of the bunks. Sleep came quickly.

Grafton bought my breakfast at the base cafeteria. Our badges dangling around our necks got us in, and we scooped scrambled eggs, bacon, sausage, potatoes, biscuits and gravy onto plastic trays. Normally I don't eat a lot of carbs and fat, but I had the sneaking premonition this might be my last meal, so what the hell. I figured my robe in the angel choir would cover my tummy bulge.

Apparently a lot of other people felt the same way. The place was packed with sailors, marines and civilians, men and women, and they were loading their trays. After putting mine on a table, I went back for two cups of coffee.

Grafton said little, just forked food. The pile on his tray was more modest than mine. Maybe he planned on being alive tomorrow. If he was, I wanted to know how he hoped to pull off that feat.

I asked, but he wasn't telling. He had a Do Not Disturb look on his face.

I was tired of him and tired of the suspense. "After scattering Anna's ashes, I have been thinking about cremation, but I was hoping to put it off for a few more years," I told him.

Grafton was ignoring me. Outside I could see the fog turning gray. Dawn. Oh boy.

I pushed my tray back when I had eaten all the grub I wanted, which was only about half of what I had taken. My stomach didn't feel right. Maybe I was gonna upchuck.

I was ready for a last cigarette and a blindfold.

I hadn't had a cigarette since the tenth grade. Didn't like that one, way back then. However, the world had turned, not for the better, and now I was ready to give cancer a chance.

About that time Grafton's radio squawked to life. He listened a bit—I couldn't make sense of the words.

He stood and motioned to me. Outside he said, "They've got a dead guy who looks like he's Chinese over at Little Creek. Woman who looks the same way, alive with a concussion. They drove through the gate and somebody shot the guy and one of the sentries. McKiernan is sending a car. He wants me to go look."

We certainly weren't going to fly over there. The fog was so thick you could have sliced it and spread it on toast. I'd never seen anything like it.

With lights and siren going, the driver still took forty-five minutes to make the trip in a gray navy van.

At the Little Creek dispensary, Grafton was taken in to see a woman who said her name was Sally Chan. I trailed along. She spoke English as well as I did. Maybe better. She was distraught over the death of the Chinese man, who she said was named Choy Lee.

The doctor whispered to me that Choy had been shot in the back.

Ms. Chan talked for two or three minutes, then answered a half-dozen questions. Chinese spies, Zhang Ping, a boat.

Grafton got busy talking into his radio.

I went outside. Puked up my breakfast in the grass. I was standing there by the van trying to get my stomach to stop doing flips when the sailor who had driven us, a petty officer, lit a cigarette. I bummed one. He lit it for me.

The sailor wanted to talk. "Boy, these Internet rumors are a real laugh, aren't they?"

"Oh, you bet," I agreed, and puffed on my bummed weed.

"A nuke at the naval base! What a fuckin' crock! I can't figure out how shit like that gets taken seriously."

"Oh, you know," I muttered. The cigarette was making me a little light-headed.

While he yammered on about rumors and crap on the Net, I finished the cigarette right down to the filter and tossed it out onto the asphalt. The fog was the color of wet concrete, and almost the same consistency.

Another car pulled up, and Sal Molina got out. He had a little radio, too. He looked at me and asked, "Where is he?"

"Inside."

Molina disappeared through the door.

"Ms. Chan, this is Sal Molina. He's an aide to the president."

Sally Chan wasn't impressed. "What president?"

"Of the United States."

"That plays golf all the time? That asshole?"

"Yep," Molina said. "That one."

"Oh." She looked at Grafton. "And who are you again?"

"I'm Jake Grafton, interim director of the CIA."

Sally Chan was trying to control her tears. They had told her Choy Lee was dead, and she was trying to handle that and listen to these people, what they had to say.

"You people have been doing a really shitty job," Sally Chan said, and burst into tears.

My mouth tasted like an ashtray smelled. At least it didn't taste of vomit.

The sailor was still running his mouth when the admiral and Molina came out of the dispensary ten minutes later. Grafton motioned to us to mount up. I climbed in the back of the van with Molina, and Grafton climbed in beside the sailor.

He was talking on his radio. "Cart, this shootout occurred a little after ten o'clock last night. Eight hours ago. Chinese guy named Zhang, doesn't speak English. He worked with a guy who was apparently Chinese American, guy named Choy Lee. Choy is dead, shot by Zhang.

"Sally Chan said Zhang bought a boat a while back, four or six weeks ago, a Boston Whaler. Zhang and Choy liked to go fishing. Fished all day, four or five days a week, weather permitting, almost every week."

Unintelligible babble came from the radio.

Jake Grafton motioned for the sailor to roll the van as he considered.

"I think at this point he's probably got a clock ticking on the weapon. A shootout, an abandoned vehicle with a body in it, a dead sailor—this Zhang isn't worried about being caught and prosecuted."

More babble.

"Soon. Probably when that carrier comes into the bay. *Lincoln*."

The sailor was staring at Grafton with his mouth open; the van was sort of on its own. Grafton noticed, let go of the transmit button and said to him, "Drive the van, sailor."

After a few more back-and-forth transmissions, Grafton put the radio in his lap and turned around to face me. "They'll get some choppers and jets searching for this boat when the fog lifts in a few hours. I doubt if they'll find it. He's long gone. Probably triggered the thing and boogied."

"Guess we better find the weapon, huh?"

"Yeah," Grafton said to me. To the driver he said, "Let's drive on the beach. From the edge of the naval reservation here at Little Creek westward."

"That's illegal, sir." The kid had more juice in him than I thought. Of course, exploding a nuclear weapon was also illegal, but I kept that remark to myself.

"Just do it, son," Grafton told him.

Grafton got back on the radio, called for a boat to pick us up off the beach. Looking back on it, I think he probably knew then how the bomb had been triggered and where it might be. Of course, he never made a comment to that effect. Not Jake Grafton.

I glanced at Molina to see how he was taking all this. He was looking out the window beside him, apparently paying no attention. That pissed me off a little. He didn't look to me like he was thinking about all the people who were going to die if the bomb went off; him, me, the winos asleep in the gutters, women, kids, illegals, everyone. All of us. I wanted to slap him. I wanted everyone to get as worried as I was. I wanted to scream.

That's when Molina told Grafton, "The National Security Council decided to turn the cell phones back on here in southeastern Virginia."

Grafton turned his head to stare.

"It's political pressure, Jake," Molina added. "The governor and Congress people are getting crucified."

The admiral didn't say another word to Molina. Got busy telling the sailor driving the van where to go.

I sat there sympathizing with those unhappy voters, who weren't going to be political problems anymore if they were dead.

The boat that picked us up on the beach was a Coast Guard boat. It loomed out of the fog like a ghost. I didn't realize it was there; then it materialized. It had a red inflatable rail around it, a little square white cabin in the middle and a machine gun mounted on a swivel on a post on the bow. They put it almost up on the beach, but not quite, so Grafton and I had to wade out to the thing and climb over the rail.

The guy who helped us aboard was going to be the commandant some-day. He said, "Hello, Admiral," to Grafton and ignored me and Molina.

I was wet from the knees down and in an unpleasant mood. Perhaps the fact that I knew we were all going to hell together in very short order had something to do with it. A man ought to be able to pick those he dies with. I had these damn stumblebums and Jake Grafton.

Grafton and Molina went into the little wheelhouse, and I went forward to where the gunner was sitting on a tiny stool beside his machine gun, which looked like an M-60 and had a belt in the breach.

The sight of that gun made me feel better. We were ready to kill somebody, sure as shooting.

I glanced at the gunner, who looked maybe nineteen. He had on an orange life vest.

"Put a life vest on, buddy," the gunner said. "They're inside."

"Naw. I'm not going swimming."

"I said put on a fuckin' life vest, asshole," the gunner snarled, "or I'll personally throw you over the side."

Everyone was having a bad morning.

I heard the motor throttle down. We drifted up to a thing that stuck out of the water on a wooden piling or post and had some kind of three-dimensional triangular thing on the top of it. The motors of the boat reversed, and we stopped dead right beside it. Jake Grafton came out for a look. He had on an orange vest, too.

The thing on top of the pole had four triangular pieces of metal welded together into a pyramid, which was turned on its side with the open end facing east. Another similar pyramid faced west, and one north. Nothing to the south. Jake Grafton inspected the thing, then made a motion to the helmsman on the other side of the glass, inside the little superstructure.

"What the hell is that?" I asked him.

"Radar reflector," he said. "They mark the channels. Radar waves are reflected back to the emitter, and the reflector appears on a scope as a bright blip." He went back inside. I tried to find a place to sit. Finally I sat on the inflatable edge of the boat. The water was pretty flat, so it was unlikely I'd fall in.

Five minutes later we were stopped at another radar reflector. Grafton examined it and waved the helmsman on.

The fog was getting thinner. The day was moving right along. I looked at my watch. Nine minutes before nine o'clock.

We went westward along the beach, doing all the radar reflectors. They marked obstacles, entrances to channels that went into estuaries where the developers had been busy, fishing piers, etc.

What he was looking for I didn't know. Nor was I curious. I was waiting for the big click. I wasn't going to hear a bang. Just maybe a little click, and I would find myself standing in an anteroom someplace with a whole horde of other folks, waiting for my turn to go up to St. Pete at the podium and go over the list of my sins. I actually had a pretty good list. I'd been a busy boy since I went through puberty. I didn't know if I'd get into heaven, but in my favor was the fact that I bought Girl Scout cookies every year since I got out of law school. I hoped that was in ol' Pete's computer. Sins shriek and virtues whisper. He was more likely to know about the former than the latter. Preachers never talk about how great their congregations are. Nope. They talk about what sinners they are. It's the human condition. Religion, anyway.

The fog was lifting. Visibility was up to at least a mile. We could see the radar reflectors on their pilings from a good ways off. Now the coxswain merely slowed and Jake Grafton stood beside the wheelhouse and looked at the reflector as we went slowly by. Then the coxswain poured the juice to the motors and we roared down to the next one.

I tried to remember any other virtues I might have. Something to tell St. Pete. A dollar or two here and there given to charity. A beer for an alkie. Couldn't remember a single old lady I had ever helped across a street. Virtues . . . virtues . . . I knew I was light in the virtues department, but since I normally didn't think about stuff like this, I didn't realize how desperate the situation was.

Truth is, my mom could have done with a better son.

Zhang Ping was awakened from a sound sleep by the ringing of his cell phone. He heard the noise, had to look around for a moment, perhaps five seconds, until he knew where he was and what he was hearing. He rolled out, dashed up the stairs to the cockpit, picked up the phone and looked at it. Forty-seven missed calls. The phone was ringing now, though.

He turned it on and made a noise. More like a grunt. The fog was lifting a little bit. Several hundred yards visibility here. No wind.

A male voice speaking Chinese said, "Commander Zhang?"

"Yes."

"This is Neptune." Zhang recognized Admiral Wu's voice.

"This is an unsecure line."

"I am aware of that. The decision has been made to abort the mission. I repeat, abort the mission."

Zhang Ping took a very deep breath and exhaled completely before he said, "Code Purple." That meant the device was armed. "I repeat, Code Purple."

The admiral didn't hesitate. "Turn it Green," he said. "Green! Acknowledge." Green meant safety the device.

"I can only try, sir. No promises."

"Yes."

The connection broke. Zhang Ping held the phone in his hand a while, looking at the houses and little boat docks he could see in the diffused sunlight coming from an uncertain overcast sky.

Beijing had chickened out. They had decided not to detonate the device.

They had the right to make that decision, Zhang told himself. After all, it was their bomb, and if it went off, they were going to have to live with the consequences.

He glanced at his watch—9:37

Well, he had plenty of time.

God, what a waste! All the blood and angst, and Beijing *chickened out.*

Maybe he should just ignore Beijing and let the bomb explode. After all, what were they going to do? Court-martial him? *He would be dead.*

But . . . no. He couldn't do that. He was an officer in the PLAN. Obey or die trying.

Zhang Ping got busy. He started the outboard motors, inched forward, put the motors in idle. Then he walked forward along the bow and raised the anchor, pinned it in its bracket. It was muddy, but so what? Once in the cockpit, he backed the boat into the middle of the little estuary, stopped all motion and let the boat drift a bit as he fired up the iPad and connected it to the radar.

He was going to go out into the York, go east and run down the bay toward the naval base, get the radar reflector on the scope, cancel the detonation order . . . then what?

Get out of the country, Admiral Wu said. Right! As if bodies lying all over weren't going to get the Americans in a tizzy.

Zhang went below for a piss and the shotgun. Checked that the pistol was stuck in his belt, got into the seat behind the wheel. The engines were idling, the props motionless.

The Americans had had all morning to hunt for the bomb. If they thought it was armed, they would pay little attention to him in his Boston Whaler . . . but if they didn't know, the Hampton Roads area and lower bay would be heavily patrolled to keep strange craft out. As heavily patrolled as possible in this fog. He would have no chance to get close enough to disarm it.

The truth was that he would probably be dead in a couple of hours, whether the bomb detonated or not; then none of this would matter. Those idiots in Beijing whose courage leaked out through their dicks could face the consequences.

The fog had lifted somewhat, and the visibility was two or three miles, I estimated, when we reached the radar reflector on old Fort Wool, the southernmost terminus of the Hampton Roads tunnel. We cruised up to the radar reflector; Jake Grafton took a look and raised a closed fist. Stop.

I went over for a look. Saw a wire leading up the wooden post to the reflector, and some kind of little antenna sticking up in the middle of the pyramid that faced east, toward Fort Henry and the Atlantic.

"This is it," Grafton announced. The bastard looked happy. He leaned in the open door of the helmsman's domain, told him to anchor here, right here, then came back out on deck. Molina was right there holding onto a wire railing, looking like a tourist in a whorehouse.

"Got a knife, Tommy?"

"Nope."

He turned to the nearest sailor. "Got a knife?"

The sailor produced one, a folding knife with a three-inch blade that looked as if it had been made in China. Grafton handed it to me. "You do the honors. Cut the wire that runs down the pole."

I stood on the inflatable gunnel, then grabbed the pole, as the boat seemed to move away, and started sawing on that wire. Got the insulation off, but the wire looked like copper. Terrific. The knife wasn't very sharp either. I got a grip on one of the reflector's braces with my left hand, wrapped my legs around the pole and sawed away on the wire with my right hand while trying not to fall into the water. If I did, I wouldn't drown because I was wearing my orange life vest.

I heard Grafton on the radio calling for SEALs. Just about the time I got the wire sawed in half, he shouted, "Ten minutes. They'll be here in ten minutes."

The coastie coxswain maneuvered the red inflatable rail back under me, so I stepped down on it and let go of the reflector. I handed the sailor back his knife.

I flopped down beside the machine gun. Maybe we were going to live a bit longer. I tried to analyze how I felt. Damn, I didn't know.

It wasn't even ten minutes, maybe eight, when an inflatable boat roared up containing a couple of guys in wet suits. They had scuba tanks on their backs and flippers on their feet. They put the mouthpieces where they were supposed to go, jumped into the water right by the pole and went straight down. The coxswain moved the boat so they wouldn't surface under it. I was glad that I wasn't a SEAL.

I surveyed the fog bank, now maybe a couple miles away. I could just make out the Hampton end of the tunnel, Newport News. Helicopters were hopping up and down from Chambers Field on base. I could see the two carriers lying beside their piers, and of course the stop-and-go traffic trying to get into the tunnel.

In a moment the SEALs came up, two of them holding a device about the size of a laptop, flippering to keep themselves on the surface. They passed it to Grafton.

"It's the trigger," Grafton said, giving it a good look-over with his glasses in place. The divers had cut the wires. SEALs carry serious knives. Grafton motioned to the SEALs. Down. Find the bomb.

Grafton handed the thing to me. It was waterproof and heavy, at least ten pounds, because it contained batteries and, no doubt, a capacitor. I tried to pass it to Sal Molina, who looked but refused to touch. I gave the thing back to Grafton, who looked as if he were going to get it mounted to display in his office or den.

So we were all going to live, after all.

If there was only one weapon.

The divers came back up and, hanging on to the side of the boat, shouted at Jake Grafton. "The bomb is there. A few rocks had been shoved over it, but when we moved them, there it was."

"What do you need to raise it?"

"Some kind of harbor crane."

The admiral got on the radio. I flaked out by the gunner and gave him an expansive smile.

Oh baby, we were going to live at least until dinner. Unless there was another bomb. Yet I suspected—knew—there was only one. Two doubled the chances that one would be discovered, two were at least twice as hard to plant, and two wouldn't do any more damage than one. After all, a nuke? How big do you want the smoking, radioactive hole to be?

So, after cogitation, I convinced myself there was only one bomb . . . and, by God, here it was with the fuse pulled. Ain't life terrific?

Grafton might have been with me on this. Maybe. But he sent coasties in boats hither and yon to inspect radar reflectors. He got the navy involved, and before long patrol and harbor boats were looking on the Eastern Shore and Hampton and Newport News and up the James and Elizabeth Rivers.

When he finished with his radio, he had the coasties put us ashore on the nearest rock, the breakwater of old Fort Wool, and go off to examine the reflectors in the navy yard. The coasties willingly marooned the three of us: Grafton, Molina and me. Two over-the-hill paper pushers and one young stud looking for an action movie. I gave the gunner his life vest back, shook his hand and sent him on his merry way.

I felt so good that I actually sat on that wet, greasy rock and leaned back and studied the sky. The clouds. The water. Boats and stuff. This being alive was pretty damned great.

I didn't get a chance to talk to Grafton. He was more or less continuously on the radio. Molina ignored me. He took out his phone a time or two, and apparently the last time found he had service. He climbed precariously across rocks until he was well out of my hearing, then dialed. Someone somewhere was apparently willing to talk to him, because I saw his lips moving. Maybe he was just saying the rosary or reciting poetry. I didn't know and I didn't care. I got out my cell phone. It logged right on to the Net. So they had turned it on again. I put in a call to Sarah Houston. She answered it almost immediately.

"Hey, kiddo. It's me. We found the damn thing."

"Oh, *thank God,*" she exclaimed, and I had to agree.

The fog was lifting somewhat as Lieutenant Commander Zhang Ping came south down the bay with the city of Hampton off to his right. He was passing Buckroe Beach when he saw a Coast Guard patrol boat come out of the fog heading northward.

Zhang cut his speed to a few knots, well off the plane. He watched the patrol boat approach. It had a machine gun on a swivel mount in the bow, manned. Another man on the fantail, now walking up the port side by the little wheelhouse. Third man at the wheel.

The boat slowed, and the man amidships shouted something. Zhang waved his arms. The patrol boat slowed and came alongside.

Zhang pulled the Beretta from under his jacket and shot the man on the bow first. The man amidships second. Now the helmsman, right through the glass. Three shots for the helmsman.

The engine of the patrol boat was at idle.

Zhang Ping turned his boat, put it alongside, idled the engines and scrambled aboard carrying the iPad. The Whaler drifted away.

He made sure each man was dead, then checked the machine gun. It had a belt in the breach. He pulled the bolt back and let it go home, chambering a round. Engaged the safety. Then he went into the wheelhouse and added a bit of throttle. Turned the boat slowly to a southerly heading and removed his iPad from its case. Got out the wires. Looked at the radar presentation.

Everything was different from the Boston Whaler. He was going to have to find the radar equipment and trace out the wiring to install the iPad.

No time for that now.

He added throttle and checked the radar presentation. Willoughby Spit was quite plain, as was Fort Wool. Five miles ahead. The reflector at Fort Wool beaconed brightly on the screen. Too brightly. Zhang realized something was wrong, but what?

He had gone no more than a mile when the fog disappeared completely, as if a curtain had risen. He glanced behind him and saw gauzy gray. He had cleared the fog bank.

And he could see everything. The carriers at the naval base, Willoughby Spit, the apartment and condo complexes, the shoreline eastward . . . and heading this way, another aircraft carrier. She had two destroyers in front of her and at least one behind, offset a little to the left. What a fine sight they were, home from the sea.

Now Zhang Ping looked at his watch. Thirty minutes until detonation. He had timed it nicely. The carrier would be almost here by then. The other two would go, the shipyard at Newport News . . . the naval base and all the ships there . . .

Overhead were helicopters, charging along on unknowable errands. Two jets up high—fighters.

More patrol boats near the channel over the Hampton Roads tunnel. They seemed to be along the shoreline, moving slowly.

He aimed for Fort Wool. Saw that a tugboat and a barge with a crane were beside the post that held his radar reflector. All that metal was reflecting radar energy.

So they had found the bomb!

Now they were raising it. There would be no explosion.

Zhang Ping passed Point Comfort on his right. He was only a mile or so from the tugboat and barge, so he eased the throttles back. The channel over the tunnel was empty.

Grafton and Molina stood on the rocks watching the divers hooking the weapon up to cables dangling from the crane prior to raising it. As usual, Grafton was on his radio and Molina on his cell phone. Sitting there beside them trying to eavesdrop on what Molina was telling the big boss in Washington, I saw the Coast Guard patrol boat coming from the north. It was exactly like the one we had ridden in a couple of hours ago, with red inflatable rails, a wheelhouse and a machine gun mounted forward.

Only there were no sailors visible.

I got my Kimber 1911 from my shoulder holster and lay down in the gravel between the stones. Rested the butt of the pistol on a handy rock and watched the boat come. It was slowing.

The patrol boat turned a little and drifted to a stop about seventy-five yards from me, perhaps twenty from the tug, thirty or so from the barge, pointed at the tug. No one on either boat paid any attention to it.

A man came out of the wheelhouse and walked forward. Reached for the handle of the machine gun with his right hand.

That's when I shot him.

The butt of the pistol was resting right on the rock. I had both hands on the grip and a perfect sight picture when I squeezed the trigger . . . He sank down on the deck of the boat.

I kept the pistol steady, ready, in case he got up again and reached for that gun.

Jake Grafton heard the shot and turned to me.

"What happened?"

"I shot a man on that patrol boat."

"Why?"

"He wasn't wearing a life vest."

CHAPTER TWENTY-FIVE

The supreme art of war is to subdue the enemy without fighting.
—Sun Tzu

The president flew down to Norfolk that evening in Marine One. Standing with the Chinese ambassador to the United States, the chief of naval operations, the governor of Virginia and the mayor of Norfolk, he held a press conference with the facade of the Chambers Field ops building as background. I was curious, so I watched some of it. First, he denounced the Internet rumors and resulting panic that had poisoned the public, despite the government's statements that the rumors were groundless. That the rumors had a hard core of fact and the government was telling lies was not mentioned.

He segued on to the bodies scattered around the southwestern Virginia area. "Terrorists have been attempting a major coup," he said, "and we have thwarted them. I wish I could say more, but I do not wish to compromise ongoing investigations or preclude the successful prosecutions of those responsible."

There was more, of course. The message was that it was safe to come home. The governor and mayor got a little mike time, and they confined their remarks to that point.

When it was over and the television lights were extinguished, I sat watching Grafton and Molina with their heads together, talking in low tones. Those two were a pair. If they swore it was Monday, I'd check the calendar before I believed them.

Technicians had been busy all afternoon on the nuke's trigger. The thing was armed and ticking down, they concluded. The iPad on the Coast Guard patrol boat with Zhang Ping's fingerprints all over it had a program that coded a radar transmission. The radar reflector had acted as an antenna and had passed the coded signal via a wire to the trigger resting under the surface of the water, near the weapon, which was essentially buried under loose stones so it couldn't be found with sonar or a quick visual scan from the surface, if the water was actually clear enough to see through.

All in all, the weapon and setup were simple and deadly.

After the press conference, Molina climbed aboard Marine One with the president and they choppered off to Washington. Grafton came over and sat down beside me. I was working on a cup of coffee. "You ready for some dinner?" he asked.

As nutty as it sounds, he got behind the wheel of a navy sedan and away we went, through the main gate and out into the wilderness of Norfolk, all the way to the Chans' Chinese restaurant. The place was practically empty, with only three other couples dining tonight. Sally Chan was behind the counter.

She sat down with us. She didn't look well. It had been a long day, but she said she couldn't stay home. The empty rooms pressed in relentlessly.

"Did you see the president's press conference?" Grafton asked.

She nodded.

"Obviously, you can say anything you want to the press," Grafton said, "but the fact is the government will call you a liar if you say anything that contradicts the president's version of things."

Sally Chan just stared at Grafton. "Our relations with China."

Grafton nodded.

"You people aren't just going to let them get away with all this, are you?" she demanded hotly.

"I don't run the government," Grafton replied, a bit evasively, I thought. "But I hope not."

"Are you really the interim director of the CIA?"

"Yes."

As we ate dinner, Sally talked about Choy Lee. "He thought of himself as an American, there toward the end," she said. "After he became suspicious of Zhang, he was so conflicted."

She chattered on, speaking directly to Jake Grafton, who looked like the father you wished you had had. Nonjudgmental. Understanding. A man you could talk to.

He looked that way, anyhow. And maybe he did understand people, with all their diverse emotions and motivations, strengths and weaknesses. Yet a harder man I have never met. I thought Choy Lee and Zhang Ping were lucky that they were already dead.

Grafton gave Sally a hug as we were leaving. She hugged him back fiercely.

Grafton stayed in Norfolk for a few more days, and I went home the following morning on one of the endless stream of helicopters that plied back and forth between Norfolk and Washington.

Before I left I saw Grafton talking to the CO of the base, Captain Butler Spiers. After a few minutes Grafton shook Spiers' hand, then came over to wish me good-bye.

"Thanks for pulling the trigger on Zhang," he said. "If you had waited a few more seconds, more people would have died."

I didn't say anything to that. If I had shot a coastie, even Grafton couldn't have saved me. The safe course would have been to wait until the guy started squirting bullets. Maybe the truth was I no longer gave a damn about playing it safe. If that were true, I wasn't long for this world.

"How is everything with Spiers?" I asked, because I had to say something.

"He's waiting for the shoe to fall. NSA is doing a study of the Internet traffic that spilled the beans about the possible threat to the base and triggered the panic. They'll have the result in a couple of days. Someone started the rumor, and it won't be that difficult to track down that person."

"It could be anybody," I suggested.

"Oh, no. That was a very tightly held secret. And hot. Smoldering. Someone found it too hot to hold. We'll find out who. See you back at Langley."

We shook hands, and I climbed aboard the giant eggbeater. When it lifted off, Grafton was already out of sight.

Sarah Houston was in her office when I rapped on her door. She let me in, then sat back down and stared at me.

"Did I forget your birthday?" I asked.

"I thought you were soon to be gone. Permanently gone. Now you are back. I am trying to figure out how to deal with that."

"There's no way you rationally can," I admitted.

"I'm beginning to understand that."

"Wanna go get some lunch?"

"Not today. Maybe tomorrow. Or the day after. Ask me then."

"Sure."

I hit the road. Closed the door behind me. Stood in the hallway feeling like dog crap for a minute or so. Perhaps this was a good thing. The truth is I was womaned out. Maybe celibacy would be good for me. At least for a while.

Grafton's executive assistants, Anastasia Roberts and Max Hurley, were glad to see me. They were full of curiosity about what had actually happened in Norfolk, but since it was all classified to the hilt, they didn't ask. And I didn't tell them. We talked about holiday plans.

I stirred through the stuff on my desk, decided I didn't want to deal with any of it and gave myself a meritorious day off.

That afternoon Willie the Wire and I made the rounds of the used car lots. At the third one we visited I fell in love with a 1974 Mercedes 450SL, a hard-top/ragtop convertible, in a pale robin's-egg blue. Willie was appalled.

"That thing is already forty years old, Tommy. Can't you drive somethin' younger than you are?"

"Hey, this baby only has a hundred and forty-two thousand on it. It's just getting broken in."

"That odometer has probably been around the world more times than a hooker on crack," Willie observed.

When the paperwork was finished and signed, I dropped Willie at the lock shop and took my new ride out on the road. I was feeling perky. Headed north, toward Philadelphia.

Didn't actually get into the city. Stopped at a truck stop on the edge of town and bought a postcard of the Liberty Bell. I took it into the little diner where the truck drivers eat and sat at a booth.

Using block letters, I addressed the card to Cuthbert Gordon, Mom's boyfriend, out there in California. I noodled my message for a while, then wrote, "FISH HAS THE CONTRACT." It was doubtful, I thought, that Cuthbert knew of Fish's recent disability. I signed the card "A FRIEND." That was a stretch because ol' Bertie probably never had any friends, but you never know.

I bought a stamp, peeled the thing off its backing using my fingernails, and affixed it to the card. Then I rubbed the front and back of the card on my jeans to smear whatever prints were on there.

After I mailed it, I hit the road back to Washington. I liked the way my new ride handled and resolved to trade cars every ten years, whether I needed to or not.

. . .

When Jake Grafton got back to Langley, he called Sal Molina. "We need to talk," he said. "McKiernan and I want to see the president."

"Maybe you and I ought to visit first."

"Yeah."

"Come over to my house this evening after dinner. We'll have a beer."

"Okay."

So Jake drove to Bethesda and said hello to Mrs. Molina and followed Sal to the basement. When they each had a cold beer in hand, Jake got to it. "We're going to have to do something that teaches the Chinese they can't screw with us."

"Jesus, we're like the Mafia now?"

"The Chinese decided to try to wipe out the Atlantic Fleet's capital ships. They saw an opportunity and leaped for it. The murders and the shootdown of Air Force One were all diversions intended to keep our eyes off the ball. And it was going their way when, for some reason, Zhang decided, or was told, to trigger the bomb with only three carriers in port. Perhaps the Internet storm panicked the people in Beijing."

Molina nodded and sipped beer.

"The question that we can't answer is why Zhang was returning to the radar reflector that he used to trigger the bomb."

"Maybe he wanted to die."

"He could have done that anywhere."

After a bit, Molina said, "Okay. Answer the riddle."

"I think he was probably coming back to safety the thing. I think Beijing changed their minds."

Sal Molina rubbed his forehead and eyes. "Got anything to substantiate that think?"

"There is no other logical explanation. His superiors ordered him back. NSA has a recording of at least one Chinese-language conversation that took place on the cell network that could be the one. Zhang died two and a half hours later."

"Which gets us where?" Molina asked.

"We must convince them that we know that they did it. We know that they intended to kill a couple million Americans and cripple our navy, even if they did change their minds at the last minute. And they had better never try something like this again. Not even think about it."

"How do you propose that we accomplish all that?"

Jake Grafton told him.

. . .

In the days that followed the president's press conference and the arrival of the final two Atlantic Fleet carriers in Norfolk, the world got back to normal, more or less. Most of the people in southeastern Virginia went home, Christmas came and went, the politicians flanged up another deal to raise the federal debt ceiling, and in January three of the carriers and their battle groups sailed away.

Captain Butler Spiers' grandson arrived in the world in the usual manner, more or less on schedule.

He and his wife, Kat, talked repeatedly by telephone in the evenings. Finally he asked her, "Did you send any e-mails telling your friends to evacuate Norfolk?"

She denied it, of course, and he knew she was lying. He knew her. He didn't press it.

The fact of the matter was that he had betrayed his trust by revealing classified information to her. *He* had! At the time he thought he had a good reason, and no doubt he did. And so did every other single person who was entrusted with the secret. Most of them didn't reveal the secret, but he had.

He wondered if the NSA investigation of the e-mail trails would get back to his wife. Perhaps. Or perhaps not.

Regardless, the fact that he had betrayed his trust weighed heavily upon him. Numerous people, twenty at latest count, had died in car wrecks trying to get out of the Norfolk/Virginia Beach area. He hadn't caused the car wrecks, yet still, he wondered if in some small way he wasn't responsible.

It could go either way, Spiers thought. Someone, his boss probably, would call him in and say NSA traced it to your wife, Kat. Or to Ellie or that dweeb Harold. We're going to interrogate them under oath, ask Kat if she got the information from you, ask Ellie and Harold if they got it from you or Kat.

On the other hand, the word would filter down that someone else was the leak. Either way, the bald fact was that he, Captain Butler Spiers, commanding officer of Naval Base Norfolk, had leaked classified information to a person not authorized to have it. If the Chinese agent had been able to read English and had seen and heard the mass panic, he might have detonated the bomb then and there. It was a miracle he didn't. Regardless of who got blamed, Spiers knew he had seen the ghost and failed. As a man and a naval officer.

One evening Butler Spiers sat at home brooding over all this. He drank a Jack Daniel's on the rocks, then went to the basement and found a good piece of rope that he'd used several years ago to tie up his small fishing boat. He stopped in the kitchen, poured one more drink, then went to the garage and got out his big stepladder.

His wife's car was missing, of course, so there was plenty of room in there. He erected the stepladder, climbed up on it and tied the rope to the highest beam he could find. He tied a noose in the rope and let it dangle.

Butler Spiers climbed back down and finished the drink as he eyed the height of the noose. He was going to have to keep his knees up. He put the glass on a little workbench he had against one wall. He climbed the ladder, put the noose around his neck with the knot under his left ear, took a deep breath, remembered his knees and jumped.

He had figured the drop just right. The noose snapped his neck like a dry twig and he died instantly.

CHAPTER TWENTY-SIX

War is very simple, direct and ruthless. It takes a simple, direct, and ruthless man to wage war.

—George S. Patton

In early January, Captain Joe Child was summoned to the Pentagon for a classified briefing. To Child's surprise, the briefing wasn't classified Secret, but Top Secret.

There were at least six admirals in attendance, and the CNO, Admiral Cart McKiernan. The interim DNI was there, along with Jake Grafton, the interim director of the CIA. They sat in the back of the conference room and didn't say a word.

"Captain," the CNO said, "your mission is to sink a ship, the Chinese aircraft carrier *Liaoning.*"

That ship was, Child was told, the former Soviet carrier *Varyag.* After the breakup of the old Soviet Union, Ukraine inherited the *Varyag,* a ski-jump carrier of about fifty-nine thousand tons when fully loaded. But money was impossible for the Ukrainian navy to find, so she was stripped of engines and equipment, and the hulk was finally sold to a Chinese consortium from Macau that intended, they said, to turn her into a floating casino. That didn't happen, but the PLAN got hold of her and decided to rebuild her as a carrier.

The briefer went into all of this at length, then got past the history lesson and discussed the PLAN's first aircraft carrier. "She's operational now, with an air wing and a capability that is superior to anything in the Philippine or Vietnamese navies."

"You want me to sink her?" Child said incredulously.

"Yes."

Joe Child turned to McKiernan, who was sitting off to one side. "Sir, may I ask why?"

"You know about the nuke we found at Norfolk" McKiernan said. "We are going to try to convince the Chinese navy that messing with us is a bad idea, and they'd better not do it again."

Four days later Joe Child was in Pearl watching two high-speed stealth Sealions, being off-loaded from two air force C-5M Super Galaxies. A SEAL team had arrived a day earlier from Naval Air Station North Island in San Diego.

Sealions were experimental stealth commando boats and had never become operational. Each boat measured seventy-one feet long and required two sailors to operate it. Each was a semi-submersible, which meant that once loaded with SEALs and weapons, it could submerge until only the pilothouse, a stealth shape that dispersed radar waves trying to locate it, was above water, and carry its commandos and their weapons into a beach or other landing without the enemy being aware of its presence. Good for about forty knots in calm water and a bit less in an unsettled sea, Sealions were the armored personnel carriers of the naval commandos.

Captain Joe Child was in charge of the operation. The two Sealions were checked and, after necessary minor repairs were accomplished, taken out for night runs in Pearl Harbor. After more repairs and a minor modification to the internal lights, Joe Child pronounced himself satisfied, so the Sealions were loaded aboard USS *Hornet,* a Wasp-class amphibious assault ship.

While this was going on, USS *Utah,* a Virginia-class attack sub, got under way. Roscoe Hanna, still the skipper, was delighted to get the chance to take the boat to sea one more time. The destination was the Yellow Sea, near the Qingdao naval base, home of the Chinese Northern Fleet.

Hanna consulted his charts and fretted over the problem. The Yellow Sea was shallow, and the naval base was at the end of the saltwater equivalent of a saucepan. *Utah*'s job was to make sure that there were no Chinese submarines near the area that might interfere with the SEALs' mission.

Naval intelligence didn't think the Chinese had either acoustic sensors at the mouth of the harbor or submarine nets. The Chinese did, however, have patrol boats equipped with sonar and searchlights, plus small depth bombs that were certainly adequate to kill submerged swimmers if they were detected or suspected, and all the usual machine guns and submachine guns.

"The problem," Hanna explained to his officers, "is that the bottom is damned shallow way out into the Yellow Sea. The Chinese don't think any fool would bring a submarine into water that shallow, and believe me, this fool wouldn't if there were any other way."

"Why don't we just wait until the carrier sails, then torpedo her?" the XO asked.

"Orders. Washington wants demolition charges. SEALs will plant them. Washington wants them detonated under the keel, so the ship can't be raised and repaired."

"Sitting right at the pier?"

"Minimize the loss of life, yet break her back, sink her. That's the mission."

"Who did the Chinese piss off, Captain?"

"Just about everybody who is anybody." Hanna didn't know why Washington wanted the Chinese carrier sunk, but he suspected it had something to do with the recent debacle in Norfolk. No one had ever mentioned that a nuclear weapon had been found there, a fact that was highly classified and would never be confirmed by the United States government. But where there was that much smoke, one suspected there was at least a little fire of some kind.

"People way above our pay grade decided on this mission," Roscoe Hanna told his officers, "so we're going." Orders are orders. Aye aye, sir.

While *Utah* ran across the western Pacific fifteen hundred feet below the surface at twenty-five knots, *Hornet* and her three escorts, all destroyers with guided missiles for protection from Chinese fighters, prepared to get under way.

Already in the East China Sea was an aircraft carrier, USS *United States,* with her battle group. Her aircraft were aloft day and night, around the clock. E-2s, satellites and shipboard radars were watching all the aerial traffic over that ocean, and the ships that sailed those waters. Every plane and ship was assigned a track number and watched. During the day, F/A-18 Hornets did flybys and photographed the ships, and occasionally intercepted aircraft that were thought to be Chinese military.

All this was out of the ordinary, and the admiral in charge of the battle group, Rear Admiral Toad Tarkington, worried that too much vigilance would make the Chinese suspect that something was in the wind. Still, with the recent aggressive moves by the PLAN against a P-8A Poseidon on patrol, and at Scarborough Shoals, maybe this was the expected U.S. reaction. He hoped so, anyway, and kept signing the operations plan.

· · ·

The northern Pacific in January was a stormy ocean, with cold air, clouds, snow or rain, high sea states and low visibility. Many of the sailors on the ships in the small task force centered around *Hornet* became seasick. Captain Joe Child was one of them. He found the endless pitching, rolling and heaving of the amphibious assault ship impossible to endure inside, so he went to the flight deck and found a place behind a mobile crane where he could huddle out of the wind. The cold air and the openness seemed to help somewhat, but the howling wind and snow made even that refuge a miserable place. Finally he went to the doctor and got some pills. Threw them up. The third time he kept them down, and they seemed to help. The nausea stopped.

For the first time in four days, he felt like eating. In the wardroom he ran into the doctor, who asked, "How you doing, Captain?"

"Better, I think. The pills are working."

"I thought I gave you suppositories."

"Pills."

The doctor nodded distractedly, as if trying to remember. "Okay. But I can't remember whether I gave you placebos or the real stuff. You might just be getting used to the ride."

"Thanks, quack."

"We're trying to do our part to keep medical costs down."

Grafton called me in one day and asked if I wanted to go to Singapore. I told him I didn't. He told me why he wanted me to go, so I said, "Sure." As if I had a choice. The brass can send you anywhere on the planet by nodding their heads. Grafton was just being polite. I was just being me.

Singapore. I thought maybe I could stop in California on the way home and visit with Mom for a day or two. I stopped into Sarah's office and popped the question.

"Wanna go to Singapore for a few days? Stop in California on our way back? Meet the family?"

She gave me the eye. "Really?"

"Yeah." We had been dating a little bit, off and on, and sleeping together occasionally, but I was pretty much living with Willie at his place in the bowels of Washington. I was going to have to do something about that one of these days, but I thought Sarah and I should get our relationship figured out first. "Be a chance for us to get to know each other better," I told her.

"This is so damned romantic I can't resist," she said, tossing her forearm across her forehead. "You've swept me off my feet. Okay, I'll go."

So the government sent me and we split the cost of Sarah's airfare. There was an odd penny left over, which I paid so she wouldn't think I was cheap.

We flew to LA, and from there all the way to Singapore. One thing was certain: Sarah and I knew each other a lot better when we staggered off that flying cattle car.

The hotel was everything I hoped for. A monstrous high-rise with a vast atrium, it was over-the-top opulent, perfect for well-heeled embezzlers seeking to get away from it all or Japanese businessmen on generous expense accounts. The rooms were actually two-room suites; the bed was king-sized. We were on the twenty-third floor, and the view out the window took in most of the downtown. If God ever gets out this way, he'll probably stay in this hotel or one like it.

Two days after we arrived, on the morning that Sarah had a visit to the spa scheduled, I went to the city morgue and asked to view a body. I gave them the number of the cold tray. They led me into a meat locker with lots of drawers. They pulled out the drawer with the number that I had given them, and I took a look. Yep. Zoe Kerry. Someone had put a bullet into the side of her head. She didn't look good but corpses rarely do.

Just to be on the safe side, I asked for an ink pad and a couple of sheets of paper. Inked up the tips of her fingers on the right hand, pressed them against both sheets. Thanked the attendant and left. Didn't make a formal identification, didn't ask what they were going to do with the body—none of that.

I took a taxi over to the American embassy and asked for a fellow whose name Jake Grafton had given me. At my request he gave me two envelopes. I put the fingerprints in them, addressed one to Jake Grafton and one to Harry Estep at the FBI. The envelopes would go into the diplomatic bag.

I strolled out of the embassy feeling rather bucked with life. Zoe Kerry had gone on to her reward. I speculated about who might have popped her. The Chinese were the most likely suspects, I thought. She had been in the game for the bucks and knew too much. Loose lips sink ships, or so they say.

After Sarah came out of the spa, we had a leisurely lunch and drank a bottle of wine at a window table in the four-star restaurant on the top floor of the hotel, then went downstairs to spend the afternoon naked in bed. I was just another civil servant on per diem. It's good work if you can get it.

Just after dusk one miserable late January night in the Yellow Sea, the amphibious assault ship *Hornet* opened her rear doors and two Sealions carrying

SEALs backed out of the well. They circled around a time or two, checking systems, then joined into a loose formation and headed west. The coxswains flooded tanks until the decks were below the waterline and only the small, stealthy pilothouses were above water. Above water occasionally, because swells washed over the small pilothouse windows from time to time, obliterating the coxswains' view.

Down and aft, the SEALs in their wet suits tried not to puke. The motion of the semi-submersibles was rather severe. Some of them lost their cookies anyway.

Captain Joe Child was doing okay—no doubt because he took two of the doctor's antinausea pills a half hour before embarking. He too was wearing a wet suit, just in case, but he was not going out unless he had to. He was the commander of this operation, with three encrypted satellite phones available to call just about anyone on the planet, including Admiral Toad Tarkington aboard USS *United States,* the admiral in charge of the *Hornet* task force and headquarters in Pearl and Washington. He knew there was a nuke sub prowling around out here someplace, USS *Utah,* but since she was submerged, he had no way to communicate directly with her. Before he left, however, he had read the latest report from SUBPAC, which said that *Utah* had found no Chinese submarines operating in the area.

The Chinese had been tracking *Hornet*'s little task force with aerial reconnaissance and radar, of course, but the official word, released in South Korea and the States, was that the task force was part of the American contingent in these waters to participate in an annual combined Republic of Korea/U.S. military exercise held at this time every year since the Korean armistice in 1953.

Captain Child and the five SEALs in his boat settled down for the four-hour ride to Qingdao.

The officer in charge of the second boat was Lieutenant Howie Peavy. His team's task was to actually plant the demolition charges under the keel of *Liaoning,* as near the center of the ship as possible. He had four hundred pounds of explosives stored in the bottom of his Sealion, broken down into fifty-pound waterproof bags equipped with electromagnets to hold them in place. No doubt *Liaoning*'s hull was encrusted with barnacles, seaweed and rust, so a conventional magnet wouldn't be able to get a grip. Without some way to attach the charges, the team would need a lot more explosives.

Just in case, Captain Child's Sealion also carried four hundred pounds of demolition charges, which all concerned hoped would not be needed.

Riding just awash, with only the little cockpit above water some of the time, the Sealions pitched and corkscrewed through the sea. The smell of vomit filled the air.

Child stood behind the coxswain in his raised chair to see what he could see. The photonics mast was up to full extension; the picture from that was displayed on a multifunction display in front of the coxswain. There wasn't much to see on the MFD or through the windows—it was really dark out there. Water from every swell washed over the bulletproof glass surrounding the coxswain. The coxswain had electronic help to stay separated from the other Sealion and a GPS to keep him on course. No radar, of course. If a ship or boat should loom out of the night, the ride would get very exciting very quickly.

Child checked his watch for the hundredth time and looked at the GPS presentation and once again took his seat. He tried to relax, to think about the mission and all the myriad of contingencies, which were things that could go wrong.

He leaned his head back and closed his eyes. No good. The boat was writhing like a living beast. So he sat and rode it, just like the six men sitting behind him in the dark.

Waiting is the hard part. Seems like most of life is spent waiting.

What was it the admiral had said? "Your mission is to sink that aircraft carrier. The Chinese will know we did it, so do whatever you must to make that happen and get all your people out. You can't leave anyone behind. We can't give them a live man or a dead body to display to the press. That is of utmost importance."

"SEALs don't leave people behind," Child answered brusquely.

Rear Admiral Hulette "Hurricane" Carter scrutinized his face and nodded. "Do what you have to do to accomplish your mission and bring your people back. Whatever it takes."

"Aye aye, sir."

"Good luck," the admiral said, and shook his hand.

Whatever it takes. God, they were really pissed at the Chinese.

It was about ten in the evening, local time, when the coxswain blew the water from the tanks of Joe Child's Sealion, lifting it from its semi-submerged condition and exposing the full length of the deck. The SEALs opened the hatches and came out on deck. They were wearing black wet suits with a balaclava, and goggles that magnified ambient light or saw in infrared.

In short order they inflated two rubber rafts, called Zodiacs, got them in the water, and began passing weapons to the man in the boat. One of the SEALs went into the water carrying a rope. He swam ten yards to the rocks of the breakwater, the mole, that formed the outer edge of the harbor, climbed up on it and began pulling a loaded Zodiac toward him.

Ten minutes after the Sealion arrived, the SEALs had a Browning .50 caliber machine gun mounted on a tripod on the mole and ammo belts ready. A petty officer manned this gun and Child was his loader and backup. The other four spread out. One carried an M-3 Carl Gustav recoilless rifle, a "Goose," that fired an 84 mm warhead—portable artillery—while his teammate carried a half-dozen warheads and a silenced submachine gun. The other two SEALs carried a .50 caliber Barrett sniper rifle with a starlight scope.

Their job was to keep any Chinese patrol boat that found the other Sealion occupied, if necessary, as a diversion.

Joe Child stood by the machine gun and used binoculars to examine the ships in the harbor, which were lit with night running lights, as usual. The carrier was quite prominent, easily the biggest ship in the harbor. She was about a kilometer away, moored against a long, well-lit quay filled with warehouses and cranes.

Other naval vessels were at other piers—three destroyers, some patrol craft, several supply ships.

Joe Child turned on his portable com device. The screen was backlit, as were the keys. He could type a message and the device would scramble it, then send it in a burst transmission to bounce off a satellite, or he could receive scrambled burst transmissions, which would be unscrambled and displayed in plain English on the screen. Finally, he could just use the device as a conventional handheld radio.

He typed in his message, a mere code word that told all recipients that his team was on station and all was going as planned. He hit the SEND button, which fired it into cyberspace.

Aboard USS *Hornet,* Admiral Hurricane Carter looked at the message on the big computer presentation in the Combat Information Center, and nodded. Aboard USS *United States,* Admiral Toad Tarkington did the same thing. Then both officers asked their aides for another cup of coffee.

Both ships were at Flight Quarters, which meant the flight decks were manned and flight crews were dressed and standing by in their respective ready rooms, ready to fly. *Hornet* had six AH-1Z Viper attack helicopters, sometimes called Zulu Cobras after their SuperCobra parent, armed and ready to launch.

Carter asked his operations officer, "How far are we from Qingdao?"

One hundred twenty nautical miles, he was told.

"Close to a hundred," he said. With a full combat load, the Zulu Cobras would sweat every mile if they had to launch. Carter prayed that they wouldn't be needed.

Aboard the large carrier, sixteen F/A-18 Hornets and two EA-18G Growlers were fueled, armed and ready for engine start. *United States,* call sign Battlestar, was just south of Cheju Island, northeast of Shanghai. Qingdao was within the combat radius of her air wing. Still, she had two tankers on deck, ready to launch if necessary.

Half a world away from the Yellow Sea, in Washington, it was midmorning. At Sal Molina's request, Jake Grafton joined him in the White House Situation Room, which was, appropriately enough, in the basement of the executive mansion. Admiral McKiernan and the marine commandant were there, as well as the chairman of the Joint Chiefs. The president was not in sight.

Jurgen Schulz, the national security adviser and erstwhile Harvard professor, was in a foul mood. He lit on Grafton like a starving mosquito. "*You* talked him into this," he said accusingly, the "him" of course being the president.

"You gotta take your medication every morning," Jake said. "Don't forget those pills." He turned his back on an enraged Schulz and wandered over to the coffeepot.

"Where's the prez?" Grafton whispered to Molina.

"Fund-raising in California. Squeezing in a little golf."

"Great."

Peter Ciliberti, the coxswain of the Sealion that was supposed to deliver the demolition charges to *Liaoning,* informed Howie Peavy that there was a problem. "They got a net around this thing, sir. We can't get any closer."

Lieutenant Peavy looked at the picture from the photonics mast. "We're still, what? A hundred yards away?"

"About that, I think."

"Seen any patrol boats?"

"One. He went by the carrier as we were coming in and went on toward the dry dock off to the north."

"Well, better lift her up so we can open the hatches and get the charges out. If you can put us alongside the net, we'll hop over it."

He and Ciliberti rotated the photonics mast in a 360-degree circle, looking at everything they could see in ambient light, then did it again in infrared. The carrier was tied up sideways to the quay, her bow to the south, Peavy's left, and well lit up. In infrared she had all the usual hot spots, as did most of the ships at pierside, but nothing seemed out of the ordinary, alarming.

Magnifying the image, Peavy could see two machine guns along the rail, one forward, one aft, each manned by one sailor. The guns seemed to be on swivel mounts, so they were probably of a fairly large caliber, the equivalent of a .50 caliber Browning machine gun. The problem was the gunners. He wondered how vigilant they were.

The carrier's masthead and deck lights were behind the gunners, so they couldn't see more than fifty or sixty yards from the ship, he thought. However, there were four lights on cables dangling from the catwalks, hanging down to about twenty feet above the water. Each cast a nice circle of light on the water. If a swimmer came up in one of those circles of light, and the gunner saw him, well . . .

They would have to stay submerged. Or take out the gunners.

"Take us up," Peavy said to Ciliberti, and patted him on the shoulder. "And keep an eye out for that patrol boat."

As the coxswain did his job, Peavy briefed his team: six men in black wet suits, wearing flippers over their dive boots, and LAR V Draeger rebreathers on their backs, so they would not release bubbles of exhaled gases into the water as conventional scuba gear did. The rebreathers used a pure oxygen system and filtered carbon dioxide from the exhaled air.

Up on deck Peavy took another look around. The night was dark as the inside of a coal mine, overcast, cold, with a stiff breeze blowing those swells lapping against the hull of the Sealion. The divers were going to have to work with headlamps to plant the charges. Peavy would need even more light to set the fuses and timer. Using lights was a risk, but as black as the water was under that ship, there was no way they could do the job by feel. The good news, Howie Peavy thought, was that the reduced visibility in the water, probably about two feet, and the spotlights hanging from the catwalks over the water would mean that no one on the surface would see the lights. He hoped.

He slipped into the water inside the net, made sure his rebreathing gear was working properly and reached up for the first fifty-pound demolition charge. It almost drove him to the bottom, but once it was in the water, it became much easier to handle. He turned, sighted on the middle of the carrier, checked his compass and began swimming toward it on the surface, towing the charge. Fifty yards from the carrier, he submerged.

Standing on the mole jutting from the land to form the entrance to the harbor, Captain Joe Child could see the harbor patrol boat making its rounds. He watched it through binoculars. The boat had running and masthead lights and some kind of deck light. He could see at least four men on the thing. One of them was using a large spotlight, playing it across the water randomly. If they found something, it should be obvious, he thought. So he watched.

After that Sealion ride he thought he would never want to sit again, but after ten minutes or so of scanning with the binoculars, he decided he did. He lowered himself to the damp concrete and braced his elbows on his knees, which steadied the binoculars somewhat.

"We have a subsurface contact, Captain," the sonar operator, a first-class petty officer, said to Roscoe Hanna. "Sounds like an attack boat. Relative bearing three-three-zero degrees. Perhaps six thousand yards."

Hanna looked at the computer plot. The contact was on the plot now, but the range was just an estimate, and would be until the contact could be tracked for a while through various bearings.

They were fifty miles east of the Qingdao naval base, running north at three knots. The other boat was heading southeast, in the general direction of the American task force. This close to the Chinese mainland, that was inevitable, perhaps.

"Are we alone?" Hanna asked everyone in the control room. The sonar operators were listening, and all agreed that the submarine at three-three-zero degrees relative was their only contact.

The sea was so shallow, sound bouncing around . . .

"It sounds like a Chinese attack boat, Captain. Nuclear."

"Let's get behind him," the *Utah* skipper said. "We'll let him cross our bows, then we'll fall in behind him." Hanna glanced at his watch. In two or three hours the Sealions would be coming out of Qingdao. "Let's make sure this boat is the only Chinese sub out here, people," Hanna said, "or we're going to be the guys with egg on our faces."

Hanna was assuming the crew of the Chinese boat hadn't yet heard *Utah*. If they had, they wouldn't mosey along as if they were alone for very long. He would soon know.

Swimming underwater towing demolition charges, moving them into position, activating the electromagnets that would hold them in place, all the time working under the vast black bulk of the aircraft carrier—it took tremendous physical exertion from every member of the team.

Peavy had to swim from the bow to the stern, watching his watch, then reverse himself and swim half that time to find the midpoint of the ship's hull. All this took time, yet while he was doing it, other team members were assembling with explosive charges.

The water was as black as the grave under that huge ship. The turbidity of the water prevented any light from the dangling spotlights from reaching the keel. Howie Peavy and his team members used headlamps—they had to. It was absolutely critical that they got all the explosives as close together as possible, and right on the keel, the deepest part of the ship. Determining just where the keel was in that dark, opaque water was a difficult task. The roundness of the hull certainly didn't help, because there was no way to determine exactly where the deepest part was.

Peavy and his team worked until they thought they had it. Every man got a vote, by gesture and light.

When the charges were all placed, Peavy and one other diver began rigging the fuses and timer.

It was the harbor patrol boat that caused the ruckus. Joe Child sat watching it, and was appalled to see that it was coming south working right along the antitorpedo net that had been rigged to protect *Liaoning*.

Of course, the coxswain of Peavy's Sealion saw it coming. Ciliberti had a great view on his photonics display, and if he didn't trust digital magic, he could turn in his seat and look north at the real thing coming his way. Ciliberti had already flooded his tanks and submerged the boat as far as it would go, which was down to the glass of the pilothouse, but the patrol boat was coming lazily on, perhaps at two or three knots, with the spotlight swinging back and forth, back and forth.

He had to do something, so he got his Sealion under way and turned ninety degrees to seaward, to clear the net. Perhaps he could allow the patrol boat to go by, then turn in behind him and join on the net again.

What Ciliberti couldn't do was abandon the SEALs that were now under *Liaoning*. He keyed his portable com unit, which was in a bracket glued to the instrument panel.

"Gold One, this is Blue Two. I have a problem. I'm clearing the net, but this boat is coming down on me."

"Roger," Joe Child acknowledged. The patrol boat was only a hundred yards or so from the Sealion's last position on the net. Child glanced at his watch. The divers had been in the water for over an hour. How much longer before they were ready to be recovered?

"How far?" Child asked the gunner on the Browning, who was holding a laser range finder up to his eye.

"Gonna be about eight hundred meters, sir," the gunner said.

Child used his com unit. "Gold Four, give them a Goose round. Gold Six, use the Barrett on those machine gunners aboard the flattop if they fire a single shot."

Mike clicks were his reply.

Fifteen seconds later, the M-3 spit out its round.

Watching through the binoculars, Joe Child saw the little shaped charge explode on the front left quarter of the patrol boat. The boat began slewing as if it were out of control. No one forward now on the gun. The spotlight wasn't sweeping anymore. That had been an armor-piercing round, one that would kill a medium-sized tank. Child wondered what it had done to the hull of the boat.

Now it straightened out and accelerated. Child could see the bow rise onto the plane. The boat's heading began to wander. The helmsman was probably wounded or dead.

"Hit 'em again," he said on the radio.

This rocket missed. The boat continued on, closing the distance. Captain Child tapped the machine gunner on the shoulder. "Take 'em out."

The machine gun began squirting short bursts. The gunner knew his stuff. Through his binoculars Child could see sparks where bullets were hitting the boat and pieces flying off. On the fifth burst the boat exploded. As the fireball rose into the night sky, illuminating the area around the boat, the wreckage drifted to a stop. The fire quickly went out as the boat sank. The harbor was dark again.

Except on the ships berthed against the piers and quay. Searchlights came on, klaxons wailed, Oriental voices could be heard talking over PA systems. The crews were being called to action stations.

Joe Child wondered how much more time Howie Peavy needed. He wondered how quickly the berthed ships could be gotten to sea. He wondered how many more patrol boats were sitting at a pier, ready to cast off. He wondered if he should alert the admirals in charge of the task forces.

He decided to alert them with a message on his com unit. Typing it would keep him busy doing something productive.

USS *Utah* slid in behind the Chinese hunter-killer sub at about four miles distance. If the Chinese boat was towing a sonar array, Roscoe Hanna didn't want to hit it. Once safely behind the Chinaman, Hanna accelerated a bit to match his speed. A submarine's stern was its dead zone, the sounds behind it hidden by the turning screws and disturbed water of its passing. The boat they were trailing would undoubtedly turn sooner or later to clear his stern, his "baffles," but probably not for a while.

"Any other boats around?"

"No, sir." None had been reported, but Hanna thought it never hurt to ask a direct question and make everyone look again.

Hanna checked the plot. The two subs seemed to be heading for the *Hornet* task group, which was only forty miles away. At ten knots, they would be there in four hours if they held this course. Of course, *Hornet* was moving, too. For whatever it was worth, they were already in *Hornet*'s vicinity.

"How are the sound conditions?" Hanna asked his sonar guru.

"Not good. Too shallow."

The sound conditions would be equally bad for the Chinese boat, Hanna thought.

The clock on the bulkhead was ticking off the minutes. Captain Hanna sat on a stool where he could see the automated plot and waited.

As the SEALs got their demolition charges attached, they went back in pairs for the last ones, until all eight fifty-pound charges were attached under the keel. Then the two superfluous pairs of divers swam back to the

Sealion, which had returned to the net after the passage of the harbor patrol boat.

It was very difficult working in the blackness under the ship, with only ten feet of water between the bottom and the keel, with visibility about a foot. Howie Peavy and his mate, Petty Officer Second Class Macon George, installed the fuses in each charge, attached the timer to the ship, and ensured the clock was working. Peavy was ready to set the timer when George grabbed his arm and motioned that his rebreather was going bad. Together the two men swam upward toward the surface.

They came up right against the hull of the ship. Lights dangling from the catwalk forty feet above lit the surface and dazzled the divers, whose eyes had not adjusted. Still, it was doubtful if anyone on the catwalk was looking straight down at the waterline.

"We can't stay here," Peavy told George. "You stay here, and I'll go back and set the timer. Then we'll share the mouthpiece and swim back together."

A thumbs-up.

Peavy turned and flippered down . . . just in time to feel the whap of a bullet hitting the water near him. Very near.

He grabbed Macon George's feet and dragged him under. George was using his hands to help get under the surface, so the two went down together.

Peavy took a deep breath, passed the mouthpiece to George, who put it in his mouth, spit the water out around the edge, exhaled, took a deep breath and passed it back.

The two men swam back down to the keel—and had to hunt for the damned charges. They had drifted too much toward the stern, Peavy realized, and turned George and swam back along the keel.

Taking turns breathing, they set the timer for thirty minutes. Then Peavy checked his compass, and they swam away underwater in the direction of the Sealion.

The cold water was getting to both men. They were very tired, lethargic.

They couldn't quit. They swam on, holding hands, trading the mouthpiece, checking the compass every few strokes in that dark, cold, wet universe.

Although they didn't know it, the Chinese sailors at the machine guns on the catwalks had opened fire on the surface of the water. They had no target, just sprayed bullets back and forth.

Petty Officer First Class Jack Brumlik was settled in with the Barrett sniper rifle on the mole. He was lying prone. He turned the rifle and aimed at the muzzle flashes. Touched off one of those .50 caliber rounds.

The muzzle flashes stopped. He waited for the starlight scope to adjust, saw the gunner looking wildly about and put the crosshairs on him. Squeezed ever so gently and felt the rifle smack him in the shoulder. When he recovered from the recoil and looked again, the man was not visible.

"The other one," his spotter said. "Shoot him, too."

Jack Brumlik aimed and touched off his weapon. A first-shot hit.

"Let's move," the spotter said urgently. "They'll be shootin' back."

Brumlik scrambled up and grabbed the rifle, and they ran fifty yards along the mole, closer to the Sealion and the machine gun on a tripod.

When Howie Peavy and Macon George got to the net and surfaced, they found the Sealion was fifty feet or so to the north. Holding on to the net, they worked their way along it, then climbed it to the deck.

The hatch was open. Peavy shoved George in, then shouted down, "Count off."

Five men answered. Peavy made six. Plus the coxswain. Peavy took off his rebreather and mask, dropped them through the hatch, then climbed down and dogged the hatch behind him.

"Let's get the hell outta here," he roared at the coxswain, and then counted heads again. Yep, he had everyone.

He went forward and climbed up beside the coxswain. "Message the ship. Give them the code. Mission complete, exiting the area."

"Yes, sir."

Peavy smacked the coxswain on the shoulder, then went aft to check on his men.

Aboard *Hornet* and *United States,* the admirals ordered the ready sorties to launch. The Sealions might need air cover on the trip back to *Hornet.*

Aboard the Sealion that was clearing Qingdao Bay, Howie Peavy looked at his watch. Seven minutes to go.

Meanwhile Captain Joe Child was supervising the reloading of the Zodiacs, then the transfer of the weapons to his ride, the Sealion with coxswain Peter Ciliberti at the helm.

It took a while. Child was about ready to go down the ladder and dog the hatch behind him when the charges under *Liaoning* went off with a thud. He could feel it through the water first, then the air. Not too loud.

He stood mesmerized, watching the carrier tied to the quay through his binoculars. Her lights were still lit. Some water had been squirted aloft, and he could see the cloud of it illuminated by the decklights. Then it dissipated.

Nothing happened. The lights stayed lit.

Child didn't know what to expect. Obviously she wouldn't go down like a torpedoed freighter in an old *Victory at Sea* movie. But shouldn't she be doing something?

Maybe they got the charges in the wrong place. Maybe they didn't use enough explosive. Maybe—

Then he realized the middle of the ship was lower, the bow and stern higher. Slowly, agonizingly slowly, the middle settled and the bow and stern seemed to rise.

Liaoning was only going to do a little bit of that, Child realized, before the middle of the ship hit the bottom mud.

Her keel was broken. She was in two halves.

Child jabbed a fist aloft, went down the ladder and dogged the hatch, and shouted exultantly, "They did it! Broke her back! Let's get the hell outta here, coxs'n."

Child personally typed the success code into his com unit and hit the SEND button.

When he finished, he turned and saw that every man there was grinning widely.

Yessss!

Aboard *Utah,* the sonarman had the audio of his gear on the control room speaker, with the volume turned way down.

It was here that Roscoe Hanna and the control room crew heard a sonar ping from one of the destroyers around *Hornet.* One ping, pause, two pings, pause, two more. Then silence again.

The success signal. That meant the two Sealions were on their way back to *Hornet.*

Hanna glanced again at the plot. The Chinese attack boat was still four miles in front of them, still heading a little south of east toward the *Hornet* task group.

Hanna decided to wait until the Chinese boat heard the oncoming Sealions, which weren't quiet. When the Chinese heard them, they would do something.

Hanna didn't know what, but the unknown sound coming from the direction of Qingdao might tempt the Chinese skipper to take his boat to periscope depth for a look around.

It would be at least an hour before the Sealions were close enough to hear. Roscoe Hanna took a head break.

It was midafternoon in Washington when Rear Admiral Hurricane Carter notified the Pentagon and White House of the success of the SEAL mission. In the White House Situation Room the civilian staffers and bigwigs made a happy noise, then wandered out. Finally only the permanent Situation Room staffers were left . . . and Admiral Cart McKiernan and Jake Grafton. They sat side by side in chairs at the back of the room.

Those two didn't get excited when the news was announced. They wouldn't get excited until the SEALs were back aboard *Hornet.* They wandered over to the coffeepot, helped themselves and inspected the stale doughnut and bagel selection.

McKiernan paused to whack Grafton on the arm with his fist. Grafton gave him a grin. Then each took a chunk of carbohydrates and a cup of sour coffee back to his seat and tried to get comfortable.

Utah heard the Sealions at least ten minutes before the Chinese attack submarine in front of her reacted by turning so her right flank was fully exposed to the noisemakers. Silently, slowing carefully, *Utah* entered a gentle turn so that her bow remained pointed at the Chinese sub, which was heading off to her right. The helmsman kept the turn in. The result was that the angle between their headings increased.

Roscoe Hanna knew precisely what he was going to do. The only thing he worried about was the timing. When? So he waited until the oncoming Sealions were about five miles away at two o'clock relative to him. They were going to cross in front of the Chinese boat, with the closest point of approach being three miles.

"Now," Hanna said, and the sonarman flipped the switch to active pinging. Ping, the sound went out, and returned. The Chinese sub blossomed on the screen. Another ping. And another, regularly. The Chinese sub was pinned.

"Noisemakers," Hanna ordered, and three acoustic bouys were launched from small tubes in the sail. They shot away from *Utah,* then slowed and began making wonderous amounts of noise, noise that would overwhelm the sensitive listening sensors of the Chinese sub, at least for a few moments.

The result of all this, Hanna hoped, was confusion. At the least, he thought the Chinese skipper would forget about the surface contacts he had detected and worry about the origin of all this noise. No doubt it was from another submarine, but where?

"Open outer doors on Tubes One and Two."

The fact that *Utah* was going to shoot two torpedoes had been briefed and rehearsed. Now the sailors went right down the checklist. The torpedoes would travel a buttonhook path so that they approached the Chinese submarine from her beam.

"Fire One."

Everyone in the control room felt the jolt of the big torpedo being ejected.

Ten seconds later, "Fire Two."

The second torpedo went into the water.

Now Hanna ceased pinging and turned his boat to port to present its stern to the Chinese boat and open the distance.

Aboard the Chinese sub, confusion reigned. The active pinging of a subsurface sonar so near had come as a shock to the entire crew. Then the noisemakers.

They knew where the other sub was, or thought they did. But why all the noise?

While the skipper was trying to figure it out, the sonar operator called, "Torpedo running. Active homing. Approaching . . ."

The Chinese sub wasn't even at action stations. The OOD in the control room smacked the collision alarm with his palm and the noise rang in every compartment in the boat.

The captain grabbed the headset from the sonarman. Put one pad against his ear. He could hear the distinctive gurgle of the approaching torpedo. He grabbed the volume knob and turned. The torpedo was close. Seconds from impact. He could hear the pinging of its seeker head.

"Surface," he shouted. "Emergency surface." He tossed the headset back to the sonarman, who flipped a switch to put the audio on the loudspeaker system.

Bedlam in the control room. Everyone shouting and reaching for knobs and buttons as the torpedo closed. The sound of the approaching torpedo was rising in pitch and volume as it sped toward the submarine. The pinging from the seeker came faster and faster as the range diminished.

Then . . . *whump!* A noise like the impact of a huge hammer. The torpedo struck the outside of the boat and didn't explode! The noise from the seeker head and the pump-jet propulsion system fell silent.

But . . .

There was another torpedo in the water! Like the first, it roared in with its pinging head probing for the sub, whining louder and louder.

Whump!

Silence.

Two duds.

Or two practice torpedoes . . .

"Level off at this depth," the captain roared. "Get the boat under control. And where is that Yankee sub?"

While the ocean floor was shallow here, Roscoe Hanna thought he could safely take *Utah* a little deeper, so he had the chief drop her down another hundred feet. Perhaps he would get a bit of help from a thermal layer, if there was one, or a discontinuity in salinity.

A minute passed, then two. "More speed," Hanna told the chief of the boat. "Twenty knots."

"Aye aye, sir. Twenty knots."

The noisemakers had hidden the sound of the practice torpedoes, but he figured he got two hits at the end of running time. And gave the Chinese skipper the thrill of his life.

Hanna turned the boat so he was heading straight for the center of the *Hornet* task group.

Now the Chinese boat went active on its sonar. Ping.

It was turning toward *Utah.*

If the Chinese skipper fires a torpedo, this will be World War III. But he won't, Hanna told himself. *He's been surprised, humiliated, lost a bucket of face, but he won't pull the trigger. I hope.*

"He's accelerating, Captain," sonar reported.

"Range?"

"About five miles, sir."

"Give me a real hard starboard turn, Chief. I want to turn and point our nose right in front of him and go charging in like we're going to ram."

"Yes, sir."

"Start pinging, sonar. I want to go close, but I don't want to trade paint."

"Yes, sir."

The deck tilted as the chief had the helmsman bring *Utah* hard starboard. She came around like an airplane with her planes and rudder biting the water with a fierce grip. Then she straightened out.

"Faster, Chief. Another ten knots, I think."

The Chinese boat was a bit to the left and perhaps fifty feet above them. The distances became stark as the two submarines rushed together, now at a combined speed of almost fifty knots, about sixty miles per hour.

"When we are one mile apart, we turn her, Chief, to port, go down his starboard side. We will fire more noisemakers as we pass."

And that is what they did. They fired three more noisemakers as they were abeam the Chinese sub, then hit the turbulence she had left in her wake. The boat bucked and writhed. No doubt the Chinese sailors were also getting bounced around in *Utah*'s wake.

"Passive on the sonar," Roscoe Hanna said. "Turn us to the south, Chief, and let's get the hell out of here as fast as we can go."

When the four Zulu Cobras from *Hornet* rendezvoused with the eastbound Sealions, two sections of F/A-18 Hornets were already overhead. The helicopters were under the overcast, flying at about one thousand feet. Their position lights twinkled in the vast darkness over the night sea.

Above the overcast, the fighters were probing the night with their radars while being illuminated by Chinese search radars. The pilots could hear the baritone tones as the radar beams swept over them. This information was datalinked to an E-2 Hawkeye in an orbit at thirty thousand feet over *United States,* and from there passed to the Combat Information Center and Flag Plot aboard the ship. From there it went by satellite to the White House Situation Room, where Cart McKiernan and Jake Grafton were watching.

Real-time text messages from Captain Joe Child and Lieutenant Howie Peavy scrolled across one of the large projection screens. The SEAL raid had been a success; all the men were coming out; they had egressed after sinking a harbor patrol boat and taking out several machine gunners aboard *Liaoning.*

"A nice job," the CNO muttered. At the duty desk, one of the officers was on the telephone, no doubt briefing Sal Molina.

Grafton and the admiral watched as two bogeys climbed away from an airfield near the Qingdao naval base in real time, rendezvoused and headed out to sea, eastbound and climbing.

McKiernan looked at his watch. "The SEALs cracked that keel two and a half hours ago. Since then the PLAN has been trying to figure out what happened and what to do about it."

These two had discussed all this, of course, before they went to see the president for approval of the SEAL raid. "The Chinese will be surprised, embarrassed and probably outraged," Grafton argued, "yet they won't shoot unless they are fired upon. No Chinese officer is going to take the responsibility for starting World War III."

"You hope," Jurgen Schulz glowered.

The secretary of state, Owen Lancaster, cleared his throat. He was a white-haired Brahmin who had been helping hold up the New England end of the establishment for at least fifty years. Although no one knew how he voted, if he did, he had been routinely appointed to key ambassadorships by thirty years' worth of presidents. This president had elevated him to run the State Department, to the relief of a great many Americans who expected another party hack.

Lancaster was no fan of Jake Grafton, with whom he had crossed swords several times in the past. Still, he eyed McKiernan and Grafton carefully, then spoke to the president. "The Chinese need to be taught a lesson. That bomb in Norfolk was a gambit approved at the very top. We can't let it pass. If we do, sooner or later we will be in a shooting war in the Far East or we will be run out of there with our tails between our legs. We must make our choice now. Tomorrow will be too late."

The president deferred to Lancaster. "Do it," he told Cart McKiernan.

So Grafton and McKiernan had gotten their permission. Now they sat in the back row of the White House Situation Room watching jets rush together over the Yellow Sea and hoped they had correctly predicted the Chinese reaction.

Yet neither man was really worried. Even if some Chinese pilot opened fire, he would quickly go into the sea, and cooler heads would prevail in Beijing. Political provocations are wonderful PR for the home folks, but when one encounters naked steel, it is time to reassess. Are you ready to fight?

The two American sections of Hornets, two fighters in each section, turned so that the Chinese formation went between them; then they turned hard to come in at an angle from each side, a classic rendezvous. But as the Chinese pilots knew, the Americans were in their rear quadrant pulling lead. If the Americans chose to shoot, they were perfectly set up for it.

The flight leader reported that the Chinese jets had their external lights on, as the American fighters did. Rear Admiral Toad Tarkington passed that comment on to Washington immediately, and both McKiernan and Grafton relaxed a bit when they heard it. The Chinese pilots had not been sent to shoot down an American plane or two. If they had, they would have never let the Americans get into a firing position.

McKiernan slapped Grafton on the shoulder again and dug a pack of chewing gum out of his pocket.

When the last of the helicopters and fighters were back aboard ship and *Hornet* had recovered her two Sealions, McKiernan and Grafton stood, stretched and strolled out of the Situation Room. They met Sal Molina coming in.

"We're going over to the Willard for steaks and drinks," Grafton told the president's man. "You want to come along?"

He did. Late that night the Willard valet at the door hailed taxis to take all three men home.

CHAPTER TWENTY-SEVEN

If we desire to avoid insult, we must be able to repel it; if we desire to secure peace, one of the most powerful instruments of our rising prosperity, it must be known that we are at all times ready for War.

—George Washington

Not a word of the events in Qingdao harbor or the Yellow Sea that January night ever made it into print, the Internet, or broadcast radio or television. It was as if *Liaoning* were still afloat. Satellite reconnaissance showed that she probably wasn't.

Three days after the event, the Chinese ambassador, who spoke excellent English, called on the State Department to deliver a note from the Chinese government. He was ushered into the office of the secretary, Owen Lancaster.

"Before you deliver your note, sir, I have something to show you," Lancaster said. "Then, perhaps, you and I can have a private, off-the-record discussion."

Lancaster's limo was waiting. Without a word being said, the driver headed for Joint Base Andrews, the air force side. The limo was waved through toward a hangar surrounded by air force MPs wearing helmets and sidearms and carrying assault rifles. Some of them had dogs on leashes.

A colonel escorted Lancaster and his guest into the hangar, which was empty except for a bomb dolly in the middle of the thing. The colonel let Lancaster and the ambassador proceed alone. Lancaster stopped beside the bomb dolly.

"This, Mr. Ambassador, is a Chinese nuclear weapon. It was recovered from the Norfolk naval base, where it was submerged near the entrance to the harbor."

"Mr. Secretary, I am unfamiliar with weapons. I have never even seen one. I have no idea what nation produced this one, if it is indeed a weapon."

"Your government has been less than forthright with you, sir," Lancaster said. "This weapon was armed and within two hours of detonating when it was found. You were there in Norfolk, sir, and had it exploded, you would now be dead, along with several million Americans."

"I repeat, sir—"

"Don't bother," Lancaster said, holding up his hand. "I feel somewhat certain that you called today at the State Department to lodge a protest about the sabotage of your aircraft carrier, *Liaoning,* at the Qingdao naval base, several days ago. Rest assured, sir, that the United States government knows no more about that incident than the government of the People's Republic knows about this weapon you see before you."

The Chinese ambassador said nothing.

Lancaster continued. "However, it must be said, unofficially and off the record, privately from me to you, that certain people in our government thought it would be fitting and proper for this weapon, made in China, to be returned to China, placed under *Liaoning,* and detonated." Lancaster made a gesture. "Although I know nothing about any of this, I assume that since I have not heard about a nuclear detonation in China, and since the weapon is physically right before us, such counsel was wisely rejected."

"Quite so," said the ambassador, who felt called upon to wipe his forehead.

"Unless you wish to take a photo or inspect the weapon more closely, I suggest we return to my office, where you can present your note."

But when they returned to Foggy Bottom, the ambassador decided not to present the note.

A week after the *Liaoning* incident, the Chinese government made a routine announcement: A new officer had been named head of the PLAN. What had happened to Admiral Wu wasn't mentioned, but intelligence agencies later learned that he was arrested on the order of the Paramount Leader, shot and quietly buried.

Sarah Houston and I flew home across the big pond. The truth is I was sort of tuckered out from all the vacationing. I have never had all the sex I wanted, but when we boarded the plane in Singapore I was perilously close to having had all I could stand. And I was kinda almost in love with Sarah Houston.

I had been really in love once before with Anna Modin, and I knew the signs. I was having a devil of a time keeping my eyes off Sarah. Just looking at her and hearing her voice delighted me. It wasn't love yet, but maybe in time it might be. Anna was still a living presence with me, but she was gone . . . forever. Life is for the living. Somehow I was going to have to get my head around those realities. Someday.

We got off the plane in San Francisco exhausted and jet-lagged to the max, retrieved our luggage, signed out a rental car and set forth upon the highways. Sarah got busy with her cell phone as I drove. After a while she announced, "The president nominated Jake Grafton for director of the CIA. Sent his name to the Senate."

We rode along silently, each of us thinking about that. We talked about what Grafton might have each of us doing.

Mom seemed to like Sarah. She wanted to know all about Singapore, so we told her some lies. In fact, we hadn't seen much of it outside the hotel. I didn't mention the morgue.

"I've got a new boyfriend," Mom announced. "He'll be here for dinner, in about an hour, to meet you, Tommy, and of course Sarah."

I tried to be casual. "What happened to the old one, Bertie What's His Name?"

"We broke up right after you were here the last time, Tommy."

"Oh," I managed.

"Then he left a week or so ago, moved away apparently. They haven't seen him at the country club." She shrugged. "I hope he wasn't devastated by the breakup, but these things happen."

Sarah nodded sagely, and I said "Oh" again.

When I had recovered a bit, I said, as casually as I could, "So tell us about the new guy."

"You'll like him," she assured me. "He is reasonably good-looking, athletic and very talented. Extraordinarily so."

"Talented at what?"

"He's a body artist," Mom told us, as if it were a secret.

A vision of some kinky sex thing flashed before my eyes. After all, I knew my mother. But maybe I was going too fast. "What's a body artist?" I asked.

"He does tattoos," Sarah told me with her eyebrows up.

I gave Mom my best lying grin. "I hope it works out for you," I said. Sarah patted my arm.

— BETTY —

A GLAD AWAKENING

Betty Ford

WITH CHRIS CHASE

G.K. HALL & CO.
Boston, Massachusetts
1988

With gratitude and love to my family,
who were there when I needed them.

Published in Large Print by arrangement with
Doubleday & Company, Inc.

G.K. Hall Large Print Book Series.

Set in 18 pt. Plantin.

Library of Congress Cataloging in Publication Data

Ford, Betty, 1918–
    Betty, a glad awakening / Betty Ford with Chris Chase.
      p. cm.—(G.K. Hall large print book series)
    ISBN 0-8161-4397-8 (lg. print)
    1. Ford, Betty, 1918– . 2. Ford, Gerald R., 1913– —Family.
3. Presidents—United States—Wives—Biography. 4. Alchololics—
United States—Biography. 5. Large type books. I. Chase. Chris.
II. Title
[E867.F657 1988]
973.925'092'4—dc 19   87-32144

And, through and over everything,
A sense of glad awakening.
Edna St. Vincent Millay

ACKNOWLEDGMENTS

I want to thank all my friends, especially those who contributed so much to this book: Leonard and Nicky Firestone, Meri Bell and Dell Sharbutt, Pat Benedict, Clara Powell, Muriel Zink, Dolores and Bob Hope, Ed and Helen Johnsen, John and Joan Sinn, Bob Barrett, Sheika Gramshammer, Jim and Joan Kemper, Paul and Mary Jane Jenkins and Wallis Annenberg.

I want to thank the many groups who have shared with me in my recovery: the women from Laguna Beach who were there in the beginning, the members of the Eisenhower Medical Center Auxiliary who help us at the Betty Ford Center and also with the Alcohol Awareness Hour and also, those special friends from the Coachella Valley, Denver and Vail.

I want to thank the physicians, clergymen and others who, working in the field of alcoholism and drug addiction, helped me to understand this disease. Among them are Dan Anderson, Vern Johnson, Joe Cruse, Joe Pursch, LaClaire Bissell, Father Joe Martin, Sheila Blume, Stan Gitlow, Max

Schneider, Bob Niven, Ian MacDonald, Stephanie Covington and Joe Takamine.

I want to thank the Board of Directors of the Betty Ford Center, John Schwarzlose, our executive director, Jim West, our medical director, and all of our able and dedicated staff at the Betty Ford Center.

And special thanks to John Sinn, President of Eisenhower Medical Center. Throughout the years, he has been my strong advisor, always available and willing.

I want to thank Chris Chase, whose talent and patience allowed us to collaborate so effectively.

Additional thanks go to Loretta Barrett of Doubleday, whose encouragement and enthusiasm convinced me the time was right for this book.

I want to thank Ann Cullen, my assistant. She has provided a sounding board, she has shared with me good, bad and indifferent moments and has been like a member of my family and, most of all, she is my friend.

I want to thank my brother, Bill Bloomer, and his wife, Betty, for helping me know how pleasant it is to share memories with a sibling.

And once again, I want to thank my family—Jerry, Mike and Gayle, Jack, Steve, Susan and Chuck—for their love.

AUTHORS' NOTE

Where names of real people have been used, those people have given us permission.

All other individuals are composites. Physical characteristics, and details of the stories of doctors, nurses, patients, patients' families and friends at Long Beach, the Betty Ford Center, group meetings, etc., have been altered in order to protect their privacy.

But in this world another hope keeps
    springing
In an unexpected place . . .
      T. S. Eliot, *The Family Reunion*

When I was in treatment at Long Beach, the naval hospital where I went to get clean and sober, I was required to write what they called an autobiography—a few pages was all the therapists wanted—detailing where I had gone off the track.

I could not do it.

I suppose I was so wrapped up in the image I had been presenting to the public that I didn't see anything wrong with my life. I was married to the perfect man, I had four perfect children, I had a new house and, after thirty years of married life, all new furniture. As far as I was concerned, everything was going along just fine, and I didn't know why these therapists should be suggesting anything different.

It seems quite clear now that I did not want to open the closet door, and have everything tumble out. You can't deal with

everything coming at you all at once. You're afraid you'll be overwhelmed, maybe drink or use again, maybe even take your own life in your desperation to escape.

You know something's wrong, but you say it's all fine. My friend Muriel Zink describes this as "honest self-deception."

You face what you're able to face, and more is revealed to you when you can handle the revelations.

In Long Beach, I couldn't handle much, and certainly I could not write the truth.

Now here I am embarking on a different kind of autobiography, and I'm not sure I can write this one either.

"What is she *talking* about?" you're saying. "She *wrote* one autobiography, didn't she?"

Yes, she did. Let me explain. *The Times of My Life*, published after my husband and I left the White House, was not—except for one chapter added at the last minute—about my drinking or my pill taking. There was a lot of "honest self-deception" in it, though there was a lot of truth too. But basically, it was the story of a girl from Grand Rapids, Michigan, and her marriage to a man who later became the thirty-eighth President of the United States.

I know more about that girl now, and I know what I want to do with this new book. And what I don't want to do. I don't want to write what we alcoholics call war stories. Testimonials to the horrors of drinking. You listen to some of them, and you think: My God, if my life was like that, I'd drink too.

This book is going to be about recovery, mine and other people's. And how recovery works and how sometimes it doesn't. I would like it to be funny, not sad, and I would like anyone who reads it to understand that while I know something about alcoholism, I am no authority on the subject. I can't tell anyone how to get well. I can only carry the message about how it was for me, and the things that helped *me* to get well.

At first, I wasn't willing to share these things except in groups of other alcoholics. The idea of leaping into print bothered me. I have a husband who supports me, and I didn't choose to make money out of my recovery. That would be counterproductive to the program I live by, a program that says, if you want to keep it, you have to give it away.

Then I realized that was no problem. I give away the fees I'm paid for making speeches about alcohol and drug addiction—

they go to help support the Betty Ford Center and other treatment centers—and I could do the same with any monies from a book.

What was more, a book could reach so much further than my voice in a speech, or my words in a letter.

At Long Beach, I got sacks of letters asking for help. This person had lost his faith, that one had been brought down by drugs, alcohol, depression, illness,

At the time, I didn't know how to answer them. I had to get home before I could write and say, see your clergyman, go to your local council on drugs and alcohol, find a support group.

It was general advice, and there was nothing wrong with it. But what I didn't understand then, and do understand now, is that there is joy in recovery, and in helping others discover that joy.

Sometimes I'm asked if I feel I have a mission. I don't. I'm not that presumptuous. I don't think God looked down and said, "Here's Betty Bloomer, we're going to use her to sober up alcoholics." But I do think people relate to someone who has the same problems they have, and who overcomes them. And I think God has allowed me— along with thousands of others—to carry a

message, a message that says, there's help out there, and you too can be a survivor. Look at us. Look at me.

Since my survival has often depended on others, there will be other voices heard here. I am going to turn to family and friends for help in reconstructing this journey of recovery. Some of them saw me more clearly than I saw myself, and all of them loved me until I could love myself.

1

I will lift up mine eyes unto the hills,
from whence cometh my help.

Psalms 121

There are mountains all around the Betty
Ford Center, blue-gray in the distance, massive and enduring. Once in a while even a
patient who doesn't believe in God will admit that if you look at those mountains long
enough, you start to suspect there's something out there greater than you, you're filled
with a sense of wonder.

Wonder is what I was feeling on October 3, 1982, the day we dedicated the Betty
Ford Center.

There was the 15th Air Force Band from
March Air Force Base, and the U.S. Army
Chorale, and a tent for the invited guests. It
was a huge tent that held four hundred people. And the sun was shining, and there
were buildings waiting for our first patients,

and all I could think was, three recovering alcoholics did this. Joe Cruse, Leonard Firestone and Betty Ford built this out of Joe's dream, and a patch of desert.

We didn't do it alone, but we did it.

I took a lot of teasing on Dedication Day.

When Leonard Firestone got up from his seat on the dais to make his little speech, he accused me of being a slave driver. "I remember early on," he said, "she called me about every day. 'Have you done this? Have you done that? Have you followed up on this?' And I think it may have been after the second or third call one day, I said, 'Dammit, Betty, I'm doing the best I can.' I thought that might get her off me, but it didn't."

Then Leonard turned to Jerry. "Mr. President," he said, "you're damn lucky you're not an alcoholic!"

Vice President George Bush razzed me too. He said my assistant had told him I was a busybody, and that "not long ago, when this building was still a skeleton of girders and beams, she saw Betty out here thrashing around wearing a hard hat, and if that day Betty had not only inspected the place, but tightened a few bolts and welded three or four joints, no one would have been the least bit surprised."

I guess it's okay, as long as he didn't say *smoked* a few joints. After all, we're talking about a rehab center.

Bob Hope stood there in front of the very patrons and benefactors I'd been soliciting for cash, and accused me of having had my hands out "palms up for the last two years.
. . . She's extracted so much money from people around here that next year she's going to be poster girl for the IRS."

In her speech, Dolores Hope, chairman of the board of Eisenhower Medical Center (the Betty Ford Center is a corporate part of Eisenhower), was not respectful either. But she pronounced herself impressed. "I did not see this facility until today," Dolores said, "and I can't believe anything this good could have been done without me."

My husband wasn't funny. My husband, who, when I told him he would be very important in this book, said, "No, I'm just a minor character," told the audience that he was speaking for our kids and our grandchildren as well as himself. He said, "We're proud of you, Mom . . . we want you to know that we love you." And when he talked about my recovery, he broke. He'd only done that in public one other time, after my

mastectomy, as he'd faced the press and said I was okay, that I would be okay.

Ask people who were there what they remember best about the Dedication of the Betty Ford Center, and most of them say Jerry.

"Your dear little husband cried," Dolores Hope says, ignoring the fact that my dear little husband is over six feet tall. "His dear little eyes filled up, and oh, God, it really knocked us out. It was beautiful, and we went to the Dedication dinner, and talked about it."

My son Steve says, "My strongest memory of the day is how proud Dad was when he got up there. He talked about you, and he fought back tears, and I just saw the love between you."

Steve remembers that I looked loving, John Sinn, President of the Board of Eisenhower Medical Center, remembers that I looked anxious. They are both right. John Schwarzlose, the executive director for the Center, reminds me that I sat on the dais between Dolores Hope and George Bush, "and everybody was watching you, and twice, President Ford started to choke up when he was talking. I don't think most people were aware of

how much the day meant to him because it meant so much to you."

Joe Pursch (the doctor in charge of Long Beach during my stay there) agrees that many listening to Jerry "felt a tug at the throat." Dr. Pursch says he was also touched by the miracle that "this thing was really happening." He compares helping alcoholics to delivering babies. "A baby is trapped in the mother's body, very isolated, and an alcoholic who is still drinking is imprisoned in kind of the same way—in the apartment, lights low, phone off the hook, television on, but not watching, cigarette in one hand, drink in the other, and that's the whole world. In either case, delivering a baby, or helping an alcoholic stop drinking, you're in at the creation of a new life."

Dr. Pursch saw the Dedication as a portent of marvels to come. "The media were there," he says. "The Vice President of the United States was there, so it was all out in the open, it was laying the foundation for a place that would deliver many babies."

Our friend Ed Johnsen, a builder who's on our board of directors, says for him, also, Jerry's speech was "the most significant. He just stood there and offered a tribute from the heart."

5

Meri Bell Sharbutt, my teacher and guide since Long Beach—she is thirty years sober—was experiencing mixed emotions. "I saw the first slabs of cement in this thing," she says. "I saw the first plans when it had no name, it was just a vision of Joe Cruse. And then you got well, recovered, and you gave your permission to call it the Betty Ford Center. And I sat there at the Dedication wondering: Are you strong enough to withstand the onslaughts of people from every side? People who would be thinking of the Betty Ford Center as an extension of your sobriety? Or as an aggrandizement of your sobriety?"

Meri Bell knows the dangers of arrogance. A priest once said, "Meri Bell has humility, and she's proud of it," and Meri Bell says that, for six months, she thought that was a compliment.

It's even worse when you're in the public eye. People crowd around you and ask for advice and tell you you're wonderful, and you can easily build up a false sense of your own importance. Which is why, at Long Beach, Joe Pursch had put me in a room with three other patients, instead of giving me the private room I'd demanded. Right off, he was telling me, hey, lady, you may

have been the wife of a President, but in here, you're nothing special.

My son Jack says the Dedication was less of a high to him than to "some of the people there who had been involved with the project. Because to me, the real victory was what had happened with Mother."

For several of my colleagues at the Center, the Dedication wasn't such a big deal either. Our opening, next morning, was what they were pointed toward.

"The staff was geared up, looking forward to Monday, and the first patients arriving," John Schwarzlose says. "So for us, it was like, well, it's an honor to be at the Dedication, but just wait till tomorrow."

Dr. Joseph Cruse, our founding medical director, says he was thinking that "we'd come a long way. The actual floor plans for the Betty Ford Center are from some slides I made in 1966, when I wanted to build a cancer hospital where the families could live with the patient. And I came to California drinking, with this dream.

"For somebody who had wandered up and down Wilshire Boulevard with a hip flask in one pocket and a letter from President Eisenhower in the other (the letter said what a good idea a live-in cancer hospital was), try-

ing to raise money and drinking every night, this was quite a culmination."

For me, too.

Good Morning America was there, shooting a special segment, and my assistant, my right arm, Ann Cullen, was standing at the back of the tent with David Hartman's producer, pointing out notables. "That's so-and-so, you might want to talk to him. Or her. Or them."

Of my children, only Jack and Steve, the California contingent, came to the Dedication. The two from the East didn't make it, they didn't want to travel so far just to take part in a packed-with-people weekend. They won't come when we have a golf tournament either, because we're too busy running the tournament to talk to them. Susan and Mike said they'd visit when the Dedication was over, and we'd have more time together.

More time. It's a family joke. Jerry and I used to drive past when they were building the Betty Ford Center, and I'd say, "I'll be so glad when we get it up and open, because then I'll be free."

I couldn't imagine how seductive the Center would be for me, how much of my life it would take over.

At the Dedication, I had to speak, and I was scared. George Bush introduced me, and

I tried to say a little about how I had felt coming home after treatment to the desert, to the serenity of these mountains that I loved. And I thanked everyone who had given us donations, or supported us in any way that had made the Center a reality. And I explained to the audience that one of the problems of alcoholics is that they tend to be perfectionists.

"The other day," I said, "I came over here to check, in my perfectionist way, on the last-minute details. Were the windows clean? Was everything in place? And as I walked up the path, I noticed that, thanks to all the water, fertilizer, peat moss and seed we'd put around, the grass was beginning to come up. You can see a wonderful green haze out there, it sort of looks like the stubble of a new beard, but it's beautiful. And I couldn't help but think, this was a pile of sand, and we've made it come alive. And it's going to be even more alive, because people will come here for help; there is going to be a way for them, a new life."

Later, after the music, the speeches, the congratulations were over, people drifted out onto the campus. At one point, Leonard and I were standing there, and we looked out across the still raw landscape. We had been

through so much together, traveling the country pleading for money, fighting for new legislation, trying to foist off the presidency of the place—"You do it!" "No, you do it!" —on each other, and we had come so far.

The basic buildings were up, the trees were planted, we had assembled what we thought was the finest staff a rehabilitation center had ever put together, and they were all set to go. I said to Leonard, "Can you *believe* this?" and he said, "Hell, no, I really can't." And we laughed, and then we cried. For happiness.

And I thought about a morning four years earlier when I had cried for shame, out of weakness and fear. I was dying, and everyone knew it but me.

2

In the middle of the journey of our life
I came to myself in a dark wood where
the straight way was lost.

Dante Alighieri

April 1, 1978. We had been in our new
California house just two weeks. I sat on the
green-and-white couch in the living room,
my husband's arm around me, and I cried. I
didn't say a word, just listened, and cried.

We were having an intervention, starring
me. My husband, my children, two doctors,
a nurse and a couple of friends had gathered
to tell me they were concerned about my
failing health, and thought I had a problem
with alcohol and drugs.

I'd never heard of an intervention, and I
would just as soon have kept it that way. I
didn't want to hear *any* of what my family
was telling me.

My makeup wasn't smeared, I wasn't disheveled, I behaved politely, and I never

finished off a bottle, so how could I be alcoholic? And I wasn't on heroin or cocaine, the medicines I took—the sleeping pills, the pain pills, the relaxer pills, the pills to counteract the side effects of other pills—had been prescribed by doctors, so how could I be a drug addict?

I had done everything in my power for my husband and our four kids I had loved so much. I had done everything in my power to help my husband's career. In my own mind, at least, I had always been there for them, and I truly believed I had given a hundred percent. My mother's voice was always in my ear—"If you can't do it right, don't do it at all."

And now I was hearing that I had failed. You have to understand that my family was *not* saying this (there were no pointing fingers, no accusatory remarks), my family was saying I had a disease. They were saying, "Mother, you're sick, we love you and we want to help you." But what I heard was that I had let them down.

My self-esteem was nonexistent. I did not understand how much love it took for them to risk this confrontation with me. For months, I had been withdrawing. As I got sicker, I gradually stopped going to lunch, I

wouldn't see friends, I was putting everyone out of my life.

So far as my family was concerned, a crisis point had been reached a few months before, at Christmas. The children say it was the worst Christmas ever, but I was completely oblivious to their distress. I thought everyone was happy. We were up in Vail, where we'd always come for the holidays, there was a lot of good snow, we were together, and I had my pills.

I did notice that anyone who prepared a drink for me kept it very light, and I would say, "Oh, for heaven's sake, if you're going to make me a drink, make me a real drink, or else just give me plain tonic." But that was the extent of my awareness that I was being watched.

Our oldest son, Mike, reports that was the week the children went to Jerry. And since I was pretty much *hors de combat*, I'm going to depend on the fighters who were *not* disabled to fill in what happened.

Mike Ford: "We said something's wrong here, but we were in the dark about drug dependency and alcoholism. We didn't know what we were up against, we just knew Mother was manifesting a lot of unhealthy

13

signs, being incoherent, kind of shuffling around, not eating right. And the slurred speech, the not getting dressed until late in the day, had become a lifestyle. You could tell she was a sick woman, but none of us—not even Dad—knew what to do. We all just kind of said, 'We'll try to spend more time with her, be more in touch with her.' And Dad said he wouldn't travel as much."

Susan Ford Vance: "Even earlier, in the desert, I had talked to Dad. He was as frustrated as I was. It was one of those 'Well, sweetheart, you find the solution and I'm with you,' but he didn't know what to do either. It was like there was this disease, and who do you talk to about it?"

Jerry Ford: "Susan had been talking to me about 'Mother's problem,' but I guess she was somewhat intimidated by me because she never really came out and said, 'Dad, you've got to do something.' "

Finally, it was Susan herself who did something. Through the grace of God, I guess, she got involved with helping Joe Cruse—Dr. Joseph Cruse—up at Turnoff, which is a rehabilitation center for chemically depen-

dent kids. Dr. Cruse was our gynecologist, and a recovering alcoholic, and he had hired Susan to take pictures of Turnoff so he could raise some money for it. On their way up there, they discussed my case.

Susan Ford Vance: "I said, 'Dr. Cruse, I've got this friend, and she's got a problem,' and he said, 'Susan, your friend is your mother, isn't she?' And I said yeah.

"He said he could help me put an intervention team together, and I said, 'Well, let me go back to my dad, because I couldn't okay anything without him.' I wasn't married yet, Chuck and I weren't even engaged then.

"So I went back and talked to Dad, and he said, 'That sounds great,' and then he took off on a trip. So I called Clara back in Washington. Clara Powell had worked for our family all the time we kids were growing up, she had been our second mother. And I said, 'Clara, you've got to come out here. Mother is taking pills, and I can't stand it anymore. The boys keep telephoning and asking how she is, and I don't know what to tell them. I don't even want to see her every day because it frustrates me.'

"I was upset when I did see my mother,

and my mother was upset when I didn't see her. I wasn't living with my parents, I had my own place, and when I'd go over to my dad's office, Mother would hear I had been there, right next door, and hadn't stopped by the house, and she'd get hurt.

"Clara promised she would come out—ostensibly to help Mother get everything in the new house unpacked and settled—and I talked to Dr. Cruse again, and he said, again, 'We can do it if your father is willing.' "

Dr. Joseph Cruse: "Almost as soon as we got in the car to drive to Turnoff, Susan grabbed my arm and said, 'Can you help my mother?' Just blurted it out.

"I said yes, and about a week later, I got a call from Bob Barrett, who had been President Ford's Army aide in the White House, and who, as a civilian, still worked with the family. He asked who I was and why I was involving myself in the Fords' personal affairs. He really raked me over the coals, and I thought, who needs this? But I explained what Susan and I had been talking about, and the next night, Barrett had me come over and explain to the President what an intervention was."

Before Jerry could make up his mind one way or another about the wisdom of a full-scale intervention, Susan and Joe Cruse attempted a mini-intervention of their own.

I was in the study when they arrived, and they brought with them Clara and Caroline Coventry, who was my secretary. And Joe started sharing with me the history of his drinking problems, and I thought, what a bunch of pips they are to have dreamt this up. It seemed so underhanded for Susan and Clara and Caroline to gang up on me, and bring in a stranger. Of course, I knew Joe Cruse as a gynecologist, but I already had an internist I saw every Tuesday at twelve noon, and nobody had sent for him. Now suddenly this Dr. Cruse comes out of the woodwork, and the only thing in my mind was, let me get rid of him.

Joe Cruse: "I had put on a tie, which you don't normally do in the desert, in order to go and see Mrs. Ford. I went over and spent an hour and a half telling her my story, and just as I was getting to the point I thought might sell her, she fell asleep. I woke her up and told her the rest of it, and I said I thought she too had a chemical dependency

problem. She was very gracious, and thanked me for my interest.

"Then Susan and Caroline and I went out on the driveway, and I said to Susan, 'You better go back in there and hug your mother, I just threw a big bunch of stuff at her.' So Susan went tearing in, and came tearing out again, and she said, 'She's hugging Clara, she doesn't want to hug me, and she wants you off this property and don't you ever come back!' "

Susan's recollection diverges from Joe's in at least one respect. It doesn't include an iota of graciousness on my part. According to her, our meeting was a disaster.

Susan Ford Vance: "We told Mother she had to stop, and she said, 'Well, I am stopping, I've cut out this pill, I've cut out that pill,' and she got so mad at us, and she was already so high anyway—we didn't catch her early enough in the morning—that she looked at me and Caroline and Dr. Cruse and she said, 'You are all a bunch of monsters. Get out of here and never come back.'

"She kicked us out.

"I was devastated. Here Dr. Cruse had promised me that we were going to help my

mother, and all we'd done was fall flat on our faces, and my mother had kicked me out of her house.

"I went home and later that night I called Clara, because at that point, Clara was the only person Mother would talk to. And boy, was I glad she was there. She said, 'Don't worry, Mother's fine. I've got her settled down.' "

They had me settled down and settled up and settled. Two days later, they did the intervention. The real thing. Thursday to Saturday was all it took for them to put it together.

Bob Barrett: "Everybody had been trying to figure out the best time to have the intervention, but they were also sort of avoiding it. We were in Rochester, where President Ford had been speaking, when we got the call. Mrs. Ford had to go into treatment right away. It was very late Friday, but the President phoned Mike and Gayle and asked them to fly to Palm Springs right away. President Ford was supposed to speak in Virginia the next day, and in New York City the day after that, but he got Henry Kissinger to agree to fill in these dates, and then we flew

home in a private jet, arriving in the early morning. The Ford kids were already there, and at 7:30 A.M. in the President's office, we were taught how to conduct an intervention."

Jerry Ford: "It all came to a head after Susan and Cruse had gone to Betty and she'd thrown them out. It was obvious something had to be done. I recognized the intervention was a gamble, but at that point, I felt the risk was worth taking."

Bill Bloomer: "My wife and I were out in Palm Springs when they did the intervention on my sister Betty. And Susan got hold of me and said, 'I've gone through this preparation, and we're going to confront Mother, and she is going to immediately call you for help. And I just hope you won't give her any.' And I said, 'Oh, no, I agree with you a hundred percent. And I think I should talk to Jerry, because he is so in love with Betty and so protective and I've got to tell him he's going to have to be tough.' And I did tell him that, and he said he knew. He said he realized it was going to be probably the hardest thing he ever did."

Dr. Joseph Pursch: "It was on a Thursday that Joe Cruse called me at the naval hospital and said Mrs. Ford needed to have an intervention. He told me how much medication she was on, and I knew she would need to be detoxed slowly, but I thought it could be done perfectly safely in her house. Because Dr. Cruse's office was close by—he was right in Palm Springs—and he'd explained that the Fords lived only minutes from the emergency room at Eisenhower Hospital if anything should go wrong.

"I said I would come to Palm Springs the next day, Friday, and I would bring my nurse, Pat Benedict, with me. There were several reasons for this. Pat was under my command, and I could have the naval hospital give her a set of orders, no questions asked, so this would not become a public matter, and Pat could live at the Ford residence.

"Also, Pat was a fully trained nurse, and a recovering alcoholic. She could help Mrs. Ford to understand the disease concept."

Pat Benedict: "Dr. Pursch called me and asked me to come by his house. It was a Thursday night. When I got there, he took me into the living room, and asked me what

21

I knew about Betty Ford. I said I didn't know anything about Betty Ford, and he looked at me like I was weird. He said he had been talking to Dr. Cruse and we were going to do an intervention, and we would take it a step at a time.

"I went on emergency leave—Pursch told people at the hospital that my mother had had a heart attack, so for days my mother was getting get-well cards, and wondering where I was—and on Friday, we drove to Palm Springs, and went directly to Joe Cruse's office. Cruse and Susan and Clara were there, and Clara said, 'Looks like we have a team.' I spent that night at Dr. Cruse's house, and it was arranged that we would all meet early the next morning in President Ford's office."

Joe Pursch: "Because we met with Clara and Susan that Friday afternoon, I had a chance to fill them in a little before the rest of the family arrived. 'What we want to do tomorrow,' I said, 'is have this lady in a position where she won't run out. So there must not be any heated discussions or arguments. We want to present to her, lovingly but firmly, brief facts about two things—how her illness

22

is affecting and destroying her, and how her illness is affecting and destroying you.

" 'And how, as her daughter and her friend, you can no longer stand by and watch.' Then I asked what they could fill me in on, and Susan said, 'Well, she's on medication, and she's taking it for pain. I know that, but it makes me angry and it makes me worried, and I'm afraid she'll die.' And I said, 'This is what you need to tell her.' "

Susan Ford Vance: "When I met Pat Benedict, it was like somebody had just taken a hundred-pound weight off my head. Because she understood what I was going through. I mean, I'd tell her stories and she'd heard them all before, and she convinced me that my mother was not the strangest person I had met in my entire life.

"And Clara's being there was good too. I think it was Clara who finally called my brother Jack and convinced him to take part in the intervention. He was the one most against it, but Clara said, 'We've got to do this for Mother. If we lose, we lose, but we will have given it our best shot.' So finally, Jack came around."

Jack Ford: "After you've buried somebody

three times over, you're probably a little reluctant to start shoveling dirt again. I had
given up hope that the problem would ever
be corrected, and I didn't want to hurt her
gratuitously, I guess."

Mike Ford: "Susan was the one who said we
just could not go on like this, she was the
one who told Dad, get your rear end home,
Mother is in a bad way. When Dad called
Gayle and me, he said, 'We want to do this
right away. Can you fly out?'

"He said we all needed to be there to
make a unified presentation, that the intervention would be an act of love to help
Mother and the family.

"I was scared of Mother's reaction. I knew
we had to face up to the problem, but I was
deeply unsure about what the results of this
step would be.

"Then, I think, with the advice of Dr.
Pursch and Dr. Cruse—we needed some
coaching—we began to understand the nature of chemical dependence, and how it had
taken over her life, and at that point, I was
really prepared to march in there and lay it
on her."

Steve Ford: "I hadn't been around that much,

I'd come visit, but Susan lived in Palm Springs, and that's why she stirred the pot up. She got burned the worst. The rest of us were off in our own areas, and didn't have to be personally involved. It's hard to live with anyone who has a drug or alcohol problem. They don't think rationally all the time, they don't act rationally, they don't understand.

"We as a family were frustrated with it, but we never made the initial push to do something about it. We kept avoiding it. We had never given Mom a chance to have our support in solving her problem.

"If she hadn't wanted to correct it, well then, we would have had to say, 'Mother, we love you, we're there for you, but we can't do this for the rest of our lives,' and we would have had to move on. But we'd never even given her the chance, we'd never tried it. I think there was some guilt about that.

"I was not educated in the treatment of alcoholics or drug abuse. I wasn't sure what was going to happen. When I drove down to the desert that Saturday morning, I wasn't sure what the whole thing was about. It wasn't until we got together over in Dad's office with the doctors and my brothers and sister that I found out what we were going to do."

Pat Benedict: "They had just moved from a rented house in the desert, everything was still in boxes in the new house and the office. When President Ford came into the office, the kids were already there. The President looked very stern, very much in control.

"I don't remember whether it was Pursch or Cruse who explained about telling their mother their feelings, but it seems to me we were not there very long.

"It was brought out that if Mrs. Ford understood and agreed to treatment, I would stay with her until her treatment was decided on, and when Dr. Pursch said, 'Doesn't anybody have anything to say?' I said, 'I have one thing.' And I said to President Ford, 'I will do all I can to help your wife,' and he just looked at me and said thank you."

Joe Pursch: "During the pre-intervention, Jack Ford was the one who needed reassurance that this was necessary. He said to me, 'You know, you haven't met this patient,' and that was true. But I told him I had seen the list of medications that had been dispensed to her."

Bob Barrett: "Before they left the office, Pursch had given them all instructions, and they got a little nitpicky like people do. Everybody started taking shots at one another, and I have a big mouth, so I got into it. I said, 'I just don't think you should all be after one another, assessing blame, I just don't see that working.' I talked to Pursch later and he said, 'Those people are scared. They've never done anything like this before. The idea is to get them comfortable enough so someone does some risk taking, gets a little more eloquent than he normally is, makes a good point in a kind manner.' "

Joe Cruse: It took us only about fifteen minutes down in the President's office to train the family. They were so ready. Pursch and I handed them pieces of paper and said, 'Now you have to write down some event and how you felt about it, and then another event and how you felt about it.' And they were all writing, and then one of them would read aloud what he had written—his mother had fallen asleep in front of his friends, and he'd had to take her upstairs, something like that—and one of the others would say, 'Dad, do you hear that? Do you hear that?' And

the President just listened, really listened to all of it."

Jerry Ford: "The doctors literally gave us a set of instructions, guidelines we had to follow to make the intervention successful. And they warned the kids in advance, 'Now your mother's going to get mad, your mother's going to cry, she's going to resent it, she may even get up and walk out, but you have to be firm, you have to be straightforward, and you can't let her intimidate you because that's what she's been doing, she has browbeaten all of you.'

"And that was true. I had turned into an enabler myself. I was making it possible for Betty to continue to drink and take pills. I would make all kinds of alibis about why we were late getting someplace, or why Betty didn't show up at all. And it was getting worse, not better. My pleading with her was not helping. In fact, it was exacerbating the situation, because she would resent it as though nothing was wrong, and I was being a nitpicker.

"So this intervention was a last chance. I knew I would hate the things I had to say, but I was relieved too. I was convinced this was the only way the situation could be

turned around. It was a dead-end street, the way we were going."

Joe Pursch: "After the pre-intervention session, I gave the family a coffee break, to get their nerves settled. I told them Joe Cruse and Pat and I would meet them over at the house in ten minutes, and we would hold the intervention.

"Sometimes, you have to hold several of these pre-intervention sessions. If the family you're working with is very disjointed, if there are several people there who have drinking problems, if the sick person's husband or wife already has some other wife or husband in mind. Then you hold these meetings over a course of a couple of weeks, and you make your decisions—we can't use the maid, we can't use the sister, the husband is iffy. But the Fords were really right there. They had been dispersed all over, but they came together like a magnet.

"When the President walked into his office so early that morning, he was tired. He said, 'This is not going to be pleasant, is it?' And I said, 'No, it's never pleasant, but it's the only thing to do. When it works, it works beautifully and is life-saving.'

"At the end of our little training session,

he spoke again. 'Are you sure this needs to be done? And that she can be helped?' I said, 'I'm positive about the first, and I'm highly optimistic about the second.'

" 'In that case,' he said, 'we'll go.' And he put down his pipe, and stood up."

When the whole family trooped into the house, I had no clue what was coming. I thought Mike and Gayle had flown out to visit because I hadn't been feeling well, and I was absolutely delighted. Until Jerry sat me down on that couch and said, "Mother, we've got something to talk to you about, and we want you to listen, because we love you."

I listened, but I didn't hear that they loved me. I heard that I had failed.

Steve Ford: "She never failed. I can understand how she could think that, when this thing happened, but she never failed as a mother. At the intervention, I only told one story, of a weekend when Dad was gone, and he didn't want Mom to be alone, so Melanie, the girl I was going with, and I drove to Palm Springs. And when we got there, I made dinner, I fixed vegetables, salad, the whole thing, and took it in to

Mom, and she said, 'Oh, thank you, but I really don't feel like eating,' and I was hurt. I'd gone to the store, done the shopping, put the silverware on the proper sides of the plates, and she went and got another drink.

"When I told that at the intervention, she cried. You know, there were a lot of things coming out that had never been said before."

Jack Ford: The only point I made at the intervention—it was a point I felt very strongly about—was that I hadn't liked to bring friends home. If somebody came by the house, particularly if we'd gone out to the movies first, something like that, I was always kind of peeking around the corner into the family room to see what kind of shape Mother was in."

Mike Ford: "I told Mother that, being the oldest, I thought I probably saw more clearly the strain on her of having been a wife in Washington, and the mother of four children, and all the pressures and demands that had created her environment. But I said she had got to the point now where her lifestyle was very destructive, she was hurting her relationships with her husband, her family and her friends, and that those relationships

were too valuable to lose, and that her life was too valuable to let go.

"Then Gayle said something that hit really hard. We had been married about four years, and Gayle's comment to Mother was that we wanted to start a family, and we wanted our children to know their grandmother, and not only know her but know her as a healthy, loving person. At that point, she had no grandchildren, and the prospect of not living to see her grandchildren, or living in such a miserable state that the grandchildren would be afraid of her—that really knocked her flat."

Bob Barrett: "President and Mrs. Ford were sitting in front of the window, their backs to the golf course. They were the only ones on the sofa. Then all around them in a circle were Mike and Gayle, Jack and Steve and Susan and Clara and the doctors and the nurse.

"Mrs. Ford looked small, almost like a doll, lost in the cushions, and as her husband made his opening remarks, you could see the confusion in her face. He was saying she was chemically dependent, 'and the doctors want to talk to you,' and then Dr. Pursch

said, 'Mrs. Ford, you don't have to be alarmed, all these people care for you.'

"Then Mike spoke. It had begun. The game was on, and you could see Mrs. Ford reeling. Here comes this avalanche of love, and yet with it a devastating appraisal of the person's shortcomings. I looked at Pursch because I thought, I'll bet that's what's supposed to happen. And the President moved even closer to Mrs. Ford, and she got even smaller.

"Jack talked, Steve talked, and then it came to Susan. She was the youngest, she was the girl, she was responsible for bringing this whole thing together, she thought she was going to have everything to say, and then she totally broke down. Up till then, everyone had been tender, but no one had broken down. Susan turned to Clara and put her head on her chest, and Clara just stroked her, and said, 'Now, now.' "

Susan Ford Vance: "Dad started by saying the reason we're here is we love you. Everybody kept saying the reason we're here is we love you. Pursch had told us if she got any feeling of animosity, forget it. And he'd also told us to write down the things we wanted to say so we wouldn't forget them. So I had

written down the fact that she'd always been a dancer, and I had always admired her for being a dancer, but these days she was falling and clumsy, and she just wasn't the same person. And I had talked to her about things that were important to me, and she hadn't remembered them, and it had really hurt my feelings.

"I had never said any of this before, but it had been building up in me for a long time. I guess I had been aware that Mother took pills when we were in the White House, but I hadn't thought twice about it until much later. When I dropped out of college and came home in the spring of 1977, I began to notice that since she'd moved to the desert, she had no close friends anymore. And I thought, poor Mother, isn't she lonely here by herself?

"Then I really started to see it. Once she fell in the middle of the night and cracked her ribs and chipped her tooth.

"I had started dating Chuck—he was at that time one of my parents' Secret Service agents—and he was with her on different assignments, protecting her, and he would come to me later and say, 'Susan, you've got to do something about your mother, she's slowly destroying herself.' I was getting pres-

sure from him because his father was an alcoholic who eventually committed suicide. It caused terrible arguments between us, and now I look at him and think, thank you for keeping after me about it.

"I remember going to Las Vegas with Mother to see Tony Orlando in a show. And Chuck and I had to just about carry her upstairs to her room. Everybody covered for her, we were perfect at covering for her, and all the while we were thinking, what are we going to do?

"At the intervention, it took me a long time to get any words out, not just because I was crying, but because Mother was crying so hard, and that bothered me, but at the same time, it was almost healing for me, it was like peeling away all the layers, for once it was out in the open."

Pat Benedict: "When Susan talked, she crumpled. I scooted my chair over beside her—I had met her the day before, which made a difference—and she took my hand and squeezed it so tight she damn near broke it."

Joe Cruse: "When we all went into the house, Betty was surprised to see Mike and Gayle, and she hugged them, and then she realized

there were these strangers along with her family. And the President sat holding her, and I was wondering, 'Who's going to start?' and Pursch was wondering, 'Who's going to start?' and Pat Benedict was wondering, 'Who's going to start?' and the President started. Betty already knew me but the President introduced her to Joe Pursch and Pat Benedict. He told Betty the family loved her and was worried about her, 'and we have people here who are going to help us, and we want you to just sit and listen.' Then he flipped around and pointed his finger and said, 'Mike, you start.'

"The President took over and ran the intervention. I said zero, Pat said zero, Pursch said zero. And that's a miracle."

The whole thing was a miracle. It's a miracle I didn't just not wake up some morning from all the drugs I was taking, and it's a miracle my family didn't just let me slip away.

I think the intervention worked because we are so close. Even when the kids were small, and Jerry and I wanted to buy a place in Vail, we asked their opinions. We wanted to be sure Vail was where they'd enjoy

spending every summer, every Christmas vacation.

Any major decision has always involved all of us, and my recovery involved all of us, because my disease involved all of us.

But I also think if any one of the kids—or Jerry—had tried to intervene, I could have turned it around. I could have said, "I'm glad you told me, I'll take care of it, don't worry." And gone on getting sicker and sicker because I'd have been adding guilt, and compounding the problem.

But they all came together, and they came before I had completely destroyed myself.

Which does not mean I enjoyed the intervention.

When Pursch said, "Well, I guess you don't have any brain damage," I was flabbergasted. Brain damage? My God, brain damage. It was something I'd never thought of.

When Steve did that bit about cooking for me—"and you had one drink, two drinks, and wouldn't come to dinner"—I thought, that kid has a lot of nerve. I was *used* to having two drinks before dinner.

When Susan came off as the perfect daughter, I felt some resentment about that too. As I look back, I realize I had no comprehension of my disease. My denial was at

its peak, and denial is a cornerstone of alcoholism.

And I didn't enjoy Jerry's reference to the night I fell and cracked my ribs either. One of my points of pride was that I didn't ever fall down. Could I have been having blackouts from time to time? Not remembering what had really happened?

Jerry said how slow I was, how tardy. "You were in second gear," he said. And he said it had become "increasingly difficult to lead a normal life."

I believe my husband had got to the point where he thought he simply had a wife who was no longer a strong woman (after all, she was seeing a doctor every week, and the doctor wasn't telling her not to come back), and having had all those babies had worn her out, and she'd had that bad experience with the pinched nerve in her neck, and she'd been in and out of hospitals; she was just one of those unfortunate women who were going to fade away, and there was nothing he could do about it.

It was easier for him to travel. He said it used to upset him to watch me get up in the morning and take that handful of pills, and then take another handful at night, on top of a couple of drinks, before we went to bed.

A lot of the time, he just turned away, pretending not to see, his denial of my condition as firmly in place as my own. While we were still renting, while our house was being built at Thunderbird, he would try to speak optimistically to the kids. "Well," he would say, "she'll be better when we get down in the house on the golf course, because she'll have the dogs, and she can walk them on the golf course, and that will be good for her, and keep her occupied; she'll have something to do."

As for the boys, when Susan first went to Joe Cruse, I'm not sure her brothers didn't resent her interference, though that interference saved my life. Or maybe what saved my life was that the intervention made me see how much they all cared about me.

When you're suffering from alcoholism, or any other drug dependency, your self-esteem gets so low you're sure nobody would want to bother with you. I think intervention works because suddenly you realize somebody *is* willing to bother, somebody cares.

Not that an intervention could work if the patient were dead set against it. The family can't say, okay, we're going to physically put you in this hospital and lock all the doors and windows and you'll stay there till you're

better. Something in me had to respond, to think maybe there is something wrong, maybe I do take the wrong pills, or too many of them, maybe I am getting dependent on them.

At the end of the intervention, Dr. Pursch asked me if I was willing to go into treatment, and I said yes, but Bob Barrett claims I didn't sound wholehearted. He says I was using my "professional political smile," and uttering hollow-sounding platitudes about how I wanted to be well.

Dr. Pursch said, "That's fine, Mrs. Ford," and then Pat Benedict crossed the room to me, and I wondered what she wanted. I'd had to agree to let this woman stay with us.

Pat Benedict: "It was my understanding that number one, we've got to get her detoxed, and number two, we've got to get her into treatment. I didn't know if she would be going to Hazelden, or the naval hospital, or China.

"I knelt in front of her, and I didn't say a word about alcohol, only about drugs. I said, 'Betty, I have had a problem too—I took a lot of amphetamines in Vietnam, and some Valium to level the nerves—and I will help you.' She looked at me like, I don't really

40

give a damn, and I said, 'Betty, I also have had a breast removed,' and she reached out and patted me on the cheek. That got her attention."

Before they went to lunch—they left me alone with my family for a while—the doctors told me they'd be coming back with some friends, and for me to get dressed. Naturally, I wasn't dressed, I was in a robe. And they said they would be collecting all my medications and prescriptions and taking them away.

I got dressed, and put myself together to prove how really well I was. I also swallowed a bunch of pills. I'd show them. They were going to confiscate my supply? I'd just gulp down the four or five pills I normally took at noon; I might need them before this day was over.

In the afternoon, some people came and showed us how support group meetings work. They all told their stories. About their alcoholism and their recovery and how changed their lives were now.

Still sedated to the teeth, I was perfectly amenable. I thought, isn't this nice? And I remember one of the women had brought me a box of Kleenex tied up with colored yarn, and she said, "Here, you'll need this

when you go to treatment," and I thought, I'm not going to cry anymore, I'm cried out, I'm numb.

After this group meeting, Dr. Pursch gave us a lecture. Using a blackboard, he listed every drug I was on, how many milligrams a day of each, and when he added them all up, the amount was staggering. He said over the years I had developed an amazing tolerance for this medication.

When they confront you with that kind of evidence on a blackboard, you have to be a real dummy not to realize you're in trouble.

Jerry Ford: "My apprehension about the amount of medication had been growing. I never counted the pills, but I knew she took a lot; I saw the bills from the pharmacy. I was more concerned with the drugs than with the alcohol, because the amounts she was drinking didn't seem abnormally high. It was a couple of vodkas before dinner, and after dinner she would want a couple of bourbons. But I did not know how the combination of alcohol and pills multiplied the impact until Pursch showed us that chart. It was the first concrete evidence I'd seen."

Pursch said that once I was detoxed, there

were several alternatives for me to consider, so far as treatment was concerned. I could go to meetings of Alcoholics Anonymous, and learn to live a sober, drug-free life, but that would take longer than if I went into a concentrated treatment program. Hazelden, outside of Minneapolis, was suggested, and so was Dr. Pursch's rehab unit at the naval hospital in Long Beach.

I chose Long Beach because I wanted to stay in California. Steve was in Laguna, Jack in San Diego and Susan in Palm Springs, and I didn't want to be far away from them.

Susan Ford Vance: "So then the process began of going through the whole house cleaning out the drugs. Dr. Cruse and Caroline Coventry and I took everything and anything we could get our hands on, even over-the-counter stuff. There were bottles and bottles and bottles. We threw them into a box, and Cruse took the box away.

"Everything went like clockwork. Mother didn't like Pat at first, but she cooperated. A movie projector arrived, and they started bringing in educational films about alcohol and drug dependency for all of us to watch so we could begin to figure out what was going on.

"Clara, I remember, made pot roast that night, and we all had dinner together. It was like the family was a family once again. It was like everything had been torn down, and there was nothing to hide anymore."

Pat Benedict: "Jack and Steve put up a rollaway bed for me in the study close to the Fords' bedroom. When Pursch went back to Long Beach, he didn't even say goodbye to me, he just left me down there. Didn't say lots of luck or anything. He was my boss, and he just left. He had Cruse and me go to Eisenhower and get the medicine to detoxify Betty at home. I've said to Pursch since, we were either very brilliant, or very lucky. She could have died."

Steve Ford: "Mom was a very scared woman, left naked to say she was addicted. And in fact, forced to say it, we kind of didn't give her a choice. When I look back, I see this vision of her shaking. Someone came in and took all the pills from her bathroom and dressing room, all the things she could hide behind. When she first started down the road to recovery, I don't think she had any idea where it was going."

I didn't, oh, I didn't.

That week of detoxification, I shook so much I didn't need an electric toothbrush. And in bed at night, my legs kept moving, I couldn't lie still. I kept saying the Serenity Prayer—"God grant me the serenity to accept the things I cannot change . . ." I did it by rote, as I struggled through the chemical withdrawal that brought on the agitation. Repeating it over and over gave me a sense of the now, it seemed to calm me.

It took a lot of prayer, a lot of exercise, a lot of soaks in the jacuzzi, to get me ready for sleep. Sometimes I couldn't sleep anyway. I'd be up before anyone else in the morning, and I'd put the coffee on. I'd wander through the house, I'd stretch out on the floor, I'd watch the hummingbirds wake up outside the windows. And what I found out is, you don't die from lack of sleep, you'll sleep when your body is ready. My body wasn't ready.

There are still nights when I wish I had a sleeping pill, but sleeping pills are from another life, and I've learned to do without that crutch. I get up, have a glass of milk and a graham cracker, read a while. It would be easier if my husband weren't so sane and

put together. He makes me furious because when I'm lying there worrying about some problem, he will say, "You can't do anything about it tonight, you may as well go to sleep so you'll be rested, and can tackle it tomorrow." He's wonderful, and I want to smack him.

I think now it was rather chancy for them to try to detox me at home the way they did. I think I should have been in a hospital, and Pat agrees with me.

Pat Benedict: "I don't know why Pursch and Cruse didn't take her over to Eisenhower. I wouldn't be surprised if she still had some anger over that. I know I was very scared, I thought, what am I doing here? I'm not even a Republican! Sick as she was, they felt this was what she needed, they don't think they abandoned her, they think they did what was best for her.

"The very first day after the intervention, she was really sick. She kept throwing up."

Susan Ford Vance: "I came by, and Dad was there, and I said, 'How's Mom, can I see her?' And he said, 'Oh, she's really sick to her stomach, I wouldn't go in and bother her.' And I thought, if I'd known what she was

going to have to go through, I'm not sure I would have voted for it."

Pat Benedict: "President Ford was scared too. He wanted to know why Betty kept throwing up. I said, 'Mr. President, this is the worst day she'll ever have. I will have her up and bathed and walking tomorrow.'

"Next day she and I did go for a walk on the golf course—we went past the President's office, and she waved to him. She was wearing a blue skirt, and she had a bandana around her head, and I carried Valium and a syringe and a tourniquet in my pocket, in case of an emergency. And as we continued along the path, all of a sudden she reached over and put her arm around me. And I thought, we're going to be okay.

"She wanted to get well, and that's half the battle."

The week passed. Pat was on the phone to Dr. Cruse and Dr. Pursch about my blood pressure, about my shots, about my dry heaves, the whole business. I took my last Librium—you're weaned away from your pills by slow degrees—at midnight, Friday, April 7. Steve was there, and he and Pat and

I celebrated in the kitchen with glasses of cranapple juice.

Saturday was my sixtieth birthday, and I was supposed to go next door to the Firestones' for dinner. I didn't want to do it. I knew there would be a cocktail hour, and I didn't want to face that, and I was having terrible neck pains, and of course I had no pain medication.

Pat Benedict: "The pinched nerve was hurting her, and they had this dinner planned, just Leonard and Nicky Firestone and Dolores Hope and the President and Betty. And Betty just said she wasn't going to go. And Clara and Caroline and I looked at each other, and then I called Dr. Pursch and said, 'She doesn't want to go.' He said, 'I want her up and dressed and at that party.'

"So we got her up and dressed, and once she and the President crossed the lawn to the Firestone house, Clara and Susan and I went into town. It was the first time I'd been out since I came down there. Clara bought our dinner, but I was worried the whole time. I thought, God, I know she isn't going to stay at that party. Well, she did stay. All evening. And when she came home, she said, 'It was

really a nice evening,' and I thought, I could just kick your tail."

Nicky Firestone: "She called and said she didn't think she could make it to our house for her birthday dinner. I said, 'Betty, you're among friends. If you swing from the chandelier, nobody's going to think anything of it. Do what you can. We very much want you to come. If you don't feel up to the whole evening, fine, do any part of it.'

"She came, and when dinner was announced, she stepped right up to the table, and she and Jerry never went home till eleven o'clock."

It happened just that way. I not only stayed through the cocktail hour, I stayed through dinner, and I marveled that I was able to eat some soup without shaking and slopping it all over the table.

On Sunday, Pat packed my bag for Long Beach. I would be going there the next morning.

I'd had my last drink on March 31, the night before the intervention.

It was more than forty years since I'd had my first.

3

They are not long, the days of wine
  and roses.

                              Ernest Dowson

Listen, they're long enough.

It takes a long time for alcohol and/or
pills to kill you. Somebody once told Robert
Benchley the liquor he was drinking was
slow poison, and Benchley shrugged. "So
who's in a hurry?" he said.

It took a long time for me to get where I'd
got, trying to decide what kind of clothes to
take so I could go hang out with a bunch of
sailors. I even insisted on shopping for new
slacks so I could go looking my very best.

I don't intend to offer here an unabridged
chronicle of my using and my drinking. Still,
it might be edifying to take a short look back
down the road that brought me, finally, to
the naval hospital.

For openers, a lot of the journey seemed
enjoyable.

I think of the first beer I ever had. It was at Bennington College, where I went to study dance the summer I was eighteen. My roommate and I, convinced we were drunk, ran around the campus acting crazy in the moonlight. Because we were happy, and thought we were such big stuff.

I think of my first trip to Europe, in 1956, and a train from Italy to Austria, and Jerry and me drinking our whiskey out of paper cups. We iced it with fresh snow we scooped up off the windowsill of our compartment, and laughed ourselves to sleep,

I think of a New Year's Eve in Vail. Watergate and my mastectomy were behind us, we were surrounded by people we loved, and we toasted in 1975, and drank enough to take care of several other years while we were at it,

I think of vacations, christenings, rituals, festivals, of lunch drinks and dressing drinks while we were preparing to go out, and nightcaps before bed. I think of that first sip of an icy martini, I think of Jerry and me sharing wine out of a German betrothal cup at our wedding rehearsal dinner.

Drinking was a way we relaxed, a way we celebrated, and it was good until it went bad. If you're not alcoholic, it doesn't have

to go bad, but I'm alcoholic. I just didn't know it for thirty years,

I first tasted liquor when I was twelve or thirteen in the pantry of a girlfriend's house in Grand Rapids. Three or four of us kids tried it, said, "Oh, how awful," and went our ways.

In fact, as a teenager, I was a bit of a Carrie Nation. One time Bill Warren, the boy I later married, slipped away from a dance to go have a nip in the parking lot, and when he came back, I slapped his face and told him not to call me anymore.

At nineteen, I had my first unpleasant encounter with alcohol. It was a cuba libre at a hotel in Grand Rapids. I had modeled in a fashion show, and some friends took me out afterward, and later, when I got home, my mother found me moaning in the bathroom and said, "What in the world is the matter?" and I said, "Oh, I just feel awful, I had a rum and Coke, it's called a cuba libre," and she said, "Thank goodness that's all that's wrong."

I was cured of cuba libres, but if my illness was a warning, I didn't recognize it as such.

Act Two. When I was living in New York and studying with Martha Graham, my room-

mate and I went to a college bash in New Haven. The boys served us something called purple passion, which was probably grape juice and grain alcohol. I had a kind of blackout. There were a few minutes when everything was sort of numb and vague. Again, I didn't take it as a warning.

Back home in Grand Rapids, I went to a Christmas party at five o'clock one afternoon, and the hosts served planter's punch. It had oranges floating around in it, it tasted like fruit juice, and it made a lot of the girls sick. It didn't make me sick, but I did get sort of tight.

I had to teach a class in ballroom dancing at the high school later that night, and my date took me home to his mother and father, who gave me black coffee. I thought how worldly they were, and was reasonably pleased with myself because I was still on my feet, when so many of my companions were out on theirs.

I disapproved of passing out; it was foreign to my nature to be out of control.

I drank on dates because I wanted to be part of the group. Then as now, young people responded to peer pressure. I can remember a beach party where we had kegs of beer, and we played ball, and somebody

passed around manhattans—they looked interesting, with cherries in them—and they made me so sick I never did drink another manhattan.

At home, my parents always served cocktails, come five o'clock. It was a habit, like brushing your teeth in the morning, Now, with the 20/20 vision of hindsight, I can see alcohol did not agree with me, but in those days, we didn't even know alcoholism was a disease, or that it might be inherited. We also didn't know that some alcoholics are born that way (in trouble from the very first time they drink) whereas others achieve alcoholism through years of working at it. We keep abusing the system until the system breaks down. We keep trying over and over to handle party drinking, like trying to handle the social mores of how to eat raw oysters on the half shell, or escargots. It all goes with the game, and it seems important to be good at it, to be accepted.

My father was alcoholic, though I never knew it until after he died, and so was my brother Bob. My brother Bill is rather baffled about how he escaped. "Drinking doesn't agree with me," he says mildly.

Wise brother Bill. I was less moderate than he. In my early twenties, I got myself

engaged to one of his lawyer friends, but the romance didn't last long. I liked boys, I liked parties, I liked to stay up late and flirt, and the lawyer disapproved of all these enthusiasms. "He was a very sober fellow," I wrote in my first book. Sober didn't appeal to me, I thought it was synonymous with stuffy. I played with a wild bunch, or as wild as it got in Grand Rapids in the early forties.

So I married Bill Warren. Nothing stuffy about him. He had blond curly hair, he danced, he played tennis, and he was very popular.

Remember the old folk poem, "There is a tavern in the town, and there my true love sits him down, and drinks his wine with laughter and with glee, and never, never thinks of me"?

That was the story of my life with Bill Warren.

Still, when we went out together on Saturday nights, I drank right along with him and if, at the end of the evening, somebody suggested one for the road, I didn't say no. I didn't feel I had to have a drink, but I very seldom turned one down.

Eventually, I divorced Bill Warren. For all my rebellion, my yearning to break loose—

hadn't I gone to New York to be a great dancer?—I was my mother's child. Hadn't I come home again? If I was going to be married, I wanted domestic tranquillity and babies, or why bother?

The marriage had lasted five years. For a while afterward, I was prudish about men and about liquor. I even stopped keeping liquor in my apartment. My brother Bob, who was by then a recovering alcoholic, and very active in helping others, used to come by with people he was trying to sober up. He said he liked to bring them there because he knew there was no beer in my refrigerator.

I can remember those fellows going out into my little kitchen and searching the shelves, hoping they'd find something, anything, even a bottle of vanilla extract. But if you wanted to drink when you came to my place, you had to bring it with you.

As for Jerry Ford, the most eligible bachelor (football hero, lawyer, ardent skier) in Grand Rapids, when I met him he scarcely drank at all. It just wasn't high on his list of priorities. At thirty-four, after four years in the Navy, he was again living at home. I think he just found it convenient to let his mother do his laundry.

The fall we got married, he made his first run for Congress, and he won a seat in the House of Representatives, and we moved to Washington. In Washington, there is more alcohol consumed per capita than in any other city in the United States. A prodigious amount of entertaining is done, and as a congressman, you are invited to most of it. Lobbyists give parties, so do senators and cabinet members and ambassadors. There are cocktail parties, receptions, dinners, fund-raisers, sometimes three a night, every night.

I probably encouraged my husband to drink. He was such a reserved man it was difficult for him even to tell me he loved me—he had proposed by saying, "I'd like to marry you." I wanted him to loosen up, so when he got in from work, I'd encourage him to have a beer or a martini to relax him. This kind of social hour had never been part of his experience, although he enjoyed it. But he never drank alcoholically, to make things better.

In my own mind, my drinking was simply convivial, and conviviality was fun. I liked our dinner guests to get a little mellow before we sat down to the table because it made for more successful parties, or so I thought.

Most of the time that Jerry was in Congress we lived in a nice family neighborhood in Virginia. Practically everybody belonged to the same Episcopal church, our kids were into everything—Scouts and Little League and Sunday school. And most of their activities seemed to take place at our house. I was in the PTA. I was a den mother. I spent days in the car ferrying children to the orthodontist and the eye doctor. Very middle American ordinary. From the outside, our life looked like a Norman Rockwell illustration.

The only thing wrong with the picture is that somewhere along the line, alcohol became too important in my life.

I just don't remember when I went from being a social drinker to being preoccupied with drinking, but I'm sure it was pretty gradual. If you go to enough cocktail parties, you start anticipating cocktail parties, and then when you aren't going to a cocktail party, you want the same kind of lift at home.

Virginia was a local option state, so in a restricted county, you had to buy liquor in state stores, and if you were entertaining at the country club, you took liquor with you, or kept it in a locker there. When Jerry and

I went with friends to a resort for a week-end, we all packed bottles. I told myself Jerry liked to have a drink before dinner. It was the "in" way to travel, a perfectly accepted way to behave. People gave each other nice leather carrying cases with room inside for a couple of bottles and some glasses.

When Jerry was away—and as he became more important in Congress, he was often away—I'd have my five o'clock drink at a neighbor's house. Or even by myself, while talking on the phone with a neighbor, I'd have another while I was fixing dinner and then, after the kids were in bed, I'd build myself a nightcap and unwind by watching television.

There were danger signs, but I buried them in my subconscious and only dredged them up years later. Sure, I didn't drink in the morning, but as I got more honest with myself, I was able to remember occasions when I had put a tablespoon of vodka into my hot tea, and it gave me a warm, mellow feeling.

Did I know instinctively that this would help relieve my emptiness, just as it had soothed me when I was a teenager, and my mother had put me to bed with a cup of tea

fortified with whiskey to help relieve a cold, or cramps?

Maybe it is that first drink that is the important one. Maybe it was as an adolescent that I first realized what pleasure and escape a drink could bring.

This is a point I want to make about alcoholism. It isn't the amount you drink, or the brand, it's how it affects you. It's the thing that happens to you psychologically, when you drink because you like the feeling it brings.

The person who is not alcoholic doesn't worry about whether they're going to serve drinks where he's going. I did worry about it. My husband would never have thought of drinking by himself. Obviously, as I look back, there were times when I not only thought about it, I did it.

The children were still young—Susan was five years old—when I developed a pinched nerve in my neck. The pinched nerve required many days of hospitalization in traction, physical therapy, hot packs, massage, acupuncture—and drugs. I remember telling one of the doctors at George Washington Hospital that I worried about going out. "I'm so afraid the pain will start."

"Don't *let* the pain start," he said. "Keep

your medication with you, take it every four hours."

If I developed a tolerance for one drug, the doctors gave me another. I hated feeling crippled, I hated my body's rebellion, I hated that I was hunched over and had to go to bed at night in traction, so I took more pills. It doesn't matter whether it's pills or alcohol, it wipes out your pain.

Now I know that some of the pain I was trying to wipe out was emotional.

Jerry became Minority Leader of the House, and I was proud of him, he was doing a magnificent job. But I was beginning to feel sorry for myself. It was poor me, who do they think is making it possible for him to travel all over the United States giving all those speeches? He gets all the headlines and applause, but what about me?

On the one hand, I loved being "the wife of"; on the other hand, I was convinced that the more important Jerry became, the less important I became. And the more I allowed myself to be a doormat—I knew I was a doormat to the kids—the more self-pity overwhelmed me. Hadn't I once been somebody in this world?

Underneath, I guess I didn't really believe I had been somebody. My career with Martha

Graham hadn't been a huge success—I had talent as a dancer, but I wasn't a great dancer—and my confidence had always been shaky. If I was pledged to a sorority in high school, I'd say, "Oh, that's because I've got two older brothers, and the girls like my brothers." Or, "That's because I can dance, and I'll be an asset when they do a show."

I couldn't accept that people liked me for myself. And I was self-conscious that I didn't have a college degree, though I figured if I acted smart, and looked smart, maybe strangers would think I was smart.

Uneducated. No Pavlova. And not half the woman my mother had been. I was always measuring myself against impossible ideals—Martha, or my mother—and coming up short. That's a good recipe for alcoholism.

My mother was a wonderful woman, strong and kind and principled, and she never let me down. She was also a perfectionist, and tried to program us children for perfection. My mother never came to us with her problems, she just shouldered them. And she was my strongest role model, so when I couldn't shoulder my problems, I lost respect for myself. No matter how hard I tried,

I couldn't measure up to my own expectations.

None of this did I know while I was living it. But because drinking relieved me of my feelings of inadequacy, I leaned on alcohol. There are a lot of women like me—I want to do a whole chapter on women alcoholics later in this book—who have done the church things and the book fairs and fixed meals and supervised homework, dedicated their days to their husbands and children, and have no selves, no sense of self.

I was a controlled drinker, no binges. When I went to parties, I was on my best behavior. I drank, but never too much. I always knew there would be more available at home. One of the reasons my drinking didn't have to escalate was that I had begun taking so much medication. If you get up in the morning and swallow a pill, you don't need a drink. The pain pill does the same thing a drink would do, it steadies your nerves. And God help us, it's a great deal more respectable.

In 1965, about a year after I began mixing pain medication with alcohol, I snapped. I packed my bag one afternoon, and decided to drive to the beach, take Susan with me, and let my whole ungrateful family worry

about where I was and whether I was ever coming home. Poor Susan thought I was crazy, and was humiliated by the idea of having a madwoman for a mother. I don't know if there was any connection between my chemical dependency and my crack-up, and as crack-ups go, it wasn't major, but it sufficed. It got my family's attention.

I talked to a psychiatrist, and he said I'd been too busy trying to figure out everyone else's needs, that I'd had no time for Betty. He said I had to start thinking I was valuable, not just as a wife and mother, but as myself. And to myself.

The psychiatrist didn't particularly encourage my drinking, but he didn't suggest I stop drinking either. If he had, I probably would have blanked that out. Anyway, he wasn't treating me for alcoholism, he was treating me for low self-esteem. (Many psychiatrists think if they get to the bottom of the emotional problem, there won't be a drinking problem. That's backwards. You have to get rid of the alcoholism before you can treat the emotional problem.) Besides, I saw no reason to discuss my drinking. I preferred to pretend everything would get better if I went back to dance class, or did

some shopping, or took an afternoon off to write letters.

Jerry, who has always been supportive, blamed himself for a good deal of my misery. He once admitted to a reporter that, because of his schedule, I'd had to be both mother and father to the children. "In election years, I'd go to Michigan after Congress adjourned, be away for three weeks, come home for the weekend, go back to Michigan and my constituents for another three weeks. We always tried to take family vacations at Christmas and in the summer, and those were wonderful times. Still, much of the year I was gone."

I think, as I've already said, I was born alcoholic. The pressures of my life didn't suddenly *make* me an alcoholic, it just took a few years for the disease to develop and surface in force. At one point, I even stopped drinking for two years.

I was hospitalized for stomach trouble. The doctors checked stomach, gallbladder, kidneys, and they couldn't find anything wrong. Then they brought in a specialist who diagnosed my illness as pancreatitis. He said, "Young lady, if I were you, I would just stay on the other side of the room from the bar for a while."

I said fine. If he'd told me I should stay on the other side of the room from the bar for the rest of my life, I would have been deeply offended, and I would have questioned him. As it was, I took his advice.

Jerry asked some of my doctors whether drinking had been the cause of the pancreatitis. They said it was a possibility. "Which shows you," he says, "what enablers the medical profession are. The overwhelming evidence is that drinking is a prime cause of pancreatitis, but they all sort of avoided that, and so I avoided it too."

I don't even remember how or where I started drinking again. It was probably a glass of wine at a dinner party. (Meri Bell and her husband, Del, once quit drinking for a year, and after the year was up, they bragged, "Aren't we great? Let's go celebrate." And they went right to the country club and got smashed.)

My brother Bill says he talked to Jerry about "Betty's problem" back before the White House. He remembers saying, "She takes one drink and she's affected by it. Either she's combining pills and booze, or it's something else." And Jerry reassured him. "If it gets serious, we'll do something."

Nobody wanted to admit it was serious.

Friends who loved me denied the evidence of their own eyes. Sheika Gramshammer, who lives in Vail and has known us since the late sixties, says, "Okay, we saw sometimes she had one bourbon too many, but everybody does that once in a while. And the drugs she took were because of the pain. We all thought, poor darling, she can't get through an evening without pain pills. But we never thought of her as being alcoholic."

Pressed about whether or not she noticed my condition deteriorating over the years, Sheika still makes excuses. "When I first met Betty, she had such a vitality and personality, but I think it must have been a very hard life for her as a congressman's wife, and she had problems with her neck, and nobody ever gave a damn how is the congressman's wife doing, and she couldn't load her problems on him, and then all of a sudden he became President, and she was pushed into the public eye, and that is the cruelest eye anywhere, and it frightened her."

Truthfully, it was *better* in the White House. I flowered. Jerry was no longer away so much. And I was somebody, the First Lady. When I spoke, people listened. I could campaign for women's rights and against child abuse. I began to enjoy a reputation for

candor, and was able to do some good; when I discussed my mastectomy, women all over the country went in for breast examinations.

But the neck problem got worse, so my pills were always with me. Susan talks about "this little black case the doctor kept perpetually filled." Still, I did not drink alcoholically in the White House. There was too much at stake, too much responsibility, I was too heavily scheduled. What little drinking we did was confined to Camp David on a weekend, or drinks upstairs—there was a bar in the President's quarters—before we went to bed.

For anyone who thinks otherwise, let me tell you being an occupant of the White House is no breeze. You have no private life, the demands on your time are constant, you are under terrible pressure. We traveled fast. Often, abroad, exhaustion and pain would take over, and I would have to go to bed with hot packs and pills only to get up later to go to a state dinner. But those dinners and the honor of representing our country meant a lot to me.

It was when we left the White House and moved West that things got worse. Maybe they would have worsened anyway, I don't know. But I was bitter and depressed at

Jerry's having lost the election after twenty-eight years of faithful service to the country. I thought the American people had made a big mistake.

In a sense, I was out of office too. As First Lady, there had been a lot of demands made of me. I had been equal to most of them, performed well and enjoyed my moment in the sun. People with low self-esteem crave reassurance from the outside world.

Now we had abandoned the place where we had spent our entire married life, the children were gone, even Susan had her own condominium, which we helped her buy in Palm Desert, and nobody needed me any longer. At least that's what I thought. And even though, in the early days of our marriage, I had sometimes resented all that needing, now I missed it.

After all the action I'd seen, it was an emotional shock to suddenly be home alone again at night, with my husband gone. Because Jerry's retirement was a fraud; he might as well have been campaigning, he was away teaching, lecturing, serving on the boards of ten or more business or charity organizations.

I'm not trying to make excuses, but I think when you are genetically predisposed

to alcoholism, and you get caught up in just the right circumstances, your controls fall away, and the progression of your disease takes over. When the kids were small, and I was feeling put upon, the circumstances were right. Then I quit drinking for those two years, and later Jerry was Vice President, and then President, and I was too busy—and too much on display—to drink any appreciable amount.

In Rancho Mirage, the circumstances were right again.

We were staying in a leased house while our own new house was being built, and I started working on my autobiography. The constant pain in my neck and back made it unpleasant for me to get up or get dressed or exercise, but somehow I got through the spring and summer of 1977. You can reminisce lying down, if you need to.

At the same time I was collaborating with a writer on my book, I was collaborating with a decorator on fabrics and colors and wallpapers for the new house. It was going up right next door to the house of Nicky and Leonard Firestone, who were close to us in more ways than one.

Nicky wanted me to go see a doctor at USC who had helped one of her daughters

with a knee problem; she thought he might be able to do something about my neck. She made the arrangements, I went to see the man, he ran tests and then phoned Nicky. "I'd be glad to treat Mrs. Ford," he said, "but until I could detox her from all these drugs she's taking, I couldn't do a thing."

He didn't say it to me, he said it to Nicky, and she never told me until much later.

As usual, nobody was telling me anything. They were afraid I *needed* all those drugs. So I went on having pain and taking pills. And feeling guiltless. Pills are infinitely preferable to alcohol if you're trying to convince yourself you're an innocent victim. Doctors prescribe pills, you don't have that excuse with alcohol.

Though I still mixed my poisons. I'd read the labels on pill bottles that said, "Do not operate heavy equipment or use alcohol while taking this medication," and I didn't operate heavy equipment, so I was 50 percent of the way home. As for the rest of it, I thought, well, those labels are for people who don't know how to drink. That's how insane I was, I thought I knew how to drink.

In the fall of 1977, I made a trip to Russia.

I had been hired to narrate the *Nutcracker*

ballet (Jerry and I had signed contracts with NBC that called for each of us to appear on a certain number of television programs), and Bob Barrett accompanied me to Moscow. It was only September—the show was to be aired at Christmastime—but it was already very cold in Russia. I slept with my fur coat over me, and if Barrett and I needed to confer, we sat in the bathroom. It was warmer there.

I remember being driven through town in a limousine, siren screaming, and it didn't matter whether pedestrians were in the road or not, they just had to scatter. I was in terror that we would hit somebody. If the indifference of our driver to the possible injuries of his fellow proletarians made me anxious, so did my assignment. It was fun to visit the ballet school, but sitting in a theater box with all those cameras directed at me was worrisome. I was not a professional, I had no idea how I was coming off, and our three directors—a Russian, a Frenchman and the NBC guy—spent hours yelling at each other. There was vituperation in several languages.

I'd sit for ages in that box, and when they excused me, I'd head for the ladies' room

and take another pill. I could hardly read the cue cards, I was so scared.

When the *Nutcracker* was broadcast back home, the press called me "sloe-eyed and sleepy-tongued," and they were right. I was so overmedicated. I didn't read the notices myself—they were so bad nobody brought them to me, and I certainly didn't search for them. I did watch the tape. Once. I have never had the nerve to look at it again.

Only recently, I asked Jerry if he'd been embarrassed by my appearance. "I knew it wasn't up to what you could do," he said. "It was so slow and deliberate and sedated. But I never told you, because I loved you and I didn't want to hurt you and I didn't want to face the facts."

Wherever I went that fall, I was in a fog. Sometimes a euphoric fog, sometimes a depressed fog. Dolores Hope invited me to serve on the board of Eisenhower Hospital in Rancho Mirage and I faithfully attended meetings, but I didn't contribute a thing. Dolores, who chaired those meetings, says friends were "mumbling" about me. "You were kind of a zombie," she says.

As your physical ability to function deteriorates, you deteriorate in all ways. The synergistic effect of pills plus a drink or two can

be tremendous. Dr. Pursch used to tell us at Long Beach, "The impact isn't two plus two equals four, it's two plus two equals twenty-two."

Jerry believes that Steve and Jack, our two bachelor sons, stopped coming down to spend weekends with us because of "the disagreeable atmosphere that existed."

I tell him I don't like his use of the word "disagreeable," it sounds as though we quarreled, which we didn't. All right, he says, let's say "strained." "Both of us made a big effort to appear to be happy and getting along, we didn't advertise our difficulties, but the atmosphere was strained."

One of the things that drove him crazy was how long it took me to get dressed. I was like a record being played at the wrong speed. Nicky Firestone stopped asking me to lunch because I ate so slowly the other guests got tired of sitting there while I worked my way through a first course. Nicky said it could take me an hour to finish half a sandwich.

It was probably a relief to everybody when I started saying no to invitations. Sometimes Jerry did it for me. "I'd tell people you had the flu," he says. "I was making all these excuses an enabler does. It wasn't that you

74

couldn't go because you were drunk, it was because you weren't healthy; you'd lost your enthusiasm for going to dinner or anywhere else."

I, a controller who had wanted to run the world, was so tranquilized I had become totally passive. Unless I got upset, and then I was very vocal. I was terribly sensitive, easily hurt. If somebody said anything critical to me, I was shattered, I knew nobody liked me, and why should they? Inside, I was empty.

But every week without fail, I went to the doctor's office to be weighed, measured and given a B_{12} shot. And every week I was making progress in the wrong direction, getting thinner, weaker, canceling myself out.

Then Christmas came, and my family got together and decided Something Has to Be Done about Mother.

The funny thing is that in the three months between Christmas and the intervention, I was more energetic and effectual than I had been in ages. I came back to Rancho Mirage from Vail and proceeded to get our new house ready to move into.

Even though I was sick, I was excited. I'd never owned a house in California before, I'd never had a decorator before ("All I knew

was you liked green and white and blue," she says, "and that's what you got"), and as I mentioned earlier, I hadn't had new furniture in thirty years.

Everything was still a mess, the beds weren't in—I'm not sure the bedrooms were —and Jerry was traveling most of the time, and then we lost our lease on the house we'd been renting, so I had to spend the night wherever opportunity presented itself. I stayed at the Firestones' until their kids came for a visit, then I moved over to Susan's condo, but I couldn't stand her cat. Every night, that cat would come in and wrap itself around my neck, and I couldn't sleep. So I moved up to one of the golf cottages at Thunderbird Country Club. My code name (the name used by the Secret Service) has always been Pinafore, but the agents took to calling me Gypsy.

Every morning at six o'clock, I got up and went to the new house and unpacked. We had three huge moving vans filled with possessions from our house in Grand Rapids, possessions from our house in Virginia and personal things we had taken to the White House, all of which had been sitting in storage.

There was no organization, it was awful.

Caroline Coventry helped me, and Clara was there at the very end, and we tore through boxes, me saying, "I want this in the study," or "This goes in the living room," I was determined to be finished before the fifteenth of March, when Jerry came home.

We had no space for half the stuff we unearthed. We piled it in the driveway, the garage. The dining room was solid with boxes —luckily, we still had no dining-room furniture—and the pool was just a big hole in the ground.

But we got the place into good enough shape so we could at least camp out there.

And two weeks after we moved in, they did the intervention. I kid Susan about it. "You waited till I got the whole job done, and then you sent me off to the hospital. Don't you have a twinge of guilt?" Susan says no. "You needed to go. You were sick."

I was sick. It took me sixty years to get to Long Beach, and every one of those years was deeply instructive. It was my life, I probably could not have done it another way, and nobody else was responsible for it. But now I had to change. Or die.

There's a saying among alcoholics that goes, you can take a bottle away from a man

a thousand times, but he only has to put it down once.

At Long Beach, I would learn to put all my bottles down.

4

Extreme remedies are very appropriate for extreme diseases.

Hippocrates

Pat Benedict tells me I fell asleep on the way to Long Beach. She was saying it was a real pretty drive, the sun was shining, but I wasn't very excited about it, I had a lot of anxiety, and sleep was an escape. (Joe Pursch says I slept because I was denying my alcoholism, and he's a psychiatrist, but I have never understood what that had to do with it.)

As we drove onto the hospital grounds, there were cameramen taking pictures, and that upset me. I remember looking out the window of the car and thinking, I'm just not going to show them that I see them. I wondered how they knew I was coming, and I

was ready to blame Pat or Pursch or the hospital, and I thought, they're waiting for me to issue a public statement, and I'm not sure I'm going to do it.

Dr. Pursch: "I knew getting her into the hospital would involve security and agents and telephone lines. And I also knew that alcoholism treatment is not like broken leg treatment, it has to involve other people. And when a group is meeting, for therapy, the door has to be closed. You can't have a Secret Service guy sitting in the group there with a big gun under his coat, and I knew she couldn't have what she normally had, a private room, a room for all the flowers people send, a room for her secretary.

"I believe you have to treat VIPs like any other patients, so there were no officers wearing their medals to greet her when she arrived, as there had been at Bethesda, when her husband was President. And I think this frosted her. She walked in like any other woman would, came up in the elevator, and stepped out into the hall."

And I almost turned right around and got back into the elevator. Because there in the hall was this huge sign that said "Alcohol

79

Rehabilitation Center." I was not ready for that. I had a pill problem, was my position, don't make it sound worse than it is.

I balked at the sign, and I balked at the room they had put me in. There were four beds in that room.

Dr. Pursch: "Pat Benedict came running into my office and said, 'Oh, Captain, that nice lady has turned mad on you, she is going to leave, she won't even sit down.'

"I went into the room, and the nice lady was sitting down, but very straight, on a hard-backed chair. She had this little press release all coiled up in her fist like a diploma—it was going to tell the world why she was here—and she glared at me. 'I am accustomed to having a private room, Doctor,' she said. 'I have been in hospitals before, I'm a good patient, I do what doctors tell me, but not in this setting. Furthermore, you cannot have my statement, I will not release it.'

"I said, 'If you persist in isolation, I am going to tell the other three ladies you don't want to be with them, and they will have to move out.' I knew she couldn't permit me to move her roommates someplace else."

I had the paper with my statement on it—it had been written by my husband, Bob Barrett and me—and I threatened Dr. Pursch. I didn't want to go into a four-bed room. I thought the least they could do was give me a two-bed room. But he stood his ground. Poor Pat just wanted to fade into the background; she says I was very tough.

But Pursch called my bluff. "I'll have the other women come and get their things," he said, and I said, "Oh, no, you're not going to make anyone move for me," and with that, it was settled. I took the bed that was free.

(In each building of the Betty Ford Center, there is a four-bed room. Its occupants refer to it as the Swamp, supposedly in honor of my stay at Long Beach. And it's amazing how some of the people who need it most end up there; it's not a matter of assignment, either, it's just the luck of the draw. We had one very self-important woman arrive from New York—she announced she was a politician's wife, she wasn't going to stay, she was going straight home, she would not be stuck in any four-bed room. She was pretty loaded when she arrived, and giving the admissions people hell, and I said to John Schwarzlose, "If you want me to, I'll be glad to talk to

her. I'll say, 'I know how you feel, but being in a four-bed room can be a great learning experience. And if I, coming from the White House, could manage it, I'll bet you can manage it too.' " I never had to do it. Apparently, the lady rethought her position, and showed up for breakfast the next morning mild as milk.)

My Long Beach roommates had been told I was to be treated just like anybody else, which was only sensible. A couple of them were young, regular Navy. There was one girl who had joined the Navy at eighteen, hadn't been in long, and was shipped home from overseas because she had such a severe drinking problem. She was very lonely. She used to sit on her bed a lot, and was difficult to get to know. She wouldn't open up even to the extent that I would. The third woman was older, much closer to my age. She was an admiral's wife and had been a recovering alcoholic. She'd gone for some root canal work, the dentist had given her Valium, she'd become addicted to Valium, and started drinking again.

Alcoholism is a chronic disease. You'll hear people say, "I was cured," but they're never cured. Alcoholism is treatable, but not curable. And it's progressive. You can abstain

for forty years, and if you start drinking again, it's as though you had been drinking all those years. You will become more desperately alcoholic more quickly.

I was not a model patient at Long Beach. I had a bit of the celebrity hang-up. I considered myself a very special person who had been married to a President of the United States, and I didn't think I should have to discuss my personal problems with just anybody. So group therapy was difficult for me. It was beneficial to me to hear the other people. I related to the feelings they were expressing, but I couldn't let anyone know *I* felt that way.

Dr. Pursch: "On the ward, the other patients were kind of tentative, watching to see how this President's wife was going to react, and she blended in very nicely. Forty-five minutes before she arrived, I had called all the patients together and told them a VIP would be coming in. I gave them a quick lecture on the VIP syndrome. I said it was their chance to be human, and to see that this otherwise privileged lady got at least an ordinary person's advantage. I said, if we treat this lady as somebody other than ourselves, she won't get well. So even though she has lived in the

White House, she will be here on a first-name basis, as someone who has an illness, just like the rest of you.

"I said I also don't want any of you to call your wives whom you haven't talked to for six weeks because all of a sudden you have something to say. And I said, you counselors, I don't want to see that all of a sudden your wives have to come to the hospital to have lunch with you. The food is lousy. Am I making myself clear? I said I was going to be around all day, and the first man or woman that behaved like a schmuck would hear about it from me. Then I said, let's go about our business."

I don't remember much about treatment, but how could I? I was still sick. They told me it would be more than two years before I was completely free of all the chemicals I had used. Prescription drugs are much worse than alcohol that way, they have a very long half-life. So I would sit through lots of lectures and meetings and groups just listening, and trying to pick up one little thing that might make sense to me.

Most treatment programs are fairly simple, but it takes a smart person to work one. In the beginning of my sobriety, for instance,

I had no idea what "let go and let God," meant. It's only five words, and I understand it very well today, but at that time, I was directing God, telling Him what I wanted. I probably gave Him a list.

At Long Beach—as at the Betty Ford Center, and Hazelden, and most good rehab places—patients are required to work the twelve steps of Alcoholics Anonymous. Also at Long Beach, we were required to go to an AA meeting every night. Anyone can go to an open AA meeting, you don't even have to be an alcoholic. Closed meetings are for alcoholics only. It was enough to make me punchy, but I guess I'd been punchy for some time. Meri Bell, whom Dr. Cruse had brought to meet me the week before I came to Long Beach, indicates as much.

Meri Bell Sharbutt: "The first time I saw her, her lips were quivering. She was terrified. She was very gracious, very polite, which you expect a public figure to be, and I talked to her and I talked to the family and then I wrote her a letter. Because when you're afraid, when you're in pain, it's hard to remember things that are said. You remember the gist, you remember the hope, but not the details.

"And the thing I wanted her clearly to understand was that I had been brought into her life because of a mutual disease. I was not a social climber. I said, 'We travel in different circles, our mutual alcoholism is the only thing we can build on. If friendship develops, that's one of the graces we receive. But it need not, it really need not. If you want to live, I am with you to the ends of the earth; if you want to drink, drink on your own time, don't talk to me.' "

It was Dr. Pursch who brought Muriel Zink into my life. He asked her to visit me at Long Beach because she was not only a recovering alcoholic but very well known in the alcoholic rehabilitation field.

Muriel Zink: "I have a feeling Dr. Pursch had some other women come in to meet her before me, but she and I just happened to click. I think he was not getting through to her completely on some levels, and he needed to bring in someone with whom she could identify. We didn't talk so much about alcoholism the first time we met. I told her a little bit about myself, and I didn't ask too many questions.

"I knew it had been Susan who had blown

the whistle on her, and I told her about my own daughter. She said she had once been able to silence Susan with just a look, but this time, Susan had persisted, and how hurtful it had been. We talked a little bit about intervention. After I left her that first day, I did a lot of soul-searching about whether I really did connect that much with her and did I really think she was that neat, or was it because of who she was. Was it that I liked the reflected glory? And I decided as long as I was being myself, and not trying to impress, it was okay.

"Later I got a call from Dr. Pursch saying, 'Mrs. Ford really enjoyed her visit with you. I wonder if you could come back down again?' And I said sure. And he said, 'Listen, would it be possible to bring a women's meeting over here to her? Because the meeting here has swelled considerably since she's come, and I think a smaller group would be helpful.'

"So we came, about fourteen women, and we held a meeting. She was gracious, like a hostess, distributing and picking up the ashtrays. She was not terribly self-disclosing. After that, she came to my home in Laguna for a women's meeting, and we took meetings to her in Long Beach again. She has

since said that the support of these women meant a lot to her.

"Now she talks so easily about her alcoholism, she can say 'drunk,' she's down-to-earth and specific, but back then she had to use euphemisms, explain that her medications had been prescribed by a doctor. She couldn't say, 'I am an addict.' But I don't think that's unusual. I believe as time goes by you begin to understand more, and see more clearly, and identify yourself more with others."

I really liked Muriel, and I wanted to hear what she had to say. I wanted to listen, I'm sure I didn't want to talk to her, I didn't want to talk to anybody, but I thought she was a classy lady, and would be a nifty friend, and if they wanted me to get acquainted with somebody, she was the somebody I was going to pick. She was not threatening. I didn't feel she looked down on me. The first thing she said to me was "You're unique, but you're not unique." I had been a President's wife, but I was also a woman like her, we both had daughters, she came across warm and friendly.

All the women in that support group did, I will be forever grateful to them; they drove

an hour from Laguna to Long Beach, and an hour back, just to meet with me once a week, and each one talked about her recovery, and the things she had done in denial of her alcoholism. When I heard one who was president of some Republican women's group say she had always laced her coffee with vodka on the bad days, I thought of myself back in Virginia, and knew, even if I wasn't ready to admit it, I was like that woman under the skin.

Muriel is right that I wouldn't say I was a drunk. That was beginning to bother a lot of them at Long Beach. Including Dr. Pursch.

I've thought about this a lot. I could *not* say I was alcoholic. I didn't relate to any of the drunk stories I heard. I had never had an urge to hang out at bars, I wasn't about to get kicked out of the Navy if I didn't shape up, nobody was suing me for running over their cat while under the influence.

I knew there was something wrong with me, or my family wouldn't have done the intervention. But there's an enormous difference between other people's thinking you're alcoholic and your thinking you're alcoholic. I was perfectly happy not to drink, I wasn't making a big deal out of not drinking, I was longing for pills, not Pilsener.

I kept asking for medication, and they wouldn't give it to me. I complained that my arm and neck were bothering me. It didn't do me a bit of good. They wanted me to exercise. Well, I was too old and too fragile to play volleyball with the rest of them, but I had a physical therapy program, and I had a walking program. I learned to walk a mile in fourteen minutes. And it was pretty bleak walking—out to the baseball diamond and back. Because Long Beach is a city, all the views from the hospital were of office buildings, empty lots and traffic, and the weather was sad and overcast that April.

We all wore name tags, and wherever I walked, the sailors would yell out, "Hi, Betty." I was sixty, and certainly the oldest patient there at the time. In spite of the fact that they were supposed to treat me normally, I sort of became a pet.

In a sense, I was like a child born into recovery with a gold spoon in its mouth. How could I fail? I had the whole country behind me. Sailors, family, friends, even the press. Not everybody in such a situation gets that kind of support.

When I went into treatment, I was a very slow learner. I said the things I was supposed to say, but no great light went on in

my brain. Example: It was suggested to us patients that a power greater than ourselves could restore us to "sanity." I took offense at that. My first reaction was, well, these people must be much worse off than I am, because I certainly am not insane, and never have been. The idea that you didn't have to be insane to commit an insane act—like insisting on driving while drunk—didn't register with me.

I didn't understand about "self-honesty" either. Wasn't I as honest as the day is long? When I was a child, and charged penny candy on the grocery bill, hadn't I come downstairs that very night and told my mother about it because it was on my conscience? And hadn't she spanked me for it? I never forgave her, and it was a wonder I was ever honest again, but I was. When my counselor talked to me about getting honest with myself, I thought, what the hell does he mean?

But at least I listened. I knew I'd better listen, because I hadn't done a very good job on my own. There's a saying you hear in recovery, "Bring the body, and the mind will follow." I brought the body and wondered if the mind would ever understand.

Then something horrible happened. It

was about ten days into my treatment. I'd been in my regular therapy group, Group Six—we called ourselves the Six-Pack—and I'd thought we had an excellent session. My notes say, "Really good meeting. Dr. Lew's thoughts about the First, Second and Third steps. . . . A discussion of Jim's problem last night. He was curled up crying. Things are really moving along, with everyone openly sharing." Except, probably, me.

Anyway, after our individual small groups broke up, there was a big meeting of all the groups. Jerry was there that day, and went to the meeting with me, and Joe Cruse spoke, and I was pleased to see him.

Lunch followed, and then Jerry and I were summoned to Dr. Pursch's office. There were Pursch, Cruse, Pat Benedict, my counselor and another doctor.

Dr. Cruse: "Pursch had noticed that Betty was getting a little cocksure, she had begun to pull back and get into her denial again, she wasn't as bad off as a lot of the sailors and wives and so forth. That's what the disease does. So he called me to come over, and the President and Pat and Betty's counselor were there, and we just sort of redid the intervention. That's the first time she

really broke down and sobbed, rather than crying silent tears as she had in the first intervention."

Dr. Pursch: "She was scared and angry and frightened and puzzled. She was hoping to continue to reserve for herself the right not only to drink but not to be labeled a drunk. I said, 'We are here because something needs to be faced, and that is that you are also dependent on alcohol.' The President said nothing, and Betty said, 'If you're going to call me an alcoholic, I won't stand for it.'

"I said, 'So far, you have only talked about drugs, but you are going to have to make a public statement saying you are also dependent on alcohol,' She said, 'I can't do that, I don't want to embarrass my husband.'

"I said, 'You are hiding behind your husband, and if you don't believe it, ask him,' And she kind of looked over at the President and said, 'Well?' And he said, 'No, you won't embarrass me.' She was hyperventilating, flushing, blanching, flushing, her blood vessels were going crazy."

Pat Benedict: "I had not been allowed to spend much time with Betty at Long Beach because Dr. Pursch wanted to transfer her

dependence 'from one person to a group, an idea, a system.'

"Treatment was out of my realm, anyway. I had been asked to take her to the women's meeting at Laguna—in order to protect her privacy, we went through a back alley to get there—and I remember saying, 'Betty, before I met you, I used to walk in the front door of these places,' and she laughed and said, 'Well, you hang around me, you've got to go through the alleys.'

"I was still on chemotherapy—I'd only had my mastectomy a few months before—and I was sick in bed on the morning when Dr. Pursch's secretary phoned and said he wanted me in his office at one o'clock. I said, 'I can't.' She said, 'He wants you there.' So I got up and put on a pair of slacks and went over.

"Pursch confronted Betty on her alcoholism, and he was kind of ruthless. I was sitting next to her, and I remember her little eyes were filling, her little nose was running, and I put my arm around her and just held her. They didn't want her to get over pills and keep drinking, and that's how Pursch does things, but I thought, damn you, this is kind of like being raped. It was very hard on her because he isn't tender. To me, that

second intervention was the more painful, and of course, I had grown to love her very much."

Jerry Ford: "Pursch was very tough. I think he felt Betty wasn't responding, she was in denial, she had probably been trying to shut herself off, and he thought he had to shock her. I thought she was going to stomp out of that office. She was mad as hell. I don't remember what I said except that I never considered embarrassment a problem. I never felt any embarrassment, period. Afterward, I got her back to her room, and she lay down. She was still in tears, and I tried to console her, encourage her, strengthen her resolve."

I probably wasn't having anything to do with him at that point. I was real mad and hurt that he hadn't spoken up to defend me. He hadn't allowed me the out I was looking for. I had cried so hard my nose and ears were closed up, my head felt like a balloon, all swollen. Jerry called a doctor to come listen to my chest, and after a while I simmered down. I think it was more the way Pursch did it than what he did. Maybe he should just have said, "Well, Betty, you hide. You're very alcoholic, but it's hidden in your sick-

ness. You hide behind it, you lean on your back or your neck or something."

I don't know, that might have infuriated me just as much. The thing he said that really made me mad was "Betty, you're just as alcoholic as anyone can be, and you're using your husband to hide behind."

I didn't believe I was alcoholic for a minute and I certainly wasn't hiding behind my husband, but I finally figured, if that's what they wanted me to say, then I would say it. If I made enough Brownie points, maybe they'd let me go home early.

They gave another statement to the press the next day. I wrote it out in longhand, and my husband added a couple of corrections. It said in part, "Due to the excellent treatment I have had here at the Long Beach Naval Hospital, I have found I am not only addicted to the medication I have been taking for my arthritis, but also to alcohol. So I am grateful for this program of recovery . . . and pleased to have the opportunity to attend it. I expect it to be a solution for my problems."

What I expected—or hoped—was now they'd all get off my back.

I kept a kind of diary—not regularly, but

from time to time—at Long Beach. Here are a couple of entries:

April 21: "Phone call from Jerry. He filled me in on the progress of the house, new driveway, office, etc. Now to bed. Hell, these damned scratchy blankets. Little did I know when I signed in here it was going to be so rough. It's a good program, but mighty hard for anyone 20, let alone someone who was 60 two weeks ago. Two weeks into my sobriety. Oh well, just one week more, and I get a weekend pass. What in the hell am I doing here? I've even started to talk like the sailors, but I can't sign out. I want it too badly, guess I'll just cry."

April 28: "Hurray. I go home for the weekend. What a relief. Jerry will be there tonight. Now just to get through the day—reveille, breakfast, muster, group, lecture, meetings, physical therapy, lunch."

Jerry Ford: "At the end of three weeks, she came home for a weekend, and there was a tremendous difference. She was just a totally different person."

One part of this totally different person was not entirely adorable. I was on a short string,

my nerves were raw, only three weeks into treatment. People don't understand the mood swings of a recovering alcoholic. I went to the beauty parlor, and the operator cut my hair very short, and I didn't realize what was happening until one side was finished. "What are you doing?" I asked. She said, "Oh, Caroline told me you wanted it short so you could swim in the pool."

I went home with blood in my eye, and screamed at Caroline Coventry, "I could kill you for doing this to me!" I really carried on. Luckily she was as much friend as secretary, and a diplomat to boot.

(I remember back one time when I was making a speech and Caroline said, "Mrs. Ford, please don't take your pills until after you get through with your remarks, because I notice sometimes you don't sound as believable or real as you could." She was trying to be delicate, so she didn't come right out and say you're tripping over your tongue. Friends and family protected me from self-knowledge even as I protected myself. I think this is what happens. You develop a shell that prevents anyone's seeing your true self. You work so hard to prevent anyone else from seeing it that pretty soon you don't see it either.)

On that weekend at home, I was struck by how beautiful everything was. Our decorator, Laura Mako, had done a marvelous job, the dining room was finished, the pool and the Jacuzzi ready, the fountains going. All in three weeks.

On Saturday morning, Dr. Cruse came by to check my blood pressure, and I did some brooding over one of my mates in the Six-Pack, a guy named Hal. You might think I had enough to do, dealing with my own inadequacies, but I was crazy about Hal, and he seemed to be doing all the right things, he spouted the vocabulary, he'd been in treatment before, yet Pat thought he was going to drink again. (Indeed, he did drink again on his way home from Long Beach.)

The most obvious reason you worry about your teammates, aside from affection, is that they mirror your own recovery; if they can't make it, how will you be able to?

For my fourth and final week of treatment, I came back to Long Beach with a box of Kleenex, some Lipton's tea and some quarters for the soda machine.

That last week, I was much more active in my group. During the first days, I had acted as an observer; I had a measure of disdain for the people who didn't speak up so I

could listen and learn. Because *I* didn't want to speak up, I liked those who did, who were open and aggressive and up-front and had lots to say. The more they told their colorful stories, the more they kept the focus off me. I was scornful of the ones who hung back. I thought, they just don't want to admit they've got this problem. Yet I didn't identify myself as one of them.

Nobody ever yelled at me, or said *you're* hanging back, not even the counselor. Maybe they were a little afraid to do it to me, maybe I had them conned. I was a pretty good con artist.

Though sometimes you're not quite so clever as you think. I remember in the Laguna women's group announcing that I never drank much, just a little bit, socially, and they all kept perfectly straight faces and said, "That's right, that's what I thought too, until I began to get well." They were kind, but they weren't conned.

To step back a bit, it was in my second week at Long Beach that I was finally shocked into admitting to my peer group that I was alcoholic. It happened at a family session where a young woman got up and said she didn't know why her family was making such a big deal about her drinking.

The family sessions were much more open than, say, the Six-Pack sessions. Doctors could walk into them, so could any family members. My husband and Steve and Susan all took some family therapy while I was at Long Beach.

"My drinking hasn't caused my folks any trouble," this girl said. And I was well aware that her drinking had caused her folks a lot of trouble, and it was my turn to speak next and suddenly I was on my feet, and I said, "I'm Betty, and I'm an alcoholic, and I *know* my drinking has hurt my family." Because I thought, by God, if she isn't gutsy enough to say it, I will.

It surprised me to hear myself and yet it was a relief.

I had some trouble relating to the very young sailors—men or women. There was one little girl, just a peewee in size and age, and she talked about sniffing crankcase grease to get high, and I had never heard of anything like that, I only related to nice social settings with lovely tall crystal glasses.

And pills. One of my fellow inmates for whom I felt particular sympathy was a young doctor from Bethesda. Before he came to Long Beach, he'd been writing himself narcotics prescriptions, and having them filled

all over a sixty-mile area, and he knew he was getting down to the line, that pretty soon the authorities were going to catch up with those numbers on his prescription pads.

Being in there with all those Navy men made me think about my brother Bob. During World War II, he'd served in the South Pacific cleaning out Japanese machine-gun nests, and he came home not only a hero but an alcoholic. Yet he managed to sober up and go on to help a lot of other drunks. At his funeral, my brother Bill and I were moved by the numbers of people who showed up just to express their love for Bob. "That church was absolutely filled," Bill says, "with poor Indians and ministers and people that flew in on their Lear jets."

In the end, whether or not I could identify with the habits of a twenty-year-old mechanic who'd gone around slurping up the dregs out of grown-ups' glasses since he was eight years old, I could identify with his disease. We were all suffering from the same thing, and it didn't matter where we came from or how we got here. If we could have done something about our sickness on our own, we'd have done it, and stayed out there where the rest of the people are. We stay out there a long time anyway, because that's where we

think the fun is. It's one of the reasons re-covery is so slow.

So we had a lot in common, and we began to listen to each other, and examine our mutual puzzlement. Because most of us *were* puzzled. We didn't know how we got here, we didn't plot our lives so that at seventeen, or twenty-three, or sixty, we could go into treatment. It isn't like setting your sights on a trip around the world.

But we helped each other in countless ways. And we laughed a lot while we were at it. There was a game called Lifeboat—very psychologically revealing, I'm sure—where a bunch of us were supposed to be in a life-boat together, and the boat was going to sink unless a couple of people got out. You had to justify being allowed to stay on board. After we'd heard from everybody, we voted on which unfortunates to jettison.

Some people were noble, and announced that they should be the ones to go because they were the heaviest, or the oldest, or the most useless. Others, with more survival in-stinct, hung on and justified their presence.

I was one of those. I said, "As long as you have me on board, the Secret Service will keep looking till they find us." Not nice? Never mind, the Bloomers are tough.

During our free time—of which there was not a great deal—there were card games, and kibitzing of card games, and drinking of coffee. We all ate together in a cafeteria on the ground level in back. We read, we tried to answer our mail.

I got lots. Not only asking for help, but offering help—understanding, encouragement, praise. I appreciated people's caring, but was astonished at the amount of newspaper coverage, the editorials commending my heroism, my candor, my courage. I hadn't rescued anybody from a burning building, I'd simply put my bottles down. It was my family, not I, who had been "candid" and "courageous,"

Dr. Pursch says he got calls all day long from reporters who said, "I know she's dying to talk to me, and they won't let me get to her." There was even one TV crew that rented a bread truck and drove in and opened the truck's doors, and a TV camera started taking pictures.

I was still telling myself—foolishly, perhaps—that even if I'd gone public with my alcoholism, my recovery was a private matter. Or at least a matter between me and my family and my doctors and my fellow patients. Which got me into another mess.

I had finished my first book. It was already in galleys. And I didn't see any reason to go back and stick in a lot of stuff about alcoholism and drugs.

Dr. Pursch: "I used to talk to her in one-on-one sessions. I remember two incidents. One was the book. She was bragging to me—it must have been the first or second day of her stay at Long Beach—about it. She said, 'My book is coming out,' and of course I'd heard about it, I said, 'What do you mean, it's coming out?' She said, 'I just told you, it's finished.' I said, 'Yeah, but is it complete?' And she looked at me like, God, this guy doesn't talk English good.

"There was another thing like that a couple of weeks later that may not sound as though it related to the book, but it did. I had brought her a little audiotape. It was of a famous politician giving a talk on alcoholism at some meeting or convention. He was then seven years sober. She pushed the tape back at me and said, 'You might as well know, I will never do stuff like that, so don't count on my running around the country talking about how I am an alcoholic.'

"She was still too proud, she couldn't go

105

back on her image, she was saying, don't push me into public view."

I wasn't ready to talk about my alcoholism or my drug addiction. I was having a hard enough time addressing it myself.

When the publishers said a chapter on Long Beach had to go into the book, I said, "No, I won't do it, it has nothing to do with the book."

Jerry Ford: "If my recollection is accurate, it was a crisis. The publishers were uptight, and we had to very delicately convince Betty that it was a proper conclusion to *The Times of My Life*. There was no other responsible way to end the book. I felt the request of the publishers was legitimate, and the problem was to prevail on Betty, make her believe that she could, in her early recovery, be forthright and go public."

Dr. Pursch: "She had physically become very small, and crumpled into herself, but mentally, she was undiminished, and she had the same problems many intelligent people have, she had some anger at existential forces, the fickle finger of fate. Why does this have to happen to me? What did I do? I was no

worse than a lot of people I know. But she didn't have the ego slippage—in a psychiatric sense—where she lost track of conversations or she couldn't remember things. And she had a kind of interesting clinical stubbornness. She wanted to make sure that nobody would subvert her or take over her life."

In the instance of my book, my stubbornness was to no avail. I finally had to agree to add a kind of postscript to my story, and at this point, I can say I am glad I *didn't* win the argument. Too many people have written to tell me how that brief chapter gave them the courage to go for help.

As for my ability to remember conversations, I'm not so sure about that, but I am single-minded. Laura Mako says when we were choosing furniture and fabrics, there were times when I would take my little pill, and drift off, and she'd sit there and wait for me to come back. And some days, she would have to go over the same ground she'd traveled the day before, but she says, "You'd pick the same thing all over again. You had a one-track mind."

It wasn't so much that I knew what I was doing as that I knew what I wanted.

I have been asked how my family feels now that they can't control me anymore, when I'm no longer this nice dopey pill pusher, sitting around nodding. Well, Jerry says they couldn't control me *then*, that in my weakness, my sickness, whatever you want to call it, I controlled everyone. They were all out there fronting for me, covering up, making excuses, and some of them were more resentful than others. Susan found out about her own anger when she came to Long Beach for that week of family therapy.

Susan Ford: "Dad was there for a while, and when he left I went and took his place in a small group. Pete was my counselor. You kind of go in and tell your story, and Dad had taken credit for getting the intervention together, and I was absolutely furious. I said, 'No way. I did it. I'm the one who put the pieces together. Without him, I couldn't have done it, but where does he get off taking all the credit?' Getting that off my chest was a good experience.

"Then one morning, for some reason, nobody wanted to talk, so Pete read us a short story called 'Warm Fuzzies.' It was something about how somebody took a warm fuzzy away from somebody. Well, it was like

taking my heart and pulling it out, it was like the way I felt about my mother, and how she had taken everything away from me, I never had a chance to be a kid, I was always covering for her, and was it really fair, and when was it going to be my turn? That sort of thing. And nobody wanted to comment. And Pete finally said, 'Hey, guys, Susan is asking for help, and nobody wants to say anything.' And then everybody started talking and it was fine. It really made me feel so much better."

Steve Ford: "I was scared to come around at first. I was pretty young, and once Mom got to the naval hospital, I had the sort of feeling that, okay, the doctor's got her under control, and I'll give her some calls and stuff, but I don't need to show up there. Pat Benedict and some other people reassured me that I did need to go up there, that it was important, and I shouldn't be scared, it was part of growing.

"I'll never forget one group session. They talked about if your parents were alcoholic, then it was very likely that you could become alcoholic, and I made the dumb statement, 'Oh, no, I'll never be an alcoholic'— you know, when you're twenty, you think

you know everything—and they jumped all over me. 'Do you think your mother decided to be an alcoholic?' And I had to accept it, yes, I have a good chance of becoming alcoholic, because of my family background.

"The thing I remember best about Long Beach is that Mom was treated like everybody else. She had been First Lady, and that was part of the problem. Her doctors would prescribe whatever she wanted, because they didn't want to make a First Lady mad.

"When I came to Long Beach for the first time, I went down to the cafeteria, where Mom was having something to eat with some of the boys, and they were telling off-color jokes, and I was a little offended. I thought, hey, what is this? Guys telling off-color jokes to my mom here, the First Lady?

"There were admirals and seamen all mixed up, and they were telling these jokes, and she was laughing and having a good time. And it wasn't till later that I realized she needed to be in a real world where people didn't care who she was. That was one of the most important things to come out of Long Beach. It got her back in touch with what people are all about."

Jerry Ford: "I was in a group of five or six who were recovering alcoholics. I spent about five days in all. And I went to a number of meetings with Betty. For the first time I learned about alcoholism. Its being a disease. I saw officers and seamen in my group, and they all had alcohol problems. I went to lectures with fifty or a hundred patients and their families, co-dependents like me.

"It was very educational. I learned that I was making all these excuses an enabler does."

When you have four weeks in a recovery program, your first goal is sobriety. And then you have to find reasons to *stay* sober. I feel better, my life is better, drinking doesn't fix my problems. You say the words, but your understanding is far from perfect.

The body recovers first. As I became freer of the drugs, even my skin began to tingle. The shock of feeling all this is rather disconcerting; your physical body is coming alive again just as the emotions you had medicated away come alive too.

When I first got to Long Beach, I was so shaky I couldn't go down the hall to get coffee. And they wouldn't even let me take vitamins in pill form, they made me take

them in a powder I could shake on my cereal.

But treatment, whatever length it may be, is just that first good swift kick in the pants that's supposed to get you back on the track a little bit.

True sobriety is built more slowly. True sobriety is freedom, and not having to white-knuckle it twenty-four hours a day, worrying that you may drink, or use.

True sobriety is living by a program that helps you handle your emotions so they don't get you in trouble. I was a long way from there when I went home.

But I was sober, and I was beginning to eat right, and exercise. And I was beginning to be happy again.

5

Heaviness may endure for a night, but
Joy cometh in the morning.
                    The Book of Common Prayer

I said in the preface to this book that there is
joy in recovery. Right from the beginning.

I was on a high because my life was all
coming together, everybody was happy with
me, I'd gone and done something about my
alcoholism and drug dependency, I was the
apple of everyone's eye.

It didn't stay that way. I had to prepare
myself for reality. There would be dips in
that happiness, there would be, from time to
time, anger. There would be many adjust-
ments.

I thought I had it made, and the truth
was, I didn't have it made at all, I had only
taken the first step. It was a big step, but the
trip was only beginning. At first, the eupho-
ria was enough. I think of myself numbed
by so many drugs I can't even remember

their names. I had been flat for so long I hadn't heard much of anything, and here I was, body and brain coming alive again.

I began to see the world I'd just been walking through, sleeping through. For me now, there was joy in waking up in the morning, just being able to put my two feet on the floor and go where I wanted to go, even with a bad neck and a bad back and all the rest of it.

I was grateful. I had friends who were dead. From drinking, from cancer. I could have been, and I wasn't. And I had an ego that made me believe I was still young and competitive. Put me on the beach at Maui with a bunch of people in their forties, and they're body surfing, and I think, why shouldn't I body surf?

Body surfing is easy. It's working a recovery program that's hard. It's the reading, the studying, the going to peer group meetings. I had come home without any great enthusiasm for joining any support group. I figured, after my twenty-eight-day crash course, I didn't need to be in meetings every day of the week. And that was where Meri Bell came in.

I spoke to her every day. She didn't permit me to retreat into my old manipulative

style of ducking out of whatever I didn't want to do. Jerry was helpful too. Sometimes I'd try to skip a night, and he'd say, "You always feel better if you go," and I'd go, fuming a little, but I'd be glad later.

Meri Bell was a tiger. She glared at strangers who came near me in meetings. She was aggressive, protective, she said she didn't want my sobriety threatened by a lot of clamor.

It was my habit to be gracious to anyone who approached, but she said, "You're not here to play former First Lady, you're here for the same reason the rest of us are here, to stay sober and work the program to the best of your ability."

Meri Bell Sharbutt: "By the time Betty came back from Long Beach, I had already told a group of women with whom I was associated that a public figure would be coming into our group, and that she was alcoholic, just as I was, as they were. And that's why she was coming, and she should not be treated any differently than they would like to be treated, and if I saw anybody doing that, I would call them on it. I told the ones who were a little pushy, 'Don't treat her like a

celebrity, help her find out what being an alcoholic means.'

"A lot of people put Betty on a pedestal. She couldn't stop that. But what she could do was not put herself on a pedestal. During that first year, she listened to me, and did not speak publicly about recovery. I said you ought not to speak of recovery until you know what recovery is. There are people in the field who say, 'Oh, you can help so many people, you can do so much.' And you want to, and before you know it, you're drawn into this trap of talking glibly with head knowledge, but not heart experience. And there is a big, big difference.

"Betty is a public figure. She is acquainted with arthritis and cancer from personal knowledge. And now alcoholism. And whatever she says may be taken as gospel by a lot of people.

"The big secret, it seemed to me, was for her to keep quiet long enough to find out where she was going."

It was easy for me to keep quiet; speaking out was what terrified me. I used to go to meetings at the last minute to make sure no one would know I was going to be there, for fear they might call on me in some way. And

then I got to this one beginners' meeting, and the leader said, "Betty," and like a dumbbell, in sheer panic, I spoke up and said, "Oh, yes, I'm Betty and I'm an alcoholic." And what I didn't know was there were several other Bettys in the room, and if I'd just kept my mouth shut, I wouldn't have had to speak.

Speaking is frightening not so much because you're uncomfortable talking, but because you're afraid you're going to make a fool of yourself by saying something stupid. And we all have this great wish to prove ourselves the brightest, most capable, most erudite. It's a terrible feeling when you join a new group and you don't really know them and they don't really know you. You're so unsure of yourself.

When we would read aloud from books on alcoholism, we'd go around a table, and each of us would take one paragraph. I'd be counting heads, trying to figure how many paragraphs before they would get to me. Of course, that meant I didn't hear anything that was going on; I was too busy rehearsing my part. Not only did I miss the whole point, I invariably got caught, because somebody would decide she didn't have her

glasses, and she wanted to pass, and I'd be all prepared with the wrong paragraph.

I had to learn I was okay, that I didn't have to be perfect before someone would like me, that it was even okay to be number two, like Avis, as long as I was trying harder.

For me, going to a beginners' meeting is special now. I realize that, after a few years of sobriety, I've forgotten those shaky, scary feelings, and it's good to be reminded of what it's like for the new people.

I went to a beginners' meeting a little while ago. There was a boy there who said he came from nothing, off the streets, but he wasn't drinking anymore, and he wasn't shooting up, and he felt good. "I'm working now," he said. "I never had anything before. If I had anything, I sold it to get drugs. Now I'm starting to buy things, and I just sit in my room and look at them. I got a disc player, I got a TV." He held up a wrist-watch, and everyone cheered. "It isn't mine," he said. "I bought it for my girlfriend. I never bought anybody anything before. Except maybe a bottle of Thunderbird."

And then he said this great line. "If I was all there, I wouldn't be here. But I'm okay."

Clean and sober. The jubilation of it. There was a woman at that meeting who said she'd

just got through the worst day she'd ever lived. Her car had broken down, her little girl had chicken pox, an old boyfriend she detested had shown up, fresh out of jail, on her doorstep. "But I didn't take a drink," she said. "And I didn't do a line. And I'm happy."

There was another young woman who was just out of treatment, and terrified to go to a shopping mall or a movie. She'd been okay in the treatment center, a protected place, but the world outside seemed too big and threatening. "So I came to this meeting," she said, "and it makes me feel whole."

Street kids, jet setters—alcoholics come from all walks of life. There was a foreign girl who had just finished a stint at a treatment center, and she made us all laugh. She said she'd been on holiday on the Riviera, and in the middle of a drink, she had set down her glass and gone to the phone and called the international operator and asked to be connected with the rehab. When she reached admissions, she asked how long treatment lasted. She was told four to six weeks, and was appalled. "I can't stay forty-six weeks," she said.

A boy who was still in treatment at the BFC—we bus them to an outside group once

a week—came up to me after the meeting. "I fight the program," he said. "I don't understand it. But in spite of myself, I'm coming back to life. When I was a kid, I talked a lot. Then, with the drugs, I drew back into myself."

"You'll talk again," I said. "I promise you."

The terrors of those first meetings, and the wonders of those first meetings. Once in a while, during the first year of my sobriety, I felt like a Martian. I sat on the sidelines and listened to young women punctuating their sentences with four-letter words, telling of making their bread on the streets, prostituting themselves to get drugs or alcohol or take care of babies whose fathers were gone.

I had come from such a different milieu; my experiences did not encompass slashing my wrists, or being rescued by the police after swallowing a bottle of whiskey and putting a gun in my mouth. I simply could not see any reflection of myself in those women. *I* wasn't suicidal. But the more I listened, the more I thought about it, the more I wondered, was I really so different?

I hadn't literally closed up the house, but inside myself, I had been pulling down the

shades. It had been my form of suicide. It had been what I wanted.

In those rooms, amidst a sea of Styrofoam coffee cups and a fog of cigarette smoke, I began to understand that I did indeed share those women's disease. And their hopes.

In the beginning, you are more fragile than you—or other people—realize. I came home from Long Beach—they had cameras there to televise my leaving—and discovered I was on instant display. I had been twenty-eight days in treatment, I was still going through drug withdrawal, which takes one to two years, and I found I was expected to greet a lot of Republicans who were having a reception at my house. Not only that, but NBC was coming in to do an interview.

I broke down and cried, I begged not to have it happen. But the TV crew had already arrived from New York. Nobody had consulted me, nobody had consulted my doctors; it was typical leftover White House programming. There's going to be a television interview, we expect you to be ready. Finally, I agreed to sit in the study on the couch next to my husband, and the TV people asked me how I was, and I said I was just fine, gritting my teeth behind my smile.

To me, it was a cruel intrusion; it was as

if they had bought a piece of my life that I had no intention of selling to them.

There was no way I should have been put under such pressure. I was upset with my husband, with politics, with everything and everybody. But something good came from that. Now when I talk to patients at the Center—and I often talk to patients and their families together—I say, 'Stay out of each other's way. You're all very fragile, it's too early to try to run each other's lives.' The person who has just gone through recovery is responsible for himself, and the family members have to realize they must stop trying to manage the alcoholic—who can't be managed anyway. That's terribly important.

In your fragility, you sometimes lose your sense of humor. The first summer after treatment, we were, as usual, in Vail, and since I couldn't have medication, I was taking hot showers, hot packs, electrical treatments for muscle spasms, and so forth. At one point, when I was lying on the hot packs, I saw a little mouse come out of a closet and run around the room and go behind the television set. I was worried he might hit a cable, get a shock, but he was fine; eventually, he ran back into his closet.

The first day I saw him, I didn't think

much about it. We were up in the mountains, in the woods, and we had lots of critters there. Well, this little guy apparently went home and told his dear ones it was okay in my bedroom, and next day he came back with a girlfriend.

When I went in to lunch, I said to my husband and the caretaker, "Do you realize we've got mice? They come out of the closet, run across the room, behind the television, over the draperies, and then go back into the closet."

Jerry turned to the caretaker. "Jon," he said, "she must be drinking again."

I did keep my mouth shut, and was proud of myself. I thought, that's pretty good, I didn't jump down his throat in front of Jon. But later, when we were alone, I told him how I felt. "I know you're kidding," I said, "but you have no idea how raw my wounds are. So please, don't ever say anything like that to me again, particularly in front of someone else. Because it hurts."

P.S.: The next day, they set mousetraps. I was sorry to see the little fellows caught.

We're delicate in our recovery.

And we don't like to be patronized either. Sometimes, on an airplane, a flight attendant, knowing my history, will pick up my

wineglass without even asking me whether or not I want wine. Early in my sobriety, that bothered me. The attendant is trying to be helpful, but it doesn't help at all. In fact, it's quite disturbing to someone newly sober who has been told, "It's your choice, you have the right to drink or not to drink, and only you can make that decision."

When I first came home from Long Beach, I just wanted to get on with my life. In my mind it was like, I've done what I was supposed to do, now let me enjoy my beautiful new bathroom with the sunken tub. I couldn't wait to use the swimming pool, I couldn't wait to entertain.

And we entertained a fair amount that year. We had guests from Washington who sat in the living room and said, "Betty, you just can't be alcoholic. Oh, sure, we all had a few drinks, but you always went home in good shape." Or, "Betty, you never had a problem. I never saw you when you were out of it." I had a lot of work to do, just to sit there and say, "I know you didn't see me when I was out of it." Because I had never allowed *anyone* to see me looking unladylike.

Jerry was no help either. He would say, "Well, you know she never had any trouble with alcohol until she got tangled up with

those pills." This was dangerous stuff for me to hear. I had to turn it off and go back to my support groups. Because the voice of the siren, murmuring, "You were never an alcoholic," fed my own denial. I was like the girl who's a teeny bit pregnant. In my own head, if I was alcoholic, it was just the teeniest bit.

In the groups, they said, "Keep coming back," and, "It works." So I kept coming back, still thinking I wasn't exactly like them, but I had no place else to go.

Sometimes, at night, I would get into bed, and when my husband put his arms around me, I would dissolve. "I just don't understand how I could have done this to you and the children. I'm so ashamed." Jerry would be very calm, and say he was grateful that I was recovering, and alcoholism was a disease, it wasn't something I'd tried to go out and get.

The changes involved in coming home, the emotional relationships with your husband and your family, are difficult. Because all you have done so far is learn a little about your disease, and on sleepless nights you brood over how you've been away for treatment of something that has a stigma associated with it, and you wonder what people are thinking about you. You haven't yet

learned to wonder, what am *I* thinking? I had so much guilt, I blamed myself so much, I badgered Meri Bell as well as Jerry. "I'm an intelligent woman, and I love my family. Why would I do a thing like this? Why would I disappoint them?"

And she would say I was an alcoholic, and if I had not been an alcoholic, then I probably would have been aware of the invisible line that you cross when you move from social drinking to alcoholic drinking. But how? If the line is invisible, how do you see it?

I would guess that I didn't really accept my alcoholism until I was almost a year in the program. But even though I thought I was different, I felt closeness with the other recovering people. All of us had known what it was like to have our lives out of control. In a little black book I treasure, I found a very important message. It said there are two days we don't have to worry about. One is yesterday, because it's gone, and we can't live it over. The other is tomorrow, because we don't know what it will bring. Today, this day, is all we have, so we should make the best of it.

At first, I was so literal-minded this made no sense to me. I would say, "That's just not

possible. If I'm going to visit somebody, I have to let the people know I'm coming, I have to make the plane reservations. I don't understand this program."

Now I understand. Make plans, but don't project how those plans will turn out. Live in the now, live this minute. You only *think* you can control what's going to happen. You may step off a curb and get hit by a car and never make your plane, so it's better to quit second-guessing God, and trust in Him.

That first year of recovery was confusing. I've said there was joy, I've said there was terror, I've said there was denial; sometimes I'd go through all of them in a few hours. I'm thinking of a day in New York. It was the first time I had come East since my treatment, and I was nervous. Jerry and I were still involved with the NBC contract, which we later bought ourselves out of, and we were staying at the Pierre. We were to give a dinner party there for Fred Silverman, who was the new president of NBC.

I was beside myself with anxiety, agitated in mind and body. I wanted desperately to take a tranquilizer because that was the only thing I knew that could help. Then I remembered Dr. Pursch telling us in lectures

that tranquilizers have the same effect as a couple of dry martinis.

At that time, Jerry was still drinking martinis, and a pitcherful had been delivered to our room. There it was on the service cart, with a bucket of ice and a couple of glasses. It was a huge pitcher, and I knew if I took just a little bathroom glass and poured until it was about a third full, the liquor would never be missed. And I would be calm and cool and able to greet and entertain our important guests.

No one would ever know. But I would know. Honesty means self-honesty.

I didn't drink the martini. And the evening went beautifully. I realized I could do it without my old crutch. The growth of something like that is the growth of sobriety. Sobriety is progressive, the same way alcoholism is progressive. That one event has given me the strength to face many others.

There was other growth in our family. In September 1978, Gayle told us she was pregnant, and we rejoiced that we were going to have a grandchild. That same month—on September 14, I remember the date—I had my cosmetic surgery. We were just back from Vail, and I was feeling so good inside I decided I'd like to look just as good outside.

The surgery caused a minor storm. Some women who had admired me for my frankness about cancer and alcoholism pronounced themselves appalled by my vanity. This happened more on the East Coast than on the West, where people have their faces lifted as casually as they drink iced tea.

Three weeks later, the new face was unveiled—I was a centerfold in *People* magazine—and I went to a big bash honoring Fred Astaire in Los Angeles. Then Jerry and I celebrated our thirtieth wedding anniversary, and I accepted a humanitarian award in New Orleans, and there was a party at the Waldorf in New York to mark the coming out of *The Times of My Life*.

All this happened in less than two months. I can hear Meri Bell's voice in my ear: "You're doing too much, you're doing too much, you're doing too much. Please stop."

I didn't stop. And much of the time, I was having fun. I loved the book party at the Waldorf. Henry Kissinger spoke, and so did Pearl Bailey and Flip Wilson. Clara Powell came up from Washington. I wore a peach-colored chiffon dress, smiled at the press, noticed that a couple of people I knew were pretty tight, and thought, gee, that's too bad.

Which was a big step up from gee, I wish

I had a brandy. Interviewers are always asking me if I'm ever tempted to take a pill or a drink. Sure, I've been tempted. I liked alcohol, it made me feel warm. And I loved pills, they took away my tension and my pain. So the thing I have to know is that I haven't got this problem licked; to the day I die, I'll be recovering.

From time to time, in these early days, there was publicity that hurt. Once I picked up a magazine that had an article on women and alcoholism, and there was a drawing of a woman completely disheveled, passed out on a couch, hair all over her face, clothes in disarray, beside a table with a bottle of liquor and pills spilled all around. And the first two words of the article were "Betty Ford." I closed the magazine and put it back, and I wondered if I'd been outspoken once too often, if maybe my alcoholism and recovery would have been better kept more quiet. All I could think was, so this is what they believe about me.

Thanksgiving of 1978 was eventful in many ways. Susan issued a bulletin. She said she and Chuck Vance were planning to be married. Jerry and I were not thrilled, and one of my greatest regrets is that we showed it. Susan was only twenty-one, Chuck a divorced

man with adopted children, and while we said we would support their decision, we also said we thought they ought to wait a while. Susan was our youngest child, our only girl, and we didn't think anybody was good enough for her.

Once the romance became serious, Chuck had to be transferred from our Secret Service detail because it's frowned on for an agent to be dating the daughter of his protectee. He and Susan were angry about that, and when he was transferred to the Los Angeles field office, she went along with him. It was a case of, I'm twenty-one years old, and I'll do as I please. Then they came to us and said they wanted to be married. Well, I suppose we should have heaved a great sigh of relief, but we didn't have the sense.

Susan Ford Vance: "There was no fondness there, between my mother and Chuck. Even after we were married, she would say, 'Well, if things aren't going okay, honey, you can come home anytime.' And that really irritated me, that she had no confidence in my choice. I guess probably after about two years of my marriage, my parents finally gave in.

"The best thing they did—and we still laugh about this—was to go to Jordan right

before the wedding, to visit King Hussein. And since Chuck and I moved the date up, we had only six weeks to plan everything, so Mother hired a social person who knew all the photographers in the desert, and where to get this and that, and then Mother took off for Jordan, and I planned the wedding with this gal. And Mother got back late enough so that anything I had planned she didn't like, she couldn't change.

"So instead of its being my mother's wedding, which is the way most daughters' weddings are, it was really mine. So many times, Chuck and I came close to running off to Las Vegas, saying, 'Let's just elope, and send them a telegram and tell 'em we got married, and forget it.' But we felt that just wouldn't be fair."

I did not want to go to Jordan. I was apprehensive. Not just about Susan's wedding. I was comfortable in my house, I didn't want to go out and test the waters. This would be a semi-official visit to the Middle East, and I wasn't ready for a lot of responsibility, I felt it was too soon.

Jerry put his foot down. "Make up your mind," he said. "You're going."

Jerry Ford: "It was not just a trip to Jordan, we were to visit Israel, Saudi Arabia, Egypt, and I insisted that Betty come. I felt it was good for our marriage to do things together. And during that early part of 1979, I would not have been comfortable going away without her for two weeks. I was concerned about leaving her home alone. Also, she had received a personal invitation from Crown Prince Fahd to come to Saudi Arabia, and I told her the State Department was anxious that she accept. Because for the Saudis to recognize a woman this way was a real breakthrough."

I was still taking orders then, I hadn't yet become assertive. So I abandoned my only daughter—that's the way it seemed to me—and went off on that much-dreaded trip, and had a perfectly fascinating time. History was being made, and one more time, I had a front-row seat. And one more time, it was totally by accident.

We went to Aswan with President Sadat of Egypt and his wife, Jihan. It was the night after the Shah and Shabanou of Iran had made their escape. We were unaware that they had fled till we met them at Aswan. President Sadat had had an entire hotel evac-

uated, and it was completely surrounded by soldiers. There was nobody there but the Shah and his wife, the Sadats, Jerry and me and all our staffs. We had dinner in this big empty room. There was a very deserted, spooky feeling to it.

The Shah was bitter, his wife despondent. I said something about skiing—she'd visited us in Vail—and she said, "Well, it will be a long time before I'll ski again."

In Jerusalem, Menachem Begin gave a dinner for us, and Jerry and I walked the streets Jesus had walked.

In Saudi Arabia, I sat at a sumptuous dinner table between Crown Prince Fahd and Oil Minister Sheik Yamani, who were not accustomed to breaking bread with an American woman visitor on a state occasion.

In Jordan, King Hussein and Queen Noor picked us up at the Amman airport, and he drove us away in his own car. He had two or three jeeps following behind him with machine guns. The next day, we boarded a big plane, which Hussein piloted, for a trip to his beachfront hideaway at Aqaba. Flying over the desert, we could look down and see Bedouins with their tents and camels, and an occasional fancy car. And when we got to

the sea, King Hussein took us out on his yacht, and he steered that too.

We visited the ancient city of Petra, riding camels through a crease in the mountains. Someone brought a camel over to me and dared me to kiss it on the nose, and I did. I've often thought how lucky I was that the dumb thing didn't bite my chin off. The military had flown us to Petra (I had half expected King Hussein to do it, as he'd done everything else) in funny little bubble-nosed helicopters. You sit right up in the bubble, and feel as though you're out in space; those helicopters are like mosquitoes, buzzing up and down.

Across the centuries, Petra's sandstone bluffs have eroded into strange and marvelous shapes; from the east, you approach these ruins by way of a narrow gorge called the Sik.

Glorious, the whole experience I had wanted to avoid. I was still having sleeping problems, and I'd even worried that I wouldn't be able to sleep on the plane going over. As it turned out, none of the things I had feared came to pass. I went through the two weeks sober, clear-eyed and able to appreciate everything. And I thought about other times when my schedule had been

heavy, and I had leaned on drugs and alcohol to keep me going, and later, could not remember half of what had happened.

One year earlier, I couldn't have made that trip, I had been too sick. Now I was physically well, I had some stamina, and I had been relieved of the obligation to keep up with whatever social drinking was being done by my companions. And I thought to myself, hey, I'm doing all right.

I had moments like that in recovery, when I was scared something terrible was going to happen because I felt too good.

We got home ten days before Susan's wedding. Everything was going swimmingly without me. The invitations were out, the designer, Estevez, had finished Susan's dress, arrangements had been made for the church, the orchestra, the caterer, the tent outside the house where the reception would be held.

Because Susan had panicked at the idea of a big wedding, she had switched from a large to a small church, but she hadn't sufficiently cut down the guest list, so not all the people who had been invited got into the small church. The day of the wedding, I spent a good deal of my time fretting about those left standing outside. Gayle, seven months pregnant, was matron of honor, and

she spent a good deal of her time trying to get her bouquet to lie flat against her stomach.

The wedding and the few days right before the wedding are a jumble in my head. We were no sooner unpacked from our Middle Eastern trip than I raced over to Pasadena to help Pearl Bailey do a benefit. Then wedding guests started arriving from all over the country. We got through the rehearsal, and the rehearsal dinner, and the bridal breakfast, and the wedding itself at two-thirty in the afternoon, and the reception followed, replete with dancing and drinking and general merrymaking. Although my son Steve contends that I was not so merry as some of the others.

Steve Ford: "The reception was very hard for Mom. She couldn't stay in the tent the whole time, and I can remember going into the house and sitting with her. I'm sure she wanted to have a drink. You know, most of these guests were people she had not seen since the intervention, and this was a big day for her, a kind of coming out. It was a big deal, you know, your baby's getting married. I sat in the house with her and held her hand."

Susan Ford Vance: "She didn't even have a year of sobriety when we got married. The wedding, I think, was very hard on her. She told some friends of mine that until the moment I walked down the aisle, she never expected me to do it."

To some extent, I suppose both Steve and Susan are right, though I don't agree that I wanted to have a drink. Everything had been moving so fast, I was upset about losing our only daughter, and what I probably wanted was a few days of peace and quiet, which I couldn't schedule. I had board meetings at Eisenhower, there were lunches and parties and a lot of television shots because there was interest in my book, and I was required by contract to make appearances and do the talk shows.

And maybe it *was* all too much too soon. Because in the spring of 1979, I fell into a depression I couldn't shake off in one day or two or three. A while back, I discovered evidence of this in an old notebook.

"I seem to be in a cycle of negative thinking," I had written. "Why? My health is good, summer is coming, we will get away to Vail, I'm a brand-new grandmother [Sarah

Joyce Ford had been born in April], what more can I ask?

"Have I been thinking about myself too much, and not enough about those less fortunate? Has playing the martyr become old hat? Am I looking for more worlds to conquer, and not finding any? Have people built me up too much? I am so far from being perfect, from perfecting myself, and it always surprised me when I was perceived as a heroine. Still, I have enjoyed helping others; maybe I need a new cause, a new challenge."

Then, on my sixty-first birthday, a new challenge came my way. Though I did not instantly recognize it. It began with a phone call from Nicky Firestone to tell me that she and Leonard would not be coming to our house for dinner. "Leonard's in terrible shape," she said.

6

Even in our sleep, pain which cannot forget falls drop by drop upon the heart until in our despair, against our will, comes wisdom through the awful grace of God.

Aeschylus

Leonard Firestone: "I think all alcoholics have a tendency to be suicidal. I used to wake up in the morning and feel so lousy, and I'd get up, go get a couple of drinks, get back in bed and know I'd pass out soon. And I'd think, oh, if I only wouldn't wake up again, this whole damn thing would be over. I didn't have the guts to do anything to myself, but I wished I would die."

Pat Benedict was staying with us that weekend. She had come to help celebrate not only my birthday but the first anniversary of my sobriety. When Nicky called, I said, "Why don't you talk to Pat?" Nicky was reluctant.

"I hate to bother her," she said, "she's just down here for a couple of days' vacation."

Nicky Firestone: "I said I didn't want to bother Pat. 'That would be a busman's holiday,' I said. 'She's here for fun and your birthday party, she doesn't want to be mixed up in this thing, he's a mess, and I can't impose on her.' 'Well,' Betty said, 'she'd love to see Leonard.' "

Pat Benedict: "Ordinarily, I don't hang out in Palm Springs. I work at a juvenile hall with street kids. But I was down there for Betty's birthday, and I was in the Fords' pool, when Betty came to the edge. 'I hate to ask you,' she said, 'because you're supposed to be down here resting, but Mr. Firestone's in trouble.' And I said, 'So?'

"I had only met Leonard once. That was when I was taking care of Betty, Steve and I had been out walking, and we met him, and Steve commented to me. He said, 'I think Mr. Firestone's been drinking.' And I said, 'Steve, he's not only been drinking, he's drunk.' Leonard and I laugh about that now."

Nicky Firestone: The first time I met

Leonard, he was drunk. That was back in 1965. It was at a party, and he had a glass in his hand, and I asked him, 'What's that?' and he said, 'Vodka. And don't give me any of that God stuff.' (The friends who introduced us had told him I was a Christian Scientist.) I told him the vodka wasn't going to do him a bit of good, and walked away. Shortly after that, he went to Menninger's, and he was there two weeks and he came back to Los Angeles, and started going to meetings. After we married, he was sober for a long time."

Leonard Firestone: "In 1965, I woke up in a hospital and my three kids were standing at the foot of the bed, and they said, 'You have to do something.' 'Okay,' I said, 'I'll go to Los Angeles and join AA.' They said no, I'd tried that once and it hadn't worked. And finally, my daughter said, 'Will you do something you don't want to do? Just for us?'

"Well, you know, I was so beat and hung over, and you have to be a real low-down not to respond to three loving kids when they're so concerned, so I said yes, I'd do whatever they wanted me to. They said they wanted me to go to Menninger's, they had a com-

142

pany plane outside, and in ten minutes, I was on my way to Topeka, Kansas.

"In those days, there was great secrecy surrounding the subject of alcoholism. My secretary said to my son, 'I'm very careful not to tell anybody where your father is,' and Brooks said, 'I don't think Dad would care, there's no shame in doing something about your problem, the shame is in not doing something.' That was profound, but at the time, I don't think it made much impression on me. I was a little frightened, I just had the feeling I didn't want everybody to know I was going in for treatment.

"After I came back from Menninger's, I went nine years without a drink, and then I thought I had it under control, that I'd built up a tolerance. So I started again with a little sherry, and then some martinis. For about eight or nine months, I got away with it. Then one night, boom! Down the drain I went. For a couple of years.

"The point—and I try to make this point to patients when I lecture at the Betty Ford Center—is that an alcoholic is never cured. There is no way an alcoholic can build up a tolerance that will permit him to drink. I found this out the hard way."

There's a story Leonard tells in his lectures. It's about the driver of a sixteen-wheeler truck who has to take an oral test before the state will renew his license. "You're coming down a steep grade in the truck," the examiner says. "What would you do?"

"I'd just keep going straight ahead," the driver says.

"You're carrying a load of dynamite," the examiner says. "What would you do?"

"Just keep going straight ahead," the driver says.

"You're almost to a railroad crossing, and you look down a hill and see a slow freight going across the tracks at the bottom of the hill. What would you do?"

"Jam on my brakes."

"You don't have any brakes. What would you do?"

"I'd wake up Ambrose, who is sleeping in the cab next to me."

"Why would you wake up Ambrose?"

"Well," says the driver, "Ambrose is just a country boy, and he's never seen the kind of wreck we're gonna have."

That was the kind of wreck Leonard was headed for, in April 1979, a scant year after I'd had my own crash. He was very dear to Jerry and me, but it was up to Nicky and his

144

family to take action, and Nicky was reluctant.

Nicky Firestone: "Back then, I didn't realize what intervention meant. Betty had talked, but it's like sharing someone else's experiences that you don't really understand. Still, when she urged me to go speak to Pat, I did. And the next thing I knew, Pat was saying, 'Could I see Mr, Firestone?' I said, 'Surely, but he's in terrible condition.'

"We walked across the lawn and into the guest room. I had Leonard out in the guest room, and I'd put the liquor there too. With an alcoholic, it doesn't do any good to take it away, they'll find it, and I didn't want him marching around looking for it, and falling into the pool.

"Pat talked to him, and she came out and said, 'You'll have to do something, he's in very serious condition. I don't know what his blood pressure is because I don't have my tools, but I can guarantee it's abnormally high.'

"Through Joe Cruse, we got a doctor who came immediately, and the minute he walked in, Leonard dismissed him. In a very imperious manner. He said his good friend Pat

Benedict—whom he had just met, by the way—would take care of him."

Pat Benedict: "When Nicky came over to talk to me, for some reason I remember she was wearing a pair of white slacks and a blue shirt and a white hat. She was panicky. I said, 'I'd be happy to go see him, but that's all.' She said, 'What do you mean?' I said, 'My talking to him won't work if you need an intervention.' I went across to the house with her and she took me in and said to Leonard, 'You remember Pat,' and he said, 'Oh, my old friend Pat.' Hell, he didn't remember me from nuthin'. The doctor arrived, and said Leonard's blood pressure was way up 'and we're going to put you in Eisenhower.' 'Oh, no,' Leonard said, 'my old friend Pat will take care of me.' And I thought, God, here we go again.

"I stayed with Leonard in the guest room. That evening, I went over to eat Betty's birthday dinner, and when I went back, Nicky was out on the patio. I said, 'How's Mr. Firestone?' and she said, 'Why, he's sleeping,' and I said, 'No, he isn't. Look, he's over there in the icebox, getting a drink.' Nicky hadn't even heard him.

"Nicky hired a night nurse. Leonard fired her. He said, 'Pat will take care of me.'

Nicky Firestone: "His 'good friend Pat Benedict' did take care of him, and the doctor started him on medication, and we took the liquor away. Len was beginning to be detoxed, and the next thing I knew, Betty had got hold of Joe Pursch, the intervention had been set up, and I felt I'd been railroaded. I didn't have time to think. I said, 'I can't take full responsibility for this.' We were dealing with someone else's life. And he was an adult. True, he was in bad shape, but he was perfectly competent to make a decision.

"Finally, I phoned Leonard's son, Brooks, and I gave him Dr. Pursch's number. I said, 'You call him and talk to him and you make the decision. I feel your father has to have help, but I want us all to be in accord.'

"Brooks came down—his father didn't know he was here—and the next day, we had this surprise intervention."

Pat Benedict: "The next morning, I got Leonard dressed, and I was sitting on the divan rubbing his feet, and in walked President Ford and Betty and Nicky and Brooks

and Joe Pursch. And Leonard looked at them and he looked at me and he looked at them and he looked back at me and he said, 'I think I know what's coming.' "

Leonard Firestone: "When they all came in, I was lying on the couch, I was being detoxed, and Pat began to rub my feet. I loved that, I thought she was doing it to be nice. She was doing it to hold me on the couch so I couldn't go and get a drink, and I'd be there when the intervention came.

"In the old days, they thought you had to get in the gutter before you could get help. Well, I was in a mental gutter. I'd never be in a literal gutter. I have too much money and too many friends, and they could take care of me and find me doctors and hospitals. But the mental gutter is just as bad, and when your friends and family point this out to you, you've got to accept it, and say, 'What do you want me to do?' "

Nicky Firestone: "Basically, Leonard knew he was alcoholic, because he'd had other treatment. But he tried to wiggle out of it. He knew the minute we walked in what was going on, because Betty had had her intervention the year before. And as he wiggled,

the doors closed, one after another. None of them gave. It's terribly emotional because you speak very honestly, you say what you feel, what you as a person can put up with and what you can't put up with.

"Intervention is tough because it's relentless, but it's kind. You don't scream at each other, but you don't give up, you keep hammering until the alcoholic gives in.

"It's the most wonderful concept. Every alcoholic used to kind of feel he or she was the only one. A friend of mine said she thought she was the only person on Park Avenue that had a drinking problem, and she was so ashamed of it she used to hide her bottles in her bedroom and then take them down to the bottom of the apartment house and put them in the garbage because she didn't want them on her floor. Now there are just miraculous things for people to do, places for them to go. The knowledge you get, the knowledge that other people have the same problem, it's all coming together."

Pat Benedict: "When Leonard said he would be willing to go to AA, Betty said, 'No, no, no, Leonard, you're going to go to treatment.'

"The President and Betty were great, you would have thought they did this every day. President Ford said, 'You're my best friend, Leonard, and I'm not going to let you lie over here and die.'

"Leonard's son Brooks did a beautiful job too."

Dr. Pursch: "Leonard was not delighted to have this thing sprung on him, and he was obviously bowled over by the President and Mrs. Ford's being there. He wondered how it all happened; he wondered, when he saw me, 'Who is this guy?' After it was set that he would go for treatment, I said, 'You have just made the right choice,' and he said, 'You know, I don't really like you. You act like you've got the only way.' And I said, 'No, no, only the best way.' "

Dr. Pursch says the reason Leonard's intervention didn't take long was that by then we were all experts. It did work pretty well, and Leonard and Nicky got bundled up into the car and went on over to an alcoholic rehab that Dr. Pursch (who had by then retired from the Navy) was running.

Leonard Firestone: "I didn't like Joe Pursch

at first, but after treatment, I realized he was one of the best friends I ever had for what he did for me. When I went to treatment—it was my second go after nine years of sobriety—I was very ashamed that I fell down again. I went there and got detoxed, and when I had to call friends, and cancel some business appointments, and a golf match, I told everyone, 'I'm down here at a rehab,' and if they said, 'What's that?' I'd say, 'Well, I'm doing the same thing Betty Ford did.' It was a crutch, you know? I wouldn't do that today. I'm not proud of the fact that I'm an alcoholic, but I'm not ashamed of it. I mean, I have the disease, and that's it. Betty took a lot of the stigma out of it."

Nicky Firestone: "When Leonard came out, he and Betty got together with Joe Cruse, who had done a lot of the groundwork, and they began working on plans for a place that eventually became the Betty Ford Center."

At Long Beach, there was no idea in the back of my mind that I was going to go home and start a treatment center, any more than there had been an idea in my mind as a young girl that I was going to go out and be an alcoholic.

That first year of my sobriety, I just wanted to get my own life turned around. But always there was the mail. "I need help." "Please help." "How did you do it?" "Tell me the formula."

I wasn't ready to get involved. And then came the weekend of my birthday and Leonard's intervention, and I *could* offer help to another person who was a dear friend and a good neighbor.

And it worked. Leonard found his recovery, as I found mine, and together, we started out to try and give something back.

7

Thanks be to God, since my leaving drinking of wine, I do find myself much better, and do mind my business better, and do spend less money, and less time lost in idle company.

Samuel Pepys

In the next three years, Leonard and I probably did lose less time in idle company, and

spend less money; we were out *collecting* money to start an alcohol and drug rehabilitation center; friends saw us coming with our hands out and sighed deeply.

Let me say a little more about Leonard here. To put it simply, he's a great man. Once he retired from the big industrialist game, he went into public service. He served as our Ambassador to Belgium; now he labors not only for the Betty Ford Center but for other rehabs in the desert—Turnoff (the place Joe Cruse had Susan take pictures of), which is for kids, and Lost Heads, which is a place where people with limited funds can go.

The only thing that can deter Leonard even briefly from good works is a golf game —he's been described as a gentleman hustler—and for all that he's hung out with crowned heads, he is plainspoken, unpretentious, funny and, most of all, dear.

I'm thinking back to April of 1978, and the dinner party I hadn't wanted to attend at the Firestones', the one Pursch insisted I get over there for, right before I went into treatment, Leonard had told Nicky he wanted to buy me flowers. "I want to get her an orchid wrist corsage."

"Ladies don't wear wrist corsages any-

more," Nicky said. Leonard was adamant. "I don't care whether they do or not. That's what I want to get her."

A year later, we packed him off for treatment, and when he came back, there was something different about him. The change was so apparent to his friends that Walter Annenberg cross-examined him. Leonard seemed to have an inner peace, and Walter wanted to know where it came from, what Leonard had done to get it. "What did they give you in treatment? What is it that you have found?"

Leonard, who is never pompous, even about weighty subjects, said, "I found I was allergic to alcohol, You might say I've got a busted filter. I used to be able to drink but I can't drink anymore, so I've learned to let go. And I've learned I needed love and understanding and help from counseling and a Higher Power."

After that exchange, Leonard called me up in great excitement. Walter (who is trustee emeritus of the Eisenhower Medical Center) had suggested that Leonard and I put our heads together and come up with a plan for starting an alcoholic treatment center at Eisenhower.

Well, I had already been trying to help

Joe Cruse get a treatment center started in the area. Once we went to see an old ranch he thought had possibilities. The White Sun Guest Ranch and Country Club was a place where people used to come to honeymoon, it had been there a long time, and Joe believed it could be developed into a facility like Hazelden. He had also attempted to convince the board at Eisenhower Medical Center that Eisenhower should include a rehab facility. He didn't have much luck.

The feeling Joe got was that the board wasn't ready. I don't know. But I do know that with my recovery, and Leonard's recovery, and Walter Annenberg's awed response to Leonard's serenity, everything changed.

At this point President John Sinn suggested to the rest of the board, "Let's take a look at whether or not this idea of Betty's and Leonard's is a good and logical one."

They took a look. And confirmed our opinion; the Coachella Valley had more than its share of drinkers. More treatment centers for alcoholism were needed in the community. There was only one, although records showed that many of the county's automobile accidents were alcohol- and drug-related.

It used to be that alcoholics were given four or five days' treatment in an acute-care

facility, and then released. The alcoholic would leave, stay sober for maybe thirty days, then start drinking again. It was a revolving door. Sometimes they couldn't even get admitted to a hospital unless they had a stomach problem, or a chest problem, some illness the hospital felt competent to deal with.

Dolores Hope: "I was excited that this issue was going to be addressed, that somebody was going to do something about it. We were having a problem at Eisenhower because we were getting alcoholic patients, and under the provisions of an acute-care hospital, we weren't really supposed to take them in. We were getting criticism from Medicare and other insurance outfits about giving alcoholics beds. Betty, God bless her, told the board alcoholism was a disease, and it had to be treated as you would treat any other disease. But not necessarily in an acute-care hospital."

Well, we—John Sinn, Leonard and I—went out to see if we could raise funds for this thing, and in the beginning, our biggest contributors were the McCallum Foundation and Leonard himself. Each gave half a million dollars. And I had some good luck, though

not the usual kind, in Las Vegas. Walter Probst, who's on the Eisenhower board, flew a bunch of us over for a Sammy Davis opening, and there was a big dinner, and gambling, and then the show, and everybody was drinking wine, and having a good time, and all of a sudden somebody said to somebody else, "You mean you haven't given any cash to Betty's project?" and they started pledging, and by the time it was over, I had people signed up to the tune of a quarter of a million dollars.

Most of these donors were on the Eisenhower board, and I was encouraged because I felt that meant we really had their blessing.

We decided that anybody who gave half a million dollars could have his or her name on a building, and discovered we had some friends who didn't want their names on buildings, they wrote the checks and let the credit go.

Leonard and I got a lesson from the CEO of a large oil company when we went to him for money. "How much do you want?" he said. "Fifty thousand dollars," we said. We were on a private plane, flying back from a golfing weekend in Augusta, Georgia, and we were the CEO's guests, so we felt a little

sheepish about hitting him up for a donation, even in a good cause. He shook his head at our ineptitude. "Don't ever go in asking for what you want," he said. "Ask for twice as much, and maybe you'll get it." Then he gave us a hundred thousand dollars.

We traveled around. We went up to Hazelden, one of the oldest and best-known rehab centers in the country, and took bookkeepers with us to look over how they kept their records; since Joe and Leonard and I had all been to different treatment centers, we borrowed freely from every one of them. We invited experts onto our task force. Ed Johnsen, a builder and developer, came in with us and helped us more than I can tell.

Ed Johnsen: "They have a tendency, in society projects, to have a lot of committees that meet. Sometimes you need a few people on those committees who say, 'Let's do something, not just meet and schedule another meeting.'

"Having put up many homes and commercial buildings, I was able to help a little on the plot plans. Dolores and the top level of trustees at Eisenhower had offered us a portion of the Eisenhower campus; we had the choice of the northeast corner or the

158

southeast corner, and we picked the southeast. It was close to eight acres. We drew up the schematics, the land layout was accepted, the concept was accepted, and a very good commercial architect went to work on the first buildings. They were a bit blockish for my taste, so we put some trees on a couple of the blank walls."

We got our money relatively quickly. We had three million dollars by the third anniversary of my sobriety. And all this time, we were also working on getting legislation passed so we could go ahead and build,

We contended that we could maintain quality recovery at about a third the cost of what was being charged in acute-care hospitals, but there was no licensing in the state of California for the type of bed we were proposing. We had to convince the state, which meant getting a bill introduced in the legislature. Fortunately, I had a friend who was well connected.

Jerry Ford: "I contacted Governor Brown and members of the state legislature. We got hold of a key senator who was in a position to help, and it was his parliamentary skill, along with later help from a member of the

California assembly, that got the bill through. The Senator managed to have it added as a rider to some other piece of legislation, and then I called Jerry Brown to make sure he didn't veto it.

"The sequel is that a year later, after the Center was built and operating, this senator was running for reelection, and he called in his chips. He asked Betty and me to come up and participate in a fund-raising event, and we had no choice. We were indebted to him."

The bill went through in thirty days, but that was only the beginning. Then a committee had to prepare the regulations. For a year, we went back and forth, to and from Sacramento, and met with other people who were running treatment centers, and with state officials, and with doctors working for the state. One of the big arguments was whether to have nurses around the clock. We said we didn't want that.

Nicky Firestone: "They had to go through this legislation because the center was to be a freestanding unit—that is, it wasn't physically connected to a hospital. It would still have all the medical protection of a hospital,

160

but not the expenses, because they didn't need, for instance, to have oxygen in every room. Or trained nurses around the clock. They could get oxygen and emergency care in the flick of an eye, at Eisenhower Hospital. Quicker than you could in a lot of big city hospitals. You could go across the grounds from the Betty Ford Center and be in emergency in two minutes.

"Leonard and Betty worked for months and months with committee members, haggling over details. Deciding whether the proper word in a given phrase should be 'to,' 'for,' 'if,' 'it' or 'but.'

"Then they got it put together, and they hired the staff—Joe Cruse was in charge of that—and all of a sudden, there it was. A miracle. Of course they had loads of help, but it was a miracle anyway."

We were to be on probation for a year, because we were a pilot project. If it hadn't worked, if we hadn't done what we said we were going to do, if we hadn't proven ourselves, they would not have given us a license. When the year was up, we had our license and we were accredited. We had established a type of care, a type of bed, that

the state—and insurance companies—found acceptable.

Sometimes, as we struggled through those endless sessions in Sacramento, I was so grateful for John Sinn, who was our anchor. As a hospital president, he had such vast experience in the ways of government bureaucracy, and hospital administration. All hospitals are run by books of regulations; there's a regulation about how they take out the trash, there's a regulation about how they dispense medication—Leonard got bored with the procedure. He just wanted it to be over and done. "We've put it together," he said. "We know we can provide quality care in a non-institutional setting at a low cost. What's the problem?" It was the cry of a man who'd successfully run a big business banging his head against a bureaucracy. But we made it.

Somewhere in the middle of the process, Leonard, Joe Cruse and John Sinn asked if they could call the new facility the Betty Ford Center. I said I was honored, but I didn't think so. "What are you trying to do," I said, "paint me into a corner? I'll never be able to drink again!" They convinced me that it would be beneficial to our cause if I allowed my name to be used. It

was definitely not my desire. What's more, they made me president of the board. I love the work, and it gives me a chance to lord it over my husband. I say, "Honey, you're just a former president, I am an acting president."

It was a hectic sobriety I was going through while the Center was being built. I was a recovering alcoholic who wanted to have a say in every decision, to have her finger in every pie. My perfectionist spirit coming to the fore again.

When Leonard and I were not on the road drumming up funds, I was traveling with Jerry. We went around the world—to Paris, Tokyo, half a dozen other places. We went to Grand Rapids for the dedication of the Gerald R. Ford Museum. We went to Detroit for the 1980 Republican convention.

In Detroit, I said a lot of prayers. Along the lines of "God, it's in Your hands." Because it looked as though Jerry might be talked into running with Reagan. I knew I shouldn't try to force on him my feelings of not wanting to go back to Washington, of wanting to stay in the desert. I thought of leaving behind the Betty Ford Center, with our work so newly started, and the familiarity of my support groups, and I turned it

163

over. I absolutely let go. I kept repeating, "Thy will, not my will," all the while hoping He might see fit to exercise His will in an agreeable direction.

Jerry Ford: "In 1979, there had been a lot of support for my going after the Republican presidential nomination. I looked at the pluses and minuses—I could lose the nomination, and even if I won the nomination, I might not be elected—and it just made more sense not to get into it. It would have been a replay of the 1976 confrontation between Reagan and me, bitter, counterproductive, and in the end, would have jeopardized the possibility of a Republican victory in November.

"In June of 1980, after I had made the announcement to the press that I would not run for the nomination, President Reagan called and said he'd like to come talk to me, and we met in my office, and he said he hoped I would consider being on the ticket with him. I said I didn't want to be Vice President. 'I can do more good for you by campaigning,' I said, 'and I will.'

"I thought the matter was settled. Then Betty and I flew to Detroit, and the day after we arrived there, President Reagan again

asked if he could see me. And when he came over—it was right at the time of my birthday—he brought a peace pipe as a present. Again, he said they wanted me to be on the ticket. I said, in deference to his request, I would reconsider. We selected four people— Henry Kissinger, Alan Greenspan, Bob Barrett and Jack Marsh, all of whom had been in the Ford White House—to meet with four from the Reagan staff, and they tried to put into writing what my responsibilities as Vice President would be.

"After about thirty-six hours, it became obvious that it was impossible, and I said to President Reagan, 'I think we ought not to try to do this.'

"Betty's recovery was never talked about, but if I had run—for President or Vice President—and in the process it had interfered with her recovery, I would never have forgiven myself. So even though it was not discussed, subjectively it was a factor."

I was more than grateful for the way it played out. I was relieved. My new life in recovery was precious to me and I was glad to be done with politics. I had eaten enough creamed chicken and sat through enough speeches to have earned a presidential par-

don. At one time during my husband's administration I made the smart-aleck remark that a First Lady ought to be paid, she had a full-time job, and I'm not sure I wasn't right.

When your husband is serving, you're an extension of him, you can't always express the way you feel, and I'd never been good at keeping my mouth shut if I had a strong opinion. In the White House, I had embraced the Equal Rights Amendment, I had said I'd been to a psychiatrist, many of my public statements might have mortified a lesser man than Jerry.

Even in Detroit, I was still having to be careful. I had come to Michigan knowing that there was going to be a march for ERA—I had packed a white dress, because the marchers had been asked to wear white—and I wanted to be a part of it.

I can't tell you how many Republicans came to try and talk me out of it. They said it wouldn't reflect well on the party if I marched. I was mad at the party anyway. The Republicans had been first to support ERA, and now they were dropping the ERA plank from their platform. But finally Jerry himself asked me not to go. "As a favor to me," he put it. He didn't *tell* me not to, because the minute anybody tells me I can't

do something, I have to prove I can. Though I'm getting better, the longer I'm sober.

So I didn't march. I stood there in the window of our hotel suite, and watched the parade go by, a dutiful wife and a disappointed feminist in one quivering package.

Other days, there were other wonders outside that window.

Ann Cullen: "The Renaissance Center Hotel is three great glass towers. It's so big you need bread crumbs to find your way around it. While we were there, a wild storm came up, and the management called us from downstairs and said to pull the blinds shut so that if the windows broke, they wouldn't cut anyone, and then to go hug an interior wall.

"I plastered myself against an interior wall, and looked around for Mrs. Ford, and she was pressed flat against a window, peering out."

Well, I'm a fatalist. And it was a wonderful storm, a wonderful freak of nature, and I wanted to look around and see how far it went. I wouldn't have missed it for the world.

Ann Cullen: "She is a fatalist. During 1980, there were not only dozens of task force

meetings about the Center, but there was also a full swing of speaking events for Mrs. Ford, and on one plane—it was a small jet—going from Westchester to Florida, we flew through another terrible thunderstorm. The President was with us, he was on his way to talk in Boca Raton, and Mrs. Ford was going to give a speech in Fort Lauderdale for the ERA. The lightning was everywhere, you couldn't get under it, you couldn't get over it, sandwiches were flying all around the cabin, at one moment a bolt of lightning flashed right through the plane. And President and Mrs. Ford were sitting quietly, holding hands, and she said to him, 'Well, honey, maybe this is it.' And I said, 'Great, but did you have to take me with you?' "

It does go through your mind: I wonder if this is going to be the last flight I ever take. Once when I was young, like Ann, and it would have been more serious—we had four little kids at home—we flew out of Aspen in a blinding snowstorm. This was an exception for us, since we usually went on separate flights. We were heading right into the mountains, and you couldn't even see the tips of the plane's wings, it was like being in a bullet. Nobody said a word, we all just

watched the altimeter and willed the plane to for God's sake get up, get over those mountains.

You have to have a sense of humor at moments like that. There's an end to everybody's life, and there is not much we can do about it. It's no use to say, 'Stop! I'm not ready.'

Terrible things happen. I was standing in my kitchen when my husband called and told me President Kennedy had been killed. We were in Tokyo when we got word that President Reagan had been shot. When Jerry was President, two different lunatics tried to murder him. Qaddafi has threatened that he has terrorists right here in the United States. But I don't waste time worrying about the possibility of disaster. A golf ball could come over my roof and hit me on the head while I was out picking roses. I believe when your time is up, your time is up, and you will proceed to the promised land. You hope.

Jerry feels the same way. He is incredibly matter-of-fact in the face of danger. When he was shot at in Sacramento, he was en route to pay a courtesy call on Governor Brown. After the incident, he just continued on his way, walked into Brown's office and never

uttered a word about what had happened. "Why should I?" he says.

In Detroit, in 1980, there were events to which I wasn't invited, and I survived. I went ahead and made other plans. The reason I tell this is that I feel it demonstrates a measure of recovery. Once, I might have been humiliated at not being on certain guest lists, but I had already built enough self-confidence so I could face the fact that I wasn't a favorite of everyone's. And that was all right. Not everybody is a favorite of mine.

You get well gradually. It doesn't happen overnight. It's like Muriel Zink said, "Treatment is really just your major detox, it gives you some tools to work with."

It isn't that I never get angry anymore, it's just that I try not to be consumed by my anger. Alcoholics don't handle anger well, but you learn in your program that you can't allow yourself to wallow in it.

And once again, I was realizing how much more fun it is to travel when you're straight. I was seeing, hearing, tasting with a sharpness I thought I'd lost. Sometimes, what I tasted was unexpected, as in Tokyo. It was in 1981 that Nancy Kissinger and I traveled to Tokyo with our husbands for what Jerry

describes as "a thoughtful discussion on foreign policy."

Among the events for which the two men had promised to show up was a television talk show. To analyze matters of state, they assumed. But when we got to the studio—Nancy and I went along—the hosts said, "We want you to come sit down, and we are going to serve you Japanese food."

All four of us were ushered in, seated and offered various Japanese delicacies, and then we were requested to say what we thought of them. It was very hard on Henry's ego. One of the great minds of the Western world, and instead of asking his opinion about world affairs, the interviewers wanted to know what he thought of raw fish.

There was another trip—an around-the-world jaunt on which Leonard and Nicky also went. We were in Chungking, China, when someone in our group said, "We haven't had any rice yet. Why not?" and our guide said, "Rice is for working people and tourists, not for banquets. If they do serve rice at a banquet, it comes at the end, and the protocol is to say, 'Oh, no, thank you, I've had quite enough.' It's an insult if you take rice after they have given you their finest cuisine."

Well, Nicky hadn't heard this conversation. And that night, at the end of dinner with the mayor of Chungking and all the top brass, they brought out the rice. And I said, "Oh, no, thank you, I've had quite enough." And the next thing I heard was Nicky saying, "Oh, rice, I just love rice, and I haven't had any on this whole trip." And she started filling her plate, and it was hard for me not to burst out laughing. She had no idea she had just broken all tradition.

We went for a wonderful boat trip on the Yangtze River, and just to stir things up, the Secret Service agents told us there would be nine hundred people on board, and only four bathrooms. This so alarmed Nicky that she ran out and bought a little cooking pot with a handle on it. She was going to be prepared. Well, it turned out that our comparatively small party was assigned one entire enormous deck of the boat, and there were plenty of very adequate bathrooms. When we disembarked, Nicky left her cooking pot behind. Or tried to.

She had no sooner started down the gangplank than a Chinese steward came chasing after her crying, "Missy Firestone! Missy Firestone! You forget pot!" She couldn't lose that thing.

When Jerry was President, and we went to China in 1975, it was very cold. Packing for the trip home, reporters would try to leave torn panty hose in the wastebaskets, or long underwear, because they didn't need it anymore. Television people buy long underwear for a trip, charge it to their networks, and then, rather than wash it, abandon it. But you can't abandon goods in China. The Chinese had been so poor they didn't understand how anyone would throw anything away, and furthermore, they were so honest, they just packed up the panty hose and long underwear and mailed them to their owners at the next port of call. So there was no way "Missy" Firestone was going to leave behind a brand-new, unused pot!

We had good times, the Firestones and the Fords. We'd had good times in our drinking days, and we had good times in our days of sobriety.

In Paris, I procured my first and only Chanel suit.

In Jakarta, I fed gorgeous tropical birds and never realized until later that what I had been plunging my hand into was a bowl of fat white grubs.

People drank all around us; it didn't bother Leonard or me. One of the things we'd both

learned in treatment was, it was our choice to drink or not to drink. Although sometimes somebody chooses for you, and you find yourself surprised. I remember that one time at a dinner party in a restaurant—we were guests, so were the Firestones—an ice was served, after a fish course.

Everybody started eating, and once I'd had a couple of spoonfuls, I realized it was champagne, straight champagne, frozen, and then mushed up.

I sat there, spoon raised, thinking, this is absolutely divine, and I looked across the table to where Len was sitting, and he had his spoon raised too. Now it was early in his sobriety, it was his first year, and our eyes met, and we both smiled, said, "Um-hmm," and put our spoons down.

For a recovering person, it's very dangerous to take that first bite, sip, slug of anything alcoholic. Abstinence is the only guarantee of sobriety. Besides, for some people, one drink is all it takes. They wake up a week or two later, after a total binge, and they never again come back to a support group.

Even if you're an "episodic" alcoholic, that first drink is dangerous for what it does to your head. You start thinking, gee, I didn't

fall down or turn green, maybe everybody got too excited about my being sick, maybe I wasn't so sick. If you should be unlucky enough not to get drunk with the first drink, the next week you're saying, well, that glass of wine last week didn't affect me, so I think I'll have another one. And when the second one doesn't affect you either, it's too late, you're on your way.

That's why they say it's not the tenth drink or the twelfth drink or the hundredth drink, it's the first drink you have to watch out for, it's the first drink that causes the turnaround and begins to undermine the truth. Which is that alcoholics cannot drink, ever, if they expect to stay well.

On September 18, 1981, a little more than a year before the Betty Ford Center was dedicated, we dedicated the Gerald R. Ford Museum. Only a man as well liked as my husband could have pulled such a crowd to Grand Rapids. The Reagans came, and the Bushes, and the President of France, and the Foreign Minister of Japan and the Prime Minister of Canada and the President of Mexico and Lady Bird Johnson and Teddy Kennedy and Tip O'Neill and Bob Dole and Margaret Truman.

Bob Hope did a television special from

Grand Rapids—I was his partner in a brief soft-shoe number—and the whole University of Michigan Marching Band performed, and there were banquets at night and parades in the daytime. The festivities were many and colorful.

I rode a float, and the weather was freezing, and the crowds were so large it took mounted police to control them, which is pretty unusual for Grand Rapids. In fact, my agents and I were caught out in the middle of the mob when I was supposed to be at the Museum with my husband, greeting the Reagans. We couldn't get through. *C'est la guerre*.

The networks came and did television for two days, and there was so much security in the hotel with all these heads of state that you couldn't get up or down in an elevator.

The Museum turned out to be absolutely splendid. Built on a riverbank, in the middle of a huge clear park, it's filled with memorabilia gathered from the State Department. And from me. I went through many old trunks looking for Jerry's baby shoes and baby clothes. His mother had saved his Boy Scout uniforms, and his Navy uniforms, and that's one of the nicest things about his mu-

seum. It's not a monument to greatness, it's a monument to the average man. It's a museum in the town where Jerry grew up, the town that knew him as a schoolboy, as a football player, as a son of the middle class who grew up to be President. It sort of says, this can happen to anyone.

One of the most beautiful things in it is a complete full-scale reproduction of the Oval Office in the White House. It's perfect in every detail, down to the acanthus leaves carved into the door moldings, with the draperies, the appointments, the furniture reproduced as they were when Jerry was President, clock, books, family photographs in place.

People come in there, and they suddenly fall quiet. It's unbelievable, like being in the real Oval Office.

There were many trips in 1980, '81, '82. Some were for pleasure, some were for duty, most were to raise money for the Betty Ford Center. Always, there was the ongoing business of the Center. I wanted to be involved in everything. I helped choose the chairs, the carpeting, the pictures on the walls, the colors of the bedspreads. I also helped to hire personnel.

John Schwarzlose: "I first met Betty in Feb-

ruary of 1982. I was a consultant to the Hazelden Foundation in Minnesota (I was also running a program for alcoholics back in Peoria, Illinois) and the people at Hazelden had recommended me to Joe Cruse. Joe was medical director of the BFC, and they were looking for a program director. This was before the center was open.

"When Betty interviewed me, we discussed my feelings concerning treatment but in particular how I would assimilate the AA program and ideals into the BFC treatment program. I could see her wondering if I, as a non-alcoholic, would be able to run such a program.

"She asked me other questions too. 'What is important to you?' 'What are your outside interests?'

"A month later, I got a phone call offering me the job.

"I already had over ten years in the field. My experience dated back to 1972. While finishing up a master's degree in psychology, I'd had to spend some time at a state hospital in Illinois, and one of the units they put me on was the alcoholic unit. Then I spent a couple of terms on a mental health unit. The contrast was startling. On the alcoholic unit, there was a positiveness, you could see the

men and women getting well. So I got very excited, but at that time, professionals with academic degrees didn't want to have anything to do with alcoholism. One of my professors said, 'John, you have such a bright future, don't waste your life with a bunch of drunks.'

"To this day, that is not an unusual point of view. A doctor recently visited the Betty Ford Center and he told us that in his city 90 percent of the alcoholic and drug treatment beds are in psychiatric hospitals. That's where the authorities believe they should be, and this is 1986!

"Most of the time, those patients aren't there voluntarily, but the point is, if that's where treatment is happening in that city, it shows how far we still have to go.

"The other people taking the tour that day were filled with amazement that ours was an open campus, that patients were free to come and go within the campus area.

"It isn't only out-of-towners who have odd ideas about alcoholics. The dietary staff asked if we were going to give the patients knives and forks, and as we were getting ready to open, we found ourselves fielding all kinds of questions from interested citizens. Was Eisenhower Medical Center going to have to

increase the security on its campus? Was it safe to have so much glass in the buildings? They would say, 'Didn't you see *One Flew Over the Cuckoo's Nest?*' That was their image of alcoholics, that they were crazy and we were going to have to lock them up.

"When I was hired by Hazelden to run a hospital program, they brought me to Minnesota and had me enter as a patient for five weeks. They said, 'Even though you're not addicted, see how the steps of AA apply to your life.' And it was then I first started working the program for myself, accepting that I don't have control over how my life is going to go, and God does.

"It was a very good lesson. At the Betty Ford Center, we also put all our staff through treatment so they can get a feel for the patients' experience.

"By September 7, 1982, we had assembled a staff of twenty-four, and we proceeded to give them five weeks of intensive training. Hazelden sent a couple of people to help, and Betty came over the first day to meet everybody. She was wearing her hard hat because the buildings were still being finished. She shook every staff member's hand, and let them know how important they were in her eyes."

We were set to hold our Dedication ceremonies on October 3, and open our doors the following morning. A few days earlier, we scheduled what we referred to as a dry run, a phrase we thought was quite appropriate. A group of people from Eisenhower (nurses, nutritionists, bookkeepers), plus some of us alcoholics (volunteers from AA, and Leonard and I), came in for a test. We played the roles of patients, and the staff got to practice on us.

8

I have seen flowers come in stony places . . .

John Masefield

There were about twenty of us in the guinea-pig group for the dry run. We were asked to give our opinions of the food, the beds, the way the showers, as well as the therapy, worked. It was only for three days and two

nights, but we all got an incredible boost out of the experience.

John Schwarzlose: "I had to decide who was going to room with Betty, and I picked a young therapist from Eisenhower Hospital. She was just kind of low-key. I didn't want someone who was going to sell her story to the *National Enquirer.* I also told the counselors, a couple of whom were quite intimidated by having Betty there, that they didn't have to get into deep therapy with her or Leonard."

Deep therapy or not—who had time for deep therapy?—Leonard and I were plenty busy. We were opening not only a new building but a new program, and everything had to be shaken down. Did the doors work? Were there bottlenecks at the food lines in the cafeteria? Were some of the instructional movies boring?

I was the Granny—there's a Granny for every residence hall—and he or she is supposed to make sure everyone else does his or her job assignments. If you have a problem, you go to the Granny. If your bed isn't made correctly, the Granny is supposed to strip it. At least, they didn't make me clean the

showers—at Long Beach, they made me clean the showers—but the idea of somebody who could never get anyplace on time being responsible for getting nineteen other people to places on time had its comic aspect.

We went through the whole drill, let the admissions people take our histories, signed a dozen different forms, checking for possible glitches in the routines. The counselors tested their lectures and tapes on the twenty of us, and we wrote out criticisms and turned them in. We didn't sign our names; we didn't dare.

One of the lectures I most admired was given by John Schwarzlose. It was on recovery. John said that, with a cold, you know you'll feel better in a few days, while with major surgery, you know it's going to take longer. But with a chronic disease—arthritis, diabetes, chemical dependency—there's no clear beginning, no clear end. You can't say, "On March 6, I got arthritis; on March 5, I didn't have it." It doesn't work that way.

He told us that alcoholics have to develop a continuing recovery plan, a blueprint for what's going to happen in our lives.

The world of treatment, as anyone who goes through it discovers, is unreal. You wish

all that hugging and mutual support did go on in the real world, but it doesn't. Sitting around at night in your bathrobe with three other patients in bathrobes, all trading stories and life experiences, can be more important than group therapy, lectures, anything.

On the third day of our shakedown—we'd come in on a Tuesday and were going home on Thursday—we had a medallion ceremony. Ordinarily, at the Betty Ford Center, you get your medallion when you have completed your four or six weeks of treatment. Everyone in your hall comes, counselors and patients, and the bronze medallion—about the size of a half-dollar, with the serenity prayer on one side and the five-star emblem of General Eisenhower on the other—is passed from hand to hand. Each person takes it and holds it, while saying something about the patient who is leaving.

We had guests come in for our medallion ceremony, people from Eisenhower, including President John Sinn, and his wife Joan. Some of our husbands and wives showed up too.

It was moving. A man—an administrator at Eisenhower who had been one of our pseudo patients—said, "I learned how to be

myself here." And he thanked his counselor "for reminding me that in losing we win."

Not bad progress for three days' work.

Leonard's counselor said at first he'd thought Leonard was going to fly the coop. "I came to work at eight o'clock yesterday morning and here's this guy standing on the side of the road, and he had some long story about packing two pajama tops and no bottoms, or something, and his wife was bringing them. Whatever that was all about, you stayed with us, Len, and it's been good."

Leonard agreed. He said when the trustees had asked him and me to head up the task force to put this project together, we'd had three concerns: whether we could raise the money, how the physical plant we'd envisioned would work and whether we could get the right counselors and director, because without the right people, we wouldn't have anything.

"It looks to me," he said, "that we've got a terrific program. And what encourages me even more than my own thoughts is the fact that those non-alcoholics who were here for the past couple of days have been so impressed and thrilled and excited about what *they've* gone through."

At the end of the medallion ceremony,

John Schwarzlose introduced "the head coach of our team, Joe Cruse," and as Joe walked up to the front of the room, one of the counselors yelled out, "Keep it short!" and Joe laughed along with everyone else and said, "After five weeks of training, they start getting sassy."

Joe said our counseling staff and support staff were like racehorses kicking at the gate, eager to break away, he spoke of patients having made reservations for next week, and then he talked directly to our guests. "You can see that in a very short period of time, a real spiritual sharing can take place." He said lives were going to be "turned around in this place."

At the end of the program, we formed a circle, joined hands and said the Serenity Prayer. Contrary to what many people think, the Serenity Prayer did *not* originate with —or in—Alcoholics Anonymous. It's the work of the Protestant theologian Reinhold Niebuhr, an intellectual whose scholarly writings are not easily followed by the average reader. Yet this prayer is as clear and bracing as water from a mountain stream.

It reads:

God grant me the Serenity

to accept the things I
cannot change;

Courage to change the
things I can; and

Wisdom to know the
difference.

Most support groups end each meeting
with those words, but there are more. The
prayer goes on:

Living one day at a time;
Enjoying one moment at a
time; Accepting hardship
as the pathway to peace;

Taking, as He did, this
sinful world as it is, not
as I would have it;

Trusting that He will make
all things right if I
surrender to His will;

That I may be reasonably
happy in this life, and

supremely happy with Him
forever in the next.

                 Amen.

And again, amen. To take the world as it is, one day at a time, is advice alcoholics need—it isn't bad advice for anybody—and I needed it more than most, as the medallion ceremony came to a close. It seemed to me there were still a million details that had to be taken care of before we could open this place.

It was the little things we might have forgotten that haunted me. We discovered the bathrooms were underequipped, and I went out to a shopping mall, Secret Service agents in tow, and ran around collecting soap dishes and toothbrush holders and glasses. There was no time to order them. It was like, we've got to get this thing done today, patients will soon be living in those rooms.

I had no anxiety about the big things. I knew we had great counselors; we'd interviewed extensively, and drawn them from all over the country—Minnesota, Louisiana, California—and we'd looked for the healthiest people we could find. Some were recovering alcoholics, some were not.

John Schwarzlose: "Alcoholism counseling is a big burnout field because people get so involved. I remember the first time one of my patients committed suicide. The guilt just overwhelmed me. It was in Peoria, a woman who was struggling in early recovery. She'd been sober seven or eight months, and she shot herself.

"You go through some terrible things. You think, if I had been a little more responsive, if I had done this or that. And then you're at the funeral, and nobody there knows you, the family doesn't know you. And you're crying, and everybody's wondering, who in the heck is this guy?"

It's the primary counselors who have the hardest job learning not to take their work home with them. They walk into a building every morning where they have seven to ten patients, each at a different place in his treatment, and what they must be able to say to those patients is: "I hear your pain, I understand your pain, but I can't take it over. It's yours. I want to help you feel it and then let go of it." Sometimes it's hard to make a new counselor understand he can't save the world, he can only be a guide.

When I say we looked for people who

were healthy, I don't mean people who didn't have problems, I mean people who were working on their problems, people who were growing emotionally. And we had got them. And now they were raring to go.

The night before the Dedication of the Betty Ford Center, Jerry and I went over there—it was already dark out—and walked through the three completed buildings: Firestone (administration), McCallum and West (residence halls). All the dignitaries who would be coming to the Dedication would also be offered a guided tour of the premises, and I wanted to make certain no doorknobs came off in their hands. My proud husband by my side, I wandered, switching lights on and off and straightening the pictures on the walls.

There was so much curiosity out there in the world about what we were doing, and I wanted it to be presented in the best possible way. It's funny to think of now, because the Center has changed so much since we first opened. As I've changed. As anything grows.

A break in the campaign swing—our rehearsal dinner.
The candidate arrived for dessert!

Couple of experts on U.S. foreign policy discussing not ships, strategy or "Star Wars," but sushi, sashimi and tempura. (P.S., I'm not one of the experts!) [Photo courtesy of Kansai Television, Japan]

The dedication of the Betty Ford Center, October 3, 1982. The dais guests included: (from left) Joan Sinn, John Sinn, Bob Hope, Barbara Bush, Vice President George Bush, Dolores Hope, Nicky Firestone, Leonard Firestone. [Photo courtesy of the Eisenhower Medical Center.]

Jerry and I are very fortunate to have four children who became such fine adults. (Mike, top, Jack, left, Steve, right, and Susan Ford Vance.) [Photo by Russ Ohlson.]

This is the campus of the Betty Ford Center, which is located at the Eisenhower Medical Center. [Photo courtesy of the Eisenhower Medical Center.]

9

Do you know what it is as you pass
to be loved by strangers?

Walt Whitman

The day we opened, we admitted two patients, and three the day after that. Within a week, McCallum Hall's twenty beds were filled.

John Schwarzlose: "The way the Betty Ford Center took off caught us all by surprise. We had high hopes, but we foresaw a gradual growth, not a boom. And I watched Betty and wondered how you stay humble when everybody's saying, 'Mrs. Ford, you saved my life.' But she always saw that it was God working through her. She said the way she had become First Lady had been a stroke of fate, and this new chance to help other recovering alcoholics through her own recovery was also fate's intervening.

"In the early days, she was a people

pleaser. She couldn't tell anybody no. Some-one would call and say, 'Mrs. Ford, you may not remember me, but I have this brother-in-law in New Orleans, could you get him into treatment?' and she'd be on the phone to me. 'We gotta get him in right now.' And I'd say, 'Betty, there's no emergency in chemical dependency. If the guy needs med-ical treatment, let's put him in an acute-care hospital, and as soon as we have a bed, we'll bring him here.'

"We don't push anybody aside in order to make room for apparent VIPs, or relatives of VIPs. Everybody goes on the same waiting list, and is notified when a bed comes free. We think Joe Schmoe who's out of work in San Diego is just as important as a friend of somebody on our board. Betty's expectation is that everyone gets VIP treatment at the Center.

"During the first year, we were feeling our way, trying to cope with so many things we hadn't expected. We'd thought we would fill up gradually, we'd thought most of our patients would be from southern California, we hadn't expected so much interest from men and women all across the U.S. and from many other countries.

"One day, Betty and I were touring the

Center with some representatives from a large corporation, and one of them turned to her and said, 'This place is so beautiful, we're going to send our executives here.' And I was so proud of her. She looked at this man and said, 'Unless you'll send us your truck drivers, we don't want your executives.' "

Blame it on the Navy. I had taken my first, tentative steps toward getting well along with a crowd of sailors who didn't have trust funds. Pat Benedict, on whom I had leaned so much for strength and goodness of heart, spent her Thanksgivings in the barrio, feeding the homeless. And I was determined that our program not become a program for the rich and famous. It had to be for everybody, or it would not work.

Sometimes I thought it wasn't going to work anyway. We'd been going about six months when, at a meeting, the board asked John what kind of reports he was getting on how patients were doing. John said the reports were "fair," but there were a couple of local people who, after they got out, had used again very quickly. About local people, news travels fast. This disturbed me. I took every failure personally. I told the board I

was worried. "It will hurt our reputation. It reflects on the Center, it reflects on me."

Leonard reached over and put his hand on my arm. "What if I worried," he said, "about every tire with my name on it that went bad?"

The group broke up laughing. But the Center's name has been burden, as well as honor. Because even if nobody else holds me responsible, I hold myself responsible.

A while ago, I went to a meeting of a support group, and a woman spoke up and said, "My husband and I are both alcoholics, and we went through Betty Ford." I cringed. At moments like that, I wonder why people can't say, "We went through treatment," but I'm fighting a losing battle. Even John refers to "Betty Ford." "Here at Betty Ford," he'll say to someone on the phone. And there's a group of alumni in New York who call the Center "Betty's place," as in "Have you got this month's newsletter from Betty's place?"

It's hard to make anyone understand what it's like to have your name on something, to be given credit for things you haven't done. I've been at meetings where someone turned and thanked me, and I hugged the person and said, "Don't thank me, thank yourself, you're the one who did it. With God's help."

From the beginning, we have wanted every patient at the Center to feel, "I'm important here, I have some dignity." The same with the counselors. We consider them as important as any doctors; they're the ones who are guiding our patients in treatment and recovery.

Alcoholic counseling isn't a very old field, and it hasn't been remunerative, either. We were determined to change that. Our counselors are well paid—not by the criteria of big business, but compared to the rest of the field—and we ask a great deal of them. Our standards are high. We won't interview a counselor unless he or she has had three full years' experience. We've been asked to franchise other centers, but that won't happen while I'm alive. It's enough to try to make this one the best it can be. When the Fisher building opens, that will give us eighty beds, twenty in each of four halls, and that's as many as we want.

Our staff cares. Along with the counselors, there are doctors, nurses, clergymen, psychologists, an exercise specialist, a nutritionist. Each patient has ten to fifteen people looking out for his heeds.

But the patient still has to do the work. It's not easy for a sick person to understand.

Everyone is used to going to a hospital and lying there while people do things to him. At the Center, we have to say over and over, "We're not going to do anything to you, not going to give you a shot, not going to give you a pill, not going to work any voodoo, you've got to do it. And if you listen, and watch, and let yourself feel, you'll find out how."

Some other places have more liberal guidelines—phones in the rooms, overnight passes, visitors seven days a week. We say, "Hey, you're not here to go on a pass." Our treatment is intensive. One magazine described us as a boot camp, which I don't think is fair. But we are serious about our program, it isn't a house party.

That's why the patient who wants to come here has to call our admissions office himself. We don't let your mother or your girlfriend or your husband put you in. You have to really want help. On the rare occasion when some chemically dependent person is coerced into treatment, it usually ends badly. I know of one young woman whose husband said he would leave her if she didn't sober up, so she came, filled with animosity, to us, and every night, when it was her turn to use the pay phone, she called her husband and

complained. "'They're a bunch of Moonies, they're brainwashing me, come and get me." That kind of thing is no good for the patient, and it's no good for the Center.

Patients have told me they have never felt so much concern and love as they get from the staff at BFC. Everyone who comes in has a complete physical examination given by Jim West, our medical director, or one of three other doctors. Within five days—once they've come to know the patient—the whole treatment team gets together to discuss the new arrival's individual problems. This group of therapists decides what to do, and how long it's going to take. Some people stay twenty-eight days, some stay six weeks. You have to be ambulatory, able to get around to classes, to meals, to lectures, before you can start treatment.

It isn't that we reject you if you're in withdrawal. Most patients are in some stage of withdrawal, but if the patient has a history of seizures or serious medical complications, he's put in an acute-care hospital. When the Betty Ford Center opened, we didn't take patients who had been using street drugs, though there were probably people who smoked marijuana. But the times change; many of our younger patients are

now cross-addicted. In fact, cocaine is the second-leading drug of choice of our patients. You hear them at support group meetings saying, "I'm an addict-alcoholic."

In July 1983, the Betty Ford Center became a separate not-for-profit corporation. We had our own hospital license. We were still a subsidiary of the parent Eisenhower Medical Center, but now our board functioned independently, and we had our own budget. (Not-for-profit means if you collect more money than you spend, what's left over is put right back into the place.) All the donations sent to us—as distinguished from the fees charged by us—have gone for buildings and equipment, not for operating costs.

When we opened there was a tremendous amount of publicity attendant on our every move. Reporters swarmed to the campus, and it seemed as though we—Joe Cruse, John Schwarzlose, various counselors and I—were appearing on television shows, network and local, night and day. Finally, we called a halt. For one year, there was a moratorium on wisdom issuing forth from the Betty Ford Center. Partly because we didn't have the time to accommodate everyone who wanted to visit, partly because we needed to concentrate on the work we were doing and quit

taking bows for how great we were. Especially since our greatness had yet to be proved.

I tried to stay on an even keel, and not be swept away by a vision of myself as "the lady with the lamp." I remember Leonard calling from New York one day to ask if I'd be willing to accept an award from the National Council on Alcoholism. He started telling me that my acceptance would be so helpful, such a benefit to mankind, stuff like that. "Ah, Leonard," I said, "you sound like all the rest of them. You know me too well to give me a lot of soft soap."

"Yeah, but it's true," he said. "If you show up, we will get a crowd."

"Okay," I said. "That's honest. But don't try and tell me how wonderful I am."

I couldn't afford to have Leonard—or Jerry or Meri Bell, any of the people closest to me—con me; there were enough strangers willing to lay on the flattery, and I'm as susceptible to sweet talk as the next one.

I had to keep remembering that while I was being written about and honored, there were volunteers over at the Center doing the dirty work. Nicky was one of them.

Nicky Firestone: "When Leonard went to

treatment, it was a terrifically emotional experience. It just gave a different meaning to our lives. You look at something and think, my, that's interesting, why didn't I see it before?

"I was vitally interested in the development of the Betty Ford Center, but I didn't have any role in it. Then, after it opened, I signed up as a volunteer. That's the part I love more than anything. I just go over there and do what needs to be done.

"The patients and the counselors think I'm funny, they think I'm a nut. I hate messiness, so I pick up litter. They used to call me the Bag Lady because I'd go over with a big plastic bag and gather up whatever trash I could find. One day, I cleaned out the icebox, and that amused them very much.

"They tease me a lot, but the Center means so much to me, I just want it to be perfect. I feel very close to the counselors, I admire them tremendously, I admire their dedication. And I love to see the change in people who've gone through treatment. They come in, faces bloated, they're suffering the ravages of alcohol or drugs, and when you meet them again at an anniversary reunion, a year

or two later, you don't recognize them. Even their facial expressions have changed.

"The uninitiated feel that alcoholism is a moral issue, a willpower issue. If you want to do something, by God, you can do it. I used to feel that way. But it has nothing to do with willpower. When an alcoholic says to himself, 'I'm only going to have one drink tonight,' it doesn't work.

"Some people can't leave chocolate alone. If they have one piece, they have a box. But chocolate isn't going to kill you, or kill someone who gets in the way of your car.

"The thing that's hard to understand is that alcoholics don't want to do what they're doing. The periodic alcoholic is so contrite, so apologetic, he makes all kinds of promises, and means them from the bottom of his heart. And then it happens again. Until the drinker finally comes to the realization that he just can't touch alcohol.

"When somebody says to Leonard, 'Do you feel that you can never have another drink?' he says, 'I can have a drink anytime I want to, but I'm going to pay a price for it, and I don't know what the price will be, and it may even mean my life, so I'm not going to risk it.'

"He doesn't feel he's depriving himself, he

feels he's saving himself. He doesn't drink, and he doesn't go out and take poison either.

"It was exciting to me when Leonard put up the money for Firestone Hall. I was happy he had the means to do it, and wanted to do it. I love to see money used in a good cause.

"And it is a good cause. I have been phoned by people at the Center and asked to come right over because someone thought I could help, and even though I was dressing for a dinner engagement, I've found myself saying, 'Why, certainly I'll be there.' I thought the heck with it, the dinner is not important. Life is tough. And people helping people is the only thing that I think is worth anything in this world today.

"It doesn't matter how tired you are, it doesn't matter what you're doing—you get mixed up in this racket and you're like a firehorse. You pull yourself together and run if you're needed. It is the most wonderful work."

Even when you believe with Nicky that the work is wonderful, you sometimes have to hang on with both hands. At the start, I would become anxious and resentful when I saw tabloids mocking the idea of treatment. At least that's what it seemed to me they

were doing. What else would you call a headline screaming out, "Big Star Goes to Betty's Booze Tank"? (That isn't exactly accurate, but it'll give you the idea.)

Eventually, I realized it didn't make any difference. Highly visible people in theater and television are role models, and if somebody comes to the Center because a well-known politician or movie star has said he or she got clean and sober there, then all the rest of it is unimportant. It doesn't matter by whose hand a life is saved. It's always the hand of God anyway.

Often, people are curious about how celebrities and the big rich mingle with the other patients. What if a big shot comes in and doesn't care to be part of the crowd? It's simple. If he doesn't settle in, he's asked to leave. Sometimes, somebody who thinks he is very important in business—or art—is unhappy when you tell him there will be no phone privileges for five days. He'll say, "Nobody is going to tell me that, I'm much too important not to have phone privileges for five days, the world can't go on without me." Then we say, "You'd better go back to the world and take care of it."

A woman is just as likely as a man to be guilty of false pride—think of my trying to

former-First-Lady myself out of a four-bed room at Long Beach—and Leonard is fantastic at knowing how to cope with the wheeler-dealers. Because he was an industrialist, accustomed to power and money and a private plane, counselors at the Center send for him when they have a tough nut to crack, a newcomer who thinks he or she doesn't belong in a place with a bunch of commoners. I remember one lady who wanted Leonard to identify with her, and he did, but not in the way she expected. She was going on about how many racehorses she owned and how prominent she was, and Leonard shook his head. "Gee," he said, "I thought you were just another drunk like me."

Nicky, too, was unimpressed by the legends in their own minds. "I have a hard time with the high achievers," she said once. "I think it started when we were in the Embassy. I can't bear people who try to intimidate other people."

We've had patients who flunked treatment, so to speak, who never earned their medallions, and sometimes it's nothing more than a snobbish attitude that gets in their way. One woman said her priest had urged her to go to Hazelden, but she'd said no way. "If

I'm going anywhere, I'm going to Betty Ford, because she's like me." It was a kind of idea she had that I was a lady who drove around in a nice car. Poor silly woman. She could have got help anywhere. Or nowhere. Because help is help, and a drunk is a drunk. But unless she could break through her prejudice, she was not going to get well.

We've had celebrities who went through the Center and stayed clean and sober, we've had celebrities who left and drank and used again. Sometimes you get kind of snooty about your own recovery, and forget there are people who have to try more than once to find the sobriety that will give them long-term recovery. One top television executive who came to the Center went home and seemed to be doing well. Then he started using cocaine again. His station—in a major market—gave him leave, and I thought it was probably going to be a permanent leave. But I've since heard that he was going back to work, which gave me hope. He's a fine man, recovering from cocaine addiction.

We've had celebrities who were helpful to other patients, warm and loving and motherly, and celebrities who were a major pain. We've had celebrities who left the Center

unchanged, and celebrities who experienced spiritual awakening.

One young woman, a very public figure who had been in treatment for a couple of weeks, became angry because her therapy group was beginning to focus on her, and she found that scary. She said, "I'm not putting up with this anymore," walked out of the group straight to the pay phone, and called the 800 toll-free number of one of the airlines.

"This is so-and-so," she said. "I want a flight to New York tonight." Now, an 800 toll-free number is probably handled out of a room with forty different operators, so the one you draw is left totally to chance. And this operator who picked up the phone said, "Oh, Miss so-and-so, I can't believe it's you. I'll get you the reservation in a second, but I need to tell you first that I've been in the AA program for almost eight weeks, really struggling, and when I found out you were in the Betty Ford Center, that gave me the reinforcement I needed to go on."

This patient of ours said, "Thank you, never mind the reservation," hung up the phone and walked back into group with tears streaming down her face. "I guess my Higher Power knows where I should be," she told

the group. As John Schwarzlose says, "Anyone who can hear that and doesn't know God is in a place like this is missing the point."

Moving from the sacred to the profane, let me return briefly to the subject of money. The Center was built, the Center expanded. We want to be able to continually upgrade our program, by sending our counselors for advanced training, by improving our physical plant, and, in time, by providing a professional in-residence program. That takes money so I'm still putting the arm on anyone who will stand still long enough to listen to me. But it doesn't mean we gather up cash without looking at where it comes from.

John Schwarzlose: "Last year, a patient stuck a check for ten thousand dollars in my hand. It was made out to the Betty Ford Center, and this man said his company would double the donation. He was going to work it out with his accountant and his attorney. I returned the check. 'I appreciate this,' I said, 'but we can't take it until you are no longer a patient, and we figure that's a year after you leave here.'

"When I reported this exchange to our board, some of the members gulped, but

everyone agreed that we could not afford to let a single thread of integrity be lost.

"A Medicare official came out to the Center and told Mrs. Ford and me that the government would only pay for sixteen to twenty-one days of treatment, and he asked how we would handle that. Betty said, 'We'll swallow the rest of it.' 'What?' the guy said. 'If a person needs twenty-eight days, that's how long he'll stay,' Betty said. 'We'll find a way to cover it.'

"For me, it's worthwhile to work here, knowing Betty and the other people on the board stand up for what they believe.

"During that first year she was still somewhat of a people pleaser, grateful that the BFC had been built, busy thanking everyone. But early on, she really began to emerge as president. She became a part of the regular in-patient and out-patient lecture series, and began to spend time with patients. She wanted to know everything they went through in a day, what they thought needed to be changed.

"She never interferes with treatment, but she will spend hours in the coffee lounge kibitizing with patients.

"We have a meeting on the first Monday of every month, a meeting with all the clini-

cal counselors. Betty often comes to that. In the beginning, she took home organizational charts and worked on them. I'd get a call at ten o'clock at night, and it would be Betty asking questions."

There were high points in those early days. When we discovered we needed an additional building which could also serve as a family treatment center, John, Leonard and I flew down to San Diego to talk to Joan Kroc about it. Joan, the widow of Ray Kroc, the founder of McDonald's and owner of the San Diego Padres, is a philanthropist who's given away millions. She is not only generous; she is highly respected among those working in the field of alcohol and drugs.

In 1976, she established Operation Cork (Cork is Kroc spelled backwards), a program to educate the public about chemical dependency and its impact on the family. Joan gave us a huge check and we used it to help build our Cork Family Pavilion.

Large contributions and small, we have welcomed every one. We offer twelve scholarships a year, and we take twelve charity cases a year. We help families who can barely afford to put a patient through treatment, let alone come to the family program themselves.

We get funds from foundations, from alumni, from individuals who have lost family members to alcoholism, from individuals who have *almost* lost family members to alcoholism.

Two years into my sobriety, my husband gave me a pink-and-white piggy bank for Mother's Day. A note stuck out of the slot. It said, "This is my Mother's Day recognition for my First Lady." And inside the note, there was a check to the Center. The pig and the note are still on my desk. They show the kind of support I've had.

About a year after I quit drinking, Jerry stopped too. He came home from a plane trip one night, and I said, "A nightcap will relax you. Let me make you one." And he said, "No, thanks." "Come on," I said. "It will make you feel so much better, and I really don't mind." He said no. "I don't want one."

I was puzzled. "We always used to have a nightcap before we went to bed."

"Yeah," he said. "And I never really enjoyed it."

I was even more puzzled. "Then, why did you do it?"

"Because," he said, "I didn't want you to drink alone."

Right or wrong, mistaken or not, it shows the kind of support I've had.

10

I was, being human, born alone;
I am, being woman, hard beset;
I live by squeezing from a stone
The little nourishment I get.

Elinor Wylie

The emotional support I've been talking about is not there for all women.

These are the statistics I have heard. Nine out of ten women stay with their alcoholic husbands. Nine out of ten men abandon their alcoholic wives.

Not only did Jerry not abandon me but I have also been the recipient of a great deal of goodwill from strangers. Many have a feeling of understanding based on shared tribulation.

Somebody once said to me, "These days, you seem to be even more popular than your husband," and I said, "Well, my husband

didn't have all the trials that I had." When I go through crowds, I have to be careful, because a woman will come up and give me a hug or grab my arm and say, "You know, we're recovering from the same disease," and frankly, I don't know which disease she's talking about, cancer or alcoholism or arthritis.

Whichever one it happens to be, I always hope she isn't trying to squeeze nourishment from a stone, but has a husband like mine. For a while after my mastectomy and the subsequent chemotherapy, I grappled with low self-esteem. I've never been very secure anyway—if I walked into a room, I was always sure that half the people there didn't like me. And losing a breast makes you feel disfigured psychologically as well as physically, less adequate as a marriage partner. You've failed to live up to the physical perfection you've wanted, not just for yourself (you can live without it) but for your husband.

My operation came at a time when some women were going without underclothes and wearing sheer blouses. Everywhere I traveled, I was aware of beautifully built females, and I suffered over having let my husband down.

To Jerry, this was nonsense. He was always reinforcing me—"Oh, you're much more beautiful than she is." In more than thirty years, he has never belittled me or made me feel I was inadequate—even when I was taking pills and drinking—and that's unusual. At support group meetings, or over at the Center, I hear women say, "I have lost my family. My husband couldn't stand to be around me. My children would not come home."

So many women had individual problems that the Center was not very old before we made some changes. It was Dan Anderson, the president of Hazelden, who steered us in a new direction. We had opened West Hall a month after McCallum, and North Hall after that. All the buildings were coed, until Dan came out and looked us over. His review was mixed.

In a conversation with John Schwarzlose and me, he said, "You're doing a great job, but do you want to be just another sixty-bed treatment center? You have an opportunity to do something special here. There are clinical differences between alcoholic men and women that need to be addressed in treatment, and because of Betty's reputation, half your patients are women. Why not separate

them from the men?" (Hazelden was then the only treatment place we knew of that practiced this separation.)

Dan said he could foresee the day "when the Betty Ford Center could become a standard-bearer, known for providing good chemical-dependency services to women. Services they haven't had in the past."

In that meeting, it was clear to us that he was making sense, so we talked to our board of directors and our professional staff to find out how they felt about the idea. The staff split nineteen to nineteen, and I broke the tie. It was decided West Hall would be an all-women's building, and we've never backed off from that decision.

Yes, we got some arguments. All of the staff, as you can tell by the split vote, was not entirely open to the idea. They questioned why women needed anything different from the regulation treatment that men were getting. Even trained counselors did not always comprehend the greater anger, the more intense feeling of resentment women have about being alcoholic.

Alcoholism had always been a macho disease. "It's a good man's failing," the Irish used to say. When he comes of age, a man is supposed to learn to drink, and he can drink

a lot—go to lunch, have a couple of martinis, drink after work—and still get his job done. A woman can't have a small child and be drinking. Not if she wants society to accept her as a good mother.

Most of the treatment centers across the country had been geared to men. Men were the ones who came forth, admitted they were alcoholics. They went into treatment—their bosses sent them, or they sent themselves—because they found their ability to make a living threatened, whereas women drank at home, hidden and protected by their families. They didn't find their way to treatment. And the few who did often resented—as I had done to some extent at Long Beach—the fact that it was a man's treatment.

Fortunately for me, the group of women from Laguna—Muriel Zink, Pam Wilder, several more—came in from the outside and shared. They made the early steps of my recovery less shaky and less threatening. It was comforting just to be with other recovering women.

I know my friends and I were not engaging in something unheard of before the mid-1970s. I know a lot of women who have been recovering for twenty, thirty years. But twenty years ago, a woman who went to

treatment received treatment that focused on men. Even the big book of Alcoholics Anonymous was slanted toward men.

Twenty years ago, most women just toughed it out, tried to straighten up on their own, for fear of shaming their children or endangering their husbands' jobs. The same way many women have to work twice as hard as men to prove themselves in the business world, so I think these women had to work twice as hard to gain their sobriety.

Women aren't weak. Bearing children, rearing them, running a household can't be done by weaklings. Neither can recovering from alcoholism. But over the centuries, a stereotype developed of what a woman was supposed to be, a creature on a pedestal whose man would carry all of life's burdens on his broad shoulders. One who didn't need to think; her thinking would be done for her. With no cares, how could such a creature be depressed, or uncertain about who she was?

This is who she was. Somebody's daughter, somebody's mother, somebody's wife. Her identity as an individual was almost non-existent.

Stephanie Covington, a specialist in female alcoholism and sexuality, developed a work-

shop project that is very interesting. She asks a group to imagine that, as they are growing up, most of the voices they hear on radio and television are the voices of women, that the bases of power and economic strength rest in the hands of women, that the government is administered by a wise, all-knowing woman.

After establishing these ground rules, Stephanie asks her students for their reactions. Generally, the women express feelings of strength and power and pride, the men express feelings of fear and confusion and helplessness.

And one hopes, at the end, a little enlightenment.

Women have been receiving negative messages all their lives, and they bring negative attitudes with them when they come to treatment. They have lived in the stereotype of what they should be as women. And when they cannot achieve everything that the role demands, they are quick to believe there is something wrong with them. Only now are we beginning to see that perhaps the error was not in them, but in the stereotype. The distorted vision is changing, but it may take a long long time.

The female alcoholic has more emotional

problems, more health problems, more parenting problems, makes more suicide attempts, than the alcoholic man. The female alcoholic can endanger her unborn baby because of alcohol and drugs passed through the umbilical cord. Prenatal exposure to high levels of chemicals can cause death through spontaneous abortion or stillbirth, as well as malformation, growth deficiency, retardation. This fetal alcohol syndrome is the third leading cause of birth defects.

Women alcoholics have to deal with other physical problems too. Our bodies have more fat tissues than men's. This means we absorb drugs and alcohol more rapidly, and have more toxic reaction to a given amount of alcohol. Our internal organs are more susceptible to the damage that can be done by chemicals we use. The changes in a woman's estrogen level can heighten and prolong the effect of alcohol. The mood swings that may accompany hormonal changes can be intensified by using chemicals. More women than men experience sexual dysfunction. Many use alcohol to overcome this, to relax, loosen up. Unfortunately, alcohol is a depressant and an excessive amount of it will only heighten any already existing dysfunction.

There is an adage in recovery that says,

"If you don't want to slip, stay away from slippery places." That's easier for men than for women. Men don't *have* to go back to the bars where they got in trouble, they don't *have* to phone the cocaine dealer. But in a large percentage of cases, a woman's slippery place was her own kitchen, her bedroom, her bathroom. And the people around her when she was drinking or using weren't pushers, they were the members of her family. After she leaves treatment, she is returning to her slippery places and the very same conditions under which she came to grief. She has to learn to be wary, if she's going to be able to continue with her recovery.

There are still women out there who are afraid to ask for help, but fewer than there used to be, in this age of assertiveness training, and female doctors and lawyers and bank presidents and airline pilots and members of the plumbers' union.

There have, of course, always been women who went into the marketplace, some from necessity, some from ambition. But in the past, it was no easier for the alcoholic working woman to get help than it was for her housebound sister.

Because in the boss-employee situation you found old boys talking man to man. "Bud,

I'm worried about you, you're getting be-hind in your work, and a lot of days you don't come back after lunch," etc. With a woman, it was more embarrassing. Rather than confront her, they'd fire her.

The average woman who comes to the Betty Ford Center is forty-four years old, married, has children and a job. (We've had them from eighteen to eighty-four.) And she does better in therapy when her group is all-female. In a group that is coed, we have found, she tends to remain in the nurturing role of mother or wife, she hangs back, urg-ing the men to do all the talking,

In an all-women's group, she's not allowed to sit back. Another woman will say to her, "What about *you?* How is this affecting *you?* How do *you* feel?"

There are also intimidating subjects, per-sonal subjects—sexual abuse, incest—that women are more comfortable talking about with other women. They're fearful of ex-pressing their anger about these things in front of men. Besides, they're still trying to please men. So, although there are excep-tions to every rule, women don't get well as fast in mixed groups.

The woman alcoholic is less apt than a man to be caught driving while drunk, she is

less apt to be arrested on the street, less apt to end up in jail, and she has a much better chance than a man of dying without ever having her disease diagnosed.

At least a third—and maybe half—of the alcoholics alive today are women.

One of the reasons I started openly discussing my own recovery was that I was so flabbergasted by what I had learned about the extent of women's dual dependencies on alcohol and prescription drugs. Eighty percent of American women who are alcoholic—more likely the ones over forty—are also dependent on one or more prescription drugs. And that chemical combination is explosive.

Another reason I started talking (when many felt I should keep quiet) was my mother. I've said that my mother was strong and kind, but she was also free, a liberated woman, as was her mother before her, so it was inevitable that I would grow up to be vocal about women's issues. My mother cared for three children practically by herself. When she went to work selling real estate during the depression, it was a perfectly ladylike thing to do, but nobody in her set had ever done anything like it.

Eleanor Roosevelt was another important role model for me. I admired her ability to

speak out in support of her beliefs, although I didn't always agree with the causes she championed. I wouldn't be surprised if Mrs. Roosevelt had also fueled my mother's independent and self-confident way of thinking.

While I was still at Long Beach, I got a letter from an elderly cousin who said he knew I was going to make it because my forebears had the right stuff. He said he had always thought of my mother "not only as one of the nicest persons I ever knew, but also as a person who overcame the rough times."

That stayed in my mind when I started trying to do something about female alcoholics. I didn't need a cause. I was already involved in raising money for the American Cancer Society, and the Arthritis Foundation, and mental health and underprivileged children. But the plight of alcoholic women pulled at me.

Sometimes, as I've mentioned before, I'm called over to the Center and asked to talk with a woman who thinks she's too well-bred to be an alcoholic and doesn't realize she has just come from different circumstances, that she is just another child of God, that her problem is not so different from the problem of the young girl who's been prostituting

herself on the street to get drugs. The girl on the street simply hasn't had the advantage of being able to get her stuff legally, from doctors.

Still, I don't push myself on people. When I do one-on-one counseling, it's because a patient has asked for me. I am not qualified to be a professional counselor—what I don't know about medical matters is a large amount —but I can answer a cry for help.

If a woman has had a mastectomy, and she's having a hard time because she's never come to terms with it, I can share with her my own knowledge of that experience. Her mastectomy is an issue that's separate from her drinking, but in recovery from either, sexual anxieties abound.

The mastectomy may have made the woman feel physically undesirable, and the drinking may have made it possible for her to accept herself as a sexual being. Some women have never gone to bed with their husbands without having taken a few drinks or pills, so they are terrified of what the adjustment will be when they go home from treatment. They are afraid they will fail at sex.

You counsel them not to expect it to be easy, to take the time to get comfortable,

because everything's different in abstinence. You assure them that this burden of guilt they are carrying around because they've caused so much trouble will eventually go away.

And you hope that it means something to them, because you believe they can make it.

A woman alcoholic who gulps her sherry out of the kitchen cupboard is, medically speaking, as much at risk as the woman alcoholic who does her tippling at a singles bar. Though, philosophically speaking, the woman in the singles bar is more apt to lose her reputation along with her liver. Because the double standard still exists. If a man goes into a bar, has a drink, watches a football game, tells some lies to some other men, nobody thinks anything of it. If a woman goes into a bar, she's looking for trouble.

The French writer Simone de Beauvoir declared in her book *The Second Sex* that feminine characteristics were socially acquired. "One is not born, but rather becomes a woman," she said. "It is civilization as a whole that produces this creature, intermediate between male and eunuch, that is described as feminine."

Whether or not you want to sign off on that, it is nonetheless true that we have a

civilization that doesn't like to admit nice women drink, a civilization in which the idea of an alcoholic woman's needing special attention is still fairly new.

Not only employers and uneasy husbands have turned their backs on the fact of women alcoholics, so have doctors.

Muriel Zink: "I went to my own physician and said, 'I believe I'm an alcoholic,' and he said, 'Muriel, what's it going to be next, Zen Buddhism?' A lot of professional people attached so much stigma to the idea of alcoholism that, in their minds, a woman who drank too much was disgracing motherhood, apple pie, and America.

"My husband was the same way. If I got tight, he would be right there with the excuses. 'Louis really loaded your drink,' or 'You were very tired,' or 'It wasn't good liquor,' or 'You haven't been eating right.'

"A friend from New York who had quit drinking came to a party beside our pool, and I made her iced tea. Because I was going to protect her from temptation. Another guest, the wife of a movie director, said, 'You must try the daiquiris, they're absolutely marvelous.' And my friend said, 'No, thank you, the iced tea will be just fine.'

And the director's wife kept raving about the daiquiris—'They put something in them that makes them taste like almonds—' and finally my friend said, 'No, thank you, I don't drink, I'm an alcoholic.'

"I was horrified. I took my friend aside and apologized for the director's wife, and my friend said, 'Honey, it's all right, I have a hard time not letting everybody know I'm an alcoholic,' and I thought, oh, my God, she's had brain damage.

"But she was the friend I called when I finally admitted I had a problem. 'I think I'm an alcoholic,' I said. She didn't say, 'It took you a long time to see it.' She said, 'Well, honey, try it on for size. Wear it like a loose garment. You know, we get what we need when we need it.' "

Sometimes, what women need is the help of other women. A patient at the Center remembers, "I walked in frightened, and I discovered a lot of women as frightened as I was. That made it easier. It was a case of 'Coward, take my coward's hand.' "

One well-known entertainer has described recovery as "belonging to this big huge club. Recovery is a unique process and people who are successful in recovery have a camarade-

rie, we have a little edge on 'normal' people. You can't survive out here without that connection."

The fellowship of recovering women cuts through all kinds of barriers. I read in a book called *A Woman Like You* testimony from a woman who identified herself as Lulu F.

"Even when I go to meetings now," she said, "there often aren't black people unless I bring them with me. But it just doesn't bother me. I talk and share just the same because AA works no matter what the color of your skin. I was never taught to be prejudiced. But when you're looking for an excuse not to change, the first excuse the black person has is 'I can't identify with or relate to those white people.' I heard Betty Ford talk one time, and we felt exactly the same way; she just had more money to spend than I did. Thank God I didn't have it, or I would have been dead."

Most of us female alcoholics do feel "exactly the same way." To sum up, we feel guilty because we haven't been able to fulfill the role society has established for us, we feel depressed by our failures and our inability to cope without chemicals, we feel angry because we lost control of our lives. The

227

disease impacts on women faster and more intensely, so when we finally seek help—and we hide in our denial longer than men do—we're sicker, physically and emotionally. Once we leave treatment, we may need intensive aftercare. But what we will have learned is that, wherever we go, there will be other women who will understand.

For a long time, despite my previously stated interest in women's issues, the women in my life always played secondary roles. I had girlfriends in school and while I was working, but like most young women, I preferred to be with men. Later, the women I knew were more or less appendages of men who were friends of my husband. We came along with the men, we shared a very little of our lives with each other.

Since my treatment—and within my recovery—I have learned how wonderful and special women are. We're a unique and sometimes mystifying breed, and I am reminded of this every time I go to the Center and talk with the women patients.

One of those patients, a friend who went through treatment last year, gave me her diary and said I could use it any way I liked. She and I both thought a few pages might

give the reader an idea—if only a sketchy one—of what a patient's first days are like.

She lived in West Hall.

11

Nine P.M. Bed. A book, V. Woolf's letters. Lights out, sleep not quite right away. No Valium. The night passes in black chiffon.

James Schuyler

Monday: Camp Betty. That's what they call it.

I read in *Parade* magazine how this rehab consisted of patient units that rival "luxurious condominium accommodations." Right. But in luxurious condominium accommodations, you don't generally have some guy come and take away your hair dryer to see if you're hiding stuff in it. They also take away your vitamin pills and aspirin and certainly anything stronger than aspirin that you have been foolish enough to bring.

Got in late, almost 4 P.M., and met my

roommate. Fresh-faced kid, but she has been doing drugs since she was twelve. Lots of acid. She is the Granny for our hall, and right now she is outside bellowing, "Circle!" I wander out to see what this means. What it means is that before supper—or any other activity—we, all twenty of us on the hall, go out the front door and form a big circle, arms around each other's shoulders, and recite the Serenity Prayer.

Supper is at 5:10 P.M., so early I wonder when these people have lunch. The cafeteria is big and bright and two women invite me to sit with them. I notice the men from North Hall seated together. It is explained to me that the women's hall and the men's hall do not mingle. You not only don't eat with the men, you aren't supposed to sit with them at lectures, or hang out with them at night. No fraternization allowed.

There's another new girl today. She is not nervous like me, or maybe she is nervous, but she could be a stand-up comic. She says she was shocked when the authorities took away her mouthwash and her perfume. After that, a counselor said, "Come on, Eve, I'll take you to your room, you're in the Swamp." (The Swamp is what they call the four-bed room.)

"They think I'm going to drink my perfume," she says. "And they sleep in a swamp. These people are crazier than I am."

After supper, there's a lecture by John Schwarzlose, who runs this place. He tells us 85 to 90 percent of the people in the United States who need treatment will never get it.

Won't their families help? No, the family's denial is as strong as the patient's.

Won't the doctor help? No, he's not trained in chemical dependency. He couldn't fix your car either.

What about your clergyman? No, he's more apt to lay a sin trip on you, tell you if you'd been going to church, you wouldn't have ended up in here.

When I get back to my room, I am supposed to write down my daily feelings in a notebook to be turned in to my counselor the next morning. We have been given so many books to read, questionnaires to fill out, things to think about, I don't know how I am going to be able to do a written assignment too. And I want to keep this diary, just so I'll remember what I saw and heard and felt when I was here.

"Feelings" is a big thing in this place. There must be people who can't express any feelings whatever, because the kit of materi-

als we are issued includes a whole list of "feeling" words to draw from. Like for anger, we're given "contemptuous," "resentful," "irritated," "grumpy" and, I swear, twenty-four more!

Well, I'm feeling grumpy. But I think it is only that I am very tired from the long day, and overwhelmed by the amount of reading I am expected to finish, and tomorrow I hope to be more cheerful. The women on this hall are very sweet with each other, and there is a good feeling of comradeship and a lot of gallows humor.

I am worried that I have to go through a physical, which I always find embarrassing, tomorrow.

Tuesday: They get you up at the crack of dawn. Breakfast is at 7:20, and then you have to walk for almost an hour, and then there's a lecture. Three lectures a day, morning, afternoon and evening.

I have a blinding headache and go to the nurse to ask for a pill—any pill. I am turned down.

Anyway, I'm in the right place for my physical examination (it's very thorough, thorough enough so I miss the 9 A.M. lecture), and at ten there's group therapy.

The members of my group include a fashion plate, an anorexic redhead and a middle-aged lady with a broken arm who says she is not an alcoholic. There is also an intellectual whose vocabulary is awesome, and a woman who seems so regal I can't imagine her tipsy, no matter how I try.

We discuss our chemical dependencies. Intellectual says she always kept a flask in her office, Regal says she always had brandy in her car, Anorexic says she was always out looking for fixes. Broken Arm remains serene. "This doesn't refer to me, I didn't drink at all during the day."

Our counselor, a soft-voiced, gentle woman, asks Broken Arm why she persists in her denial. "Your family brought you here because they love you, and they say you drink a fifth a day, and take sleeping pills."

Broken Arm is not impressed. "Everything they said is not necessarily true. I did take sleeping pills, and I did drink two shots of whiskey every night. But I did *not* wet the bed, and I did *not* have to be picked up off the floor."

"You're fighting something," the counselor says. "Quit fighting. Surrender."

This counselor is fantastic. Very pale-skinned, wears frilly blouse, but nothing frilly

about the way she hooks right into every patient, kind, but direct, her eye is like a laser. She says the first year she counseled, "it was sink or swim. I got so involved with my patients, I was available to them twenty-four hours a day. Now I have a kind of shield around myself."

She says we all "use" for a quick fix, to be able to walk through the pain, walk through the fear.

This is an exciting day. I can't believe how fast you start to care about twenty strangers. You form a bond that's almost mystical, and it happens in a matter of hours.

Several times a week, the Center brings in AA meetings. At the beginning of a meeting, they go around the lecture hall and everyone gives his or her name. "I'm so-and-so, I'm an alcoholic." "I'm so-and-so, I'm an addict-alcoholic." Whatever. When they get to Broken Arm, she looks up brightly. "I'm so-and-so," she says, "and I'm not an alcoholic. Yet."

One guy gets up and says, "Cocaine loves me."

Another patient gets up and says he's afraid when he goes back to work—he works in a hospital—"they won't trust me with the keys

to the narcotics cupboard." I'm sitting there thinking, well, I should hope not.

There's a man who's been drinking forty years, and says he didn't want to come into treatment until he'd emptied his liquor cabinet. He says, "Nobody else is going to drink my brandy."

After the meeting is over, a woman from our hall announces, "I've had such a good time, I can't remember when I've had such a good time," as though she's been to the movies, and the man who is leading the meeting says fine. "When you go home, call AA."

My head still hurts, but I am happy. I like the safety and the structure, of which there hasn't been much in my life, and the process. I really have begun to love these people. I have worked hard for a long time at the cost of having no personal relationships. Or maybe because I wanted to avoid personal relationships. Except with scotch, or Demerol. I feel myself becoming humanized.

Wednesday: These days are almost too packed. If you can grab five minutes to go outside your room and sit on your terrace or patio or whatever they call it and look up at the mountains, and smell the trees, it

stretches your soul, but those breaks don't come often. Every afternoon, in addition to lecture and exercise—sometimes aerobics, sometimes pool—and book study, there is also a medallion ceremony for graduating patients

Today, little B. got her medallion. She is on my hall, but not in my group, and I like her a lot. She is as crazy as I am. Goes into the pool in tights, so nobody can see her fat thighs. She is leaving tomorrow, and everyone here thinks she is going to be fine, but she is going back to a domineering husband, and I worry about her. I also worry about whether my roommate has the will to stay off drugs. Does this mean there is still hope for me as a connected-to-others human being?

Little B. says at medallion ceremony that she had thought for a long time her counselor didn't like her, because he always seemed to disappear when she had a problem. "I didn't want you to lean too hard," her counselor tells her now. "I didn't want you to ascribe any magic to me, because I'm only an alcoholic, just like you."

Today, for the first time since Broken Arm has been here, she wasn't totally negative in group. The counselor said, "What do you

think of the treatment here?" and she said, "Some of it is nice."

Thursday: The cocaine addicts get to use the pool at night. They're hyperactive, and it's supposed to calm them down. There's a certain amount of fussing from people who would *like* to use the pool at night but are just plain old alcoholics, so find it off limits.

Following are a few interesting things I've heard in lectures these past four days:

Shame and guilt are different. Shame is "I am bad." Guilt is "I have done something bad." (I'm still working on that.)

Depression is anger turned inwards, and can result in arthritis, colds, flu, cancer, heart attack.

Dr. West, who's the medical director here, lectured on the personality of the alcoholic. He said alcoholics have low tolerance for frustration, they are woundably sensitive, and they are isolated. "You have to break out, take the risk," he said. He also said there was no such thing as returning to limited use of alcohol or drugs. "If one day, fifteen years from now, you see a drunk and say, 'Oh, how awful. *I'm* not like that anymore,' it won't be true. You're just not *doing* it anymore."

And he told us there are two things necessary for mental health. (1) You must have a sense of your own worth. (2) You've got to relate to at least one other human being openly, unconditionally and unguardedly. If you lack either of these, you're mentally ill.

At the end of his talk, Dr. West promised something beautiful. "In recovery," he said, "we're given floods of grace."

We are kept very busy here. We are given no time to look at a newspaper, watch TV (except on weekends, they tell me), listen to music. We are supposed to spend every moment possible "interacting," because addicted people are egocentric babies, and we have to be forced to focus on other people.

Before you leave treatment, you're supposed to write your autobiography, and then gather your therapy group together in the lounge and make them listen to it.

The lounge is nice, there are easy chairs and plants and a big fireplace, and up two steps, there's a coffee machine, and cold drinks and fruit, but for three nights now, I've seen Intellectual trying to drum up an audience. You think you're afraid to share your guilty secrets with others, because they'll listen with sick fascination and then spread the news all over town. Then you find out

that you can't *force* others to come listen to them. That really struck me funny.

Everybody is so exhausted by evening, and they have their own journals to write. If you can stay awake past nine o'clock, you find yourself sitting up pretty much alone. Even people who are used to sleeping pills are falling asleep without them.

Friday: A counselor on the evening staff has given me an assignment. I am to share my chemical-use history with six peers and ask them for feedback. I am supposed to record the chemicals I have used in my life, the amounts I used, the frequency with which I used, run this past my peers and record the insights I gain from the exercise. I can only buttonhole four peers. (What? Only four people want to hear about the night I had my stomach pumped?) But I lay out my whole sorry saga, and one at a time they point out that I'm not a damn bit different from anyone else. I have fears, low self-esteem, I want to be admired, drugs and liquor make me feel less scared and more likable.

When I get back to our room, my compassionate roommate has brought me a chocolate bar. It tastes fantastic. I feel accepted.

Today in group, it was Intellectual's turn in the "hot seat." She is told by the rest of the group that she's melodramatic, judgmental, manipulative, a self-justifier, willful, sorry for herself, angry, aggressive and threatening, as well as smart and talented and likable. She agrees with most of this, and says she took drugs to "quiet down the frenzy."

She is told she mustn't talk for twenty-four hours. Not to anybody. Not a word. A plaque is hung around her neck to advise passersby not to engage her in conversation.

"In recovery," the counselor says, "we have to keep things simple. They tell you when you go home, if you do the first step of AA perfectly, you will not use or drink again."

Well, it's easy to admit you're powerless over alcohol and drugs and your life has become unmanageable when you're safe in here, because you get a lot of reinforcement; outside, it won't be so simple.

During this week, I have had meetings with a psychologist and a clergyman. The clergyman says he's not here to push religion down people's throats, but to help people to the spirituality of the program, and to seek a power outside themselves. He is a recovering alcoholic, and it took him a long while to get

the message because he didn't identify with other alcoholics. "*I* didn't have a divorce, *I* didn't abandon my children, *I* wasn't a skid row bum."

Identifying is the crux. In one meeting, a woman says, "This sounds snobbish, but I don't relate to a bunch of farm women bawling because a cow kicked over the pail," and the counselor says, "Try to relate to the *feelings* of those women, not to the women. Don't you relate to disappointment? Dashed expectations?"

Tonight, they brought in some alumni of the Betty Ford Center for a panel discussion in the lecture hall. The first man said he came to treatment to save his marriage. "But it wasn't like the TV ad. 'John, I think you've been drinking too much.' 'Yes, but it's all right, dear, I've signed up to go to Betty Ford.' "

An alumnus who's skin and bones—he was twenty pounds thinner when he was on drugs—says nobody who's recovering should plunge into an emotional relationship for at least a year, because you're just not strong enough. Lots to think about. Almost too much to think about.

What a week. Games, exercises, lessons, lessons, lessons. Sermons in stones. Next

week, I'm planning to be stronger, smarter, and maybe I'll even understand more of the things I'm being told. I asked one middle-aged lady why she had chosen to come here, rather than going someplace else, and she said it was because of Mrs. Ford. "I once heard Betty Ford speak," she said. "And there was such a look of serenity and peace on her face. And I thought, if I could get that look, I would be happy."

I saw Mrs. Ford briefly today—she came and talked to the patients—and I told her what the lady had said because I thought it would please her. "She doesn't know how long it took me to get that look," she said.

12

Independence? That's middle-class blasphemy. We are all dependent on one another, every soul of us on earth.

George Bernard Shaw

I was not struck with "a look of serenity and peace" on my way home from treatment. I

had to struggle, one day at a time, to maintain my balance. We all have to. But it can be done.

It's hard for the chemically dependent person to believe there is life without substance abuse. Any addict who's tried to stop drinking or using for a day, or even a few hours, and who, as a result, gets the shakes or the screaming meemies or simply suffers from a sense of impending doom, thinks, there's no way I can make it.

You can make it. But it's easier if you don't have to do it alone.

In an essay she wrote back in 1951, Katherine Anne Porter talked about the richness of the relationship "between a man and a woman who are good lovers, good friends and good parents; who belong to each other, and to their children, and whose children belong to them: that is the meaning of the blood tie that binds them, and may bind them sometimes to the bone."

Gorgeous writing, but a simple thought. Belonging is necessary to most of us ordinary human beings. And in recovery, you begin to belong again, you come out of the isolation where you lived with—and for—your particular drug, and rejoin the world.

But you have to learn belonging means

being part of, not owning or being owned. I see it with my children. I've let go. Today, I don't try to control my children. They have their lives, and what they choose to do is their business. I try not to intrude unless I'm asked. I've brought them up, and released them, and the more you let go, the more you love them for what they are, the more they love you for letting them be what they are.

Jack Ford: "I've never been that good at keeping in touch. I think that's more my problem than anyone else's. But it's obviously more pleasant to go home now.

"I feel closer to Mother. I think, also, her recovery taught us a great lesson, that nothing is hopeless, that you can face up to whatever bad thing happens in your life. As bad as it was for the family, Mother's problem has been a hundredfold worse for her. But she's like a whole new person. She really looks forward to living each day, whatever glitches occur don't put her in a negative attitude. You know how some people sort of live from problem to problem? Instead of from good moment to good moment? To me, that's the difference in Mother now.

"I think she and I are both oversensitive. I think we can seem very smiling and open on

244

the surface, but both of us have a tendency to keep a lot of things to ourselves. That can be agonizing, and I think it's one of the things Mother has been able to put behind her. And someday I hope I can duplicate her success in that regard."

Mike Ford: "I'm overcome by the changes in my mother. In her alcoholism, she was very self-centered, she was very, very sensitive to what you said, what you did or didn't do. For her, everything was viewed in terms of her own well-being. And she had no real interest in other people's needs. That is all changed. What has been so remarkable is that here I have a person writing letters, phoning, going out of her way to find out how we're doing. She's very attentive, very alert to what's going on in our lives. Gayle and I were talking about it, it's almost as though we are getting to know a whole new person. It's kind of like I'm getting to know my mother for the first time. I think it's a real miracle that her life has been transformed as it has.

"A while ago, she came out to Wake Forest University, where I'm on the staff, to give the Founder's Day lecture, the convocation program. She had worked very hard

preparing to say something that would be from the heart and challenge the community here. There was a huge gathering, two thousand or more—students, faculty, people from the outside.

"Interestingly, there were literally hundreds of women in the audience who were looking to Mother for hope and courage. I know because of notes that were passed to me, and messages and calls that came later. Many of these women had suffered through cancer, or an alcohol-drug problem, so they came to hear her story. And I was sitting there in the front row, and she got up to speak and it was the most emotional, overwhelming experience I have had since the intervention.

"I looked up at this woman who is my mother and thought to myself that eight, ten years ago, there's no way she could have done what she was doing at that moment.

"What she was doing was in a very personal way articulating how the healing of a person involves the body, the mind and the spirit. Hers was a message of holistic healing. She related some of her own pilgrimage, her own struggles, how she had hit bottom and come face to face with death and by the grace of God had been brought back again.

And that it was not only a medical or physical transformation as she got off the drugs and felt better, it was also an emotional and spiritual experience. She was able to love herself again, able to love her family again, able to experience, in a spiritual way, God's love for her and His acceptance.

"It was such a powerful message. To me, it represented the complete circle of healing. That she, sick as she had been, was now up there speaking these words of great hope and encouragement to many others who were struggling."

Steve Ford: "I can't imagine trying to run our family the way we used to. It would be terrible if we had to go back to the way it used to be, knowing how wonderful it is now. Because you can't have a family with one person missing. It's like you don't let one person play the game. That just doesn't work. I guess we could have kidded ourselves the rest of our lives, but something made us want to change, and it was Mother's strength that finally got us over the hump.

"She was never a bad person. She always wanted to be a good mother, but I think there were times drinking got in the way.

She was not able to function sometimes as a thinking human being, and we kids took advantage of that, we learned how to get away with little things.

"Somebody asked me if I blame my father at all. I don't. When he met Mom, he was the all-American guy, college football, law school, Navy, Yale, good-looking, running for Congress, the whole shot. Who wouldn't want to be married to him? That's what dreams are made of. But Dad is one of those guys that delegate responsibility. Everybody has his responsibility, and you put your head down and get it done. He never starts a project and quits, and he expects other people to be the same way.

"After they got married, Dad expected to serve the country, and I think he expected Mom to raise his family, and it all went fine for a long, long time.

"But when Dad became a leader in the House of Representatives, and Mother started developing a problem with drinking and the prescriptions, it got real complicated. Because Dad didn't look back. He kept going. He had a job to do, and he expected her to get done whatever she was supposed to get done.

"Dad has tunnel vision, he's set in his direction, and Mother sort of got left by the

wayside, not because he didn't love her, but because he didn't understand.

"He was not one to backtrack and pick up people that couldn't keep marching. He kept going, she stumbled, and the wonderful thing is that he finally came back and got her. He slowed down enough to reeducate himself, to find out what was the problem. Mom helped herself a lot, but if Dad hadn't turned around and come back and got her—

"Everybody's got a little piece in this thing, but to me, theirs is a wonderful love story."

Not only do my children like me better since my recovery; my husband and I have never been so close either. Which is a paradox, since we are so often far apart. It used to be that he was running all the time. Now we're both running. On our thirty-seventh anniversary, we had our first breakfast together in a week, and I said, "Well, maybe it's good that we just have a lot of changing scenery all the time. At least this way we don't have time for changing partners."

Jerry's an inspiration to much younger people. He can be out playing golf, come home, have dinner, fly to New York, make a speech, attend a banquet, get back on a plane and fly to Texas in time for a board

meeting the next morning. (He never believed that sleep accomplished much; when I married him, he thought anything over five hours was an absolute waste of time.) Sometimes I say to him, "I can't possibly keep up with you, you ought to trade me for a newer model, honey," and he says, "I don't want a newer model, I'm happy with you." I don't know. If you turned in a sixty-eight-year-old, could you get two thirty-four-year-olds? That wouldn't be bad.

We appreciate each other more these days. I no longer resent his traveling, because he's very understanding about my traveling, and when we get home we're both ready to put our feet up; neither of us is nagging the other to go dancing. Sometimes our schedules are a joke. Once, we were both in Columbus, Ohio, on the same day, staying at different hotels, because we were on different projects. We had to phone to say how much we missed each other.

He's always called me every day from wherever he's been. He's a very thoughtful man. But as I have grown in my recovery, so has he. I've said that, in the early days, he could never tell me he loved me. He was too much the lawyer, so programmed and efficient. I had to know in my heart how much

he cared, because the words just weren't there. He was ambitious, he was aggressive, he wanted to be successful for his family—I still wonder sometimes if he knows he's successful—he wasn't a sweet-talker. Now it just knocks me for a loop that he's learned to express his feelings. He calls me from halfway around the world—"I had six hours' sleep, I feel pretty good, I'm getting ready to go to the board meeting, and I just want to tell you that I love you and I miss you."

Jerry Ford: "It isn't just her family that loves Betty. She's far more popular than I. Many people think she could have been elected President of the United States in 1976.

"I often acknowledge this after somebody has got up and announced me, with a lot of flowery phrases, at a banquet. I say, 'Well, I'm deeply grateful for your generous words; I need the morale boost. The reason I need it is because of an introduction a master of ceremonies made in southern California a couple of weeks ago. But before I tell you how he introduced me, let me give you a little background.'

"Then I talk about Betty's public acclaim, and I say our second son, Jack, has been a TV commentator and is a prospective politi-

cian in the San Diego area, and our third son, Steve, is a star on the daytime CBS soap opera *The Young and the Restless*. At that point, any little girls in the audience titter. Then I say, 'Well, with that background, let me tell you how this man introduced me. He got up and said, "It's my pleasure to present Betty Ford's husband, Jack Ford's dad and Steve Ford's father." So I thank you for helping my morale.'

"Seriously, Betty has always been talented. But the challenge of the Center brought out special skills that had been kind of hidden. She not only raised most of the money, but she is a hands-on chairman of the board. I tease her about it. I say I'm jealous because she spends so much time over there that I feel neglected.

"But to have seen the Center go from an idea to a successful operation gives her tremendous satisfaction, particularly to see people come in very sick and leave a few weeks later totally different, healthy, vigorous, with a future ahead of them.

"Betty has changed so much. Now when she addresses an audience, she has confidence that her subject matter is of interest to them. She's more articulate, more persuasive. She was always well-intentioned, but

now, whether she's talking about her individual recovery or about alcoholism, she has become a professional speaker, and everybody is impressed, including me.

"And she is a much more meaningful partner on a day-to-day basis. When I say, 'We ought to do this or this,' she wants to know why, she asks tough questions. So it's a more equal relationship than it used to be.

"Somebody asked me if I ever got tired of her talking about alcoholism. I said no, not at all. I think it's good for other people, and I think it's good for her.

"She has a big audience out there in the country. Whether I go to Tennessee, or Tallahassee, women come up and say, 'I sure wish Betty was here. Where is she?' and I have to tell them, Salt Lake, or Midland, Texas, or wherever she happens to be.

"In the course of her recovery, I've become healthier myself. I stopped drinking a year after she did. I realized I'd never really enjoyed it, it was just that I had become socially addicted.

"It was relatively simple for me to stop. I didn't want to drink alone, I wanted to lose some weight, I had no craving for liquor, and I saw how much benefit it was for her.

It would be much harder for me to stop smoking a pipe."

Never mind his pipe. His real weakness is dessert. When he was trying to lose weight, he said, "I'll give up my martinis before I'll give up my ice cream." Now that's not an alcoholic speaking.

We never stopped having liquor in the house as some people do. We *did* stop having various medications in the house, because any mood-altering or addictive drug was more of a temptation to me than alcohol. If I was in a lot of pain with my neck, with my back, with arthritis, I wouldn't be apt to go take a drink. But the drugs were seductive; I knew they could give me relief, as well as the euphoric feeling that nothing mattered, that the house could burn down and it would be okay because somehow somebody would fix it.

I know pain can be emotional too, and I know a drug is a drug is a drug, and alcohol is just as mood-altering as a tranquilizer, but I was more frightened of medications, more frightened that I might use something and get hooked on it. (After I'd been sober for three years, Joe Cruse said, "Well, Betty, maybe I should bring back all those pills we

cleaned out of your medicine cabinet and let you have a look at them." And I said, "Sure, Joe, bring them over." And he said, "Well, you'll have to wait a little while because there were so many I'm going to have to go over to the market and swipe a grocery cart to carry them all.")

Back when we began this book, my daughter Susan said, "You could do a whole chapter on the healing of a family," and I kept thinking about that. You hurt your family when you're sick; when you recover, so does the family. If you are lucky, their injuries mend along with yours. But not always right away. Susan, who had done so much to bring me help, was not altogether pleased by the mother who emerged from treatment.

Susan Ford: "I saw a change in her immediately, and at first, I didn't like it at all. I couldn't stand it. All of a sudden she was aware, all of a sudden it was 'Where are you going? With whom? What time are you going to be home?' And I was like, get off my back, you never paid attention before, why should you start paying attention now?

"It was like watching a brand-new rose bloom, and it was really beautiful, but it was a pain in the neck too. I had kind of done

everything, and all of a sudden she was taking over the reins again.

"Now it's fine. We can be honest with each other and not hurt each other. I can tell her things I could never have told her before, and they don't bother her, she accepts them. She's interested in what I think, what everyone in the family thinks. She came to us kids when they were first talking about naming the Center, and she said, 'Do you want them to name it after me?' We said that was no problem. She said, 'Well, after I die, I want one of you always to be on the board and participate. And your children are going to grow up with a grandmother who has an alcoholics' hospital named after her. Is that going to bother you? Because if it is, I don't want it to happen.' We talked about it for a long time."

I also went to the family before I agreed to appear on all those TV shows when the Center first opened. I said, "I'm not going to do any of this if you guys don't want me to, because I don't want anybody embarrassed." The children said they were proud of what I was doing. "We've got you back healthy, and if it's going to help other people, and

you want to do it, you should be able to do it."

Looking back now, I don't think my husband or the boys ever had the resentments Susan had. She was the one who rescued me, but she was also the one who most felt the hurt of my illness. Always. Beginning when she was little and didn't know what was wrong with me because I was so emotionally drained and upset. She didn't think I was alcoholic then, she thought I was crazy, and she didn't want a crazy mother.

After she married, she and Chuck moved to Huntington Beach, just a couple of blocks away from Pat Benedict, and she had a lot of help from Pat in working through her problems with—and about—me.

Meri Bell once told me she'd gone to a meeting of a support group for families of alcoholics. "And all I could think," she said, "was what damn fools they are. They put up with stuff from their alcoholics that I would never have put up with from anybody." Still, she said, "you can't go on manipulating your family forever. Eventually your kids know you are conning them. Other people know it too, but your kids have to live with it, whereas the other people can walk away."

Well, I did manipulate my family, but I

didn't know any other way—if I didn't want to do something, I traded on their love or their sympathy to get me out of doing it. And then I think Susan just got fed up. The family of an alcoholic *has* to get fed up.

It took time for me to accept that I had taken advantage of my family. After all, I reasoned, nobody else was affected by my alcoholism or drug dependency, it was just something I did to myself. In those early days of recovery, I knew meetings with other recovering alcoholics were important. I made myself attend them, and gradually, I began to hear a little, and understand a little. Still, when I listened to people talking about being hurt or angry or resentful or guilty, I was confused, because I really couldn't feel much. I didn't know what feeling was, I hadn't done it in a long time.

Since I've been active in the field of treatment, I've learned how even little children—six, seven, eight years old—are affected by the alcoholism of their parents. They are ashamed and guilty, they wonder what they did to make their parents drink. There's a lot of agony in that. If we can get a child into treatment at the same time that his mother or father is being treated, we can help him begin to understand it's a disease,

and it isn't his fault. In Al-Anon, children are told that, eventually, they will have to learn to ignore the alcoholic and go about their own lives. It's a hard lesson.

For anybody, not just children. We knew people, a very proper churchgoing couple, and she was a periodic drinker. If they had an important social engagement, he would telephone one of her friends and say, "I want to pick up R. at five o'clock. We have to go to a reception and dinner. Will you stay with her till then?" The friend would have to spend the day, make sure R. didn't start drinking, so she would be in shape for the evening's business. And if R. was home alone, and got herself absolutely blotto, passed out on the floor, her husband had learned to deal with that too. He'd come in, take one look and step over her, go watch the news, get up, go out, get some dinner and come home again. By then, maybe she'd picked herself up and crawled into bed. You should not be responsible for the mess an alcoholic makes of his or her life.

When I came home from Long Beach, my family—except, maybe briefly, for Susan—was ecstatic because in their minds everything was okay again. They had all been to Long Beach themselves for bits and pieces of

treatment, but not through a real family program. At Long Beach, wives, husbands, children of alcoholics were in therapy right along with their alcoholics, rather than in separate groups.

At the Betty Ford Center, family members are regarded as patients. You don't get to just sit around and bitch about what it's like at home, and what a dirty deal you got having to live with that creature all these years. You have to talk about yourself, and why you feel the way you feel, and sometimes it sort of comes out that maybe you are not perfect either.

Alcoholism is a family disease. We tell this to our inpatients, and we tell it to their parents and their children and their mates. We would tell it to their uncles and their cousins and their aunts, if those relations came around. It's important for everyone to know the extent to which the disease affects all those around it.

During the four to six weeks that a patient is in treatment at the Center, we ask family members to spend five days there too. Sometimes, they don't want to. One of them will say to the counselor who has contacted him, "Why should I come? *I* don't have the problem."

They're right. They have a different problem. Family members are in denial. They don't communicate with each other or the patient. And they don't know they're sick. But enabling is a sickness. An enabler's addiction is to the alcoholic. And usually, everyone in a family is required to be an enabler, to cover up, to mop up. Your twenty-year-old son is arrested? You pay the fine. Your husband is drunk? You don't go out to dinner.

That's the sickness, that's the family disease of alcoholism. It's as if your hands are tied, you don't know what to do, and you're scared to do anything, and you hope if you don't do anything, maybe it'll all go away, clear itself up.

"Alcoholism is like having an elephant in the living room, and we don't talk about it," is the way one of the counselors at the Center describes the denial.

Why don't we talk about it? That's easy. We're quick learners. We know that if you confront the alcoholic, you get back so much rage it isn't worth the effort.

Enablers, co-dependents, whatever you want to call those who live with chemically addicted people, have to step back and look at the disease, and realize they didn't cause

it, they can't control it, and they can't cure it.

We tell the people who come to family treatment that they *must* let go. But it can be hard to let go, because the person who cares for and takes care of the sick person is also sick in his or her own way.

In five days of therapy, family members are not going to get as heavy a program as the inpatient does, but what they do get gives them a handle on their situation. And that's what they're asked to concentrate on, *their* program. They're not even allowed to spend time with the inpatient. They can wave when they pass on the campus, and they're welcome at certain lectures, and they see the same movies the patients see, but they're all supposed to be working out their new lives separately.

For the alcoholic, the first step is to admit you're powerless over alcohol and other mood-altering chemicals, and your life has become unmanageable. For the family member, the first step is to recognize, and accept *on a feeling level*, your powerlessness over addiction, dependency and an addicted, dependent person.

In the family program at the Center, the family member is forced to face his preoccu-

pation with the chemically dependent person, the devices he's been using to try to punish the chemically dependent person—insults, silent treatment, laying on guilt—along with covering up the problem, enabling.

Some enablers are drama junkies, and when the alcoholic starts to get well, the excitement goes out of their days. They have to face this; there are people who do not want the sick person to get better.

Many women who divorce alcoholics turn right around and marry other alcoholics. They're attracted to people they think need help.

And then the children come along, and they are affected. They are embarrassed, and don't want to bring their friends home after school. They are confused, because one minute Mommy is throwing out Daddy's bottles and haranguing him, and the next minute she's calling his office to say he can't come to work; he has a cold or the flu or a toothache.

Kids see all this convoluted love-hate, and they get into the act too. The children of alcoholics play many parts, Quite often, the first-born plays the hero, is a good student, takes over, tries to help fix the damage. Then

there's the scapegoat, who misbehaves to get attention (he's the one who may end up in trouble with the police; he's defiant, withdrawn, the most apt to use drugs, the most apt to commit suicide). Then there's the mascot, who tends to be hyperactive, clowns, tries to distract the family from its troubles (and covers up his own feelings), and there's the lost child, who hides out in his room.

These are all survival roles, and all of these children are preoccupied with the alcoholic. The alcoholic is running things, pushing everybody's buttons, watching them react, keeping the family off balance, making them bounce around trying to compensate for the disruption.

Dr. Pursch always felt if you could get the rest of the family into treatment, even when the patient would *not* go for help, you could do some good. When you teach a family to walk away, and not to let the alcoholic upset them, you reach the alcoholic too. Because once he is no longer the center of everyone's attention, he says, hey, what's going on here? He can't push their buttons anymore.

Family treatment is similar in many ways to the in-patient program. The family members struggle in group to find their identities

and to learn how best to survive their co-dependency.

To give you an idea of the exchange of feelings that goes on in a family program, let me suggest a hypothetical group made up of composites of patients I have known during my eight years of sobriety:

Patient One: A woman still angry about an accident she's had eight years before (her husband, off drinking, was not with her when she drove herself to the hospital).

Patient Two: A woman whose addict son blames her for his father's desertion of the family.

Patient Three: A young rock musician whose father is an inpatient, but who realizes he has a drug problem of his own. "In the end, I can't blame my pot on anyone else," he says. "It's my ass, nobody else's."

Patient Four: A middle-aged gentleman who is horrified by some of the language he hears in group. He has come to family—his son is a drug addict—and has grown fond of his fellow patients, but the vernacular of the young ones still shocks him. When a girl stands up one day and says, "Well, I think it's important to call a spade a spade," the middle-aged gentleman just shakes his head. "In this group," he says, "they don't call a

spade a spade, they call it a f—ing shovel."
Then he blushes.

Out of such disparate groups comes the
same kind of bonding we find with the
inpatients, and it's even more mysterious
since these people aren't together twenty-
four hours a day. At the Betty Ford Center,
family is a more or less nine to five business,
the sessions start after breakfast and end
before dinner. The program is intensive—
films, lectures, group therapy—and if you
want to come back after dinner, there are
meetings and Al-Anon meetings. Local par-
ticipants commute from home, while most of
the out-of-towners stay at a nearby motel
which provides bus service back and forth.

With family members, the same as with
inpatients, much of the learning process goes
on during breaks. People gather in the
lounge, where there are soft drinks, coffee,
fruit and cake. The fat ones eat pastries, and
the skinny ones smoke, and everyone ex-
changes stories and discovers he or she is not
so different, so alien.

What the counselors try to do is teach the
families to love the alcoholic, not his behavior. Recently, a woman came, reluctantly, to
family. Six months earlier, her husband had

ɔeen through treatment, but in spite of his present sobriety, she was still very angry.

"He wasn't the sweet old man you see here, when he was drinking," she said. "And if he was breathing, he was drinking. I had ten terrible years because of it.

"I was so mad. My husband never understood why, 'What do you want?' he would say. 'Why don't you go buy yourself a fur coat?'

"I don't understand this program. Nothing happened until I told my husband, 'I'm through.' Then he came and got help."

It was pointed out to this woman that when she had said she was through, she had stopped enabling, and this surprised her. She had never heard the word before. At the time her husband had come for treatment, she had refused to go through family. "I've put up with his drinking all these years," she said. "There's no reason I should go and find out it's my fault, or something."

By the time she went home, she had changed. "I found out I didn't have to be the general," she said. "I found out I was not alone."

Sometimes there is so much bitterness or lack of interest that out of six family members, only one is willing to show up and be

counted. We had a pilot who had almost no support (his wife had divorced him), but his little boy came to treatment. He was only six or eight years old, and I remember his drawings of all kinds of airplanes, because planes were a big thing in his father's life.

There's plenty of black humor in family too. One mother and father whose son was in North Hall said, "We gave him a gift certificate to Betty Ford for Christmas."

People who have never confided in anyone at all suddenly break through in family therapy sessions, pouring out the pent-up sickness of years. "I hate my husband, he's a drunk, he doesn't give me any money, he says I'm a mess, my clothes aren't coordinated right, I'm a joke. And I'm angry at my daughter because she joined a religious cult, and now my darling little grandsons aren't allowed to celebrate Christmas."

In treatment, people stop intellectualizing, stop rationalizing, and start feeling. They start to see that if your alcoholic totals the car, you shouldn't be saying it wasn't his fault, there was a tree in the middle of the road.

Co-alcoholics lie to themselves a hundred ways. One of our counselors invents an example. "My uncle's alcoholic. He has a tat-

too and is in the Navy, so everyone who's alcoholic must have tattoos and be in the Navy. My aunt was not alcoholic because she didn't have tattoos, and she wasn't in the Navy. She died at forty-two of cirrhosis of the liver, but—"

Most family members who come to us believe they are here to support the alcoholic. We emphasize that they are here for themselves.

Another counselor who has worked very effectively with children says that the first question kids ask her is how they can get a parent to stop using. They're guilty, they think it's their fault. Older children suffer guilt when they feel they have abandoned an alcoholic parent. "I couldn't stand to see him like that, so I'd leave. I'd say I had a date, even if I just had a date with my dog," one boy said, breaking down in group because his father had died and it was too late to fix anything anymore.

We families who get help in time to fix things are the ones who have been blessed.

I remember Mike and Gayle at my intervention saying they wanted a healthy grandmother for their children. I had no grandchildren then, I have five now. Susan

and Chuck have two little girls, Mike and Gayle have three. I went back East for Hannah Gayle's christening in February 1986, and Jerry and I spent a couple of days with Mike, Gayle, Sarah, Rebekah and the new baby. And I got to put six-year-old Sarah to bed. She is accustomed to being tucked in with a song and a prayer, so after I sang "Jesus Loves Me," she said, "What about the prayer?"

"Well," I said, "I usually say the Lord's Prayer. Let me teach you that one." And I got as far as "forgive us our trespasses," and she said, "Gramma, what's a trespass?" Time out. Ten minutes while I'm trying to figure how to explain to a six-year-old what a trespass is. "It's like when you're mean to one of your friends or classmates, and hurt their feelings," I said. "Because then you hurt God's feelings."

Three weeks later, I was talking to Mike on the phone, and I could hear Sarah yelling something in the background. He said what she was yelling was "You gotta tell Gramma I've put all the information about trespassing on my tape recorder."

Sarah is not going to hurt God's feelings if she can possibly avoid it.

With Susan's children too, I relish being

270

"Gramma." I was in Virginia in February 1983, right after Heather, the second Vance baby, was born. Chuck was away on a trip, and there was a storm. It turned into a real blizzard, and we were snowed in. I couldn't get back home—where I had a speaking engagement—because the Washington airport was closed.

It was a wonderful adventure. We had to have wood brought in to keep the fires going, and it was so cold Susan and I ended up sleeping together. There were three generations of us, mother, daughter, granddaughters, in the house. I took snapshots of Tyne, who's three years older than Heather, lying on the floor coloring with crayons, and she went out with me to shop at the supermarket, and I cooked. I made meat loaf and pot roast and roasted chicken. I was the mother taking care of her child again, this child who had so courageously taken care of me. And here was this new baby who was such a wonder. Susan and I were happy, sharing so much love and gratitude. I think we were realizing the circle of life.

The healing of a family, Susan had called it. It can be a chain reaction. Wellness spreading from one to another. And you don't need to have gone through the family pro-

gram at the Betty Ford Center to get there either; there are many roads back to sanity, and sometimes one person's resolution to be healthy again is enough to carry a whole crowd along. Mike and Gayle got a firsthand example of what I'm talking about when they visited the Center in March 1985.

Mike Ford: "Gayle and I went West to a conference, and spent the night with the folks, and then, on a Saturday morning, Mom took us over to the Betty Ford Center. We had missed the Dedication—it came at a time when we couldn't get away—so this was the first time we had been there.

"We walked all through this wonderful facility, saw the rooms, met the staff and some patients, came out again and were about to get into the car when these two kids rode right up in front of the Center on their ten-speed bikes.

"It turned out they were on spring break from San Diego State and they'd backpacked their way across all those miles. They were wearing cutoffs, and they were all sunburned and windblown from the long trip. It was a pilgrimage of sorts for them. They were coming to the place where their father had found

272

recovery, and they just wanted to go in and see it and experience it for themselves.

"They were brother and sister, their father was an alcoholic, and in fact the sister was an alcoholic too, and they had had terrible domestic problems at home. They weren't expecting to see Mother, but they rushed right over to her and introduced themselves, and the words of gratitude poured out.

" 'We just need to tell you what you and this place have meant in the lives of our family,' the boy said, and the girl broke in: 'We have gone through hell. My father came here as a last resort, he went through eight weeks of therapy, and he's now been sober for a year. He came back and helped me get into AA, and there's been so much reconciliation and healing in our home because of this experience we just have to tell you how grateful we are and how much we love you.'

"Gayle and I were standing back watching and listening in amazement, and these kids were crying. I got all choked up, and Mother didn't know what to say. But to me that scene represented the feelings of a lot of people who have been touched by Mom's experiences, and by the Center. It was both a thrilling and enlightening moment for me."

13

O Rose, thou art sick!
The invisible worm
That flies in the night,
In the howling storm

Has found out thy bed
Of crimson joy,
And his dark secret love
Does thy life destroy.

William Blake

Like the invisible worm that eats at the heart of the rose, drugs and alcohol are dark secret lovers that destroy. I have heard those patients who say, "Cocaine loves me." It wasn't until 1955 that the American Medical Association finally said—out loud, and in print— "Alcoholism is a disease." Not that this was accepted with wild acclaim by the entire medical establishment.

But I don't want all the doctors in the United States mad at me, so let me add that

society in general is even less swift than its doctors to recognize that sick people are not just out there making trouble.

Joe Cruse wrote a fascinating parable called "When the Stigma Is Gone." Here it is, somewhat abridged:

"She had been concerned about him for a long time. He was acting differently, he was missing more work, he had lost his vigor, he was quick to snap at the kids, and most distasteful, in bed at night he would sweat profusely, waking her with his mumbling and restlessness. Next day, he would have no recollection. On occasion she sent him to their dear friend and physician, who backed up his allegation that 'he had the flu again.'

"On one occasion, she confronted him with her diagnosis and he exploded and hit her, for the first time in their marriage.

"Their daughter was engaged to the son of a very prominent family, and it was a foregone conclusion that if the future in-laws became aware of his disease, there would be no marriage.

"He couldn't face the thought that he might have that disease. People who had it lost jobs, families, had to be sent away to one of those places for 'the cure,' and there were no funds or insurance to pay for it.

"His boss had approached him and said he was concerned about his absenteeism, decreasing job performance and increasing inability to get along with his fellow workers.

"He considered moving to another state. When he was particularly bothered, he would isolate himself, and only return when he had control, but still appearing much the worse for wear. Then one morning the bed was full of blood. His wife immediately took him to the physician, who finally had to tell him that, in this new year of 1911, he was suffering from advanced tuberculosis."

Isn't that amazing? The physical symptoms, the social stigma, the doctor's unwillingness to tell the truth—but Joe is talking about tuberculosis, not alcoholism. Where tuberculosis was in 1911, alcoholism was in the thirties, the forties, the fifties. And still is today in some places.

It was in that year, 1911, that Dr. William Oursler wrote that as long as science looked upon the spread of TB as "a behavioral problem," it held out "small hope of recovery to the stricken one."

In the matter of alcoholism, not only has science looked upon drinking as "a behavioral problem," some doctors have not cared to look upon it at all.

Shortly before Christmas of 1985, the New York Times ran an article headlined "Doctors Learning to Diagnose Alcoholism." In it, journalist Nadine Brozan wrote of a depressed college dropout who went to see a psychiatrist. The psychiatrist said the girl was suffering because she had been small as a child. "I told him I was drinking and taking drugs—marijuana, LSD—but he didn't want to discuss that at all," the onetime student informed Ms. Brozan.

A year later, the same girl went to another psychiatrist, and he announced that she was simply going through an identity crisis. And "although she candidly described her dependence on alcohol and drugs," reported Ms. Brozan, "the doctor dismissed it."

So did several other doctors. "Six more years elapsed, and finally a psychiatrist—whose name she had found in the Yellow Pages—said, 'Do you have a problem with alcohol?' and referred her to Alcoholics Anonymous." Where she found her sobriety.

But Ms. Brozan, who interviewed a good many doctors in the course of her research, wrote, "The stone wall this patient encountered is not unusual."

Too many psychiatrists and other physicians contribute to addiction and help main-

tain addicts in their habits. Because while they don't dispense alcohol, they do write prescriptions. Mostly for women. And women, more than men, become dependent on their doctors and on the drugs they prescribe. A woman thinks her doctor can help her emotionally as well as physically. And we love those prescriptions. We've spent a long time waiting for the appointment, we've got dressed and gone to the office, we're going to have a hefty bill to pay, and we don't want to go home without that little white piece of paper covered in hen tracks; it's the return on our investment of time and money.

Let me recap my own medical history. As a young housewife in Washington, D.C., I began taking daily medication for a pinched nerve in my neck. The pills eased my pain as I chased four active little children.

My children grew, and so did my pill habit. Then came pancreatitis, tactfully shrugged off as a gallbladder or stomach disorder. In all my years in Washington, no doctor ever specifically made a reference to my misuse or abuse of alcohol. And I never made any connection between drinking and a health problem.

I now believe some doctors choose to be

uninformed about chemical dependency and to ignore the impact of combining alcohol with pills.

I had a gourmet collection of drugs—I did a little self-prescribing; if one pill is good, two must be better—and when I added vodka to the mix, I moved into a wonderful fuzzy place where everything was fine, I could cope.

If, as Dolores Hope says, my friends were talking about my "problem," and noticing that my health was deteriorating, I still did not blame myself, disavowing all responsibility. For years, doctors had been giving me pills, and I had never questioned them. In my early recovery, I was angry with all of them. But as I grew in recovery, and began more fully to understand my disease, I realized I was responsible, it was my body that was being assaulted, I was the one who was feeding it pills and drinks. I could have asked questions about what I was taking, but I didn't. The fuzzy feeling was too nice.

There was enough blame for all of us, the doctors and me. They were of a generation faced with a proliferation of new, mood-altering, miracle drugs. They hadn't been taught about alcoholism and addiction, and even when they recognized the symptoms,

they turned away. Addiction was just too messy to try and treat.

Often, these doctors were angry with patients who had so little "willpower," and many of them were still committed to the hypocrisy of the double standard—women couldn't be alcoholic, and certainly the wife of a former President couldn't be involved in anything so disgusting.

It was a generation of doctors who felt it was easier to write a prescription for a woman than to listen to her complaints and try to find her real problem. Diagnosis on a more serious level could take hours. And women were neurotic little things, and the waiting room was full of patients.

Today, things aren't quite as bad as they were a few years ago, because more women are going into medicine, because through television and newspapers and magazines, the public is learning more about the epidemic of chemical dependency which has swept the country, and because some medical schools—Dartmouth and Johns Hopkins, to name a couple—have begun to concentrate on alcohol education.

But it still is not enough. More medical schools have to offer more courses, require more study, and teach what is now learned

for the most part only by accident and through intuition.

Joe Cruse is a recovering alcoholic. So is Jim West, who became medical director of the Betty Ford Center when Joe decamped for a job with another treatment center. We regretted his leaving, but Joe is a visionary, he is always searching for the next challenge. Without him, the Betty Ford Center might not have happened.

The personal experience and empathy brought to us by Joe Cruse and Jim West were invaluable, but it's my view that all doctors ought to be trained to recognize alcoholism, even if they themselves have never hoisted a glass.

Jim West: "I am a surgeon by specialty, but back in the seventies I also taught substance abuse in the Department of Psychiatry at the University of Chicago. At that time, very little was known in the medical profession about alcoholism and drug dependence.

"Alcoholism and education about it has been kind of a confusing issue to the medical community. They're not for it or against it, they just don't understand it.

"In 1975, because I recognized what chemical dependency had done to me (I stopped

drinking in 1958), I started a Program for the Impaired Physician for the Illinois State Medical Society. We trained medical staff, informed them as to what chemical dependency was and also drove home a message: If you cover up for an impaired physician who is functioning poorly, you are helping him to commit suicide. If you love your brother physician, you must get him help. This kind of led the way for doctors to intervene on other doctors. More importantly, perhaps, this program served to protect patients of impaired physicians.

"At the Betty Ford Center, I give the patients three lectures; they are a condensation of the best lectures I gave to my medical students, because I think alcoholics are so smart there is little they can't understand.

"Our treatment here is eclectic; we've taken the best techniques from everywhere and incorporated all the things that have been learned about chemical dependency that work. I think everybody who works here likes working here, and this enjoyment spills over onto the patient. There is a special feeling between the staff and patients that may also exist in other good programs but doesn't exist in other aspects of medicine. (As a sur-

geon, whether or not I liked the patient had nothing to do with my effectiveness.)

"We treat everyone the same. Superstar types adjust in about one half hour, because if they look at themselves as too special to follow our program, we will help them find another place, but we will not adjust to them.

"The bonding that goes on here is magic, indescribable. Having said that, I will now try to describe it. In psychiatric terms, we have people in extreme distress, they are terribly vulnerable, their defenses are dropping away, their ego boundaries are gone, it's like they are falling in love with everybody.

"Those defenses were the only things left in their survival kit. We've already taken away their drugs. The idea is, we trust the person but we don't trust the illness.

"For me, this place is a tremendous gift. I was blessed in my sobriety to do this work I love. I am seventy-two years old, and if it weren't for the BFC, I would probably look and act like eighty-two, instead of feeling like forty-one."

There is a full-time medical department at the Center; Jim West has three other doctors to assist him in giving physical exams. But

Jim is as good a teacher as he is a doctor. He never talks down to patients. He *does* believe alcoholics are smart enough to understand whatever he says, no matter how technical it gets. I like to hear him lecture. He says he spent most of his life in green pajamas and a surgical mask—"I was a repairman"—and he's still repairing people.

He tells patients, "This disease is chronic, and this disease is primary. It isn't that people have something *else* the matter with them, and that's what makes them drink; it's that they have a psychological lesion—we think the site is in the brain—and it's genetically transmissible."

He says that every recovering alcoholic must always be aware of the possibility of a relapse into drinking, because our personality traits are like "a snake who lies back in a dark corner of the mind and who, every now and then, maybe every three or four years, will open one eye to see if the alcoholic is still on guard."

Every patient who comes to the Center gets a physical examination and a psychological evaluation, along with a chest X ray and a full spectrum of laboratory tests.

In time, we want to reserve a couple of beds in each of our residence halls for medi-

cal students, and maybe administrators of other hospitals, and nurses, have them actually go through the treatment process as part of their education. We're just going to have to feel our way along in this, but we know the need is great.

Over and over, we see the evidence. When I was in Long Beach, the Navy had made it mandatory for all Navy doctors to go through treatment, so they'd recognize the disease when they came up against it. Well, out of every group that went in for training, a couple of people discovered that they themselves were alcoholics, and elected to stay on as patients. I think they would have been reluctant to seek treatment on their own. Just as in their professional lives, they were reluctant to diagnose and refer to treatment other alcoholics and addicts.

Jim West: "Recent research (*Alcoholism: An Inherited Disease—NIAAA*) makes it increasingly clear that heredity is a major contributing cause of alcoholism. Findings in these studies lead to the conclusion that there are two kinds of genetic predisposition to this disease. One is termed Milieu-limited Alcoholism and the other is called Male-limited.

"Milieu-limited Alcoholism is the most

common form of this illness. It affects both men and women and its severity is thought to be determined by environmental factors in genetically susceptible persons.

"Male-limited Alcoholism is a much more severe type of the disease, transmitted by the alcoholic father to the son. It is not influenced by environment and frequently develops in adolescence. It is thought that about 25 percent of male alcoholics fall into this category. Male-limited susceptibility in a family does not increase the risk of alcohol abuse in daughters.

"There are promising studies which may one day identify neurophysiological and enzyme markers to help us understand the genetics of alcoholism and help us design strategies for prevention in susceptible persons."

Eternal vigilance is the price of sobriety.

Alcoholics can't drink. It would be nice if they could, but they can't. Except in the fantasy worlds of the certain mistaken "experts."

I have nothing against fantasy. If Jerry comes into the study and says, "It's doubtful that your son is going to survive. He was shot twice in the abdomen, and he's

losing blood," we can laugh, because Steve's wounds were actually inflicted on the character of Andy Richards during the course of *The Young and the Restless*, and the blood is fake.

But doctors and other scientists who have tested their theories of "controlled" drinking on alcoholics have failed miserably to prove their points. And too many of the alcoholics who tried to drink again, died. It wasn't a soap opera where, after the lights faded, the murdered actors got up and went home.

Still, the medical profession can't be blamed for all the woes of the alcoholic.

I myself have had too much help from doctors—Dan Anderson, Joe Cruse, Stan Gitlow, Vern Johnson, Joe Pursch, Max Schneider, when we were getting the Center started—to be churlish about the profession. I've leaned on doctors, and so has my family.

Steve Ford: "You know, at Long Beach, the one thing I really put my faith in was the doctors and the staff around Mom, because I wasn't sure medically how serious her problem was, and what she had to do to lick it."

None of us was sure how serious my prob-

lem was, nobody knew what I had to do to lick it, but Steve's faith was not misplaced. And since my recovery, I've encountered many other fine doctors who are helping men and women to live drug-free. I just think there are still plenty of them who need to learn more.

In November 1985, I offered this opinion to a whole auditorium full of doctors. We were all attending a conference at the Annenberg Center at Eisenhower, a conference labeled "Alcohol, Drugs, and Primary Care Physician Education."

I was asked to speak, and I did. I told the history of my disease and my experiences with doctors. I closed by saying, "A doctor's ability and willingness to recognize the symptoms of alcoholism or drug dependency, to make the diagnosis and then offer viable recommendations for treatment can save lives!" And they listened. That's what I call progress.

14

A change of love: if love is a
   groping Godward, though blind,
No matter what crevice, creek, chink,
   bright in dark, the pale tentacle find.
                  Robert Penn Warren

Before we abandon the subject of the medical profession, did you know that alcoholism is an equal-opportunity disease? And that doctors, lawyers and clergymen have just as many problems with alcohol and drug dependency as anyone else? They're all in caretaking professions, they're trying to save other people, and they experience a lot of stress.

Some of them work too hard, put in terrible hours, are fallible human beings to whom we attribute supernatural powers. We lean on them, demanding what they can't give. But who's taking care of the caretakers? And why don't they lean on God? For some rea-

son, this is a subject that makes many modern people uncomfortable.

It's relatively safe, unemotional, to discuss the addict's physiology—lesions in the brain, genetic aberrations—but you can't treat the flesh without taking into account the spirit. Which, sick itself, is often unwilling to be taken into account. Many addicts view the chemical as God. They don't need other help, except from the bartender or the pusher or the doctor.

Ralph Waite, the actor, and a recovering alcoholic, tells a story that makes this point. It seems there was a man up in Alaska who ran into a priest. For all I know, the encounter took place in a bar. Anyway, the man walked up to the priest and said, "Father, I hate to tell you, but I've lost my faith in God and the power of prayer."

"Why is that, my son?" the priest asked politely.

The man explained. A couple of months earlier, he had been hunting in the Alaskan wilderness, and he had become separated from his friends. It was terrible, all alone out there. "I was in danger of freezing to death. So I prayed and I prayed to the Lord to save me, but nothing happened."

The priest was perplexed. "But you're here

telling me your story, so obviously you were rescued,"

"Oh, yes," the man said, "I was rescued, but the Lord had nothing to do with it. I was saved by an Eskimo."

Millions of us are saved by Eskimos, and don't see the hand of God in it.

This doesn't mean I don't believe we should take all the earthly help we can get. Some people may have found recovery in a church, a synagogue or a mosque, but alcoholism is a disease like cancer and arthritis, and I'm not sure praying more would have helped me avoid any of them. (Jack Benny once made a speech after having been given an award. "I don't deserve this award," he said. "But then, I've got arthritis, and I don't deserve that either.") Still, I believe that even if praying doesn't prevent our afflictions, it helps us get through them.

Meri Bell says God is very tough with us. "He gave us free will, and then sat back and watched what we did with it. A lot of times, we destroyed ourselves, and He stood by and let us. But if we turned around and said, 'Hey, will You help me?' He was there."

I've had personal experience of this. When I was hospitalized for my mastectomy, I thought, this could be it, and only God can

help me. Through prayer, I let go and turned it over. This was before I knew I was alcoholic, before I had ever heard these phrases. Tension dissolved, my mind and my whole body relaxed, it was as though a huge weight had been lifted from me, as though a light had gone on. God was in my life, He would take care of me, and I was going to be all right. That day, my faith in God was reaffirmed in such a strong way that it has never really faltered since.

For me, the acceptance of a Higher Power was easier than it is for many alcoholics. Religion had always been part of my life. For the people who come into treatment wanting no part of God, it can be harder. Because almost all treatment programs are based on the twelve steps of Alcoholics Anonymous, which has a spiritual foundation. Step One simply requires us to admit we were powerless over alcohol, Step Two says we "came to believe that a Power greater than ourselves could restore us to sanity," and the third step says we "made a decision to turn our will and our lives over to the care of God *as we understood Him.*"

In a world that glorifies science and provable fact, these steps can be stumbling blocks for atheists and agnostics, even though the

phrase "as we understood him" offers a lot of leeway. As one of the books published by AA says, "Some of us *won't* believe in God, others can't, and still others who do believe that God exists have no faith whatever He will perform this miracle." (The miracle of removing our obsession and giving us sobriety.)

Patients can accept that they wouldn't be in treatment if they could have got well on their own, that they need help. And they're able to ask for help from the staff of a treatment center, so they've already begun to turn their lives and wills over to something or somebody outside themselves. But for many, it's a giant leap from counselor to God.

Still, "God as you understood Him" is a phrase with wide latitude. It means you can choose as your Higher Power whatever gives you comfort, the mountains, a river, a rock, even your therapy group, the consensus of the group. The journey is spiritual, no matter what road you travel. Muriel Zink, for example, is going to Russia with a group of recovering alcoholics, and they plan to hold meetings there to share their recovery.

Muriel Zink: "We are going with sanction by

the Ministry of Health, and we have to be very careful, because we are not there to proselytize, we are not there to say, 'This is the catechism, and this is the way you should do it,' we are there to share something that happened to us.

"Treatment is adaptable. The American Indians, for instance, use the concept of the Great Spirit, and they have a beautiful program that they have evolved to fit their needs.

"I think in Russia we can make the term Higher Power understandable by explaining it's like the good conscience of the collective. What I want to get across is that alcoholism is a disease and we didn't know we had it, until it almost did us in and we can share our experience in recovery and our strength and hope with you. It doesn't matter that you're Russian, and I'm a Scotch-Irish American, what matters is that I'm an alcoholic, and I have been lost."

My guide, Meri Bell, also speaks of having been lost, not because God failed her, but because she thought, in her drinking, she had failed God.

Meri Bell Sharbutt: "You see, the spiritual goes first. You go away from God because

you think you shouldn't have a hangover, or you shouldn't have behaved badly; it was because you got drunk. And gradually, you stay away from church, you stay away from prayer, or you continue to go through the motions, but there is this vague unrest inside that says something is missing, something is going away.

"Alcoholism is a baffling disease, it turns you into somebody you don't know. One of the spiritual gains in recovery is that women begin to share more with other women, and that increases our courage. I have a feeling that most women isolate themselves from each other as they begin to develop façades, and that changes when they suffer enough pain to break down those defenses, those walls. You look at another woman and you find out you've been denying your own sex.

"I used to think I was a man's woman. I didn't like women. I didn't trust women. That was a lie. I was the woman I didn't trust. Women alcoholics become friends as Betty and I have become friends. We don't make demands of each other, we accept each other where we are in today's pattern, knowing each of us has so much to learn, and so much to find out.

"I lost my way a long time ago. We lose

our way by not maturing. We have a lot of fun and a lot of pleasure, and then we have a lot of pain and a lot of shame. We have a lot of pain getting sober. We have a lot of mental attitudes to change. We have the physical recovery. And then we begin to recover the laughter and the joy and the pleasure of not having to pretend anymore. And then we begin to find our souls."

We journey blind on our way back to family, to faith, to God, as we understand Him. But the blindness is a requisite part of the process. We can no longer control, we have to trust.

Not necessarily in any formal religion, but in a spiritual program. The people who started AA knew this. Bill Wilson, a cofounder, stubbed his toe on dogma when he first tried to get sober. Bill joined the New York-based Oxford Group, which practiced what they called "aggressive evangelism," and found the emphasis on religion too oppressive.

In 1940, after AA was established, Bill explained why he had left the Oxford Group. He found their appetite for personal publicity dangerous to recovering alcoholics, and while he admired their "Four Absolutes—

absolute honesty, purity, unselfishness and love," he believed more tolerance had to be emphasized. "We can never say to anyone (or insinuate)," he wrote, "that he must agree to our formula or be excommunicated. The atheist may stand up in an AA meeting denying God, yet reporting how he has been helped in other ways." (Years later, Bill corresponded with the psychoanalyst Carl Jung, who, in the 1930's had attempted to treat an alcoholic at his sanitarium in Switzerland. Jung had also come to believe that some kind of spiritual conversion was necessary, if an alcoholic were to stay sober.)

There are people at the Betty Ford Center who say they don't get the spiritual part of the program, and I'm sure there are people at AA who say the same thing, but it does unfold gradually, as our own cobwebs lift. It's very hard to tell even ourselves, let alone God, the wrongs we have done. It's very hard to make the appropriate amends to those we have harmed. You have to be careful not to inflict more pain while you're trying to fix something. You shouldn't say, "Since I'm supposed to make amends, I better tell you I slept with your boyfriend a couple of times while you were out of town. I'm really sorry about it and I won't do it again."

I kept trying to make amends to my family by saying I didn't understand how a person as intelligent as I could be such a total failure and a mess, do this to them, embarrass them this way. The emphasis was still on me and what I had done wrong.

I had to learn to forgive myself if I expected them to forgive me. And I couldn't forgive myself until I could believe God had forgiven me.

The Lord's Prayer says, "Forgive us our trespasses, as we forgive those who trespass against us." That was the beginning.

But it was still hard to let go of the controls, to work the program of "Thy will, not my will." I also had trouble with a prayer that says you must be willing for God to have all of you, good and bad. When I first heard that, I was *not* willing. Give myself to a power greater than I, sure. But why the bad part? It was hard for me to think that the bad part of myself would be acceptable, that God didn't expect me to be perfect, or to walk on water.

I have had so much to learn. And many people have helped me learn it. Everyone fails from time to time, but in my case, it isn't for lack of trying. My understanding is that God wants me to look at facts straight,

to be honest, to abide by my convictions without imposing them on anybody else.

For a long time, I couldn't look at anything straight. I was so self-blaming, I was so disappointed at what I had done to myself, my family, my body, my mind, at the way I had emptied myself, spiritually, emotionally. I had always maintained a dependence on God, but I had expected God to do everything for me.

In my early recovery, I heard Joe Cruse talking about himself, saying, "I had to finally realize that I couldn't allow my eyes just to focus inward on my problems. It was time for me to turn my eyes outward, and see other people."

That's a lesson in recovery that anyone can understand. When you find you're feeling sorry for yourself, it's time to get busy and start helping somebody else. Soon, your self-pity and self-centeredness disappear, and you feel healthier. I know it works for me.

Though there are traps in that direction too. You can't save the world. I have on occasion become too involved in counseling someone, only to find that person was not ready. I finally had to free myself of my involvement with one friend. Tell her I loved her, but I couldn't fix her, and if she wanted

to drink, she must go ahead and drink. I cannot turn anyone else into a recovered person. All I can do is share my own experience, and if someone wants to make use of it, that's fine.

Recovery can't be easily defined. Certainly, there is no recovery without abstinence. You have to stop drinking and using before you can start trying to get on with your life in a constructive way. It's later that the spiritual growth begins, and it comes along slowly. You turn it over. You find out that you are not the greatest power, not the greatest controller, not the greatest person. I went through the whole business of accepting the fact that I was alcoholic, that my life had become unmanageable. I surrendered to the fact that I couldn't fix myself, and I turned my life over to a power greater than I that could lead me to sanity.

I learned in recovery that we must try to love unselfishly, and not expect anything in return. I was never good at that, but people can change. Susan said that Chuck and I were not natural companions, we would not automatically have sought each other out. But because he's important to Susan, I love him, and now we're good friends.

I know this sounds almost simpleminded,

but most truths are simple. When I autograph books for alcoholics who ask me to, I write, "Sobriety is joy."

Nobody gets recovery overnight, and in treatment, we don't demand that the patient believe, but we ask him to have an open mind. There are so many ways to faith.

Every once in a while, a friend who goes into treatment credits his or her recovery to Leonard and me. We don't accept the credit. Again, we know it's God working through us. One thing is for sure, nobody should go to treatment just to please his wife or his kids or Leonard or me. Unless the alcoholic wants to be sober, he might as well skip it. Leonard and I can sometimes find the words, share the phrases that a patient needs to hear, whether or not he wants to hear them. And God gives us the strength to be willing to face the person's anger when we confront him with truth. That's tough love,

At the beginning of my recovery, I read everything I could find about alcoholism and treatment. I read inspirational material and statistical material. I read pieces that made me think, and I read pieces that made me angry. A friend put me on to a collection called *The Great Texts of the Bible,* and, searching the index for some reference to

alcoholism, I found Numbers 32, Verse 23—
"Be sure your sin will find you out"—expli-
cated at great length. The author went on
and on about how a drunkard's sin brought
its own punishment. "The sin looks out of
his bloodshot eyes and grasps his hands until
they tremble as with palsy." Well, this trea-
tise was written in the early 1900s, when
they didn't know alcoholism was a disease,
and not a sin. Today we believe the sin is in
not doing something about it.

I have found sobriety brings balance, and
balance brings serenity. In recovery, I have
sometimes lost this balance, and it usually
happens when I am neglecting my spiritual
program. Then all the chronic symptoms—
envy, resentment, self-pity, anger—of my
disease reappear. Like most alcoholics, I handle anger badly, and I try to deal with this
by writing out what is making me angry,
and when I put it down on paper, I realize
how I'm allowing it to disrupt my life. And
this realization permits me to move along. I
really do believe that God never gives us
more than we can handle. But I also believe
He expects us to do the footwork, we can't
just sit back and wait for Him to dump
everything in our laps.

All the women who came to Long Beach

to help me signed the book they brought me. One of them wrote, "May He hold you in the palm of His hand."

I think He does.

15

My problem is how not to will;
They move most quickly who stand still;
I'm only lost until I see
I'm lost because I want to be.

W. H. Auden

Just to confuse the issue, a postscript to the spirituality discussion. Jim West says no data have ever really been collected to show whether or not people have more difficulty recovering if they can't conceptualize a Higher Power in their lives. He says that, over the years, he's known a great many agnostics, they're making it just fine, and most of them have done it through AA.

Jim West: "I think people are motivated to get better for whatever causes—terrible phys-

ical condition, psychosocial condition, occupational condition—there aren't too many of them. And different people interpret Higher Power differently; it doesn't have to be a theological power, it can be the group, it can be a kind of great unknown. The agnostics have to admit there is no proof that there isn't any God, and as far as they are concerned, that's good enough.

"That's why the AA program has endured since 1935, and believe me, it has been battered and pushed and pulled at."

Which reminds me of a joke I sometimes tell in the course of a speech. Mrs. Jones's husband, who was alcoholic, died of the disease. Standing at the graveside, Mrs. Jones received condolences. One casual acquaintance, a Mr. Smith, offered his sympathy and asked the nature of her husband's illness.

Mrs. Jones said Mr. Jones had drunk himself to death.

"Oh," said Mr. Smith, "was he a member of AA?"

"Of course not!" cried Mrs. Jones. "He was never *that* bad!"

Sometimes it's easier to die of drink than to admit to alcoholism and live. If you opt for living, meetings are your lifeline. When I

speak at the Center, I tell the patients that. "If you don't do anything else when you leave here, get tied into a good support group. And if you don't like one group, find another or start one with friends who are also recovering. But go, and keep going."

There are self-help groups of all kinds. There are groups for people who can't stop eating, for people who can't stop gambling, for people who are emotionally disturbed, for people who have experienced sexual abuse, for battered wives, for drug addicts and for alcoholics who are *not* affiliated with AA.

The guidelines used by most of these groups are based on the Twelve Steps of AA. And most of these groups practice anonymity. In the case of AA, there were a couple of reasons why this tradition was established. One was to prevent any single individual from purporting to speak for an organization which has never had official spokesmen. People say, "How can it exist?" and the answer is: "Nobody knows." There's a joke about a drunk who was asked, "How does AA work?" "Fine," the drunk said. "Just fine."

Anonymity also protects the reputation of the organization itself. If somebody joins AA,

and fails to stay sober, skeptics might say AA is no good. Besides, when the world was younger, and alcoholics were considered the lowest form of animal, nobody mentioned he went to AA because it would have harmed him socially and in the marketplace. It was all right to fall into the gutter, but you didn't dare admit you needed to do something about it.

Because it is non-judgmental, because it doesn't ask for a penny from its members and because it works, AA's program has spread all over the world, and we who run treatment centers borrow and steal from its wisdom.

Dolores Hope has been so impressed by the progress of patients at the Center she thinks the program should be given to everyone. "Whether they're alcoholic or not," she says. "There are people suffering, trying to cope with life. And they have to admit there are certain things they are not able to do, certain situations they cannot handle, certain personalities that are diabolical for them to be exposed to. If there was some way that you could treat yourself like an alcoholic, get into this program, that would be wonderful."

Some members of Alcoholics Anonymous

do not think treatment centers are necessary for every alcoholic. I've met many alcoholics who have told me they recovered simply by going to AA, without the ministrations of psychiatrists or nutritionists. But because of my own experience at Long Beach, I believe that the concentrated attention you get in a rehab helps do the job faster.

Thirty years ago, there were very few treatment places in the United States; now there are thousands. And they are vitally important because some people who won't go to AA will go to a treatment center where they hope they can be taught how to drink. When they learn this is foolishness, they either leave or hang around and begin to save their lives.

But once they're home again, they need a group. Most of them do, anyway. They need the reinforcement of a group, the sharing of a group, the acceptance of a group helps them to accept themselves as recovering people.

I've told about my first year of meeting with a group of ladies and being afraid to say anything, afraid to sound stupid or foolish. I would walk through the door and my stomach would start to do flip-flops because I was afraid I might be asked to read aloud.

Meri Bell did not indulge me in my terrors. "I'll see you in the morning at ten, won't I?" she would say. I was more scared of her than of my stomach, so I would get there by ten. Well, maybe ten-fifteen.

There is almost never a meeting where you don't encounter miracles. I remember a little girl who was new to the group standing up to tell her story. She said she had been dead drunk six months before, and knew she had to quit, "in order to save my life. And I had to leave the man I loved or the man I thought, in my sickness, I loved. He died of alcoholism two months later. And I didn't take a drink. I've been sober six months, and I'm grateful."

Six months may not sound like much, but it's a good start. There are people who never make six months. They come to meetings faithfully, and then around the fourth or fifth month, they get squirrelly, and go off and drink, and then they come back and try again.

Trying is what it's about. When I got out of Long Beach, I would have been happy to believe the friends who told me I didn't have a drinking problem, it was just the pills that had messed me up. I went to meetings where I was so tense I couldn't hear much that was

being said. And then I began to clear and realize that what they were talking about related to me.

Now it's different. I see the other people. We've been through something together. The same way I share a certain understanding with women who have had mastectomies, I share an understanding with recovering alcoholics. I have known what it's like to have my life out of control. There is no support group anywhere in the world where I would feel like a stranger.

That first summer after Long Beach, we were in Vail, and a few women who were recovering alcoholics came up from Denver, and we formed a kind of intimate, friendly group. Some of the women had eight years' sobriety, and to me in my first summer, that was a lifetime. I couldn't imagine anyone who had gone eight years without taking a drink.

The second summer, the group came to Vail again, and we spent a couple of days together, and one of the women, who was working in the field as a counselor at a treatment center, got on the subject of self-honesty. I was still telling myself I had been no more than a social drinker, and all of a sudden, I had an awakening. I knew that my

"social" drinking was a fiction, "honest self-deception." I didn't drink to be social, I drank out of a compulsion I didn't understand. That's alcoholism. And I thought, that's okay, that's what they mean when they say, "More will be revealed to you."

We're still meeting every summer. Each year, the group grows more important to us. We call ourselves the Denver Dolls, and it isn't all talking about recovery either, we spend a lot of time eating, gossiping and shopping.

Eight years ago, there was only one meeting a week in Vail, on Wednesday night. Now there are nineteen in the area. There are meetings at night and at high noon. And when I see that, I'm happy so many more people are finding help.

But the battle is never won. An alcoholic needs an ongoing support system. I remember hearing a woman speak at a conference, and her story was so moving, she was so convincing, so dedicated, and later she drifted away from her support group, drank again and eventually committed suicide.

When you're bereft of your chemicals, you have to learn to cope with that void. You fill it with people, with love, with meetings.

It took me a long time to quit being juve-

nile, acting immature in my recovery. I kept pulling all these little group-pleasing things to make everybody think I was getting it— oh, yes, look at me, I'm getting it.

Alcoholics are great manipulators, they think they fool people, and I suppose my way of dealing with my inadequacies was to try to look put together and in control. And all the time, I was worrying through everything I had to do, feeling insecure. I was very aware of being just a simple old girl from Grand Rapids, Michigan. I wasn't ashamed of it, but I didn't feel I had the worldly experience and knowledge to be going around meeting queens and maharajahs. I was perfectly well equipped, I'd lived in New York, earned my own way, danced with Martha Graham, but how could I believe it when I did not have—horrors!—a college degree?

Feelings of inadequacy are part of the alcoholic personality. An alcoholic can appear to be very conceited, full of braggadocio, but this is a front. I covered my own feelings of inadequacy by trying to appear very sure of myself.

It worked. Unless you remember that I had to spend my sixtieth birthday in a rehabilitation center.

During those many early meetings, I was advised to be quiet and listen—I didn't really need the advice, you'd have had to horsewhip me to make me take center stage—and I remember certain book study meetings where the paragraph under consideration dealt with self-pity, or anger or resentment. Sometimes the words would hit me right between the eyes. It was like that ad for men's shaving lotion where the guy slaps his face and says, "Thanks, I needed that."

Bring the body and the mind will follow. It can't be repeated often enough. You aren't sure what people are saying, but the information is getting into your computer, and after a while, you have a nice awakening, you begin to understand.

People ask whether or not I had any friends left once I sobered up, whether the people I knew who were still drinking were self-conscious about being around me. Well, my experience is different from the experience of younger people in my support groups. At sixty, most of my friends were not having wild parties.

At home, we still had a bar, we still served drinks, and when I was out with drinkers, it wasn't a problem for me. For some people this can be tough. Most treatment centers

advise putting the liquor out of sight and availability until you become more sure of yourself. I remember a big fund-raising event for the Eisenhower Hospital—it was a spring fashion show—and I ordered a tonic and lime, and when I went to drink it, there was vodka in it. I simply asked the waitress to take it away and bring me a plain tonic. I was comfortable with that, because I had gone public. Somebody who hadn't made public the fact that she had stopped drinking might have been intimidated, might have thought, I don't dare send this back because somebody will notice.

If I'm served a dessert like ice cream, and they've poured Kahlúa or crème de menthe over it, and all that liqueur is going to gather in the bottom of the dish, I just leave it and say no, thank you. I don't make a big thing about it.

And I don't turn my glass down. I think it's rude at a nice dinner table set with somebody's good crystal; I just watch for the person who's serving and tell him I don't care for any wine this evening.

You say no, thank you, to spinach if you don't like it, you say no, thank you, to straw-berries if they make you break out, what's

wrong with saying no, thank you, to a glass of wine?

Anyway, I seem to have kept my old friends, though few of them do any heavy drinking around me. Perhaps it makes them uncomfortable. It doesn't make me uncomfortable.

When I first went to meetings, I had been told that these were going to be the people who would mean the most to me, who would always be there for me. I didn't get it. How, all of a sudden, was I going to become a part of this group, when I still had all my old friends and an entirely different life out there?

In time, the question was answered. The men and women in my support groups *have* become very important in my life; they're the ones who understand me when I'm hurting, they're the ones who know what it means to be alcoholic. If I ever felt I was in trouble, they are the people I would go to.

Which doesn't mean I warm to everybody in every group, at every meeting. There are those with whom I will never be friends, and that's all right too. There are people who don't follow the rules, people who gossip. Alcoholics are no different from the general run of human beings. Meri Bell says if you sober up a man who was a horse thief before

he started drinking, he may still be a horse thief when he quits drinking.

Meri Bell Sharbutt: "You hear a lot about high-bottom drunks and low-bottom drunks. The only difference between them is economic. The alcoholics you used to hear about were skid row drunks who drank under a bridge, or in a gutter, but there were also little old ladies who passed their days drinking Lydia Pinkham's Extract, which was 60 percent alcohol.

"The bottom is actually soul sickness. When you have gone as far as you can go with your pretense and your façade and you are willing—in Betty's case, with intervention—to get sober. Some people go to AA, some people go to treatment, some people turn to Christian Science, some sign up for aversion therapy, where they give you ipecac, and then make you drink, and you have to watch yourself in a mirror getting sick and throwing up. I think people get sober anywhere, anytime.

"But alcohol is cunning, it will wait for you forever. If I took a drink today, I would be thirty years along in the progression of my disease. So I go to meetings because that's the way I remind myself that by my-

315

self I could not stay sober. Many people have tried. They've done my research for me."

Meri Bell was forty-three when she got sober, and I was sixty. Now we have people sixteen coming to our meetings, because the loose structure of our society allows a sixteen-year-old to destroy himself in a very short time.

We see so many new people coming into groups now, and there isn't always enough time given to the beginners, to tell them the things that will help them, to make them understand that sometimes they have to stand still when they don't want to. They're used to going full tilt, and when they learn that's not the way you get sober, it's at great emotional cost.

It takes so long to learn that you can't have it all at once.

I have a friend—he's *not* a youngster—who confided in me one evening at a dinner party. He told me how he had stopped drinking. He said he couldn't bear to continue to wake up in the morning embarrassed by what he remembered he had done the night before. And it was just as bad when he couldn't

remember at all, when he had a total black-out.

He'd heard about AA, and the book they considered their bible. He bought a copy, read it and worked a program on his own.

He was a very disciplined man, and he was able to do this, but he might have found an even richer experience if he had joined with other recovering people.

We can understand our disease and accept it more easily when we are with people who understand *us*.

I remember the first time I was asked to lead a meeting. I thought I was expected to tell my story and I sat up until two o'clock in the morning writing about what it was like then, what had happened, what it is like now. The next morning when I got up to be Madam Chairperson, I read through the agenda, and I saw the part where I was to start the meeting, but nowhere did it say a word about my telling my story.

I told it anyway. I said, "I stayed up until two o'clock in the morning writing this. If you don't want to hear it, leave and come back later."

I have learned from all kinds of groups, from meetings with conservative middle-aged women and meetings with drug-using kids

who have come right off the street. That's sort of like walking into a jungle, when you're not used to it. The four-letter words are just like you hear in the movies. What they're saying is okay, but the way they say it puts me off. It takes me about fifteen minutes to settle in. At one meeting, a girl who noticed Meri Bell looking disapproving came up to her later and said, "You don't like the way I talk, do you?" Meri Bell said no, she didn't. "If you're going to clean up your life," she said, "I think you should clean up your mouth."

On the other hand, the conservative-appearing ladies used to amaze me too. You'd see these women who looked like they had never done anything risque or out of the mainstream, and they'd start talking about their drinking, and how they used to be pretty wild in their heyday. One of them whom I admired from afar—she made profound, all-encompassing statements about recovery and staying sober and getting your life in shape—always intimidated me. I thought she was so stern. And then I heard her telling a woman who had slipped not to worry, she was doing great, and I thought, how loving she is, and how easy it is to read somebody wrong.

You can find a meeting no matter where you are in the United States. You can find a meeting anywhere in the world. Some of the people who come to the Betty Ford Center for treatment go back to Australia, Italy, France, and they join—or start—support groups of recovering alcoholics.

On the anniversary of the day I had been sober seven years, I went off to my women's group, and afterward there was the usual monthly luncheon. As the day approached I hadn't been very impressed with the idea of seven years—so it's another year—but when I got up to speak, to thank these comrades, these other recovering women, I was just overcome with love and gratitude. I could hardly talk, the tears were welling up in my eyes, my throat was tight, and I thought, God speaks to us in such strange ways.

The learning in meetings never stops. I've heard Muriel, with twenty-seven years of sobriety, and Meri Bell, with thirty, say, "I just can't believe that more is still being revealed to me."

It comes over you like a wave. Suddenly you know something you could not have accepted knowing a year, a month, even a day before.

My early drinking became clear to me in

such a wave. I had done most of it when I was alone at night. Why hadn't I read good books? Why hadn't I developed my mind? Why, at the end of the day, did I watch television, and drink?

Because I was physically exhausted, that was why, because I'd been charging around after four kids all day, because I wanted to be lazy. The idea that I might *need* to be lazy had never occurred to me, I didn't like to think of it; I am so much an A personality, so energetic, so determined to get things done and keep going. But in one of those times of revelation, I was finally able to forgive myself for watching Lucille Ball when I could have been reading Spinoza. The hell with Spinoza, say I.

I read an interview with Richard Pryor in which he told how meetings had changed him. He said that even after his accident, free-basing cocaine, despite the fact that he'd been scared he was going to die, he had not stayed clean or sober. And then he went to visit a friend. "He was in the hospital for drugs. They had these group meetings. I was sitting there listening to all the people talk and I *heard* something. And I said, 'S—t. This is good here. Remind you of anybody, Rich?' And the more I went to visit, the

more I was like a clandestine participant in the recovery of a drug addict. And one day I stood up and said I was a drug addict."

There it is. You hear it when you're ready, when you're able. For people who aren't sure, but who are making the first tentative steps toward deciding whether or not they're alcoholic, or addicted to some other drug, the Alcohol Awareness Hours that are held over at the Annenberg Center can be instructive, not to say lifesaving.

I first learned about the Alcohol Awareness Hours when I came back from Long Beach. They were held on Saturday mornings by Joe Cruse and Del and Meri Bell Sharbutt. They had been doing this for several years, in order to teach the community at large about alcoholism—what it was, and that recovery was possible.

Meri Bell Sharbutt: "The first three years of its existence, Joe, Del and I footed the bill for the Alcohol Awareness Hour. We called speakers—recovering alcoholics who were well known—and said, 'Here is what we're trying to do. Will you help us?' They came. We had no money, so they came at their own expense. We had them stay at our

homes, we arranged golf games for them, we took them to dinner.

"That was about ten years ago. Our Alcohol Awareness Hour was the first, and now there are many, all over the country. Ours is a community effort. It is free for everyone. I don't care if you are social dynamite or at the bottom of the heap, you are welcome. We are education and information. We are trying to remove the stigma from the word 'alcoholic,' and the fact that we're still in existence means we're doing something right.

"We get the major part of our funding now from the Eisenhower Auxiliary and we reach people who would be frightened or embarrassed to go to an AA meeting. They come, and often, they come back."

A friend of mine remembers the first time he went to an awareness hour. He was wearing sunglasses. "I think everybody walks into the first meetings with sunglasses," he says. "You think, 'They'll never know me,' even though you might look like a truck. A truck with sunglasses."

"I went, and I was looking at the directory downstairs, and a little old lady, one of the hospital volunteers, came over and said, 'Can I help you, son?' And I said, 'Yeah, I

was trying to see where they're gonna have the Alcohol Awareness Hour.' 'Oh,' she says, in a voice I was convinced at the time carried clear to downtown Rancho Mirage. 'You mean where all those alkies meet?'

"I cringed. It was just like somebody threw a bucket of water on me. 'They meet on the second floor,' she said, 'take that elevator.'

"So I said thanks, and I skulked down to the elevator, got on, and a couple of people came aboard wearing these big round buttons that say, 'Some of My Best Friends Are Alcoholics.' I stood in the back of the elevator, I didn't want to associate with them.

"But anyway, I went to some of those meetings, and they were very good. A marvelous informational thing. They always ask people to put up their hands if this is the first time they've been there, and always about half the room puts up hands.

"Out of those meetings comes a lot of awareness—literally. That was a fantastic thing that Joe and Del and Meri Bell started. They have athletes, actors, doctors, excellent speakers. And anybody can go. From anywhere. It's marvelous."

Every time there's a new book on alcoholism, Del and Meri Bell snare the author as a speaker. Many of the doctors they bring in

to lecture are themselves recovering alcoholics, and the Auxiliary of Eisenhower serves coffee and doughnuts; showing up for the Awareness Hour has become a popular thing to do on a Saturday morning.

In no way does it intimidate. It's just "Listen to what so-and-so has to say, it will help to educate you about the disease."

Del Sharbutt always greets the audience, and says something like "Please don't call us reformed alcoholics, you wouldn't talk about a 'reformed' cancer patient, or a 'reformed' heart patient." Or he may explain that, according to the U. S. Department of Agriculture, Americans drink more alcohol than milk. And another Alcohol Awareness Hour is off and running.

Once, speaking at an Awareness Hour, Leonard summed up the dynamics of the thing in a brilliant way.

Leonord Firestone: "Last winter, I was asked to speak at a dinner at the Monterey Country Club, and my subject was to be the Bob Hope Cultural Center. They told me about ten days before the dinner that they had a hundred reservations. Right after that, somebody put up a golf cart as a door prize, and they got another hundred reservations.

"On the night of the dinner, I said to the crowd, 'I don't know how many of you came to hear me, and how many of you came to win the golf cart.' But it really didn't make any difference, because they were there, and they got the message. And in some ways, I think the Awareness Hour operates a little on that kind of basis.

"We don't know exactly why people come. Some may be alcoholics, and want to see if they can get help; others may think they might be alcoholics, and come to see if they can learn something. Or they come because a friend is in trouble, and they'll learn something that can help the friend. In any event, they come. And they get the message."

That's what all of us, in our separate ways, try to do. Pass along the message. And it is through this sharing, through our own joy in recovery, that we attract others to the program we embrace.

It doesn't matter whether you start interacting with a group at a treatment center or in AA or during an Alcohol Awareness Hour; it doesn't matter whether you come through the front door or the side door or the back door; it doesn't matter whether you meet in a church basement or in a community cen-

ter—there is help out there for anyone who wants it.

16

The wine of Love is music,
    And the feast of Love is song:
And when Love sits down to the
        banquet,
    Love sits long:

Sits long and arises drunken,
    But not with the feast and the
        wine;
He reeleth with his own heart,
    That great, rich Vine.

James Thomson

I'm here to say that *you* can reel with your own heart and your own brain too once you quit believing that only alcohol or drugs can make you joyful.

Sometimes, I'm almost sorry for people who *haven't* been alcoholic, because I know things that a person who's never been sick

doesn't know. I had to climb over hurdles. I had to experience the disease, be sick with it and then experience recovery.

I've said this before, but it's worth repeating: When you recover, you are weller than well. Your life takes on a different quality. You are able to accomplish more than you ever dreamed you could. In the eight years since my recovery, I have not needed to use drugs or alcohol to help me live my life, I have been free to make choices, and there has been such an exhilaration in that, such an inner feeling of self-fulfillment and self-worth. I can't imagine anything more valuable, more satisfying. In recovery, you have a completely new lease on life, and that's what a person who's never been sick has not experienced.

Sometimes, in your wellness, it's hard to credit how sick you used to be. When Joe Cruse finally brought back the mountain of pills he had taken away from me before Long Beach, I put them in a closet off my bedroom lest I forget. After a while, I could smell that odor of old drugs. It was noxious, so I moved them to another closet in a spare room. And the aroma still grew. Finally, I put the whole mess in a huge plastic bag and stored it outside in an old storage cupboard,

so I would always remember how sick I had been. It's strange, the odds and ends of your life that wind up in those cupboards,

I'm grateful that's all behind me. Sheika remembers when I returned to Vail that summer after treatment.

Sheika Gramshammer: "It was like you opened the door, and the sunshine came in, and the warmth with the sunshine. And the thing which was sheltered and covered up for so long, her identity, came through.

"There were times when we had said, 'Betty, why don't you lie down?' or 'Why don't you get help?' But this is something she had to do herself, she had to be ready for it, and I think the time when she did it, it was her time to come out."

Since I've "come out," I've talked so much there may be people who wish I'd go back in, but I need to share the sunshine and warmth that came through when the door opened.

Leonard feels the same way. We both know there are other treatment centers that accomplish as much good as the BFC, but you don't hear about them as frequently, so we talk them up too. One of them—Turn-

off, which I mentioned in earlier chapters—
is run by a man named Sam Hardy and his
wife, Ann.

Leonard Firestone: "There are, I think, different kinds of rehabs. Now Sam Hardy takes
kids under eighteen. A lot of times, they're
referred by the courts. Sam is a green-thumb
kind of guy, he just knows kids, and he gets
them straightened out. He sent one boy down
to a lady who needed housework done and
was going to pay by the hour. The boy came
back, the lady called Sam the next day and
said, 'I think this boy you sent down stole
my clock.' Sam said, 'Okay, I'll find out.'
He asked the kid, and the kid said yes, he'd
done it. Sam said, 'Well, let me tell you
what you do. You take that clock back to
that lady and you tell her you're returning
her clock, you did steal it, you're sorry, and
you want to make amends. And then you do
whatever she asks you to do. And when
you've done that, forget it. It's finished.'

"A judge wouldn't do that, I wouldn't
think of that, but that's what Sam told the
kid. The kid had been terrified he'd have to
go back to Juvenile Hall, but Sam let him
handle it, and he came back and got straightened out.

"Turnoff is filled with every leftover sofa and chair that anybody would contribute, but it's cozy, it's clean, the kids are great-looking, and they have dignity. It's exciting to see that kind of operation. It's in an old house, but anybody could be happy staying there."

Lost Heads is another wonderful rehab. It's in the high desert, and when Rick Mesa took over the management, it was a mess. Nobody had kept books, there wasn't any money, Rick didn't know how he was going to be able to feed the patients. He said they had four cars, three of them didn't run, the buildings were leaking, there weren't enough beds, and he was looking to see how they could get some people who had public visibility interested, and also get some financial support.

My first thought was the people I had worked with in getting the Betty Ford Center started. I made appointments. I went to Leonard and Ed Johnsen and said, "This guy needs help. What do you suppose we can do for him?"

It was right up their alley. Both of them wanted to work on a place that might provide treatment for the less privileged, for

those who could afford to pay little or nothing. They came out, took a look and began to figure out what had to be done.

Ed Johnsen: "There was nothing there but a couple of old shacks; one was the size of a three-car garage and six ladies were living in it with one bathroom and one little gas heater. The cold hung on there, the ceiling was falling, and there was no privacy. It's pretty tough to get dignity out of a situation like that. You're already feeling pretty down on yourself for having got into that situation.

"We put up two new buildings in one weekend. We began work at dawn on December 7, 1985. We had a lot of help. A fellow donated two fireplaces, a lady I know who has a carpet mill in Idaho gave us five hundred yards of carpet, a lumberman donated $15,000 worth of wood, and dozens of people contributed their labor.

"It was like a barn raising, neighbors getting together and saying, let's go over and help old George. And it was a thrill. I remember seeing one man who had just checked in the night before, and he was in bad shape. He was a former builder, a carpenter, but on Saturday all he did was watch. He was detoxing right then. By Sunday af-

ternoon he was bending over, picking up some scrap and taking it out of the way. Two weeks later, I went over, and he had his leather belt on, he was stripped down to his shorts, and he had organized a team to build auxiliary wardrobes to go alongside the lockers.

"On the morning of December 7, some ladies volunteered to come over and cook breakfast, and we had about eighty people show up to work. We worked all day Saturday and all day Sunday, and by Sunday night we had both buildings erected, each big enough to hold twenty beds. What would have cost over $300,000 as a commercial project ended up costing only about $75,000, due to the wonderful spirit of the community.

"We did pay some people. You can get carried away with the romance of volunteer help, and we knew we had to have enough people there to make sure the things went up properly. They're really very nice-looking, well-constructed buildings. They'll be there forever. The patients are walking on five feet of air. I'm pleased. I think we'll have a dedication after a while."

It was such a good endeavor. One couple gave Rick cash for a van, and Jerry and I

sent money at Christmas. I wrote to people I'd normally have sent Christmas flowers and said we were making a donation to Lost Heads Ranch in their names. Then Lost Heads wrote to thank everybody, so now the Lost Heads mailing list is a good bit longer. I thought that was better than my sending flowers to a lot of people who didn't need flowers. It was a little manipulative, but it was for a good cause.

In addition to manipulation, one of my character defects is that I'm always trying to be what I think people want me to be. Which is available. I've had to learn there are going to be more people asking for my time than I can possibly see or please. I have to get used to that. I'm not the only one there for those people, there are plenty of others who know more and can counsel better, and I have to accept that, and so do they.

Still, I think wanting to respond to other people is a strength. If someone comes over to talk to me, I don't believe in cutting that person off short. I try to listen. I've learned a lot that way.

Despite ourselves, we learn. I've learned to recognize when I'm not working my program. Anger interferes, and so does overload. Sometimes I get short with those closest

to me, like Ann Cullen, who has worked with me for almost six years and whom I love as I love my own daughter. Yet I know I have hurt her at times by being impatient, by expecting too much, or because I was having resentment about something else and I had to take it out on somebody. Somebody I knew I could take advantage of. And then I regret it. Because whatever it was wasn't important enough to get that upset about.

Mostly, these things happen when I'm too busy, when I'm trying to do too much in too short a time.

I don't think I'm as crazy as I was in the first years of my sobriety. I remember the weekend Leonard went off to treatment, and he and Nicky had been expecting house-guests—Pat and Al Haig—and Nicky said to me, "Will you please take over the entertaining?"

When I went to bed Friday night, I had a hundred things falling all over each other in my head. The next day, I wanted to get up and go over to the Awareness Hour, because Muriel Zink was speaking. And then I would have to rush home and be hostess at a luncheon for the Haigs, and I was concerned with the flowers, the menu, the china, the place mats, everything.

In addition, Saturday night, we were going to a black-tie dinner, to which the Haigs were also invited. It was in honor of some of Queen Elizabeth's entourage, one of them a lady-in-waiting who had accompanied the Queen when she visited us in Washington in 1976.

I couldn't sleep. I was worrying about what to wear the following night. At three o'clock in the morning, I got up and went into my closet and looked at my evening dresses. I didn't want to be caught in something I'd worn at the White House during the Queen's visit. It was silly, but typical of me at that stage of my recovery. These people were special guests of the Annenbergs, and I didn't want to show up in the same dress I'd worn three years before.

At three-thirty in the morning, I was still trying on clothes.

I don't do that anymore.

There are other things I don't do either. If I have a problem with household help, I don't upset my husband by complaining to him over the phone when he's thousands of miles away. I assume responsibility, because I'm supposed to be able to run my house.

A while back, one of the people who worked for us quit when we had houseguests

coming the next day, and I said to myself, let it go, you can't do anything about it. At an earlier stage of my sobriety, I would have been so consumed with anger it could have made me physically ill.

Even though Jerry is my main support system, these days I try not to burden him. He was gone when our dog Liberty died, and I told him because he was anxious about her and was asking. But I try to avoid running to him with trivia, the way I once might have.

Susan always said I was good in a crisis; it was the little everyday things I couldn't handle. When Jerry was defeated for the presidency in the election of 1976, I had to fill in and make the concession speech and the remarks on television and so forth. The kids were very upset, and Jerry had lost his voice in the final days of the campaign, so it was up to me. Now I'm trying to learn to handle the little everyday things as well.

When I told Susan that Liberty had died, she cried, and then Tyne cried, but I didn't. Lib was a very dear old dog, and I was glad she wasn't suffering anymore.

I've had to learn to let go of creatures I've loved, people I've loved. I guess even my

attitudes toward death have changed with sobriety.

I had no serenity when my mother died as the result of a cerebral hemorrhage. I was angry. I cried myself to sleep nights because I hadn't been able to reach her before she died. My plane was delayed because of mechanical problems, and I damned the circumstances. I knew my mother would never have been happy living as an invalid, but her death came soon after I married Jerry, and I had a lot of guilt about that. Maybe I had required too much of her, put too much stress on her at the time.

I don't really believe that myself; she was crazy about Jerry, and she did everything she could to make the wedding the way Jerry and I wanted it. But afterward, I worried that I had been more demanding of my mother than I was of Jerry, that I expected more of her.

When my children were born, they had no maternal grandparents, and that bothered me, because my grandparents had died before I was born. It took me a long time to let go of all that anger and guilt and resentment.

But because grandparents have always seemed special to me, I'm now living out the role of grandmother with delight. I love my

five little granddaughters, I hope someday to love my grandsons. I don't want to spoil and ruin them, but I want to get right to the verge of it.

The last Ford baby, Hannah Gayle, was born in September 1985. We were up in Colorado, and all day I kept calling Gayle's mother. (Gayle was to have a caesarian section, so the date was set.)

"Have you heard anything from the hospital or Mike?" I would say, and Gayle's mother would say, "Not a word. I just can't imagine what's going on, but maybe the doctor had some emergency he had to take care of first."

I finally went out and had my hair done, and while I was gone, Mike called the office and spoke to Jerry's assistant. "Do you think they'll accept another girl?" he said, kidding.

We accepted her. Gladly.

In 1985, the whole family came up to the house in Beaver Creek for Christmas week. We built the place in the mountains, a few miles from Vail; it started out to be small, but we kept adding on—a recreation room, an office, a playroom, bedroom and bath in the loft for the grandchildren—until we achieved absolute magnificence.

It was the best Christmas we ever had,

and I keep contrasting it with the Christmas seven years earlier when the children were pussyfooting around and whispering to each other in corners about what they were going to do with me, their alcoholic parent.

In 1985, everybody got along. There was no undercurrent of conflicting personalities. And that's surprising when you think there were fourteen people living together. Steve had brought a friend, there was a brand-new three-month-old baby, and not everybody was thinking about eating at the same time, or going to church at the same time, yet it all worked.

The kids played games and enjoyed having dinner together, and I was entirely relaxed in spite of the fact that they were drinking our very best wine, at forty-five dollars a bottle, and leaving the cheap stuff. The argument was: "Well, we wanted to leave a lot of one kind for you, Mother, so you'd be sure to have enough for a big dinner party. We're drinking up the rare bottles because there are only two or three of them."

I was able to laugh and be comfortable with their drinking, I didn't feel I needed to be in control of the situation, I could let them have their good time and contentedly go off to bed with my husband.

I was well enough to let my children run their own lives.

There were so many special things about that week. On Christmas Eve, while I was out doing some last-minute shopping, it began to snow. It always takes a few flakes on my eyelashes to make me feel really Christmasy. Later, at home, the little girls, Tyne, Heather, Rebekah and Sarah—everybody but Hannah—came downstairs in their pajamas and robes and hung up their stockings. And we put out carrots and lettuce for the reindeer to eat, and cookies and milk for Santa Claus and his helpers. Early Christmas morning the girls found an empty glass and plate with a note from Santa that said Uncle Jack and Uncle Steve were bad boys and weren't going to get anything. They loved that, even though they worship Uncle Jack and Uncle Steve. They call Jack the Tickle Monster.

We went caroling too. We rode in a hay-filled wagon over to the Children's Fountain in Vail. We were bundled up in big fur blankets, and we sang all the way. At the beginning of the Christmas program at the fountain, one of the grandchildren pushed the switch to light the tree. We've been lighting trees in Vail ever since Jerry was Vice President.

Santa Claus was waiting at the tree, and at first, our girls wouldn't have anything to do with him. One of them grabbed my arm and said, "He's not going to ho-ho-ho, is he? I don't like it when he ho-ho-ho's."

By the time we got back in the wagon, Santa was their best friend. It was a question of who was going to sit next to him, and they never let him have a minute to himself or let any other—non-Ford—kids get closer than necessary.

Before we left for Vail, there had been more serenading from small girls back in Palm Springs. John Schwarzlose took his daughter Rachel and her Brownie troop (there must have been a dozen six-year-olds) to the Center to sing carols for the patients. I'd invited them to stop by our house afterward and perform for us. So they came, and stood on the front steps and launched into "Rudolph, the Red-Nosed Reindeer." I came out to listen, and after the song, I congratulated them, and Lisa Schwarzlose, John's wife, asked each little girl to introduce herself. Then she gestured toward me. "Now do all you girls know who this is?"

"Mrs. Ford," one of them said.

"But do you know who Mrs. Ford is?"

"She's the lady who's named after the Betty Ford Center," said the little girl.

Sometimes I feel that's true. The Center runs me, rules my life. But I like it that way. Though sometimes I stand back and look at myself sitting in some tycoon's office, trying to interest him in an assistance program to help his alcoholic employees, and I think, why couldn't I have taken up golf? Then at least I'd be outside on this pretty afternoon.

Almost everyone has some alcoholism in the family. But lots of executives don't believe they could possibly have it within their business organizations. I had a conversation with a clothing magnate—he has thousands of employees—and he said, "Oh, we just don't have alcoholics in our business." And I thought, this man doesn't drink, so he doesn't see any drinkers. After we got through talking, he said, "Well, you know, I have been sort of blind. I'm going to take another look." There are some companies that don't want to be aware of the problem, because they don't want to deal with it. Their policy is to fire the alcoholic rather than offer rehabilitation, even though it is financially more sound to rehabilitate a trained worker than to let him or her go.

But I keep badgering them and hoping.

I've turned into a splendid haranguer of all kinds of audiences, even though I'm still terrified when I speak. Always, I anticipate the possibility of falling on my face. Always, I know there comes that time when you don't do well. And I want to do well. I think whether or not a speech comes across has to do with my preparation, and my conviction that what I'm telling the audience is something they need—and want—to hear.

Jerry was a big factor in convincing me that I knew more about my subject than my listeners, so why should I be scared? (Somebody once asked Ethel Merman if she was scared when she went on stage. She looked dumbfounded. "Why should *I* be scared?" she said. "If they could do it, *they'd* be up here.")

At this point, I've had to educate myself in order to educate others. I've spoken to people in the insurance field, to doctors, to religious groups. I started a whole new career when I was sixty years old, a career of recovery.

The nice thing is that now I know I can make a mistake or two before I'm through with this world, and it won't mean I'm unfit to live. I'm just not as frightened as I used to be.

Ann Cullen: "When I first started working for Mrs. Ford, she was about to hit the trail to raise money for the Betty Ford Center, which gave her the impetus to get out there and start doing a lot of public speaking. But she was scared to death. If she had to talk for more than five minutes, she would not sleep for the three nights before the event, and she would be sick to her stomach. She would just be a wreck. Now, she talks for forty-five minutes, and it's 'No, no, they can't take me off yet, I still have things to tell these people.'

"She's much more comfortable now standing up in front of a group, she is more sure that people will listen to what she has to say."

There is something about the challenge of public speaking that's similar to the challenge I once felt about whether I should or shouldn't take a drink or a pill. For me, it was a little like living on the edge, and I liked that in my life.

Today, I get that same kind of exhilaration from standing up and trying to give a good talk, or interview, from trying to erase the stigma associated with the words "alco-

holic" and "addict." If I could help remove even one dot above one *i* in those words, I would feel I had proved myself.

Ann Cullen: "I think a lot of the old anxiety was camouflage. She thought if everybody saw the perfect outside, they wouldn't ask questions about what was going on inside. There were a couple of times when hair was the ultimate thing that happened around here, and Mrs. Ford almost lost some of it, because I was going to snatch her bald.

"Seven years ago, she had two hair appointments every week, every Tuesday afternoon, every Friday afternoon. She would not go out the front door if there was a hair out of place, or something the matter with the way she was dressed, or her purse did not match her shoes or whatever. Now she can do with one hair appointment a week, and if she misses that, it's no big deal. Last year, when she went to the Bob Hope Classic Ball (she had been busy getting ready to have her foot operated on), she actually wore a dress that was wrinkled. To a big social event! That was a major breakthrough."

I always thought if I looked good to other people, then I must be okay, and that got

me off the hook of having to realize that maybe I wasn't okay. Working through support groups of recovering people, I have learned the value of *being* okay, rather than just *looking* okay.

It's funny, back when I had a little sobriety, I had a discussion with one of my oldest friends in Washington and she said my hair always looked exasperatingly perfect on television. "Why don't you come on with it messed up once in a while?" And I thought, defensively, well, I wouldn't go on television with my hair looking like yours usually does.

But I like my hair less structured now, a little easier, which I suppose is also symbolic of letting go. I did attend the last Bob Hope Ball in a wrinkled dress. It was a gold lamé affair and it had a voluminous skirt that takes forever to press. Ann offered to do it, but I said, "No, they'll just think it's pleated," and she couldn't believe her ears. She said a couple of years ago, I'd have been hysterical if my dress had been in that condition, and I'm sure she's right.

My priorities have changed, and I guess your personality changes with your priorities. I wasn't going to make any grand entrance at the Bob Hope Ball, it wasn't a Betty Ford party, Jerry and I were going to

be there as support for Bob and Dolores, because they were our friends.

The changes that come with recovery come in every area of your life. I no longer care so much about people pleasing, I tell the truth to—and about—doctors, I've stopped denying I'm an alcoholic, I even travel lighter. Jerry used to say, "*I* don't have to take ten bags to spend two hours like some people I know." Even in my early sobriety, I needed a backup dress for a speech, because what if the zipper broke, or I caught my heel in my hem. Now I just pick a dress and go. It's a small thing, but a sign that I'm more self-assured. Even my brother Bill, who always thought I was nice, thinks I'm nicer now.

Bill Bloomer: "She has a great thoughtfulness and consideration of people, and she's always had that to some extent, but now more than ever. And her life has got meaning and direction and stability beyond my greatest imagination. You know, there are a lot of alcoholics in this world, 10 percent of the people in our country are chemical dependents, and so few of them turn their disease to some good. Or as much good as she has.

"Jerry is so proud of what she's doing; he sat in this room in Scottsdale and all he

talked about was what Betty was accomplishing. When I tell people I'm Betty Ford's brother, they say, 'I just love your sister and what she's done,' and it makes me feel good."

If only everyone could speak so wisely!

But seriously, I think these last few years have been my best years, and that in itself is success. Everything keeps getting better.

Scenes with the grandchildren play in my mind. Hannah's christening. A birthday party Tyne and Heather gave for Jack, during which Tyne pushed Jerry, fully dressed, into the pool. When he surfaced, glasses, watch, wallet dripping, he swam silently to one side, walked up the steps, water sloshing out of his shoes. "That wasn't very nice, Tyne," he said. I was tickled. It was his dear, darling Tyne who had done it, and he never can get very mad at her, or any of his granddaughters, but Jack swears the temperature in the pool rose ten degrees.

You can sit outside our dining room and look across the pool and the fountain at two layers of mountains, dark ones in front, light ones behind. There are olive trees and palms and oranges and lemons and grapefruits and roses growing under a bright blue sky. It smells sweet.

And there are other sweetnesses in my life. A while ago, I got a letter from my friend Betz Hutchison. She enclosed a check to the Center. She wrote, "The folk art business did very well this last year. I had been putting a bit aside for a nice piece of Georgian copper. Then I did some long and hard thinking. An old piece of copper is just a thing. It is people, not things, that are life's most valued treasures. Betty, I hope this will help someone, even in a very small way, to regain control of his or her life."

Something like that makes me want to work harder.

There have been blows as well as joys. Last year, Pam Wilder, one of the women who brought the group to me at Long Beach, died of cancer, and so did my darling Nicky Firestone. I think about Nicky every day, not because she was perfect, but because we were neighbors, and relied on each other, and loved each other.

Just before Christmas, Nicky became critically ill. The doctor told me no one but family could see her, and there was nothing I could do. Jerry advised me to go on to Beaver Creek, where our children and grandchildren were coming for the holidays, and where he would join me later.

I flew to Denver. It was one of those days when the air shimmers. The sun was shining, and at one point, the clouds separated and it was almost like a pathway to heaven. I sat there in my quietness, in my love of Nicky, and I felt she had been released.

I had to let go, and let God.

A long time after I had been in treatment at Long Beach, Joe Pursch had a patient come to him at Care Manor. He was a big burly beer distributor, and he said, "I'm here because of Betty Ford. My wife said, 'Look, if even a woman can do it, you ought to be able to do it.'"

Even a woman can do it. A man can do it. A teenager can do it, and so can an octogenarian. At our Third Alumni Reunion last November, more than eight hundred former BFC patients who had done it came together, and that was a weekend I will never forget.

17

Because the birthday of my life is
     come . . .
                    Christina Rossetti

We took 840 reservations for the Saturday-night dinner—840! It was unbelievable to me that we could have that kind of turnout for an anniversary. They came from the desert close by and from faraway places. We filled the Grand Ballroom of Marriott's Rancho Las Palmas. To me it was absolutely astounding. I saw BFC alumni from Hawaii, from New York, from Florida, from Canada, and the celebration of everyone's sobriety made us all buoyant, we bounced along the whole weekend on a giant high.

Saturday morning, the Awareness Hour was held in the Annenberg Center Auditorium, which seats maybe 450. It was full.

Right at the beginning, I thanked the alumni for coming, and said how good it made me feel to look out and see all of them,

and then Leonard spoke, and Del Sharbutt spoke, and so did the president of our alumni association, who had been sober for two years. He said he had come to the Betty Ford Center "basically to learn how to drink and work on my tan. And I was only able to accomplish one of those two objectives."

After the formal program, volunteers stood up and told how their lives had changed, they just stood and talked, without mikes, from wherever they were in the auditorium, and it was wonderful.

One after another, they shared their stories.

A man said he'd first come to the Center out of fear, but that in the midst of all his fear, there had been a seed of hope, small as a mustard seed, and that hope had grown, and he had found recovery.

A woman said she'd been wrestling with a drinking problem all her life, "and was scared to death somebody was going to find out I was an alcoholic." Then she'd read about my going into treatment, and said, "One of these days I'm gonna have to do that myself."

She remembered making New Year's resolutions every January 1. "I would say, 'I hope I'll find some happiness this year,' but I never had much happiness. Now I do. I

have been sober for nine months, and it's wonderful. I have been frightened, scared, afraid, the whole nine yards, but I have finally found some peace of mind."

There was a girl who'd had a drinking and a drug problem, and had never thought "that I was good enough, or that I helped enough, or that I got enough." She had found out through treatment that "it's okay to feel good, it's okay to smile, it's okay to love and be loved."

There was a young man who said he'd been so desperate to come into treatment that when he'd been told the fee was "fifty-five," he'd said, "Fine, fifty-five thousand dollars is no problem, I'll pay anything." Advised that the fee was fifty-five *hundred* dollars, he'd been shocked. "I thought it was a mistake, because of the movie stars who had come here. I thought this was *the* place, and you had to pay a lot of money."

When he went home after treatment, he was still in trouble. "I thought I had a very secure job. I was president of a company that my father owned. But within fifteen minutes of my being back in the office, he said, 'I don't want you around here anymore, you're fired.' Two days later, the girl

I was living with left. She took off with another guy."

This young man said he had started going to support group meetings—"I averaged a hundred eighty meetings in ninety days"—and through them, he had begun to experience "a clarity. And the talent I didn't think I had came back." He said he'd been able, in recovery, to change the "negativity I've had all my life" into something positive. "Now, when I put out positive, I get positive back."

Every story revealed a marvel.

There was a very pregnant girl who had been in treatment with her husband. You could see their joy, and without recovery, it's a joy they might have missed. The husband said he'd used alcohol and drugs from an early age. "They seemed to diminish those pains I was feeling inside. And everyone would say, 'Look at him, he's so together,' and on the inside, I'm going, 'Hey, man, I'm dying, there's something killing me.'

"But this recovery is contagious. I had a friend who came into the program several months before I did, and when I got to the point where I just didn't want to live anymore, something brought me to his office, and we sat and talked, and three hours later,

I was here at the Betty Ford Center seeing if I was sick enough for them to help me.

"They told me I was okay, and they loved me. When I went home, weeks later, I had an idea I'd have a sweet, warm, wonderful relationship with my wife, but it didn't quite work like that. I had to recover from my disease of alcoholism and drug dependence, and then I had to recover from the disease of emotional dependence on that other person. As time goes by, I've come to realize I can be in love with someone without being emotionally dependent on her, and that's just part of the freedom and joy that this program has brought me. If I hadn't come to the Center I'd probably be dead, but today I'm alive and real glad to be here."

The weekend was filled with events. There were brushup workshops at the Center, and we had the groundbreaking for the new, twenty-bed wing to be called Fisher Hall, and everywhere, you could see former patients milling about, embracing with bear hugs, greeting one another.

On Saturday night, the ballroom looked beautiful for the dinner. My friend Mary Fisher—she and her family contributed toward Fisher Hall—had done a terrific job with the decorations. Each table had a BFC

medallion set in the center on a round, flat mirror, and the lights of the room bounced off the mirrored centerpieces and flared upward, so that every few feet, on the ceiling, there appeared a big, diffused image of a medallion. Those reflections must have come from the angle of the lights, but there was something almost mystical about it.

And there were balloons, and people dressed in their best, and again we heard brief talks—inspiring, touching, funny—from those who had been asked to tell how their lives in sobriety were going. One drug addict said he'd learned humility while working in a cemetery. "There's forty thousand bodies in that thing," he said, "and a lot of the young people were there because of alcohol and drugs, and that scared me. It made me realize how serious this disease is. And when I was at the Betty Ford Center, I really learned the tools to recovery."

People thanked the counselors who had seen them through their ordeals, they thanked their families, they thanked us listeners for letting them share. "I'm grateful to all the people associated with the Betty Ford Center," said one woman. "For the love and acceptance I felt from the first day. And I'm grateful to God for staying with me

when I was lost, and leading me from the depths of hopelessness to the joy I have in recovery."

A former cocaine addict said he had believed he could wing his way through the Center and get back to his drugs. He was shocked when a counselor searched his suitcase and took away his Old Spice. "I said, 'What's the matter? You don't want me to smell good in here?' He said, 'There's alcohol in this Old Spice.' I said, 'I'm a drug addict, I don't drink, especially not Old Spice.' He took it anyway.

"Then I went to see the nurse, who dug out my last gram of cocaine from where I'd hidden it. Thank God."

Instead of getting back to his drugs, he'd gone on to save his life, his marriage, his career. "It's wonderful to be home," he said. "And the Betty Ford Center for me is home."

For me, that night, the Grand Ballroom of the Marriott was home. I was moved to see people, some of whom I remembered as gray-faced, blotchy, burnt-out, now thriving, pink-cheeked, clear-eyed, happy.

But a great poet once said—and I'm paraphrasing—that it's easy to resist riches, fame, power, what's hard to resist, the most insidious of temptations, is the temptation to saint-

hood. And as I listened, swelling with pride because the Center had been able to guide these people back to meaningful lives, I reminded myself one more time that it was God, not Betty Ford, who had made these miracles. Inwardly, I thanked Him for including me.

When it came time for me to speak, I tried to say this. "I'm really proud of this Center," I said. "And I'm grateful for my own recovery, because with my recovery, I was able to help some other people come forward and address their own addictions. And I don't think there's anything as wonderful in life as being able to help someone else. But believe me, it's through the grace of God that I'm able to do it. It's not me, it's all you people put together, and a great staff, and my Higher Power that gives me the strength to try and keep it going. I love you all for that, and I thank you."

Winning a victory over drugs and alcohol doesn't mean you can rest on your laurels, you have to win again tomorrow. And I wished for all the people at the party that they would make it again tomorrow. And I hoped that they would wish the same for me.

What I remember best about that exultant

evening is something said by a woman who told us she was forever getting herself into trouble. "But I just keep coming back," she said. "I just keep showing up for my life."

Showing up for life. Being blessed with the rebirth that recovery brings.

One day at a time.

Authors' Note

No one needs to suffer alone and help is only a phone call away. Contact Alcoholics Anonymous, Al-Anon—the fellowship for relatives and friends of alcoholics—the National Council on Alcoholism, a clergyman or the local police department for help. Information about alcoholism or drug addiction can be found in your telephone book.

The publishers hope that this
Large Print Book has brought
you pleasurable reading.
Each title is designed to make
the text as easy to see as possible.
G.K. Hall Large Print Books
are available from your library and
your local bookstore. Or, you can
receive information by mail on
upcoming and current Large Print Books
and order directly from the publishers.
Just send your name and address to:

G.K. Hall & Co.
70 Lincoln Street
Boston, Mass. 02111

or call, toll-free:

1-800-343-2806

A note on the text
Large print edition designed by
Kipling West.
Composed in 18 pt Plantin
on a Xyvision 300/Linotron 202N
by Genevieve Connell
of G.K. Hall & Co.

ACKNOWLEDGMENTS

For their kindness in reading and commenting upon various portions of the manuscript, the author wishes to thank Gilbert F. Pascal, Jerry A. Graham, and RADM Daniel H. Stone USN Ret. A special thank you to Deborah Jean Coonts, who read every word of every draft numerous times and didn't surrender.

The author also wishes to acknowledge the wisdom and seemingly infinite patience of his long-suffering editor, Charles Spicer of St. Martin's Press. Thanks, Charlie.